CITY OF REFUGE

STARHAWK

Books by Starhawk

FICTION:

The Fifth Sacred Thing

Walking to Mercury

City of Refuge

CHILDREN'S FICTION:

The Last Wild Witch: An Eco-Fable for Kids and Other Free Spirits

NONFICTION:

The Spiral Dance: A Rebirth of the Ancient Religion of the Great Goddess

Dreaming the Dark: Magic, Sex, and Politics

Truth or Dare: Encounters with Power, Authority, and Mystery

The Pagan Book of Living and Dying: Practical Rituals, Prayers, Blessings, and Meditations on Crossing Over with M. Macha Nightmare

Circle Round: Raising Children in Goddess Traditions
with Diane Baker and Anne Hill

The Twelve Wild Swans: A Journey to the Realm of Magic, Healing, and Action with Hilary Valentine

Webs of Power: Notes from the Global Uprising

The Earth Path: Grounding Your Spirit in the Rhythms of Nature

The Empowerment Manual: A Guide for Collaborative Groups

CITY OF REFUGE

STARHAWK

CALIFIA
PRESS

CITY OF REFUGE

A Califia Press Book

PUBLISHING HISTORY
Califia Press special Kickstarter hardcover edition December 2015
Califia Press special Kickstarter paperback edition December 2015
Califia Press trade paperback edition February 2016

Book and Cover Design by Diane Rigoli, rigolicreative.com

Printed on 100% recycled paper by Worzalla,
a worker-owned cooperative.
Printed in the United States of America.

Library of Congress Catalog Number on file.
Available from the publisher by request.

Trade Paperback ISBN: 978-0-9969595-0-6

Califia Press
PO Box 170177
San Francisco, CA 94117-0177
califiapress.com

starhawk.org

TABLE OF CONTENTS

Declaration of the Four Sacred Things

The earth is a living, conscious being. In company with cultures of many different times and places, we name these things as sacred: air, fire, water, and earth.

Whether we see them as the breath, energy, blood, and body of the Mother, or as the blessed gifts of a Creator, or as symbols of the interconnected systems that sustain life, we know that nothing can live without them.

To call these things sacred is to say that they have a value beyond their usefulness for human ends, that they themselves become the standards by which our acts, our economics, our laws, and our purposes must be judged. No one has the right to appropriate them or profit from them at the expense of others. Any government that fails to protect them forfeits its legitimacy.

All people, all living beings, are part of the earth life, and so are sacred. No one of us stands higher or lower than any other. Only justice can assure balance; only ecological balance can sustain freedom. Only in freedom can that fifth sacred thing we call spirit flourish in its full diversity.

To honor the sacred is to create conditions in which nourishment, sustenance, habitat, knowledge, freedom, and beauty can thrive. To honor the sacred is to make love possible.

To this we dedicate our curiosity, our will, our courage, our silences, and our voices. To this we dedicate our lives.

PART ONE

THE AFTERMATH
OF THE
OVERTHROW

Chapter One

How to Make a Revolution: I

Tinder dry, these times we live in. Resentments and injustices pile up like brush, awaiting a spark to set them alight. Any fool can toss away a smoldering butt and start a blaze.

Before you do, consider: How will you survive the inferno?

A firestorm creates its own wind, makes its own weather.

Be like the redwoods.

Let it go, that tangle of underbrush, that overgrown field of bracken. You don't need it. Release it.

Sing up the old Gods of storm and rain, Oya, Orisha of the whirl-wind, of sudden change. Learn to love lightning and thunder.

Disruption, destruction are the necessary agents of renewal. Embrace disturbance.

Guard your heartwood, turn your attention underground, to the root mass, the mycelial threads that link tree to tree.

The wall of flame will pass. And even if all that remains above are blackened posts, retain your faith.

Life renews itself from below, from what is hidden.

Out of seared bark poke new shoots. Green gauze covers the charred land.

And a trill breaks the silence.

High atop the skeleton of the tallest tree, perched on a scorched limb, one defiant bird lifts its head to the sky, and sings.

A Century of Good Advice:
The Autobiography of Maya Greenwood
Yerba Buena: Califia Press, 2049

A BROKEN-NOSED BEAUTY, THAT'S WHAT WE ARE, THOUGHT MADRONE as she picked her way through the tangled maze of torn-up trees and chunks of paving left by the Stewards' Army in their latest invasion.

Punched in the face, eyes blackened, lips split. But we're tougher than we look. We simply spit out a couple of teeth, and go on.

All around her lay the evidence of destruction. And all around her, as she wove her way through the tangle of paths and torn-up gardens, teams were at work, clearing away the rubble, digging new beds, pruning damaged trees.

She stumbled on the deep track left by a bulldozer and came out onto a cleared space overlooking the grounds of the healing center. Before the invasion, the old brick building had been surrounded by lush gardens filled with herbs used to staunch wounds or treat illnesses, and flowers to refresh the spirit, for the medicine of the City integrated the ancient knowledge of root-women and cunning men into Western allopathy, along with acupuncture and Ayurveda and the physic of the East.

Now the plants were trampled, the ginkgo grove was a waste-ground, and the myrtles and chaste trees of the Women's Grove overlooked a ruin of torn-up leaves and shattered stalks.

The Stewards' Army had taken a special delight in destroying gardens and uprooting sacred groves, as if beauty and abundance offended them.

We chose not to fight with bullets, but to make beauty itself our prime weapon, Madrone thought. Offering it to the invaders, beckoning ... Join us, become us, taste our fruits. Until, in the end, the soldiers of the Southlands fell into our embrace, and were undone.

No wonder they went after fruit trees and flower beds! They recognized our true arsenal.

It hurt Madrone to see the destruction of this most sacred of all places. She was a healer, and these gardens had for so long been her place of sanctuary, her place of rest and comfort in all the crises and epidemics. She missed that refuge now. In the month that had passed since the people of Califia defeated the invaders from the Southlands, the demand for a healer's skills had been unrelenting.

She mounted the steps of the building slowly, feeling her fatigue. Her shift had not yet begun, but she was still tired from the day before, and the day before that. At the top, she paused to survey the scene below.

The worst damage was in front where the temple had stood, a pillared pavilion draped with fragrant vines. Here, where convalescents once had come to meditate in peace, where family and friends of the sick would bring their hopes and their offerings to lay in the niches dedicated to Hebe, Asclepius, Brigid, Mother Mary, or Kuan Yin, now lay a ruin of shattered rubble.

But the temple was being rebuilt. As she did her healing work inside the wards, the work crews of the City would be healing the grounds and gardens outside.

We are resilient, she thought. We'll use broken concrete as the base for new sculptures and benches to rest upon, and melt down shattered glass to make new vessels. We use everything, even our injuries.

She sighed. Resilience required energy, and hers was flagging. She felt far older than her twenty-nine years. Ready to be a crone in a rocking chair, or if not that, at least ready for a little vacation, camping in the quiet of a high mountain lake. With no one around to need her. Well, maybe Bird ...

Just for a moment, she let herself imagine it, the two of them swimming naked in pristine water, diving and surfacing like a pair of seals. As they had in their teenage years, exploring each other's bodies on beds of cedar boughs.

And then suddenly she spied him, in the midst of the workers. Bird was stripped to the waist, his milk-chocolate skin glistening with sweat in spite of the fog that chilled the summer air.

Bird, her lover, her best friend, her miraculous proof that some thread of beneficence still wove its way through the snarls of unlucky fate. The air thrummed with the joy of it: that he had come back to her, out of the prisons and the dust of the Southlands, that after all the battles and the journeys and the devastating mistakes, against all odds, they were together.

She watched him squat and lift the huge log, and the song shifted into the high whine of anxiety. There was a gray tone under his skin, a tremor in his bad leg. He would injure himself beyond repair if he kept on like this. Something would rip him away again, and she would lose him forever....

Stop it! She told herself. Just go inside. Your shift is about to start. You have patients who are asking for your help. Leave him to deal with his pain in his own way.

Push through the doors, and trust. That was what she should do. Her hand was on the door ...

Mierda! The man was as worrying as a carbuncle!

⁓

Bird trudged up the slope and set his log down at the landing stage with a secret sigh of relief. He was pushing himself too hard, way beyond any need, and he knew it, carrying loads too heavy for his damaged hip, stressing a body that was barely recovered from the last round of beatings and hunger.

But the physical labor, the sweat, eased other tensions. When he was pushed to the edge, there were no questions, no need to examine what he was doing or why, no impossible dilemmas to review with harsh judgment.

His leg ached, but the physical pain drove away a deeper pain. This work was not so different from what he had done in the prison camps of the Southlands. He could tolerate much worse. And he had.

The grounds of the healing center swarmed with activity. The work crew around Bird began a rhythmic chant as they aligned themselves along the length of a fallen tree trunk. He joined in, his clear, musical voice still hoarse a month after the final battle. His bad leg trembled, but he ignored it and took his place.

"One, and two, and three, and LIFT!" they chanted.

Bird put all his strength and breath and muscle into the lift, and the log rose. Pain shot through him, a sharp moment of agony as if someone rammed an icicle up inside his thigh and deep into his guts.

Familiar as a neural probe to the base of the spine. Unbearable.

Yet each time he bore it, he confirmed again that he *could* bear it.

Then someone took the weight of the log from him, and the pain passed. The relief was sweet! A feeling of well-being washed through his body, and just for a moment he closed his eyes and basked in it.

Yes, it was over. Truly over. He had survived.

He opened his eyes to see Madrone glaring at him. She was the one who had stepped in and shouldered the weight of the log, and now it pressed down on her.

She fixed him with the Look, the raised eyebrows, pursed lips, and expression of general disapproval he had so often seen, as a child, on the face of her grandmother Johanna. He gave her a rueful smile.

She was growing into it, he thought, her cinnamon skin flushed, her full lips pressed together, her wild cloud of dark hair bouncing on her shoulders as she sadly shook her head.

"You want to break that hip all over again?" she said, but he heard what she didn't say out loud, and the theme was "idiot!"

She was right. He knew that. But that didn't mean he would admit it. And now everyone was looking at him. He had been so happily anonymous only a moment before. Now they were all remembering who he was, what he had done, his whole litany of failures and betrayals.

"You think you need to bear my load as well as your own?" he said. "Carrying the whole blasted City on your shoulders isn't enough?"

"Don't change the subject!" Her dark eyes shot sparks at him. Her brow furrowed, enough to pucker the small scar in the center of her forehead, the mark of her initiation by the bee priestesses, the Melissas of the Southlands. "Go ahead and say it: You're right, Madrone."

Bird took a long breath.

"You're right, Madrone." It wasn't Bird who said it, but Kria, the *responsable* of the work crew. One of the many in the City who transcended the binary polarities of he or she, Kria smiled at Bird from a delicate-boned face while taking the log from Madrone with a pair of arms muscular as a bodybuilder's. "And he's right. The rebuilding won't be done in a day. We've all got to pace ourselves. But it won't get done at all if twenty people need to wait here with a log on their shoulders while the two of you argue."

"Sorry," Bird said.

Madrone, embarrassed, brushed loose pieces of bark off the shoulders of her healers' robes, wishing she'd just left him alone.

"There's lunch at the canteen," Kria said. "Go get yourselves some."

Madrone followed Bird over to the canteen line. Now that she thought about it, she supposed she was hungry, and it would be good to eat before beginning another long shift. She had a little time. And it would be good to spend it with Bird. They didn't get enough time—they would never have enough time to make up for the lost years while he'd been in prison in the Southlands and she hadn't known whether he was alive or dead.

A warmth filled her like a shaft of sunlight melting ice, and she slipped her hand into his to let him know that she'd forgiven him.

He took her hand, but he was still irritated.

Frag it, maybe he knew what he needed better than she did. Maybe it was worth a bit of pain to deflect that other, deeper ache.

But he felt a balm flow from her hand to his, bathing it, releasing some of the pain of fingers that had been broken and never correctly healed. She was looking at him with those dark luminous eyes, and he was lost in the grace of her generous mouth, the smooth curve of her cheek. Even the scar looked to him like a flower, not a blemish.

He couldn't stay mad. He squeezed her hand.

The canteen was crowded with workers, sweaty and dirty, packed into a line that crawled beside the long table where helpers dished out plates of salad and vegetable stew. At a second table a big dispenser held a vat of iced herbal tea.

Bird debated just getting a drink and going back to the work crew. He was hungry, he supposed, but he didn't feel hungry. He'd been on short rations for so long, it was hard for his body to comprehend the abundance of food the City offered. But Madrone was watching him, expecting to share a sweet moment with him, eating together in the midst of an exuberant crowd. One of those moments they had both fought hard for, and should treasure.

Makeshift tables and rough benches hewn from logs filled the cleared area in front. At a far table sat a clump of sojuhs, the former soldiers of the Stewards' Army whose mass desertion had bought the City's victory over the invaders.

"There's a place set for you at our table, if you will choose to join us," Bird muttered to Madrone. That was what they'd said to the Southlander troops, and now they were indeed sitting at the table, playing cards and drinking the iced tea, though they scorned the food. Instead, they passed around packets of chips, the pressed soy wafers laced with vitamins and drugs that had fed the Stewards' Army.

If they favored chips over real food, they had to be breeds—the sojuhs born in the breeding farms, Bird thought. They had never tasted real food before they'd defected, and looked upon it with suspicion.

In contrast, the croots—the unfortunate recruits pressed into the Stewards' Army for petty crimes or unpaid debts—ate avidly. There was a table full of them on the other side of canteen, laughing raucously and coming back for seconds.

Madrone and Bird took their place in the line, and he continued to observe the table of sojuhs, somewhat warily. They worried him. The breeds clung together in their old units, alarmed and overwhelmed by the complexity of the City, exhibiting an apparently infinite capacity for cards and chips and liquor, for kicking back and letting others do the work. They seemed to be always waiting for orders that never came.

A young woman server brought a tray of food to the sojuhs' table. She set down plates of salad and bowls of stew.

"Dig in," she said with a big smile on her round freckled face. She had wide innocent hazel eyes and white, even teeth, and Bird imagined that in her life she had never known a reason to feel less than good about herself. "This is for you!"

They shook their heads.

"This unit don't eat that shit," said the largest and strongest.

She looked hurt.

"It's good," she said. "I helped to make it myself. Try it!"

"Got food," said a skinny sojuh, thrusting forward a packet of chips. "Try it!"

She reached for a chip, took it gingerly between her fingers, nibbled at the edge. She made a face.

"It tastes like chemicals and salt," she said.

"Taste good!" the big sojuh said, running his tongue over his lips and leering at her as they all laughed.

I'm going to have to do something, Bird thought. I know how to reach them, how to talk to them. I've been among them. Somebody is going to have to do something, before this idleness and restlessness turns nasty.

Madrone watched him monitoring the situation. He was always on alert these days, always wary. Bird had come back, but he was not Bird, not the beautiful boy, the golden-voiced singer, the laughing lover, the kind protector, the cocky, arrogant, full-of-himself but oh-so-charming magician she'd fallen in love with at sixteen. He was a man in pain.

And I'm a healer who can't make it better.

Madrone and Bird reached the serving station, and filled their plates with quinoa vegetable stew and salad. With a glance at Madrone to see if she would acquiesce, Bird steered them to seats at the end of the sojuhs' table.

He's still pulled to the front lines, she thought. It must be some kind of guard dog instinct—place yourself where trouble is likely to break out. But I guess I share it, too. Goddess knows, I've healed enough breeds to know how to handle myself around them.

The big burly fighter across the table glared at them. Madrone smiled back.

"Whassup?" Bird asked mildly, in the sojuhs' own staccato, truncated speech.

He received a grunt in reply from the big sojuh. They must all be from the same unit, Bird decided, for they all looked alike, pale-skinned, with blond crew cuts. The Stewards' Army was strictly color-divided: sojuhs ate, slept, and trained with others who looked pretty much like them. Bird wondered if they kept breeding records—how many of the breeds were literally half brothers? Surely this crew all had a family resemblance, their jaws square and their blue-gray eyes deep-set. They had unit tattoos on the backs of their necks, bar codes enclosed by a catlike form that must be their mascot.

Bird grunted back. The big sojuh stared at him, and he stared back, taking each other's measure, wary but not hostile. He could risk the next move.

"You down to help with the cleanup?"

The big sojuh laughed. "This no packa humpers! Fighters!"

"Fighters are strong," Bird said. "We could use strong men to help us rebuild, now that the fight is over."

Now the skinny soldier laughed. "Fight go on," he said. "This unit chill for the next round." The food the young woman had brought sat untouched on the table. The sojuh pushed it away. "Don't eat trugger food."

"Why don't you try it?" Madrone suggested. "You might like it. And sooner or later, we're gonna run out of chips."

The big sojuh turned his back on her.

"Trugger food grow in the dirt!" the skinny sojuh objected.

"Could have bugs on it," the big sojuh agreed. "Roach spit. Spider shit."

Bird opened his mouth to respond, then shut it again with a soft sigh. Where to even begin? Dare he tell them that their beloved chips were far more likely to be full of frass and ground-up roaches from the unregulated factories that made them?

"Ai, stallion," the big soldier said to Bird, while pointedly ignoring Madrone. "Heard that squab bitches got sideways slits. True?"

He's looking for a fight, Bird thought, and stole a glance at Madrone, who merely looked amused.

"Anatomically, there's no difference," she said.

They looked at her blankly.

"Down in jungleland, all the same," Bird translated.

"A hole, a hole," remarked the skinny sojuh philosophically.

"Got to taste some pigeon meat!" said the big sojuh.

"City women all know how to fight," Bird said. "You got to persuade them."

"No fun in that. Hey, why the yarbo bigsticks close the rec rooms? A fighter got needs!"

"So do the former pen-girls. They have needs of their own."

"Need drillin'! This unit got the tools for the job."

Laughter rippled down the table. The big sojuh slapped down a card, and attention turned back to the game.

Bird observed his salad with distaste, but forced himself to eat it, bite by bite. Set an example. The stew was full of vegetables and chickpeas. Tasty, if everything didn't taste like wood to him. But he made himself eat it all. To waste food was the worst of sins. There were times when he would have killed for that vat of iced tea, this plate of vegetables. He should feel grateful. He should enjoy it, instead of forcing it down like medicine.

He kept a wary eye on the sojuhs as he ate. No doubt about it, they were a catastrophe waiting to happen. He should do something about it. But he didn't know what.

Smokee had been walking since the early morning. She'd woken up in the unfamiliar softness of her bed and felt the walls of her room confine her too closely. The city had assigned her a small apartment after her liberation, just a room with a tiny kitchen and a bathroom, in an old building in the heart of town. It was the biggest space she'd ever had to herself, as big as the apartment she'd shared with her parents and brother before her own relinquishment. And she treasured it, the wide bay windows where the sun came in, the tiny kitchenette like a doll's kitchen with stove, sink, coolbox, and cupboards full of rosebud china and fat blue mugs and a set of cast-iron frying pans. Most importantly, a door she could lock from the inside, and open at her pleasure.

At night she slept with the key clutched in her hand, to remind herself, when she woke from the nightmares, that she was free.

But at times any walls around her felt too much like a cage. Then she would walk, hour after hour, striding through the torn-up gardens lining the green streets and dodging the rubble, trying to walk off her rage.

Years and years of bottled anger bubbled up, spilling over and coloring all she saw. Every bright bloom dancing on the breeze, every cherry hanging red from the bough, every beckoning frond seemed to mock her. Here, see, this is your birthright, what you should have had and never did. This is the world your lost child should inherit, and will never see.

There were children in front of her now, chattering away so fucking happily as they played in a fountain the Stewbos somehow hadn't managed to destroy. She wanted to yell at them to shut up, yet they were only happy children. Not their fault that her own child would never turn her face up to the spray and laugh with delight.

The child. Smokee was haunted by her—her delicate fingers, her sweet, trusting eyes that had known only the comfort of Smokee's warm body until the Terrible Day.

Smokee turned away from the park and forced herself up one of the city's many hills that rose up like a rounded belly behind her. The path was steep, and it took all her breath and concentration to make it up to the top. She was still weak from confinement and long hunger, but growing stronger every day.

Don't think about the child. Just feel the blood pumping, and try to claim it as a triumph. Feast your eyes on the color and the beauty. Try to let it in, the healers had told her, and she'd tried. But when she let down the wall of numbness, all she could feel was a pure red rage.

She crested the hill and continued down the south slope, where she found herself at the healing center canteen. Lunch was being served, and a long line of workers stretched out into the torn-up garden. She wasn't hungry; her stomach had shrunk down to almost nothing in the days of starvation and captivity, but she'd promised the healers that she would eat when they released her from the wards. And they checked on her.

"Are you eating?" "Are you sleeping?" "Would you like to take a meal with a family from time to time?" "Would you like to join a Learning Group, get trained in some new skill?" "How can we help you?"

"Fuck off!" Smokee wanted to cry but some faint echo of her own mother's voice held her back, reminding her to be polite.

"No thank you," she said instead.

Yes, she'd had a mother once, and a father and a baby brother, too. She couldn't bear to think about his fate. When she thought of her parents, her mother's screams echoed in her ears. She saw her father's arms reach out to her as the billie's club smashed down on his skull and the Relinquishment Squad dragged her away. She could still hear the crack, and the moans fading to silence.

She put her hands up to her ears to block the sound of those memories, shook her head to clear her sight.

"Are you okay?" A face bent over hers, another Glossy, all smooth and shiny with bright white teeth. Well, not all smooth. There was a small puckered scar in the center of the forehead. Another fucking healer!

"Fine!" she grunted, and turned away from the eyes that followed her with concern.

Madrone had seen the girl looking strained and tense and gone to her. More than that, she had felt the distress, scented it on the breeze. The bee initiation she'd received in her own hard journey to the Southlands had gifted her with an awareness of smell and touch and pheromones and deeper energies. Scents informed her, aroused her, alarmed her. Now they spoke of damage and pain.

"Just leave me the fuck alone!" Smokee growled.

Madrone debated. She recognized the young woman now. She had tended her after the liberation, when the victorious Cityfolk had found her near death from starvation and abuse. Should she back off? Or push in with offers of the help she so clearly needed?

But her wounds come from violation, Madrone knew, from the battering down of all her protective walls. I can't help her by shoving through her boundaries.

Madrone returned to the table, where her stew was growing cold. Bird still kept a wary eye on the sojuhs, Madrone on the former pen-girl. This is our downtime, Madrone thought, but we're still on duty.

Smokee made her way to the back of the food line, and stood with her arms wrapped around her chest, glowering at anyone who tried to make conversation.

The line moved slowly. Smokee caught wafts of fragrance on the breeze, something hot and savory. At least it would be real food, not the chips, those thin little slices of artificial vitamins and nutrients fried in enough grease and salt to make them palatable. The chips and the sweeties were the only food offered in the pens and the other girls devoured them eagerly. It had taken Smokee a long time and immense hunger before she'd given in and eaten them.

The tables were already crowded, and she hoped she could take her tray and find a spot to sit by herself, where no one would bother her, as far away from the nosy healer as she could get. She wasn't in the mood to talk to anyone right now.

The line brought her close to a table full of sojuhs. They made her sick. She had to push away the drugged, hazy memories of something heavy and bad-smelling pawing and mauling her while she thought of the sea. She thought of it now, the light sparkling on the waves and the lace patterns of foam and the sharp, salty smell of the air. That was where she lived, that memory, while the sojuhs grunted and drilled. That was where she went now, when the anger threatened to burn her from the inside out.

She turned her head away from the sojuhs, not wanting to recognize any of them, to remember their pig grunts and their smell. She was standing in the sand, with the waves pulling away and the feeling that she was rushing backwards, rushing back to some other time, before, before....

"Aya, spillrag! Squirt gun need a target!"

The wave crashed. The anger broke through. She was aware of a leering, pale face. And she was no longer imprisoned, no longer caged and drugged and strapped down, helpless. On the table lay a knife.

⁓⁓⁓

Bird heard the jeer, saw the fury in the green eyes, the red flush in the pale, freckled face of the woman in line. A flash of metal ...

Before he could think, he was down on the ground, gripping the wrist that held a knife. The woman wrenched her arm back but he hung on like a bulldog. She clamped her teeth on the back of his hand. He heard a voice yell—it might have been his.

Then other hands grabbed her and pinned her arms. She twisted and swore and kicked.

Bird let go and nursed his wounded hand.

Madrone looked from Smokee to Bird, not sure who needed her more. His hand! His strong, supple, so very skilled musician's hands that were already battered and broken and permanently stiff from torture in the Stewards' prisons. He'd worked so hard to regain even a measure of his former skill! And now...

But the girl—for she was truly no more than a girl. Terrified, beneath her bravado. The air hummed with the subsonic whine of her fear.

She walked over and stood beside the girl, not touching her, not even looking at her, just being there, close by. Madrone closed her eyes, and thought about peace, and sunlight on petals, and the scent of honey. A drop pooled in her bee spot.

Calm. Safety. She sent the thought out, a scent that quivered gently in the air.

A crowd had gathered, some who were done eating and others who'd been close by in line. They crowded around, buzzing with shock and outrage. A slim woman with a tight mouth and a jutting chin pointed at Bird.

"He had a knife!" she said in a voice dripping with righteous indignation.

"Me?" Bird said. Since the knife was still clenched in the hand of the angry woman, it seemed a remarkably poor use of the rules of evidence.

Madrone snapped out of her reverie. "He did not!"

"She took it away from you!" Cress, anchor of the Water Council, stepped forward, his dark eyes smoldering with anger. He tossed his shock of black hair back and strode forward.

Fuck, Bird thought. Cress. His primary foe in the City, his self-appointed judge and prosecutor. Well of course, it would have to be Cress. And the slim woman beside him was his girlfriend, Flo.

Kria gave Cress a firm shake of the head. "That's not what happened!"

"Justice circle!" someone called out, and people began moving tables and arranging chairs.

Madrone's eyes snapped open. A justice circle? *Diosa*, she didn't have time for that! It could last all day. She hated to abandon Bird at this moment, but she was already late for her shift.

But the girl? Maybe she would need an ally, someone to stand by her. Madrone sighed, and thumbed the crystal that hung from a leather thong around her neck. It glowed a luminous pearly white, and she quickly whispered a message to her work team, warning them that she'd be late.

Bird was relieved to see Salal step forward. She was one of the City's foremost mediators and facilitators, an older woman with a square patient face under a surprising thatch of bright red hair.

"Sit down and behave yourselves," she said to the crowd, and took charge of the circle.

"My name is Salal," she said. "I'll volunteer to anchor this justice circle, if that's agreeable to everyone." Most everyone nodded or raised their hands and wiggled their fingers in a gesture of approbation. "Okay, so what just happened?"

"Crazy fuckin' bitch went ballo with a knife!" said the skinny soldier. He jerked his chin toward Bird. "Saved this sojuh's sorry ass!"

"Who saved your sorry ass—sorry, who saved you?"

The soldier pointed at Bird. "That stick."

"And who attacked you?"

"Slit right there."

"What's your name?"

"Don't got one. Number's four thirty-seven eighteen fifty. Unit call this sojuh Fifty."

"Okay, Fifty, I realize you're upset but I'm going to ask you to speak respectfully in this circle and use respectful terms for women."

Fifty looked deeply confused. Bird repressed a smile and the urge to explain to Salal that the poor tubo had probably never heard "respect" and "woman" combined in the same sentence before.

Salal turned to the woman.

"And what's your name?"

The big sojuh snorted. "Slit don't got no name, got an address. Hall C, Pen Thirty-Eight."

"Shut the fuck up, you filthy piece of bankersnot. I don't got to take shit from you or anyone!" Smokee retorted.

"Enough!" Salal said in a soothing but no-nonsense voice. "Sojuh, I expect you to be quiet unless you're called on, you hear?" She turned to Smokee and fixed her with her eyes. Salal had a gaze like a good herding dog, Bird thought, intense, penetrating, hypnotic.

It worked on the woman, who sat down meekly.

"My name is Smokee," she said. "Smokee Ann Dawson." Saying her name restored some tiny splinter of pride. She wasn't sorry for attacking the sojuh. Foul-mouthed clone needed to learn some manners. The eyes of the circle were trained upon her like a barrage of searchlights, and while she wasn't scared, exactly—she thought nothing that could possibly happen to her would ever scare her again—she was aware that there would be consequences. She gathered herself together and stared back defiantly.

Salal looked up at the growing crowd.

"Don't you people have work to do?" she asked. "Unless you were directly concerned with this incident, I suggest you get on with it!"

No one moved. Salal amped up the Gaze, folding her arms and cocking her head.

"Are we having an epidemic of deafness? This is not happening for your entertainment. So please, unless you were involved, get back to work! Come on people, we've got a city to rebuild here. Go haul some pavement!"

Reluctantly, much of the crowd began to peel away, leaving a small circle behind. Madrone stayed close to Smokee.

"Okay, anyone else see what happened?"

Kria stepped forward. "That sojuh made a really crude, sexual remark and this woman, Smokee, just seemed to snap and go after him. She grabbed the bread knife from the table but Bird caught her wrist and blocked her. Then it just got crazy."

Salal turned to Smokee.

"Is that what happened?"

"I don't have to take that shit from him or his monkey-dick clones. I don't have to take that shit from nobody!"

Salal nodded. "Can you tell Fifty how his remark made you feel?"

Smokee stared at Salal as if she'd just been asked to dance like a penguin or compose an operatic aria. Salal stared right back.

"Feel like I'm gonna slice his moldy balls into little thin pieces, fry them up for chips, and stuff them down his throat!" Smokee said finally.

Bird suppressed a smile. His hand throbbed where Smokee's teeth had left their marks, but he was enjoying watching Salal try to cope with the situation.

"I'll take that to mean 'angry,'" Salal said. She turned to the sojuh.

"Fifty, can you understand how mad your remark made this woman?"

"Thass no woman, thass a spillrag. Got a twat the size of a tank!"

Smokee started to rise but Kria pulled her down. A murmur ran through the crowd. Bird could feel its sympathy shift to the woman's side.

"Not any more," Salal said firmly. "There are no more pen-girls in this City, no one who exists to be used by others. We're all people here, every one of us. Deserving of respect."

She swept the crowd of sojuhs with a stern glance like a beam from a lighthouse, and in response they assumed blank expressions of deference.

"Nonetheless, Smokee," she went on, "you've responded to words with violence. That's not acceptable. You've used a weapon. That's grounds for banishment, or a long stay with the mind healers."

"Fuck you!" Smokee said, not helping her cause. "I never asked to come here!"

Bird found himself suddenly moved to stand in her defense.

"With all due respect, Salal, these aren't normal times."

"We know that," Salal said. "But we can't have outraged former pen-girls knifing sojuhs all over the City! Smokee, if you were angry at the soldier, or felt threatened, why didn't you ask for help?"

Now Bird was angry. Ask for help? Fuck you, Salal! he wanted to say. You can't ask for help if you've screamed your lungs out night after night begging for help that never comes. You can't ask for help from a bunch of strangers who have no fucking idea what it's like to be locked up and caged and assaulted and battered and have no way out! He bit it all back, clamping his mouth shut. He was getting close, too close, to all that he never talked about. And this was not the moment to break that silence.

He whirled on the sojuhs.

"Listen up, tubos! It's over—the p-girls, the rec rooms, all that shit. You got needs, you find some other way to meet them. You see any woman on the street, anything remotely resembling a woman, any former pen-girls or camp followers or anything, you keep your fucking mouths shut! And that's an order. Understand?"

From behind came the sound of soft applause. Bird turned to see Isis, the pirate who had ferried him back from the Southlands when he'd escaped from prison. She was standing with her lover, Sara, another Southlander, who'd run away from her rich and brutal husband. They understood something of traps.

He was gesturing as he talked and he became aware that a fine spattering of blood lay over the table. His hand was seriously bleeding—not just from the bite but also from a deeper cut on the palm. He must have grabbed the blade of the knife in the struggle.

Madrone whipped out a bandanna, and quickly wrapped the cut tightly. She pushed Bird's elbow up to elevate the hand.

"And you, Miss Hellcat," Bird turned to Smokee, "lay off the knives and the fists and the street brawls. Some asshole says something stupid, you just close your ears and walk away. You understand?"

Smokee nodded.

"Okay, that's done," Bird said. "Can we go now?"

"That's not enough!" Flo objected. "She pulled a knife. That's got to have a stronger consequence than just 'don't do it again'!"

"And why are you defending her?" Cress demanded of Bird.

"Maybe because I understand a few things that you don't!"

"Like what? Like you understand the enemy mind so well because you've been one?"

Now Madrone was mad. She felt the air vibrate around her, as if she were giving off a hum of alarm.

"Stop it!" Salal thundered. "Cress, you're off topic! We're not going there!"

"Then where are we going? She just gets to walk away after attempted murder?" Cress sneered. "Because *he* says so?"

"You understand her so well, Bird—you should answer for her behavior," Flo said.

Bird hesitated. He didn't want to take on the woman—he could barely answer for himself. But he couldn't say that in this circle. Admit any weakness, and Cress would be sinking sharp teeth into his throat.

Madrone opened her mouth to volunteer, then shut it again. No, she couldn't carry this woman and all the demands of her patients and an ailing Maya and a wounded Bird. She couldn't. But as the silence lengthened, she felt herself wavering. Maybe, just maybe, if she...

Sara stepped forward.

"We'll be responsible for her, me and Isis," she said. "We're from the Southlands. We know what Bird is talking about."

Flo glared at her. Cress rolled his eyes. Madrone let out a long, reprieved breath.

Smokee looked at Isis suspiciously.

"You a stud or a puss?" she demanded. Indeed it was hard to tell. Isis was dressed for the sea, with rubber-soled shoes and loose cargo pants covering her runner's legs. Her shoulders were broad, her arms bare, her muscles sculpted and well-defined. A spiral pattern was shaved into her close-cropped hair, and her narrow, square-jawed face had prominent bones, a broad mouth, and intense dark eyes. There was nothing conventionally feminine about her, except for a slight curve of breasts under the tight singlet, its sparkling whiteness contrasting strongly with her obsidian skin.

Isis gave her a smile full of mystery and promise. "I am Isis," she said. "Thass all I need to be."

Sara, beside her, was slim and graceful in her own rough work clothes. Her shirt was unbuttoned down to the valley between her own swelling breasts. She had toughened up in the last months, Madrone observed. Her face was wind-burned, her blond hair sun-bleached, the delicate-boned hand that stroked Isis's arm work-roughened and callused. But she still managed to look as pale and graceful as a Madonna lily.

Isis sported a gold ring in one ear, as if to announce her pirate status. Its twin graced Sara's pink, translucent lobe. They stood close together, brushing arms.

"What do you say?" Salal asked Smokee.

Isis winked. "Come on, jib-girl. We go sailing."

Sailing. Once long ago, before her relinquishment, Smokee's family had made a pilgrimage to the sea. She thought of it that way, because it had taken so long, so many changes of buses and long waits and walks in the glaring sun.

She had found a twenty-dollar bill on the street that morning, and brought it home in wonder. And her father had said, "We should put that toward the debt." But her mother said, "We've been in LA for over a year and we haven't seen the ocean yet. Let's go, Jake. Let's take the kids and go to the beach."

"The debt," her father said again, but she could tell by his voice that he didn't really mean it.

"We'll always have the debt," her mother said. "It doesn't matter how much money we put toward it. So let's steal just one day for ourselves, and give the kids a memory they can treasure."

Smokee remembered that day, the roar and hiss of the ocean, the great waves tumbling in. She and her little brother splashed in the shallows. They didn't own bathing suits, but her mother let them swim in their undies and T-shirts, while she and their father rolled up their trousers and waded. The little waves had rolled in with light dancing on their backs. Her mother showed them how to build sand castles, and they built towers and moats and channels to the incoming tide, and watched them wash away.

That was the one memory that never hurt her, that always offered refuge. She went there, when the tubos drilled her body. She filled her mind with the hiss of the tide and closed it to the sounds around her, trying to be hard and impervious as a pebble rolling in the waves.

And now this heeshee was offering her the sea?

There were beaches here in the City, Smokee knew, and great levees that held back the rising ocean, but she had never gone to them. She wouldn't go, she told herself, not without her family, not alone. It would be too unfair for her to enjoy the sun and the sand and the salt smell on the breeze when they could not.

But to sail—to float on the waves, surrounded by light reflecting back from every direction like a thousand stars, yes, if she had ever wanted anything at all, she wanted that. Even if she were selfish and bad for wanting what her mother, her baby brother, her own lost child would never know.

"All right, then," Salal said. "Anchors away, pirates! She's all yours."

And before Smokee quite realized what was happening, she was walking away between the heeshee and the slim, pale woman, her arms held kindly, but firmly.

Madrone caught Bird's eye, and smiled with relief. But red blood was now soaking her bandanna.

"Come on," she said. "Got to fix that up!" Still supporting his bleeding hand, she helped him up the stairs into the healing center.

Isis and Sara steered Smokee out of the canteen, past the work crews restoring the damaged wing of the healing center, down through walkways still fragrant with summer flowers and around the base of one of the City's towering hills. Over a boardwalk that spanned the wetlands where the rising sea had taken bites out of the eastern edge of the City, down to the basin where bright boats lay docked. Amidst the reds and blues and greens, one sailboat was painted black. It was hung with a rag-tag collection of solar panels and windspinners, and sported a black flag with a death's head emblazoned in white.

"Welcome to the *Day of Victory*," Isis said as they went aboard.

Chapter Two

"HOW A BREED GET TO BE A REAL PERSON?"
Maya looked up at River, who trailed behind her as she wiped counters in the big, open kitchen of Black Dragon house. They were cleaning up, in the aftermath, the aftermath of the overthrow. She liked the sound of that, the soft *f*'s and *th*'s. A suspiration of relief. A relaxation of the tension, after the battle.

They were alone in the big house, and she suspected that the big former sojuh had been assigned to babysit her for the afternoon, while Madrone was off at the healing center and Bird joined a work crew. At the age of ninety-nine, she supposed that a babysitter was perhaps not a bad idea. Or maybe they should call it an eldersitter. Biddy-sitter. That would be the word.

I'm probably drooling on the sponges as I wipe the counters, she thought. Ah well. At this stage in life, I'm entitled to a little drool. I've cleaned up after so many battles. This one will be the last.

"How a breed get to be a real person?" River repeated patiently. She didn't really know how to answer him. There he stood: River, formerly the sojuh Ohnine, bred to be the worst of the Stewards' ruthless combatants, a cold-blooded murderer. Clumsy but eager to please as a puppy, his skin shiny-dark, his stocky body hard-muscled but somehow as brittle as the chips that he'd been raised on. Her own pet killer, now doing battle with crumbs.

There's a place set for you at our table, if you will choose to join us. It was my own idea, my hubris, Maya thought, to tell the occupiers that. My vision to meet them with an offer of welcome, not weapons. And now here the invader stands, taking the sponge from my hand.

Her table was a beat-up old antique, round, made of oak. It was looking good to Maya, the chair beside it looking even better. River steered her gently into a seat.

"Sit there, Mama," he said. "Watch."

Maya didn't mind that he called her Mama. The soldier-defectors called every older woman Mama. It was the only term of respect for a female they knew. Torn from the arms of their own caged dams when they could barely talk or toddle, they only half-remembered some blissful time of love and nurture.

She looked around the kitchen, the house where she'd lived for so long that it had become something like a second skin. Long ago she'd come to this home as to a refuge, and Johanna had taken her in to her arms and her life. She'd fed Johanna's daughter, Rachel, at this table, and her own daughter, Brigid, so many years later. There were the scars where Brigid's eldest, Marley, had practiced his drumbeats with wooden spoons. Across from her, Bird had sat in his high chair, warbling his toddler songs, dead on pitch even at nine months old, humming along as she sang that old classic:

> *"Today is the day we give babies away,*
> *With a half a pound of tea.*
> *If you know any ladies that want any babies,*
> *Just send them round to me."*

River was looking at her strangely, and she realized she was singing out loud. She winked at him.

"Getting old," she said. "I don't recommend it. Although I suppose it beats the alternative."

He looked even more confused.

"Never seen nobody old before. Sojuhs die young."

"The young are inscrutable," Maya told him, although she was well aware that he had no idea of what she meant. "Your faces so smooth, blank, opaque. When you're old, your face tells your story. Each line records how you've met the events of your life, with fortitude or feebleness, with humor or with hatefulness, with smiles or sneers."

There was a stew on the stove for dinner that Bird had put together before he and Madrone left for the day. Maya thought about getting up and stirring it.

"It's no fun," she admitted. "Things hurt. You lose your faculties. Getting up from the table becomes a project. But there are compensations."

"Whass that mean?" he asked as she carefully positioned one hand on the table, the other on the chair back, and pushed herself up to her feet, knees groaning in protest. He swung around and offered a hand as she stepped toward the stove. She took a wooden spoon from the jar on the counter and began to stir the stew.

"You know who you are," she said.

His brow furrowed.

"You Maya!" It was a struggle for him to get it out. The breeds rarely used personal pronouns.

"And who is Maya?" Stirrer of stews, wiper of counters and noses, mother, grandmother, teller of tales, maker of trouble for all these long years. "Who is River?"

As he paused to think, Maya became aware that the spoon was dripping on her hair. River gently took it from her and put it back in the pot. He squeezed out a rag in the sink and, with a look of daring in his eyes, gently wiped her head.

His touch was hesitant, a soft swipe with that big killer's paw—then he pulled back, waiting perhaps to be scolded for his presumption. Maya took his hand and held it for a moment. The underside of his trigger finger was still hard with calluses.

The marks of the past, she thought. Not easily erased. And where, she wondered, did this gentleness come from? No one, as far as she knew, had ever offered any gentleness to him. Beaten into submission from toddlerhood, raised and honed to be a soulless, ruthless killer—who would have suspected that deep inside lived a potential for kindness? Yet it was there. Buried deep like a dormant seed that sprang into life when exposed to wet and warmth.

Maybe this feather-light touch was a faint echo of a mother's hand on an infant's cheek, the ghost imprint of a caged woman who had nothing else to love.

"You are somebody," Maya told him. "You have a name."

"Never had a name before. Was born and bred to be a sojuh, not a real person. Maybe I half a somebody."

"Somebody enough. You have the foundation of somebodiness. Now you can build the rest."

"How?"

River held her hand like a soft-mouthed setter holds a bird.

"Choices. The somebody you become is the sum total of the choices you make."

She was thinking about her own choices, the nicks and scars of them on the tabletop, the battered couches covered now with bright throws where she had cuddled a succession of lovers and children, the stains on the rug from a cavalcade of dogs. Choices that led to happiness; choices that led to despair. Choices, some of them, that had led to this moment of freedom, where further choices awaited.

Her options, now, seemed so limited. To push her aching body and frail wrists to stir, when she could be sleeping. But stirring and swiping and cleaning were part of her somebodiness, mother Maya, grandmother Maya, or more basic than that. Somebody Who Does Her Part. Who still has something to offer.

Bird was standing at the kitchen door, watching them. He heard Maya speak about choices, and wrenched his mind away from the memories of his own, that threatened the peace of this moment. Late afternoon sun streamed through the big, west-facing bay windows. The thermal-lined chintz curtains were pulled back. Maya had made them long ago, to replace a set of drapes that his brother Marley's pet rat had eaten through. How mad she'd been! He felt a sudden, sharp longing to have Marley back with him now, his older brother, someone to lean on. The epidemics had taken him, when Bird was imprisoned in the Southlands, and he'd never even had the chance to say goodbye.

The curtains were getting a bit threadbare, he noticed. It made him sad, for Maya was beyond making curtains now, even if anyone had leisure to think about such things. The paint on the ceiling was peeling in patches where rain had soaked through from a blocked gutter. The bright pink sofa that had once belonged to Johanna's mother had faded to a dusty soft rose, and sagged in the middle. A shabby room, but comfortable. It was home, and he'd spent enough grim hours locked away from it to be grateful now simply to be here.

He gave Maya a peck on the cheek, and steered her back into the chair, giving River a nod and smile. The room was filled with the hearty smell of the stew. A basket of ripe tomatoes sat on the counter, and he brought it over to the table with a knife and a cutting board. Salad would go good with the stew.

Maya sat looking around the room, her eyes vague but her face beaming. Bird wondered what she saw. Was it this room, filled with cooking and conversation, just the way she loved? Or was it this room in some other time, with some other configuration of lovers and babies, Johanna stirring soup, his own mother Brigid feeding his brother or himself?

She was slipping away, he thought. Not so much losing her faculties, but shifting their focus from now to then, from here to the other side. He was filled with tenderness toward her. She was ninety-nine, she couldn't be eternal, but he couldn't imagine the house, his life, without her, anchor and heart.

He placed a tomato on the cutting board and took up the knife. But the bandage on his right hand made slicing awkward.

"What happened to you?" Maya asked, her eyes snapping into focus.

"I got between the sound and the fury," he said.

"Whass that mean?" River asked as he stirred the stew.

"Sojuhs' brawl," Bird said. "Tried to break it up."

River muttered something under his breath.

"What was that?" Bird asked.

"Not the smartest squab in the roost, Birdie-boy." River shook his head sadly at Bird.

"I noticed," Bird admitted.

"It's a problem," Maya said. Her eyes cleared now as her mind came back into sharp focus. "The Southlanders. We succeeded in subverting their army and bringing the sojuhs over to our side, but now what do we do with them?"

"Sojuhs trained to take orders," River said.

"We could order them to start helping out, and stop leering at the women," Bird said.

"But that won't change them," Maya said. "They've got to want to change, to choose it."

"No way will they ever stop wanting to leer," Bird said. "But a few timely kicks in the *huevos* might teach them not to do it."

"Sojuhs don't make choices," River said.

"You did," Maya retorted.

River stood, looked suddenly dumbstruck, as if the thought were a shock to him.

River had made a choice, Bird thought. The big sojuh had gunned down an entire family, father, brother, sisters, one by one. That was what sojuhs were trained and programmed to do.

But then River had stopped. He'd shot an eight-year-old girl through the head, but when her baby sister and toddler brother stood before him, crying, something had broken inside him. He'd collapsed, screaming and wailing as if all the cries the army had beaten out of him were breaking free at once.

Bird had watched it all, dressed up as one of the sojuhs but in reality, their prisoner, bound by their control. Sometimes when he looked at River the nauseating taste of that helplessness still rose up in his gorge.

If our choices make us who we are, Bird wondered, what do we say about those bitter times when we have no choice? Does helplessness destroy us?

In the end, River had thrown down his gun and opened the door to his own transformation and the City's victory.

Maybe, just maybe, Bird could lay claim to part of that choice. Forced to live and work with the sojuhs and wear their uniform, he had still resisted as he could, reaching out to the sojuh Ohnine that River had been. Maybe that thread of connection had become an umbilical cord, nourishing the sojuh's embryonic self. And that would mean that he, Bird, was in some small measure redeemed.

"I made a choice," River said slowly. "Me. Chose to join you."

I, Bird thought. He says I. That's progress.

"That choice earned you your name," Maya told River. "And your freedom, to make more choices. To construct yourself, choice by choice. Who do you want to be?"

"Gotta be a somebody, to want," he said with some wisdom.

"Got to want, to be a somebody," Maya replied.

"How many tonight?" Bird asked, getting hand-thrown, stoneware soup bowls down from the shelves.

"Just us, and maybe Holybear," Maya said.

"He should be getting off shift," Bird said. "Just saw him—he helped Madrone repair the damage." He cradled the bowls a bit awkwardly in his sore hand. "She'll be late, as always."

Maya shook her head. "They're running her into the ground."

"Believe me, I've noticed," Bird said. "But she likes it that way. What about Katy and Mary Ellen and the little ones?"

"They moved into the mother's house, today," Maya told him. "Housing Guild found them places, and they jumped on it."

Bird nodded. When Madrone had come back from the Southlands, she'd brought a train of refugees back with her. For a while, they'd filled the house with life and babies' cries and dirty diapers, like the old days. But it was a lot of noise for Maya, and, he admitted, for him. He appreciated the quiet.

River set a spoon down in front of Maya, another in front of Bird. "Sit down with us," Bird told him. "Eat."

He still has to be invited, Bird thought. He doesn't yet really understand that he is a part of this household.

River sat, and held out his hands. Madrone always insisted on a blessing, and River expected it. Bird joined his good hand to River's, and Maya gently rested her fingers on Bird's bandages. He looked at Maya, but she simply smiled and nodded to him to begin.

"Thank you, Mother of Life, for this food, and for all the lives of all the creatures, the plants, and the animals that go into it. Thank you to the human hands who grew it and tended it and brought it to us, and cooked it for us. Blessed be."

The door banged downstairs, and they heard swift feet ascend the stairs. Holybear opened the kitchen door, peeling off his white medical robes and revealing the gauzy pastels that he favored beneath. They clashed with his red hair, and the heavy work boots he wore weren't quite the right footwear. But he stood for hours on his shifts at the healing center. Although his true calling was biological research, he was medically trained and filled in now, when the need was so great, working alongside Madrone.

"Just in time!" Maya gave him a smile.

"Excellent! I am hungry as the proverbial bear for whom I am named!" He quickly washed his hands at the sink and joined them.

"How's the hand?" he asked Bird.

"Hasn't fallen off yet. In spite of your best efforts. What'd you use to clean the wound, porcupine skin?"

Holybear smiled.

"Thoroughness is my watchword." Holybear helped himself to a big dish of stew. "Had me worried, there. The human mouth is a cesspool. And I'm not just talking about the language Madrone said she used."

"What are you talking about?" Maya asked.

Bird told them the whole story, as they ate the fragrant stew. It was hearty, full of squash from the garden and the shredded meat from an

"I thought you wanted me to be cautious and sensible and safe?"
Maya batted his uninjured hand. "Not on the table! Barbarian!"
"Why not? It's already as scarred as a battlefield." As I am, he
thought. But she's right. I want to go back.

He got himself a cutting board from under the counter and resumed
his slicing.

"I didn't say that," Maya went on. "I just want you to be strategic.
You and I both know what needs to be done."

Bird met her eyes. They were sharp and clear. She saw his desire, and
what he wouldn't even admit to himself, his fear.

"Doesn't take a military genius to figure out that they'll be back
again, if something doesn't change down there," Maya said. "Even a
fuzzy-headed old woman can see that through a cataractal fog."

"You're about as fuzzy as a laser."

Maya laid a gentle hand on his bandaged hand. "Afraid?" she
asked softly, so that only he could hear. "That's normal. Nothing to be
ashamed about."

"No. Or at least, yeah, of course I'm afraid, I'm not an idiot," he
admitted. "But that wouldn't stop me." How to say, I'm afraid you're
dying and I don't want to leave you alone? "It's just that I want to savor
this time we have together."

"But the time to go is now," she said.

"Then let someone else go!"

Maya gave him a long, steady look from beneath her brows.

"No one else can do what you can do."

"What?"

"How are you going to liberate a bunch of people who have no idea
what liberation means?" she asked.

"I don't know. Believe me, I've thought about it!"

"You're my grandson," Maya said. "Tell the story. Sing the song."

Chapter Three

SMOKEE SAT IN THE PROW OF THE *DAY OF VICTORY*, WATCHING IT PLOW through the waves and leaving trails of foam behind. Her head was cold, and the wind fingered the stubble of her hair, just beginning to grow back from the last shaving in the pens. She raised the hood of the soft gray sweatshirt Sara had loaned her.

The wind smelled good, wild and free, and the light played on the water, making a sparkly track between the boat and the sun. No matter how fast the boat went, or what direction it turned, the track remained, a road of light leading to a great, white blaze.

Something taut and hot within her began to dissolve. But instantly, she was on guard again, clenching tight to all her reasons for rage and despair. If she let herself relax, if she allowed herself to be flooded by this beauty, how could she ever bear to lose it, as she surely would?

Yet without something, some taste of happiness, no one could live. She had pictured that one day at the beach again and again, feeling the soft sand that burned her bare feet and her little brother padding back and forth to the water with his small pail, laughing as the waves covered his toes. That was where she went, while her body was used for service. Her refuge in the worst of moments. Her sanctuary. If life offered her nothing else of joy or grace, at least she had that.

And this, this unexpected day on the water. She could double her wealth of memories in a day, if she dared to. Memories were better than hope. Memories could not disappoint you.

But did she want new memories? Did she want this new life that was dropped on her?

At first, after her relinquishment, each breath had seemed like a victory. Each morning when she opened her eyes, still alive, she vanquished the forces that negated her. And, even caged as she was, she continued to cherish a small nugget of hope that she might yet find a chink in the bars.

But hope was the cheater, the deceiver. It had begun to desert her in the breaking pens, that nightmare of pain and violation and utter helplessness. It trickled away with her sweat in that airless, sweltering cell, leaked out through the ache of her arms as they wrenched against the shackles that bound her day and night, gusted out with her screams when they "disciplined" her with the neural probes that left no marks but triggered tidal waves of overwhelming pain. When they'd decided she was sufficiently softened up, they let the grunts have her, one after another, hour after hour, and each thrust had pounded the hope out of her, until at last they hammered into her deepest, most intimate places the truth—that there was no escape, no refuge, no barrier they could not breach, no sanctum they could not despoil.

And then, when hope was utterly gone, they replaced it with her first sweetie—a bun of spongy cake wrapped around synthetic cream.

After weeks of nothing but salty chips, her body greeted the sugar with joy. She ate one and began to feel a delicious sense of release and relaxation, a warmth and languor running through her limbs. She ate another, and then another.

Into her euphoria came an awareness of something heavy on top of her, grunting and sweating and stinking of iron and blood. But she didn't mind. She felt beneficent, floating somewhere high above the rutting of her body. And when it was over, and she began to feel the bruises and the pain, there was another sweetie to take away the edge.

Occasionally, she woke in the middle of the night, when the drugs wore off, and she stared out at the darkness in horror, as if it were a mirror of the void that she'd become. She wanted to refuse the sweeties, but each day when they came, her body betrayed her, craving the sweetness and the release. With each mouthful, she despised herself more, until in her brief moments of consciousness she wanted not to live but to nullify the last fumes and vapors of Smokee. Then another sweetie would come, bringing blessed oblivion, and away she would float until it no longer mattered.

Until one day she felt something new, a spark inside. Something growing. Battered, raped, shackled, bruised though she was, she held within her the power of Gods. She had created life. And there was within her a sudden flutter of pride awakening again.

At first it was her own secret. Cradling that flicker of life within the confines of her body, she once again became distinct. She had borders, and even when they were breached the very sense of violation proved to her that there was somebody there to be violated. She had a will, a volition, separate from their usage and ends.

The sweeties began to disgust her. No longer could she stomach their chemical sweetness and cloying grease. She shredded them up and flushed them down the toilet with her wastes.

Without them, the service sessions were almost unendurable—the stink, the heavy weight crushing her thin body, wringing out all her will and volition like dishwater from a sponge. Yet she endured. While the sojuhs used her body, she went to the sea, built castles of sand and watched them wash away.

When her pregnancy began to show, she was given a respite. She then understood why the pen-girls were so eager to get pregnant. The condition brought with it new perks—time in the rec room with the other girls, never talking much for they had little to say, but watching the vidscreen in company. Exercise, walking around and around the "yard," a wasteland of asphalt surrounded with barbed wire, but with sky above, and sometimes clouds making shapes and patterns. Months of relative comfort before the birth.

When her due date came, she was strapped down to a table, given drugs to induce her labor on schedule, given other drugs by needle to produce a haze of unconsciousness while the baby was pulled roughly from her womb. When it was over, she awoke sore and in pain but with the comfort of the child itself to hold, to nurse, to cradle. Something alive and precious to love.

The child generated her own fog of anesthesia. Holding her, watching her, mirroring back her baby sounds and expressions, smiling and watching her smile back, was more euphoric than any sweetie. In spite of her better judgment, in spite of the sure knowledge that what awaited them both was pain, Smokee found herself adoring the small being who'd come to her and from her. The lack of any other source of comfort or pleasure only heightened the miracle grace of the child's every gesture, the wondrous music of every coo and cry.

Even though it was forbidden, she gave the child a name. She herself was named after mountains, the Great Smokies of Tennessee where her family came from. But she would name her child after the sea. Azure, she called her, a word that she knew meant "blue."

All the while, a fate hung over her that she simply would not let herself see. She would have time—two years at the least, until the child could walk and talk, maybe three. Sometimes they left them until they were three. They'd found, through experiments she wouldn't let herself think about, that babies taken too early simply failed to thrive and died, that it was more cost-effective to let the mothers feed them and nurture them and teach them the rudiments of language and humanity before moving them on to their ultimate destiny.

A stronger woman, she thought, would kill herself and the child before accepting the fate that was certain for a girl child. She thought about it, considered how to do it. She could fold her ragged blanket into a pillow and gently, firmly press it down over Azure's face. She would croon to her, "Mommy is sorry, so sorry, but it's better this way. Don't cry, child, don't suffer, just sleep. Sleep." Could she really do it? She would do it! But not tonight, maybe tomorrow....

She had time. Something could still happen. She could find a way. Hope seduced her.

But then suddenly she had no time. She'd been sleeping, the child wrapped in her arms, and dreaming of walking with the child on the beach. Azure ran ahead with her funny lurching toddler steps, and fell just at the edge where the dry sand turned to wet. Falling, she laughed, her round blue eyes taking in the bright sunlight dancing on the backs of waves, the marks of wet sand on her chubby knees. She looked back at Smokee with her adoring gaze.

"Bye-bye," Azure waved, and Smokee briefly wondered how she'd learned the word in this place where the one saving grace was that she never went bye-bye.

"Bye-bye," Smokee waved back, smiling, filled with a warmth and a lightness that she slowly, cautiously allowed herself to identify as happiness. They'd waved and smiled and laughed for a long time.

And then a wave came up from the sea, pulling Azure in, sucking her out with the tide.

Smokee awoke, heart pounding. Her arms tightened around the warm, sleeping child. She had one sweet moment of relief, just a dream ... waking back into a day which would be just like any other day, horrific but familiar.

The cell door clanged open. Suddenly two rough billies were holding her down while another grabbed the child and shoved her out the door into a mam's cold arms. She was gone, just that quick—no waves, no smiles, no bye-bye.

Azure had cried and Smokee cried out "No!" She screamed as if she could tear out her throat, as if her guts were pouring out of her mouth, as if she could expel the last of her breath and die. She'd wanted the child to hear her protest. She'd wanted Azure to understand in some deep place below memory that her mother had resisted this rupture with every fiber of her being.

One of the soldiers smacked her across the mouth. Against her own will, she gasped and took air in.

"Shut the fuck up," the soldier barked. "Make another noise, gonna pull out the whelp's arms one by one."

Another scream was rising in her and she swallowed it, for the child's sake, swallowed back all the rage and immense loss, and shoved it harshly down somewhere deep inside.

And now it was as if that swallowed scream was still there, still trying to push its way out.

Maybe now was the moment to let it out, she thought. Yell it out to the waves and let it fly like a tattered banner on the wind, a great No! No to this fucked-up world and all that was in it. No to this beauty that hurt her because her child would never see it, never trail her small hands in the water, or cry Look, Mommy! at a jumping fish.

But the scream remained stuck. The waves were turning colors now, the golden light deepening, casting shadows of purple. The sky was streaked with orange and fuchsia as the sun dipped down to the horizon.

Isis and Sara came up behind her and stood together, their hands entwined, watching as the sun went down. The golden ball sank into blue, became half a ball, a blazing arc, a single star of light. And then, just like that, it was gone.

"Let's eat," Isis said.

Smokee followed them down to the cabin below decks. As ragtag as the *Day of Victory* looked above, it was meticulously neat below. A small stove and sink took up one end of the galley. A table on hinges had been let down between two bunks that doubled as benches. It was set with colorful plates and heaping platters of food—hunks of chicken, newly harvested sweet corn, and a big bowl of salad. The cabin was filled with the inviting fragrance, and Smokee suddenly realized that she was hungry.

But to eat was to live, a commitment she was not sure she wanted to make.

After they took the child, she'd tried to die. A big sojuh had slugged her in the stomach and bound her hands behind her. The billies had bundled her into a van with her night dress and her day dress and toothbrush, and then she was in a cargo truck packed with other girls, listening to a mam give them a lecture on their new opportunity to serve. They were going to the North, with the army of the occupation.

Her breasts cried out for her child. Huddled in a corner of the van, buffeted by every turn and slammed against the wall when it made sudden stops, she willed herself to die. But hope came again, and cheated her. The child was gone, but maybe, just maybe on this trip there would be an opening. Some small crack, a window of escape. Once free, she would become a fury, never resting until the child was restored to her.

So she watched, and waited. In the van, she had found one small hole, a tiny spot where rust had eaten through the metal walls. She could twist around and glue her eye to the hole and watch the landscape roll by, green hills and brown, things that had once been familiar to her and now were only part of her dreams.

But there had been no opening, no escape. In the middle of the night, they reached their destination, and suddenly there was a gun at her head and shackles on her wrists and she was locked into a new cage.

Back in the Southlands, the pens had been long barracks lined with rows of windowless cells, each with its own small vidscreen and wide bed, its tiny alcove with toilet and sink and shower. Pen-girls were required to be clean, to shower between each session. The cells were deadly quiet, soundproofed so no one could eavesdrop on the sojuhs as they grunted in release, or hear a woman's cries of fear or pain.

But in the North, the pens they'd set up to serve the army of the invasion had been far more primitive. A circle of screened cribs, jerry-rigged in an old concrete building that was always cold. Each one held a bare bed and a bucket for wastes, behind a locked door. Pressboard walls separated one from another by sight although they couldn't conceal the sounds. That encouraged the sojuhs to vie with one another, boasting of their prowess and comparing the shrillness and duration of their victims' cries as they drilled and battered their way through living flesh.

Grunting and heaving and endlessly pounding, pounding, driving home into the bowels of her castle the truth that she was nothing, no one, a rag to wipe up spill.

And so she had rebelled against hope. Hope was more potent than fists or drugs at keeping her in chains. She would root out hope, and take the only road of resistance left to her.

She stopped eating. She shredded up the chips and sweeties and crumbled them into a bucket of slops. She grew weaker, but she welcomed her weakness.

But the mams noticed. They noticed everything. When the billies came for her, she fought back, kicking and biting with all the fury in her and all of her waning strength. When they beat her, she welcomed the pain, eager to die. But she didn't. The billies wanted to force-feed her, but the bigsticks said no. Instead, they would make her an example. They would cage her in the center of the rec room and let her slowly starve to death, in view of the others.

"Go ahead and beg for food," the top mam said with a smile as cold as a Final Notice. "You won't get it."

But she didn't beg. She lay on the hard floor of her cage, imagining her body cushioned by warm sand, the tide rolling in and ebbing away, filling moats and wearing down the turrets. And when the last of the walls washed away, she would be free at last.

When the Day of Liberation came, there was not much left of her. A low mound on a smooth beach that one last ripple could demolish. Dimly, she'd become aware of shouting and banging, of screams and yells and in the distance, shots. But she was far, far away on the receding tide, and it meant nothing to her.

"No matter how long you stare at that chicken, it ain't gonna say a word," Isis broke into her reverie. "Might as well sit down and eat it."

"Maybe she can't eat real food," Sara suggested to Isis in a low voice. "Most of them can't."

"I'm no breed!" Smokee said, stung into motion. She sat down. Not a breed, but a breeder, she thought bitterly.

"White meat or dark?" Sara asked. Smokee stared at her, uncomprehending. "Which part of the chicken do you like?"

She couldn't remember the last time she'd had chicken. In the years before the relinquishment, they'd mostly eaten beans, trying to stay on top of the debt. Were there different parts, and what was the difference? She had no idea. She shrugged, and Sara put a breast on her plate.

"White wine or red?" Isis asked. Smokee shrugged. She'd never tasted any kind of wine. Before the relinquishment, her mother said she was far too young. Winos drank it in the alleyways, and she was dimly aware that Primes drank it in their gated estates, but her family contented themselves with water and saved their pennies to put toward the debt. Fat lot of good it did them.

"Try this." Isis poured her a ruby glass full. She picked it up and took a gulp. It was odd-tasting, kind of sour and bitter. She'd thought it would be sweet, like fruit punch. She remembered fruit punch, suddenly—her mother made it from a powder and said it was good for her. It was a treat—both sweet and tart.

"Sip it slowly," Isis said. "Hold it in your mouth. Savor it."

Smokee took a smaller sip and held it. She still didn't much like it, but as she swallowed she felt a warmth steal over her. Her arms were still tight and clenched as if they'd never completely let go of her lost child. With one more sip, they began to relax.

She found herself staring at Isis, the sculpted arms, the long legs striped with muscle. Isis observed her gaze and gave her a long, slow smile.

"A racer?" Smokee asked.

Isis nodded proudly. "Top ten of the Valley Valkyries, three years in a row. On track to run in the All-Region Championships."

"So you're a breed, then," Smokee said to take her down a peg. Fuck her, she thought, why be proud of being a bigsticks' toy. "How'd you get out?"

"Clear your plate, and I might tell you."

Smokee obeyed, partly because she was curious, and partly because she was hungry. And the food tasted better than she wanted to admit.

"Had a sweet stick," Isis went on. "Used to go sailing, just Daddy and his favorite filly, while Mrs. Trophy went to church. Then one sad day, overboard went Mr. Sweet and sugar gal turned pirate."

"And a fine buccaneer you turned out to be!" Sara raised her glass in a toast. "Me, I was a Trophy myself, a breed of a different order. Married to a Prime. Had it all—the big house, the gated estate, the water garden. Hated every minute of it. So I ran off, with a mad healer and a beautiful pirate, and here I am!"

She clinked glasses with Isis, giving her a long promising smile, then turned to Smokee. "How about you? What's your story?"

"Same story as a million others," Smokee shrugged. "Family had debts. Couldn't pay them. When they passed the Relinquishment Law, we didn't run fast enough."

Silence fell. Sara rose and cleared away the plates. Isis poured out the last of the wine. Smokee sat nursing her anger.

She had never found her opening. She had never made her fate. Her only attempt to do so, her last act of resistance, had been thwarted by liberation, and while she knew that she should be grateful, right now she was simply mad.

She had felt good dying. Liberation, in the end, was just another thing that was done to her.

Sara set down small bowls filled with raspberries and covered with cream. Smokee stared at the red berries, the white cream, the pale pink of the china bowls. Yet another good thing her child would never have. But she ate them, savoring the sweet-sharp taste of the berries, the smooth, rich cream.

"So, what you gonna do with yourself?" Sara asked Smokee.

Smokee shrugged.

"It's a different world up here," Sara said. "You could get an education. Become an engineer, or, I don't know. A poet. A sculptor. Whatever you want."

"Don't want anything," Smokee said.

"Give yourself time," Sara said. "You will."

"Or you could fight back," Isis said.

Smokee looked at her. Isis was licking her spoon and smiling like a cat with a secret. "How?"

"You a fighter, sailor. Saw that at the canteen. Ain't killed your spirit."

"Not that you can go around knifing former soldiers at the lunch table," Sara said, spooning another serving of berries into Smokee's bowl. "Richly though they might deserve it."

Isis shrugged. "One chipster more or less, no loss to the world, and his mama already mourned him. But there's better work for a girl like you. Got a little moment here, a breather. Stewards run home with droopy tails. But it won't last. Sooner or later, got to go down there and finish the job, or the sharks come back up here and finish us off."

"We're going to need fighters," Sara said.

"And not just squirts and jellydicks," Isis said. "Women are smarter."

"And meaner," Sara added.

"Don't know anything about fighting," Smokee said.

"She'll train you," Sara said, looking at Isis. "She'll train us all."

Isis was no longer focused on them. Her head was up, her ear cocked toward the open porthole. She waved them quiet.

At first, Smokee heard nothing but the lapping of the waves. Then she became aware of a low vibration, like the thrum of a faraway engine.

"Hear that?" Isis asked. Sara nodded.

Isis opened the door and went up on deck. Sara and Smokee followed.

The last glow of summer twilight lingered on the horizon. The bright stars cast light from above, just enough for them to make out something squat and ungainly coming toward them. The thrum grew louder.

"What the Jesus is that?" Sara asked.

"It's big," Isis said. "And it's coming from the south. Let's go take a look."

"How? Not much wind tonight for a sail."

"Plenty juice in the batteries."

Smokee watched as Isis and Sara quietly rigged a light air sail to catch the slight breath of wind. Isis fired up the electric outboard, and took the tiller. The boat began to skim toward the sound.

The dark silhouette grew and resolved into geometric shapes, long, low, boxy, big as a football field. It was hard to see details in the dim light, but it had the prow of a warship cobbled together with the flat field of an old aircraft carrier. On its back was a huge array of some kind of equipment, a parabolic disc, like a radar disc, and a metal tower.

"They're back," Sara said. "I think we'll find in the morning, if not before, that we're in radio silence again."

Smokee heard a high whistle, barely audible, and suddenly Isis jammed over the tiller and gunned the engine. The boat scooted forward on a diagonal path away from the warship, just as the sea exploded behind them.

"Grab hold!" Isis yelled as the wake of the blast tossed the little boat up and down and sideways. Below decks, china crashed and glass tinkled. Smokee grabbed the rail and clung hard as the deck bucked beneath her feet. A wave washed over her, drenching her to her waist. Then the boat lurched to starboard and set a zigzag course away from the warship.

"Now is that a friendly way to say hello?" Isis shook her head.

"How'd they see us?" Smokee asked.

"Must have good radar. Wonder what the range of their guns is?"

"We're about to find out," Sara said, as another shell whistled overhead. Isis banked sharply, and it missed them by a hundred yards, but this time the wake of the explosion pitched them sharply up into the air.

"Duck!" Sara yelled as the boom came about. Smokee fell flat and it swung over her head, but then the deck seemed to drop away beneath her. She was falling—but then it rose again, slamming into her. For a moment, she couldn't breathe. Another wave washed over her, leaving her drenched and shivering. She was filled with a sharp, primal terror as she fought for breath. Her hands scrabbled on the wet boards of the deck and caught hold of a post. She clung on as the aft deck dipped down into the trough of a wave only to be caught by the wash of another explosion on their right. They were sinking. She was drowning. And she was on fire with rage because she knew, now, how much she wanted to live.

Ironic, how hard she'd worked to die. But she wanted to sail and fight and search for her daughter, to rescue her if she were still alive or avenge her if she were dead. And yes, she wanted more for herself too, more days like today on the peaceful sea. One fucking day of happiness was not enough for a lifetime.

"Fuck you!" she screamed into the wind, and became aware that the boat had righted itself and nosed its prow into sweet air. She gulped it eagerly. How good it felt in her lungs! She drew it in, deep, and then she was laughing as the boat pulled forward. Another shell boomed behind them, but they were beyond the range of danger now, the wake was soft as a lullaby compared to what had gone before.

"You okay?" Isis asked Smokee.

She stood above her, the water plastering her clothes to her sculpted form, with Sara beside her, blond hair dripping, her wet shirt clinging to her.

"You know, back in the day, I always fantasized about having adventures," Sara said. "But nobody warned me that they'd be cold and wet."

Smokee pulled herself up to her feet. "Let's do it again!"

"That's the warrior spirit!" Sara smiled back, and handed her a life jacket. "Remind me next time we go chasing warships to put these on first. Can you swim?"

Smokee shook her head.

"We'll teach you," Sara said.

"Teach me to fight."

Chapter Four

BIRD SAT AT THE PIANO IN HIS OWN BEDROOM. AROUND HIM WERE the mementos of his boyhood: guitars, pictures on the wall, an old catcher's mitt, and a basketball stuffed in the corner. The room was small, and the baby grand took up most of it. There was no room for a bed. He shared Madrone's, in her room, or threw a sleeping bag down on the floor if he needed privacy.

He tried a scale. His bandaged hand hurt. All of his fingers were stiff with old breaks, relics of his last tour of the Southlands. But he had made Holybear and Madrone leave the fingers free so he could play. His hand would heal with more flexibility if he exercised it, although he would never have the skill and flexibility that young Bird had taken for granted. But he forced himself to practice daily, even when it hurt.

Whatever else he did or didn't do, he could do his scales. It was an ongoing act of resistance, a refusal to let them take away more of who he was.

Every now and then, as he ran up and down the keyboard, boring himself with the simplest of finger exercises, he would hear something, some echo or trace of the Great Music. When he did, he would pick up the tablet that lay on the piano top and sing into it, and it would record his voice and notate the tune. Then he could program guitar or rhythm or keyboards. The synthed instruments didn't have the tone, those slight variations that gave a live performance its vibrant quality, but they allowed the music inside him to come out.

He sang, punched in a rhythm backup, and listened. Not bad. He could add orchestration, and that would make it richer.

He heard a knock on the door. Madrone slipped in without waiting for an answer and sat on the bench beside him.

"What's the point of knocking if you're just going to come in anyway?" he said, without stopping his practice.

Why am I pushing her away? he wondered. When what I really want to do is just wrap my arms around her and bury my head in her breasts and never move again.

"What's the point of coming in if you're not even going to stop playing and look at me?" she retorted.

"I will in a minute, as soon as I finish this."

Because if I give in to that desire, I'll never have the strength of will to pull myself back from that sweet distraction to this frustrating tedium, this continual reminder of what I'm not.

She leaned against him. *Diosa*, she was so tired! She breathed in his scent, absorbing some vital energy from his presence. He was so focused, so concentrated on his exercises. For a moment she felt like she was eight years old again, kicking her feet in boredom as he endlessly practiced, trying to get him to come out and play. She plunked an experimental finger down on a key.

"No you don't!" he said. It was their game. Let's pretend we don't need each other so desperately, that we don't listen for the door, keep an ear always cocked for some new catastrophe. Pretend that we have so much time to squander we can afford to waste it.

She snatched her hand away, but a few minutes later, she banged a key again.

"You're pushing it!" he warned.

"My, you are Mister Growly Bear." Madrone began to play chopsticks, the only tune she knew.

"Now you're living dangerously!"

"It's a big piano. Learn to share!"

"This piano ain't big enough for the both of us."

"Hog!"

"You want to learn to play, I'll give you lessons." He inched closer to her, slid his arms around her.

"You did, when I was eight years old. This is what I learned." She sped up the tempo and banged out the chords of chopsticks with gusto, laughing as he tried to grab her hands.

"You never practiced." Now he had them, placing his fingers over hers, his bandaged paw against her delicate hand, her body warm against his, the scent of her hair enfolding him.

"How could I practice when you were always so far ahead of me?"

"Now I'm back to your level. We could start again."

"I could think of something else we could start." It really didn't matter what they said. They were like mated songbirds, peeping back and forth to confirm one another's presence. She was happy just sitting next to him, feeling the comfort of his nearness. She'd spent hours here when she was a little girl, restless but not wanting to leave his side. Something about him, even then, made her feel safe when she'd so badly needed a sense of safety. When the City and the house and Maya and her grandmother, Johanna, and her grandfather, Rio, were all strange to her, and she had ached with longing for her mother, who was dead.

She'd tried to hide under this same piano as a child on the day of the Uprising, when the soldiers of the then-newly formed Stewardship marched in. Bird had coaxed her out, and given her his favorite shell.

"This will protect you," he said, and all the while he was gathering his catcher's mitt and his skateboard and heading out into the action. And in some sense, the action had never ended, not for him, not for her. More than two decades later, and she was exhausted from a day spent mopping up the wounds of its latest round.

"What are you thinking?" she turned toward him and nuzzled his ear.

"I'm thinking about discipline. Will power. And what an undermining influence you are."

"I'm being very restrained," she said. "What if I did ... this?" She took her hands out from under his and ran her fingers up along his back, stroking the nape of his neck. She felt him shiver under her touch.

Resolutely, he returned to his scales.

"Or this ... " She played a scale on his thigh, then continued up to feel a hard swelling in his jeans.

He stopped playing.

"Don't let me interrupt your practice." She pressed her hand against him. He was warm and hard and full under her touch.

"A fighter has needs," he breathed.

"Are you a fighter?"

"I could be a lover."

"Shall we give it a try?"

───

There are so many ways that making love restores the soul, Madrone thought as she pulled him into her bedroom. Not just the animal passion, but the choices. Clothed or unclothed. Gentle or rough. She lit a candle, then pulled off his shirt, and ran her hand over the hard muscles of his chest and belly. He was as nicked and scarred as a battered old tomcat, but under her touch his skin felt new, electric, innocent.

He unbuttoned her healer's robes, folded them with the care a soldier might fold a flag at the end of day, and laid them on a chair. He unbuttoned his own jeans and dropped them on the floor, standing before her proud and ready. She lifted her undertunic over her head, peeled down her tights. For a long moment, they just looked at each other in the flickering light.

We're still young, she thought. With all that's happened to us, all we've done. We still have so much life in us.

His lips found hers. His tongue traced a snail-track down her throat, around her breasts, over the slight mound of her belly, flicking in and out of her navel, leaving a trail of fire. Deep inside her, a hot coal smoldered and as he pulled her down on top of him, as he probed her with tongue and lips and hot breath she blazed with need and desire. And then she was riding him, beyond thought, plunging herself down deeper and deeper as if to draw his heat into her very cells. It was life itself, pulsing through her, flame licking flame until two fires were one.

Heat filled her, genes and cells smoldering with a primal desire—to kindle new life. A baby, she thought. I want one. One of my own. Our own.

She cried out, with the joy of it, and his cries joined with hers in a great, shuddering flare. Then she lay in his arms, basking in that sense of comfort and peace.

All those hundreds of babies I've delivered, she thought. Now my body craves one of its own. She scanned her own womb, using her healer's senses. Had she already conceived? No, it was the wrong time of her moon cycle. But had it been just a few days later ...

They would have to talk, she realized. But not now. Now he had drifted into a peaceful sleep, sleep that he needed so badly and found so hard to achieve. Her own exhaustion came back to her as well. She nestled in his arms, and let herself drift away.

Bird and Madrone stood on the shores of a blue lake, cradled in the green arms of the high mountains. They were standing, naked in the sunlight, their hands up and their palms touching. And his hands were whole again, undamaged, full of fluid strength and control.

So that was all it took, he thought, for the healing. They smiled at each other. He was filled with peace.

But then their hands were on a table in a cold, concrete room, and a faceless guard stood above them with a hammer.

"What's it going to be, slime, you or her?"

"Her!" he cried out, and the hammer came down. He heard the bones crunch, heard her scream as her healing hands were smashed into jelly and his own voice kept crying, "Her! Her! Not me, not me!"

He sat bolt upright in bed, sweat cold on his naked back, and she was stroking him and soothing him.

"It's okay. It's okay, Bird. It's just a dream."

But her touch pained him. He felt as guilty as if he really had betrayed her. Surely he had betrayed someone, something, to earn this deep remorse.

But I never did, he reminded himself. Every time they had us in that room—not Madrone but Rosa, poor unlucky child—every time they faced me with that choice, I said me. Whatever else I did, or didn't do, I can hold to that. And if I'm faced with it again, in the changing fortunes of these wars, I can remember that there is some small part of me they never broke.

But his sense of guilt remained.

I'm a healer, Madrone thought. I accompany my patients into the worst of their pain, even to the edge of the dark pillars, the final threshold. It's my job, to stand beside them, so that when the worst comes at them they are not alone.

Yet she couldn't accompany Bird into the places he had gone. The doors were locked with secret combinations she couldn't guess.

Would he ever open them? The nightmares were getting more frequent. The war was not over yet. She suspected that he was trying to work up the courage to go back, down to the Southlands again. That if he could indeed ever truly come back home, he would do it only by dragging the liberated Southlands behind him.

The thought terrified her, for she knew that if he went, she would want to accompany him on that perilous journey.

And what about having a baby? she thought. I couldn't go down there if I were pregnant, couldn't risk having a child who could suffer an unimaginable fate. Yet if he went, I couldn't stay behind, safe in the garden with his child.

Now is not the time for a baby, she admitted to herself reluctantly. Even to talk about it would be to lay another unbearable burden on him. He carried enough guilt.

Yet to not talk about it, to keep the singing desire to herself, created one more locked door, one more hidden chamber. Something else to hide.

But that's part of my burden, she thought. Healers by nature are secret keepers.

"You want to talk about the dream?" she asked gently. "It can help."

He shook his head.

"You can't do this," he said to her bitterly. "You can't heal all day and fuck all night and then wake up before dawn with my fraggin' nightmares."

"I'm a healer," she said, her fingers tracing a tender circle over his third eye. "I can do whatever it takes to make it better."

"Some things don't get better," he said. "Some wounds don't heal."

Chapter Five

GENERAL DEMARCUS JOHN WENDELL HAD A POUNDING HEADACHE. He had stood in the blazing sunlight for over an hour as the Primes made speeches and the Retributionist preachers droned and the ceremony marking his promotion to general dragged on. He considered himself a deeply religious man, but where in the Bible or the Book of Retribution was it written, he wondered, that one must pontificate at such great length when the heat was stifling? He, of course, had to stand at attention, stone-faced and imperturbable, no matter that he was just out of the hospital recovering from the injury which was even now causing his head to throb.

He supposed he should be grateful, and bless the pain. If he hadn't been blown unconscious in the final battle in that godless city, he would undoubtedly have felt it his duty to stay beside General Alexander, the fool, until the bitter end. And now be lying in a northern grave, or worse, a demon-haunted prison cell.

Instead, he'd awakened three weeks ago from a five-day coma in the military hospital of the Slotown garrison where the remnants of his army had brought him as they fled. Had he been in a state to give orders, he would have demanded they stay and fight to the last skittering sojuh and blundering breed. Unconsciousness had bought his defeat, but also his life.

He sighed, and sat down gingerly on the hope chest at the foot of the king-sized bed he shared with his wife, Pammela. Slowly, he bent down toward his shoe, but the motion set off a bout of vertigo, like someone was pounding a spike into his forehead. He moaned softly.

It had been hard to stand there silently, listening to Head Prime Mather Culbertson spout lies. "A great victory!" he had proclaimed. If only that were true! A complete and utter rout would have been more accurate.

Never mind. Wendell benefited from the lie. They'd had to promote him, in part to help to maintain the illusion that the war on the North had been anything other than an absolute failure. Besides, no one else was left who had the experience and know-how to step into Alexander's empty shoes. The promotion was more than he could have expected in any other circumstance, since he and his family clung to their Old Church beliefs instead of jumping on the Retributionist bandwagon, or should he say, chariot. He appreciated that Alexander had always protected Wendell's church, First Faithful, from the Retros' drive to gather in every flock from all the old denominations. Now he would be in position to do the same.

And there were side benefits. They could expand the house, like Pammela wanted. Paige and Palin could each have their own rooms, and they could get Landry a car.

Pammela was a good wife, modest and selfless. Had they turned Retro, he could have added a few concubines or a stable of Trinkets who officially had no immortal souls, if he'd been so inclined. With this promotion, had he wanted to, he could have put her away and gotten himself a Trophy.

But he didn't approve of that. A wife was a wife, to his mind, as Old Church doctrine held, and he mistrusted the dispensations the Retributionist preachers were eager to hand out to powerful Primes and commanders. Pammela wasn't the youngest thing around, and she was no great beauty, not at her age, although she'd been pretty enough when they first married. Blond curls that now he suspected would be tinged with gray if she didn't color them. Generous breasts now grown flaccid with childbearing. But she'd given him six children, four of them boys, and she was quiet and easygoing and looked after him.

No, it was his duty to stay with her and keep her.

As if she'd heard him thinking, she appeared, knelt gracefully at his feet and untied his shoes. She slipped them off, and peeled off his socks. He favored her with a little nod, indicating that he was open to conversation. That was one of the things he appreciated about her. She didn't burst into a room assaulting a man with every half-brained thought in her mind, but waited instead to feel out whether or not he was in the mood to talk.

"How's the headache, dear?" she asked in her low voice. It irritated him, sometimes, that she spoke so softly he had to strain to hear her. But now it was soothing to his throbbing skull.

"'I am the anvil, God wields the hammer,'" he quoted. It was from the Book of Retribution, not the Old Christian Bible, but it spoke to his condition.

She looked at him with concern. "You should rest," she said. "I'll bring you a nice glass of cold water and your pain pills."

The bed at his back was tempting as sin, but he knew he had to resist a little while longer. He started to shake his head, then winced.

"Is Livingston here?"

"He's in the study. But he could come back later."

"Better now. Just help me out of this circus suit, and you can bring us drinks."

"You know what the doctor said about drinking with the head injury ... "

"Don't nag. I'm not an imbecile! Ice water for me, whiskey for him. Now get me out of this over-ornamented straitjacket!"

Wendell had given Pammela free rein in the decoration of his study, and she had gone full force for the wood-paneled, old-leather atmosphere of an English men's club. The dark walls dimmed the blaring light of a Southlands' summer afternoon, and Wendell was grateful for that, and for the comfort of the winged chair that enveloped him. His wife dutifully brought them a tray with a pitcher of ice water and a selection of stronger drinks for his companion, along with cheese straws and pretzels and a cool pillow which she gently molded to support his head. He should get her something, he thought, to celebrate his new status. Maybe a nice piece of jewelry, or that antique mirror she'd set her heart on.

And then, as a good wife should, she left.

Naval Lieutenant Adam Livingston was standing by the fireplace, looking at the Greek vases that lined the mantel. They were the pride of Wendell's collection, or at least, they were the ones he deemed safe for public display, with no overt nudity or perverted sex acts depicted. Those, which might be heretical but which he still considered very beautiful, were safely locked away in his inner sanctum. He'd rescued a lot of them from museums during the Retributionist purges.

These vases marched across the mantelpiece in soldierly formation, befitting the scenes of long-ago battles and victories from ages past that adorned their sides.

"I see you're something of a connoisseur, General," Livingston said, turning toward him. Blond and boyish-faced, he loomed above Wendell. "Congratulations on your promotion, by the way."

"In a kinder, gentler world, I would have made a good archaeologist," Wendell said. "Sit down."

Livingston folded his lanky body gracefully into an armchair, and observed Wendell through cool, gray eyes that looked amused by some secret only they knew. Wendell waved at the drink tray. "Help yourself."

"Thank you, sir." Livingston poured a dollop of whiskey into a glass already supplied with ice. He raised it up.

"To the newest commander of our army, your health!"

Wendell raised his glass, and Livingston leaned forward and clinked his against it.

"And to our great victory in the North!" Livingston added with an ironic twist to his smile. Wendell was not at all sure he liked him, but he'd reviewed the files and Livingston was the brightest of the rising young men of the navy, top of his class in every test of potential or performance.

"Let's not waste time," Wendell said. "I've read your files, and I know you're not an idiot. I assume you know what the true situation in the North is?"

Livingston nodded, and his smile deepened as he lifted his glass.

"While I was unfortunately incapacitated," Wendell went on, "the posterior orifices in charge of the navy decided to send a new warship up there. Must have been AWOL on the day the Good Lord handed out brains!"

"I won't quote you on that, sir," Livingston said.

"You won't quote me on anything," Wendell assured him. "But believe me, they know my opinion. Meatheads! We only have three destroyers in the fleet, we've got privateers from the Gyre slathering their jaws to attack our shipping, we just got our asses seriously kicked and they send a third of our fleet off into hostile waters, for what? What the dickens do they expect it to do?"

"I believe the strategic goal is to keep the North under radio silence, sir."

"Bull deposits! For what? five minutes? Now that they've had a couple of weeks to make contacts and set up shortwave bands and codes? What would you do if you were the North?"

"Me, sir?" He gave a smile and a shrug. "Either I'd capture it and use it myself, or I'd blow it out of the water."

"Exactly. And that's exactly what we can't afford at this moment." Wendell took a sip of the water. The icy coldness made his headache worse. Dear Jesus, you should have kept me in that coma longer!

"I won't lie to you, Livingston. You're a smart man. You must know that our defenses are stretched thin as a supermodel. I'm not kidding when I say that if the North decided to attack us now, we'd be in bad shape to fight them off."

Livingston nodded. "So, what can I do for you, sir?"

"We need to know what their plans are. We need a spy in their ranks."

Livingston set his drink down, stood up, and turned back toward the mantel. He picked up one of the cups, examined the red-figure portrait of combat between two heroes with shields held high and swords raised.

"I'm looking for the right man to send north. To join the crew on the warship, and then find a way to defect."

"Sounds like a dangerous assignment," Livingston observed.

"Not really. They love defectors, the squabs do. Take them in, open their wormy trugger hearts, and throw their arms around them in a big, fat hug. Biggest danger would be lice, to my mind, or suffocation. But a smart man would be able to report back on all their plans. Would that be you?"

Livingston set the cup down.

"Heroes, the Greeks were," he observed. "Imagine the blood and stink and mess of it—battles with bronze swords and chariots."

"You are my top choice for this mission. But I won't order you to do it. It's the kind of thing a man can only do of his own free will."

"I'll give it my deepest consideration, sir." Livingston turned and favored Wendell with an earnest smile.

Wendell nodded. "As I said, I've read your file. Your father manages a chip factory. Your mother has social aspirations. You and your brothers are all navy men, but you'll never make top command even though you're ten times smarter than that crew of paddledicks. No, you're from the wrong class. Never rise higher than XO to some dunderhead captain. But that could change. War provides opportunity for a military man."

Livingston gave another long, slow smile, and raised his drink to the General.

"I understand. Sir, it would be an honor."

The General raised his own glass. "Here's to honor!"

"Here's to victory!"

Chapter Six

WAKING AND DREAMING ... DREAMING AND WAKING. THE EDGE between them blurred for Maya these days. But she was awake, lying in a warm bed with feeble rays of sun attempting to push their way through the blanket of summer fog. Or maybe she was dreaming.

She was lying on an edge. Edge of the sea, with the small waves of the turning tide sneaking in. Naked, nothing between her skin and the wind and sun and sand. Oh, she was young, flesh still bursting with juice, smooth as a nectarine. Rio was with her, young and strong and unbroken, muscles swelling in golden arms, that thin yellow fur of his covering his back like the fuzz on a baby chick.

They were making love at the water's edge, sun on his butt-cheeks, his hands probing her secret pools and outcroppings. Desire rose in her, swelling like the moon-pulled tide, and she rolled atop him and rode him like the wild horses of the sea until the great wave peaked and crashed down.

She must be having a sweet dream, Bird thought, with that look of bliss on her face. He didn't have the heart to wake her. He took the tray of soup and a cheese sandwich back to the kitchen, with his worries. Madrone was at the healing center, as always. Today was River's day to be out and about in the City. And he was here, cleaning up as best he could with his wounded hand. Nursing one old woman, whom he loved. And yet he felt that love as a tether. His deepest tie, his constraint!

A warship! Isis and Sara had reported a warship out beyond the Golden Gate. It had begun.

As if they'd learned nothing from the last invasion, the City continued in its slow, deliberative way. Tending flowers, planting seeds as if nothing might uproot them. Debating and ruminating in all of its intricate layers of councils and guilds and work groups.

The techies laughed at the blanket of silence the warship broadcast over the Bay. It amused them. They picked holes in it, undetectable by the Southlanders' instruments. When they felt like it, they claimed, they could crash the system entirely.

Let it sit there, was the general sentiment. Let them think they have us under surveillance. The warship we see is easier to cope with than what else they might send if we turn it back. Let them think they have us under their control.

But Bird was not so sure. The warship they could see might just be a cover for spies or worse assaults that they couldn't see.

He took his restlessness and his worries out to the garden. Well-mulched, well-tended, the beds offered little opportunity to lose himself in physical work. He ripped out the few weeds he saw as if they were the outliers of an assault force, took up a pitchfork and attacked the compost pile.

The garden took up the whole center of the block of old Victorians. Long ago, Maya and her neighbors had combined backyards, taken down fences, dug ponds and built beds and chicken runs and islands for ducks. It was a beautiful, fragrant space, filled with flowers and ripe squash and tomatoes, rich with greens. The late afternoon light made the crimson cannas glow and turned the red-veined leaves of chard to stained glass.

He became aware of a shadow that ducked quickly away. He turned, and set the pitchfork down.

Rosa, who lived with the Sisters in the convent next door. Rosa, whom he had tried so hard to shield from the Stewards' tortures. Rosa, whom he had so badly failed.

"Hey." He gave her an uncertain smile. She turned away.

Why wasn't she with her Learning Group? Was she still recovering from her imprisonment?

"Want some tomatoes?"

She fled, pounding up the stairs and slamming the door.

That hurt. But he didn't blame her.

He stared at the tomato plants, bowed down under the weight of scarlet fruit. But he no longer saw them. He saw the old, scarred linoleum on the floor of the cell where the Stewards had kept him, those last weeks of the invasion after he'd been captured. After he'd been tortured, pressured between beyond his ability to resist, after he'd given in and recanted and given in again.

His cell had been improvised from an old office building. Between bouts of torture, he'd lain on the cold floor that was covered with battered squares of linoleum. At first he had counted them, left to right, up to down, just to keep the fear at bay. And then he had stopped counting, because it sickened him to be a creature who spent his days counting square after square to keep from going mad.

Maybe madness would have been preferable to that stalwart effort to keep it back. But he had tried madness before, during his time in prison in the Southlands. Or at least, he had tried locking away his mind, turning his memories to stone to shield them from the Stewards' probes.

It had worked, partially. He'd kept silent under interrogation, then, even as they'd broken his hands. He'd convinced them they'd broken his mind as well.

And maybe they had. That was his secret fear. When he woke sweating from his nightmares, he couldn't always convince himself that they hadn't.

And so, when they'd captured him again, he couldn't take refuge in madness, feigned or real. No, he was like the boy in the story with his finger in the dike to keep out the rising sea, and the wave that threatened to swamp him was no ordinary swell but a tsunami. If it hit he would go under, and never surface again.

So he'd resumed counting. Fifty-three to the right, forty-seven down if you don't count the one that was broken, with that gouge in the edge. You could use up a lot of time pondering the shapes that it made, trying to decide if it were the angry face of an outraged god or the laughing face of a conqueror.

He grew to hate the damn squares. After a time, instead of keeping fear at bay, the sight of the floor brought back not the pain, but what was worse—the sick nausea of pain's anticipation.

Yet he couldn't stop himself from counting. There was nothing else to do.

He'd gone to see Rosa the day after the victory, when she was still in the healing center. She had wounds that were being treated, and other damage he didn't ask about. They'd shorn her beautiful chestnut braids, and shaved her head in the Stewards' prison. With her bruises and the dark hollows under her huge, dark eyes, her face so painfully thin, she looked like a refugee from a concentration camp or a cancer victim.

He'd brought her roses from the garden, a bouquet red as blood, and he'd entered her room and dredged up a smile, a shard he'd had to excavate from some long-buried deposit.

She returned it with a stretch of the lips, then turned her head away.

"How are you?" he had asked.

She didn't answer. He'd added the roses to vases already overfilled, tucking their thorny stems in, feeling them abrade the softer stems of lilies and cornflowers.

"Can I get you anything? Do something for you?"

She'd turned her head to the other side, and closed her eyes.

"Soon you'll be better," he'd tried to sound hearty and cheerful, but even to himself it seemed a lame attempt. "We could get back to your piano lessons, if you still want to."

At that she sat up. She spat words at him. "I hate the piano!"

He understood. He had failed to keep her safe, and now his presence would always be a living reminder of her violation.

He was her linoleum.

Rosa watched from the back window until Bird left the garden, and then crept back down to sit in the sunlight. She liked the garden because it felt enclosed and safe, a quiet oasis of peace and stillness. There was always something to do—chickens to feed or check for eggs, rabbit poop to rake up and compost, new seedlings to set out. Something she could do without having to talk to anyone or see anyone.

She didn't know what to say to people. She'd tried to go back to her Learning Group but she couldn't stand the way they looked at her with those pitying, sickening looks. Or worse, glanced away and wouldn't look at her at all.

In fact, she didn't quite know how to be with herself. She wasn't quite sure who she was.

It's as if everything that happens to you makes you a different person, she thought. She had learned that first when her father died in the big epidemic, and she had changed overnight from being lucky and happy little Rosa to someone that other people looked upon with pity. Her mother, too, had become a different person, not the laughing, cuddling, cozy mom she loved but a silent and weepy mom. And then she too had died, and the baby whose birth would have made Rosa a big sister had died, and she had become someone else again, an orphan who lived not with her own family any more but with the Sisters, who lived next door to Bird and Madrone and Maya. Sister Marie, her mother's friend, had founded it long before Rosa was born as a satellite to the much larger mother house where now the former pen-girls lived.

It was Sister Marie who took her in after her mother died, and now she too was dead, and the other Sisters were more like friendly strangers than family. They looked at her with that pity in their eyes, and she tried hard to be good because she felt like she was their guest. Maybe after a few more years it would have worn off and she would have begun to feel at home, but before that had had a chance to happen, the army marched in. And everything changed again.

She wished she could talk to Maya about it. But Maya lived in the big house with Bird, and she couldn't bear to see him or to go over there again. A different Rosa had loved to sneak over and talk with Maya at the big kitchen table. She had always been begging to play Bird's piano, before he came back from the Southlands. On the wall, facing the piano, hung his picture, dressed in camo, smiling with bravado and confidence, the brave warrior who'd gone down to the Southlands to fight and never come back. She'd liked gazing at it while she played his songs, and imagining what it would feel like to be a hero.

She had wanted to be like him, like she thought he was. Someone brave, who faced huge dangers and laughed at them. But then he did come back, not the hero she'd imagined but a haunted man, who taught her piano with broken hands.

Oh, she had been stupid, stupid! She had led them out, that awful day and they had thrown themselves in front of the Stewards' victims because they didn't believe the soldiers would harm children. But they had.

She had survived. So had Bird, somehow. Not by being a hero, but by giving into them, wearing their uniform. As she had given in to them. He said he was sorry and he tried to smile at her as if he were glad to see her, but she knew he wasn't. He haunted the music room like a ghost of himself, and she didn't want to see him, didn't want to play his piano or any piano ever again.

He hadn't been a hero, and neither had she. Heroes weren't real. They existed in stories, but not in real life. In real life was only pain, until you gave in.

He was ashamed of her, she was sure, for not knowing that. He'd tried to warn her. And was mad at her. Because she had been so stupid.

She couldn't look at him, because when she did all she saw was his face, trying so hard not to scream as they hurt him, and they hurt him because of her.

Who we gonna work on, her or you? they would ask. He would always say me, and she felt ashamed that never, not once, had she brought herself to say me instead.

Even though they had, they had hurt her in ways she had never known people could be hurt. Then they had made him do terrible things, and she knew he did it to try and protect her, and how could he not hate her for making him become a traitor? And she was ashamed of him, even though he did it for her, and maybe even more ashamed of wanting him to do it, wanting to beg him to do whatever they asked him to do, anything, because the pain was so great and she was so, so scared.

At Maya's there was warmth and laughter and people who wanted to be her friends. But Rosa couldn't go there.

For her there was only the garden, the gossipy clucks of the chickens who were not picking over her stupidness but only remarking on the bugs they found and the scraps they foraged. If there was comfort to be found, it was here, in the silence of the roses waving gaily in the breeze, the sleepy, nodding sunflowers on their tall stems. Only here.

Maya watched Bird as he did his daily rounds, as in spite of his wounded hand he tackled cupboards that had not been cleaned since the first Gulf War, pulled the stove away from the wall to evict a multigenerational family of mice, scoured out the compost buckets. The kitchen had not been so clean in years.

"I see what you're doing," she said. "I know. I cleaned, too. When Rio shot the TV, that's exactly what I did."

"Rio shot the TV?" he asked. He emerged from under the sink, where he'd fixed a leak in the drain, the trap now watertight again. He'd heard the story a dozen times before, but he knew she liked to tell it, so he pretended it was new to him.

"It was back during the war. Some war. The Vietnam war. And his brother had died in it, and Rio got a letter from him, after he was dead. Jim, that is. Rio's brother. He got drunk and he took the guns we'd been stockpiling for the revolution and he shot the TV. And every mirror in the house."

Stories were spilling out of her like the last dregs of wine before the bottle is empty, all the things she might have once concealed. As if she had no more need for concealment. I'm losing her, he thought. But I'm not ready.

"Ah, it was an insane, bloody mess and a smart woman would have walked out then and never looked back. But I wasn't so smart in those days. What can I say? I was raised to be a girl. To stand by your man, and make excuses, and cover up the messy spots.

"So I cleaned. I cleaned up the mess and the broken glass and the blood where he'd cut his hands, trying to gather shards of mirror and put them back. I cleaned and cleaned because if you clean enough, you can pretend it never happened. That everything is really okay, you know? Hide the evidence and you might even convince yourself that nothing is broken.

"Women have always had this. It's kept us sane. It's also kept us trapped—but it's how we survived the traps. Small things that you can accomplish. Maybe if I clear up the dishes no one will notice the bruises. Maybe I didn't save the world today, or liberate the oppressed, or end world hunger. But I got the laundry done, and that's something. That's something."

"Exactly," Bird smiled. "And in the end, it's better to die in clean underwear."

"I'm sorry," she said. "I wish I had left you a better world. I wish it was easier for you."

"You have nothing to be sorry about."

"Or everything."

There were tears in her eyes, and he hugged her. He crouched so that he could put his arms around her where she sat, and a beam of sunshine played with her corona of white hair. She felt frail in his arms, as if she were slipping out of his embrace. And I can't protect her, he thought. Who can protect the old against the coming of death?

"Ah well," she said. "You do what you do, and in the end, you hope the good outweighs the bad in the balance. And the things I'm sorry for, mostly, are the things I didn't do."

"Like what?" He sat down, savoring the moment, the light coming in through the window, the halo of her hair, the white roses on the table illumined. These ordinary moments were so precious to him, bright oases of simple pleasures—a cup of tea in the morning, a clean kitchen, a conversation in the golden hour while the sun was still bright on the road to darkness. The more so because he knew they would not last, as the ordinary, for him, had never lasted.

"I didn't go overland to India in 1972, when you could. I've always regretted that. I'm sorry I didn't fuck more when I was young, although Goddess knows I fucked every chance I could get. I'm sorry I didn't have a dozen kids and fifty grandchildren, each one exactly like you."

"I don't want you to die," he said abruptly.

"Why not? You'll inherit the house, not that that matters anymore. And my literary estate. Not to mention the Prince Charles and Lady Di historic tea tray. Although maybe by rights that should go to Madrone."

"I want you to live forever."

"Ah, what a curse that would be!" She leaned over and kissed him on his forehead. "You're a dear boy, in spite of all the times you put the compost in the city bin instead of taking it out to the yard. And that time you broke a lunchbox over Andy Corbin's son's head in middle school. And painting my grandmother's silver mirror with red nail polish."

"That wasn't me, that was Madrone," Bird smiled.

"You were in on it. But it doesn't matter. I forgive you." She gave his bandaged hand a little love pat.

"Don't!" he said involuntarily, not because it hurt but because her forgiveness felt so final, like a goodbye.

Her eyes went soft and faraway again. "Try to forgive yourself."

Chapter Seven

MOST DAYS, WHEN IT WASN'T HIS DAY TO MIND THE HOUSE, RIVER gathered at a corner café on the block with his old unit. They played cards and gambled for stones and baubles, watching the city people work. Waiting, as sojuhs always waited. For orders, or action, or a target to attack.

That day might be coming soon. Warship in the harbor, sooner or later even these soft city pigeons gotta figure out what that meant. But they seemed barely concerned, still focused on planting and cleaning up and making everything pretty.

"Maybe this unit help these people out," River suggested one morning. The truth was, he was bored, tired of dealing out game after meaningless game. He was feeling healthy, full of energy from eating the real food of the city, and his body craved to do something physical.

"No orders," countered Threetwo as he shuffled.

"What bigstick gonna give orders? General dead. The rest dead or run away back South. City people tell us sojuhs free."

"Somebody got to be in charge."

"Maybe these fighters ... maybe *we* that somebody," River said. "Maybe we each got to be our own commander."

The faces looked up at him blankly. They were his unit mates, his familiar companions. Together they had been beaten into submission as children, taught to stand and march in formation, to use their weapons, to endure and inflict pain. Yet something separated him now. He had a name.

River stood up. A teenage boy was struggling with a big chunk of concrete he carried balanced on his head. With a sense of trepidation, of daring, River took it from him.

"Where to?"

The boy smiled. "Follow me."

The other sojuhs watched with some alarm as River disappeared around a corner. But soon he was back, heading off with the boy and a group of older teens to the stockpile of concrete chunks salvaged from the invading army's many demolitions.

The rest of his unit watched him make trip after trip. Ohnine was smiling.

"Why chipster smiling?" Threetwo asked the others.

Fiveforty shrugged. "Feelin' good, maybe."

"Carryin' that heavy shit? That dòn't feel good!" Seveneighty objected.

"Why the tubo not order this unit to help bear the load?" Threetwo asked.

"Heard what the stick say—no more bigsticks," Fourteentwenty said.

"Whass that mean?" Threetwo asked.

"Means a fighter want to bear the load, do it!" Fiveforty stood up and walked over to a group of diggers. A beautiful young woman handed him a shovel, and he winked back to his companions. They stared at him for a moment, then they got up and joined in the work.

River was feeling good. Each heavy load he carried seemed to strengthen the somebodiness inside him, as if it were a muscle that developed with exercise. Perhaps it was. He had destroyed a lot in his time, and that was one way to feel power. To make another somebody cringe or cry out in pain, to shut a pair of eyes for good and wipe out that somebody—he had always enjoyed that, because by comparison he felt alive, felt for one moment that these muscles, these bones, this hand and the will attached stood out together as a unit of its own.

But this was a different sort of pleasure. Slower, deeper, watching the wall slowly rise, concrete chunk upon concrete chunk.

"Whass this for?" he asked a young boy.

"We're building a raised bed, so the elders can garden without having to bend and kneel. When we're done, we'll fill it with earth and compost."

River liked that. He thought about Maya, imagined her down on the street, planting a flower with her papery-skin hands. The workers around him, he noticed, were mostly young teens and even small children. The adults were working on structures and buildings, leaving the garden repair to the younger ones.

In the center of the garden stood a red sphere on a pedestal.

"Whass that?" River asked one of the older girls.

"That's Mars." She looked up at him, her dark, straight hair framing an owlish face.

"Whass Mars?"

Thick glasses hid her dark eyes. Her blouse hid new-budding breasts, River noted, but he tried and failed to imagine how she would be in the rec room. She was a bit on the old side to be broken in, recently blooded, maybe, but already she had the eyes of the Califian women, looking straight into his with no fear nor submission. As if she were a person looking at another person—one she didn't think much of.

"It's our neighbor planet," she told him.

"Whass a planet?"

She looked at him sharply, as if she suspected he were joking. "We're standing on one. The Earth is a planet—like a giant ball, circling the sun."

"Crazy shit!"

"It's true."

"How come we don't fall off, then?"

"Gravity holds us on."

"Whass gravity?"

"Gravity is the Earth's love for her children, holding us close," she said as if repeating something she'd memorized.

"Hey, tubos!" River shouted to his old unit. "Come hear this!"

The girl called her friends over, and the children soon discovered that the sojuhs knew almost nothing about the world. They had been taught to read, write, and count, mostly for the convenience of their commanders, but they had never been given storybooks or even textbooks on anything other than weapons and the simplest of military tactics. Their entertainment came from vidscreens, vidgames, and failing that, cards. They didn't know that the Earth turned around the sun, or that compost made soil. They knew nothing of history, and were unaware that Califia and the Southlands had once been part of the same state, one of fifty in the same country.

They had rarely seen the night sky before they made the long march to the North, and it hadn't occurred to most of them to wonder what those pinpoints of light in the heavens were. Stars had to be explained to them.

"Help us rebuild this Learning Track," the girl said. "And we'll teach you things."

"Thass an order?" Threetwo asked.

The girl frowned. "If you want it to be. It's an offer."

"An order," River said firmly.

The girl held out her hand. "I'm Jasmine. What's your name?"

"River." He took her hand and stood looking at it, not sure what to do with it or why she extended it to him. She grasped his, pumped it vigorously and let it drop. "These other chipsters here, don't got names, just numbers," River told her. "So whass this track thing about?"

"It's how we learn, here. There's different tracks that run all through the City, with different learning stations. Right now we're on the Solar System Track, and this is the Mars station. The next one out would be Jupiter, and then Saturn. It's like a giant scale model. This ball is how big Mars would be if the sun were as big as the giant model of the sun that used to be in the Central Plaza. And it's as far away as Mars would be if it were this big."

River and the other soldiers just looked at her, mystified. So Jasmine explained that on the Solar System Track, every planet had a learning station. Mars had its sphere, and around it were gardens with herbs that belonged to Mars and flowers in martial colors along with statues of war Gods from many cultures, Ares and Chango and Thor. Each had a port for the intelligent crystals that the children wore around their necks. When they touched them to the ports, holograms jumped out with stories, myths, and explanations. They could listen to the Greek and Roman myths, or hear the Scandinavian Eddas, and then compare them to the Marvel Comics Thor and the movies. They could watch video from the early Mars rovers or access the scientific reports from expeditions the scientists had mounted back when people could still do such things, before the collapse.

In their Learning Groups, they might delve further into the mysteries of space exploration, or write and perform their own Mars space opera, or read Mars-centered science fiction, or create a strategy game about a Mars expedition.

River understood little of her explanation, but he gathered that the children had taken on the project of replanting the gardens and cleaning up the tracks, while the techies repaired the smashed electronics and the Artist's Guild rebuilt the sculptures. In the end, Jasmine offered to meet them on the following morning and take them to the outer planets that hadn't been damaged in the invasion. There they could see what a fully functioning station was like.

Madrone, on her way out to the healing center the next morning, was charmed by the sight of two ten-year-olds flanking a big burly sojuh on a bike careening wildly down the path, yelling his head off in panic. Jasmine and her Learning Group surrounded a group of the former soldiers astride an assortment of bikes borrowed from the City's stock. In normal times, there were racks of white-painted bikes in every neighborhood that could be freely used and left at the next depot. Some of them were rebuilt from older parts. The newer ones had bamboo frames and only the gears and steering mechanisms were made of scarce metal.

The sojuhs were looking at the bikes with a mixture of suspicion and alarm. Apparently cycling was not part of the army's training program.

Madrone felt her own pang of alarm at the thought of the City's innocent children in such close, unsupervised contact with the sojuhs. But then she noticed that a dark-haired man weeding his garden kept a close eye on the group, and a strong-looking woman with her gray hair in mediator's braids was knitting on her doorstep with the group in clear sight. The watchful eyes of the City were upon them, and the children and sojuhs would be kept under scrutiny.

As she watched, a stringy sojuh mounted a bike, wobbled dangerously, then found his balance and zoomed on down the path. A huge smile
broke over his face, and he laughed, a sound fresh as a first rain, as if he'd
never before laughed with pure enjoyment, free from derision or mockery.

A healing laugh, as the other sojuhs joined in with him.

Maybe I don't have to do all the healing myself. Maya would tell her
that, and Doctor Sam, who headed up the Healers' Guild and ran the
center. The children, the watchful eyes of the grown-ups, they were the
City's immune system, at work on the sojuhs, changing them.

Just for a moment, she had a wild desire to jump on a bike and join
them, to ride the City's paths with her hair streaming behind her, laughing and laughing with the joy of it.

But she had patients awaiting her, and a shift to cover. Reluctantly,
she turned away down the path.

By lunchtime, the children assessed that the sojuhs were fit for the journey. Jasmine handed out packets of sandwiches, and they all picked
plums and berries from the trees that had survived the Stewards' assaults.
The sojuhs shook their heads at the food, but under River's stern glare,
they put away their chips and took it.

Then with their bikes they all boarded a transport in the shape of a
giant dolphin. They'd had their choice between that or a giant birthday
cake or a pirate ship. It took them far out to the edge of the City and
beyond the San Bruno Mountains, where they found the Pluto station.

Here were statues of Pluto, God of the Underworld, and here the
crystals still functioned. They explored the planet's surface and watched
in amazement as a hologram told the tale of Pluto's abduction of the
maiden Kore and her mother Demeter's wrath. Then they rode the long
way back to Neptune where they rode animated statues of the Sea-God's
wild horses erupting from the waves. By then it was dinnertime.

They met again the next morning to cover the ground from Uranus
to Saturn with its rings, to giant Jupiter, and back to Mars.

"Whass this shit matter?" Threetwo grumbled. "This unit ain't goin'
to no planets."

"You got to be a real person now, not just a tubo grunt, and real
people, they know things," River told him. "Besides, it's somethin' to do."

Something to do, he thought, until the time for action would come
again. And it would. He felt sure of that. These weeks in the beautiful
city, this time to learn shit as if he was a real person entitled to learn,
it was like rec room time between training sessions, R & R between
battles. He had no doubt that dust and smoke and blood awaited him,
soon. But one thing every sojuh learned early was to take each moment
of pleasure as it comes.

The children held their own Council once a week, and Jasmine made
a successful proposal that each of the Learning Groups adopt a unit of

the sojuhs. Soon gangs of burly fighters were daily being shepherded, ordered around, and lectured by gangs of kids. They stared at models of DNA and squatted to observe frog habitat on the biology track. They followed the History Track that traced a long line of struggles for justice, from the Chinese debt rebellions two thousand years ago, to the medieval peasants' rebellions, to the Uprising twenty years before. At night, they would stand and stare at the skies, looking at the stars.

Always, silently in the background, a quiet guard was kept. Not interfering, but present in case of any hint of danger.

Some of the soldiers were bored, some restless to get back to their card games and their lounging. There was a high rate of attrition. Some succumbed to frustration, overwhelmed by more information than they were equipped to take in. The adults who hovered near the learning groups broke up the occasional fight and stopped more than one sojuh from kicking the guts out of some animated sculpture they couldn't comprehend.

But many of the former soldiers eagerly soaked up information, hungry for everything the City could teach them. Not all the units were made up of breeds. Some were croots, conscripted into the army for stealing water or because their families had defaulted on debts. Many of the conscripts had rudiments of an education, but in the Southlands advanced learning was reserved for the Primes and the Subprimes. So the croots saw education as a luxury that had always before been out of reach, and many were eager to indulge.

The children found simple books to loan the sojuhs, and encouraged them to read. At Black Dragon house, River was surrounded by books. Shelves and cases of them lined the walls and spilled out onto the floor. Even the bathrooms were well-supplied with reading material. River took to borrowing picture books left over from children long grown, to puzzle out the stories for himself.

He was filled with wonder and rage. "All this shit in the world—and we never knew! Nobody told us nothin'!" he said to Maya, waving a toddler's picture book about bats at her. "Didn't even know what there was to know!"

Maya smiled at him. "And now you do. Now you know how much you don't know, and in that you are wiser than a professor."

River looked at her, confused.

"The world is a vast place of mysteries," she said. "Education can give us the mistaken impression that we know a lot. But if we're wise, we admit that none of us really knows jack shit about the universe. We're a speck in the arm of an immense galaxy, a drop in a boundless sea."

His frown deepened, then softened. He gave her the look she was beginning to get used to from so many sources—the kind smile, the tone one might use with a small child or a puppy.

"Wantin' a nap, Mama?" he asked her. "Gettin' tired?"

"That's just your way of saying I've wandered into the thickets of dementia," she snapped. "But I haven't. Maybe you don't understand me now, River. But you will. Mark my words, you will."

River had been trained as a fighter, put through boot camp, learned to march in time and run laps until he dripped sweat. But never, before coming to the City, had he been a walker. There was never before any place to go.

Now he discovered the joys of walking over the pathways that wound through the City's green streets. His vision seemed sharper, colors more bright, if only because in the City there was always something to see. Turn a corner and a bright mural decked an old wall. Down a side street, and there was a giant snake covered with bright mosaics, big enough for small children to walk on, with toddlers clambering up its back.

He felt himself growing strong on the good food. His bones didn't have the ache inside that they used to, his stomach never had the low burn, his mind felt less fuzzy. His stride lengthened and his arms began to swing with the easy motion of a free man.

Walking eased the tension he felt creep up inside him. Not a pain, not exactly an itch, more like a sense of dislocation. Like he wasn't where he was supposed to be. Or who he was supposed to be. He'd changed. And that was good. All good. But not comfortable. Not familiar. Like a new and different uniform he wasn't used to wearing. Or a new pair of boots not yet broken in.

Boots he didn't believe could last. He was afraid to get too accustomed to them, for deep inside he knew that sooner or later they'd get shabby and worn on a long dusty track. Back, back to the Southlands, where there were battles yet to be fought.

The people around him—they were worth looking at, too. They liked to costume themselves up in bright colors and decorate their skin with elaborate tattoos. The women always had fresh flowers in their hair—and the men, too, for that matter, not to mention the ones you couldn't tell was a man or a woman or an inbetween.

That woman in front of him, now, with her red hair flying like a flag in the breeze, and her little apple-cheeked butt twitching left, right, left right. Be nice to have an hour with her in the rec room!

But City women were off limits. Bird had explained that carefully to him. If they want you, he'd said, they'll approach you themselves. You try, you're likely to get an eye gouged out.

He sighed. A sojuh has needs, and he was aware of his. One good thing about the army—always a rec room down the hall in the barracks. So long as he wasn't on punishment detail, he could meet those needs. Now it was complicated.

But watching the red-haired woman, he began to wonder what it would be like to have a filly who wasn't a pen-girl, who maybe had made her own choices. Who chose him.

Suddenly the woman ahead of him stopped, so abruptly that he nearly bumped into her. He stopped himself, just in time, conscious of how near their bodies were, how they had almost met.

"Sorry," he said.

She turned and scrutinized him closely. Now he could see her face, ivory covered with freckles. Her small, pert mouth seemed to be holding back a smile. She had some kind of squiggly shell tattooed on her forehead, and her gray eyes were cool, assessing him.

"You were looking at me," she said. "I could feel your eyes."

"Couldn't help it. You right in front."

She gave him a long smile of appraisal. "Do you consider yourself a brave man?" she asked in a low voice with a purr in it almost like a cat's.

River stared at her, confused. "Nobody call this fighter a coward!"

She tossed her long hair in the breeze, and slowly undid the top button of her diaphanous blouse.

"How brave?"

River gulped. He was suddenly terrified, although he didn't know why.

She undid another button. He didn't know what to do. The curve of her breasts drew his eyes like a tractor beam, and he couldn't seem to pull away, even though he thought maybe he should. But they were in the middle of a public street. People could come by and see her. Didn't she mind? Didn't seem to. What was he supposed to do?

"Well?" Her smile deepened, as if she were amused at his discomfort. She looked him up and down. He could feel the hot swelling in his trousers and her eyes lingered on it thoughtfully. It grew under her gaze.

"Has anyone ever taught you the art of love?" she asked.

"Don't need no teaching. Natural."

"Eating is natural, yet fine cooking requires knowledge," she said, not smiling now but serious. "How would you like me to take charge of your education?"

River felt a deeper sense of panic. What was she proposing?

"On my way to market—got to get some fresh fruit," he hedged.

"I can give you peaches, and ripe strawberries," she did purr now, and her breasts rose, the nipples hard under her blouse and thrusting forward, as if they were the fruit she offered. "Unless you're scared?"

"Never been scared of no filly!"

She held out her hand. "Then come. Let me take you to the Temple of Love and Desire."

"Who are you?" River held back, still suspicious.

"I am a devotee of Aphrodite, mistress of love. And a priestess of Oshun, Goddess of the river."

"River my name," he told her with some pride.

"I know," she nodded. "Now let it be your destiny."

The Temple of Love lay just beyond a high wall that bordered the pathway. The red-haired woman opened a discreet gate and led him into a courtyard, scented with jasmine and overhung with roses. Within were blue pools, some steaming hot, some crystalline cool, some with herbs steeping.

A small room opened off the corner of the courtyard. Inside was a soft chair, where he sat down. The walls were decorated with voluptuous nudes and scenes of lovemaking in many different styles. Not quite like the porn-pacs the sojuhs could buy with their scrip, these were drawn or painted or sculpted, what the squabs called "art." Still, they were doin' it from the front, from behind, upside down and every which way, mouth on drill, tongue on pooch—River wasn't quite sure what to think.

The door opened and a woman walked in. She had gray hair and a full, rounded belly, with huge swelling breasts under a flowing, silky robe. Not what River would have thought of for a priestess of love—more like a commander with her air of authority and her ancient face.

"Soldier," she addressed him. Her eyes looked him up and down like searchlights. "So you wish to be educated in the ways of love?"

"Uh, yeah," he said, although mostly he just felt nervous. Maybe this was all a big mistake.

"Are you willing to pay the price?"

"Whass it cost?" he asked anxiously. Let her name a fee, and he would say that he had no money, and that would be the end of it. Maybe better so.

"No money," she smiled as if she read his thoughts. "Not even your work credits. But your time, and your willingness to submit to our discipline and to agree to our rules. Understand, if you go through this you will not be the same man at the end."

"Uh—how long?" he dropped his eyes. "Supposed to bring home some food for dinner."

"You won't make it home for dinner. Not for many nights. But we will feed you."

"This fighter's people—my people—gonna worry." And suddenly he realized that was true. It made him feel strange to think about Bird and Madrone and the old woman, all worrying about him if he didn't show up. Almost like he was a part of something, a different kind of unit. Almost like a real person.

"We will send them a message."

River took a gulp of air. This was a choice, he thought, like Maya said. Say yes, and he might become a different kind of somebody. Say no—fuck it, only a limpdick mallet-head say no to that red-haired filly.

"Yes," he said and with that answer suddenly he knew something more about himself. He was a chooser. A risk taker. He had chosen to leave behind his life as a breed and say yes to the City, to Madrone's healing, to a place at the table. He had said yes to the children when they offered to guide his unit on the Learning Tracks. Now he had said yes to this, and whatever it turned out to be, it was now part of the self he was constructing, yes by yes.

It could never feel comfortable, that self, not like the old Ohnine who had been a number and had just existed. It would always mean more risk, more danger. Yet he had been born and bred and trained for danger. They had instilled terrible strengths in him that now he could use for his own ends.

Just for a moment, he felt that he liked that new self. The idea startled him. Liking himself—it was almost obscene, like whacking his own drill, an activity the army discouraged as it disturbed the quiet of the barracks at night. And with a rec room always available, there wasn't so much of a need.

"Here's the rules," the old woman said. "You will submit to what we do to you. Some of it will seem strange, and some may seem uncomfortable. If there comes a moment when you want something to stop, all you have to say is no. But we encourage you to stretch your limits. That is how we learn.

"If you are doing something to someone else, and they say no, you will stop. Instantly. No arguments. And believe me, we will test you on this. If you want to do something you are not instructed to do, ask. You will learn how to give great pleasure, and how to receive pleasure you have never imagined. Do you agree?"

River gulped, and nodded.

"Say yes."

"Yes," he said in a voice barely above a whisper.

"Then come with me."

She took him to a small dressing room, where he was instructed to take off his clothes and shower. A velvet soft robe hung on the door, and he put it on. He stepped out, and the red-haired woman greeted him and handed him a cup of a ruby-red liquid.

"Drink this," she said. It tasted sweet and fruity, and even as he swallowed it he began to feel strange, as if his senses were heightened and his inner wariness decreased. He noticed how the soft robe caressed his bare skin, how the stone felt warm under his feet as she led him back into the courtyard.

The priestess plucked his robe from his shoulders and he felt the chill air on his skin. He took a step down into the middle pool, and another, slowly submerging. The water felt warm and silky, and smelled fragrant, like spice and flowers.

"Close your eyes and lie back," she said, slipping off her robe and sliding in with him. "Let me cradle you."

The pool was deep enough to float, and she held him and rocked him back and forth, crooning a song that sounded like a lullaby. Soft hands were stroking him, rubbing some smooth lotion into his skin, caressing every orifice. There was a mouth on his cock, not sucking but humming a deep, sonorous vibration. And then there were uncountable mouths on him, each humming a different tone into belly and nipples and forehead. He risked a quick peek—and was shocked to see a crowd of priestesses, women and men and heeshees. He froze, but the rocking went on.

"Relax," said a deep male voice. "Do not fear the pleasure brothers and others can give to one another. Take a deep breath, and let go of your fears."

He took a breath. The rocking and humming resumed.

"Let us cherish you, for this is our worship," the red-haired woman whispered in his ear. "We worship the living God hidden within you. Let us rock you and bathe you like a mother bathes a child."

He couldn't remember his mother. He doubted she had ever bathed him in anything more than a bucket in a cell. Yet maybe she had cherished him, in her own way, as the pen-girls do love their babies. Maybe she had cried when they took him away, as he had heard so many cry. Suddenly that seemed sad to him, so sad. His eyes began to leak tears, tears he had never cried before. The humming and stroking broke open some barrier within him, and he was gulping for breath and crying out, deep, groaning sobs, all the pain he had never before been able to feel.

"Good boy, brave boy," the priestess crooned. "Let it out. Let it go. Let the sadness flow, for if you hold it back, it will block the pleasure. Breathe."

"Drink this," the red-haired priestess told him a long time later. He sipped something dark and velvet, bitter but not unpleasant. They drew him out of the bath and laid him down on a blanket in a patch of sunlight. Relaxation stole over him. He couldn't move his limbs. He was not paralyzed, but so deeply relaxed that he couldn't summon up the will to raise an arm or shift a leg. Even the effort to form words in his mind began to seem too much. They slipped a soft blindfold over his eyes.

"Now you will relearn the most primal of senses," they whispered, and slid muffs over his ears.

In the darkness and silence, there was only touch. They began with the toes and worked up, massaging, stroking, stimulating every part of his body. He was aroused but far too languid to rise; he lay limp and passive as a baby. At times their touch was painful, when fingers probed deep to release a knotted muscle, but more often it was sheer pleasure, the velvet stroking of hands on oiled skin.

When the sun began to fade he felt many hands lift him and carry him inside to a soft bed. He felt each of his feet grasped by a pair of hands that rubbed and probed and massaged the soles. The touch sent electric currents up through his body. Then he became aware of a delicious fragrance. Rich and sweet and fruity, it seemed to steal in through his nostrils and caress him from the inside. Just when his nose got used to it, soft fingers parted his lips and slipped in a ripe strawberry. The taste exploded inside his mouth like a burst of ruby light, as another soft hand ran the softest of feather-light touches down from his lips to his groin. Then a soft breeze shivered through the room, the air cleared, and a new scent surrounded him. Flowery, savory, spicy ... they taught him the full range of fragrances, and between the perfume of roses and the aroma of fresh mint came the scents of arousal, of sun-warmed flesh, of the body's moist, secret places.

And then they rolled him onto his stomach, and slid the muffs off his ears. Music surrounded him, soft and lilting, while he felt someone straddle his buttocks and begin to work the muscles on either side of his spine. The fingers moved in rhythm to the music, gathering energy and moving it up and up as the muscles in his back seemed to melt. The music built in rhythm and power, and the hands followed, while voices whispered to him things he had never heard before. "You are holy. You are sacred. You have a shining, immortal soul."

The music touched the sadness that washed through him, and he cried again, softly this time, tears soaking into the pillow, crying for his lost mother's grief when he was torn from her arms, crying for that big, beautiful world that had for so long been concealed from him, crying for all that he had never known before. A memory came to him, clear and vivid. He was small, very small, and he was missing her, the warm arms, the smell of her, the soft breasts with their sweet milk. He was standing in line with a group of tiny boys, and the sun was too hot and he was tired and he had to pee. He opened his mouth and began to wail, and a huge hand slapped him across the face. The pain and shock made him cry harder, and the hand slapped him again. The more he cried, the harder he got hit, until finally he understood and choked back the tears.

He had not been the only child to cry: they all did. They all got slapped, and beaten. Then they took the smallest of them, the one who couldn't stop his tears, and they'd put sticks into the hands of the others, and told them to beat the boy themselves. With a great swing, he had been the one to put out the light in the boy's panicked eyes, because he couldn't stand to look at them, filled with pain and terror that mirrored his own.

He remembered the crunch of the bone. And then it was like a great noise stopped, and there was silence and peace.

They gave him a sweetie, for delivering the killing blow. The sweetie was soft and sugary, and something in it soothed his sorrow and made him feel just a little bit like he had in his mother's arms.

So he had learned to be a killer. And over time, he had learned to enjoy it.

Now a rage flooded through him and pushed him up. He threw off the hands and reared up to his knees and then onto his feet. Words were pouring out of him. He screamed them out, shouting and bellowing. Someone shoved something into his hands. A club. He crashed it down again and again. But it was soft, somehow, and everything around him was soft. Still blindfolded, he couldn't see. He couldn't seem to hurt anything, and that made him more enraged. And yet at the same time he felt safe, held. He screamed and cried and beat the walls until at last his rage was spent. It flowed out of him, and behind it came an even deeper grief. All the years of unshed tears poured out, as the music bathed him in sounds that felt like forgiveness.

"You will be whole," the voices murmured. "There is a precious jewel within you that was never crushed. Cherish it. Cleanse it. Bathe it in the river of love."

At last, exhausted, he fell into a deep, dreamless sleep.

He awoke in the morning, still blindfolded. Invisible hands guided him up, to the toilet, to an outdoor shower where warm water washed away the sweat of the night, to a table in the sun where they fed him soft eggs and bits of toast with sweet jam and held up steaming cups of herbal tea for him to sip. Then they removed his blindfold at last and placed him on a deep, comfortable bench.

"This morning," they told him, "you will just rest, and watch."

He was enclosed in a bower of roses, sweet-smelling but thorny. Through the branches, he had a clear view of a raised bower, and there a young woman and a young man stood, their eyes fixed on each other, their hands raised, palms touching. They wore shiny tights and leotards that revealed every curve and muscle of their bodies. Again he heard music. They began to dance.

Their movements were liquid and graceful, not overtly sexy and yet there was an erotic undertone to all they did, the way their hands caressed the air, the way their eyes followed each other. As the music shifted the dancers left the stage to be followed by other combinations, a man with a man, a woman with a woman, dancers who seemed neither man nor woman but inhabited some magical state in-between or different than either. There were dancers of every shape and age and color, and the movement shifted from graceful ballet to rhythmic flamenco to pounding African dance.

At first, River felt soothed but just a little bored by the dance. He was still raw inside from the emotional storms of the day before, and deeply weary. He dozed, in and out of waking, falling into erotic dreams where dancers turned into naked lovers. But when he opened his eyes, he realized the dance had changed. The dancers no longer wore leotards and tights, but filmy tunics that revealed naked bodies beneath. Now glances led to touch, touch to strokes, strokes to kisses. And then the dancing became lovemaking, slow and graceful. He was wide awake now, riveted by the display of every gender and combination and position. There were slow dances and wild, rough, faster ones, acrobats who twined each other into unthinkable positions, and aerial dancers who swung in on ropes, coupling in midair. He was almost too amazed to be aroused, but soon his cock began to rise and his hand groped for it. Then from behind him he felt a naked woman's body press up against him. She slid her arms under his shoulders and her hands grabbed his.

"Resist the temptation to give yourself release," she breathed. "You must learn to tolerate pleasure."

Her fingers interlaced with his. Her thumbs caressed the back of his hands, his palms, reflecting the movements of the dance before them until his hands seemed to swell with desire. He was throbbing with a need that was almost beyond bearing.

"Breathe into it," she whispered into his ear. "Learn the power of restraint, for it will intensify your ultimate pleasure. Breathe with me."

He could feel her breath rising and falling, pressing her breasts into his back, her soft moistness rubbing over the base of his spine. She drew him back down onto the chair and wrapped her legs around his thighs. He couldn't see who she was, and somehow that excited him in a different way.

"Breathe," she whispered, and her teeth gently nicked his earlobe. He took in a deep breath, matching her rhythm, and they breathed together, their in-breath pressing them closer, tighter, their out-breath giving just enough of a space to make him anticipate the in-breath more. And she was right—this was better, deeper, the pleasure a thousand times stronger than anything he had ever experienced in the quick ruttings of the rec room.

Then he felt her hips rocking against him, rocking and thrusting, and he realized that she was pleasuring herself. He could feel soft little motions, as if the lips of her pooch were giving him soft kisses at the base of his spine, and they sent shivers up his back. He wanted to face her, to turn and take her and help her, but she was surprisingly strong, holding him pinned to immobility, murmuring only, "Breathe! Breathe!" Her breath quickened, as his followed. They were breathing together, one breath, strong and fast as the music quickened and the dancers rocked in unison.

Energy pulsed through him. The music reached a climax. He could contain himself no longer, and with a great, shuddering cry he felt the seed spurt from his cock, as she let out a deep moan and pressed herself hard, hard into his back.

"Let this sojuh see you," he pleaded as their mutual breath subsided. "Me. Let me look at you."

"Do you really want to see?" she murmured.

"Yes!"

She released his arms, and turned him gently to face her. He looked into her eyes with shock, for she was not the red-haired priestess but the old woman he had seen at the beginning. Her eyes had creases at the corners. Her full breasts hung down. But he was still aflame with desire for her, and at that moment she was the most beautiful woman he had ever seen.

"I am Oshun, Goddess of love," she said. "I am ancient and deep as the river."

He was feeling things he'd never felt before: tenderness and gratitude and a deep sense of wonder. Nothing in his life had taught him how to express them. He did something he had seen Bird do to Madrone. He bent over and kissed her lightly on the forehead. He remembered how, watching them, he'd felt some deep-buried ache that he was hardly aware of. But now he knew what it was, that longing to have some hint of this, what real people had.

"Thank you," he whispered.

He looked into her eyes and felt himself floating, flowing down a river, awash in her love. Deeper than human, she knew him, knew all that he had done, and she forgave him. More than that, she saw something in him, possibilities and gifts he did not yet know he possessed.

They left him alone, that afternoon, to bathe in the hot pools or swim in the cool pool that took up most of another courtyard. "Rest," they said. "Integrate what you have learned so far. If you want to talk, come to this window and a priestess will come to you. If you want to be silent, that's good too. For tomorrow, your instruction intensifies. That will require work from you, and concentration."

He didn't want to talk. He couldn't talk. He dozed, and swam, and dozed again. I don't have to become real, he thought. I am real. I always was. They tried to make me into a thing, a killing machine. And they did. But all the while, the real me was hiding underneath.

It's not a different uniform. This sojuh's—I—I've taken off the old one, thrown it away. This is me, my true skin.

⁓

"Call it the flower," the red-haired priestess said. She sat before him, her legs spread wide. "And here, these are the petals of the flower. And this, this is the hidden jewel in the lotus. And now I will show you the different ways you can polish the jewel. You will watch, first, and then we will practice. For today you will learn to be a giver of pleasure."

And so his instruction began. Throughout that long day, he learned all the pleasure points of the body, hers and his own. She taught him the many ways to touch and stroke, to pulse and vibrate, to sniff and taste, how to read the signs of arousal, how to alternate the delicate and the strong like the movements of a symphony. After the first hour, a dark-skinned young man came in and began to demonstrate possibilities of the male body that River had never imagined. He watched, breathing through his own arousal, and then he did what he was shown, rewarded when he did well by her quickened breathing, his gaping mouth.

He received no touching back in return. The time to receive would come. They limited him to hands and mouth, for, they said, when the time came to use his shaft, he would be giving and receiving at once.

From time to time they tested him. "Stop!" they would cry out, and he was expected to stop, that instant, whatever he was doing. When once he failed to do so, they simply left the room, leaving him alone for half an hour. When he did, he was praised and rewarded by being allowed to give some more.

No one had ever told him that pen-girls were supposed to receive pleasure, or indeed, were even capable of it. They were there to service the sojuhs, receptacles, not partners in love. But to give, to see her eyes grow misty, her breathing heavy, her flower open to his touch, filled him with a sense of power. He was real: her gaping lips proved it. "You are a giver of pleasure, an artist, a God," they whispered, and he began to believe them. Giving and giving until he knew that giving was receiving, until the tides of pleasure rose within him and could not be contained.

On the fourth day, they led him into an innermost courtyard, a wild, fragrant garden with a ring of apple trees in the center. In the midst of the trees lay a deep hollow filled with mud. Again they covered his eyes and laid him down in the mud. He began to panic—there was dirt covering him, touching him, burying him alive!

"Breathe," the voices said. "Do not fear the embrace of the mother."

He gulped air. But the fear remained. They would bury him alive. The fear built to panic. His chest was heaving. He was gasping, shaking with a primal terror. He couldn't control his face, his body. With a great heave he pushed himself up, rolled onto his hands and knees. To be afraid was to be a coward, unworthy to be a sojuh. He was trembling like a beast waiting for the death blow. They would strike him down, his blood would mingle with the mud. Breathe, they said, but he could no longer breathe, his chest worked in empty spasms.

Then there were bodies pressed against him, chests rising and falling, soft breasts pushing into him. They were breathing for him, he could feel their own slow heartbeats against his hammering chest. His clenched throat released, and sound burst out of him, a bellow that became a shrill child's scream. He screamed and shook as hands massaged him, arms held him, voices murmured, "It's okay. It's okay."

The storm of fear subsided and his breath began to come, deep and full, reaching down into places that had always before been barricaded against it. It felt fresh and cool, caressing his lungs, bringing with it the scent of living earth.

"Give yourself to Air," they murmured. "First of the four sacred things, element of life, our most intimate lover. Air will penetrate your blood and into every cell of your body. Open to it. Open deep." And he opened, filling the hollow place where fear had been with the touch of air, opening every pore and orifice until he no longer knew what was stroking him, touching him, probing into him except that it was all life, the great gift of life.

They laid him back down, hands covering him with mud, rubbing it into him, sculpting him anew out of clay. He felt the earth embrace him, and he was no longer afraid.

"Breathe. Give yourself to Earth, another of the four sacred things, our Mother. Feel the weight of gravity, her love pulling you close." It seemed as if the earth, now, were breathing with him, a living being who held him in her arms, a deep voice who murmured, "I am your Mother. They cannot take you from me, ever. I hold you close. I will never let you go."

He rested there for a long time, feeling a deep sense of peace. The barricades had fallen. He no longer had to maintain them or to fear what lay behind. For the first time since they had snatched him away from his mother's arms so long ago, he could truly rest.

After a long time, they roused him, sluicing him with warm water, another form of caress. Then followed hot streams that ran down his spine and cleansed the creases in his skin. And then the shock of a sudden deluge of cold. He gasped, but suddenly every pore in his skin felt electric, alive.

"Drink," he heard, and a cup was put to his lips filled with cool, clear water. Suddenly he realized how thirsty he was. He drank and drank, and when he drained the cup another appeared. Then he had to piss. He ached with the need, but he didn't know how to ask. It seemed such a mundane need that it would break the spell. But if he didn't, he was going to burst, or piss all over whatever he was standing on.

"Gotta piss," he finally made himself mutter. Now they were laughing at him. Not in a mean way, but as if they understood.

"Of course you do. Don't be ashamed, we all piss," the dark man murmured.

They guided him to a spot where he felt earth under his feet, and smelled the fragrance of herbs and flowers. "Let go," they said. He couldn't see, didn't know where to point himself but hands reached up and pointed his cock for him. He throbbed with the touch and spurted out his stream, feeling it flow through him with a relief that felt sensual. At the same time, other hands held the cup to his lips. Water flowed in and flowed out.

"You are a vessel," they murmured. "Give yourself to Water, sacred Water, womb of life. Let her heal you and cleanse you."

Then suddenly he was cold, shivering. They guided him out, into the sunshine. He felt its warmth, and turned his face to it.

"Open to the light, to the sun," they said. "Give yourself to Fire, kindler of life, the last of the four sacred things. Let it warm you, heal you."

He spread out his arms, opened his mouth, felt the sensual heat on his bare skin. He turned, slowly, to let it caress every part of him. He heard music again, slow and melodic, and he was turning in time to it, moving in its rhythm. The beat grew faster, the melody more intense, and he was whirling and turning. He was dancing, he, River, who had never done such a thing before. There was music in the barracks, pounding beats that jacked them up before a battle, but nothing like this.

Then hands pulled off his blindfold. The red-haired priestess stood before him. They were alone in the garden. She was wearing something flowing and diaphanous, that followed her movements as she twirled around and held out her hand. And then they were dancing together. He made a move, and she mirrored it. She swayed, and he followed. The dance was a promise, a tease. He was learning her, and she him, until at last there was no leading, no following, only their bodies moving in unison.

He didn't need to take her, he thought. He didn't even need to touch her smooth skin. This was enough. But even as he thought that, he began to imagine how her body would feel, swaying against his, how her breasts would feel under his hands. He began to throb and rise, and she smiled at him, drawing him close and pressing up against him so their bodies moved together, then teasing him as she swung away. And then back again, tighter still, her hips making a circle against his groin. He pulled her close, wrapped his arms around her, sought her mouth.

She put a finger up to his lips.

"You can have what you want," she said. "But you have to ask for it first. And say 'I,' River. And 'you.'"

"Can I kiss you?"

"Yes."

She tasted sweet. Her eyes were open as his tongue probed hers, and suddenly he saw something there, as if he could look through her eyes and see a soul, another person with her own thoughts and feelings and desires. I am a real person, he thought. And so is she.

He wanted more, suddenly, than just to taste her and pleasure her and take his own. He wanted to know her.

"Who are you?" he asked, breaking off.

"I am Lilith," she said.

"But who are you? Want—I want—to know who you are."

"I am a priestess." Again she gave him that knowing smile, that curve of the lips as if she were in possession of deep secrets. It aroused him more than anything, that smile.

She touched her forehead. "We train to put our personal selves aside, so we can become a vessel and bring forth the healing power. In this grove, I am Goddess."

He sat down, suddenly, on a stone bench. He could smell lavender, and could still smell her own rosy, spicy scent. But he could feel his cock shriveling. He was no longer aroused, but confused, feeling a different desire, not to take her like he had once thoughtlessly taken the pen-girls, not even to practice his new-learned art of arousal and satisfaction. He wanted to know what she ate for breakfast, and what made her mad. He thought about Bird and Madrone, how they would argue and fight and make up. That was what being a real person meant.

"Don't want the Goddess," he said. "Just want to know who you are."

"Ah, sweet boy, you want the one thing I cannot give you here." She smiled at him. "But if that is what you truly want, then we have done our work well. You are healed. You have found your immortal soul."

"Don't understand."

"Here in this temple, we worship the primal force of love. It's beyond the personal. When we take the oath of priestess, we forego that kind of individual, romantic love. Here is my sigil, a mark of my pledge, the scallop shell of Aphrodite. So you can't fall in love with me, nor I with you. But what you learn here in the grove can open your heart to find love outside."

He shook his head, even more confused. But he felt one burning question rising up. "Just tell one thing. You want to do this? Someone making you?"

"Yes, I want to," she leaned forward and touched her lips lightly to his nose, smiling. "It's my calling, and my great pleasure to give and to teach and to open hearts."

"Why'd you bring me here?" he asked.

"I liked your looks," she teased, but then her voice grew serious. "But that's not the whole story. The truth is we've been debating what to do about all you sojuhs and pen-girls. We could see that you were deeply wounded, and the wounds were like festering sores that were breeding nasty stuff, things that we haven't had to deal with here in this city for a long time. We thought we might have something to offer. So we decided to do a trial run."

"With me? This sojuh the experiment?" he said, angry now. He felt betrayed. No, this wasn't what he wanted. He wanted what he saw in Madrone's eyes when she looked at Bird. He longed for someone to look like that at him.

"We know your story," Lilith said, pulling back slightly as she sensed his anger. "We know that you have killed many, and that you chose to stop, that you are capable of change. And you brought the army over to our side, much of it. We owe you a debt of gratitude."

"How can you know this ... know me? Don't even know myself!"

"I know a great deal about you," she assured him, running the tip of one finger down the length of his arm. "I've watched you now, for four days. I would say you're maybe the most courageous man I've ever met."

"Me?" River looked at her in surprise. "This fighter? Nothin' but a howlin' mess, just this morning."

"Courage isn't about not feeling fear," Lilith said. "It's about facing fear. Letting yourself feel it fully, but not stopping. Over four days I've watched you touch deep wells of pain, but never once did you turn away, or say stop."

She took his head between her hands and gently turned it to face her. "You're brave. And I sense that in your deepest soul you are kind."

"No," River said. "Not kind. Never had a chance to be."

"And now you do," she said. "So the question is, do you want to go on?"

He took a breath, and forced himself to push out a sentence using both "you" and "me." That still felt wrong to him. But it was the only way to ask what he wanted to know.

"You want me?"

No fist came crashing down. He let out his breath.

"Yes, I do," she said firmly.

"Want to see the experiment succeed?"

"I want you, River. The Goddess wants you for her own. But more than that, underneath, I admit that I, as a woman, want you. I want to taste you and know you in the deepest intimacy. I believe it will be a gift to me, one of the crowning experiences of my life." She looked up at him, her eyes now wide and soft and silvery with tears. "So? Do you want me?"

"Oh yeah!" he smiled.

She smiled back, her eyes teasing again. "Then let's play a game. I'll ask you for something, and then you can ask me. Either one of us can say 'no' at any time, or 'yes.' But I want you to describe in detail everything you want to do to me, and everything you want me to do to you. It will heighten the pleasure. Do you agree?"

"Give it a try."

"Then ask me for something," she breathed into his ear. "And say 'I.' Always say 'I.'"

"Can I kiss you again?" he whispered softly.

"Yes."

Kissing. They had never bothered with such preliminaries in the rec room. But he liked it. His lips touched hers, his daring tongue sought the cave of her mouth, a foretaste of that deeper cave.

After a long moment, she pulled back and in a husky voice asked him, "Will you caress my nipple with your fingers, through my gown?"

They played a duet of request and fulfillment.

"Kiss you one more time? With your eyes open?"

"And now unbutton my gown, if you will, and do the same on my bare flesh ... please ... "

"And can I touch your ass?"

"And would you now stroke the fringes of the flower ... "

The game went on for hours. The sun went down, and Lilith drew him inside, into a candlelit chamber with a big, soft bed in the middle and mirrors on the walls. River found that the talking and describing slowed their lovemaking to a maddening pace. But then he relaxed into it, and began to enjoy it. He experienced everything twice, once in the describing, once in the doing.

Until finally she asked him, "May I prepare your shaft to enter the chamber?"

"Oh yes!"

She slipped a condom over him, stroking him as she did, and murmuring what sounded like a prayer: "I place this here as a sign of our deepest love and respect for the great powers that generate life. I place this to honor the act we are about to do with reverence and care for one another, for our health and safety. All acts of love and pleasure are my rituals!"

She drew him into her. Their eyes locked.

"Now, no more talking," she said. "No more need to ask. I am yours. You are mine."

Their eyes locked, their bodies moved, arching in the dance of dances. He plunged into her, searching her depths, his own depths, her pleasure his, his power hers, straining through flesh to touch her soul and in that connection restore his own. She was breathing in him as the earth had breathed with him, her body warm and radiant as the sun. He moved into her as air rushed into lungs, dissolved in her, pleasure rushing through him like a dancing stream full of rills and ripples, a rapids of dancing waters, a cataract that plunged over the edge of the world and spilled out into her ocean.

He slept, and awoke ravenously hungry. He realized that he hadn't eaten all day. She woke when he did, and brought a tray full of fruit and bread and cheeses. When he had satisfied his first rush of hunger, she fed him tidbits off her fingers. Then they made love again, all through the night and long into the dawn.

When morning came, she kissed him one last time.

"Sleep now. Today is a day to rest, to integrate what you have learned."

"Will I ever see you again?" he asked, suddenly filled with panic.

"Don't fall in love with me." She kissed him on the forehead. "Fall in love with you."

He spent the day in the garden, walking and thinking, smelling herbs and looking at flowers with new eyes. He was filled with a poignant sadness. He had received more than he had ever imagined. New worlds were open to him. But in spite of what she said, he loved her. She was the first woman who had ever wanted him, who knew what he was and still desired him. Would there ever be another? He missed her already, missed her touch, her scent, her voice.

Why couldn't he find her and hold her and keep her? Why did every-thing sweet have to end?

Yet he understood somehow that he was learning the final lesson. For everything sweet did end. That was life. Either you fought that, and tried to bind and cage the sweet stuff, killing it dead before its time, or you accepted it, and that made every moment of love all the more intense.

"So, what have you learned?" the old priestess asked him. They sat in the garden, over a table laden with an abundant lunch. He was hungry again, his body craving energy to make up for all that it had expended.

He looked into her eyes and realized with a shock that she, too, was a real person. She had hidden thoughts and feelings and judgments that he would never know.

He smiled and shrugged. He couldn't begin to answer her question, to put everything he'd experienced into mere words.

"Now that you've been through it, do you think the experience would benefit your brother soldiers?" she asked.

He gave her a long, slow, knowing smile.

"The army know about this, don't need no other weapon."

Chapter Eight

THE EARLY MORNING SUNSHINE STREAMED THROUGH THE BIG BAY window of Maya's bedroom. Her bed lay in its embrace, and the pale morning light caressed the grooves and ridges of her soft skin, the silver thicket of her hair spreading out over the pillows.

Madrone set the heavy tray down. It was a relic of another era, the metal surface so scratched and dented that the faces of Prince Charles and Lady Di were nearly obliterated. On it, a teapot steamed beside a cup and saucer embellished with rosebuds and a delicate china pitcher held milk. On a small plate rested a slice of toast. Once Madrone might have scrambled up eggs from their chickens or made a big pot of oatmeal for Maya. But these days the old woman ate little.

Madrone was tired. It had been her rotation on night shift, and she was ready, now, to go to bed. She could have woken Bird, let him get Maya's breakfast, but he was catching some late, restful sleep after what she suspected had been another night of horror-show dreams. And she savored this time with Maya, these rare moments of quiet.

How many more mornings like this will we have? Madrone wondered. She was a healer and midwife. She could see what was happening to her *madrina*. It's as if she's getting into position. The cervix is opening, the head engaged. Soon she'll be birthed into some other dimension.

And then, what will I do? Who will I talk to while the sun rises and I feel just like an empty teapot, nothing left inside but the dregs?

Maya muttered softly. What was she dreaming about? Was she cuddling in the arms of Grandma Johanna, her longtime lover? Or Grandpa Rio, her other longtime lover? Madrone smiled. They must have had a few stormy arguments, forming that trio! But as a child, she saw none of that. By the time Rio brought her up from Guadalupe, the three had long settled into peaceful companionship, and they had been her rocks of stability in those few peaceful years between the death of her mother and the Stewards' first invasion.

Maya opened her eyes.

"You think I'm sleeping, but I'm not. I can feel you staring at me."

"If you're awake, sit on up," Madrone told her. "I brought you some breakfast. Nice hot tea."

"Black?" Maya raised her head hopefully.

"Black! Just the way you like it. Sonoma County's finest imitation of English Breakfast."

Maya pushed herself up, and Madrone adjusted pillows for her back and set the tray down in front of her. Maya picked up the lid of the teapot, bent her head and sniffed.

"It's not the same as a good old cup of Yorkshire Blend or PG tips. But it'll do. It'll have to. At least it's not some bland herbal swill."

"Watch it, old lady! You're talking to an herbalist," Madrone smiled.

"You're talking to an elder, I'll have you know," Maya retorted. "Show some respect!"

She raised the teapot with shaky hands, and Madrone steadied it for her. The brew was rich and brown. Maya added milk and stirred.

"I bow to your superior taste in tea blends, O elder!" Madrone said.

Maya snorted. "Not that it means much. As soon as they started calling me an elder, I knew they were no longer thinking of me as a hot babe!"

Madrone laughed. "I don't know about that. You seem to me to be smoldering a bit, even now."

"Nah. Doctor Sam was my last wild fling. And that's over. Faded away into mere affection. The dangerous end to old people sex."

Madrone perched on the side of the bed, grateful for a few moments of tranquility as Maya sipped her tea.

"Do you miss your wild youth?" Madrone asked.

"Makes me sad to think I'll never do the dirty thing again. But makes me tired to think about actually doing it." Maya set the tea down, and fixed Madrone with eyes that were suddenly sharp and clear. "But what about you? What's happening to your wild youth?"

"I'm not so young. Almost thirty."

"Thirty! Ha! At thirty I was just getting going. While you and Bird— you're looking more and more like an old married couple. It's been a while since I've heard those happy thumps and moans of a group orgy in the attic."

Madrone smiled. "Well, half of the *compas* are scattered, or focused on other things. And—I don't know. With Bird, it's like, intensified."

He was wounded, was what she didn't say. His needs and those of her patients together drank up all the energy she had to spare.

Maya gave her another sharp look. "Don't make him the center of your life, that's all."

"What do you mean?" Madrone felt a flash of anger. "He's not the center of my life!"

But he is, she admitted to herself. How could he not be, right now? My love, my heart, my own resurrected miracle.

"Isn't he? I see you watching him, with that look on your face."

"What look?"

"The woman look. The 'Is he okay? What more can I do for him? How can I adapt further to his moods and soothe his pain and spare his feelings' look."

"Oh, *that* look."

"Goddess! As if I didn't fight all those years on the feminist front lines to spare you that! Ears ringing from misogynist jokes, eyes smarting from the smoke of burning bras ... "

Now Madrone was laughing. "You did not! At least not in that way. Nobody ever really burned a bra."

"How in Hella's name would you know?"

"I learned it in our Radical History Module."

"Ha! I was there, while Ms. Radical History Module was sucking her baby dum dum."

"You are incorrigible. Eat your toast."

Maya crunched down on a bite. "I just want you to be the hera of your own life."

Now Madrone was irritated. "And who went down to the Southlands? Who brought back the antidotes to the biogerms? Who went into the research center and rescued Katy and then delivered her baby? My hera creds are impeccable!"

"I won't say you haven't had your moments," Maya conceded. "But don't let it slip away. I see you getting sucked down into the endless black hole of everybody else's needs. Don't lose sight of your own."

My own? Madrone thought. But what needs do I have? Aside from a bit more sleep. I'm healthy and well and well-fed and well-loved. More than that, I'm a vessel, with power pouring through me and bee-song humming in my ears.

"But isn't that what heras do? Put aside their needs to serve some larger good? Nobody ever waged a heroic battle to get eight hours of unbroken sleep and eat a healthy, vitamin-filled breakfast."

"Just make sure you're the center of your own story. Not Bird. Not your patients. Not even me. You. Madrone. What is your vision? What do you want?"

Who am I? If I'm not healing or nurturing or feeding? I want a baby, but is that just someone else whose needs will take precedence over my own? Another gaping beak to fill? I'm not a painter or a singer or a storyteller.

I don't miss being a warrior. I could happily never taste that particular brew of terror and exhilaration and thirst and panic again.

What if my center *is* to serve others? Isn't that the essence of what a healer is?

A vessel. A teapot. Tip me over and pour me out.

"I don't know," she admitted.

Madrone was washing up the breakfast dishes when Katy came in, her baby Lucia strapped across her body with a sling. Her wavy black hair was pinned back with a rose behind her ear, and even weighed down with the baby, her carriage was regal and graceful as a flamenco dancer. She had filled out a bit on the good food of the City, Madrone noted, and while she was still slender, she no longer looked gaunt. There was a healthy, rosy flush to her dark-honey skin.

"I've come to sit with Maya for the day," she said. "Let me do that! You look exhausted. Why don't you get some sleep?"

"Not until I get a hit of that baby!"

Katy unwrapped the child and laid her in Madrone's arms. Madrone took her and sank into the easy chair in the far corner of the room, while Katy tackled the remaining few dishes at the sink. Lucia looked up at Madrone with an innocent gaze, and grimaced.

"I swear that was a smile," Madrone said.

"She knows who brought her into the world."

Madrone beamed down at the baby. Lucia crinkled her eyes and smiled back, her whole body wriggling in delight. They grinned back and forth at each other.

This is better than sleep, Madrone thought, drinking in the sheer, goofy pleasure of it, making silly little sounds and talking baby talk. My reward for being a hera. For all that fear and terror and making myself ignore it and go after Katy anyway. For those harrowing moments on Isis's boat, making their getaway, Katy moaning in pain and terror and the baby stuck. This peaceful moment, now, with Katy humming at the sink and sunshine bathing the windows, Maya snoring softly in her bed and Bird still asleep, at last, in his. And this child, charming me with her smile.

"How's life at the mothers' house?" Madrone asked.

"Blissful! Always someone there to take the baby, if I need a break. But not quiet! There's about a million toddlers underfoot, all of them well-endowed with lungs and vocal cords. It's nice to come back here from time to time. I can get a bit of peace, and feel like I'm doing something useful."

"I'm sure you're always useful."

"Maybe. Not indispensable, like I was at home in the Southlands."

In the Southlands, Katy had run the urban home of the Resistance like a combination of a mother superior and Wendy among the lost boys. Until the raid.

Katy sighed. "But in any case, now I'm dispensed and they'll just have to manage without me."

She sounded worried.

"Do you miss it?"

"Not the hunger and the dust and the fear. I miss feeling like I was doing something important. Something toward making a better day." She sounded sad and worried. The dishes were done, and she flopped onto the couch under the window.

"I miss Hijohn. I wish he could see his daughter."

"He will, someday." Madrone put all the assurance she could muster into her voice.

"When?" Katy countered, and Madrone had no real answer for that.

Many years ago, someone had hung the prisms from an old chandelier from the window frames, and now sunlight streamed in and sent rainbows dancing around the room. Lucia's eyes followed them, her arms pumped as if she were trying to grasp for them with her baby hands, her mouth worked with frustration.

Madrone picked her up and held her out so a rainbow danced over her face. She kicked her feet in delight, and favored Katy with a radiant smile.

"Chasing rainbows," Katy smiled back. "We don't get to do that in the Southlands. But ... " she stopped.

"But you can't help but feel that the Southlands deserve a few rainbows, too. I know." Now Lucia had her eyes fixed on Katy, her arms reaching out. Madrone laid her back in Katy's arms.

Katy gazed down at the child and pulled her close.

"I never intended to get pregnant with her. It was crazy, insane. But it happened."

"It does."

Could it happen to her? Could it be just that easy, no long discussions, no agonizing choices. Just a happy accident?

Katy went on, "And I thought, 'Well, she'll be a child of the Southlands, always in danger, always in want, but she's chosen to come into this, and maybe she's got a role to play.' I accepted it. But now ... now there's a choice. And I can't choose to bring her back into that danger, when she could be safe, here. But ... "

"But you want to go back," Madrone said softly.

Slowly, Katy nodded. "I want to go back. Some days I think I'll go mad with it, sitting in the garden, Lucia nursing and looking up at me with love, and part of me wanting to wrap her up in a sack and follow the noon sun back to those dusty hills."

"I know."

"You feel it, too?"

"Bird feels it. I can tell." And what would Maya have to say about that? Okay, I admit it, I'm doing it, the woman thing. She asks me what

I feel, and I tell her what he feels. Nonetheless, she continued. "And if he goes, I'll want to go with him."

"But what do you want?"

"Everyone keeps asking me that today!" she snapped. "But what does it really matter what I want? I'll go where I'm needed!"

"You'll be needed wherever you go," Katy said. "So you might as well decide for yourself where you want to be. Or you'll end up one of the those whining, bitter women—'I gave up everything for you, and this is the thanks I get? I gave up my dreams, my ideals, my revolutionary career, my ...'" Her voice faltered.

"You aren't giving it up," Madrone assured her. "Maybe putting it on 'pause' for awhile. Or maybe you could trust that you'll be learning things here that eventually you'll put to use, when you do go back."

"When? How old is old enough, safe enough? Another ten years? A dozen? When will she ever be old enough to be safe from the Stewards' breeding pens?"

"When we free the Southlands, and there are no more breeding pens." It came out of Madrone's mouth like a vow.

Is that my task? If the need for a healer is great here, what will it be like if I go back down there? And the more power I gain, the greater the need for it.

But Katy was right. Maya was right. She couldn't just follow Bird down there, if he went.

She had to find her own gravitational pull, her own sun to revolve around.

Chapter Nine

THE COUNCIL DOME HAD BEEN ONE OF THE STRUCTURES THAT suffered the most damage under the Stewards, who had blasted its geodesic windows into shards. Repairs were underway, but they would take many months, not least because the Builders' Guild decided to use the opportunity to upgrade the insulation and energy systems.

In the meantime, the people of the City met to make decisions in the amphitheater on the hill used for ritual and open-air theater. A processional way wound round the slopes, past altars to Earth, Air, Fire, and Water and that fifth sacred thing that had no single name. Atop were shrines to every religion imaginable, with statues and reliquaries, banners and sculptures, dancing grounds, and a cairn of stones to honor the dead.

Far below lay the colorful tapestry of green streets, the shining ribbons of flowing streams, the colorful windspinners, and gaily waving flags. The view almost but not quite compensated for the wind that whipped off hats and snarled flowing scarves.

Bird felt anxious as he shoehorned Maya into the crowd and found her a place of honor in the front, next to Lily, her old crony from Defense Council. Maya had insisted on coming, and although Bird could think of ten reasons why she should stay home, he couldn't bring himself to muster the argument. How could he tell her, "It might be too much for you," without implying that she was now too weak to take part in the City's life? How could he say, "The whole city will see that you are getting vaguer and vaguer," without admitting to himself, and to her, that she was slipping away?

Dark-eyed Amani was facilitating, dressed in an embroidered robe of crimson red, his black hair in a hundred long braids with small bells on the ends. Bird wished it were Salal, but she couldn't facilitate every meeting. Smokee sat together with Isis and Sara, the three of them dressed in pirate cutoffs and bulky sweatshirts. Holybear sat beside Doctor Sam, still hale and hearty in his eighties, amidst a crowd of healers. Across from him sat Cress and his Water Council posse, who fixed Bird with hostile glares.

The signer for the Deaf looked at Amani inquiringly, and he nodded to indicate that he welcomed interpretation. The younger people of the City, who had grown up after the Uprising, spoke American Sign Language as easily as they did English, but even the most fluent of them sometimes found it difficult to speak both English and sign at once.

At stations marking the four quarters of the amphitheater sat four masked figures. In the East, Hawk sat covered with beak and feathers, ready to speak for the creatures of Air. In the South, Trickster Coyote would listen deep for messages from Fire. Salmon, in the West, spoke for Water and for all their long efforts to restore the waterways and bring back the sacred fish that linked the ocean to the land. In the North, Deer raised proud antlers, messenger of Earth. The speaker for the Voices, with flowing beard and swirling skirts, moved between them, ready to bend down and listen for a whisper.

Amani planted his feet, surveyed the crowd, tossed his head so his braids whipped back and forth and the bells tinkled.

"There's a warship anchored offshore," he said. "As we know. On the agenda for today—what to do about it? So far, what we've done is watch, for weeks. Is that what we want to continue to do? Or, something else? I'll take a report from Tech Guild first."

Beryl, one of the techies, stood up. Slim, pale, with shaved head and an almost genderless body concealed beneath a silver tunic, Beryl spoke with a voice that cracked and squeaked, like a rarely-used, outdated sound system. "They're jamming our radio contact with Cascadia and the Heartlands. Or they think they are. We've been able to bypass their obstruction using morphic resonance technology. So far."

A large man stood in the back of the crowd and called out in a ringing voice. "How do we know they'll stop with just jamming communications? What if they start firing shells on the City?"

The buzz grew louder, with an undertone of fear.

"They're attacking again!" a woman cried.

"We always knew they would. We've got to go down there and root them out!" a stocky man thundered.

"That's war-mongering!" came a shout from the back.

"What do you call a warship—a peace brigade?" he countered.

"Quiet!" Amani barked. He stamped his foot, whipped his braids around, and shouted it out many times before quiet fell.

"I'm going to take a stack," he said. "I'll call you one at a time, so wait your turn! Lily, you're number one."

Lily rose. She had to be almost Maya's age, Bird thought, but she was slim and erect and graceful, and although she now leaned on a cane, her spine was straight and her stance as proud as a dancer's. Her face was a contour map of wrinkles. Her dark eyes, half-moons surrounded by a web of lines, were still sharp and clear, set in a face that was a contour map of wrinkles. Her hair was still midnight black. Maya accused her of dyeing it, but Bird somehow couldn't imagine Lily concerned with such things. Her lips curved in a serene smile.

"We should approach the sailors," she said, "and offer them a chance to defect."

Cress snorted. Amani turned a sharp eye on him, and he fell silent, but raised his hand to get on the stack. Amani nodded acknowledgment and then pointed to Sara, who was next.

Cress waited his turn. It gave him time to steel himself for the hostile reception he generally got from Council. Why? he wondered, when he spoke the simple truth. But people generally don't want to hear the truth. They'd rather hear comforting platitudes and mumbo-jumbo that supported their beliefs.

"The problem is," Sara said, "we can't get close enough to the ship to offer them anything. Any boat that approaches, no matter how small, they bombard with their shells."

"Proof that they fear our strategy," Lily said. "They fear the loyalty of their troops will not withstand exposure to our ways."

Cress stood up, wrapping his arms around his torso, his blue Water Council jacket too thin to keep out the bite of the wind. He'd lost flesh during the invasion, and his clothes hung on him. He took a deep breath.

"Maybe so," he said. "But they've also figured out a good way to keep that loyalty from being tested. We've got to take it out. We can't just sit here passively and wait for them to come back after us."

He stared defiantly across the bleachers at Bird, who sat by himself in a top row. Go ahead, lunkhead, argue with that, he longed to say. Make some stirring, arrogant speech about love. I dare you!

Bird heard the impatience in his voice, and ventured a brief, conciliatory smile. He sympathized with Cress, even though the man hated him. While Bird admired Lily, at times he found her absolute, unshakable certainties to be irritating. Maybe he and Cress could make an alliance, let some of the hostility between them drop.

But Cress only glowered back at him.

He didn't look so cocky now, Cress thought. Stewards knocked him down a rung. Arrogant fool! Bird was the one who had thrown his weight behind Lily and Maya, arguing for nonviolent resistance. But it hadn't taken long for him to betray them all, sitting there in the Central Plaza, wearing the uniform of the enemy, handing out their water ration cards.

He should have been tried for treason, Cress thought. Banished to go live with the wild boar people. But while they said there was no hierarchy in Califia, that no one stood higher or lower than any other, that was not functionally true. Concessions that would not be made for an ordinary joe were extended to the grandson of Maya, the City's honored storyteller and one of the key figures in the Uprising.

He was glaring at Bird, he realized. He might have let go and forgiven him. But he clung to his smoldering resentment, a coal of warmth against the chill.

"Take it out, how?" Lily countered, interrupting his thoughts.

"Well, we can't offer them a place at our table," Cress spit out impatiently. "Not when they shoot first, parley after. Why don't we simply blow them out of the water? We've got ordnance that we captured from the Stewards."

"It was by inviting the army to our table that we won our victory," Lily said.

"Or in spite of it," Cress countered. It's the smugness that gets to me, he thought. It would almost have been worth a Stewards' victory not to have to look at that Kuan Yin smirk on Lily's face. But careful. Take a breath. Don't lay into her or you'll lose what support you have in the crowd.

"And now look what it got us!" he went on. "We've got a city full of sojuhs eating our food, sitting on their haunches at our cafés, harassing our women, and threatening the peace!"

A tall, dreadlocked woman leapt to her feet. "*Your* women?" she thundered. "Since when have the women in this city become *your* women?"

Mierda, that was a bad mistake, Cress owned to himself.

A petite but well-muscled blonde beside her jumped up. "And we are perfectly capable of defending ourselves, thank you very much."

"I didn't mean 'our' women in the sense of possession," Cress back-pedaled quickly. "I meant it in the sense of, 'we're all part of the same City.'"

The sojuh's representative was stung into wakefulness. "Fuck you!" he spat at Cress.

"Batting a hundred," Flo murmured from behind him. "Who else can you piss off?"

"Oh, shut up!" he snapped back at her. That sort of remark was why their relationship was off-again more than it was on. What he needed from a partner was support, not digs. Someone who was on his side, like Valeria had always been.

Valeria. Better not to think about her in this moment, or their child who had never had a chance to live.

"Silence!" Amani called. "People, remember, we don't do personal attacks."

Flo laid a restraining hand on Cress's arm. Cress sat down abruptly.

"The sojuhs are doing work, now," objected Allie, the guide who worked with Rosa's Learning Group. "They're helping the children rebuild the Learning Tracks. And getting an education."

"Some of them," yelled a voice from the back.

River stood. "Ain't gonna be harassin' nobody no longer," he said. "Temple of Love takin' care a that."

"Sweet," Cress said. "The rest of us are busting our veins clearing up the shit the army destroyed, while the army disports itself in the Temple of Love. What else can we do for them? Peel them some grapes?"

"You don't know," River said with dignity. "You don't know what they do. Fighters, they got to become real people before they can help you. Temple of Love, they figure that out."

"No offense," Cress said. "But is a week in the Temple of Love really going to change a gang of ruthless killers into sensitive rosebuds of peace?"

Flo pinched him.

"Makes a start," River countered. "Gotta start somewhere." He was staring back at Cress, not dropping his eyes. Cress stared at him. Like two adolescent roosters, he thought, trying to prove who's tougher. In a moment I'll begin to crow.

Flo pinched him again, but he ignored her and turned back to the crowd.

"So why is it only the sojuhs?" he asked. "What about the pen-girls? Don't they deserve some love, too?"

At this the pen-girl's rep, supported by many encouraging hands, struggled to her feet. She looked terrified and her voice quivered.

"Don't want that," she said. She glanced around after she spoke as if she expected a blow to fall. Amani held a hand up for silence. Everyone waited expectantly.

"Go ahead," Amani said gently. "If you have more to say, we're here to listen."

The pen-girl shook her head. "Just leave pen-girls alone."

"Is that all you want?" Amani asked.

The rep was small and slight, painfully thin as if she'd never quite gotten enough to eat. She had bittersweet chocolate skin, round dark eyes, and fine, delicate features. If she didn't look so scared, she'd be pretty, Cress thought. But brittle, as if she might break if you looked too hard at her. He sighed. One thing he didn't want was a conflict with the pen-girls. Just watching her quiver made him feel like a bully.

"Only one thing pen-girls want," she mumbled, looking down.

"What's that? Go ahead, don't be afraid," Amani encouraged her. "If we can help you get it, we will."

The rep shook her head, clamped her lips shut. The Council waited.

"It's okay," Amani said. "No matter what it is. You can say it here."

The girl darted a glance around, opened her mouth and shut it again.

"Take a deep breath," Lily encouraged her. "Find your courage, child, and speak."

The girl stole a glance up. She inhaled a shuddering breath, then quickly, before she could change her mind, she spoke. "Babies."

Again the Council waited.

"Pen-girls want them babies back," she blurted out.

The sojuhs' rep snorted. "Babies dog meat by now. Pet food."

She whirled on him. "Fuck off, slime balls!" The words ripped out of her. She was no longer scared, just blazing mad. "How many times shit-for-brains been in the rec room? Where them babies come from, pus-squirt? They sojuhs' babies too!"

She sat down, looking both scared and triumphant. The big sojuh was stunned into silence. He looked confused, as if a new idea were working in his brain.

River stared at the pen-girl. He, too, was struggling with a host of new ideas. He had never thought of the babies as having any connection to him, to the rutting and grunting in the rec room. But of course they did. He could be not just a person but a father. There could be any number of little Rivers, torn like he'd been from their mothers' arms, suffering the beatings and the drill. Or worse, corralled in the pens, learning to tolerate the probing and the beating and the rapes.

Suddenly he, too, was filled with a sense of outrage. How had he never thought of it, this ultimate takeover of his self, his seed, his future? It was like a storm that shook him, and when it passed, he knew beyond a doubt that he would go back, back to the Southlands. They had bred and trained him to be a fighter, well then, he would fight and they would come to regret that they had ever forged such a weapon.

He stood up. Amani nodded at him to speak.

"This fighter ..." he stopped. "No, I. I, River, will go back to the Southlands. North never be truly safe as long as the Stewards rule. But the Southlands full of people, real people, too. People that deserve somethin' better than what the bigsticks dish out.

"Time to end this mess. Any fighters that want to go with me, they welcome. But I will go, if I go alone."

He glanced over at the pen-girl. She was looking at him with something in her eyes, something like admiration. It excited him. So did her fear, her fragility. Ohnine, the breed he'd been, Ohnine could break her in pieces, and that aroused him, made him feel powerful in the familiar old way. But it also now sickened him a bit, made him feel ashamed.

Yet there was something else, a different urge that River the dancer in the Temple of Love might feel. What would it be like to hold her, to feel her body shudder under his not with fear but with pleasure? That would be a different sort of power, and the thought excited him even more.

Could he do that, he wondered? Could he teach her what the priestesses taught him?

And there was something more. She was a pen-girl, but she was a real person, too. She had spoken up—she was brave, and he liked that.

Cress met River's eye again, but this time he let himself smile at the sojuh. Suddenly he was filled with the desire to go with him. To shed this cloying city with its flower-perfumed streets, its factions that despised

him, and its grief-filled corners. Hardly a park or a bower where he
hadn't been at some time with Valeria. Not a playground or a learning
station where he hadn't imagined their child laughing and running to
him with arms outstretched.

He rose to his feet. "You won't be alone, *compa*." And suddenly he
felt light, released, clear. Yes, this was what he was meant for, what he
was called to do.

One by one, all over the theater, others stood. They came from all
the different guilds, farmers, techies, some of the younger healers.

"How many of the sojuhs do you think you can persuade to go along
with you?" Cress asked River, keeping his voice carefully calm, neutral.
There was a small flap of skin on the inside of his cheek and he realized
he was chewing it with the tension.

"Not all," River admitted. "But a lot."

"And not just the dicks-for-brains!" Smokee stood up. "We go get
our own babies back, thank you!"

"The pen-girls?" Cress said, unable to keep silent any longer.
"Really? You think they're capable of that?"

The pen-girl rep rose. "Pen-girls fight, too!"

"With legs in the air!" a former sojuh taunted. "With ass to the
sky!"

Suddenly the former sojuhs and pen-girls and half the Cityfolk were
shouting each other down.

"Quiet!" Amani cried. But his voice was lost in the pandemonium.
"QUIET!" he yelled at high volume. "Repeat after me, 'QUIET!'"

"QUIET!" thundered back much of the crowd, and quiet fell.

Isis and Sara stood up together, and drew Smokee back up with them.

"We will train the pen-girls," Isis said. "We have a plan."

"Can we get back to the warship?" Cress asked. Irritation had crept
back into his voice. He took a long, deep breath.

"Lily, I do actually respect your views," he said in a controlled,
neutral tone. "And I admit, nonviolence worked well for us in defending
this city. But it's one thing to offer the soldiers a place at our table when
they're in your back garden. How do we win them over when we can't
even see them? How do we stop them launching an attack on us from
afar? They could have anything—even an old nuclear missile."

Lily sat silent.

"Well?" Cress was losing patience.

"I'm thinking!" she snapped.

Maya stood up. "Back in the day when I was a revolutionary cadre,
with the bomb squad—"

"You?" Cress interrupted in surprise. What was she trying to pull now?

Bird gave her a sharp, anxious glance. But her eyes were clear and
focused, a slight smile on her face. It was one of her good days, when she
was fully present. He should just relax.

"I thought you were a pacifist?" Cress said. When it suits your purposes, he thought bitterly.

"There's a lot you don't know about me," Maya snorted. "I was never a pacifist—I'm not one now."

"'There's a place for you at our table, if you will choose to join us'? That wasn't you who came up with that line?" Cress wasn't sure whether to be mad, or just confused.

"That was a vision," Maya said. "I never claimed it was a dogma for all occasions. Here's what I've learned after a long, misspent life— winning over the enemy is preferable to slaughter. But it's always an experiment. I don't have Lily's pure faith. But I'm willing to try. And I believe that if we accept the necessity of slaughter, we don't push ourselves to employ our imagination, our magic, our compassion. We fall back into the old story."

"But the old story is still there, anchored offshore," Cress objected. And now he knew what he was so angry about. Why did he always have to be the one to pull them back to reality? Was he panting for war? No! Did he lust for battle, thirst for the blood of his enemy? No! He wanted to dig hollows into the land that could become vernal pools, and channel graywater to grow fraggin' flowers!

But the Stewards were taking that from him, as they had already taken so much from him, the losses he couldn't bear thinking of. And these idiots around him still couldn't seem to grapple with clear facts.

Maya sighed. "I do believe that everyone has something redeemable within them. But in the end, it comes down to choice. Not everyone will make the choice to be redeemed."

"And the warship?" Cress prompted. "How do we redeem that?"

"I'm trying to tell you, if you'll stop interrupting. Back in the day, this was the Vietnam War, mind you, when we'd lost faith in marches and demonstrations and some of us believed that stronger action was called for. We thought that by attacking the infrastructure of the system, we would reveal its weakness. We considered ourselves nonviolent terrorists—that is, we didn't really want to hurt anyone. We just wanted to blow up some of the pillars that propped up the system, like the draft boards or the weapons transports.

"In hindsight, that didn't work so well for us. The physicality of the system was its strong point. We would have done better to attack its weak point—its legitimacy."

"How would you have done that?" Sara asked.

"By exposing the violence that was its underpinning. Our biggest successes came when we made that violence visible." Sara still looked confused, so Maya continued on. "When we marched, when we demonstrated, when they sent the police to attack us, then it became clear that the system needed force to maintain itself. It couldn't stand just on its own merits. Of course with the war, people expect violence, but what we revealed was that violence was built into the system. It wasn't just the tiger cages and the executions and the children burned to the bone with napalm, although those were bad and beyond what people of that more innocent time were prepared to accept as a cost of war. It was the underlying injustice, the way the rich could avoid serving but the poor had no choice, the lies, the greed that the war served ... all of that was packed into every billy club that came down on the head of a peaceful protestor.

"Our blowing up buildings just confused the issue. Most people failed to grasp the subtle distinction between radicals attacking a draft board and not hurting anyone, and the army in Vietnam massacring civilians. But I'm digressing, I know.

"The point is, how did we do it? Keep from hurting people, that is? We planted the bomb and then phoned in a warning. Gave everyone a clear chance to get out."

"So what are you suggesting we do with the warship?" Sara asked.

"It's simple," Maya said. "Wire it up, and then give them a warning. Offer them a choice."

"How do we do that when we can't get close enough to them to talk?" Doctor Sam asked.

Maya shook her head at him as if he were hopelessly dim. "Do we not have a city crawling with techies and sound engineers?"

"And mining the ship?" Beryl the techie asked.

"We have divers," said Shakir of Water Council. "And we could use kayaks and rafts. Small enough to sneak under their radar. Go in at night, or under cover of a storm...."

A long discussion ensued, and slowly they devised a plan.

"Take out the warship, then head south," River said. "Need some time to prepare."

Lily stood up and addressed River.

"So, soldier. You propose to go and liberate your homeland—and who could blame you? But how do you propose to fight that battle?"

"Got guns. Got weapons left by the army, and these tubos—we—know how to fight."

"Guns can kill," Lily said. "And with them you may be able to damage or even destroy their forces. But guns cannot liberate. To do that, you will need to free the minds of the Southlanders, not just destroy their bodies. Or else you will simply replace one tyranny with another."

River shrugged. "Sojuh's job just to clear the way."

"Clear the way for what?" Lily asked. "How will you liberate people who have no comprehension of what liberation can mean?"

Bird sat fighting his own inner battle. What kept him hesitant was not fear for himself. He had moved into some kind of zone of deadly calm, beyond fear. No, it was more uncertainty of how to begin and what to do.

He had put down the gun. He had chosen, in the moment of the ultimate test, to put his faith in a different kind of power. He had sworn that his hands, broken as they were, would no longer kill.

Yet everything within him longed to pick the gun back up and lead the soldiers back to the South, blasting their way to liberation, ending forever the Stewards' threat. He dreamed of guns in the night. His hands ached to hold the weight of one.

He'd been down there. He knew what life was like, in their slums, in the thirsty hills, in their prisons. He couldn't draw a line around the North and say, These are my only people, no one else counts. For the Southlands were full of people, too, and while they suffered, he couldn't completely lose his own pain or heal his scars.

I'm a fighter. I know how to fight. And I know what we're fighting against.

Yet his deepest power had come to him as a singer, a maker of music. He could feel it surge within him, driving him night after night to his piano and his music sheets, hearing songs, writing them out note by note even though he could no longer play them as he heard them.

Will I blast that power into oblivion, he thought? Will it leak away with the first blood I spill? Yet how in Hella's name can we liberate the Southlands without fighting for them? We can't invite them to our table—we'll be invading theirs. We can't win over the soldiers with kindness or haunt them with guilt.

How could they possibly inspire the population to rise when said population had no idea of what a Rising was or could lead to?

And there was Maya. Tell the story, she'd said. Sing the song. Yet how could he leave her at the end of her own story? How could he not be there to sing her over when her time came to go?

─────

As the meeting broke up, River saw the pen-girl rep ducking out of the amphitheater and heading down the path. He followed her. Her head was down and she didn't look at any of the shrines, the sculptures, the trees and flowers around her, only at the path in front of her. So he was able to come up behind her.

"Aya," he said.

She turned, startled, looking around for a place to run. He held up his hands.

"Don't be afraid. Won't hurt you. Just want to talk," he said as softly as he could.

"Talk?" she said, as if she had never heard the word.

"I liked what you said." He scurried to catch up with her, and felt awkward, big and lumbering. "Never thought about it before. The babies. About—about maybe some of them mine, too."

She looked him up and down with suspicion.

"What this tubo want?" she demanded.

"Nothing." He took a big gulp of air, and thought about risks he had taken before. Saying yes to the City. Yes to the Temple of Love. They had worked out all right. What would Maya tell him to do? She'd probably say, Go for it, sojuh. What you got to lose? "Just—can I walk you back to the convent?"

How many pen-girls had he taken, thoughtlessly? Holy Jesus, why was he scared of this one, now?

"No billies to stop it," she said. He took that for a yes, and fell into step beside her.

River thought he should say something, but he couldn't think of anything to say. Finally, he forced out a soft question.

"Happy, down at the convent?"

"No complaints."

They walked on farther, down to the line for the gondolas that wafted people from hilltop to hilltop over the City.

"Want to ride, or walk?" he asked.

"Don't ride them fool things," she said.

"It's wonderful!" he said eagerly. "Like flying. See the whole city spread out down below."

"Fall out of the air, not so wonderful."

"Never happen. Promise! Want to try it?"

She gave him another long, suspicious look, but fell into line beside him.

"Got spirit. This fighter like that," he said.

"Not asking no tubo to like it or not," she retorted, but the rigid line of her spine softened just a bit, and as they moved with the line she stood just a bit closer to him.

"Name is River," he said. "What they call this ... you?"

"Hallby."

"That a name, or an address?"

"Don't got no name."

"Should have a name," he said, conscious of her lightness, how tiny her wrists were, how breakable she looked. "Ain't gonna say no address. That shit's over."

"Not askin' to be called nothin'." She stiffened and moved away from him.

There was a kitten in the garden at Black Dragon house that she reminded him of. He saw it in the yard when he went out to water the plants or tend the chickens. It was small and looked so delicate, but when it stalked a bug it was fierce, and if you tried to grab it, or pet it when it wasn't in the mood, it scratched and spit.

"Kit," he said. "Call ... you ... Kit."

"Kit?"

"Like it?" he asked. She shrugged.

They were next in line for the gondola, which swung to a stop in front of them. River hopped in. Kit hesitated on the platform.

Suddenly he found her fear irritating. He stepped back out, gripped her arm and propelled her in.

She cast her eyes down, like the pen-girls did, and he felt that same strange mixture of excitement and shame. Yes, she'd let him do what he liked with her. But was that what he wanted?

He felt an electric tingle, like a pulse, linking them, where his hand gripped her arm. Maybe he was holding her too tight, hurting her. His shaft grew warm at the thought of hurting her, and he didn't want to feel that. Fuck! He dropped her arm.

The gondola moved off with a lurch and she stumbled and fell against him. Without thinking, his arms clasped her. She froze, rigid against him.

What had they taught him in the Temple of Love? Ask!

"Okay to do this?" he asked. "Maybe feel safer?"

She looked at him, uncomprehending.

"Sojuh do what sojuh wants," she said dully.

"What do *you* want?" he asked. She simply stared, as if she didn't understand the words. But her body relaxed, just slightly. He could smell the herbal scent of her hair, new-grown since liberation, a fine, mossy cap that outlined the shape of her head. He was flooded with some of the same feelings he'd felt in the temple, the warmth, the electricity, the sweetness.

"Look," he said, pointing down to the panorama below them. Streams ran through verdant gardens. They sailed over the tops of laden fruit trees. Bicycles glided on paths and children played in the parks. He folded his arms around her, breathing with her, feeling her warm against him.

The gondola docked atop another hill and he helped her out. He walked beside her up the steep path that led to the old convent above Buena Vista Park.

At the gate of the convent he stopped. No men were allowed inside.

"Maybe come by again sometime?" he asked.

Kit looked at him with suspicion.

"This about poundin' the nail?" she asked.

"No. This about me, River, liking you, Kit. I like you." He took a breath. "Do you like me?"

She stepped back, and thought for a long moment. "No complaints," she finally admitted.

"Want me to come for you?"

"Okay," she said, and slipped through the door.

Chapter Ten

"WHAT MAKES A PERSON LIKE ANOTHER PERSON?" RIVER ASKED. He and Maya were alone in the kitchen, surrounded by buckets of plums to be pitted and made into what Maya called her world-class famous plum barbecue sauce. For so many years, it had been one of her summer rituals. This would be the last time, she thought. The ache in her bones told her that by next summer, she'd be off on a very different journey.

My legacy. Sauce for the barbecues of decades to come. And a recipe.

Actually River was doing the pitting. Maya sat with a knife, a plum, and a chopping board, staring vaguely at them, her mind wandering off in some faraway place. It hurt him to see her that way. She was like the torn-up gardens in the City, half-ruined but still in her own way beautiful. He reached over and gently took the knife from her. She stared at the plum for a long moment, then ate it absently. Slowly, as if she were calling herself back from a far country, her eyes came into focus.

"You want someone to like you?" she asked.

He nodded.

"A special someone. A girl someone?"

"Just a pen-girl. But—don't know. Somethin' about the ... about her."

He looked bashful and shy, like a little boy. Or like the awkward teenager that he actually was, Maya realized. When had the Stewards started their breeding programs? Not until after the old world fell, and then it must have taken them a while to get it up and running. Even if he was in their first cohort, he couldn't be much more than seventeen.

"Well, you have to court her," she said with a faint smile, as if she were remembering long-dead suitors of her own.

"Court?"

"Be attentive to her. Look after her well-being. You could bring her little things—flowers."

"Flowers? Flowers everywhere." River said, confused.

"True," Maya admitted. "But if you bring her some, make her a little bouquet, that's different. And then, you could ask her out on a date."

"Whass that?"

"It's when two people go out together to have some fun, get to know one another. Listen to some music, or see a movie, or have a romantic little dinner in some candlelit restaurant ... "

"Pen-girls don't eat but chips," River said, discouraged.

"Take her to the theater, then," Maya suggested.

"Whass that?"

"It's like the stories on the vidscreens, only acted out live."

River felt overwhelmed. It seemed a lot more complicated than he'd imagined, this business of liking and being liked.

"Or just ask her on a walk," Maya suggested. "Or to go someplace together."

"Asked if this tubo can come by sometime," River said with a certain pride that he'd taken that risk.

"Did she say 'yes'?"

"Took the filly home on the gondola." He smiled at the memory.

"River, just a caution," Maya said with a slight, worried frown. "Don't move too fast. If she's a former pen-girl, how do I say this? She's been battered and abused her whole life. She's never had any choices, never had a chance to develop a self or become a real person. You push her too hard, you might scare her away."

"Don't wanna just drill," River assured her. "Want the girl to like this ... me."

"Try saying 'making love.'"

"Whass that?"

"Didn't they teach you in the Temple of Love? Sojuhs hammer and drill. But real people make love with other real people." Maya placed her hand on his. "And River, she may not be ready for that. Not any time soon. If she doesn't want you in that way—I don't want to see you get hurt."

"Girl's a little thing, can't hurt me," River assured her.

"Not physically hurt. Emotionally hurt. Rejected." She felt tender toward him, as she had to her own child when Brigid was young. A bit shy and nerdy, she'd been, and far smarter than anyone else in five watersheds. Maya had had to stop herself from hovering, that first day she went to preschool. Would the other kids like her? Then she had come home crying after some girl bit her. Maya had suffered more than Brigid from that nip.

"Whass that?"

"That means when you like someone and they don't like you back."

"Oh. So how can *I* make the girl like *me?*" River returned to the point. He pronounced "I" and "me" carefully, with a certain pride in using them.

"That's it." Maya sighed. "You can't *make* her like you—you can only offer your friendship. And if it gets to the point of making love, you've got to go slow, very slow. And gentle. Let her have the control. Ask her permission, every step of the way."

"Like in the Temple."

"Yes, they're all about consent in the Temple of Love."

Bird came through the door, tossed a satchel down on the couch, and plopped himself down on a chair next to Maya. He leaned over and kissed her cheek.

"You look intense. Am I interrupting some deep conversation?"

"We're talking about dating," Maya said.

Bird smiled wearily. He'd been down at the dockyards, trying to convince the kayak club to let him join the relays of small boats keeping a surreptitious watch on the warship. So far, it had simply sat there, not attacking but not moving, the discs on its deck pumping out sonar that jammed shortwave radio waves.

The kayak club had not welcomed him. He'd been told they already had all the volunteers they needed. That might be true, but it might also be true that they simply didn't trust him. And deep in his heart he felt they were justified. He no longer truly believed that he could trust himself.

Bird shook off his gloomy thoughts and winked at River. "Got someone in mind?"

River looked down at his plum, and concentrated intently on digging out the pit.

"You do! You got a girlfriend?" Bird stuffed a plum in his mouth.

River shook his head.

"Boyfriend?"

"No!" River protested quickly. "Got someone I like," he admitted. "A girl."

"I've been encouraging him to ask her out on a date," Maya said.

"Why not encourage him to bring her home, meet the family, so we can see if she's good enough for him?" Bird took a knife and began working on the plums.

Maya snorted. "I've lost far too many potential good lays when I brought them home to meet the collective. Much worse than merely meeting the parents."

"What do you expect, when half the collective were your other lovers? But that doesn't apply in River's case. We can be a nice, neutral panel to vet her and make sure her intentions are honorable."

"How about making yourself useful?"

Bird held up a pitted plum. "I am!"

"No, I mean help him out. Maybe you could double date with him, show him how it's done. Aren't there any supper clubs up and running yet?"

"You know this city," Bird laughed. "The supper clubs were up and running before the tail end of the Stewards' Army had made it out of Daly City."

"So take Madrone, and the four of you go out," Maya said. "It'll be good for her. She can't work all the time."

"Wanna bet?" Bird said.

Madrone walked home in the fading summer light, threading her way through the ruins of the Math Park. There, in happier days, children had swung on pendulums or climbed up a helical ladder into the eye of the Fibonacci spiral slide. An enormous Aeolian harp had made music from the wind. In the center had stood a giant chessboard, with pawns and knights a child could ride that moved forward, sideways, diagonally. On lazy summer nights, in times of peace, teams would compete in chess tournaments while supporters grilled corn and baked potatoes in geometric fire pits.

Now it was all a ruin of smashed parts and torn up broccolis and sunflower seedheads. She perched, for a moment, on the remains of a sculpted earthen bench, then realized that was a mistake. Weariness washed over her, and it would take an effort of will to get up again. She was so tired!

She'd been in and out of the bee-mind since before dawn, using the powers she'd gained from the Bee Priestesses of the Southlands. All through a long night shift and an endless day, she'd tasted the sweat of her sick patients and let her body brew up just the homeopathic drop of honey that could cure. Magic. Or some science so advanced that only her intuition could follow it.

It was a gift, the healing gift that had made their victory possible. For the chemists could analyze her potions and reproduce them, and that was how the Cityfolk had been able to defeat the Stewards' engineered epidemics. And how they'd weaned deserters away from the immunoboosters that had kept them enslaved to the army, and freed them to take up the place at the table they were offered. It was the magic that had allowed Maya's vision and Lily's strategy to work.

And now it was the magic that healed the wounds and the residue of diseases. But the trance took energy and concentration. Energy to slide in, and energy to pull herself back out, to shore up the walls that kept her human self distinct from the bee-mind. She was tired now, and the walls were slipping.

A bee hummed, and a river of scent flowed over her: lavender, concrete dust, sunflowers, metal, human sweat. Two teenage girls bore away the severed horse-head from one of the huge pawns. A group of younger children were sweeping up the shards of the blown-glass beads that had been threaded on the poles of the life-size abacus. A boy gathered up the mess of springs and gears to be recycled.

She shook herself, and with an effort of will stood back up. Just take one step, then another, she told herself. Down the path through the replanted gardens—waves of lavender, whiffs of rose. Hungry! Dive in and let velvet flower petals enfold you in fragrance and soft touch. Hear the song of the bees, the song of well-being, that low, harmonic tone that hummed, *All is well, all is blossom, all is golden pollen, sweet honey, and the Queen content upon the brood.*

"Look out!" A young boy on a skateboard careened within a few inches of her nose. She jumped back. In her reverie, she had wandered onto the skateboard and bike path. A racing bike zoomed by. She shook her head and jumped over a patch of sage back onto the walking path. The cyclist left a trail in his wake, as if a hundred bicycles dopplered in and out of her range of vision. She was going to have to get a grip on herself.

But just a little while longer, she thought, and we'll have this all back under control. And I can go back to working regular hours, and get some sleep.

Then, just for a moment, the world split into a kaleidoscope of images, the laden apple tree in front of her multiplied into a thousand trees. She closed her eyes, touched her bee spot.

Madrone. My name is Madrone.

She liked to come home through the side door into the garden. It led through a narrow walkway alongside the garage, cool and dark and smelling just a bit musty. A second door opened up into a flight of steps, their risers decorated with mosaics and bits of flashing mirror, and up onto a patio with fragrant herbs growing between the bricks.

Bird was watering the pots. She stood still for a moment and watched him. The spray of the water made rainbows in the low, afternoon light, and the leaves of the chard glowed emerald and ruby. And how could she distinguish him from her, or her from the garden, when it was all light, colors playing against one another, wrapped in scent, rich earth and citrus? Bird himself was merely a sphere of turquoise and gold, laced with darker streaks. Musk and sweat and sun-warmed skin. She inhaled, wondering what elixir she could brew from this moment of perfect beauty.

A buzzing. He was talking. She wanted him to stop talking, to let her stay in this rapture of scent and color. But he was shifting now into tones of scarlet and purple fear, and he wouldn't stop talking. Even when she forced the words out past her lips.

"Stop talking."

But the buzzing and humming only got louder. She soon lost words again. There was only sound, and the brilliant colors that trailed with them. They got louder and faster, round and round, like the little boy who ran so fast he turned into butter. It was all melting away.

A blast of cold water hit her in the face and drenched her healer's robes. The shock and the chill snapped her out of the bee-mind. Suddenly the garden came clear, each leaf and stem distinct. There stood Bird, training the hose on her and laughing.

A wave of sheer fury took her.

"You pig-blind cousin to an idiot!" she screamed at him.

Bees filled the air, buzzing in fury. As she watched in horror, they converged into a buzzing, furious mass and headed straight for Bird.

He dropped the hose and ran for the toolshed, slamming the door behind him. Bees hurled themselves against it like bullets.

"Call them off!" she heard from the shed.

Madrone was shaking. She struggled to breathe, ground, calm herself. She sent out thoughts of safety, images and scents of comfort and clarity. After a long while, the bees began to calm. They left the toolshed door, and dispersed back to the late-summer flowers.

"It's okay. You can come out now," she called.

Bird opened the door a crack, peered out cautiously.

"They're gone." *Diosa*, she was shaking. The bees could have killed him, stung him to death before her eyes. *Madre de la tierra*, she was losing control!

He emerged, cautiously. She eyed him nervously. What would he say? Would all his love and passion turn to fear and horror? Would he hate her?

"Not fair," he said. "Dirty fighting."

She breathed a sigh of relief. It was going to be all right.

"Stay on my good side," she advised him.

Then she flung her arms around him, and he kissed her fiercely, pressing his body into hers. She clung to him, feeling him shake and tremble under her. Was he crying? No, he was laughing, and then she was laughing with him, laughing until her knees buckled and she sank to the ground, pulling him after. They rolled together out into the sun, still consumed with laughter. He pulled her on top of him.

"Which is it, your good side? This one?" He rolled over on top of her, pressing her down into the lavender bed. "Or this one?"

She gulped for air.

"I so need a break," she admitted.

"You so do!"

Will I ever get that break? She wondered. Would he?

Bird gathered her into his arms and sat, holding her and rocking her gently, as if she were a baby he was rocking to sleep. Maybe this was it, this time of respite between battles. For she sensed that another one was coming. Whether it came here to get them, or they pursued it down to the Southlands to fight on someone else's turf, this war was not yet won.

But not yet. Not while his arms are around me, not while the sun lights up the waving blossoms of purple cosmos and the bees sing of increase. Please, Goddess, not yet.

He held her, basking in those last long rays of the late-summer sun. She was wet and muddy, and he watched as her eyes closed and she dropped to sleep, exhausted from healing the casualties of the last battle. Garden soil was ground into her healers' whites. He should wake her and make her put on something warm and dry, before she caught a chill. But he just held her, not wanting the moment to end. These gardens, this golden light, Maya playing with plums in the kitchen. And Madrone, her even breath rising and falling. Resting, for this one bright moment, that we both know cannot last.

Madrone dreamed of concrete, acres of rubble under a blazing sun. She moved through dark passageways. She had to be silent, careful. Something stalked her. Skeletons lined the walls, their skulls fixed in the death grin. *They* hadn't been careful, careful enough.

But everyone needs a refuge, she heard. Everyone needs a place to go.

Then the tunnels opened out to a big, empty space under a blue sky. In the center, one scraggly tree struggled to grow, its leaves covered with dust, its trunk twisting up toward the sky.

Every city needs three things, she heard. *A plaza. A hearth. And a sacred tree.*

Build a city of refuge in the heartland of the enemy.

Chapter Eleven

ROSA CLUMPED DOWN THE WOODEN FLIGHT OF STAIRS CARRYING A bucket of scraps for the chickens in one hand, gripping the rail with her other. She didn't quite trust her balance—she who had once so confidently run across the high wire at circus camp. Others had tumbled into the net below, but she had laughed and danced on one foot, showing off. Now she felt like an old person, shaky and weary.

She dumped the bucket of scraps into the chickens' pen. They ran forward, clucking happily in their chickeny way. She used to find them endlessly entertaining and funny. Now she wanted to shout at them, Stupid birds! Don't you know what's going to happen to you in the end?

"Rosa, you'll be late!" Sister Elizabeth called to her from the balcony on the second floor.

She was supposed to go to her Learning Group today. She'd agreed to go. Last night, their guide Allie had come to check on her, and held a whispered, worried conference with the Sisters. Allie brought her a book that the group had decided to read: the diary of Anne Frank, about a girl who hid out from the Nazis.

"We miss you," Allie had said, perching her slim body on the edge of Rosa's narrow bed in the stark, bare room on the top floor. "Everyone's asking about you. We want you back." Allie's warm, brown eyes glowed with sincerity, and her chestnut curls bounced with emphasis.

Rosa had just stared out her window. Outside was a big palm tree that functioned as a bird hotel. Pigeons nested in its trunk, and robins. A big fat jay with a high black crest perched on the edge of a branch and scolded them as jays do.

"Rosa?"

Rosa shrugged. Allie was kind but when she thought about trying to explain to her, she just felt tired.

"Is it the sojuhs?" Allie asked. "No one would blame you for not wanting to hang out with them. But we're not with them this week. We're going to read the book, and discuss it, and take a field trip out to the country for the fall bird count."

Rosa just shrugged again.

Allie stood up and slipped an arm around Rosa's shoulders. She didn't pull away, but she didn't nestle close either, just stood, unresisting, watching the jay lecture all the lesser birds.

"We know you've been through a lot," Allie said in a low voice. "We care about you. We want you to heal, and be happy."

But Rosa wouldn't look at her.

This morning Sister Elizabeth had woken her with a cup of tea and a bowl of oatmeal, and sat on the edge of her bed until she ate it all. It was a lot of steps up with a tray for an old woman with swollen legs. Sister Elizabeth had to wear special stockings for her varicose veins, and Rosa felt slightly ashamed to be causing her so much trouble.

So she ate. Then Sister supervised her as she packed a change of clothes and extra underwear and her hiking boots, and now she was watching. If Rosa didn't go, she'd get a lecture, and not from the jays. Worse, she'd get those sympathetic, probing questions. How do you feel? Do you want to talk?

She rinsed the scrap bucket with the hose and hauled herself back up the stairs. Sister Elizabeth rewarded her with a worried smile as she placed the bucket back under the sink, washed her hands and took her pack.

"Have a good trip, dear," Sister said. "Try to enjoy yourself."

Rosa trudged reluctantly along the path. She'd forgotten the book, she realized, but it didn't really matter. She hadn't told Allie that she'd already read *Anne Frank*. Maya had lent it to her, long before the Stewards came.

And she didn't feel like camping with all her old friends, eating meals together, remembering how much fun it had been in the old days. If her mother had still been alive, if she'd been home in her own home, she would have just stomped her feet and said No way! and then her mother would have yelled at her and she would have yelled back and by the time the fight was over the ferry would be gone.

But of course if her mother had been alive, and none of the awfulness had happened, she'd be excited to go on the trip. The fall bird count had always been one of her favorite moments in the year. It took place just before the Equinox, when the weather was still warm, not like the winter count when she was always shivering in her blind. The big-leaf maples already were starting to turn lemon-gold, and the air carried a hint of rains to come. She had loved being out in the hills, the quiet moments in the forest.

That was the worst of it, she thought. Not just what they'd done to her, but how they'd ruined all her ordinary pleasures, left their nasty mark on everything.

She hopped on a bus shaped like a giant salmon. Sounds of the ocean and of running streams were playing through the sound system, along with songs about the salmon's migration from stream to sea and back. It all irritated her. Why the jacks couldn't they just have a simple bus that took people from place to place, without entertaining and instructing and inspiring every stupid minute of the day?

The New Ferry Building filled a gap in the seawall that kept the waters of the rising bay from climbing even farther up Market Street. Half a mile away, the tower of the Old Ferry Building rose from the water, a beacon for the sailboats that plied the bay. In between stood the spires of half-drowned high-rises, their upper floors a haven for seabirds and a rich source of the guano that kept the City's gardens fertile.

The high, buttressed seawalls were made of urbanite—recycled chunks of used concrete—covered with turf. Sea-pinks and thrift and low-growing lupines made a garden of their bulk. The ferry docks extended out into the bay, and the New Ferry Building itself was a light-filled polyhedron of soaring bamboo struts that reached skyward like a ship's prow.

Her Learning Group was massed on the walkway by the wide glass entrance doors. Rosa saw Allie's face light up as she hopped down from the bus and walked over to join them. Her once-best-friend Lumi gave her a small, thin smile, but the others looked down or looked away, as if they weren't sure how to be with her. It made her feel awkward and angry.

"Good, you're here!" Allie said brightly. "I'm so glad you decided to join us, Rosa. We're going to have a wonderful time!"

Rosa wasn't convinced. She kept her head down, and didn't talk to anyone as Allie shepherded her charges through the embarkation area in the lobby and out to the long docks beyond.

The Golden Gate Bridge was still being repaired from the damage it had suffered during the occupation, but ferries crossed the bay often and, like everything else in the City, they were built for beauty and pleasure as well as function. Solar sails stretched like proud banners, winking out starbursts of light. Passages from *Moby Dick* were inscribed on the gun-wales. Painted windspinners danced on the rails, and music wafted from the top deck where people were dancing to a live band.

Some of Rosa's Learning Group went up to join them, but she didn't feel like dancing. She made her way to the prow of the ferry and stood in the V where the rails came together, watching it cleave through the waters of the bay. It made her feel better somehow, watching the keel cut through the waves, leaving a trail of white foam in its wake. Leaving it behind. That was what she needed to do, she knew, just leave it behind. But she didn't know how—how to be sharp as a prow, bold as one of those old figureheads that faced into the wind. She opened her arms and the wind whipped around her, blowing her hair back, stinging her eyes.

This wasn't so bad, Rosa thought. She was crouched in a blind on a small promontory of exposed rock, with a thermos of herb tea and her notebook. Alone. Peaceful, after the noise and bustle of debarking and finding their transport bus and making camp. Below her, a small stream trickled its way down a cascade of boulders in a cranny of the hills covered with coyote bush and thickets of willow. Upslope, oaks stretched out beckoning limbs above a meadow of bunchgrasses and gone-to-seed lupines. On the ridge stood a dark line of Douglas fir, edged with tanoaks and madrones. The air was fragrant with sage, and in the distance a hawk screamed out its hunting call.

She put a mark in her book. They tallied all the birds they heard, and kept a special tally for those they actually saw. She raised her binoculars, and searched the sky in the direction the call had come from.

There! A dot high in the sky. She tracked it with her glasses. A kestrel!

The rest of her Learning Group were stationed up and down the ridge, helping the biologists get an accurate count of how many species were there at the start of the fall migration. They could compare the tally with old records, and get a feel for how successful they'd been at preserving biodiversity.

Most of the students were in groups of twos and threes, but she was glad to be alone, not to have to talk to anyone. The others still looked at her awkwardly, and she still sat alone during meals although Allie tried her best to draw her into conversations.

The long day was peaceful, but when evening came, her solitude ended. Allie pointedly made room for her around the fire, and reluctantly Rosa joined the circle, sitting quietly as they roasted sausages on sticks and ate them on crusty buns the group had made especially for the campout. They sang songs, but without much heart. Last year, Mira had played guitar and her brother Ozzie had made them all laugh with his funny songs, parodies of the anthem of the City. The soldiers had blown up their house, with them in it, while Rosa was imprisoned.

Now the music seemed to die away into the empty echoes. Charity had cooked breakfast pancakes for everyone the year before. Charity always had a thing for pancakes. She'd been hit by a stray bullet in the final confrontation in the plaza.

Where were they now? Would their souls return, riding high on the wind currents like falcons? Were they even now fighting gales and turbulence, struggling back to life and birth? Did they blame her? Hate her? Why was she still alive when they were dead?

"Okay, let's talk about it," Allie had said when yet another song had trailed away into the silence of the dark woods. "We all miss them, Mira and Ozzie and Charity. I miss their laughter and their voices and their mischief. It hurts me that they aren't here. Who else wants to speak?"

"Mira was my best friend," Keira said. Her dark eyes bored into Rosa's. She had been the prettiest of them all, with her caramel skin and her tumble of brown curls, but now a jagged scar marred her left cheek and her jaw was set at an awkward angle. She spoke with a slight slur, mark of the bullet that had caught her in the face. "Since we were babies. She should be here. Charity and Ozzie should be here. They shouldn't be dead."

"They were brave," Allie said. "You were all brave."

"We were all stupid," Rosa snapped back at her. "And I was the stupidest stupid of them all! Okay?"

"Hey," Allie said weakly, "don't blame yourselves for what the Stewards did."

But they did blame her. Rosa could see it in their eyes. She had encouraged them to think of themselves as fighters. She had egged them on, the day that she was captured. She blamed herself.

Keira poked the fire with a stick, and a shower of sparks flew up. Like souls going to heaven, the Sisters would say. But Rosa didn't believe in heaven.

She wished she hadn't come on the trip.

She didn't want friends, or counselors with sympathetic smiles. All she wanted was to be left alone, with the wild wind whipping around her hair, too fierce for thought.

Chapter Twelve

T HE BEST SUPPER CLUBS WERE DOWNTOWN, BIRD TOLD RIVER. THE
wide pedestrian avenue along old Market Street was lined with outdoor tables and small stages, the fruit of alliances between chefs and
musicians and other performers. They were lively places, always jam-
packed with crowds decked in the festive and colorful garb that Cityfolks
delighted in.

Even after a hard work day, the people of the City seemed to have
endless energy to go out, to gossip and listen to music and to dance. The
threat of a warship didn't daunt them, and the preparations underway
for an assault on the Southlands seemed only to spur them on to preen
and promenade as if the sun were never going to burn out.

There were other clubs besides the big downtown ones, of course—
informal, sociable places in the neighborhoods, run by groups of friends
who pooled their garden produce and took turns cooking and serving
and eating and watching each others' kids. A welcome alternative to
eating alone or in isolated family groups.

But the downtown clubs were for seeing and being seen. Before he'd
gone down to the Southlands, Bird would have been playing at them,
a favorite headliner who could guarantee a packed house. He'd spend
a happy hour picking out his outfit, shaving carefully, making sure his
shoes were shiny clean. He'd liked knowing that he looked good.

That night, he had simply showered and thrown on whatever first
came to hand in his closet, making the minimum of effort so that he
would not disrespect River and the girl. He spent most of the evening dressing River, digging down into chests full of old clothes left
by housemates to find a pair of black slacks that fit River well. Maya
produced a red sports shirt that had once belonged to her old lover,
Rio, and Bird carefully ironed out the smallest creases. He had not
been out to hear music since his return from the Southlands with his

damaged hands. It was too painful to listen to others playing when he no longer could.

He wasn't entirely sure why he was doing it now. They could have gone to a play or out to one of the comedy clubs. But a play would need lots of explanation to River and Kit, and he doubted they would follow the in-jokes and references in the City's comedy.

Besides, his old musician friends were playing at one of the top clubs, and he knew they'd be pleased if he came to hear them. They were trying out some of his newer songs, as well, the things he composed secretly alone at night. He'd sent them over to their fiddle player Sachiko on the Net, and she had been full of praise. If he were going to continue to write songs and create music, he couldn't hide away in his room forever and refuse to listen to it.

Madrone spied Bird and River waiting for her at the entrance to the healing center. She was late, she knew, but only by about fifteen minutes and she wouldn't make excuses for it. Bird took her arm and she felt happy, suddenly, like a kid let out of school. There were ten dozen things back at the healing center that could use her attention, but there were always things that could use her attention, and Sam had been firm with her when she asked for the night off.

"Absolutely!" he said. "You've been working twelve-hour shifts seven days a week, as far as I can see. You bet you can have a night off!"

"I think I hear the pot calling the kettle cookware," Madrone came back at him. "And you're older than me."

"Yeah," Sam agreed. "By rights I should be fishing down in Florida. If there still were a Florida, half the state underwater. But in any case, the load is easing up. If there's a new epidemic between now and tomorrow morning, I'll message you. Or we could all just die, and finally get some rest."

Madrone had stripped off her healer's robes and stuffed them into her locker. Underneath she wore a blue dress that Bird had liked ten years ago, when they were young and unscarred and she'd gone out at nights to listen to him play. The fact that the dress hung loose on her was a tribute to the stress and short rations of her own time in the Southlands, and the constant demands since. She skipped meals too often in the press of work. But tonight, she decided, she would order double portions, and eat dessert.

She was amazed, actually, that Bird had asked her to go hear his old group. He had never been willing before, and she wondered what had made him decide to face his own loss and pain.

This is a healing mission too, she thought. If he's prepared to go, I want to be with him. To support him.

River looked so different, she thought. The bright red shirt brought out the warm tones in his skin, and looked good against the trim-fitting black pants. His cap of tight-curled hair was newly clipped. Someone had taken some trouble with him, Bird most likely, and she felt a little warm thrill as she pictured him helping River primp. It was those small, human gestures that she loved most about Bird, not the hero, not the brilliant guitarist he'd once been, but the guy who would iron a shirt for his friend. She flung her arms around him and gave him a big, sloppy kiss as a reward. For her, too—a reward for finally extricating herself from the nonstop demands of others, for daring a night out on the town.

"You look beautiful," Bird said, burying his nose in her wild hair. "So nice to see you in something besides the robes."

"Well, if I left them on they probably wouldn't charge us for dinner," Madrone said. Indeed, it was hard, as a healer, to spend her stipend because the grateful people of the City pressed so many gifts and invitations on her.

"It's worth ten times the price to get you out of those things. Besides, I've got credits to burn."

He did. They all did. The more they worked, the more credits they got. The more they got, the more they needed to spend them before they expired, which they did after a year. You didn't need to save them. All the things that Maya's generation had saved for—a home of one's own, retirement, the kids' college education, medical emergencies—all those were now each person's birthright. When the surplus was totaled each year—for the City inevitably ended up with a net surplus—it was simply a measure that they had produced more than they consumed, given more than they took back.

Yet everybody had enough. More than enough—an abundance of good food and bright clothing and small luxuries.

The result was a city hopping with nightlife and replete with delectable cuisine, just a few short weeks since the invaders had been repelled.

From the healing center, they hopped a tram to the top of Potrero Hill and caught a gondola across the City to get Kit from the convent. The two men waited at the gate while Madrone went in for her.

The convent was a sprawling Spanish-style stucco edifice that took up much of the hilltop above Buena Vista Park. It contained a large parish church, a chapel, an enormous dining hall, and a hundred small bedrooms. Back in the 1920s, when it was built, it had housed a thriving community of mostly Irish immigrant girls who staffed the City's Catholic schools and served food to the homeless. They had spawned dozens of Sister Houses, including the one next door to Black Dragon house, where small communities of nuns served as teachers or nurses in poor neighborhoods.

But by the turn of the century, the young nuns had reached old age or had gone to be united with their heavenly bridegroom. Fewer and fewer new recruits took their places. In the early twenties, the Sisters had turned half the dormitories into a homeless shelter for women and children. Then, after the chaos of the Uprising subsided, the newly formed Califian Housing Council found permanent housing and work for everyone. Suddenly, instantly, there was no more homelessness.

As the shelter emptied, the nuns opened the rooms to the aged who had no families to take them in, and the infirm who needed ongoing nursing care. But still much of the complex remained empty. So when the Califians vanquished the invading Stewards, leaving behind the pen-girls who had serviced the army, the Sisters offered to care for the abandoned girls.

Madrone walked through the outer courtyard, noting how lovely and well-tended it looked now that a troop of pen-girls were there to water the lemon trees growing in pots and deadhead the climbing roses. She rang the bell beside the curved wooden door and a dark silent girl led her to the dining hall, where she found Kit the center of attention.

Apparently the whole convent had made her date their project. Kit stood on a table, in a white cocktail dress dotted with small black flowers. Two of the Sisters were frantically hemming the dress while one of the pen-girls brushed Kit's lashes with mascara.

"We're almost done," sang out a nun with pins in her mouth. "Ladies, this is Madrone, the most famous healer in the City! It's a great honor that she's come to take our dear friend out this evening. Please make her welcome!"

The speech had the opposite impact, as the pen-girls froze with awe and dropped their heads, refusing to look her in the face. One of them finally grew bold enough to offer her a cup of tea, which she declined. Another pointed at the bouquet of roses and lavender that graced the grand piano filling one corner of the dining hall.

"Sojuh bring that to this one," she said, casting her glance at Kit.

River had apparently made a very favorable impression the day before by arriving with the bouquet to ask Kit out.

The Sisters snipped the last threads of the hem. Kit was told to pirouette, and the dress was pronounced perfect.

"Remember, if you aren't having a good time, if he's asking you to do anything you don't want to do, you just come home," said Sister Camilla, the eldest of the presiding nuns. "Madrone won't let you come to any harm."

"You look beautiful, Kit," Madrone said. "Come on, the guys are waiting."

"Kit?" Sister Camilla echoed in surprise. "Is that your name?"

"Big tubo fighter say to call this pen-girl that," she muttered.

"Kit! What a lovely name. We'll all use it from now on, won't we, girls? Good night, Kit. Have a wonderful time."

Madrone took her arm and steered her down the corridor and out through the courtyard.

"And I thought it was bad for me, back in the day, when my dates would come to pick me up under the eagle eyes of my collective household. You've got a whole convent breathing down the neckline of that dress!"

Kit didn't answer, just stared at her shoes as they opened the gate to the waiting men.

"You look lovely," Bird said. He poked River, who was standing dumbstruck. "Don't you think so?"

"Yeah!" River nodded. She didn't look like a pen-girl, except for her downcast eyes. She looked like a Trophy, something far beyond his aspirations. "Like on them vidscreens!"

At this she snapped her head up. "Somethin' wrong with tubo's eyes," she said. "Vidscreen ladies all white."

"You better lookin' than all of them," River pronounced boldly. Kit just shook her head in response.

They walked back toward the gondola platform. River gently took Kit's hand, holding it tentatively as if any moment he expected her to snatch it away.

The gondola wafted them over the City. Bird slipped his arm around Madrone and River followed his example. Kit, still terrified as they swung high above the trees, accepted his embrace and clung to him.

Below, the City was ablaze with lights powered by an abundance of solar, wind, and tidal energy. They illuminated the walking and riding paths, and twinkled amidst the trees.

The group disembarked at the foot of Market Street and wandered up the wide promenade, dotted with circular gardens and towering sculptures. The artists of the City had been engaged, before the invasion, in replacing all of the old asphalt with brick and pebble mosaics. Many of these were torn up now, or still bore the tread marks of tanks, and the gardens were sparse. But the supper clubs were open, their tables spilling out from lighted doorways.

As the four of them strolled down the avenue, they caught snatches of music from each club they passed, melodious ballads or pounding dubstep, electronic dance riffs or hard-thumping snarls of sound from the punk revival clubs.

Bird steered them to one of the biggest clubs with a prominent marquee and candlelit tables sprawling out into the walkway. The entrance lobby was lined with mirrors, and Kit caught a glimpse of a strange girl in a poofed-out dress.

With a shock, she recognized herself. How did she get here, wearing a lady dress, on the arm of a tubo treating her like a sweetie that might melt away if he turned his back? She felt on the edge of panic, as if she were pretending to be someone else, someone real, someone entitled to that look of admiration on sojuh's face. Soon, soon they'd find out and then something terrible would happen.

But she stole another glance at herself. She didn't look like a pen-girl. Pen-girls don't wear pretty dresses, just rip-away shifts. Pen-girls didn't have to look good. All the same when the lights go out, they said. All the same. But now she was different.

They were ushered to a table alongside the dance floor. A large bear of a man lumbered over and embraced Bird.

"So glad to see you!" he said. He wore a sleeveless T-shirt that revealed a grizzly tattooed on his left shoulder, and a bamboo-munching panda on the right. He turned to the others. "I'm Walker. Bird and I, we go way back. Played in a band together for a couple of years. Still playing his music! You'll hear, tonight. But in the meantime, what can we get you? Tonight we've got a nice meat choice, roast lamb from the Sonoma hills with some good veggies and a salad of fresh garden greens. Or, if you prefer vegan, there's an awesome chickpea stew served with a tomato salad and homemade pita bread."

They all made their choices except for Kit, who shook her head. "Pen-girls don't eat that shit," she said. "Got chips?"

"Sorry to disappoint you," Walker said.

"Let's get her some of the chickpea stew," Madrone said.

"See that light in the center of your table? When that goes on, come up to the serving window and get your dinner," Walker said. "Wine bar's over in the corner, and the bar in the back has varietal grape juice, water with lemon, and fruit juice. We're a bit low on the wine stocks after the bloodsuckin' Stewards drank up our best vintages, but there's enough for a glass apiece and it's an excellent pinot noir from the Wild Hog Vineyards in west Sonoma County."

Bird followed Walker to the back of the room and returned with four glasses of wine. He raised his in a toast.

"Here's to dating," he said.

Madrone raised hers back. River and Kit just sat, staring at theirs.

"Now you raise your glasses, and we all clink them together," Madrone instructed them.

"Why?" River asked.

"It's a custom."

They raised and clinked.

"Take a small sip first, see if you like it," Bird suggested. River complied, and made a face.

"Sour!" River warned.

"That's how it's supposed to taste," Bird said. "It's not meant to be sweet."

Kit took a cautious sip, then pushed the glass away.

"How about I get you two some apple juice?" Bird suggested.

While he was away, Madrone studied Kit. She knew all about the difficulties getting pen-girls and sojuhs weaned off chips, and she suspected that they might actually lack the right intestinal flora to help them digest real food.

"Have you tried eating people food?" she asked. "I wonder, did it give you a stomachache?"

Kit nodded.

"I have something that will help with that problem." Madrone had prepared a vial of probiotics, and when Bird returned with two more glasses she dropped the potion into Kit's juice. "Drink this up. It'll help prevent the tummy troubles."

"Chips good enough."

"But the supply of chips is limited. As soon as we go through the last of the Stewards' stockpiles, they'll be gone," Madrone told her.

Kit looked alarmed. "Then what pen-girls eat?"

"That's why we want you to learn to eat real food. Besides, it's better for you."

"Chips nutritionally complete. Vidscreens say so."

"The vidscreens show stories. They don't always show the truth," Madrone said. "Chips, they have some nutrients, but they lack others. There's things your body needs, tiny little trace minerals, that chips can't provide. So drink that apple juice down, and try to eat a bit when it comes."

Kit hung her head again. Apparently she wasn't ready to argue with the City's most famous healer.

The band was playing dance music from the past century. Couples began circling the dance floor, doing their own creative versions of the waltz and the swing.

"You two gonna dance?" Bird asked.

"Don't know how," River said.

"Doesn't matter. Just make something up," Bird said. He pointed to two men dancing together who were simply rocking back and forth to the beat. "Look at them—that's not much of a dance but it looks like fun."

"Wanna?" River asked Kit. At first she shook her head, but as he continued to look at her hopefully, she began to feel more daring. The girl who wore the dress, that girl would dance.

"Give it a try," she said hesitantly.

"Say I, Kit," River told her. "You a person now. Not a thing, not an address. No one gonna beat you for sayin' I."

Kit held her breath. Say I, as if it were as easy as that. Say I and she might become the girl in the dress, who was an I as sure as Kit was a pen-girl. But then, if she were Kit, she wasn't a pen-girl. She was something else, someone else. It was frightening. And yet being a pen-girl was not such a wonderful thing that she should cling to it. It was just familiar, what she knew.

She'd put on the dress, she'd come on this date, she'd just said that she was willing to try a dance. Why not go one more step? She took a great gulp of air.

"I give it a try," she said, and flinched involuntarily. But River was right. No fist came out of the air to crash into her face. Madrone beamed at her with approval.

River took her hand and led her onto the dance floor. He put his arms around her, not too tight, remembering Maya's cautions. He rocked back and forth, and her body followed his. He remembered the temple, how he had danced with the sunlight there, and took a breath. He couldn't let go like that here, not with people around, watching. But he could rock and sway, and it felt good holding her.

He began to feel that warmth down in his shaft. But not with a sense of demand. No, it was gentle, like in the temple. He could savor the moment, feeling her begin to sway and yield to the rhythm.

At first Kit found it hard to tolerate him near her. What she liked most about liberation was not having to be close to anyone, to put up with their smell or the pressure of another body against hers. But he smelled okay, she admitted. Not pungent and sweaty like the fighters in the pens, but like soap and something spicy.

She dared a glance around at the dance floor. On the edges were a few other couples, rocking simply as she and River were. But in the center, better dancers twirled and spun. She watched two women dancing together. They held hands. One whirled away, and the other pulled her back.

River was holding her lightly, so lightly she could escape if she wished. She spun away from him, exhilarated by her daring, by the freedom of having no one touch her at all. He stood looking at her for a moment, then spun around in turn. To her own surprise, she held out her hand, and he took it. She felt the warmth of his hand, the strength of those great fingers. She spun toward him, and then whirled apart. Again and again she twirled, loving the sense of freedom, of being the one to abandon him and pull away. But drawn back, again and again, for the joy of feeling that freedom once more. Drawn back also, she realized, because she liked it, that sense of a warm body next to hers, not pressing but just oh so gently brushing, teasing, bathing her in a warm regard. She risked a glance up at his face. He was laughing, as if he couldn't quite believe his luck. She found her own mouth stretching out into a smile.

Bird watched them intently, like a coach watching a new batter step up to the plate. He so badly wanted the girl to like River, for him to be happy, even for a little while. They would probably only get a little while, if that, but even a drop of happiness could color a whole well of misery.

Madrone watched Bird watching them. He had been a great dancer, once, flexible and inventive. They had won contests. It had been so long since she'd been on the dance floor—not since Sandy died, she thought, that lover who had held her and comforted her during those long years when Bird was away. Another loss, another one she hadn't been able to save.

But she had mourned Sandy, and tonight was not the night to spend stirring up old grief. It was her night off, a night to dance.

Dare she ask him? What if it brought back all his pain and loss, or hurt his bad hip? No, safer not to.

But she looked at him, remembering a steamy tango long ago. Could she still bend her back almost down to the floor?

There was a little half-smile on her lips. Her eyes were dreamy. Suddenly Bird was tired of watching Kit and River dance. It was like spying on a new couple making love. Madrone was looking at him. She was offering an invitation. He knew that. Why in Hella's name shouldn't he accept it?

There comes a time with pain, he thought, unrelenting pain, when you just stop feeling it. You stop shying away and cringing, and it just becomes meaningless and oh so boring. Maybe he was at that point.

He turned to Madrone.

"I'm way out of practice," he said, "but would you care to risk a dance?"

She knew what he was telling her.

"If you're game, I am," she said. He held out his hand, and led her onto the dance floor.

We aren't going to win any contests, he thought, but we're still a banker's ass better than half these folks on the floor. Madrone was moving gracefully in his arms and he followed her, aware that while she seemed to be completely abandoned to the rhythm of the music, she was carefully plotting her moves so that he could follow without straining his hip. Their bodies were so familiar to each other. He knew her rhythms as she knew his deepest sources of pleasure and his deepest wounds. And for just one moment, he was happy.

He remembered something Maya had said to him.

"You're moping because you aren't all you once were," she'd snapped. "Well, get over it. We're none of us what we once were. We all get old. We lose the use of our knees, or our faculties. But you know what? Life goes on. And there's still plenty of it to enjoy."

So this is a victory, he thought. I can dance. I can be happy.

He was still in the light mood, later, when they sat back down, flushed and sweaty. The dance band retired to much applause, and his old friends Walker and Anna and Sachiko got up to play. When Walker called him up and asked him if he would sing one of the new songs, the one he'd written for Madrone, he didn't say no. He stepped up onto the stage, took the mic, and sang it with such tenderness that the room was in tears, followed by a storm of applause.

He enjoyed the applause. He'd missed it, he realized. Maybe it was a shallow side of him, but he basked in it. And suddenly he understood that there was no reason he shouldn't have it. He couldn't be all he was, but he could still be a musician, a singer, a composer, a songwriter. A lover. He still had so much. So much to cherish.

So much to lose.

Chapter Thirteen

THE WILD SEA-WIND WHIPPED IN OVER THE LEVEE. ISIS PULLED SARA a little closer for warmth as they stood surveying the line of pen-girls in their colorful racing shorts and jerseys. At least wind kept off the fog and allowed a bright sun to shine. Still, the girls were shivering and wrapping their thin arms around themselves as they waited to start the race.

A race! It had been a long, long time since Isis had crouched at a starting line, and she wouldn't be running in this one. But now two hundred of her protégées stood, ready to compete, and each one who crossed the finish line would be her victory.

It had been a long journey to get here and prepare the girls. The idea was born one evening in the cabin of the moored boat, sharing wine with Sara and Smokee and debating how they could turn a pack of downtrodden fleshbots into a fighting force.

"Somehow they've got to move from being terrified and depressed to getting angry," Sara said, running one of the North's best syrahs over her tongue. The winemakers had gifted Isis with many cases of their finest products as a thank-you for bringing Madrone back to the City. Sitting in the warm cabin, replete with good food and with her tongue alive to complex flavors, Sara found it hard to believe they might be going back off to war.

"Pen-girls *are* angry," Smokee had said. She was still a gulper, not a sipper, and instead of wasting a fine vintage on her Isis had made her a fruit smoothie laced with just a touch of brandy. "Biting, spitting, clawing mad! Once they lift up those heads, gonna rip out some throats!"

"But thass not the same as being a force of warriors," Isis had said, setting her own glass down with a thump. "They need discipline. Strategy."

"And to discipline yourself, you need to have a self," Sara said thoughtfully. "You need to be a real person, with a name."

"How's that gonna happen?" Isis asked.

Sara shrugged. "Maya says they need a rite of passage."

"What's that?" Smokee asked.

"It's like a ceremony. But with challenges you have to meet first. Tests. And at the end of it, you receive a new name."

"What kind of tests?" Smokee asked.

Isis was thinking. She had been another sort of pen-girl back in the Southlands, a racer, raised to run naked before crowds of cheering Primes and then service the big betters when the race was over. She'd had a name, unlike the pen-girls, for owners liked to bestow them on racers as they did on prize dogs and horses. Citation, they'd called her, after the first racehorse to win a million dollars, back in the century before. She'd renamed herself when she broke free and turned pirate. One of the hillboys she'd transported had suggested it. They liked to take the names of mythic heroes, Gods and Goddesses. And so she'd named herself after the ancient Egyptian Goddess, ruler of flowing water and love.

She had hated so much of the racers' life—her body at the disposal of the team owners and the big betters, her strength on display for a bunch of pasty-assed limpdrills to cream over.

But she had loved the racing itself, the adrenaline pounding through her limbs, albeit heightened by the drugs and steroids with which the Stewards had laced her rations. She'd loved that sense of being strong and swift and alive.

When she won, she'd felt real pride. They could compel her to attend practice sessions, yet she was the one who chose to put her heart into the exercises and strove to better her time with each lap. They could force her to run, but she was the one who chose to run flat-out, pushing herself to the limit.

And that had made her different from the pen-girls. For while the trainers allocated her winner's body to whatever Prime made the highest bid, in the end her speed, her strength, her will became her own.

The pen-girls had never had that chance, never been able to own any part of themselves.

Isis looked up. "They could race."

And so the idea was born. Training for the race, they would begin their fighters' training. Then they would run, and earn their names.

Now she looked over the line of honed bodies in their proud racing colors as they stamped and waved their arms and bent down in stretches. Just six weeks ago, she and Sara and Smokee had stood in the old convent's dining hall looking out at the crowd of painfully thin pen-girls with cast-down eyes.

Smokee had planted her feet and stood, hands on hips, regarding the bowed heads and hunched shoulders before her. They were every shade from chocolate to wheat, dressed in a motley assortment of hand-me-downs from the nuns' back closets—loose pullovers and modest shirtwaists that made them look oddly demure.

"Listen up!" she said in a loud, energetic voice. "Raise up your eyes, and look at me!"

Shyly, they peered up through wary brows.

"You want the babies back?" she asked.

For a long moment, dead silence filled the room. Then a pale girl in the front row of seats mumbled, "Babies dead."

"Maybe. But maybe not. Who wants to go and find out? Sojuhs going down to the Southlands to throw the Stewards out, make it free like this place. No more pens, everybody free. Who's gonna go with them?"

The girls stared at her blankly. Kit was sitting in the front chairs, and she raised up her head and stole a quick, daring glance into Smokee's eyes.

"Pen-girls to service the sojuhs?" she asked.

"No. If we go, we go to fight," Smokee said firmly.

Timid laughter broke out.

"Pen-girls don't fight," a small woman said.

"We can learn," Smokee assured her.

By seven the next morning, Isis, Sara, Smokee, and all of the pen-girls were doing yoga in the convent gym, led by Kerali who was one of the foremost teachers in the City. By eight, Isis had set them to run laps around the park. They'd staggered and moaned; most of them had only ever walked as far as their rec room on a regular basis, and their muscles were weak and nearly atrophied. But she'd barked orders and they obeyed because it hadn't yet occurred to any of them that an order could be refused.

At lunch, they were served soup and salad and fruit smoothies, laced with probiotics to help them digest it all. They clamored for chips, but Isis informed them that chips were no longer on the menu.

"Thass slave food," she announced. "You're free now—got to learn to eat real food to build up your strength."

Most of that first lunch went uneaten. But by dinnertime, after workouts with weights and a long session of dance aerobics, most of the girls were so hungry that they gave in and ate.

And they all survived the night, Isis thought with satisfaction. Now, a few short weeks later, they were ready to race.

~~~~~~~~

Sara was watching Isis's face. The pirate's eyes were shining, her lips parted with excitement, and just for a moment Sara saw how young she truly was. Oh, she was as cynical as a broker in so many ways, yet she was a product of the Stewards' first breeding program, which meant she couldn't be more than nineteen. Now her eyes shone with the excitement of a child—the child she'd never been allowed to be.

It's only me who will ever see the innocence in her, Sara thought. Only me who will ever see the soft core under that brittle shell. She nestled close.

"You're a genius," she murmured.

Isis snorted. "Sweet talk! I know what you want."

"What?"

"Want a hot sailor to fondle your tiller!"

Sara made a soft chortle of agreement deep in her throat.

Isis would always do that, always keep it light and deflect away real praise. But the race had been a stroke of genius. Isis understood that a sense of self must be physical before it can be conceptual.

Sara felt that, too. She and Isis had joined the girls in their training, and her own body was stronger, her own sense of who she was more sure. For Sara, the regimen was a challenge, even though she was in far better shape than the pen-girls. Back in the Southlands, in her days as a Prime's Trophy, she'd jogged on a treadmill dutifully and religiously crunched her abs and sculpted her thighs. It was part of her job, and her survival, to keep herself looking good.

But this was different.

LeeSing, the City's top instructor, had taught them *pacha-jitsu*, Califia's own form of martial arts that welded judo, tai chi, and karate with acrobatics and dance. It focused on disarming and binding the enemy, not killing. But it required muscular strength and control, and a sharpened sense of balance, along with a deep mental focus. Pacha-jitsu was a meditation, a discipline.

"Center yourself," LeeSing had told them, "and you become a channel for the flow of the universal energy. Dance with that flow, embrace it, and you become invincible."

As a counterbalance, they'd had Old Max, a former Marine instructor from the days before the Changes, now old, scarred, and battered but still an expert in what he called "good old-fashioned dirty fighting."

So Sara had learned to use her body in a new way. Not just to polish the jewel of her beauty, but to muster force and make an impact. She began to walk with a different rhythm in her steps, a sense of contained power like a cat. Her joints felt oiled and smooth, her muscles ready to spring.

At night, when she and Isis were alone, she found herself trading off with Isis, taking the lead and daring new roles.

Now Sara looked over the lists of eager girls, ready to race. Her eyes traveled up to Isis's face, watching intently, excited, unguarded. How good it would feel to make that excitement gust and billow, to fill their sails and speed their craft into the swell, taking the waves head-on.

"Tonight," she murmured to Isis, "it's my turn to steer."

Isis gave her a long, appreciative smile.

The starting gong rang out, and the first relay of pen-girls set off to the loud cheers of the crowd. Isis caught her breath, and Sara reached over and gripped her hand. It had begun.

Smokee felt her breath rasping in her throat and her muscles begin to grow warm in spite of the chilly wind. She was running in the first relay, with the other girls who had been relinquished rather than bred for the pens. They were a small group, not more than a dozen among the hundreds left when the Stewards withdrew, and they'd had an advantage in the training, for at least they had grown to a certain age free to move and run and use their bodies for something other than service.

Now the first relay ran together along the wide levee, the autumn sun glinting off the waves below them on the ocean-side, the cries and cheers of the crowd in their ears. It was a long course, half a mile, and Smokee had worked hard to rebuild her endurance and her strength, still compromised by her bout of starvation. The point of the race, she knew, was simply to finish, to feel this growing strength of will and muscle carry them through a challenge. But suddenly she wanted more than that.

She wanted to win. She wanted to prove to them all that she was not some pitiful victim, not some whining, pathetic rag. She was a champion.

There were two other girls in front, and a long course ahead. Pace yourself, Isis had said. No need to take the lead straight away. Save some strength for the finish.

Still she sped up her breathing and increased her speed.

The gong rang again, and the next relay set off, ten minutes behind the first. These were the oldest and strongest of the breeds, maybe fifteen or sixteen years old. The rest would follow in wave after wave, down to the youngest who were barely ten.

Isis took pleasure in watching them now, as they displayed the strength and stamina she'd helped them develop. In the sessions she'd led, she discovered something new about herself as well. She enjoyed coaching. It gave her pleasure to show some timid girl just how to shift her weight or breathe in rhythm with her stride. When a fearful child took a powerful whack at a dummy, when a shuffling girl with lowered eyes learned a new step and looked up with a shy smile, she felt a thrill of achievement.

She could feel Sara watching her, that constant awareness like a heat lamp, keeping her warm. If it had been anyone else, Isis would have shuttered her eyes and secured her expression. Don't let them know, not what pleases you, not what repulses you—that had been one of her earliest lessons. For they would use that knowledge against you, to solidify their control.

But Sara held her soft parts in tender hands and cherished her secrets. She had a way of saying exactly what Isis most longed to hear. Not that Isis would ever admit it.

Now Sara flashed her pearly smile, her hair a sheet of gold in the sunlight, her face beaming.

"From time to time, sailor, you come up with a good idea!"

—————————

Livingston heard the cheers of the crowd and sauntered toward the noise along the top of the levee. He'd come ashore late that night from the warship, paddling a small zodiac to the beach and landing unseen. It had been a relief to escape the close confines of ship life. Two weeks had passed since the resupply boat had made contact and left him on the big ship, with a cover story that he was a communications officer, preparing press releases for the media. He'd used the opportunity to interview as many of the men as he could corral into a drink at the canteen and a conversation, to learn everything he could about the running of the ship. He had no plan as yet, but he was starting to feel one formulate in the back of his mind, and information was power. And potentially, currency.

Still, there were some big things he had not yet decided. Might not decide, until the moment came to act.

He was also relieved to escape for a few hours the watchful surveillance of his bunkmate Kline, an earnest young officer whose pale blue eyes seemed to follow Livingston wherever he went. Kline was starting to lose his hair, and when he wasn't surreptitiously staring at Livingston he spent a lot of his free time looking in the mirror, running his hand over the growing bald spot at his crown and then over the bristles of his blond buzz cut, looking worried. Aside from that, and the way his feet smelled, he wasn't a bad sort. Livingston divided the world into Good Boys and Bad Boys and Kline was a Good Boy through and through, meticulous at obeying orders, following rules, and showing up on time.

Livingston himself was a Bad Boy, of course, but he had learned to feign Good Boy behavior when it suited his ends. And Kline, he suspected, watched him for reasons beyond jealousy of his thick, blond mane which in any case was kept too short by the mandatory military cut to show off his natural curls. No, Kline undoubtedly had a secondary assignment—to make sure Livingston didn't defect for real.

That might be an idea, Livingston thought as he neared the colorful crowd. Today was a scouting trip, to get the lay of the land, help him make some plans. He'd chosen a day when Kline would be busy overseeing an overhaul of the engines, and wouldn't miss him. But he'd have to be back by night watch.

The zodiac was weighted down with stones and buried in the sand by an old pier farther south. It would be tricky to get it out through the surf, but he was a powerful rower and he was confident of his strength. With his escape route secured, he could focus on the task of the day.

He'd stretched a wig over his cropped skull, with a fall of black hair that brushed his shoulders. The bark-lickers of the City, he had heard, liked their men to have a girlie look. He wore a pair of nondescript blue jeans, an old, beat-up pair of running shoes, and a simple white T-shirt. Nothing about him was distinctive or designed to catch the eye. His plan was to blend into the crowd and observe, looking for opportunities.

A loud roar up ahead made him pick up his pace. He shoved a pair of mirrored sunglasses over his eyes—although the day was misty, the sky more pearl than blue. If anyone was taking snaps of the crowd, they would protect him from biometric sensors.

But as he approached the cheering mass of people gathered on the levee, he began to feel more and more conspicuous. No one else seemed alone in the crowd. They were all eagerly greeting friends, or passing bottles around and laughing in packs, or standing in stations with jobs to do, like the white-robes with stethoscopes around their necks that appeared to be medics of some sort.

His very blandness was out of place. Everyone else seemed to be wearing some sort of costume that proclaimed loudly who they thought they were. Stripes and spots and patterns mingled with no thought for subtle restraint. The bright colors assaulted his eyes. He saw a feral-looking, buckskin-clad, knife-wielding huntress with long blond dreadlocks and some sort of indeterminate heeshee with a snake tattoo that ran down his/her naked back, poking a triangular snout into the top of a butt-crack. He watched a muscular redhead in diaphanous pink robes greet a dark, shapely beauty in feathers and spangles. In their company, his nondescript attire seemed to shriek, "Look at me! I'm a spy!"

Well, couldn't be helped now. Surely there must be some of the deserters from the army who hadn't yet been tarted up to look like a walking carnival. Yes, there they were, in jeans and sweats, albeit with spirals and suns silkscreened all over their shirts, their cropped hair growing out, their expressions sullen or cynical.

He had made another mistake with the wig, he realized. The squabs wore their hair short or long or razored into elaborate designs, braided, dreadlocked, tumbling in masses of curls that seemed to fit their costumes. If he was dressed most like a former sojuh, his wig was a bit too long to have grown out from a military crop in just these last weeks. But there was no help for that, now, either.

Ah well. It was a beautiful day. He would stroll over to the knots of sojuhs, and enjoy the festive scene while he pondered whether and how to destroy it.

Sweat poured down Smokee's face. There was a sharp pain in her side and she remembered Isis telling them to hyperventilate for a moment and breathe into it. Ahead of her, the pinned-up blond hair of the hindmost runner tumbled down in the wind and whipped around her face. Smokee was glad she'd kept her own chestnut locks cut short, and resisted the ministrations of the Hairapists Guild, who had offered their services to the pen-girls. "We bring out your inner beauty," they'd said, combining counseling and styling to help each girl's appearance reflect her growing sense of self. Yes, the City had spared no efforts, deploying trainers and groomers and fashionistas to help each girl choose her racing colors and sew her own jersey and shorts.

She was gaining on the blonde girl. The crowds were more sparse along this stretch, most of them concentrated either at the starting line or ahead, at the finish, and the faces flashed by as she streaked past, too quickly to catch more than a glimpse of recognition. That grubber she'd seen at Council. That bright flash of red dished out food at the canteen. Those whites—healers stationed along the route in case of emergencies.

But she couldn't afford to get distracted. She was gaining on the blonde girl, whose tangle of hair slowed her down as she pushed it again and again out of her eyes. Just one more ahead, a lanky girl with skin like black coffee and her hair shaved into geometric patterns.

Faster, Smokee told herself. You can do it. Move those legs. Almost to the finish now! Time to quit pacing and make some speed!

They were dots on the white plane of the levee path, coming closer, larger. Then they began to resolve into figures, limbs flashing, faces still too faraway to be seen.

Kit was due to run in the second relay, River knew, and he had placed himself midway, where the crowds were thinner and she would see him. He watched for her anxiously.

The first relay flashed by him, one by one. He saw Smokee, puffing along near the front, and waved at her but she was past him so quickly he wasn't sure she'd noticed. Behind came most of the girls bunched up together, with a few stragglers bringing up the rear. And then they were gone.

He would have to keep his eye out for Kit, and call to her, and make sure she knew he was there to cheer her on. Her colors were turquoise and green. It had taken them all a long time to choose, because in their lives they had so rarely been allowed to choose anything at all. They weren't allowed changes of clothing or even a choice of hairdo in the pens. If their hair was blond and fine, it was left long, and blondes serviced the officers and elite units. If it was nappy or thin or just dark, it was shaved.

Let a pen-girl make a choice, might start choosin' what tubo to service and which to reject. Might become a real person.

And if she did learn to choose? Would she choose him?

There she was, still far down the levee. She wasn't in the forefront of her relay, but toward the back, running, but not killing herself, he noted. He waved his flag and began to call her name.

"Kit! Kit! Go, Kit!"

⁓

Kit ran toward the back of her relay, not thinking about winning but thinking about food. Now that she was getting used to it, it fascinated her. The different tastes. At first they had just been alarming, unfamiliar, but now she was beginning to enjoy them, to look forward to trying something new. The Sisters encouraged the pen-girls to help with the cooking and cleaning, and she volunteered for kitchen duty each day. One of the Sisters had shown her how to scrub potatoes and peel them, and she liked to watch the rough brown skins slough away, revealing the moist white flesh below. And chopping things, that satisfying thud, as a knife slipped through a carrot, the long skinny thing turned into circle after golden circle. The exhilarating feel of the knife in her hand, a sharp edge that could draw blood if she turned it on someone. Not that she would. But she could. No one could force himself on her with a knife in her hand.

She didn't want to be a fighter. She wanted to be a cook. To know all the secrets of turning potatoes and carrots and onions and beets into those things that were beginning to taste oh so good to her.

Still, she pressed doggedly on. She heard a noise ahead of her, a rhythmic, sharp booming voice that resolved into a name.

"Kit! Kit!"

She looked around in surprise. There tubo was, big as a barracks, yelling like a mam with a hotwire up the ass. Yelling that name—*her* name. Why?

She slowed down to look at him. Grinning, big teeth flashing, head bobbing.

"You go, Kit!" he cried. "You can do it! Go! Run!"

Kit stopped, and whirled on him.

"Don't need orders!" she snapped. "Don't take orders no more!"

He looked at her, confused and hurt.

"Not an order," he said in a small voice. "Just a cheer. Means this tubo—I— I'm cheering you on."

"Don't need cheering! Runnin' just fine."

"Supposed to make you feel good," he said in that small, hurt tone. "Want you to finish. Succeed."

She stared at him for a long moment, clearly confused. Tubo cracked, she thought.

"Gonna finish," she assured him.

"Know you will."

"Then whass all the shoutin' about?"

He didn't know how to answer her. He shrugged. "Sorry."

She shook her head at him, but something warm glowed in her belly. She remembered dancing, twirling, pulling away, and coming back.

"Gotta run, not talk!" she told him, but she gave him a quick flash of a smile.

He grinned again and waved the flag.

She spun around and ran off.

Then he felt a chill on the back of his neck, a sense of menace. His fighters' instincts alerted him. Someone was watching.

He wheeled around. But nobody was there.

Who was in charge, Livingston wondered? Find the leaders, and he could come up with a plan. Subvert them, undermine them, pick them off. But it wasn't easy to tell, at a glance. He was near the finish line, so there ought to be judges. But if so, he couldn't tell who they were. There was an old lady in a folding chair, and a crowd of medics, and teenagers holding wreaths of flowers.

Surely, at the end of the race, there would be speeches? He felt himself growing conspicuous again, and decided to stroll back along the raceway to the starting point. Along the route, there were smaller knots of well-wishers, and even some solitary fans. He stood for a moment watching a dark, burly hulk of a man with the hunched-over stance of a breed who seemed to be cheering on his girlfriend. He moved quickly on before the sojuh could spot him.

There, down the way was a nearly empty stretch. A young girl stood alone, beads of fog adorning her short dark curls, her face solemn. He ambled over her way. She looked harmless enough. Perhaps he could risk a few questions.

Rosa stood alone, watching the race. She'd dutifully helped Sister Elizabeth and Sister Clare carry their folding chairs and picnic baskets, and installed them at a good spot along the raceway. They were all excited, chattering happily about how good the girls looked, how bright their colors, how strong they were growing. As soon as she could, Rosa slipped away. She didn't feel particularly cheerful, and she didn't like watching the pen-girls and remembering ... or working so hard not to remember.

She found a spot toward the middle of the raceway, where she could stand alone, gazing out across the track to the sea. If only she could run away to sea, like an old-time hero! They were reading *Moby Dick* in her Learning Group, and while she avoided joining the group she was plodding her way through that dense novel on her own, enjoying the funny, old-fashioned language. What did he say at the start? Something about wanting to step into the street and knock peoples' hats off, and knowing it was high time to go to sea. That was just how she felt.

Then suddenly, someone was standing next to her. She hadn't heard him come up beside her, and she was startled. He was a tall man, with longish dark hair, and something was funny about him. The way he was dressed, for one. Everyone else wore their best, even her. She'd put on a bright blue blouse that morning if only to avoid an argument with the Sisters, and grabbed a warm green hoodie to put over it against the chilly fog. The man was wearing what looked like his work clothes, except they were too clean, too fresh, as if he'd never actually done any work in them.

He gave her a creepy vibe. Of course, most men did, these days.

"What team are you rooting for?" he asked conversationally.

She turned and stared at him. What rock had he been hiding under, that he didn't know there were no teams in this race? Only pen-girls racing themselves, for their names. She shivered, suddenly.

"Why are you wearing sunglasses in the fog?" she asked him.

He gave her a reassuring smile. "Eye infection," he said. "Not contagious," he added as she took a step away from him.

Something about him scared her. She took another step away.

"Not feeling friendly?"

What was it? Why was her skin crawling and her stomach feeling like squirrels were nesting there?

Then the wind shifted and brought her his smell, pungent and floral like cheap soap. It hit her with a wave of nausea so intense she doubled over for a moment, then turned and streaked down the beach, outrunning the runners.

It was the smell of the sojuhs, the smell of captivity.

⁓

Madrone was not exactly on duty, but she was watchful as she stood behind Maya's folding chair at the finish line, one eye on the first wave of runners still far down the levee, the other on Maya who was beaming and waving a rainbow flag.

It was a festive day, a glorious day with the fog filtering the sunlight to a pearly glow that lent a soft radiance to the runners and the wildly cheering crowd. A day to enjoy, even as her dream haunted her. She'd had it again, after she and Bird went dancing. And again, last night.

A plaza, a hearth, and a sacred tree.

What did it mean? she wondered. But she knew what it meant. A plaza—here was a plaza, one of the many in their city, the gathering places that allowed people to come together. Here was a hearth, a source of warmth and radiance, and a sacred tree of growth and connection. Here was everything and everyone she loved.

But the dream directed her to return to the heartland of the enemy. Well, I wanted a vision of my own, she thought. But that was the problem with visions. Once you invoked them, you had to follow them.

"Here they come!" Maya said excitedly as the figures drew closer. She waved her flag with renewed vigor.

A tall woman was in the lead, her skin black as a bittersweet chocolate bar, and how Maya wished she could taste that again! She ran like an antelope, with a loping easy stride, almost to the finish line.

But behind her came a freckled girl with short-cropped, mousebrown hair, chugging away with determination, her arms pumping like the pistons of the Little Engine That Could. She was all will and fierce concentration, nothing easy about her, and yard by yard she was gaining. But would she have enough time?

"Smokee!" Bird cried from behind her. "Smoke 'em, Smokee!"

He wanted her to win, suddenly, wanted that bolt of fury to know a moment of sweet victory. She seemed to hear his voice, lifted her head, then put on a new burst of speed.

There was nothing in Smokee's world now but sweat and pumping breath and pounding feet. She ran with all the strength she could muster, gulping in air, willing her feet to go faster, faster. And still it wasn't quite fast enough. She was close to the runner ahead. She could see the sweat trickling down the dark skin of her neck and feel the grit kicked up by her shoes. Just a little more speed would do it. But the finish line was coming up now, just ahead, the tape stretched across the path, and the girl was going to get there first.

"Smokee!"

She thought she heard her own name. As if someone outside her was cheering for her, cheering her on.

She whipped her head around. Who could it be?

"Smoke 'em, Smokee!"

But she was going too fast to see. Still, as if the cheer carried a burst of speed with it, her stride lengthened just a bit, her pace picked up, and just as the finish line came up ahead she surged past the girl ahead and broke the tape. The winner!

Cheers and a roar of applause followed her as she loped down the cool-down track and back to the end stand. A medic thrust a drink into her hands, and a small girl handed her a bouquet.

"The first winner, congratulations!" Salal cried out. She hung a medal over Smokee's neck and smiled broadly at the girl Smokee had managed to beat. "And you, too, well done! What a race!" She hung a second medal on the dark girl's neck.

Smokee smiled, a little ruefully, at the runner-up. Suddenly she felt ashamed, as if she'd cheated somehow, or willed herself to some victory she didn't deserve. What if this girl, too, had something to prove? But the girl just laughed, and now another girl arrived, and another, and the cheers became a roar of joyful shouts and laughter. Smokee was still panting, and Madrone rubbed a towel over her sweating shoulders.

Bird smiled at her. "Smokee, you smoked 'em!"

She looked at him. For one fleeting moment, a smile flashed across her face. Instantly, she clamped her mouth shut and furrowed her brow in her usual angry glare.

But he had seen it.

The shouts of congratulations grew louder as relay after relay came in. Every girl received a bouquet and a medal. Every girl won.

Loudest of all were the cheers for the young ones, the girls who were only nine or ten years old. They ran last, to be greeted by the open arms of beckoning Cityfolk who cried out, "Welcome! Welcome! Come and join our family!"

None of the youngest would be going off to war. The Council had made a blanket ruling that only those who appeared to be at least sixteen would be eligible to go to the Southlands. The others would remain in the City in safety, with families who were eager to adopt them and give them a taste at least of the childhood they'd never had.

They toasted all the girls in apple juice and champagne, brought out trays of tidbits to restore their energy, handed out cartloads of bouquets. Musicians pulled out drums and guitars, and a huge party ranged all over the seawalls, stretching for half a mile from finish line to start.

Rosa stood at the tide line, watching the sun sink below the waves. She'd run down the beach, far, far down, alone until her pounding breath came in great gasps and she felt a stitch in her side. And there she'd stayed, all afternoon, just watching the waves roll in and out, and the tiny sandpipers chasing them.

The Sisters would be worried about her, but she didn't care. She couldn't go back, not yet. Not to the crowds where someone dangerous was waiting.

She should tell someone, she thought, but what could she say? *I saw a creepy guy. He smelled like the sojuhs.*

He hadn't really done anything to her. Maybe he did have an eye infection.

You've had a rough time, they would say to her with pity in their eyes that she didn't want to see. *You're imagining things,* is what they'd be thinking. *Crazy!*

Then she saw it, dodging through the waves. A dark spot, a black smudge on the water, rising and falling, making its way through the surf. A rubber dinghy, black, just big enough for one creepy man with dark hair to row, out from the shore, out toward the open ocean.

Where the enemy ship waited.

This is what victory sounds like, Bird thought, listening to the cheers and the roars of laughter and the drumbeats. Victory unstained by guilt and recriminations. Just for a moment he wished that his hip was unhurt and his leg still whole and that he could run. Run for his own victory. Run down the beach, run for miles and miles, out of the City, out of this life, away from everyone he loved and everyone he'd failed.

But where would he go? Back to the Southlands, calling out for liberation? Where he had his own history of failure and pain?

What would he do there? How could he fight that tyranny with only the weapons of story and song?

Suddenly there was a small figure in front of him, standing, head down, blocking his way. He almost stumbled into her, but stopped short with surprise when he heard her call his name.

"Bird."

"Rosa?" He squatted and looked up into her face. Was she ready to forgive him? To be friends again?

It had taken all her determination to force her feet back to the party, to wind her way through the crowds in search of him, and then to make up her mind to face him at last. But whether he despised her or whether she despised him, he was the one person she could think of who would believe her.

"What's wrong, *querida*?" he asked gently, for clearly she was in distress. Her breathing sounded panicked and her eyes darted away from him.

"I saw someone ... someone creepy," she said in a voice just above a whisper. "He was wearing sunglasses, in the fog."

Bird nodded, not daring to interrupt her. There was more.

"And he smelled ... he smelled ... " She took a long gulp of air and steeled herself. "He smelled like the soap they gave us ... after ... "

Holy Mother of all the Gods, he thought. A spy!

Well, of course. They should have expected it.

Did he dare take her hand? Would she pull away from him? Tentatively, he reached for it, felt her cold fingers in his.

"Do you know where he is?"

"I should have told you before—it was a long time ago. This afternoon."

"It's okay."

"But I saw a boat. A little boat, like a blow-up raft, in the surf. Just at sunset. And it was heading out to sea."

"You've done good," Bird assured her, although he wished bitterly that she'd come to him right away, when they might have been able to catch the troll and find out what he was up to. But it was a miracle that she'd come to him at all, that she was willing to trust him that much.

"And hey," he added. "Thank you. Thank you for telling me."

She looked up now and met his eyes for one brief instant. She, more than anyone else, had gone with him to the worst of places, and though he had failed her there, failed to protect her or keep her safe, or even to protect her image of him as the hero who would never bend, it was a bond between them.

"I knew you'd believe me," Rosa said, and her words dropped into the maw of his guilt like balm, like grace.

She flashed him the tiniest hint of a smile that vanished as soon as he glimpsed it.

A sign, he thought. Like Smokee's fleeting smile, like the look of wonder on the faces of the youngest girls as their new families led them away, like the light in River's eyes as he shyly took Kit's hand. A rainbow flag, cheering him on to the next race. A banner flapping in the wind, proclaiming the lists for the next battle.

It was everything he'd fought for, suffered for, sacrificed so much for—all he'd failed and betrayed.

It was everything he'd fight for again.

Chapter Fourteen

The Naming Ceremony took place in the amphitheater high up on Ritual Hill. It was packed with the people of the City who had come to watch the pen-girls' celebration. Maya stood at the podium and looked down over a rainbow of colorful cloaks wrapped tight against the chill of the summer fog. It was a new fashion, to weave or paint them with elaborate designs and personal symbols. *As if we were running out of walls,* she thought, *and now have to deck ourselves out in artworks.*

Sara had invited her to bestow the official certificates, but Maya had declined. Mostly, she admitted only to herself, because she wasn't sure she could stand up for such a long time, and sitting would be an admission of weakness. But she had offered to make a short opening speech.

Couldn't resist the temptation to strut my stuff one last time. And now here I am, shivering in the wind, with Isis stalking about the stage putting finishing touches to the arrangements, and Lily beaming from the wings.

Sara was backstage, helping the girls with their final primping. The members of the City's orchestra were seated in the pit, playing an upbeat tune. Maya turned with a questioning look to Bird, who stood at her side, steadying her.

"Not my music," he said. "Mendelssohn."

The music stopped. Isis gave Maya a nod, Bird handed her a carved wand topped with a crystalline microphone, and she began.

"Names have power." Her voice was soft, cracking a bit, but the sound system carried it easily over the crowd. "It's an old magical teaching, that when you know someone's true name, you can command their allegiance. For that reason, the wise keep their true names secret.

"A name confers identity. It draws a line around what is named. It says, 'I am this and not that, me and not you.' The Stewards understand this. Hence they withhold names from the unfortunate subjects of their breeding programs, the pen-girls and the sojuhs. They forbid the use of the word 'I' to them. You don't name the chickens you intend for slaughter."

There was a time in her life when she'd tried to lose names, to forego nouns and verbs and experience the world directly, without separating the tree from the forest or the mountain from the stream. She'd spent that summer alone in the mountains, not speaking, trying to lose even the inner dialogue in which we speak to ourselves. At moments, she'd achieved a state in which everything melded together into a flow, energies resolving into forms, forms dissolving into energies. It was all one song, one chord reverberating through a million strings.

She heard that chord now.

Bird squeezed her elbow.

Right. She couldn't drift off. How embarrassing! She was making a speech. Not the time to lose words, but to employ them. Maybe her last chance to be publicly inspirational.

"So a name is a victory," she said.

The crowd cheered.

But what she really wanted to say was, a name is like a balloon. Hold it on a string, lightly, let it rise up above the crowd so others can find you. But remember that it can float away on a puff of wind.

Bird squeezed her arm again. The crowd was waiting.

"Every young woman who has earned her name today has won far more than just a race. Every name is a stone, pried loose from the edifice of control the Stewards' constructed. Wiggle enough of them free, and the fortress will fall. And with them, we will build the foundations of a better world!"

Cheers again! Bird steered her gently back toward the steps down from the stage, and the cheers rose higher. Someone stood, and then another, and another, and suddenly the whole crowd was on their feet, cheering for her.

Not for my words, she thought. Not my worst speech, but far from my best.

No, they're cheering because they sense this is the end. I hold my own balloon now so lightly between thumb and forefinger. In a moment, maybe with the next breath of breeze, will come a tug. My fingers will open and let it go.

The cheers had become a roar. This is a good moment, she thought. I could stand in it, and bask in it. As my mother was fond of saying, I could die now.

But this isn't my moment. It's for the girls.

So she nudged Bird and let him help her down from the stage, so the ceremony could begin.

They sat in the front row, the place of honor, where Madrone had saved them seats.

A chorus of the City's children trooped up and sang an old civil rights song.

"This little light of mine, I'm gonna let it shine!"

One by one, each former pen-girl walked across the stage, took the mic for a moment and told the city her new name, to huge applause. Lily handed them each an official rebirth certificate, and one by one they strode proudly off.

Bird cast a quick look back over his shoulder. Ever since Rosa told him what she'd seen at the race, he'd been on hyper-alert, expecting spies in every corner. But what could they learn, here, that would help the Stewardship? Would they understand the subversive threat in this ceremony honoring their reclaimed pen-girls?

Maya was not impressed with the ceremony.

"It's like out of the Miss America pageant," she grumbled quietly to Madrone. "When do they come out in bathing suits? Or show us their talent?"

Madrone gave her a gentle jab. "Don't complain. They asked you to join the committee, and you said no."

Maya just snorted.

But as the ceremony wore on she began to find herself deeply moved after all. Instead of shuffling with heads down and eyes low, each young woman strode across the stage with pride. Each now looked unique, her hair in a new style, her clothing comfortable but in colors and shapes that brought out her special beauty. And each one spoke out clearly, looking out into the audience and holding up her head with pride.

It was a graduation, she thought. A taste of what I missed by dropping out of high school and refusing all my mother's frantic pleas to go back and on to college. But more than that. It's for all of us. Our Academy Awards of insurrection. The testament that our strategy worked, that we defeated the Stewards not by killing, but by awakening the full humanity of their rags and throwaways.

This was what I needed to see, she thought. My commencement ceremony, too. I *can* die now.

The alarm on Bird and Madrone's faces told Maya that she'd spoken aloud. Madrone gripped her hand as if to anchor her firmly in life.

"Don't say that!" she whispered.

Maya squeezed her hand. "You're a midwife. Don't be afraid of this passage."

"I'm not afraid. I'm selfish. I want you around. I would miss you so terribly!"

Maya snorted. "You have other work to do, you two. I see it."

Bird said nothing, just slipped an arm around her as if to hold her back from some precipice.

"Don't think you have to die to free us. We don't want that!" Madrone said sharply. Their low voices had risen, and people behind them were hissing "Shhh!" Maya made no reply.

After the ceremony, they walked slowly back home. The electric cart that transported the infirm and the elderly stopped for them, but Maya waved it away. She still loved to walk, albeit slowly, leaning on Bird's arm. She wanted one last stroll through the City's green streets, one last chance to savor the beauty of its summer gardens, sunflowers nodding on their tall stems, overhanging branches bent with fruit on the scattered trees that had escaped the Stewards' ravages. They grazed as they walked, Madrone picking a handful of berries, Bird stretching up to pluck a perfectly ripe plum.

Still beautiful, this city, Maya thought. A bit battered and scarred, but resilient. It would survive, and that means there is hope for us all.

Bird supported her up the flight of steps that led to the front door of the old Victorian that Maya had called home for almost three quarters of a century.

The last time, Maya thought. This could be the last time I drag this old carcass up these steps. The first time, long ago, she had been a young outlaw, stepping out of the shadows to startle Johanna as she juggled take-out burritos and papers and Rachel's small hand. Johanna had long ago made the passage that beckoned to Maya now. Would they meet soon? Would Johanna and Rio be waiting for her, their arms outstretched, their faces beckoning at the end of a tunnel of light?

She heard a snort in her ear, felt a presence.

"Been waitin' for you for a decade or more, girlfriend," Johanna's warm voice murmured in her ear. She was holding Maya's right arm, strong and vibrant and in command. And Rio supported her on the left, his blond hair flapping like a pirate's flag, his face alight with mischief as it had been on the day long ago when he'd rowed up to her in a stolen dinghy on Stow Lake and carried her off. *"Always late to the party! Got to make an entrance."*

"Say the word, and I'm ready to steal you away again," he promised. *"Any time, now."*

She stumbled, and a strong arm held her up.

"Easy, *abuelita*. No need to hurry."

But that wasn't Rio's voice, or Johanna's shoulder she was leaning on for support. For one dire moment of confusion, she couldn't remember where she was or who she was or who held her with looks of concern on their young faces. Then it came back to her. Madrone. Bird.

Her knees hurt and her back hurt and she had to stop between steps to catch her breath. Worn out, this body, like a pair of favorite shoes so well-used that the nails protruded from the soles and the leather had cracked.

Almost time to discard them, and step out on another road.

After a long dinner—coq au vin made from an annoyingly aggressive rooster—they lingered at the table. For once, they were all together, no one stuck in some long meeting elsewhere or tied up with some life-and-death emergency. Katy and the baby were staying for dinner, and Holybear and Madrone were both off-duty. Even Doctor Sam had snuck away from the healing center to join them.

They cleared away the plates, and Bird set out an apple pie he'd made earlier in the day. No one moved to leave, as if they all sensed that a moment like this might not come again.

Holybear brought out a deck of tarot cards and made Katy play what he called destiny tarot, a form of blackjack.

"Destiny tarot!" He laid down a card with a showman's flourish. "You've got the nine of pentacles," he told Katy. "The woman at home in her garden, safe and secure. Remember, destiny tarot tells you not the future that you will have, but one you could have. Will you risk another card?"

"Hit me!" Katy said, laughing.

With a wave of his hand, Holybear set down the seven of cups. "Ah, a card of dreams and fantasies, hopes and wishes. Will they come true? It all depends on Lady Luck! You have a total of sixteen now. Will you dare another card, to try for twenty-one? Or will you rest with what you now have, solitary dreaming?"

"I'll live dangerously. Hit me again!"

Maya surveyed the big common room, thinking about all the years of meals and conversations and gatherings she'd shared here. An ever-shifting cast of characters that came and went. Almost always, there'd been a baby, as Katy's baby now lay cradled in her arms. Toddlers and children, lovers and coconspirators. A huddle of cooks.

Doctor Sam, last in a long line of her lovers and suitors, relaxed in the big chair under the window. She hoped he wouldn't be jealous of Rio, who lay collapsed on the couch, back from a long shift at the soup kitchen where he fed the homeless for so many years. He looked up at her and winked. Or had she blinked? No, that was Bird, lounging there with that careworn look that settled on his face when he was unaware that anyone was watching. But surely that broad, straight back at the sink in the corner was Johanna doing the dishes, humming away to herself, and taking the singing kettle off the stove to brew a pot of tea. Maya wished she'd get on with it, so the two of them could have one of their long, sweet gossips about all the recent events.

But where had Johanna gotten that mane of hair, those healer's whites?

"*You got to lay off the weed,*" Johanna spoke firmly in her ear. "*It's addling your mind.*"

"It's not the weed!" Maya protested.

A roomful of eyes turned to look at her, and she realized she'd spoken out loud again. She smiled ruefully.

"Well, it's not," she said. "Haven't done that in years! Although I wouldn't mind some now, come to think of it."

"I could bring you some medical grade from the hospital," Holybear offered.

Bird smiled. "I have musician friends. They've got the stuff that will actually get you high. What do you want, *abuelita*? Relief for those aching joints, or a trip back to never-never land?"

"I have everything I want," she assured him. Looking around the room, she knew that was true. If there was a heaven or a Summerland, she hoped it would be like this. Not harps and angels, or even ever-blooming apple trees, but the everyday comfort of food and fellowship that had so graced her long, long life. She would never tire of it, but she was ready to let it go.

"The four of wands!" Holybear turned back to his game. "A card of feasting and celebration! Out of the peaceful garden dreams, something comes true! Banners, flags, multiple desserts! And a score of twenty. Oooh, very close! Will you dare one more card?"

"I think I'll stick with what I've got," Katy said. "Not too bad—although I was kinda hoping for the Knight of Acorns to come riding up for a visit."

"You never know," Holybear said. "Who's next? Madrone? Will you dare the knowledge of your destiny?"

Madrone's eyes were far away. Slowly she drew her attention back to the room, and shook her head.

"I know my destiny," she said. "I had a dream."

She turned to meet Bird's eyes, and gave him a little, hesitant smile, almost like an apology.

"What kind of a dream?" he asked, knowing before she spoke what she was going to say.

"That kind of a dream," she said lightly. "The kind that messes up your life. It said, 'Build a refuge in the heart of the enemy.'"

She looked so sad, Bird thought. Her wild cloud of dark hair shone like a halo in the summer evening light that streamed through the window behind her. She looked like the Goddess of Sadness, *La Llorona,* weeping. He remembered a moment from the Uprising, when they had been children. He'd been running messages from the battle in the streets to the medics who had set up a clinic in their basement garage. Strictly against his parents' orders, he'd left a terrified Madrone to help the medics, grabbed his skateboard and headed out to the street.

The medics had shown her how to wash out the eyes of tear gas victims. And that's when he'd seen her, as he zoomed in on his board, showing off a bit with a wheely. Illumined by a ray of sun that snuck through the clouds of that rainy day, she stood amidst her patients, kneeling like worshipers. Her fear was forgotten; her face aglow. And in that moment she'd transformed from his annoying little friend into his Goddess, his beacon, his north star.

And she still was. He felt a sudden flash of a panicky rage. He had struggled so hard to get back to her. He needed her so desperately. How dare she have a vision that might rip them apart again!

Because much as he longed to say, "I'll go with you," he couldn't. They couldn't both leave Maya.

And more than that, he couldn't see clearly what his role in the unfolding story would be.

"We've tried that," Katy said in a grim voice. "We've tried that over and over again. Every time we set up an urban base, the Stewards find it and destroy it."

"I know," Madrone said. Katy's eyes were dark with the memory of the nightmare day the Stewards had attacked the Rat's Nest, as they called the base she had anchored down in Angel City. For Madrone, it had been terror and chaos, screams and blood and a desperate dash through the streets with the Angels who had rescued her. But for Katy, nine months pregnant at the time, it had been the beginning of a nightmare: capture, torture, infection with the bioengineered diseases of the Stewards who used their captives as experimental animals. Madrone still sometimes caught a worried look on Katy's face, as she nursed Lucia, and knew she was still afraid that those days of horror had somehow damaged the child.

"But that's what the dream said," she went on.

"Them old dreams are only in your head," said Doctor Sam.

"I wish," Madrone said.

Sam turned to Katy. "How do they find the urban camps? Informers?"

"Sometimes," Katy said. "But most likely it's the water. We tap into city lines, illegally. It's not easy to do, but I could tell you how. But after a while, they notice. Their monitoring systems are patched together and faulty, like everything the Stewards do. But sooner or later they work, and we get discovered."

There was a long moment of silence at the table. Holybear turned over card after card, as if looking for an answer. They were all dismal—spilled cups, clashing wands, a heart pierced with swords.

And then the Ace of Cups, water overflowing from a brimming chalice.

"There are springs beneath the streets of Los Angeles," Maya said.

Everyone turned to look at her.

"What do you mean?" Madrone asked.

Maya gave her an impatient look. "I mean there are springs underneath the streets of Los Angeles. What part of that don't you understand?"

"Like, springs of water?" Katy asked.

"I don't mean bedsprings," Maya retorted. "Yes, springs of water. Hot springs. Used to be resorts back in the early part of the twentieth century. Movie stars would stay there. There was a group that revived them, back in the nineties. I gave a writer's retreat there once."

"Drinkable springs?" Bird asked.

"Ever heard of water filters?" Maya snapped. "Do we have a map anywhere?"

Madrone thumbed the crystal that hung around her neck. The Net had shut down when the Stewards invaded, for the living crystals at its heart would not cooperate in an atmosphere of fear and anger. But with the Stewards gone, the techies had rapidly gotten the Net up and working again. With a simple voice command she tapped into it and cast a holo onto the table.

Katy shook her head. "It still seems like magic to me. Down in the Southlands, computers are things with screens and wires."

"It is magic," Holybear said. "If you think of magic as the directed application of mind to matter. And the realization that there are many forms of sentience that we can communicate with."

"Bird's mother," Maya said to Katy. "Brigid, my little girl! Played with rocks when other kids played with dolls. Made up stories, talked to them. And eventually, they began to talk back to her. We worried a lot about her sanity, until we saw what she could get them to do."

"The technological advances of the old world came from breaking things down," Holybear said. "Taking them apart, focusing a narrow beam of investigation into smaller and smaller parts. But the technological advances of our City come from consciousness, expanding awareness, and opening communication and cooperation to deeper and deeper levels of being. We cooperate with the crystals, and they enjoy helping us play our little games."

"We were talking about springs," Madrone said patiently.

Maya looked at the map and frowned.

"I want an old map," she said. "One before the Collapse."

Holybear murmured into his crystal and another map appeared, one that went back to the old days before quakes and epidemics and the Stewards' takeover. Maya squinted at it, and Holybear gestured with thumb and forefinger to make it bigger.

Maya traced a line off the old freeways with her finger.

"There!" She pointed to a spot between Hollywood and the old downtown.

Holybear moved Madrone's map onto his and synched them.

"But that's the Death Zone!" Katy objected. "No one goes there!"

"All the better for a secret base," Maya said.

Madrone looked at the map. It felt right. She placed her own finger on the spot Maya had indicated, felt a hum deep within her like the song of the bees when the queen was on the brood. Destiny was indeed pulling her.

She looked at Bird hopefully. The dream had come to her, but would he come with her? He met her eyes, then his eyes darted over to Maya, back to Madrone. He shrugged, with a rueful smile.

And that was it, Maya thought, observing the distress underlying Bird's smile. The last piece of helpful information. The final bit of advice. The last ceremony, the last supper. It had been a good one, this evening, just what she would have ordered for her last meal. Nothing special, no cake, no candles, no heart-wrenching goodbyes. Just the company of those she loved for one ordinary meal that she could nonetheless savor secretly as a farewell feast.

They would cry, and grieve for her, and it was right that they should. She'd be hurt if they didn't.

But Maya hoped they wouldn't mourn too much.

Let go, she wanted to say to them. Let go of words, and names, unclench your fingers, and trust.

Trust that when the balloon sails off, the hand remains, just for a moment, illumined in the diamond light of what is truly real.

And then dissolves into radiance.

Chapter Fifteen

ISIS STILL WASN'T SURE HOW SHE'D ENDED UP IN THIS ROLE. SHE stood on the deck of the *Day of Victory*, trying to see through the lashing rain while simultaneously watching the handscreen strapped to her wrist like an old-fashioned watch. Little points of light danced onscreen. Each represented one of her fleet of sailboats and steam-powered ferries.

They'd elected her captain of the assault team. Of all of them, she had the most experience dodging and running blockades on the water. But in all those raids, she'd been alone. She had never before been in command of others, and she wasn't sure she liked it.

The driving wind made it hard to stand, and the rain seemed to find every gap in her gear, snaking down her back in an icy rivulet. Somewhere ahead, she knew, lay the warship. At least it would be hard to miss, big as it was—could hold a soccer tournament on its deck. So huge it could easily ride these swells that threatened to sink the *Victory* if Deva, at the tiller, were to let her attention slack and turn the wrong way into the wind.

She barked commands at Deva to trim the sails and run close to the wind. Whoever came up with this plan had never tried to sail a small boat in a roaring gale. She'd argued against it, against timing the attack for the onset of the autumn storms, but in the end she'd agreed mostly because she couldn't come up with a better plan.

On the handscreen, the dots were being buffeted back and forth. They sailed a wide arc around the big ship, which showed up on her screen as a black rectangle even when the driving rain prevented her from seeing it directly. The ferries and rescue boats would form an arc to the east between the ship and the City. But the *Victory* and the other attack boats would converge in the west, to let the tow craft and the divers take advantage of the incoming tide.

Each boat towed a small sea kayak, staffed by the kayak club. In happier days, its members built near-perfect replicas of traditional kayaks, umiaks, and coracles out of willow and canvas and skins. In them, they explored up and down the coast, holding races and contests to test their skills at rolls and rescues.

They were good, Isis admitted, but she shivered just thinking about it. *Better them than me, down among the waves in leaky baskets. Cold enough here on deck.*

The kayakers were zipped into their crafts, gripping their double-handed paddles and preparing to traverse the heaving sea. Isis consulted her screen again. In the dark and driving rain, she couldn't see a damn thing, but the screen told her they were near to the warship.

It was time—if they were ever going to do it. The storm was strong enough to cover their approach. If they waited longer and it got worse, it could swamp the tiny boats. If the storm eased up, clearer skies might reveal their presence.

"Launch kayaks!" she barked the command into the screen.

Behind her a dark presence moved closer. Sara, covered head to toe in the black neoprene wetsuit of a diver, slid a cold, rubber-clad arm around Isis's shoulder.

"Kiss me for luck," she whispered.

Isis kissed her, partly for luck and partly for lust.

"Good luck," she said.

"Good luck to you!" Sara responded. For a long moment, she looked at Isis, wanting to say *I love you,* but afraid that it would sound like Last Words to Remember Me By. Instead, she tried to beam love out of her eyes.

She had volunteered for the diving team, for back in the Southlands she and her Prime had often vacationed in one of the Stewards' colonies in Lower California. She'd learned to dive, and she'd loved the escape into a different realm filled with strange creatures who lived their own lives with no concern for politics or Purities.

But she had never dived in water this dark and cold, not with a biting wind lashing the deck with needles of rain, and never before with explosives strapped to her back.

She shivered.

Just do it, she told herself, and flashed Isis a final, brave smile. Then she headed back to the stern.

She checked her equipment one last time. Batteries and headlamp, okay. Homing chip. Magnetic hold-on. Incendiaries. Oxygen for two hours. Check.

The ship pitched and tossed in the roiling waves and Sara clung hard to the metal rungs of the ladder as she slid her legs and feet into the frigid sea. The bitter cold chilled her even through her wetsuit. It was a much-used suit, preserved from some earlier day, and in patches the insulation was worn thin. Her left breast felt like an icy hand was gripping it.

With a gasp, she let go of the ladder, pushed off, and plunged into the dark waves. The sea kayak pulled alongside her as she surfaced, and Mitch threw her a rope. With powerful strokes, he paddled in the direction of the warship, cutting across the swells.

Sara gripped the rope and scissor-kicked with her flippers. Whenever she rose to the crest of a swell she caught a glimpse of a dark hulk against the sky. Rumbling thunder was punctuated by cracks of lightning that revealed a square and bulky shape on the skyline. A new squall of rain came down. The wind was so filled with driving rain and moisture that it was hard to distinguish the air from the sea.

The wind whipped the swells up into a towering crest that hit the kayak broadside and knocked it over. Mitch went down and Sara gasped—but in a moment, he was rolling back up again with a grin. He whistled "Okay" and kept on paddling.

On deck, Isis watched her screen as the kayak-dots slowly moved toward the warships. They'd had long discussions about this strategy in the sea command meetings, whether to use outboards and zodiacs, whether the increased power would be worth the risk that the Stewards' ultrasound would detect the thrum of engines. But the kayakers had been confident they could handle even the roughest of conditions.

Isis was less sure. None of them had imagined the ferocity of this storm.

"Ready about!" she yelled as the wind whipped them broadside to an oncoming swell. The gale tore her words away from her, but Deva swung the ship in time so that the wave broke over its bow instead of swamping them. Isis gripped the mast as an icy tide rushed against her legs, threatening to pull her out with it. Then the *Victory* bucked and reared and leapt up, mounting the swell and coming down safely on the other side.

"Good girl!" Isis cried, not sure if she meant Deva or the ship, or both. "Yee hah!"

The kayak battled another monster wave, and suddenly the bulk of the warship loomed above them. In the driving rain and the dark, Mitch had risked going in close—no deck watch would see them, and no infrared could pick them out in this onslaught of wind. In any case, Sara thought, she wasn't warm enough to show up on infrared. Mitch whistled and raised his arm—the signal for her to drop the tow rope and dive. For a moment, she felt one wave of stark fear—and then suddenly, instead, she felt a rush of exhilaration.

She remembered the deadly years she'd spent servicing her odious husband in return for listless shopping trips and ladies' coffee parties, wondering if she would go mad from the stultifying boredom and point-lessness of it all. She'd never imagined that she'd be diving into a raging storm to blow up an enemy ship, with her wild pirate lover waiting anxiously for her return.

Whatever happened, she was happy, so happy to be in this moment, to be this new person that she had somehow become. Smiling, she bit down on her mouthpiece, adjusted her face mask, and slipped below the surface.

She let herself drift downward about ten feet before she switched on her headlamp. The homing beam did not activate—so no one had yet reached the ship to set a beacon. But the compass light switched on, pointing a sharp beam north.

Sara headed east, in the direction of the ship. She counted her strokes. Twenty-five, thirty-five, fifty ... she was there.

The bulk of the ship was like an iron wall in the sea. It was moving slowly through the water, cruising back and forth in a wide arc outside the entrance to the bay. The force of its drag through the water created a zone of turbulence that was hard to push through. Time after time, Sara swam almost to the wall only to be swept away and back. It was if a swift stream ran alongside the gunwales. Frustrated, she tried different depths and levels, and finally, revved herself up, magnetic hold-on in hand, and propelled herself forward with all her strength.

There! She felt the iron against her hand, reached back for her magnet and slapped it hard against the ship's side. It clung tight, and she gripped hold with her left hand, as with her right she clipped the beacon onto it. Instantly her headlamp was activated with a green laser beam homing straight to the beacon.

Good, that's done, Sara thought. She was already feeling a little tired, but the adrenaline was still pumping through her veins. She had another task to do.

With her left arm, she clung tight to the hold-on. With her right, she extracted from her pouch the explosive device, a pack of gel with a crystal embedded in the center. She clipped that onto the magnet and pressed the crystal to ready it to receive the signal that would trigger the explosion.

Then suddenly the ship lurched. A burst of turbulence caught her, spun her around in its wake, and slammed her head against the side of the ship. Darkness ...

"Tighten the main—bring in the jib!" Isis was hoarse from screaming commands. If she ever got off this demon-fucked ship, and out of this rain, she was done with raids. Crazy fool of a Council, sending them into this storm. "Ready about! Helms a' lee!"

Not a good idea—to have Sara down there in the water, with herself up here on deck. She herself should have been with the divers, not watching little specks of light dance on a screen while all the tantrum tears of angry sea-devils poured down on them.

One by one, the kayak lights blinked, signifying that they had dropped their divers. The screen pulsed blue—the homing beacon had been set. If the wind would only stop for a moment, she would have time to worry in peace.

There was a sick dread in the pit of her stomach, and it made Isis angry. She wasn't supposed to feel like this. She wasn't supposed to care for someone like she cared for Sara. She enjoyed dalliances, not alliances. She didn't want some she-jockey holding her reins.

Lights blinked and flashed—kayaks picked up their crew and returned out of the view of the ship's watch. But there were still four, three, two kayaks in range of the warship—and one of them, she was sure, was Mitch's. For one thing, she was sure because he was not yet back. Damn and fuck! Especially not some tyro spike-heeler bitch ... where the Jesus was that piece of shark bait? What was keeping her?

<hr />

Sara's head hurt. Slowly she opened her eyes. She was adrift in darkness, weightless, tumbling. Was she dead? No, the dead don't have headaches. Where was she?

She couldn't tell which way was up or down. She was so cold she could hardly think or feel. Her mouth tasted of blood, and something was jammed between her teeth. She spat it out, and drew in a breath. But water rushed into her mouth, down her throat, burning and choking her. She coughed and spat, water into water. A primal panic gripped her, lungs screaming for air. What the fuck?

Some instinct clamped her lips. You stupid bitch, she told herself. You spat out your mouthpiece.

She fought down the fear. Think, you idiot! She brought numb fingers up to grope for her tank, her tubes, her mouthpiece. There. There it was. She slipped it into her mouth and took a gulp of oxygen. And another. Relief flooded through her. She floated for a long time, just breathing, grateful for each breath.

Slowly awareness returned. She was in the ocean. On a mission. She was cold, bone-chillingly cold under her wetsuit. What the fuck had happened?

Her head—she reached up and felt it. The shards of her headlamp came loose and drifted up through her fingers. She watched them, uncomprehending. Then gradually she became aware that they were floating up, up toward the surface. That was up, the direction they went, and she could somewhat see them because there was a very faint amount of lightness, a gradation of dark, in that direction. And that was good—good to know *up,* to orient herself. She kicked and wriggled until her own head was pointing up, her feet down, and felt a moment of proud satisfaction.

She was in the ocean, and up was up and down was down. That was a good start. Now, where the hell was the ship? And the kayak and Isis's boat? With her headlamp and beacons busted, how the Jesus was she going to find them?

Air. Air was a problem. How long had she been unconscious? She had two hours of oxygen in her tanks—and she'd used maybe forty-five minutes that she could remember. But she couldn't remember what had knocked her out. How long did she have left, before the first explosives tore into the ship?

She had to get away from the ship. That was the first priority. And she had to get back to the surface, before her air ran out. But how deep was she? Where was the ship? She could see no sign of it in this blackness.

Sara fought down panic. No, she would not give way to it. She was having an adventure. She had always wanted to have an adventure and never thought she'd really get to have one, and by God she was going to survive it!

Panic is the worst killer, she remembered her diving instructor telling them long ago. And she thought about the breathing exercises she'd learned from their yoga instructor. Could she ground in the water? Why not—now that she knew where down was. She took some long, deep breaths.

Get to the surface first, she thought. Then, maybe, there will be light to see. Question was, how deep had she gone? If she'd been down deep for a long time and surfaced too quickly, she might get the bends. She should make a safety stop, at the very least, ten or fifteen feet down. But how far was that?

Her chronometer and depth meter were smashed along with the homing beam. She would have to take her best guess. She could count, couldn't she? She would swim up, three or four long strokes, and count out ten minutes, and then swim up again.

One one-thousand, two one-thousand, three one-thousand ... slowly, she counted out sixty, then started again. One minute, two minutes ... they seemed endless. She would lose her mind. Three minutes, four minutes ... remember her lessons. Breathing slowly, fitting the breath to the count. Don't think about anything else. Let the count and the breath bring calm.

She was going to lose it—she was going to freak out and burst up to the surface ... no she wasn't. She was going to be like those vidscreen heroes, stoic and brave. Eight minutes. Nine.

The last minute seemed like the longest ever. She was sure she felt the air in her tank growing less, gurgling on minimum.... Ten! She had done it. She had waited the ten, and now she propelled herself upwards again, three long strokes, four ... and now, yes, she could feel it, she was back in the upper zone, the increased turbulence, she could hear the splash of waves above and see the faint light of the predawn sky. So she hadn't been too far down. She could risk surfacing, gulping fresh air, looking around....

Sara swam up, up toward the growing light. She was cold to the bone and all her limbs moved stiffly. Her head broke the surface. Damn, it was getting light, the sky was no longer black but indigo, and that meant the kayaks would have been pulled out. She swiveled her head, and slowly revolved around.

Don't panic, she told herself. Isis won't let you stay lost.

Isis may think you're already dead, a little voice whispered. Isis has a mission to run.

Sara revolved slowly. No little boats—but behind her, too close, loomed the bulk of the ship. Boat or no boat, she had to get away before they gave a little wake-up call in the form of an explosion. She'd been on the west side of the ship. She knew the plan was for the boats on the western side to regroup to the east and form a barrier between the ship and the entrance to the bay. If she swam farther west to get away from the ship, it would be a long, long swim to get back around to the bay-side. Too long—she was still too cold. Hypothermia would get her even before she drowned.

But to swim around and past the ship, or under it—she wasn't sure she had that much oxygen, and the dangers of turbulence—and explosions—

Now she could see pale color in the eastern sky, behind the ship. Very well, then, she'd go west, and then swing back in a wide arc, and use the sunrise, when it came, to orient her. How far was safe? Three hundred yards, the demo experts had said, for the small explosions. Half a mile, for the big ones. Okay, she would do it—at least swimming would warm her. She set out, with long, strong strokes, to the west.

⁓

Another light blinked—another pickup made. Now only one was missing. That wasn't too bad, for such a mission in such a storm, Isis thought—except if that missing light was Sara she was going to wring somebody's neck. Damn, how had this happened to her? If she thought about that beautiful face, bloated and drowned, those fine hands ... no, she couldn't think about that. She had to run the mission. Get a grip.

The sky was starting to get light. She couldn't wait any longer, she had to pull the pickup boats out of there. She sent out the command, watched the little lines of light move out, away from center. One lingered ... but at last it, too, turned and headed back.

The boats and kayaks had all moved back out of the warship's line of sight. Isis couldn't delay. She would put that rag Sara out of her mind, and focus on the task at hand. When it was over, she would find her or mourn her, and then, if the bitch lived, that would be the end of it. She wasn't going through this again for anyone.

The wind was dying down, and the waves were no longer mountains but hills, and then simply low swells. Now, as the eastern sky grew light, a dense fog rose up from the ocean. That was good for the mission, though bad for her hopes of finding Sara if she were merely lost and not dead.

Don't think about it.

Isis gave orders to trim the sails, and catching the hint of breeze that remained, sailed into view of the big ship.

"Good morning, crew of the *Retribution*! How did you like our little storm?" The loudspeaker echoed over the waves.

For an answer, a laser-guided missile exploded in the location from which Isis had hailed them. Fortunately, the *Victory* had already fled that spot, but the explosion drenched the deck with spray and rocked the boat with a huge swell.

"Hold your fire!" Isis called over the loudspeaker. "More polite to parley. And besides that, divers got your ship mined. Every shot you fire, we blow another hole in your hull. Small ones, at first, just to show you we ain't fuckin' around. But collect enough, and your warship will do the *Titanic*."

She slammed herself down on the deck as a shot whizzed overhead. She spoke a soft command into her wristscreen, and a boom thundered from beneath the bow of the warship.

Lily, on another boat, took up the call. The sound techs had outdone themselves, Isis thought. Her voice came over the waves, resonant and clear.

"There is a place for you at our table, if you will choose to join us. I speak for Defense Council—sailors, abandon your attempts to bombard us and hold us in radio silence. Throw off your chains and join us, and you will be free members of our city!"

A missile zoomed past the prow of the *Victory* and exploded in the waves beyond.

"This is a warning," Isis called. "Surrender your ship, and we guarantee you all safety. But be aware—the ship is now mined, and you got twenty minutes to get off it before we blow it up."

"Join you demon-fucked rebels in hell!" came the raspy call of a bullhorn from the warship. If we were fighting this war with bullhorns, Isis thought, we'd have them beat to hell. She called out one more warning. "You can choose to join us—or you can sail on the death ship!"

"Fuck you!" came the reply.

And the death ship sailed.

It loomed up out of the fog and grew as it headed toward the warship, until it towered above the deck where the Southlands salts stared at it, transfixed with horror. Winking in and out as the fog shifted, in the dawn light it looked pearly, iridescent—here one moment, not the next. Larger than life, shroud-white, its hull was made of translucent bones, its ragged sails were shreds of flesh.

A ghost ship, filled with ghosts.

Ready for more ...

Chapter Sixteen

L IVINGSTON WAS OFF WATCH, TRYING TO SLEEP BELOW DECKS AS THE ship tossed in the storm. He was jolted into full wakefulness by the first explosion, which took place in the hull directly beneath his quarters. The alarm sirens wailed, and he groped for his clothes and emergency pack with the practice of long training.

Pushing through the crowds of panicked men, he made his way up the narrow steel ladders to the command deck in time to hear Isis's ultimatum, and the Captain's stiff refusal to consider it.

Livingston had often considered that he had one great gift as an officer. He wasn't the bravest of men, nor the strongest, nor the best shot. As the General had pointed out, he was certainly not well-connected. His family would remain forever Subprimes, the middle management that provided the brains while the alphas took the credit and the bulk of the profits. His father, whose talents for organization and efficiency had improved production fivefold at his factory, had nonetheless needed to go into debt to buy him this command and provide for his brothers.

Yet he had one ability that had pulled him up as far in the ranks as a man could go on merit alone and, he believed, had won him his current assignment. He could instantly assess a situation and take action.

He assessed the situation now. There were twenty or so officers among a force of close to two hundred men—men whose interests would be far better served, from what he'd seen on his scouting expeditions, by defecting to the North rather than staying loyal to an armed forces that offered them nothing but a life of near slavery.

Question was, did they see that?

An even better question was, what was best for him?

He had no great reason to be loyal to a navy that kept him subservient to men of lesser talent and brains. But, if the General was as good as his word, he had opportunities to rise. He had his family in the

Southlands, to which he still felt some loyalty and sentimental attachment. I may not be overburdened with moral fervor, he thought, but I'd like to avoid doing something that would send my dear old mother and my nerdy little sister to the breaking pens.

"We will never surrender!" the Captain shouted through the bullhorn into the fog.

Pompous bag of bilge water. Livingston himself had no desire to go down with the ship. The rankers might prefer death to dishonor, but he strongly preferred a blow to his macho ego over a watery grave any day of the week.

And that wasn't his mission. Defection, in fact, was his duty. Question was, how to work it to keep his options open?

The ordinary scrubs had no honor to lose. Already groups of them were battling their superiors for control of the winches that lowered the lifeboats. Far better to jump ahead of that wave.

He pulled out his pistol and calmly shot the Captain in the head. He watched him fall with a certain cold satisfaction. The man was a blustering idiot and a brute. Granted, he had now undoubtedly exceeded the scope of his mission, but what was the point of a secret mission if you couldn't have a bit of fun?

"Are you out of your mind?" gasped Lieutenant Kline, coming up behind him. "That's mutiny!"

"Right," Livingston said. "You in, or out?"

Kline might be his watcher, but he was as close to a friend as Livingston had on the ship, and he would regret having to shoot him, although that wouldn't stop him.

Livingston stooped, picked up the bullhorn, and called out, "On second thought, what are your terms for surrender?"

Kline was not the swiftest of thinkers. Under his thinning hair the gears inside his head turned as slowly as a hand-cranked windlass.

"But, but they'll flog you for that ... they'll send you to the breaking pens ..." Kline sputtered.

"Try thinking for a change, Steve," Livingston said. "What 'they'? We've got a handful of braids on this ship, and two hundred swabs who are armed and dangerous—or at least, dangerous and they'll be armed as soon as it occurs to them to break into the armory. None of the salts have any real reason to be loyal to the Stewards. Nor do we, except for the accident of birth that put us down there. Certainly no overriding reason to go down with the ship."

"But what will happen if we join the North? Won't they kill us? Or put us in prison?"

"Not from what I've heard. But even if they throw us in the brig— it's got to be better than being tops on the menu at the Shark Café."

One good thing about Kline—he might be a bit slow but once he grasped a situation, he took action. The XO ran up, looked down at the

Captain's body, and grabbed for the bullhorn in Livingston's hand. Kline took careful aim and shot him.

"I always wanted to do that," Kline admitted. "Asshole!"

"Now we're having fun," Livingston said. And now he had something on Kline, something he could leverage should Kline attempt to tattle on him.

"Lay down your arms, surrender the ship to us without bloodshed, and you will be welcomed into our city as free citizens, with full rights and privileges," came an old woman's voice over the waves. "There is a place set for you at our table, if you will choose to join us."

"Or take a long, cold sleep under the waves," came a younger, husky voice. "Your choice."

Livingston shouted out through the bullhorn.

"We'll negotiate. But give me a little time."

"Ten minutes," came the reply. "Cold as a banker's heart out here!"

There were brawls and shouts and fights all over the deck. The salts had gained control of one of the lines that lowered the lifeboats and paid it out—but the rankers had winched up the other side and now it hung stern-down, swinging like a pendulum. A swab grabbed a crank and smashed an officer in the head. A bigstick sprayed bullets into the crowd of sailors.

Livingston shot three times into the air.

"Men of the good ship *Retribution*!" Livingston cried. "Drop your weapons! That's an order!"

He wasn't sure they would follow him and not just shoot him, but he was betting that they would respond to a voice of confidence and command. They were used to following orders, not thinking for themselves, the minor braids even more so than the swabs. If a leader strode off in a direction they wanted to go, they would likely be happy to follow.

For a moment, everyone froze.

And then the ghost ship sailed toward them, gleaming bone-white in the fog, skulls on its prow, its sails the rags of tattered souls. It loomed above them, and the fog seemed to grow colder, wetter. An icy drop of water trickled down Livingston's neck, and he shivered.

Around him he heard gasps of fear and saw faces frozen in terror.

A laser rifle clattered to the deck. Another followed, then a rain of metal falling on metal.

"Death!" Livingston cried, throwing a hand up to hail the death ship. "Death is coming for us! Our leaders are dead, and now we have to choose whether to live or die. Well, I don't know about you, but to me, our duty is clear. As the Bible tells us, choose life!"

"Life!" Kline echoed loyally.

"Life!" the men thundered back.

"With your permission, I will undertake to negotiate with the northern squabs. Are you with me? Say yes!"

"Yes!" the men thundered back.

Livingston picked up the bullhorn. "Call off your death ship!" he cried. "We have made our decision. We will join you!"

A shimmer, a shudder, and the ghost ship dissolved.

"Lily, can you take over the surrender?" Isis barked into her wristscreen. "Towboats know what to do. I'm gonna search for Sara."

"Sara? She didn't make it back?" Lily's voice held concern.

"Not yet. But this pirate'll find her," Isis said.

Her own voice sounded far more sure than she felt.

Isis took the tiller from Deva and struck a course to the west. Sara had air for two hours, and that time was gone. If she was dead, they might never find her weighted body, or at least, not for weeks, not unless some chance current washed it up onshore, crab-eaten and bloated. Don't think about that. If she was alive, hurt maybe, or lost, what would she do? She might have made it back to the surface.

If she has sense, Isis thought, she'd jettison the weights and the empty tanks, and try to swim back. What was it—five miles? A good marathon swim. Not when you're tired and cold—but she'd know I wouldn't leave her. Wouldn't she? Maybe she wouldn't. Did I ever tell her I care for her? Did I ever say, I love you, Sara?

Shit, I don't, I hate the bitch, let her drown for all I care, others just as good spilling out of the pens every day.

Hey you, Goddess. I don't fucking believe in you, you know that— but if you exist, you bring her back to me. And then I'll tell her, I'll tell her to her fat white face, I love you, you fucking bitch.

Now go away, and don't let me ever see you again, because I don't want to feel this. I don't want to feel this ever again.

Sara heard the booms and the shots. By then she was far out to sea, but the backwash generated by the explosion still lifted her on a supersized swell high up in the air. For a moment, she was buoyed on the crest of a mountain ridge, looking down on the sea far below. Then it subsided, but the wash had carried her farther to the west.

Oh God, Goddess, whatever you are—don't let them shoot that crazy woman! Isis would be in the forefront, Sara knew ... and Goddess, you can't take her! If I survive this, you can't let her go down. No. That wouldn't be fair. Although if there was one thing Sara knew in her bones, it was that life wasn't fair.

But it's not that I'm just hot for her, Sara pleaded with fate. Although I am. It's not just the looks and the chiseled body and those oh-so skillful hands, not to mention the other parts—no, it's that I can feel it, what's inside of her like what's inside of me, the soft caramel center under that hard chocolate shell. The vulnerable girl who never got to be a girl, never sheltered, never protected.

I see that part of her because it's my mirror. I love her, down to the very depths of her, the parts she will never show. I love what she's ashamed to let me see.

And though she'll never admit it, she needs me. My love allows her to be real.

The booms, the explosions—and far in the distance, on the foggy clouds, the ghost ship sailed across the sky. For a moment, Sara saw her own doom written there. It was coming for her. Those skeleton hands would reach down, haul her aboard, and they would be off to the Island of the Dead in the far western sea....

"It's a fucking hologram!" She yelled it out loud, to give herself courage.

As if her words had broken a spell, the ghost ship dissolved into fog.

More shouts from the ship—and then the explosions stopped. The boats turned around and began to move east and north, toward the Golden Gate. They were leaving her, and she couldn't catch them. She was swimming as hard as she could, and the effort warmed her but also tired her. Her arms felt heavy. The currents through the Golden Gate were strong and treacherous—no way she could buck them in her exhausted state. She struck out straight east. Maybe she could make her way to the beach, crawl up on one of the levees. It was a long, long way, but she could make it, because she had to make it....

Then one of the boats broke away from the others, and headed out in a long arc to the west. It was Isis. Sara knew it. Isis would not abandon her. Isis needed her. Isis loved her. Now if only Isis could fucking find her!

Maybe their love could be a homing beacon. She could project it, she could send it up like a flare—

A flare! She had a flare—all the wetsuits had emergency flares tucked into their vests. She could find it, there it was, hands so numb, fingers won't fucking work—clumsy, clumsy—there! There it goes!

Isis, scanning the horizon, saw a fountain of light erupt. A joyous sight, a glorious spout of light and water. She banked into the wind, and streaked toward it....

<hr />

"Fuckin' fish-faced idiot turbot-brain! Where the fuck you been?"

Isis stared down at her from the deck of *Victory*, too enraged and relieved for one long moment to even throw Sara a life preserver.

"I love you, too!" Sara said.

Sara's lips were blue, her teeth were chattering, and her breathing was labored. Isis stripped her, wrapped her up in a blanket on the bench, pulled off her own clothes and crawled in with her. On deck, Deva had the tiller and the sails, speeding them back toward the City. She would be fully occupied, and down here, she and Sara were alone.

"Gotta warm you up." Isis pressed her own warm body against Sara's cold flesh. Cold, like a dead body was cold, with an icy chill that threatened to penetrate her heart.

"Baby, you can't do that to me!" Isis whispered. "I don't wanna feel like this ever again."

"No?" Sara murmured. "Feel this ... and this ... "

"Oh God, thought I was never going to see you again ... "

"And this ... now you tell me—is it worth it?"

"No, no it's not, not to worry about you like that!"

"And this? Feel this ... and this? Like it or not, you are gonna feel. You need to feel. You want to. Tell me you don't want to?" Sara persisted. Her teeth were chattering and she was shivering so hard she could barely talk, but she rubbed herself up against Isis, cold dolphin flesh against the warmth.

Isis felt all the blood rush out toward her skin, as if the depths of her own body wanted to enfold Sara and warm her and make her fast.

"I ... I don't ... " Isis hesitated.

"You don't mean that," Sara gasped. "You want it. I know you want it. I know you, Isis. I know the parts of you that you don't show to anyone else. I love those parts. I love you!"

"I ... oh shit. Oh Jesus, I ... "

Isis was crying. Sara cradled her and rocked her like a baby, crooning to her in shaky gasps. And then she was no longer holding her like a mother, but like a lover, sharing warmth, sharing pain, sharing the great joy that made it all worth while.

"I love you," Isis whispered. She tried it out, so softly that Sara could barely hear it. Isis thought her lips would burn, but she took a breath and tried it again, more loudly this time.

"I love you."

"Did you really say that?" Sara breathed.

"Yes. I swore when you went missing that if you were brought back to me, I would say it."

"Say it again."

"I love you."

"I love you, too."

They lay there, holding hands, in a slightly stunned silence.

"'Course I also swore that I was gonna kill you!" Isis admitted.

"Pick one or the other. I recommend love, if you have to choose."

"Well, I ain't gonna kill you," Isis conceded. "But Sara, I can't do this!"

"Do this," Sara murmured, and stroked her in the place she knew that Isis couldn't resist. "And this ... and this ... "

For once, Isis lay back and let her. Isis the doer, the giver, the one in control, she just lay there and let Sara sail the seas of her body, probe its shoals and ride its deep tides. Pleasure washed over her, like the play of windblown waves, building and curling and crashing. But underneath was something dark and cold as the hidden depths of the sea.

Chapter Seventeen

B IRD DREAMED OF A FORTRESS. IMPREGNABLE, FORMED OF COLD blocks of gray stone, it towered above him. A bugle blew. The gates opened and legions of soldiers poured out. Masked and helmeted, armed and shielded, they marched in lockstep, left, right, left, an invincible force.

"But how do we fight this?" Bird asked. "How do we bring it down?"

He wasn't sure who or what he was asking, but he heard a voice, low and toneless.

The fortress falls when the ground beneath it shifts.

A rumble ... the earth shivered and trembled under his feet. He stepped closer to the fortress walls. A shaft of light came down out of the lowering clouds, and played over the surface of the stones. It formed a rippling pattern, like the broken webs of light playing through water. But the light, he realized suddenly, was shining through the stones. The walls that looked so solid were riddled with cracks. They were brittle, and ready to fall.

And now, up through the cracks, vines snaked, and out of the stones herbs and grasses sprouted. The walls began to crumble, but the roots and the twining stems held the structure together as mortar turned to dust. Trees took root in the rubble and arched overhead, their branches heavy with fruit.

Where the fortress had stood now was a leafy hall, open, with room for the multitudes.

They towed the warship through the Golden Gate, and anchored it in the bay. The old docks and piers were underwater now, drowned by the rising seas, and they'd had no reason to build new deepwater ports in the last twenty years. The Stewards' blockade had kept any big ships from coming in.

All that might change now. But in the meantime, the warship was anchored outside the recently inundated shallows, which were treacherous to navigate with their broken high-rises like new shoals.

The sailors on board, poor salts, most of them, were drawn into the City's integration program, assigned living quarters, and given jobs to do. They were encouraged to send a representative to Council, and Livingston appointed himself. That is, he stood up at their first meeting and said, "I'd like to do it. Anyone object?"

Nobody did, in part because they were used to following leadership, but also because the swabs were still stunned by the sight of water flowing freely through the streets, by the lush gardens and the fruit trees and the many little gifts that people pressed into their hands ten times a day—a ripe pear, a child's drawing, a carving of a seabird.

Livingston was as enthralled as the rest of them, but he did not allow himself to be distracted by the sweet taste of tree-ripened figs or the glory of a border of late roses, or even the sense that he had somehow slipped down the rabbit hole into a wonderland out of some sunny children's tale of the old world.

He kept his mind on his objective, always, and his objective was power. And that lay in the Council, in so far as it lay anywhere in this strange place. The Council, he gathered, was where decisions were made, strategies planned, resources allocated. And he would need power to walk the dangerous line he had to walk.

He'd made a quick radio report from the ship while it was being towed into the City, on his own special line. They'd patched him through to General Wendell himself.

"You did what?" the General had thundered at him in a rage. "Your orders were to defect and spy, not to surrender the whole whore-loving carnival to the enemy! That's a third of our godforsaken fleet, for Jesus's sake!"

"Yes, sir," said Livingston calmly. "But the choice was surrender or let it go down. If it sank, we'd have no way to recover it. This way, I'll be in position to bring it back."

He didn't mention the part about shooting the Captain himself. That undoubtedly would not be seen in a favorable light.

"I'll do my best to report in, sir, but it might not be possible. Until I learn more about the enemy's technological capabilities, I won't risk the shortwave. They may be able to monitor it. So please, trust me, sir."

A loud snort of derision came back at him. "You have a brother, I understand," the General said genially. "A sister. Little nephews and nieces. Parents still living?"

"Yes, sir."

"Find a way to report."

"There could be spies in the City." Bird stood up before the Council and signed as he spoke. That meant his battered hands were visible, on display for all to see, but he had always prided himself on his ability to speak and sign at the same time, and if he didn't he would be giving in to his own sense of shame and humiliation.

The weather was now too chilly for open-air meetings in the amphitheater, and the Council Dome was still being repaired. So this Council was packed into the big room in the basement of city hall, and Bird had his back pressed against the cold marble of the walls because there simply wasn't any room to step forward.

All eyes were on him, some of them approving, some of them smoldering with veiled hostility.

"One was spotted, at the race," Bird went on.

Cress let out a loud snort of derision. "Takes one to know one," he sneered.

Bird ignored him. "We're an open Council—that's part of our strength. We don't want to change that. But let's not be stupid. We don't have to publicize every detail of our plans."

We can begin our anti-stupidity program by not trusting you, Cress thought.

Beryl, sitting among the techies, spoke up. "We've been picking up some interesting signals that none of our crystals recognize. Not part of any of their families. Shortwave signals, but with some kind of encryption. We're working on breaking it now."

Livingston allowed nothing but a show of mild interest and slight surprise to reach his face, but inside, he was livid. Kline, that idiot! It had to be him. Because it's sure as the jism of Jesus not me!

Kline was not at the Council. Livingston had sent him to make an inventory of the City's seacraft. He hadn't wanted the man looking over his shoulder as he played his delicate game of revelation and concealment to win the City's trust. After that one short burst of a report while the ship was being towed in, Livingston had avoided using his coms. Until he understood the City's technology better, it was too much of a risk.

But Kline was a donkey. He'd have to be stopped before he blew their cover. The techies seemed far more sophisticated in their weird, woo-woo way than he'd given them credit for, and he doubted Kline could outfox them for long. Perhaps worse, he might poison the waters back home before Livingston had a chance to make his case. The loss of the warship was going to take more justifying, and he wanted to be the one to do it.

He could turn Kline over to the squabs. What did they do with spies and traitors, he wondered? Probably killed them with kindness, spoon-feeding them some healthy gruel while smiling kindly with their perfect teeth.

For a moment he was tempted to just let the City have him. But what if Kline escaped, made his way back to the Southlands, and bought himself a promotion by denouncing Livingston as a traitor? No, he couldn't risk that. He did have family, after all.

He would have to handle the situation himself.

The conversation had moved on as he was ruminating. Now Bird stood up again.

"We're thinking about this wrong. We're planning for a war, when what we need to plan for is a mutiny. Like what happened with the soldiers, here. We just need to figure out how to make it happen on a larger scale, down there."

He saw some nods of approval, but he also heard snorts of derision. Well, there were some people who would oppose him no matter what he said or did. They would never forgive him for his role in the last struggle. He would have done better, maybe, not to have spoken himself at all, but to let others make his points. He could doom a proposal just by supporting it.

But if he let himself be silenced, then his voice became yet one more thing the Stewards had taken from him.

To his surprise, the first person to stand in his defense was Livingston himself, the naval officer who had surrendered the ship. He had positioned himself between the reps from the army and the Cityfolk, and he disentangled his long legs and rose gracefully up from the floor.

"Exactly," Livingston said. His voice was cultured, educated, and Bird's musical ear picked up the slight difference of inflection that marked the accent of the Southlands. Twenty years, he thought, and we're already starting to diverge.

Livingston went on, "The ones with the money and power might be the head—issuing directives and orders to the rest. But the head can't function without arms and legs and hands. The Stewards' head has gotten smaller and smaller, and the more it shrinks, the stupider it gets."

And that's Jesus's honest truth, he thought to himself. What do I tell them, what more do I offer, to plant my credentials good and solid?

"With less and less to offer the hands, the Stewards depend more and more on the rule of force and fear. But fear is costly to maintain. It requires more and more hands to wield the lash, to man the prisons and the guards and the army, to maintain the debt records and enforce the rules. If those hands refuse to serve its ends, the system falls."

"Why don't they rebel?" Shakir of Water Council asked.

Livingston shrugged. "They haven't thought of it. Or they're afraid. Or they don't have any idea that there could be an alternative."

"So how do we show them that there is another possibility?" Lily asked. In deference to her years, she had a chair and a front row seat at the head of the room, close to Akirah, who was facilitating. "That is our greatest strength."

"With all due respect, Lily, that's what you always say," Cress countered from the back. He'd spent all morning doing difficult calculations involving slope and pressure and flow rates for the repair of the main water line, and it was a year to the day since Valeria and the baby had died. He wasn't in the mood to listen to Lily, or to try and be reasonable and diplomatic, no matter how much Flo frowned at him. He was in the mood to get rip-roaring drunk and break things.

"And it worked," Lily smiled. "The invaders marched in, and then their army dissolved when they saw the possibility of another way of life."

"Yes, but the point is they marched in here and saw it," Cress said. His voice was a bit too loud, Bird thought. Maybe he was trying to be heard over the crowd, but it made him sound strident, almost shouting. "We're talking about *us* marching in there. What do you suggest we do—drag along an orchard, an organic garden, and a troop from the Temple of Love?"

"The battle we fight is for the hearts and minds of the enemy," Lily insisted. "Plant the seeds of our ideals and our vision, and they will sprout and grow roots that can upend concrete."

"Sometimes you have to clear away the weeds before you can sow the seed," said a young man in the garb of the Farmers' Guild.

"I don't like killing any more than you do," Cress said. "I'd far rather sashay down there, hand them a few daisies, and watch them all come over to our side. I just don't think it's going to happen that easily."

Much more of this, Bird thought, and he might lose his mind. Cress and Lily had marshaled the same arguments before the invasion, and they'd still be arguing if Genghis Khan and his hordes erupted out of the past and swept across the Golden Gate Bridge. A smart person would simply shut up and keep out of it.

But I'm clearly not smart, he thought as he found himself standing and speaking.

"There's pure nonviolence," Bird said. "Gandhi's *satyagraha*. And there's also strategic nonviolence—where you aren't so much trying to win over your biggest enemies, but to shift the allegiance of the masses who support the system. Then it's like the ground shifting underneath a concrete wall. The system can't stand."

"I see you paid attention in our Theories of Revolution unit," Cress snapped. "Too bad you slept through the solidarity module."

Bird did not respond, in part because to answer back would be to divert the discussion into charges and countercharges, in part because in some secret chamber of his heart he felt he deserved the barb.

"And how do you do that?" Livingston asked, interested.

"You've got to undermine people's faith in the system," said a short man whom Bird recognized as one of the professors from the university. "Maya said it, before. Make the violence visible, so the masses realize that violence is the only leg the regime has to stand on. Then show them there's an alternative."

Isis snorted. She sat with Livingston, part of neither the army nor the City. "No trouble with that. Violence down there plain as a whale."

"But it doesn't undermine people's faith." Sara rose. "It maintains it. Or at least, their fear. Everyone's afraid to make any trouble. The starving masses don't have a clue about how to overthrow the system or what to put in its place. And there's barely any middle class left, no tacit supporters to be turned."

"The Stewards have the biggest military machine that it's possible to assemble in these days of ruination," Livingston told them. "A huge percentage of the population is either in the army, supporting the army, or feeding the army. But that itself is a symptom of their weakness, just as the attack on the North was an expression of their desperation."

He was enjoying himself, enjoying the discussion. Deep cover, he thought. What a perfect excuse for saying the things I've always wanted to say. There could be other watchers besides Kline, he worried for a moment, scanning the crowd. Someone else could be here, reporting back. But then, Livingston was not telling them anything they couldn't find out by interviewing other deserters and defectors. And his plan would only work if he gained their trust.

"How is that?" asked Sachiko, Bird's musician friend. Bird wondered what she was doing here in a Council of War.

"They need an enemy," Livingston said. "They have no economy left, aside from war. Well, and prisons. There's been so much concentration of wealth that there's basically no one left to buy anything. Agriculture is on the rocks, literally. Yields are down, topsoil is gone from the land that used to be productive, and a lot of land is contaminated. There's nowhere to expand.

"The only entity that can afford to buy anything on a large scale is the army. Ironic, really, that this is the end of all those free-market economics. All those politicians wanting to shrink and shrink the government—well, at least they had the sense never to shrink the defense budget, because now if it weren't for the factories making guns and the farms breeding soldiers and the prisons—the threat of which keeps everyone else in line—no one would be buying or selling or making much of anything at all! Even the Primes have to have some kind of ultimate source for their wealth, and some kind of base for their power. Not to mention something to trade for the luxury goods they bring in from overseas. And more and more necessities that we don't produce."

"So how do we use that to our advantage?" Shakir asked.

"Don't attack their strength. Attack their weaknesses," Bird said.

"Which would be ...?" Cress asked.

"Food supplies. Water. Above all, loyalty."

Livingston gave him a sharp look. Who was the leader here? He was still trying to work that out, but it wasn't clear to him. This fellow, Bird they called him—he seemed to have some authority but whenever he spoke there were a lot of sour faces and rolling eyes. The old woman—a lot of people listened to her with respect, but he couldn't believe that even here in never-never land they let an old woman rule. The angry dark-haired guy in the blue monkey suit, he had a faction too, but damn if he could figure out who was actually in charge.

"But how do we win over their loyalty when they can't see what we're offering?" asked a young woman in the garb of the Builders' Guild.

"Radio Free Southlands?" suggested Logos, who was high in the Tech Guild.

"That might work, if people still had radios," Livingston said. "But private radios were confiscated back in the thirties, and the Stewards have a total lock on what comes over the vidscreens. And as for the web—unless you can pay for Prime service, you're restricted to what the bigsticks decide is appropriate fodder for the masses. And even that is agonizingly slow.

"But somewhere in all the ranks, you'll find always someone like me. Smart enough to see the writing on the wall. Generally at the midlevel ranks—where the smart kids rise up on merit and can't get any further. Stupidity floats to the top—with the right connections.

"The ones you have to worry about are the ones who are both smart and well-connected. If they had a few more of those, the Stewards' empire might not be sinking like the leaky warship that it is. But they don't. So, keep on making it easy for people to come over to your side."

That again was God's honest truth, and no more than they could figure out for themselves, if they thought about it.

Now it was River who stood up. He looked up and down the room, as if debating with himself whether to speak. It was another risk, he thought. An idea that had come to him. Should he speak it out? They might laugh at him, a breed gettin' uppity. But that was old him, Ohnine talking. River, new him, he had as much right to speak as anybody.

"Don't attack the army," he said. "Let the army sit in Slotown, that base there. On the road. Army of Califia gonna go down a different way. Valley route. Hit the plantations. Cut off the chips."

Livingston stared at him. He looked and talked like a breed, except he had lost the shuffle and the down-hanging head. But that was a smart suggestion—smarter than any breed had a right to be. Just what he might have proposed himself, if he'd been in the business of actually helping the North to win.

And what if they did? For a moment, he was tempted to help them just to see what would happen. That would certainly be an interesting turn of events. What would it mean for him? And his family?

"They still have big farms in the south end of the Central Valley," Livingston admitted. That was no state secret, after all. "Trouble is, decades of farming and irrigation and chemicals add up to salty, deeply damaged land. So the farms produce less and less as time goes on. The soybeans and corn—they keep engineering them to tolerate the salt and the chemicals, and the yields keep dropping. More and more, we have to bring them in from Lower Cal or even Panasia. I know this, because my father manages one of the factories that make the chips. He has a constant struggle to get supplies.

"Fact is, you could do nothing at all and the Southlands might starve to death in another decade or two. But they probably wouldn't starve quietly."

"So if we do this, we've got to figure out how to feed people, how to get them water," Erik Farmer said. "We can't in good conscience destroy their supply lines and then leave hundreds of thousands to die of hunger and thirst."

"We'd have to figure that out anyway, once we win," Lily said.

"*If* we win," Shakir said.

"*When* we win," Lily retorted.

"How do we transport an army?" Erik asked.

"Army can march," River said. "Thass what armies do."

"It's the driest time of year," Cress said. "And nearly the hottest. I grew up in the Central Valley, before the Collapse. I know! It can get to be over 130 degrees out there, even in October."

River shrugged. "March at night. Sleep by day."

"And what do we use for water?" Cress asked.

"There are water sources," Livingston said. "And you don't need a cast of thousands. The farms are tended by debt-slaves, who lead short, unhappy lives picking crops in the blazing sun. They pretty much all die of cancer or malnutrition in a few short years, but there's always new ones to take their places. If the plantations run short, they simply up the interest rates and that yields them a whole new crop of relinquished grubsters who no longer can keep up the payments on their loans. Liberate them, and you'll have masses of recruits."

River turned to Livingston. "You gonna lead us?" he asked.

"Me? Hell no!" Livingston laughed. "I'm a navy man."

"Navy goes down the coast, to cut off the food ships and the plastics from the Gyre and the luxuries," Isis said. "Army goes inland, down the Central Valley, cuts off the supply of chips."

"The Gyre?" Sachiko asked.

"'Turning and turning in the widening gyre, the falcon cannot hear the falconer,'" Livingston declaimed. "'Things fall apart, the center cannot hold ...'"

"The Gyre," Sara explained. "That center of the Pacific where all the currents circle, and all the plastic comes to rest. It's an area the size of a continent, filled with the detritus of a century of waste. It's where the plastic miners run their operations."

"Lawless," Livingston said. "A no-man's land, subject to no country, no government, no police. There are rumors of pirate bases, and floating islands built of plastic bottles roped together with imported soil laid atop mats of seaweed. Where the people live by catching rainwater, and fishing for tuna. The Gyre, the last free land."

Isis snorted. "Unless you get sold to the plastic miners."

"Slave ships, without even the rumor of law to keep them civilized," Sara said. "They make the plantations look like a rest farm."

"The miners sell cargo of plastic pellets to the Stewards," Livingston said. "About their only source of raw material for such manufacturing as they still do. The Stewards pay with human cargo, and chips to feed them on."

Cress was not thinking of the Gyre, thousand of miles out in the ocean, but of the Central Valley, the land where he was born. Suddenly he felt an overwhelming urge to go back there, back to that flat, ravaged valley where on rare clear days you could see the high peaks of the Sierras rising snow-capped in the East. Painful memories waited for him there, but it was painful here, too, with echoes of Valeria's voice haunting the streets and babies who were not his own jiggling on their mothers' arms.

And he had tools now, skills and knowledge he could use against the pain. He knew how to carve the land to hold water, how to capture moisture from the tule fog, and harvest the rain to replenish the springs. Together with the farmers—he caught Erik's eye—they could bring life back to the soil, plant almonds and oranges and golden fields of poppies to bloom in the spring.

It took hold of him, this new dream, grabbed him like a pit bull clamping a throat. He stood up.

"I will go with the army," Cress announced. "Back to where I was born. Who'll come with me?"

"This fighter," River said. "I will. Me."

"And me," Smokee said, somewhat to her own surprise. Part of her yearned to stay with the navy, to go with Isis and Sara and remain on the blue and sparkling sea.

But she would always have the sea, and her memory of it, clear and unstained. If there was fighting to do, and blood to spill, she preferred to stand on solid ground. And the pen-girls would need a leader. They would be no real help to the navy, but they might make a strong fighting unit on land.

"We go with the navy," Isis announced. "Head down the coast, cut off the supply lines of food goin' in and slaves and weapons goin' out. What about you, salt?" She gave Livingston a long look.

Yes, he was saying silently to himself. Yes. This is all working out to plan.

"Navy, of course," he said smiling. And that will put me in the perfect position to deliver back both the warship and the navy of the North, should I choose to honor my mission. Or not, as the case may be.

The army going down the Central Valley didn't worry him. If their ragtag band of leaderless breeds and fluffies killed a few dusters and an overseer or two, that would be no great loss to the world. If they met with any serious fighting, he'd put his money on the Stewards' troops to win. If he maneuvered himself into command, he could make sure of that.

Bird sat silent. He knew that he had a part to play, but he still couldn't see what it was. Not to stay here in safety, he was sure of that. For in truth there was no safety here for him, only a more refined form of suffering. There were days when everything was so bright that it hurt—the smiling children, the singing gardens. Hurt because it seemed to have no relation to the shadows deep inside him. Hurt because it was so hard to live here, with the condemnation of those who had no idea of the terrible places he had been.

Madrone said nothing throughout all the arguments and discussions. But now she stood. "I had a dream," she said. "In the dream, I was told to go back to the Southlands. 'Build a city of refuge, in the heartland of the enemy.'"

They were all looking at her. She could feel Bird's gaze like a sunburn on her left cheek. She gulped. This was it, the moment of commitment. If she opened her mouth and continued, she would be bound.

But I'm already bound, she thought. By the vision. My vision. Not just by Bird's restless anguish, but by my own necessity. Now let's just make it public.

"I believe that I'm called to go down there, not with the army, and not with the navy. I will go down and make a place of healing, a city within the city, a refuge in the heart of the fortress. So that people can see an alternative, there where they live."

Bird was sitting a little way away from her. He couldn't see her eyes, only her profile, the proud set of her head, the way she unconsciously squared her shoulders as if preparing for a fight. And he still felt torn by his own confusion, his terrible uncertainty.

She was looking at him, hoping, inviting.

She had backed him, held him, healed him so many times. He could never let her go alone. Now he would back her. They would do this task together, if at all. He let out the breath he hadn't realized he'd been holding.

She had given him a gift, a great gift, he realized. She was offering him a way out of his dilemma, another way to fight where guns would not serve them but where his song, his story just might.

"I will go with you," he stood and said. "I'll tell the story. I'll sing the song."

And Maya? But that was a question without an answer.

~~~~~~~

It was well after midnight by the time Livingston got back to the old yacht club, where he found Kline playing cards with a few of the sailors and a contingent of kayakers. He'd needed to make a few preparations. Now all was ready for them to head back to the warship.

They cast off their outboard, and Livingston took the tiller, threading his way expertly past the spire of the Old Ferry Building which stuck up out of the engulfing waters like the arm of a drowning man making one last bid for help. The night was dark, the wind was cold, and the bay was lonely. Livingston allowed himself one twinge of regret as he locked the tiller into position and called Kline's name.

"What?"

"Over there—look!"

Kline turned and peered out toward the bridge. Livingston grabbed the heavy metal crowbar he'd stashed below the seat and swung it with all his strength at Kline's head.

Crack! Kline slumped down and Livingston quickly pushed his head over the side so that he wouldn't bleed on the gunwales. He rifled through Kline's pockets until he found the coms unit, a small plastic rectangle with a fuzzy screen. Too dangerous to keep. He crushed it and tossed it over the gunwales, tied a bag of heavy stones he'd stashed earlier around Kline's neck, and tipped him over the side.

No one would miss him. If they did, he'd simply say he had delivered him to the ship, and hadn't seen him since. With luck, his body would never be found, or at least not until Livingston was a long, long way away.

He supposed a better man might feel remorse, but what he felt was relief. No one watching him now, second-guessing his motives, and snitching back to the Stewards about it. No one to give him away.

He leaned carefully over the gunwales and washed his hands in the salty water of the bay. Only the little riffles kicked up by the light wind broke its surface. He revved up the engine and headed for the ship.

Chapter Eighteen

One of the gifts of a long, misspent life is to leave on a note of victory. It's the storyteller's prerogative to decide when to end.

When I was young, I'd stay at every party until the bitter end, wringing the last dregs of pleasure out of every occasion. But the last ones to leave get stuck with the cleanup, and I just don't have the heart for it, not again. I've rebuilt this city once already—I've done my part. Best to go while the music is still playing and the lights are bright.

I'm ninety-nine years old, and long past my sell-by date.

Okay, I admit, I would like to see one hundred. A round and satisfying number. An achievement.

But that would mean long months more of delay before Bird and Madrone would feel free to follow their destiny, while meanwhile I lose my faculties one by one. Hearing is already half gone or more, next to go will be sight and smell and what doctors like to call the executive function, until I'm dribbling into my bib and they're changing my diapers. I'd rather go in solidarity with our old friends, the ninety-nine percent.

But how? I rule out active means of suicide—so messy and painful and easily misunderstood. I could stop eating—but never in my life have I been the sort of person who stops eating. Age and the privations of insurrection might slim me down, but I refuse to go out like some teenage anorexic, refusing the last tastes of pleasure left.

I would like to go out on one last, glorious orgasm, letting pleasure reverberate like the twang of a bowstring to shoot the arrow of my soul out into the beyond. But who could I get to provide it?

During the heat of the invasion, Doctor Sam had obliged with pleasure and comfort, but now that tide had ebbed and in any case, sex of life-terminating intensity is a lot to ask of a pragmatic medical man.

Perhaps the Priestesses of the Temple of Love would oblige? Ah, I could imagine it so well. I would offer myself to Oshun. "Pleasure me,"

I would say. "Take me to places even I have never yet been, use all your skill to carry this venerable body to heights I've never known, and don't let up until this old heart stops."

But the repercussions, for them, would be unthinkable. Ah, I could imagine the arguments in Council, the accusations of irresponsibility, the investigations. No, I couldn't do that to them.

While I ponder, I finish my last task. I had never wanted to write an autobiography. I prefer fiction to fact. It's more truthful, and no one can indict you for it. I always said I would never write my own life story until I received some terminal diagnosis, with only weeks or months to live. And if I were shot in the public square, or run over by a bus, as my soul catapulted out of my body my last thought would be, "Praise Goddess, now I don't have to write my memoirs!"

But now that it comes to the end, I would like my stories to live on. I would like others to know something of the truth of my life, or at least, have the bare facts to compare to those deeper truths of my fictions. So I write, in the early mornings, when my energy is fresh, even though every word I type is signing my own death warrant.

And so I place the last words here, this last record. It's done. A century of good advice.

I see her now, the Crone, old Serpent-Skirt, her face two snakes rubbing foreheads. Coatlicue, they used to call her.

"We met in Mexico," I say. "You're a long way from home."

Her face changes, darkens ... now she reminds me of Johanna, if Johanna had a silver web of lines etched into her mahogany skin, and eyes that opened into the heart of galaxies.

"What do you want?" she asks.

"To come to you. It's time."

She snorts. "Oh yeah? You still clutchin' to life like a stripper clings to her pole. You want to come to me, girlfriend, let go."

Let go. Easier said than done. The body struggles to go on living, long after that aim becomes pointless. The heart continues to beat, even when you tell it to stop. The breath slows, but just when you think, Okay, that's it, some spasm of the diaphragm forces the lungs to inhale.

I am prying loose my fingers, unclenching my thighs. Madrone's healer instincts bring her to my side, she's holding my hand. Bird is crooning, tears dripping down his face, but me, I'm laughing. Yes, laughing. Suddenly the whole thing strikes me as hilarious, all the petty problems and shrieking concerns of life, all the nattering and nittering and worrying and scurrying, like a bunch of frantic mice, and the fear. Fear of what? A rift, and on the other side, something luminous as a billowing cloud bank lit by the sun's golden rays.

When my own mother was dying, she said to the doctors, "How will I know when I'm dead?" The doctor truly didn't know what to say, although I thought it was a reasonable question.

"I'll tell you," I promised her, and I did, to the consternation of the nurses.

"You're dead now, Mom," I told her. "Now you're dead."

"Tell me when I'm dead," I whisper to Madrone. I think I say it, but my voice is weak and whispery and I'm not sure she could hear. I consider making a greater effort, but I am leaving effort behind and any straining will take me backwards. I consider what my last words should be. Shouldn't I say something inspiring, something they can treasure, that will be part of my legacy?

The truth is that after ninety-nine years, even dying carries with it expectations. They're watching me, the young. Oh, they're holding my hand and crying their tears and singing their chants to help me over, but beneath it all, they're watching, still asking something of me, asking, How do I do this when my time comes? Show me how to die with grace.

Yes, I can see them—Madrone intent and peaceful, though tears drip down her cheeks. Well, she's a healer, she knows death well enough. She shouldn't need me to show her the way. And Bird, stroking my hair, crooning one of his songs.

"If you sing, you won't be scared," I used to tell him. "I'm not scared!" he'd always say. Now I can't tell if I'm saying it to him, or him to me. But I'm not scared, and I see the nightmares lurking behind his eyes. Maybe he does still need me, his grandmother, to soothe him in the night.

And just for a moment, I'm pissed. Haven't I given enough, in ninety-nine years? Wasn't it enough to rear you and chide you and occasionally inspire you? To fight all the battles I've fought? But the rage passes like a hot flash, leaving peace behind. It's a gift, to be able to give something even with my death. The last grace. I give it generously.

"You are the great gifts of my life," I tell them. Of course there's also sex, and food, and the creative thrill of writing and leaving a legacy, and acclaim, and revolutionary victory, but I'm going for something memorable and inspirational, not a fucking catalog. I'm remembering the day now, the Uprising long ago, when Las Quatra Viejas, the four old women with pickaxes went out in front of the tanks to crack open the pavement and plant saplings.

Everyone deserves one day of grace in a lifetime. One day of golden light, one crazy pirate in a purloined rowboat, one mad kiss in the locker room, one soft, surprising breast under your hand that opens the gates of heaven, one strawberry placed between your lips with a brush of a fingertip and a secret smile.

One day when you step beyond fear, and commit one act of courage that can change the world.

"Widen the cracks," I say. "Just widen the cracks."

And the rift opens, and I'm standing on shore, watching a boat approach across a dark, dark sea, as once long ago in Golden Gate Park

Rio rowed up to me in a stolen rowboat and carried me away into this life I now lay down.

The boat scrapes its bow on the shores. And the Sailor reaches out an arm, as Rio reached for me, as once long ago Johanna reached for me and the world cracked open. And I step aboard. I feel it rock under my feet, hear the crunch of the hull on sand.

And then Rio is at the tiller, his hair golden again, shining in the sun, his face young and unmarred, and Johanna has her arm around me, warm and tangible, and I smell the fragrance of her hair. My body gasps for a breath, and they fade. I feel the touch of Madrone's hand, hear Bird's song. I release the breath, and Johanna is warm and close, Rio young and proud and laughing. A breath, dragging me back ... a release, letting me go, letting the boat sail forth into a sea suffused with light.

Birth, death, sex—each has its own sort of climax. A last great push, a rush, a throbbing convulsion of heart and lungs and bowels, and then—freedom! A green flash on the horizon, a great wind catches the sails, and we're off, buoyed by the current, heading into a splendor of purple and blue and gold.

"IT'S OVER," MADRONE murmured. "YOU ARE DEAD NOW, *MADRINA*. We love you."

She held one of Maya's hands, as Bird held the other. They faced each other across her body, and Bird reached up and gently closed Maya's eyes. Behind them the morning sun streamed through the curtains of her bedroom and made a halo of her white hair.

Bird couldn't speak. He felt bereft as a child, suddenly adrift with no anchor. Maya had been more than a grandmother—she had been a lodestone, a pole star, always there at the center. Without her, where was his north?

> *"May the Wind carry her spirit gently*
> *May the Fire release her soul,*
> *May the Water cleanse her, may the Earth receive her,*
> *May the Goddess take her in her arms and guide her to*
>   *rebirth."*

Madrone murmured the blessing. Maya lay, looking peaceful and serene, in the bed where she had spent so many mornings writing, where they had had so many cozy breakfasts and cups of tea. No more.

Rebirth, ha! Madrone could almost hear Maya's voice. *Not until I get a good long vacation!*

Bird stood, looking stricken.

"Sing for her," Madrone said. "Keep on singing."

He sang a requiem, a song of grief and sorrow that poured out of him. If you sing, you won't be scared, she had said to him long ago. He wasn't scared, not for her. Her face was peaceful—beatific. The look in her eyes, at the end, had been one of joy.

They sat together for a long, quiet, peaceful hour, as the golden light of a new morning filled the room. Then Madrone went and got a basin of water. She crushed some fresh rosemary and lavender into it. Bird watched as she tenderly bathed Maya's body. He stroked her face with the cloth, rubbed in some ointment that Madrone handed to him. But he couldn't touch the rest of her body in death any more than he would have in life. He simply watched, one hand on Madrone's back to support her as she bathed Maya in herbal water and tears.

That hour was the last one of peace he had for a long time. When it was over, he left Madrone to sit with the body while he sent out messages over the Net, to Doctor Sam, to Lily, to Holybear, and to their old friends Sage and Manzanita, who were upriver guarding their experimental cell lines. Then he went out to tell the household.

Katy came, with baby Lucia, and enlisted River to help her cover all the mirrors in the house. Then she began to cook. She kept River so busy helping her, chopping and stirring and rolling out pie dough, that he barely had time to feel how much he would miss the old lady. But as he scrubbed the old, round table in the kitchen, he suddenly realized that she would never again sit there and talk to him, never wave her paring knife vaguely, never again give him counsel on the hundred disturbing new ideas and feelings that plagued him.

He stopped, dead still. He was breathing in a funny way, and a tear was trickling down the side of his nose. He snuffled and jerked and choked.

He hadn't cried since he was three, except for those spasms of relief in the Temple of Love. He didn't think he could cry any more. They had beaten it out of him thoroughly, and he'd never felt the need to. But something suspiciously like a sob was trying to push through his clenched throat. He emitted a harsh, chuffing sound, like a bark. Katy was staring at him. Embarrassed, he tried to turn it into a cough.

She came over and put an awkward arm around him. Mostly she either ordered him around or avoided him, but now there was affection in her touch.

"It's okay," she said. "Go ahead and cry. Nobody's going to beat you for it."

But the urge was gone. He couldn't cry, not with a witness. He bent his head and began wiping the table.

"Grief," Katy said. "It's the price you pay for love. But it's a good thing that you loved her."

"Did I?"

"I'd say you did. I saw how tenderly you looked after her. I know you talked to her about the things you'll never tell the rest of us."

Is that love, River wondered? That sense of comfort he'd felt when he was with her, the pain he felt now. Yet it was a good pain, like the way muscles felt after a training session. There was something beautiful about it.

"She had a good life, and a long one," Katy said. "She had as peaceful a death as anyone could ask for. So mourn for her, River, but don't grieve too much. We all have to die, and her time had come."

Sam came as soon as he got the message. Bird and Madrone left him alone with Maya while they began making arrangements for the funeral. Death, for the survivors, is not a restful prospect. There were a thousand details to arrange. As soon as Holybear sent out a formal announcement to the Net, there were arguments to arbitrate. For Maya was a public figure, who belonged not to Bird and Madrone alone but to the City as a whole. And everyone in the City had opinions about how best to honor her.

Some wanted her buried in the Central Plaza, others wanted to erect her monument on the street where Las Quatra Vieja had stood before the tanks during the Uprising, planting trees. Some wanted to carry her coffin through the streets—but among those, one faction wanted to follow the Track of Literature, another the Track of Revolution.

The Jewish Council insisted her funeral should be the next day, in accordance with Jewish law. The Guild of Priestesses wanted a wake that would last for three days followed by a grand cremation, together with all her books and a pickaxe at her feet.

"She'd hate this," Bird complained to Madrone as they caught the warmth of the afternoon sun in the garden. "All this squabbling over her remains. It makes me sick!"

"She'd love it," Madrone said. "All these people who feel she belongs to them. All the fuss and attention. But in the end, you are her grandson. Just figure out what you want, and what she would want, and decide."

Holybear brought them tea on the Lady Di and Prince Charles tea tray. He also brought them a note that River had found on her dresser when he went to drape the mirror.

About My Funeral—

What I most want done with my body is to take it up into the hills and leave it for the vultures. Goddess knows, they've eyed me often enough, and I've said to them many a time, "I'm not dead yet." I owe them a feast. And if you are what you eat, then it stands to reason that you are what eats you, as well. How I will love to soar over the hills, riding the updrafts with that slightly tipsy wobble, nostrils alert for the scent of something putrid and delicious below!

But if that solution seems disrespectful, or impractical, or unhygienic, then I'd like to be cremated and my ashes sprinkled in the City's gardens. And do it fast. I'm enough of a Jew to want my body disposed of rapidly and efficiently. Don't let me lie around stinking up the atmosphere while people make a fetish of my corpse.

There were a lot more instructions, but Bird was relieved that he now knew what to do. He could not bring himself to throw her body to the vultures. However wild and feral that might be, to him it didn't feel respectful enough. And the City would have his head. Half of them hated him as it was, the rest would follow.

They couldn't do the funeral within twenty-four hours, as Jewish law required. It just wasn't possible to move that quickly. But they planned it for the afternoon of the following day, and he placated the Jewish Council by assuring them that he would sit shivah for the traditional seven days. He wanted to, in any case. He needed the time, craved it—a time out of time to integrate the loss.

He nixed the conflagration of her collected works, however. It smacked too much of the Nazi and Retributionist book burnings.

They began at the house, carrying the coffin out the front door of the home she'd lived in for almost eighty years. Bird and Madrone led the first relay of bearers, along with Doctor Sam and Holybear, Sage and Manzanita who'd come back from the mountains. But it was a long, long route and there were many strong backs eager to help with the load. They carried her past the intersection where she and the others had stood up to the tanks in the Uprising.

The saplings they had planted had grown into strong trees, only to fall to the bulldozers of the Stewards during the invasion. Now Bird and Lily and Madrone knelt and planted new starts, apples that would some-day feed a new generation.

They went on, the procession growing into a march. It seemed like everyone in the City turned out. Some were dressed in the skeleton costumes of Dia de los Muertos, some in the white of the ghosts who had haunted the soldiers of the Stewardship. Others wore their brightest, most festive clothing and sang as they carried offering baskets of flowers and fresh herbs from the gardens, while drummers held a steady beat. Giant puppets of Gods and Goddesses hovered over the crowd, acrobats did flips and cartwheels and stilt walkers performed amazing feats of balance. The procession flowed through the streets, a rainbow river.

They carried her down to the Central Plaza on the Track of Liberation, stopping for homage at the stations that celebrated rebellions and revolutions, the Underground Railroad and the anti-Nazi Resistance. Then back they came on the Track of Literature, reading poems and passages from some of her own works and her favorite authors, and finally up the processional way to the top of Ritual Hill.

Maya lay in state while the people of the City filed past, hour after hour, burying the coffin under a mound of flowers and herbs brought in tribute. Priestesses sang chants to the Goddess Maya had followed throughout her long life. Rabbis said the prayers of her ancestors. The Ohlone danced an honor dance. Drummers and dancers honored the Orishas, copal and conch shells called out to the ancient Gods of the Mayas and Aztecs, a dragon danced its way from Chinatown to circle the hill while a hundred yogis and yoginis did the Salutation to the Sun. Nuns and priests and ministers offered Christian prayers, and an imam chanted verses from the Koran as Buddhist monks sat in meditation and Tibetan horns rang out. Musicians played, and led by Bird, thousands of voices were lifted up together in the "Uprising Song" and her requiem.

At midnight, the Witching hour, Bird and Madrone together lit a torch to the pyre. It flamed up in a glorious blaze that lit the sky and burned for hours. When it was finally cool, three days later, the people of the City returned again with pouches and baskets and collected ashes that they scattered in the gardens and the greenways, among the orchards and the native meadows and the urban forests of the City. And Maya was gone.

Bird sat shivah for a week sitting on the floor or on the ground in the garden, wearing torn clothes. Madrone joined him as much as she could, but the needs of the living called her back to the healing center for hours each day. She was working, but she was also turning over her responsibilities, preparing to go.

On the third day after the funeral, Bird received a notice on the Net from the Writers' Guild, with a fat file attached. It was Maya's autobiography. *A Century of Good Advice*, she'd called it. They'd received it that morning—apparently she'd put it on a time release the day before she died. In the preface was a final note to him.

"I spend too much time talking to the dead to think that death is a final ending," she wrote. "Expect me to haunt you. Mourn me, of course, but not overmuch. I'm having the time of my life, in every sense of the word. Now go do what you have to do."

At the end of the week Bird showered and shaved, uncovered the mirrors, and slept in his bed again. Then he and Madrone began to plan.

PART TWO

A Plaza, a Hearth, and a Sacred Tree

Chapter Nineteen

D RAGONFLY!" MADRONE CALLED OUT TO BIRD AS SHE CRUISED DOWN the Stewards' rebuilt road on the brand-new bike the Transport Guild had given her.

It was a beautiful thing—the light, elegant frame was made of bamboo to save scarce metal, and the twenty gears were formed of a new alloy that the Materials' Guild had forged from aluminum mined from old landfills, with traces of other metals to give it strength. For steep climbs, a small motor assisted weary legs. Great wings of solar film unfolded when the bikes were at rest to recharge the batteries, so the bikes looked like giant dragonflies, perched for takeoff.

"Dragonfly!" she called again.

"What?" Bird yelled back.

He was just ahead of her, on his own new bike.

"I'm naming mine Dragonfly," Madrone shouted.

"Not fair," Bird called back to her. "I was going to name mine Dragonfly!"

"I said it first!"

"Why don't you call yours Damselfly?" He slowed for a moment to let her catch up with him.

"That would be gender stereotyping." Madrone peddled up to ride alongside him. "Call yours Damselfly!"

She and Bird were heading down the old Highway 280 that followed the spine of the Peninsula hills. Spread out below her, like an afghan of granny squares in every shade of green, lay the patchwork of minifarms that had transformed the ruins of the suburbs into some of the most productive growing land in the Bay Area. Gardens flourished in what once had been wide lawns and big back yards.

The Stewards, in their latest invasion, had not had time to raze the suburbs. Swaths of forest gardens lined the old avenues, their trees still tall and green. Beneath their high canopy, Madrone knew, layers of shrubs with edible berries and medicinal herbs provided cover for wildlife and offered secret paths for children to explore.

Out in the bay far below them to the east, an occasional sad spire of an office building stood like a forlorn island, crowned with colonies of seabirds. Small boats plied back and forth, painted in the green and gold of the Farmers' Guild. Madrone wondered what the long gone Silicon Valley's tech-wizards would have thought if they'd known their high-rises were fated to end as guano-harvesting towers.

Of course, they could have known, should have known. Scientists had warned the country for decades about the dangers of global warming, but still they'd built on the low ground until the floods of the '20s finally forced them to stop. There below her lay the proof that even the sharpest minds could still be pig-blind stupid.

Bird sped ahead of her, but she pedaled furiously and gained ground as the road leveled out. He coasted for a bit, letting her pull ahead, feeling suddenly happy. Riding a bike made him feel like a kid again, off on an adventure. With every mile they pedaled away from the City, he felt lighter, out from under the heavy fog of shame and blame, the endless circular questioning of his own choices, the reproach in Rosa's eyes. All of that lay like a brume of smog over the City. Leave it behind, he thought. Leave it behind.

And Maya. At times his grief washed over him like a wave. He was glad to escape the emptiness that struck him every time he stepped into the house that she'd inhabited for so long, relieved to escape for a bit the wrenching loss he felt whenever he glanced over at her chair.

She was gone. She'd had a good, long life and a beautiful death, but still he missed her dreadfully.

Out on the road, the grief was present but less sharp. She was with him, as she had always been with him on even the worst of his journeys, her faith in him like a deep vein of rock under his feet.

And now he had her memoirs, encoded into the crystal hung around his neck. Away from the City's banks of singing quartz, he wouldn't be able to easily tap into the Net. But the crystal still had many useful functions. It carried a whole encoded library, and could cast the contents of a thousand books into holos that glowed with their own light. It charged automatically from the sun, and in the dark it could shine a light or focus a narrow laser beam to start a fire or cut through an obstacle. It could play music or record a song.

So at night, if Bird wanted to hear Maya's encouragement or wisdom, he could cast the holo and read her words, or play back some of the recordings he'd made over the years of her stories. If his own past threatened to overwhelm him with guilt or regret, he could dive into hers.

And his future? Best not to worry. Their course was set, now. All they had to do was follow it. He had learned the trick, in desperate hours, of suspending time, walking between moments like dodging rain-drops, evading both fear, the underminer, and hope, the cheater. Don't look ahead. Don't look behind. Let the present encompass you, and even in the worst of times, at least for an instant here and there, you could feel happy.

Now Bird was breathing free air under a sunny sky, with a fresh wind at his back. He laughed, and Madrone turned to look at him, a smile stealing over her face. She slowed, and he shifted gears and pulled away from her. The road dipped and he cruised no-handed, opening out his arms like wings.

"Show-off!" she yelled, and put on more speed. She was happy, too, seeing him enjoying himself. She remembered him as a boy, on his bike, on his skateboard, hovering on his surfboard in the pounding waves. How he'd loved speed! He was always flying, well-named as a creature of the air.

He'd been so sad lately, his grief at Maya's death compounding his struggle with his own guilt and pain. Bearing up under it, not letting it show, but she felt it, maybe even more than he allowed himself to.

I can't carry his grief for him, she told herself. I can't heal his losses and make it all better. Yet she couldn't seem to stop herself from trying.

And where is my own grief? Maya was like a second mother to me, and now she's gone and I can't seem to really feel it. How can I be enjoying a bike ride on a day that she is dead?

Get over it! she heard a gruff voice say inside her mind. *You think I begrudge you one short hour of happiness? I was ninety-fucking-nine years old! Pedal to the metal, girl!*

She laughed, and pushed down harder on the pedals, gaining ground an inch at a time as the road rose up before them. Bird's bad leg held him back just slightly, and she pulled even with him, and then a little bit ahead. They reached the crest, laughing and panting.

"Okay, you win," Bird said. "I'm calling mine Skimmer."

The road was a smooth ribbon laid over the rolling hills. Each day, they rose before dawn, and rode on in the cool of the early morning. When the October sun grew too hot to bear, they searched for shade and water, and argued about whether to call their meal a late breakfast or an early lunch. Madrone made Bird warm his muscles in the sun, and stretch his bad leg in the exercises Doctor Sam had prescribed. Day by day he grew stronger. They made camp in meadows or small breaks in the forest, and lay together in the shade for their siesta.

It's strange, Madrone thought. We're on a mission back to hell. We might never return. Terrible, unimaginable things might happen to us, and all the odds say we're probably going to fail.

Yet she felt almost weightless, as if she were on a holiday. For the first time in a very long time, no one was depending on her to ease pain or save a life.

In those long afternoons, Madrone discovered a new awareness humming deep within her. She was hyperconscious of smells, the fragrance of flowers, the pungent scent of herbs, Bird's own sweat as he lay beside her. When water was near, she knew by the hint of moisture on the air. And sounds. It was as if every insect spoke to her. The buzz of a fly was a conversation. The song of the grasshoppers rang with erotic allure.

When she let herself go into the bee-mind, lying in the sun in some camp they made in a meadow under trees or on the edge of a forest, bees came to her and sang of the strength and well-being of the hive. She loved to hear their sweet song of well-being, the low hum that said *all is well*.

More than that—the bees told her of the joys of the hive, the oneness, the comfort of having a place and knowing what it was, knowing by deepest instinct what task was to be done, and how to do it.

What is my task, truly? she wondered. Am I meant to be part of a hive, subsuming myself in the whole? Or simply a woman doing what women so often do, letting myself be defined by the needs of others?

And yet I'm not like Maya, not a storyteller or a poet or a maker of music.

Still, somehow, sometime, once in my life I would like to make something beautiful, something purely my own. One garden. One song. One child.

The bees sang of the brush of pollen on the velvet of a thigh, the satin stroke of petal against wing. They were above all erotic creatures, and though among them only the queen and a few of the strongest drones mated, all the hive lived in a haze of honey-pleasure, vibration and scent and touch. Madrone understood all this, at a level deep beyond thought, and she found their song aroused her until her whole body hummed with longing for touch and scent and the sweet strokes of love.

Bird sensed her arousal. Wherever the sun kissed her dark-honey skin, it gave off a sweet fragrance that drew him in. He longed to lather himself with her nectar, to plunge into her and let the pungent scent of propolis engulf him.

He was hungry, suddenly, hungry for life. He needed Madrone's touch, needed her hands to ease his grief and brush his scars and erase the memory of pain. He needed desperately to become someone different than he was, someone more like he had been as a boy, more the singer and less the scarred and battered fighter. For to build a refuge, he had to embody something sweeter than martyrdom, more hopeful than pain.

In the heat of the day, they lay together and made long, slow, languorous love. They rediscovered each other, velvet petal-soft skin, how to evoke pleasure delicately, flicking a tongue into the hollow of an earlobe, stroking an anther erect.

They didn't talk about the past or the future. They simply stayed in the present, gathering the sweetness of the moment to feed them through harsh times to come.

It took them two days at a leisurely pace to reach Santa Cruz, turning from 280 to follow the winding road down through the coastal hills. Santa Cruz had been hard hit by the Stewards, but they were eagerly rebuilding. Bird and Madrone stayed in a guesthouse, and Bird talked strategy with the local leaders while Madrone consulted with the Healers' Guild and brewed them up bee potions to counter the lingering threat of resurgent epidemics.

From Santa Cruz, they set off inland down the old Highway 101. They had debated going back along the ocean through the mountains, on the old coast highway. But the road was blocked in many places by mudslides and rock falls, and in key spots, drowned by rising seas. They would have to abandon their bikes and hike down, and they would need them for transport when they reached the Southlands.

So they followed the route of the Stewards' Army backwards down the rebuilt 101 through the Salinas Valley. Much of it was deserted now—the farmers and ranchers had mostly fled the Stewards' latest assault. But it was rich, beautiful land, the rolling hills and fertile valleys sandwiched between the coastal mountains and the inland ranges.

The days grew hotter as they moved farther south. To their right were the mountains of Big Sur, to their left the Pinnacles rose and far beyond them, across the desolation of the Central Valley, the Sierras. The hills trapped heat between them, and it lay on the land like a smothering blanket. Bird and Madrone ended their rides earlier in the day and rose long before dawn, breakfasting in the dark on waybread and tea so as to be underway by first light.

After another four days, the road dipped west, back toward the coast. They began to hear the sounds of engines in the distance as they drew near to the old town of San Luis Obispo, that the Stewards had renamed Slotown.

"Who's our mother?" the sentry challenged them, rifle raised.

They were back in the territory of the Monsters. The face of the sentry who held the rifle was sundered down the middle, as if someone had taken an ax and split it open from nose almost to chin. His words were almost indistinguishable; if Madrone hadn't known the challenge and the password, she wouldn't have understood what he was saying.

"The earth is our mother," she replied. "I'm Madrone, the healer. And this is Bird. We've come back to bring you news of the victory in the North."

"I am Heph." When Madrone took her eyes off his face, she saw a slim, muscular body that looked healthy and fit. He lowered the rifle.

"We have seen the army heading back south, looking like a whipped dog. Good job!"

Madrone watched Bird's eyes take on the long stare, and knew as clearly as if he'd spoken aloud exactly what he was thinking. Good job. Two short words to sum up all that suffering and terror.

But she simply nodded in acknowledgment.

"Did you meet any scouts on the road?" Heph asked.

"Nobody," Bird told him, pulling himself back to the present. "It was all clear, from here to Santa Cruz and on up to the City."

"Good!" Heph smiled. When he did, the halves of his divided face pulled even further apart. And then there were his eyes. Hazel, beautiful as water in a sunlit stream. "We patrol the road, try to keep it open now that the Stewards rebuilt it. Where are you going?"

"South," Madrone said.

"That will be more dangerous."

"We know."

They were high on a ridge that faced west. Far, far away Madrone could catch just the glimpse of a blue horizon, the ocean. Ahead of them lay rolling hills, brown and dry in the late summer heat.

Heph led them back into the woods, through a labyrinth of coyote bush and manzanita, back to a hidden camp that sheltered under a rocky bank. By the fire squatted a hillboy in a patched camo jacket. He had nut-brown skin, a shock of sandy hair, and a wizened face that Bird recognized.

"Appleseed!"

"Bird! Knew you were too mean to die!"

"You, you old pucker-mouth, you're too dried up to bleed!"

They greeted each other with back-thumping hugs.

Over tin cups of acorn mush, they talked of old friends and losses, or routes and strategies.

"Come visit us," Heph pleaded with Madrone. "We need your healing skills."

But she shook her head. She and Bird had both met the Monsters on their journeys to the Southlands, and the temptation to return and help them was strong. But that was a diversion from their purpose, one that could tie them up for weeks or months if they let it.

The Monsters' main enclave was over by the coast. But the safest route lay inland. They could skirt the army camp that still blocked and guarded the coast road just north of Slotown, and bike through the hills on smaller, less-watched roads that would reconnect with the highway south of the base. Then, when they were back in the Stewards' territory, they would travel by night, hide out by day, and finish their journey.

"I can't come," Madrone said apologetically. "I wish I could. But I bring you a message from the Healers' Council. The road is open now. Come to us. Come visit our beautiful city, and the healers will do all they can for you. Your cleft palate, we can fix that. It'll take a series of operations, but it can easily be done. We can't fix everything, of course. But what we can do, we will."

They spent that day in camp, telling tales. Bird left it to Madrone to tell of the resistance in the North, how they had undermined the army and invited them to their table, how they had encouraged and protected defectors, and how mutiny in the ranks had brought about the City's ultimate victory. Appleseed told them how the Monsters and hillboys combined had harassed the road and the army base, blowing up road-beds, ambushing convoys, and raiding supply warehouses.

"Thanks," Bird said. "You made it possible for us to send the blood-suckers home."

The temperature climbed with the sun, and by afternoon they were muzzy with heat. Appleseed took sentry shift, while Bird and Madrone slept.

At night they set off. Appleseed filled their food pouch with acorn grits, a staple Madrone remembered from her stint with the Resistance in the Southlands. It was palatable if the acorns were thoroughly leached, and nourishing, but to her it would always taste of fear and privation.

The holiday is over, she thought, and now the danger begins.

Bird and Madrone headed east into the hills, on smaller roads that wound around past the barred and barb-wired gates of the Stewards industrial-scale farms. The waning moon was still a fat crescent, and gave just enough light that they could avoid using theirs.

The roads twisted and snaked through canyons and climbed over ridges. After dark, they were mostly empty. Occasionally a patrol passed by, but in the quiet of the night, Bird and Madrone could hear the sound of engines long enough ahead to duck into the underbrush, cover the bikes and lie low until the danger passed.

After another two days, they reached the lower stretch of 101. Now they were in the Southlands proper, and this part of the road was well-maintained by the Stewards, running smooth and broad like a black arrow pointing south. Unfortunately, it was also frequented by army convoys, by workers heading out to the fields, and transports carrying the debt-slaves who did the dirtiest of the field work.

Madrone's bee senses came to their aid. At night, her sixth sense seemed amplified. She could feel the disturbance in the atmosphere when strangers approached. She could hear the subsonic scream of misery when the transports of debt-slaves were nearby.

By day the bees were their sentries. While Madrone and Bird slept in hideaways dug into shallow banks or scraped into thickets of scrub, the bees were on guard. Even in her sleep, Madrone heard them singing, and responded to tones of alarm with immediate wakefulness.

But the alarms were few: a contingent of soldiers marching past on the highway. A transport that halted so the driver could take a leak, just across from where Bird and Madrone lay hidden. A flat tire that a pair of sentries changed on the shoulder of the road.

Madrone and Bird were too tense now for languorous lovemaking. Nor could they risk the noise, or the distraction. They were on alert, even in sleep.

At last the road headed west again, beginning the great curve around the cape that jutted out into the ocean. Out on that promontory, Bird knew, stood the old air force base and missile range, now the toxic waste recovery camp where he'd nearly lost his life, and finally escaped.

Whole chunks of his life, his youth, his memory lay lost in the Southlands.

Maybe that's why I'm going back, he thought. Maybe there is something I need to recover.

The road was no longer safe. They left it and headed into the hills, following narrow lanes and dirt roads, bushwhacking across country. Appleseed had warned them that there were checkpoints on all the major routes. The hills were infested by the rebel hillboys, and the Stewards feared their uncontrolled movement.

Bird and Madrone turned east. Appleseed had also advised they stay clear of the big lake that the Stewards had renamed Galilee West. The area around its shores was one big, gated community of second homes for rich Primes. So they left the wide highway and headed up into the hills on the forest roads.

Old logging roads from the past century formed a labyrinth of trails. A few were still kept clear as firebreaks, and there Bird and Madrone could ride and make good time. But most were overgrown or blocked by fallen trees.

Bird had brought a small ax, and Madrone carried Maya's ancient, treasured, folding pruning saw. Together they hacked away at obstructions and portaged the bikes over, under, and around thickets of brush and saplings. But it was slow going, and even with stretches where they could ride, they were lucky to make ten miles a day.

Their need for water also slowed them down, and they spent much of each day searching for it. Madrone found that she could smell it, sometimes almost a mile away—but many times after they'd scrambled up a dry creek bed, clambering over rocks and balancing on fallen logs, what they found was more of a mud hole than a clear spring. They had a good ceramic filter they'd brought from the City, but it needed liquid to work with, not sludge.

The extra week of hard labor scrambling through the hills took its toll on their food supplies, which began to run short. They rationed the waybread they had brought from the City, simmered acorn grits for dinner, and eagerly picked over the stands of blackberry that were ripe now in autumn. But all that, too, took time.

Madrone found herself slipping into the state she remembered from her time in the Southlands, the constant thirst, the nagging hunger. Lightheaded, she found her bee senses taking over. The bees were hungry, too.

The desiccated woods offered little in bloom at the tail end of the dry season. The smell of dust and oak leaves choked her nostrils, and she often found herself humming a high bee-whine of distress.

On the ninth day of their trek through the mountains, Madrone caught a whiff of something clear and sweet. The bees were singing of water.

She led Bird up a gully and across a ridge. They carried their bikes on their shoulders, and it took a good hour to clear a path through the hedge of thorny blackberries that blocked their path.

"Are you sure this is going to be worth it?" he grumbled, picking a thorn out of his thumb. "Seems like every time you get a feel for water, I lose blood."

"I know it is," Madrone said. "This one feels different."

"That's what you said the time you led us to a mud hole."

"This doesn't feel like a mud hole. Trust me."

"I trust your integrity. I don't necessarily trust your navigation. Or your obsessiveness."

In truth he was beginning to worry about her. At times she seemed very far away, listening to something only she could hear. He caught her sometimes walking with her eyes closed, nose up, sniffing, droning a strange, tuneless hum.

"I am not obsessive!" Madrone objected.

"Am!" he countered.

"Am not!"

"Am, am, am!"

"Well, if I'm obsessive, you're ungrammatical!" With a wrench, she pushed her bike out from the clutches of a twining blackberry stem. Below them lay a steep slope running down to a dry gully.

"Ah, but can you love me in spite of it?" Bird asked, hacking at a tangle of briars that had fastened itself around his wheel.

"I can love you but I can't respect you," Madrone said, her head cocked, listening. Her eyes were focused again, Bird noted. The banter had brought her back to herself.

"But then you might take advantage of me," Bird said, wrapping his arms around her. "You might lay me down right here in the dust and have your way with me."

"I will have my way," Madrone said. "My way is that way!" She pointed across the slope of the hill to the head of the gully.

Sighing, Bird shouldered his bike and followed her.

But as they drew closer, he began to hear a soft, musical note, the sound of water falling onto rock. It rang through the quiet air and reverberated through him with a song of grace. Plenty after lack. Safety after danger. Forgiveness.

They topped a small rise, and looked down a steep drop to a pool where a trickle of a waterfall flowed. The water mirrored the sky, silver and blue.

"Are you going to say it?" Madrone asked.

"Say what?"

"Say 'You were right, Madrone. I'll never doubt you again!'"

"I will if we can kiss and make up." He wrapped his arms around her. "You were right, Madrone." He bussed her lips. "I'll never, ever, *ever* doubt or question or hesitate to follow your slightest command." He plastered his lips on hers in a long, passionate kiss.

"Shut up," she said when they broke for breath, then she kissed him back.

"Water!" she said firmly as they pulled apart. "Before we bonk ourselves into terminal dehydration."

They headed down the slope, propped their bikes on the bank, plunged their heads into the pool, and drank deeply. *Diosa*, Bird thought, how good it felt to drink his fill! The water had a clean taste, alive and potent with the minerals of the rock. They drank and drank, and filled all of their water containers. Then they slipped out of their clothes and plunged in.

Madrone felt her skin come alive as she crouched down in the cold water. The pool was small, and not terribly deep, coming only up to her waist, but she let her whole body slide under, relishing the luxury of being completely immersed.

Bird watched her hair float like seaweed around her. Her nipples grew hard from the cold. It had been days since they'd had the energy to make love, oh how he wanted her now! He felt heat rush down into his cock; he was surprised the pool did not begin to sizzle and steam.

Madrone surfaced, took a great gulp of air, and opened her eyes.

"I know this place," she said. "I've been here before, with the hill-boys. We've done it, Bird. We've made it back."

"Shall we celebrate?" he asked hopefully.

She smiled up at him. "So now you want to have your way with me?"

He put his arms around her, pressing against her. She could feel his hardness, his heat warming her fish-cold skin.

"How did you ever guess?" he asked.

His hand slid down over her belly, his fingers parting the soft curls of her hair.

"What are you doing?" she murmured.

"Exploring the Southlands," he breathed into her ear. "Let's do that together."

He drew her down onto him, and they drank each other in, letting the waterfall trickle down over their heads, rocking and moaning.

She is my waterfall, he thought. She's the music of water singing over rocks, my grace, my reprieve. He began to hear the music suddenly, liquid notes trilling a song of forgiveness, an amnesty for all the mistakes of the past. And with it, suddenly, came the bite of fear when he thought about all that they might face ahead of them in the Southlands.

He needed her so much, and there were so many forces in the world that could tear her away.

She felt the shift in his mood, the chill to his heat, and clutched him more tightly.

"Don't go there," she murmured. "Stay here. Stay with me, now, in this moment."

She pulled him more deeply into her, rocking him, back and forth, on great waves of pleasure that rose and thundered and overwhelmed the fear. And he rode the waves like a surfer, balanced perfectly inside a tunnel of blue, aware of the waves of her pleasure rising and curling around him. When he could resist no longer, the wave crested and crashed down in a froth of white foam, and they floated together in that place of perfect peace where there was no more fear.

Walking and riding, the two covered the ground between the pool and the main encampment of the guerrilla hillboys in just over two hours. The hillboys were glad to see Bird, but they were ecstatic to welcome Madrone back. Madrone looked around with a sense of homecoming and familiarity. A gang of dusty boy-men and a few women squatted around the fire pit, cleaning rifles and mending gear. A rusty old fifty-five-gallon drum held water. She was glad to see a homemade bucket filter beside it. Bags of acorns hung suspended from the branches of a spreading live oak, and a pot of gruel bubbled on the coals.

She felt a sudden pang, remembering Littlejohn who had always been there before with his questions and his eagerness to help. He was dead now, killed when he gunned down the Stewards' helicopter as it raided the urban hideout where Katy had tried to establish a refuge of her own. That memory cast a chill over their own plans. They could build their city in the rubble of the old, of that she had no doubt. But could they defend it if the Stewards discovered it?

But she had little time for worrying or even thinking. There were old friends to greet, Begood and Baptist and Joan Dark, and Hijohn himself who came rushing up to them and grabbed Bird in a big bear hug.

"So you made it! Heard they caught you but they threw you back again!" Hijohn grinned.

Bird's smile froze, his face suddenly a mask. Then he shook free of his memories and forced a smile. "You know me. Too stubborn to die, too ugly to keep. And you? How many wildcat lives you got left?"

"One or two, don't you worry! Madrone, welcome back! By oak and sage, am I glad to see you!"

Hijohn's smile lit up his wizened face. He had aged, Bird observed. He'd never looked young. Chronic thirst had etched lines onto his face that made him look middle-aged at twenty-five. Now there were new creases of pain that marked his eyes. His straight, black hair was already starting to go gray, and he limped badly.

"Katy?" Hijohn asked in a low voice.

"Katy sends her love," Madrone said. "She and the baby are well and happy in the North."

She opened her pack and handed him a small crystal. "Hold that in your hand for a moment, until it gets warm."

He took it with a puzzled look.

"What is it?"

"Now open your hand and tell it to speak."

The crystal began to glow, and then suddenly a hologram appeared, a tiny Katy rocking Lucia, there in his hand. He stared at it with a look of wonder.

"Hijohn, you old badger, take a look at our beautiful baby!" Katy held the child up. Now the holo showed the child, plump and smiling. "We're safe, and well here in the North. But I miss you. And Lucia wants to meet her father. You get your dried-up little acorn ass up here for a visit! The roads are open most of the way now. And you need to see this place. See what we're fighting for. It'll put heart into you."

"Magic!" Begood breathed.

"Technology," Baptist countered. "They been workin' on holos ever since before the Collapse."

"We're coming to a place, in the North, where technology and magic meet," Bird said.

Hijohn just held the holo up to his face, and played it over and over again. Madrone was touched to see how joy and wonder lit up his battle-scarred face. His limp looked painful, and she itched with the urge to examine his legs.

Hijohn noticed her gaze and gave her a rueful smile.

"Took a bullet, in that raid on the Rat's Nest," he said. "That was the end of my dancing career."

"We can gimp around together," Bird said.

"Or you can take Katy's advice," Madrone said. "Visit her, and our orthopedic surgeons can help you."

Rocky, a stick-thin young woman in torn jeans and a gray rag of a wrap, greeted Madrone with delight and relief. She looked, if possible, even thinner than Madrone remembered, and her skin had a gray, dry undertone. She spirited Madrone away to look at some of their more worrisome cases, while Bird and Hijohn caught up on events and talked strategy.

Hijohn was not happy to hear of their plans to build a refuge in the heart of the city.

"We had our urban camps," he said. "Every single one of them got rooted out. Stay here with us. We can put you both to good use, and we're a refuge, too."

Bird was tempted. But Madrone's vision had not been of the hills, and his own dreams now were of landscapes of concrete and rubble.

They stayed with the hillboys for a week. On the third day, with the most urgent healings done, Madrone walked into the hills alone, and sent out a call to the bees. She waited, basking in the sunshine, until she heard a buzzing and a hum.

A woman walked toward her, surrounded by bees. They swarmed around her, constantly in motion, singing of both increase and warning. It was the Melissa, one of the Bee Priestesses, and even though Madrone was now familiar with the hive, the sight of the tall woman wearing a living cloak of bees was still breathtaking.

She remembered her own initiation, that transformative time in the hive when all her human senses had been stripped and new ways of seeing and sensing and healing had been conferred upon her. Now what she felt was a sense of belonging and welcome, like coming back to the hillboys' camp. Homecoming.

As the Melissa approached, a cautious scout bee circled Madrone. She let a drop of honey pool in her bee spot, sending forth greeting and welcome.

Part of the swarm detached itself and encircled her. She was surrounded by the hum, enclosed in vibration. Thousands of delicate thread feet danced on her skin, and every cell came alive. Her ears rang with overtones of contentment and delight; her nose was filled with the sweet scent of honey.

She and the Melissa clasped hands in a cloud of singing bees.

Madrone shifted into the bee-mind, feeling a deep sense of comfort and rightness. The song warmed her through to the bone. She couldn't say exactly how she and the Melissa communicated—not in words, but in some mind-to-mind transmission of smells and sounds and feelings. She sensed approval, as if the Melissa were telling her that she had done well with the power she'd been given. And she was aware of an opening. She was invited to come back, to train more deeply.

Madrone told the Melissa of the healing powers she'd come to discover on her own, how the bee-mind let her taste the sweat of a patient and, in her own body, brew antidotes to poison and disease.

The Melissa shuddered. Madrone felt her sharp sense of disapproval, and she spoke not in bee-mind but in words. "The sisters do not tolerate disease."

"I could teach you."

"The sisters do not tolerate disease," she repeated.

"But you could ... "

"The sisters do not tolerate disease!"

The song of the bees had changed, taking on a harsher tone, as if they were revving up for a battle. Madrone took a breath, and sent out thoughts of harmony and health, until the song grew serene once again, and the priestess returned to a calm smile.

"But I need help," she admitted to the Melissa. "I find the bee-mind sometimes taking over when I don't want it to. That shadow in my mind that you warned me about long ago—those painful memories—I've faced them all now and I know what they are. I know my own anger. But I can't always control it. And when I'm flooded with rage, the bees sometimes come and it's all I can do to keep them from stinging someone to death. What can I do?"

"You must come back to us," the Melissa said. "The hive is calling."

"But I can't live in the hive," Madrone said with regret. "I have another mission."

"The call of the hive is strong," the Melissa told her. "When the blocks are gone, the way is open."

And Madrone realized that the Melissa couldn't help her. The Bee Priestess knew how to open the gates, how to release the human self, and let it merge with the hive. But what Madrone needed to know was how to go back and forth, to open and close the portal, to remain both bee and self. She had already gone to places where the Melissa couldn't or wouldn't follow. She was on her own.

Chapter Twenty

E VERYTHING IS UNDER CONTROL," GENERAL WENDELL ASSERTED with far more assurance than he felt.

"Define 'under control,'" Culbertson said in his cool, clipped voice. "Seems to me we might have different understandings of what that means."

Head Prime Mather Culbertson lay back on the bench of the weight machine and gave a long, strong pull that caused his triceps to bulge. The veins stood out on his neck. He wore only a scanty pair of shorts, and Wendell could see little beads of sweat form in the graying hair on his chest.

Stinking, sweating, nearly naked—and yet he still manages to make me feel overdressed and ineffectual, Wendell thought ruefully. He was wearing his full formal uniform for this meeting, freshly ironed and crisp, his shoes carefully shined, his four stars gleaming. Yet he felt like a little boy dressed up as a toy soldier, while Culbertson oozed power and disdain from every sweating pore.

"The warship will soon be on its way back to us, with the navy of the North," Wendell assured him. "It's a brilliant strategy, and I have every faith in our agent."

Or so he wished. Why was he in this position, having to defend actions he had in no way authorized and didn't in his heart believe in? But if he were to say, "Livingston acted without my orders and I'm scared shitless he's simply defected for real," then he would look like a fool and a bumbler. He could lose his command, with its perks and welcome pay raise, just when the twins' school fees were due. Or worse. Culbertson could sic the Retro hounds on First Faithful.

Culbertson paused in his reps and turned his cold, gray eyes on him.

"Faith may move mountains," he said, tipping back his head and closing his eyes. "But it doesn't win battles or secure positions. That takes planning and competence."

Wendell resisted his instinctive urge to mumble "yes, sir." This whole setup was an insult, designed to humiliate him, to say he wasn't worthy of a conference in the war room, or even in a civilized study or dining room. No, Culbertson did nothing, said nothing, that was not an assertion of power. If Wendell wasn't careful, he'd be reduced to the status of the little towel-girl who, head down and eyes averted, rubbed the sweat off Culbertson's torso.

Well, fuck him! I'm not going to tremble like a spillrag. I'm general of the army, albeit in a station a bit above my breeding. But I survived, when my betters went down like dominoes. That's got to count for something.

"Their navy is heading down the coast, into our trap," Wendell asserted. "Their army is off to die of thirst in the Central Valley. This is the moment to make our move. The garrison at Slotown is ready to head back north—but we need reinforcements. That was Alexander's mistake. Underestimated the enemy. I won't do that. All we need is the resources. And that's where you and the Council come in."

Culbertson inclined his head slowly to fix Wendell with a cold eye.

"Ever consider a career as a comic?"

"I'm serious."

"Never make the mistake of thinking that I'm not."

He swung his legs over the bench and sat with them spread in a wide V.

It's like he's thrusting his balls in my face, Wendell thought bitterly. The little towel-girl rushed forward and Culbertson backhanded her in the face. She fell sprawling on the hard-tiled floor, without a cry or a whimper. It made Wendell feel a little sick. The Primes had their own ways, and everyone was born to a station, but regardless of what the Retro preachers said, Wendell didn't approve. The kid couldn't be more than six. And what went on in the back, the steam rooms and the baths ... no, he didn't want to think about that. He was too aware that even his own girls were not immune to that fate. Not if he continued to fail so spectacularly.

And that's why they do it, he realized suddenly. Why they flaunt their Pets and their Trinkets. To keep us in line.

But it's not the Primes I truly serve. No. They, like me, are merely tools that we must use to preserve what's left of all that makes life decent and possible. There are Destroyers and Preservers in this world, and I know which side I'm on.

The little towel-girl picked herself up and brought Culbertson a white terry robe from a peg on the wall. She was far too small to help him into it, and he took it from her without a glance at the red mark on her porcelain-white skin or the film of tears in her violet eyes. Palin has big eyes like that, Wendell thought. But hers are brimming with mirth and mischief. She was only just beginning to learn decorum.

"Armies run on money," Wendall said bluntly, trying to refocus on the objective. "If you want to protect your investments, you'll need to provide us with the resources to do so."

"Are you blackmailing me?" Culbertson said in a voice that came close to a growl.

"I'm just speaking the truth."

"We didn't get much return on our last investment in the army." Culbertson stood up now. "You owe us."

Culbertson was a few inches taller than Wendell, and the General drew himself up to his full height, but still felt the Prime towered over him.

"I was not in charge then," he said, projecting every ounce of confidence he could muster.

Culbertson simply turned his back and walked away, the towel-girl trotting behind him.

Chapter Twenty-One

BIRD AND MADRONE MADE THE TREK DOWN TO THE CITY AT NIGHT, to take advantage of the cover of darkness. They were both still in the Stewards' database as wanted criminals, and the fewer eyes that saw them, the better. Patrols and checkpoints were more stringent after dark, and they would need to be vigilant to avoid them. Hijohn assured them that bikes were fairly common in the better part of the city. In the absence of reliable public transportation, professionals and office workers who could scrape aside a few extra dollars often invested in bikes. In the poorer sections of the city, the options were to walk, or stay put. Only the rich could afford cars or taxis.

But nobody had bikes like theirs, with their solar sails and bamboo frames. They would need to use Madrone's bee senses to stay out of sight.

They headed for the university, now the city's top-flight hospital for Primes and the research center for bioweapons. Madrone wanted to visit Beth, who ran a boarding house for student nurses just outside the research center grounds.

"Who is Beth?" Bird asked as they pedaled on the fire road that ran along the ridge of mountains separating Angel City proper from the Valley. There was just enough ambient city light reflected off the clouds to see by if they traveled slowly.

"She's a friend of Sara's," Madrone said. "She was a doctor, before the Retributionists drove women out of the professions. Now she boards nursing students and runs a soup kitchen on Sundays where wealthy women come to do good and she can dole out some clandestine medical care on the side. I'd been trying to get her and the hillboys to work together, before I left."

"How'd you meet her?"

I've never really talked to him about my time in the Southlands, Madrone realized. When she'd finally made it back to the North, Bird had been a captive of the Stewards. And when he finally broke free and let loose the revolt, they'd had other, more pressing things to talk about.

"It was the day I was a Bad Revolutionary and yielded to the temptation to grab a swim in Sara's pool."

She'd been fresh from the bee initiation, dehydrated, and probably somewhat heat-stroked from the blazing sun on the fire roads of the hills. She hadn't yet learned how her new senses could flood her with scent and sound, and overwhelm her human judgment.

"That's what I love about you," Bird said. "The yielding to temptation bit."

"Well, that time it nearly got me killed. But I was lucky—Mary Ellen, Sara's maid, rescued me, and then she and Sara cleaned me up and invited me to eat with the lunching ladies. One of them was Beth."

"Were there eleven lunching ladies?" Bird asked.

"About seven or eight. Why?"

"There should be eleven, like the song . . . On the first day of Revolution, my true love gave to me . . . " he warbled. "Eleven lunching ladies . . . Ten hillboys—what would the hillboys be doing? Hopping? Harping?"

"Hoping," Madrone suggested.

"Nine Angels angsting . . . "

"You can't have the Angels angsting," Madrone laughed. "For one thing it's not a verb."

"Poetic license," he retorted. "Anyway, when did you become the grammar cop?"

"And they don't angst. They don't fret, or fume, or worry, or torment themselves with guilt and regrets. They just calmly take revenge."

The Angels. She had met them on her first trip to the Southlands. Slim, cold-eyed, their bodies sculpted, their faces with perfect, even features, they were escapees from the Stewards' sex farms. Thinking about their marble faces, their steely eyes, gave her a little shiver. She was back in that world, now.

"Nine Angels avenging . . . Eight Retributionists ranting . . . " Bird went on. She knew what he was doing. He was clutching at the last shreds of their lightness together, that relatively carefree interlude that their journey had been.

"Seven soldiers switching sides?" she suggested.

Me too, she was really saying. I don't want it to end. I'm not ready yet to pick up the mantle of fear.

"Shush. We're getting near the bridge."

There was one bridge over the old freeway that ran through a deep pass separating the western ridge of hills from the east range. The bridge no longer had a permanent guard, the hillboys had told them. With all their losses in the North, the Stewards were too short on personnel to maintain one. But it was still patrolled regularly.

Madrone remembered many crossings from her time with the hill-boys, creeping along the scaffolding that held the crumbling structure intact. She dearly hoped they wouldn't have to do that spider-walk tonight, not with their bikes precariously balanced on their shoulders.

They dismounted, and walked their bikes quietly forward along the fire road. Madrone strained all her senses to listen to the night. No bees were flying in the dark, but there were other insects, moths and mosquito hawks, and she could open her mind and share glimpses of what they perceived. She touched Bird's arm and they ducked down into a hollow at the side of the road, pulling their bikes down with them and hiding them under a stand of black sage. Brushing it released its pungent scent, which Madrone breathed in with a shiver of pleasure. Resolutely, she pulled herself out of insect mind. Stay present, she told herself. Maintain control. No mad swims tonight!

They lay quietly until they heard faint steps in the distance. From their hiding place, they could see the legs of a pair of soldiers who strode up to the bridge from the eastern side, paused and looked around, then crossed it and stopped to survey the western stretch. They stood close enough that even in the faint light Bird could see the worn heels of their boots.

We've got them under stress, he thought. Can't even keep the army in new footwear. The time is right.

Then the soldiers moved on, marching west along the fire road. Madrone and Bird waited until their footsteps died away, then waited for another long moment.

"Now!" Madrone said. They hauled their bikes out, hopped on, and pedaled furiously over the bridge and eastward along the road.

After that it was easy going. They rode along the fire road for a short distance, then dropped down onto the maze of smaller roads that wound through the canyons. The slopes of the hills on the north side of the city were covered by the gated enclaves of the Primes, but there were ways around the perimeters and routes that avoided the checkpoints. Just before dawn, they freewheeled down the street that ringed the university and the research center, and as the sky grew light they pushed their bikes into the side passage of Beth's house and gave the secret knock on her back door.

A young woman in a blue headcloth opened it.

"What do you want?" she hissed at them.

"Tell Beth her colleague from the North is back," Madrone said.

The woman shut the door on them, and they waited anxiously in the passage. A high hedge of greenery enclosed them, arching above their heads into a tunnel that sheltered them from all but the most determined of watchers. Madrone nevertheless felt uneasy as the sky grew light.

But soon Beth herself opened the door.

"Quick," she said. "Stupid girl to leave you hanging out there!"

She ushered them in, with their bikes, and closed the door behind them and slid the deadbolt back.

Only then did she grab Madrone in a fierce hug.

"You came back!" she exclaimed. "Sit down! Rest yourselves! Where have you come from?"

"The North," Madrone said. "Via the hillboys' camps."

"All that way! Seems like another world. And yet here you are, back again! I can't tell you how glad I am to see you safe and sound!"

"This is my *compa*, Bird," Madrone introduced them.

Madrone flopped down on an old sofa with broken springs, and Bird greeted Beth as he set down his pack and joined her on the couch. It felt so good, so comforting, to sit on something soft again.

Beth turned to Bird. "Welcome! Last time I saw this girl, she was all dressed up in a nurse's aide uniform, ready for her ninja attack on the research center. Jesus God if I didn't think it was just an elaborate way of committing suicide!"

Bird looked at Madrone sharply. He knew she had rescued Katy, but the full story was one more thing they'd never discussed.

Beth saw the look. "She went right in there and somehow, God only knows how, she got her friend out. It was like something out of a movie!"

Bird gave her a small nod of respect. "Always said she was more than just a pretty face!"

She stuck her tongue out at him.

"Sara drove the getaway car," Beth said. "I was watching from a safe distance. Madrone came streaking out of the door, pushing Katy in a wheelchair, guards and med students hot on her heels—then suddenly, out of nowhere, came a huge swarm of bees! The guards all dove for cover and then Sara's car was careening down the road—never knew the woman could drive at all, let alone like that!"

Madrone smiled, a little embarrassed. "She said she learned how from playing video games."

"Sara, how is she?" Beth asked.

"Thriving. Mary Ellen and the child, too. The whole family came along. And Katy is safe in the North, with a beautiful baby," Madrone told her.

"Thank God! Or Goddess, if you prefer. I want to know all the details. But first, I'll bet you'd like to shower while I cook you up a real meal." She opened an inner door and led them through into a small kitchen. "Nothing fancy, but I have some eggs and a new loaf of bread. I know what it's like with the hillboys. Man cannot live by acorn gruel alone, and woman certainly not!"

Beth had her own apartment in the basement of the house, while the upper floors and the big kitchen of the former fraternity were left to her boarders. Madrone and Bird took turns showering in the small but immaculate bathroom. Beth brought out two terry robes for them to wear while she threw all their clothing into the washing machine. It was a generous act, Madrone knew, for Beth bought water by the rationed gallon and she would probably have to forego washing her own clothes that week. Then they sat on her cozy sofa and ate potatoes and scrambled eggs and Beth's own homemade bread while Madrone filled her in on all of her adventures. It was simple fare, but after the weeks on the road and in the hills, it tasted delicious.

But when they got onto the subject of Madrone and Bird's plans to establish a refuge, Beth's eyes grew worried.

"You'll never last a week," she said. "Every time someone's tried anything like that, they get shut down and shot, or hauled off to the work camps or the pens."

"We have an army on its way." Bird said. "We even have a navy. Goddess help them, it's only a few old sailboats and one warship held together with duct tape. But we have to try. The people need to rise up and liberate themselves. And they can't do that unless they see an alternative."

"The Stewards don't tolerate alternatives," Beth said. "And what are you going to do for supplies? For food and water?"

"We brought some things to trade," Madrone said. "Holos and crystals. But we know there are underground springs in some parts of Angel City. We're going to try to find one."

"We know roughly where one is," Bird said. He told her what they'd learned from Maya.

"But nobody goes into the Death Zone!" Beth objected.

"So nobody will bother us," Bird said.

"But no one will come to you, either. How can you show people an alternative in a place they're afraid to go? They all believe the whole godforsaken sector is haunted!"

"Good," Bird said. "Ghosts and spirits—we come from a line of Witches, you know. We'll have friends."

Unhappy though she was with their plans, Beth gave them what help she could. Deep in her backyard, overgrown with thorny blackberries, lay an old wagon. Bird and Madrone spent much of the morning hacking it loose.

"If anyone asks, you're the yard man," Beth said.

No one asked. The backyards and alleyways were deserted, and no eyes observed them prune back the vines and pull the wagon free. Bird pulled a thorn out of his thumb and sucked on it as it bled.

"I feel like we're back in the hills," he complained. "If there was any part of me that escaped being scratched before, berries got it now. I think they're in conspiracy."

"Whiner!" Madrone said. "You should be grateful, we might even get a pie out of this." She was systematically stripping the prunings of any ripe berries, and by the time they extricated the wagon, she did indeed have a large bowl full.

The wagon, when liberated, proved to be old and rusted. They took it into the old garage at the back of the property, where Beth kept tools and discarded furniture. Madrone sanded the splintery wood while Bird took the wheels off and greased the axles. They painted it with a white undercoat. While it dried, they napped in Beth's back room. Then Bird made a pile of all the prunings and cleared out the overgrown weeds to open up some usable space in the garden, as a thank you to Beth. Madrone painted Retributionist slogans on the cart in a deep blood-red: "Repent!" on the back and "Fear the Wrath!" on the longer sides.

The cart was just big enough to hold their bikes, lying down on their sides. Madrone covered them with sacking. Deep in the bowels of Beth's storeroom, she unearthed a papier mâché figure of the Avenging Christ, left over from some Sunday school pageant, complete with a somewhat mouse-chewed bullwhip and a crook in his arm to hold a real copy of *The Book of Retribution*. They centered the figure atop the bikes and anchored it down. The result was a most authentic looking Atonement cart.

Beth fed them soup for dinner, cooked up from rice flavored chicken broth and a few vegetables.

"You could grow a great garden in the backyard, now that we've hacked back the blackberry invasion," Bird suggested. He was enough of a Califian that an unused patch of tillable earth cried out to him to be transformed into a productive site.

Beth shook her head. "We don't have the water."

"Why not use the waste water from your showers? And the laundry. That would be more than enough to grow some greens," Bird said.

"And herbs don't take a lot of water," Madrone said. "You could grow enough for teas and tinctures."

"Once we get our refuge underway, I could come back and put in a graywater diversion for you," Bird offered.

"Graywater is illegal," Beth said. "You could go to the pens for defiling water, as they term it."

"That's insane, of course, but who needs to know? Or you could just put buckets in the shower to catch the runoff."

"Maybe," Beth said, but she sounded unconvinced.

Bird let it drop. He would soon have enough work ahead of him, and if all went well, plenty of chances to get his hands in the dirt.

They slept that night in Beth's bed. She insisted they take it, and have one night of comfort. She slept on the couch, and woke them at dawn for one last breakfast. They veiled themselves in sacking, rubbed dirt into their skin, and hitched themselves to the wagon. Beth hung cardboard signs around their necks: Madrone wore "Sloth" and Bird "Gluttony." They each carried a small lash with which to beat themselves. In the early, predawn light, they set out.

Chapter Twenty-Two

TIGHTEN THAT LINE!" ISIS CRIED. SARA WOUND THE END OF HER ROPE over a cleat as Isis paid out another sheet. The mainsail rose, luffing and flapping, and Isis hurriedly wound it down again, swearing. One of the lines was fastened wrong, and she quickly freed it, squatted down, and retied it.

The new solar sails were the pride of her heart. Light, pliable, shining, and immensely strong, they were made of photovoltaic film that would make electricity for the sailboat's lights and the engine even as they swelled with the wind that propelled the ship.

And they were beautiful. If there were angels, Isis thought, and they had wings, they'd be made of this stuff, iridescent with pearly pinks and golds like a sunrise reflecting off clouds.

"Okay, ready!" she cried. They tried it again, and this time the sail rose elegantly upward, a gleaming triangle of light. She checked the meter. Yes, already it was gathering sunlight, making energy. Reluctantly, she reefed it, rolling it into the mast. She didn't want a stray gust of wind to catch them tied into the dock here and slam the little boat around.

"Right, now let's do the foresail," she said.

"How about a break?" Sara asked. "Want a beer?"

"Does a fish want water?"

Sara plopped herself down beside Isis on the cushioned bench that surrounded the small deck and handed her an ice-cold beer. It was one of the things Isis appreciated about the City—great brews, all done in small-scale, artisan breweries. Rich, foamy, making the mass-produced swill of the Southlands seem tasteless and bland by comparison.

"So they want me to take charge of the divers," Sara said, nestling into the curve of Isis's arm. "The training, and when we get to it, the deployment."

Isis froze, and set down her bottle.

"Training, sure," she said. "You'd be good at that. But best you stay here to do it. No need to deploy."

"You know I don't want to just stay here while you go off."

"Wanna keep you safe," Isis said, murmuring in her ear. She licked it, and breathed into it, and Sara gave a little shiver of pleasure.

"I didn't run off with a wild pirate in order to be safe," Sara said softly, nuzzling Isis's cheek and nibbling on her earlobe in turn. "I could have stayed in the Southlands if I'd wanted safe."

"Ah, but this way you got safe and satisfied!" Isis purred.

"Maybe I want satisfied, and more satisfied." Sara sat up abruptly. "Satisfied like knowing I'm doing everything I can to bring those fuckers down!"

"What about me?" Isis asked in a low, dangerous tone.

"What about you?"

"How'm I supposed to run a navy and worry about you at the same time?"

"Don't," Sara said brightly. "Don't worry about me. Let me take my own risks."

Isis pulled away and took a long drink from her beer.

"Never stopped you."

"You would if you could," Sara countered.

Isis stood up.

"Wanna be Queen of the Divers? Go right ahead."

"But?" Sara asked.

"But what?"

"That's what I'm asking you. I hear the 'but.'"

"But nothin'." Isis's eyes flashed. "Go ahead! Train divers, lead missions. Just don't think that I can live with you, sleep with you, fuck you, and not worry about you!"

"What about me, worrying about you?" Sara asked softly.

"That's different." Isis set her beer down with a thud.

"Different how?"

"Just different."

"Yeah. You're the pirate, you get to have the adventures! I'm supposed to be the little woman, staying safe at home. Well, fuck that!"

"Not that," Isis said in a low voice. She let out a long breath. "Just can't handle it."

"I thought you were the gal who was so tough you could handle anything."

"Not that."

Sara pulled back and looked at Isis, her eyes serious.

"I'm sorry. But you'll have to toughen up. I'm not going back, Isis!" She stood up and gripped the rails. "I'm not going back to being the pleaser. I spent my life doing that, and when I left Lance I swore I'd never do it again. Not for anyone! Not even for you."

"I'm not asking you to go back. Just saying ... "

"Saying what?"

Isis took a deep gulp of clean, ocean air. "Maybe we should cool it. You wanna be Queen Shark of the Sea, okay by me. You're a free woman. But then you stay with your divers." That will show her that I mean it, she thought. Then maybe she won't be so hammerhead stubborn.

"All right, then. I will," Sara retorted. I'll call her bluff, she thought. And she'll turn, and grab me, and it will be all right.

But Isis didn't turn. She bent her head over the sails, and continued to check the knots.

Sara hesitated. She didn't quite know what to do. Should she walk away, let it go? Was this the end of it? But it couldn't be. Surely what they had was stronger.

"I'll just get my things, then," she said. She went below, and began packing up her clothes, her few possessions. Isis would come down, she thought. Any moment, and she'll be down here, asking me to stay, begging me to stay, admitting that she was unreasonable.

She stuffed her pack, and dragged it up the cabin steps, deliberately making noise.

But when she reached the top, Isis was gone.

Chapter Twenty-Three

MADRONE'S SHOULDERS WERE CHAFED FROM THE ROPES. THE CART was as heavy as she imagined sin would feel if she believed in sin. Salt from her sweat stung as rivulets dripped onto her rubbed-raw sores. Her eyes and forehead itched from the sackcloth that veiled her hair, and when she ducked her head to avoid looking into the eyes of a passerby, her nostrils filled with dust that made her want to sneeze.

Once an hour, she and Bird stopped in an alleyway for a quick drink of water. But they didn't dare stop for long. If they were truly the Atonement Seekers they pretended to be, they'd be whipping themselves with knotted ropes as they walked and eschewing water to further inflame their thirst for redemption.

Madrone suspected that a fair proportion of the wandering Atonement Seekers were actually like themselves—simply adopting a convenient disguise that let them traverse the streets of Angel City while avoiding the omniscient eyes of the Lash, the secret police that kept a sharp lookout for dissidents and scofflaws. Repentance made such a good excuse for keeping your head down!

They had been walking since early morning, and they still had far to go. It was at least ten miles from Beth's place on the West Side to their goal close to the old downtown.

They tramped from the wealthy haunts of the Primes near the university, down through the wide, tree-lined streets of Beverly Hills. On they went, past giant apartment buildings that housed the techies and professionals who constituted the last remnants of a middle class. Those who were lucky enough to have work were hurrying off to their jobs, and paid little attention to Madrone and Bird as the pair trudged on through the streets.

Here and there, a few single-family homes were left in between the giant edifices. Some even had small gardens with greenery growing in front, although most yards were barren patches of dirt or had been paved over. Bird looked up at the street signs, and stopped suddenly.

"What? What is it?" Madrone asked, applying her flail as a hurrying woman, small child in tow, squeezed past them on the sidewalk.

"This is it," Bird said. "This is where Maya and your grandmother grew up."

Madrone looked at the street. It had been a corner house, she knew, but now each corner of the intersection held a big apartment building, with peeling paint and holes in the stucco. When Maya and Johanna had lived there, the neighborhood had been mildly affluent. Now, like so much of the middle class, it had gone down in the world.

"The house is gone," Madrone said. Still, she felt a little thrill of connection. Under this pavement lay her roots. She would have liked to make an offering, pour out a small libation to the ancestors, the great-grandmother she had never known. But a man in a business suit a little too tight for him was watching them with suspicion. Bird began singing a Retributionist hymn. They quickly scourged themselves, albeit without true Atonement Seekers' enthusiasm, and moved on.

The streets grew emptier as the day wore on. People were either at work or holed up against the heat. Bird and Madrone headed east along the wide avenues where a few cars prowled, army vehicles or the limos of the Primes.

By afternoon they were deep in the slums, where crowded tenements of concrete towered toward the sky. Here there was more life—ragged kids kicking a soccer ball down the middle of the street, doorways where shrill women carried on loud arguments, corners where men played cards on the tops of garbage cans and smoked hand-rolled cigarettes, tossing the butts to the ground. They took no notice of Bird and Madrone.

The streets grew emptier again as they got closer to the old downtown. Now Bird led them slightly north again. The land was flat, and they had to pick their way past empty blocks of collapsed buildings, canyons of ruins separated by dry ravines of asphalt packed with rubble, utterly deserted.

At last they came to a ruin where a once-wide avenue was crowned with a broken sign that read "Harm ny Vil lage." Behind it was a nightmare landscape of tipsy buildings leaning against one another at impossible angles. Huge chunks of concrete had fallen, blocking the avenue with a mountain range of rubble. One giant roof slab formed a triangular tunnel against the side of a relatively undamaged wall. The passage led inwards.

"Welcome to the Death Zone," Bird said. "Welcome home!"

The Death Zone cut a swath through the center of the city, along the path of the worst of the catastrophes that had struck the city during the Collapse. When the San Andreas Fault had shifted, back in '28, it unleashed an earthquake greater than any in living memory, and whole neighborhoods had crumbled, especially the newer sections built after cutbacks in regulations had opened the door to shady contractors skimping on rebar and using substandard concrete.

But the quake had unleashed something even worse, although no one was quite sure what. A stockpile of nerve gas, perhaps, in some army reserve bunker, or the toxic ingredients stored in an insecticide factory. A plume had settled on the city, bringing instant death to tens of thousands. While the West Side, bathed in the prevailing wind off the ocean, had mostly escaped its effects, whole neighborhoods in the center and eastern parts of town became instant charnel houses. No one had ever counted the full toll, and for many, many years no one would enter the area willingly.

In the aftermath of the disaster, coupled with floods in Florida and convenient rumors of a planned terrorist attack, President Brandon had declared martial law and suspended elections. His backers in the Stewards' party moved in and took over.

The country had splintered. In the northern part of California, they'd rebelled and threw the Stewards out. But the Southlands were not so fortunate. There people were desperately searching for their missing loved ones, or frantically digging out of their own collapsed homes. They'd had no time or energy to organize. And many others had lost their faith in the old democracy, disillusioned by its ineptitude in responding to the disasters. They were happy to cede power to the Stewards, who promised order and security.

Refugees and dissenters took to the hills, and their successors were still there, waging the hillboys' perpetual guerrilla war. And the Death Zone still lay deserted.

But the disaster was more than twenty years in the past. By now, Madrone believed, the air would be clear, and if not, she trusted her bee senses would smell any danger.

She stared at the ruins, fighting the urge to sit down and cry. She was thirsty and dusty and sore, exhausted from their day of self-flagellation and their long hike across the city. Her vision had been so strong—but the reality was overwhelming, the scale of destruction beyond anything she had imagined.

She and Bird could never shift these ruins. The whole sorry army of the Stewardship would need a year or more to even make a dent.

"Would you like me to carry you over the threshold?" Bird asked.

"We're not going in there!" Madrone objected.

"Isn't that why we came?"

"It's not safe!"

"Safe?" Bird laughed. "'Safe' is five hundred miles away!"

"You know what I mean. It could be unstable."

"I'd say it's found its angle of repose long ago. Look, there's thistles growing in the dirt that's blown into the cracks. I'll scout."

Before she could protest, he'd ducked into the tunnel. His flashlight gave the concrete a warm glow, but then he passed deeper into the ruins, and there was only darkness.

Don't go! Don't leave me alone! Madrone wanted to cry out, but he was already gone.

Night was falling, and the air had a bitter chill. Madrone heard skittering in the rubble, and shivered. She hated rats. She wanted to be home, in their real home. She wanted a long, hot bath, and a soft bed and a down comforter. And a cup of tea, and a good book where she could read about somebody else's blasted uncomfortable adventures.

Then he was back.

"It's okay," he said. "In fact, it couldn't be better."

"I could argue with that!"

"The tunnel leads in for about a hundred yards, and then there's an opening, and a passageway through the rubble. It should be wide enough for the wagon. Come on."

Back in the nineties, Maya had told them, the area where Harmony Village lay had been a neighborhood of old buildings from the 1920s, quietly decaying in a genteel way on tranquil streets behind a blighted strip of liquor stores and parking lots. Back in the Jazz Era, it had been a popular spa, with natural hot springs where flappers and bootleggers came to take the waters.

Seventy years later, enterprising New Urbanists had renovated the old hotel, and Maya had given writing workshops there that were especially popular in the winter with aspiring writers from the Midwest. While blizzards roared through the streets of Chicago or Minneapolis, they could sit in the garden with their laptops or gather in the evening on the terrace for drinks and talks on "Myth and Story" or "Writing as Shadow-Work."

But in the 2020s, the area became the site of one of the last great ventures of the old regime. Developers pushed out the poor people and built a shopping mall along the street front, with high-rise condos behind. Two years of construction noise had done in the spa, and the new buildings blocked the sunlight from the gardens of the older houses. Many of the more stable residents left, and the area fell into decay once more.

Harmony Village opened its doors in 2025. The developers pocketed a fortune, in part by skimping on the cement in their concrete. The shortfalls became evident when the earthquake hit. Walls crumpled, and roofs fell in. Doubly unfortunate, Harmony lay in the direct path of the toxic fumes that decimated the city.

Now Bird and Madrone picked their way through the tunnel and jimmied the wagon through a narrow passageway between cliffs of concrete rubble. After a few hundred yards, they came to an open area, the remains of the pedestrian street where shoppers had once strolled between chain stores. Concrete benches backed by planters were covered with dried husks of weeds. Some of the lower buildings had survived mostly intact, although their plateglass windows were shattered and wind and rain had done their work on their contents. Broken glass and chunks of fallen rubble littered the promenade.

They saw no bones, no overt signs of death. Anything once living had long ago been stripped and scattered by the rats they heard scurrying through the ruins in a desperate search for something left to eat. Concrete dust lay over everything like a fine, gray shroud.

They snaked around blocks of fallen concrete and wound their way between boulders of cement. The pavement buckled into ridges like the backs of giant prehistoric beasts re-emerging slowly from the ground. To the south, the pancaked floors of a fallen high-rise lay tilted like geological layers of a fossil seabed. To the north, the ground broke into troughs and peaks like crashing waves frozen in time.

They clambered over hillocks of concrete. Behind, another narrow passage between slanting walls opened to a wide space that had once, perhaps, been a park. Skeletons of trees stood black against the dim twilight. A dried thatch of dead grass covered the compacted ground like a threadbare carpet.

Madrone felt oppressed by the silence, the dust, the scale of the ruins. She had not imagined this in her vision. It had seemed so simple, five hundred miles away in the gardens with their singing fountains. But visions were conveniently hazy and vague, tricking you into trusting them. Then they delivered you into sharp, jagged reality, like this parched, concrete landscape with its scent of death.

Bird felt happy, almost giddy with relief. They had made it across the dangerous open ground of the city and evaded its patrols. This surreal landscape of sharp-toothed ruins felt to him like shelter. No eyes would pierce the concrete walls. No Lash would penetrate this wreckage to seek them out. The very scope of the devastation awoke in him some boyish instinct to explore, to poke into its dark corners and probe its secret caverns.

"Look!" he cried out in excitement. "Here it is—just like in your vision! It's alive! Your sacred tree."

A small, cement amphitheater was dug into the low slope of the ground. Perhaps it had once been meant as an outdoor stage, where a poet might declaim a verse or a singer belt out a love song. Out of a crack in the mud-caked ground grew one brave, spindly tree with feathery leaves.

Madrone found Bird's cheerfulness irritating.

"That's not a sacred tree," she said. "That's an ailanthus. It's a weed tree. Invasive."

"It's a nitrogen fixer." Bird slipped an arm around her and gave her a hug. "A giving tree. And a survivor. That's got to count for something."

She pulled away from him and sat down on one of the cracked, concrete seats. "It's not even native."

"Chinese Tree of Heaven," Bird said. "Somebody thinks it's sacred. And it was the *Tree Grows in Brooklyn* tree—remember that book?"

"It's not like my vision," she insisted.

"But it's like mine," Bird said. "The green things pushing through the cracks in the fortress walls."

"Fine, you can have it then!"

"We can camp here tonight," he said, ignoring her mood. She sat hugging her knees while he unloaded the wagon, taking out the bikes and the four five-gallon jugs of water that Beth had generously given them. He spread out their sleeping pads and bags on the wagon bed.

"Doesn't look like rain, and this will keep us out of the way of any critters that might mistake us for a last, lonely corpse. Why don't you climb in and take a nap while I make dinner?"

"You're trying to get on my good side."

"Always." He came over and put his arms around her. "Hey, *querida*, we're here. We've made it. We're still alive, and free, and together. And I still think you're the most beautiful woman around!"

At that she laughed. "Not much in the way of competition."

"Doesn't matter. You beat them all."

In the morning, after a quick breakfast of acorn porridge, they set off to explore. A night's sleep and an extra ration of water had restored Madrone's spirits, and though she couldn't feel cheerful in this place of ruin, she did feel interested in what they might discover.

She sensed death surrounding them, made all the more present by the remnants of life they passed as they explored deeper into the ruins. The severed head of a child's doll lay on the path, full of the tooth marks of some rodent who had taken a long time to convince himself that this was not flesh. Scraps of electronics littered the ground, broken housings for archaic computers. Windrows of plastic shards banked up against chunks of concrete.

A dry wind blew and the white-hot sun blazed down. Dust and sand piled up to form a new Sahara. Only a scurrying lizard broke the silence.

Bird poked into dark places, pried open long-closed doors. As a boy, he and his brother had played games, imagining themselves discovering long-lost Egyptian tombs or chests of pirate gold. Below them, he was sure, lay treasures, the resources they would need to turn this ruin into a refuge.

Bird shifted a beam, and something rattled and crashed down in the distance.

"Leave it alone!" Madrone yelled. "You'll destabilize it!"

Cautiously, he shifted the beam another few inches. Nothing happened.

"I think it's okay," he said.

"Don't think!"

But Bird had succeeded in uncovering a door that had fallen sideways, so that it now opened upward, like a trap door. He yanked it open, and shined his light down into the wide space below.

He let out a low, soft whistle. "*Diosa!* Holy Mother of all the Gods!"

Beside him, Madrone peered in. Slowly, the light revealed a dreadful tableau. Death lay everywhere, and she shivered and drew back, as if it might rush out and grab them if they exposed its works.

"It's okay." Bird wrapped an arm around her. "The air's okay now."

His crystal beamed forth a light that played over a scene of horror, like a grotesque Dia de los Muertos display of *esqueletos* and *Catrinas*, skeletons in dresses and skeletons in suits, skeleton shoppers holding crumbling bags in clawlike finger bones. Skeletons clutched their throats or crouched retching in sad heaps. One skeleton mother wrapped bone arms around the scapulae of her skeleton child, in a last, futile gesture of protection.

Madrone knew death; she would have said that she was death's intimate. But she had never seen anything like this. She shuddered, and drew Bird's arm more closely around her. It was warm and alive, and strong.

"May the wind carry your spirits gently," she murmured the prayer for the dead, and Bird joined in.

"May the Fire release your souls.
May the Water cleanse you, may the Earth receive you.
May the Goddess cradle you and bring you to rebirth."

"We can use this," Bird said when they had finished. He had a dangerous light in his eye.

"Use this?" Madrone looked at him, uncomprehending.

"The Dead will be our defense."

———————

"I'm not squeamish," Madrone told him over their meager lunch. They were back out in what they'd come to call the plaza, stewing a ration of quinoa and chia over a tiny open fire.

"I'm a doctor, for Goddess's sake! I lived with a skeleton all through medical school. We kept him in the common room in the dorm. Freddie, we called him. He was an old guy who left his body to a science. But this is different. These dead didn't volunteer to be our materials! They deserve a burial, at least. An honoring."

"What could be more honoring of the dead than giving them a role to play that will serve life?" Bird retorted. "I'm sure they'd be pleased to know that their castoffs were so useful."

"You don't know that."

"You don't know that they wouldn't."

"Maybe they just want rest, and peace."

"So ask them. Don't you talk to the dead?"

"No," Madrone said. "The dead talk to me."

And they did talk to her. They came to her as she and Bird lay in their wagon. They had wheeled it under the overhang of a suspended slab to provide some shade for their siesta. But the ruins all around them soaked up heat, radiated it back out to compete with the blazing sun, and she slept lightly and feverishly.

Use us! She heard the whispers in her dreams. *Use us. We will be your guardians.*

The narrow tunnel through the old archway provided a natural, defensible entrance to the Refuge. Here Bird planned to station their guard. The gates of death would mark the entrance to another life.

"I'll go down and hand them up to you," Bird offered. "I know you don't like heights. Or depths, as the case may be."

"I'm just a middle-of-the-road kind of gal, is that what you're saying?" Madrone said lightly, not wanting to admit how grateful she felt not to have to climb down into that charnel house herself. "Well, you're wrong. I'm a Scorpio. I live for the heights and the depths. What I don't like is rope climbing."

"As I was saying," Bird agreed. They had brought climbing lines and gear from the North with them in their packs, and Bird slipped into his harness and clipped on. Madrone belayed him as he swung down into the cavern.

"How's the air?" she asked anxiously.

"Fine."

The air smelled musty, with a little rank tang of rodent piss, but there was a fresh current that wafted through from some further opening. Bird rappelled slowly down into the dark cavern. He touched his crystal and murmured, "Light, please."

The chamber was illumined with a pearly glow, in which the bones looked even more eerie, as if they might suddenly stand up and go about their business. He shivered, then thrust the image resolutely out of his mind, and examined the skeleton that lay closest to his feet. It was still dressed in a business suit in the fashion of the last days of empire, but the gray, expensive-looking cloth was riddled with holes.

"Ready!" he called up, and Madrone let down the sling they had rigged. Gently, he picked the skeleton up, cradling it as if it were a living casualty of war. As he laid it in the sling, the head fell off and rolled, clattering, over the floor, leaving a track in the dust. Bird winced. The hollow, dark eyeholes stared at him with dumb accusation.

"Sorry," he muttered as he retrieved it and settled it firmly onto the sling with the rest of the bones. He jerked on the rope, and Madrone hauled it up.

Through a long afternoon, they continued the grisly task. Bird scavenged skeletons and Madrone pulled them up and laid them out, keeping the bones together as best she could. Some were still linked by tough tendons, but others had all their soft parts eaten away and fell into a heap at the slightest motion.

Madrone murmured the prayer for the dead over every heap of bleached bones. It was a small expiation, a recognition that each had been an individual with friends and family and dreams.

Yet even the bones told tales to Madrone's experienced eye. Here was a broken femur that had healed. Here an arthritic knee that must have hurt going upstairs or down. Here an old woman with bad teeth, too poor to afford dental care in the waning days of empire.

After a couple of hours, her arms and shoulders were aching. Bones had weight, and while she was strong, she was working muscles that she didn't normally use.

"I'll trade with you," she called down to Bird.

"I thought you didn't like climbing?"

"I don't, but my arms are going to fall off if I do any more lifting."

"Let's take a break," he suggested.

What he meant by "a break" was another laborious task, carrying the skeletons out to the entranceway of the city, arranging them to stand as guards or sit as watchers. Bird tore through piles of rubble and probed the back rooms of wrecked shops searching for posts and cords, scattering nests of chittering rats who fled in complaint. They propped the skeletons up and tied their bones together, working by the light of their crystals long into the night. Madrone was nearly dropping from weariness, but Bird was possessed by a manic energy. If they could only set up enough Watchers, as he called them, only animate enough of the Dead, they would be safe.

Their days fell into a pattern. In the mornings, they pulled skeletons out of the ruins. They cleaned up as best they could, guarding their precious water, and cooked a lunch of acorn gruel or quinoa, same as their breakfast and their dinner. It was a bland dish, and Madrone's mouth watered for spices and fresh greens. She found herself fantasizing about ripe tomatoes and juicy plums, or even a simple vegetable stir-fry with tamari. Their waning stores of quinoa and chia and amaranth were their seed grain, and they conserved them carefully against the day they would find water to start their gardens. Here and there, dandelions grew among the ruins, but the greens were tough and bitter now at the end of the growing season. Once she found a patch of lambs' quarters, and almost cried from joy. They were past their prime, already gone to seed, but she sautéed up their leaves in a little of their precious olive oil and they both thought they'd never tasted anything more delicious.

In the afternoons, they arranged their skeleton tableau. Much to her surprise, Madrone began to enjoy the project. Once she got over the shock and the sadness, the task took on its creative aspects. She had never been much good at drawing or painting, but she enjoyed building altars and arranging things. And this is like an altar, she thought. The biggest Dia de los Muertos altar anyone's ever seen.

And if she were honest with herself, she'd admit that even being immersed in death was more restful than being overwhelmed by the needs of the living.

Soon *esqueletos* stood guard at the tunnel's mouth and perched atop all the surrounding concrete precipices. Skeletons lurked in niches inside the passageway. Bird found a gift shop that held a trove of votive candles packaged tightly enough in plastic that they had escaped the teeth of the rats. He set them inside the skulls where, lit at night, they created a truly eerie atmosphere. By the fourth day, the entrance to the Refuge would have done credit to any haunted house or Day of the Dead display.

"I wish we had some marigolds," Madrone said. "And some cut-paper banners."

"I wish we had some water," Bird said.

Chapter Twenty-Four

The sign said "Vista Point." Cress stopped, raised his arm, and cried out the command to halt. "Halt!" rippled back through the column of marchers, a thousand strong, stretching out in a long line along the old Interstate 5 that led down through the Central Valley.

They were five days out from the City, still close enough that transports could zip back and forth with supplies in a couple of hours, but far enough that they were reaching the edge of Califia's settled lands. Around them, low hills lay smooth and rounded, as if a giant hand had taken real hills and polished them down to an even perfection. Green with the first rains of winter, they appeared inviting in the cool of the tule fog that lay heavy around them. But Cress remembered the road scorching his feet, long ago, under the relentless blaze of a summer sun, and was not fooled. There was a reason that this rich-looking land was still depopulated.

"Take a break!" he cried, and all down the line the former sojuhs and new recruits from the City unhooked their heavy packs and flung them down. Canteens came out, as did packets of dried fruit and nuts and jerky, their walking rations.

River came up beside him, chewing a hunk of the seedcake the cooks called "lembas."

"This shit tough as a sergeant's hide," he complained.

"Cooks say it's good for you," Cress told him. "Roughage. Builds character."

Together they headed up a cracked drive and climbed a small hillock. From the top, they could see over miles of the rolling hills, emerald fading to misty blue in the pale, foggy light.

"How far the army come today?" River asked.

"I'd say about seven miles since dawn," Cress said. "I'd like to do at least another ten before nightfall. It's still a long way to the Southlands."

They were marching on foot, as armies had marched from time

immemorial, because there wasn't enough transport in all of Califia to move a thousand troops on busses or trucks or electrocars. Nor were there recharge stations down in the Southlands. Such transport as they had followed behind with supplies.

The march had another objective, too. In the month or more they estimated it would take to move the army down south on foot, they would have time to bond it into a single force. Right now it was just a ragtag collection of defectors mixed with Cityfolk who had never held a weapon before. They needed time to season, Cress thought. Like a stew needed time to simmer.

"Pretty land," River observed, looking over the hills. "Soft, like."

"You should see it in a summer heat wave, when it's 130 degrees in the shade."

And yet Erik of Farmers' Guild believed it could be reclaimed.

"Plant trees," he'd suggested when they discussed what they would do after victory. "Mitigate the climate."

Cress recalled with some skepticism the dead orchards they had passed, rows of desiccated sticks parched to black skeletons. But his Water Guild mind was already calculating area and rainfall—maybe ten, twelve inches a year in this part of the Valley, say a foot, that would be an acre-foot per acre, captured and infiltrated with some swales and ponds. They could catch some of the spring flow down from the Sierras, reinfiltrate the dehydrated aquifers....

He realized with a slight sense of surprise that he was smiling at the thought. His anger, that sense of outrage constant as a toothache, was dulled here, as if he'd released it with the motion of marching, the commitment to action.

"Gonna have lunch here?" Smokee asked. She'd come up the hill to join them, and instantly Cress's irritation was back.

She was the third of their triumvirate of commanders. Her Valkyries amounted to about twenty of the former pen-girls, all who could be persuaded to leave the comforts of the North and head back down to the Southlands. It had been Maya's suggestion, in her last days, to name the pen-girls' unit after the women fighters of Norse legend.

River was commander of about six hundred former soldiers, and Cress was first rep for the four hundred City recruits who were willing to cede decision-making authority to him, recognizing that a war cannot be fought by bringing every decision to Council. But they never let him forget that they could withdraw that authority at any time.

Cress also carried the responsibility of arranging transport and supplies, and liaised with techies and support. He could delegate a thousand tasks, but the weight ultimately rested on his shoulders.

In spite of the meager numbers under Smokee's charge, she placed herself on equal footing with him and River, insisting on being part of every conclave decision.

He tried to cut her some slack. She had suffered from the Stewards as much as anyone, no doubt. At least she was willing to fight. Nonetheless, she annoyed him. He swallowed his irritation and replied simply, "It's as good a place as any."

She nodded, set herself down on a boulder that had once marked the edge of the Vista Point parking lot, and pulled out her marching rations.

"Valkyries wanna know, when do we get there?" she asked.

"At this rate, in about twenty days," Cress said.

"Twenty days!"

"That's if we pick up the pace to about twenty miles a day," he said. "Less than the old Roman legions used to do, but more than most of our troops are used to. And that's not counting any fighting time. It's a long way to the Southlands on foot."

"And when we come up on the plantations?" Smokee asked. "What's the plan?"

"Recon," River said. "Recon first, then decide."

"We *all* decide," she said firmly.

"That what this fighter—what *I* said," River told her. He'd gotten used to saying "I" back in the City, but it was all too easy, in this too-familiar setting of troops and marches, to slip back into old patterns. He thought of Maya, how often she had corrected him and encouraged him. He'd think about her, and then feel sad, wishing he could still talk to her, sit with her. It was an unfamiliar feeling, what Cress called "mourning."

Kit was marching with the Valkyries, and that worried River, for he didn't trust Smokee as a commander. She was too hot-headed, too inexperienced. He had tried to persuade Kit to stay behind. Much as he liked being with her, he would have preferred to know that she was safe in the City rather than worrying about her on the march or in battle.

He sighed. He still hadn't drilled—no, made love to her. He reminded himself to think in the new terms Maya and the Temple of Love had taught him. Back in the City, he'd been careful to go very, very slowly at first—and then suddenly they were in the midst of preparations for the foray south, and there was no time.

He still couldn't really tell how she felt about him. Sometimes he thought she wanted to be near him, and that was why she'd come with the army. The thought warmed him, like a swig of sauce in his belly, but also worried him, because if something happened to her, it would be his fault.

Sometimes he felt like she didn't care about him at all, that he was just an annoyance to her, a painful reminder of her days in the pens. And when he felt like that, all hot and hurt and angry, he wanted to punch her in the face and throw her down on the ground and nail her in the dirt, whether she wanted it or not. He still found that idea exciting, though he didn't want to.

Best not to think about it. Got an army to run.

"We could reach the northern edge of the Stewards' influence in a week," Cress said, "if we keep up the pace. We'll have decisions to make there, long before we get all the way down to the Southlands proper."

River nodded and stood up. Down below, he saw the Valkyries relaxing in the sun. He strode off and headed back down to look for Kit.

She was perched on her pack in the midst of the other women. River sauntered over to her, trying to look like he'd just accidentally wandered by. She looked tired. The marching and the carrying of heavy packs was hard on the girls, most of whom had only ever done one thing in the physical realm up until the Day of Liberation. But they plodded on without complaint, and it was only in these moments of rest that their exhaustion showed.

Kit was looking without enthusiasm at a handful of nuts and raisins.

"Try one at a time," River suggested. "Go down easier that way."

"This Val know how to eat," Kit informed him. She still said "I" only reluctantly, but seemed to take great pride in calling herself "this Valkyrie" or its shortened form, Val. She popped the entire handful into her mouth, and began chewing valiantly.

"Good way to choke to death," River said.

Kit shrugged.

"Holdin' up okay?" He sat down by her and pulled out a hunk of lembas.

She shrugged again, but she leaned infinitesimally closer to him. They sat and chewed companionably.

When they finished their rations, he beckoned to her to come with him up to the overlook. He reached for her hand but she snatched it away.

"Don't need no guide dog," she said.

But she walked beside him up the road and sat next to him on the big boulder. When he slid his arm around her, she didn't pull away. She even nestled into his side, and he could feel her breathing, the rise and fall of her ribs. He breathed in her scent, rank with the day's sweat but with something peachy and sweet underneath.

Cress had gone down to the troops, and Smokee with him. There was no one around, and the slope of the hill screened them from below.

Daringly, River let his lips brush her temple. Her skin was soft, the edge of her hair soft in a different way. She didn't pull away from him. More daring yet, he gave her a soft, tentative kiss right where her hair dipped down toward her ear.

"Why do that?" she asked him.

"Because I like you. Like to kiss you."

"No army up here to stop you," she said.

"But would you like it?"

"You askin' this pen-girl?" she said, her voice dropping almost to a whisper.

"Askin' you."

She gave him a long, sharp look that softened to just the hint of a smile.

"Fighter don't know till he tries," she said.

He brushed her lips with his. Softly, so softly it was like a tickle, a vibration. She didn't pull back. He pressed his lips gently into hers. A heat filled him. He wrapped his arms around her, held her tight, and their lips locked. Her mouth opened, he could feel her breath against his, her heart beating fast. His tongue slid into her mouth, he held and caressed her for a long, long moment.

Finally they broke apart.

"Like it?" he asked.

"No complaints."

"Do it again?"

She said nothing, but leaned slightly forward. River felt his whole body come alive as he held her, as if every part that touched her warm flesh were aching, yearning, electric. But this was no place for it. He wanted her, but he wanted her slow and careful and private, like in the Temple of Love, not rough on a hilltop with the army just below.

He sighed and pulled away.

"Not the place for it," he said. "Not the right time."

She nodded.

"Get them babies back," she said. "Then maybe make more."

He looked at her with a sudden suspicion.

"You don't really want to do this at all!" he accused her. "You just tryin' to make sure we go get them babies."

"Get them babies, you do whatever you want with this ... with Kit."

"Fuck you!" he said, suddenly furious. He stood up and turned away, shaking. Got to get control of himself. Got to get control. The bigsticks had beaten this fury into him, and no matter what he learned in the Temple of Love, or how many times he chose not to act on it, it would always be part of the bedrock of who he was. The thought made him feel a heaviness, what he might have called despair if he'd had the words. Somewhere deep in his memory a small boy cried for his mama. Mare threw this pup away, a gruff voice told him. He felt a blow to his stomach, but the words hurt more. Don't want this cub no more. But now the army gonna make chiplet into a sojuh.

And a sojuh he was, and would always be.

After a long moment, he turned back. She was just sitting there, her eyes in the dead, pen-girl glaze.

"Let's go," he said. "Been here too long."

She stood up, alarmed. He could see fear in her eyes and it made him angry.

"Get them babies," she said. "Be good, then. Truly."

Now all his anger had turned to a dull sadness. Why be mad at her? Wounds, the sojuhs called the pen-girls, among many other insults. And that's what Kit was, a walking wound on legs. How could she know anything about wanting, and love?

"Don't have to buy it or bribe it," he said. "Fighters go get the babies, if we can, because they our babies, too. Because they babies. Don't want the babies to go through the shit these fighters—no, you and me gone through. Don't matter if you kiss me or not, fuck me or tell me 'fuck off'! We real people now, and real people protect their own!"

He stalked off, down the hill. After a moment he heard steps behind him. He whirled around. She had followed him down, and tentatively she reached out a hand and placed it on his arm.

"You a real person," she said in a tone hardly louder than a whisper. "This ... this girl ... me ... just learning."

He bent his head, and let his lips again brush her forehead.

"Learning together," he said. "Learning together."

Day after day, they continued down the old highway. At first they passed through a landscape of low hills, a pleasant enough land, Cress thought, with the mountains rising up to the west and the shadow of the Sierras hanging on the eastern horizon like a looming cloud. Land that was once rich and fertile, and still might be reclaimed.

But the quakes of the '20s had had a devastating effect on the Valley, especially in those areas where decades of pumping had drained the aquifers, leaving a crust of land perched above great hollows below. For years, the land had been subsiding, and when the big quake hit in '28, the earth didn't just shake. It collapsed.

Now they passed through a new, hideous landscape, ancient sediments crumpled into badlands, slabs of rock perched at odd angles like huge books tumbled from the shelves of giants. In places the old road was buried under slides, dried rivers of mud deep enough to drown whole towns. To the east, Cress knew, the old cities of Fresno and Stockton lay in ruins, crushed into sticks and rubble, or burned down to blackened patches of ground where twisted columns of steel proclaimed there had once been a high-rise. The bones of his mother and sister lay buried somewhere there.

Here on the I-5, there had never been towns, but at long intervals they passed the relics of amenities that once had served truckers and travelers. A faded sign, leaning at a crazy angle, offered Andersen's Pea Soup. Broken fences and piles of cow bones marked the remains of stockyards. Here and there were old automobiles, smashed in pile-ups, their bent hoods and shattered windows frozen in time, though scavengers had scattered the bones of the drivers. They came to more than one traffic jam, long lines of cars now permanently stalled, their soft parts gnawed by rats and their steel beginning to rust.

A few still held remains, although scattered bones along the road-side told how most had abandoned their vehicles and tried to make it to some oasis on foot. But some held whole families, tiny skeletons cradled in bony arms. Many, when they'd realized they weren't going to escape, had simply turned the exhaust inward and made their cars their tombs. Cress knew. He had been there. He'd watched his own father struggle with a man who was crazed with despair, jamming dirt into his tail-pipe. There had been three children in that car, and a baby in its mother's arms, and his own dad had soon realized that he could spend his strength to prevent the suicide but he couldn't truly offer them life. It was eighty miles to the Bay, where they'd heard there were stores of water and food, and he had barely enough water to see himself and Cress through. So they'd moved on, closing their ears to the cries around them.

The remains brought it all back, the sounds he'd tried so hard to blot out. The low growl of the earth in motion, the tumbling chaos of concrete, and the screams of his mother cut short as a beam fell on her. And worst of all, his sister's high, quavering cries as she lay buried in the ruins, crying for help, crying for water.

He and his father had dug through the rubble, his father like a mad-man, tossing huge chunks of concrete aside, pulling beams out of the ruins and starting new avalanches, until he reached a solid wall of con-crete, too heavy for them to lift no matter how hard they strained and tried. Cress had gone on a frantic search for help, and brought back men who pulled themselves away from the corpses of their own families, strong men with huge trunks of legs and arms like iron bars, who dug through rubble with their bare hands until one of them pulled on the wrong end of a beam, and the slab careened down in a great crash of dust, and the cries stopped abruptly.

The worst sound of all, then, that silence.

He'd seen his father cry, sobbing for his daughter and his wife who lay somewhere in the ruins. As he had cried for his own wife and daugh-ter in turn. A family legacy, loss and grief.

But his father never cried again. After that, Cress saw only his dad's grim determination that they at least would make it out alive. They'd fled, not up this road but up the old 99, north and then west to the City, which opened generous arms and took in all the refugees who made their way there.

His father had sheltered Cress, protected him as best he could, fought for him, stolen food, dipped water out of the cracked irrigation canals to keep them alive. He'd brought Cress to safety, but he himself was broken, and soon after they came to the City he'd died in one of the early epidemics.

The ruins brought it all back. Somewhere beneath this Valley lay the bones of his mother, his sister. They had become this land, and the parched and broken earth was still crying with their voices, calling for help, calling for water.

Chapter Twenty-Five

Like so many of Angel City's poor, Madrone and Bird became water thieves. The twenty gallons they had brought with them from Beth's was three-fourths gone by the time they finished arranging the Gateway of the Dead. They were not in the Stewards' registers, so even had they wanted to spend much of their day waiting in the water lines for a meager ration, they were ineligible. Worse than that, they were wanted criminals. Madrone's face was still keyed into Angel City police rosters. Bird was still in their database as an escaped criminal.

They knew that the ancient springs lurked somewhere beneath the ruins, but knowing did not confer superpowers to shift tons of concrete and twisted beams of steel.

Bird waited for a dream, but no dream came. Madrone called on her bee powers, but could trace no scent of moisture. There were no hazels within forty miles that they could cut into a forked stick for dousing. They tried bent wires, and experimented with ailanthus branches, holding them out hopefully, waiting for a twitch or a dip. But they got no results.

They spent days searching in vain. Promising passageways led nowhere. Shafts that opened into the ground inevitably were blocked.

"A 'dozer would be handy right now," Bird said, as he and Madrone attempted to muscle a heavy chunk of concrete away from a promising opening. "Or a team of testosterone-crazed ex-sojuhs."

"Or a superpower," Madrone said.

"The bees didn't teach you to levitate concrete?"

"Not when there's all this kryptonite around."

"A simple backhoe would do it." Bird wiped a stream of sweat off his forehead. They looked at each other bleakly.

"We could go back to Beth's," Madrone suggested. She was hot, and covered with a gray dust that stuck to her skin. Her throat was parched but already she was halfway through her ration of water for the day. Beth's basement seemed like an oasis of comfort and luxury.

Bird shook his head. "It's too dangerous, for her and for us. Her house could be watched. And she can't afford to keep giving us her rations. We're going to have to use the map."

During their preparations for the journey, Bird had consulted with the Researchers' Collective, an offshoot of the Techies' Guild. They had searched back through archaic databases and come up with a precious map of the underground water lines that fed Angel City. The map was old, but the Stewards had added little if anything to the existing infrastructure. The greatest danger was that many of the lines had undoubtedly been destroyed in the disasters of the '20s.

The lines feeding Harmony Village had long been cut off, but about a mile away, a major artery ran down to the southern ports at Long Beach. That line was still functioning, or so the Researchers' Collective believed. If it were not, the ports would be dry and deserted. It was the best bet for an illegal tap.

Katy had tutored them in the techniques for tapping a water line. They'd brought with them a drill and plugs. They were prepared.

Darkness covered them like a blanket. They used no light, but moved through the city slowly as their eyes accustomed to the night. They'd left their bikes and the wagon in the Refuge. If they needed to hide, they couldn't afford encumbrances. And, useful as the wagon might be for transporting the water, they couldn't risk leaving it vulnerable to thieves while they explored underground. So they walked. The target was only a mile away, on the edge where the Death Zone merged with the merely abandoned stretches of the old downtown.

It was strange, Madrone thought, this dark void in the center of a great city that had once been filled with light and noise and motion. She remembered Maya had told them how the night sky of her LA childhood was a hazy glow, the smog reflecting back the streetlights and neon. Only a few of the brighter stars had ever been visible. Not until Maya grew up and fled to wild places had she ever seen the Milky Way.

Now the stars were bright enough to steer a course by. No lights shone in the Death Zone or the deserted downtown streets. No one was out after curfew. No one but them, and here and there, other creeping shadows, other thieves.

Madrone felt a hollow, squirrelly feeling in her stomach. She envied Bird's capacity to ignore fear, or rather, to step through it into some other zone of calm. More than that, he was enjoying this, she realized. He'd been absorbed and eager as he'd prepared their gear, like a boy excited at the prospect of adventure. But she couldn't ignore the uneasiness she felt, the sense that some dark fate lurked in the shadows that would change their lives forever.

The water pipes ran far below the original level of the streets, even deeper beneath the piles of rubble and the strata of trash and debris that lay atop the old city like a new geology. Yet here and there were openings. A few old manholes still gave access to the sewers, where the clean water pipes ran above the drains. Old basements of crumbling high-rises, abandoned for lack of power and maintenance, sometimes still gave access to pipes where the inflow had missed being turned off. There were even one or two still-functioning standpipes that had once watered lawns and shrubberies, when such things were common in this part of town.

"I won't do the sewers." Madrone had been clear on that. "Not unless we don't have any other choice. We'll never be able to carry back enough water to wash off the stench."

"The sewers would probably be the safest chance," Bird had said.

"Not so safe if we get bitten by rats, or contract some infectious disease."

"Then you can cure it, healer!"

She shook her head. "Don't bet on it. What if I got too sick to heal? Why don't we find some nice, abandoned drinking fountain?"

"Because if such a thing exists, every water thief in a fifty-mile radius will have it covered."

In the end, they settled on the ruined high-rise that was now their target. The darkness barely slowed them down, and within a short time they saw it looming above them, a rectangular shadow that blocked the stars.

It was a big complex, covering a complete city block. Madrone and Bird skirted the perimeter, looking for a way in. Sharp, jagged spears of thick glass like a child's drawing of a mountain range surrounded the ground floor.

They moved slowly, careful to stay out of sight. The circuit took them nearly an hour, for each time they heard a sound, they froze in place, waiting to hear if the footsteps of a patrol were coming their way. But the sounds proved to be rodents on the prowl, or the slight breeze shifting some old scrap of cardboard.

Finally, on the far side of the ruin, they found a chunk of wall standing with a fire door in its side. It was made of metal, painted a dark green that flaked away in sections. Rust had etched its surface with streaks of red like mysterious runes. Its electronic lock had long rusted, and Bird yanked on it with a hard pull. With a groan like the cry of an outraged beast, it opened.

"You stand sentry," Bird told Madrone. "I'll go in."

"No way," Madrone said. "We go together."

"It could be dangerous."

"Now that would be a change, wouldn't it?" She pushed past him and entered.

She choked on the smell of mold that rose up with the dust clouds from the remains of a rotting carpet.

"Stop!" Bird warned. Inside, darkness turned pitch-black. He risked a low-beamed light. Huge sections of the floor had fallen away, revealing a grid of steel beams bent and twisted as if a giant hand had squeezed them out of shape. A group of orange plastic chairs sat, incongruously marooned on an intact island of floor space, as if someone had pulled them together to hold a meeting. Perhaps someone had, for others also prowled the night.

They skirted the edges of the chasm and found a corridor that had survived with only some cracks in the once-white drywall and the doors askew on their frames. They hurried along it, looking for a stairwell down.

A sign on a gray metal door read "Exit." But when they pried the door open, the inside was a mass of fallen concrete and metal debris.

"No way through." Bird shook his head. "Come on."

Next to the stairwell were the elevators: six closed doors, three on each side of the foyer. Madrone pushed the call button experimentally, but no long-dead electrical system came to life. The doors remained shut.

Bird took a short crowbar out of his tool pack. He pried it into the opening between two of the doors, strained and pushed. The crack widened.

"Help me," he said.

Madrone added her weight to his. With a screech, the door gave way and opened.

"I can get through," Bird said. "You wait here, belay me with the rope."

No, don't leave me, Madrone wanted to plead, but she made herself stay silent, just nodding as he slipped into his climbing belt. He searched for a moment in the dark, rubble-filled foyer until he found a few small metal chinks that he jammed into the base of the elevator doors.

"Don't want them suddenly deciding to close on us," he said, smiling.

She pulled out the line they had brought, and uncoiled it as he clipped in. Wrapping it around her waist, she braced herself against the door as he squeezed through the opening and pushed off, rappelling down the shaft in a series of long bounds. She paid out the rope as he went down, until at last she felt it slacken.

And then there was only waiting. To stop her mind from imagining horrors, she began to listen deeply, searching for any sounds of life.

There were no bees within miles, no allies to save them if anyone came. She thought she could hear the creak and groan of the metal, the slight shifting of the rubble. If another quake were to come when Bird was down there—but no, she wouldn't envision that. She would think about their Refuge, the gardens they would build, the healing center she would establish. They would find water. She had to believe that.

Bird had always loved climbing, and what he had loved best was rappelling, paying out the rope and sliding down in long leaps, bounding off the sides of cliffs in the bright blue air. Once, in his younger days, on one of the Learning Group trips to the High Sierras, he and his fellow students had explored caves, after long lectures on safety from Jacquez, their instructor. Quez had made them go over and over the knots, the signals, the protocol, made them tie their flashlights to their wrists as Bird had done now.

As he descended, he felt like that young Bird again, free and weightless. In the harness, dropping through darkness in great bounds, his bad leg didn't bother him. The stiffness of his fingers was no handicap on the ropes.

Descending into the shaft was like going deep into a cave. The water pipes for the tower ran alongside him and he banged them lightly with his metal wrench at intervals, hoping for water. They rang hollow and empty. But at the bottom, he hoped to find the feeder pipe that tapped into a main line, and with luck it would be full.

When he reached the end of his hundred-foot line, he was still far above the basement level. He tugged on the rope, signaling to Madrone that he was going to add line, and with a firm knot he secured the extra fifty feet he'd had wrapped around his shoulders. The rope vibrated with her tug back, signaling that all was well.

He continued down. Care and precision, Jacquez had drummed into them. Thinking through each step. Taking precautions—so you don't lose the rope, letting it swing free and out of reach. So you don't drop the flashlight, leaving yourself trapped in the formless dark. His stomach was churning with adrenaline but he found himself grinning. Okay, I admit it, he thought. I'm enjoying this. Haven't had this much fun since I learned to snowboard!

Down and down, like in those trances Maya used to lead, down into the underworld. When the rope finally gave out, he was still ten feet above the top of a metal box, the elevator cage, which he firmly hoped was itself at ground level. There was a rusted steel maintenance ladder affixed to the wall, in a small niche that ran up and down alongside the elevator. He pushed himself off from one of the cables and swung wildly through the space until he was able to grab hold of a rung. Clinging to the ladder, he untied the rope, with some reluctance. It was his lifeline, and he suddenly felt that if he left it, he might cut himself off irreparably from the upper world, from light and air and from Madrone. He tugged on it with five sharp tugs, signaling that he was releasing it, and then tied it firmly to one of the rungs.

He squeezed down through the narrow channel and reached the bottom. Below him, in a trench, lay lines of iron pipe. One he recognized as water pipe, and he felt it. It was cool. He thumped it with the wrench, and it made the dull thud of a pipe full of water. *Gracias a la Diosa!*

He played his light over the trench. If the water was under pressure, he could make a hole in the top and it would spurt out, but it would be harder to capture efficiently and time was of the essence for filling their containers. The longer they stayed down here, the more the danger of discovery grew.

Better to make a hole closer to the bottom side of the pipe. There was just room enough below for him to squeeze down and lower a jug.

They'd had a long argument, around the hearth, about how many containers to bring. Each five-gallon jug, when full, would weigh more than forty pounds.

Bird had offered to carry two, but Madrone had vetoed that idea.

"You stress your bad leg enough as it is," she'd said. "I can carry two."

"Eighty pounds?" he'd asked skeptically.

"I've backpacked with that much."

"Not for a long while. And we'll need to move fast."

They'd compromised by agreeing to each carry one jug and trade the third back and forth between them. Fifteen gallons would last them for a week, if they were very careful, and maybe by then they would find the springs.

He pulled out the diamond drill and selected his spot, wincing at the ear-splitting whine and screech of the bit as it ate through the metal. He wondered if Madrone could hear it up above, or if anyone else could? Would it draw pursuit?

He'd made a small hole, only about half an inch in diameter. Too large a hole might register as a loss of pressure on the Stewards' monitors. But too small a hole would require a longer time to fill their jugs, and every extra minute increased their danger. Like so many things in life, it was a compromise.

He set the first jug to fill, and timed it. Four and a half minutes. He took it away, capped it, and set the second jug to fill, while he took the first and climbed back up to the ladder, tied it to the end of the rope, and gave Madrone the signal to haul it up.

"All is well," she signaled back, and the jug began to rise.

Madrone had not sat idle. When Bird signaled that he was off the rope, she began to explore, for it occurred to her that hauling forty pounds of water up 150 feet was not going to be easy. Nothing in the hallway seemed helpful, so reluctantly she squeezed through the doorway and climbed into the shaft.

Far, far below she could see the pale gleam of Bird's light. She used her own. The door opened directly to the long drop, but a small shelf beside it led to an open steel beam separating the shaft from its twin alongside. The beam was wide enough to support her. Above the perch was another narrower beam that would serve as a brace for the rope.

Don't think about it, just do it. That was what her climbing instructor had told her when she froze halfway up some cliff. Madrone repeated it three times before she finally forced herself to make the move. She signaled down the rope "Wait!" although she thought that Bird had unclipped by then, and quickly slid one foot through the narrow doorway, feeling for the ledge. Above, her hands found a grip, as if the ledge had been built for someone like her to use.

It was probably for maintenance, in emergencies, she thought. She scooted along it until she could lower herself down onto the beam, straddling it with her thighs. A metal maintenance ladder ran down the wall on the opposite side of the shaft, and she scooted across. She passed a short loop of spare line through a rung of the ladder and clipped in. There, a safety!

Balancing carefully, she paid out a long loop of the main line. She kept a firm grip on it, for if she lost it, Bird would have no way back up. She took a deep breath, and tossed the loose end over the beam above. Missed! It knocked against the beam and fell back down again. She paid out a little more rope, leaned farther out from the ladder, and threw. Yes! It whipped over the beam and hung down just far enough that she could hook a finger into the carabineer that weighted its end.

She clipped the carabineer onto the ladder. That would secure the end, and keep her from accidentally dropping it and dooming Bird. And now the beam would hold the weight of the water and serve as a fulcrum, so she could pull downward to raise the water jugs. That would be much, much easier than trying to pull them straight up.

She sat down again with a huge sigh of relief. She knew that her safety line would catch her if she slipped, but knowing was not the same as trusting. She took a breath to calm herself. Ground, she thought. Somewhere far below us is earth. Put your roots down to it, draw up solidity, stability.

When Bird gave the signal, she was ready. The jug was heavy and her arms soon hurt, but she gritted her teeth and hauled away.

At last the jug came into the view of her headlamp. She forced herself to ignore her sore muscles and pull faster. The quicker she sent the rope back down to Bird, the sooner they could be out of there. She could sense danger stalking them, like a subtle pressure on her inner ear, as if the altitude around them were changing, pushing them into the death zone.

She untied the jug, jammed it securely behind a rung of the ladder that ran up the wall, and then tied on a small piece of metal they had brought as a weight. Leaning carefully over, she tossed the rope back down, praying that it wouldn't catch on anything. With relief, she felt Bird signal back to her. All is well.

The second and third jugs had filled long before Madrone succeeded in hauling up the first. Now Bird tied another jug on and gave the rope a tug. Slowly, it began to rise.

He climbed back down and pushed a soft rubber cap into the hole in the pipe to plug it. They could come back, if need be, and it would be quicker and easier the second time. But the more often they came back, the more likely that they would be watched and trapped. That was how water thieves got caught.

By the time she had raised the second jug and secured it on the shelf next to the first, Madrone's arms were screaming. She ignored the pain. It would be worth far more discomfort to replenish their supplies of water.

Only one more to go. She tied another weight onto the rope, and dropped it down. But it swung wide, and the weight caught the rungs of the ladder that ran down the side of the shaft.

Swearing, Madrone tried to pull it away, but it was stuck. Trying not to panic, she tugged and pulled, but it wouldn't budge. She wondered if she should dare risk calling down to Bird. But what would she say? What could he do? The rope was caught close to the top; there was no way he could free it from below.

She would have to climb down and free it. The ladder extended downward into the dark. If it didn't pull away from the wall ... if the rungs didn't break underfoot ... if her hands didn't slip ... but there was no help for it. Regardless of the danger, she would have to untie, and slide down onto it.

One more tug—nothing. Swearing with every Retributionist curse she could think of, she unclipped, tied the end of the main line firmly to the beam, grabbed the ladder with sweaty hands, and started down. Don't look down. Don't think about the fall. Think about Bird, trapped down below if she failed. No, don't think about that. Too scary. Think about their babies, playing in the sand. Making sand mountains and little ponds—no, that was too distracting. It awoke too much longing in her, to go home, to be safe, to have those babies....

The rungs of the ladder were slick and her hands were sweaty. Think about their grandchildren, great-grandchildren. And her being an old, old woman, old as Maya....

Suddenly her feet went out from under her. A rung broke free, and went clattering down the shaft. She gripped tight, feeling her sweaty hands begin to slip as they took the weight of her body. She kicked out her feet, searching for the next rung. Air. Her left hand was slipping ...

There it was—her toe felt it. Did she dare commit her weight? But she had to. There was no other choice. *Diosa*, I can't do this!

But she did. She slid her foot onto the rung, moved one hand off the rung that it gripped and let it slide down the side support rail of the ladder.

And then her left leg caught on something. The rope!

Hooking one arm into the ladder, she reached down cautiously, straining to jiggle the weight free. With great relief, she felt it come loose. Thank you, Goddess! She hauled it up and leaned out as far as she dared, to drop it carefully into the shaft, letting it fall straight down.

She heard a clang down below, and a thud. The sound echoed through the dark as if it were a bell to call down upon them all the forces of destruction. Then silence.

She scurried back up the ladder. Going up was easier than feeling her way down into the dark. When she came to the broken rung, she could feel above it and hoist herself up. With great relief, she clipped back into the safety of her perch.

The rope was vibrating with Bird's signal. She gripped it and began hauling up the last jug of water.

Suddenly she froze. Voices echoed through the hallway, and footsteps. She heard grunts and thuds, as if something or someone unwilling was being shoved and dragged.

What to do? There was no time to get herself off the beam, across the ledge and out the doors, and nowhere to take cover and run even if she had been willing to abandon Bird. She wished that the door to the elevator was shut, but then of course, they would not have been able to open it again and they'd be trapped. Best to stay where she was, hidden and quiet, concealed by the blanket of the dark.

Quietly, hardly daring to breath, she lowered the jug again and tugged on the rope to signal "Danger! Quiet!"

Outside the door was a scuffling sound. She heard the padding of multiple footsteps—then they stopped.

"Godspiss, someone been here 'fore us," a rough voice barked.

"Save us time with the doors."

"Bring the Lash down, more likely."

"Get in, get out. Hook up the penspawn."

A wail echoed through the shaft. It was a child's cry, high and terrified. A loud slap cut it off.

"Shut up, whore's whelp! Close that demon-spawned mouth, or we shut it for you!"

A gasping, choking sound, like a swallowed sob.

"Better. Now, go down on the rope, quiet, or go down fast, without no rope. Whass it gonna be?"

The sobs broke free.

"Enough of this shit. That noise bring the Lash for sure!"

Another scuffling, a scream, and then something was flying past her, wailing in terror. Madrone forgot her own fear, lunged forward, and grabbed. Her momentum propelled her off the beam, but her harness held. She grasped rough cloth that began to slowly slip away. Swinging free on her own short length of rope, she flailed frantically and managed to grip a small, thin wrist. In one swift motion she yanked the child up and covered its mouth. The wails died away. A chunk of concrete thudded down, ricocheting against the walls. They swung like a pendulum in the dark.

She pressed the child close against her body, holding it tight. She didn't know if it was a boy or a girl, but it smelled sour and unwashed. She fought back the urge to gag.

"Gonna make trouble, slimepup?"

"No, sir," came another small voice.

"Get the Jesus down there, do the job."

"Sure that little creeper ain't on the wall somewhere?"

"No matter. Won't get off the wall!"

A beam of a powerful flashlight illuminated the shaft, playing over the wall just above the spot where Madrone's rope was tied. She hung still, clutching the child in terror. The light swept by her foot and pointed down into the depths.

"Too far down—can't see shit," said the second voice.

"Don't be a limpdick. Get it done and get out."

With a creaking sound, another rope was lowered with a small figure clinging to it. Down and down it went in a frozen silence, the only sound the heavy breathing and soft cursing above.

Madrone held the child she'd grabbed close to her, smothering the sound of its breathing in her shirt. She wondered how long they would have to hang there, and how she would ever get them back up to the safety of the beam. She was strong, but not strong enough to shimmy up the rope one-handed while holding the child. But if she didn't, how would Bird get back? Would they all die, herself and the child slowly swinging until her arm weakened and the child fell, or they died of thirst and dehydration? Would Bird perish alone, down below, never knowing what had happened to them?

No. She couldn't think that way. Sandcastles. Great-grandchildren. Maybe she would redecorate her bedroom when they got home. Paint the walls a new color.

She couldn't freeze. Not here, not now. Blue would be nice, restful. She had to remain alert, to listen, to be ready, once the men left, to somehow get herself and the terrified child back on their perch, and then to haul up another five gallons of water, and then Bird himself. No, don't think about that. Think about green, or maybe a nice, natural yellow ochre. And new sheets. She would sew herself new sheets. And pillow-cases. With crocheted edges. It had been years since she'd crocheted anything, but she could still remember how. She pictured the needle, wrapping the yarn around and poking it through, grabbing it and pulling it back. She could feel the soft grip, the tug, the release as loop slid through the loop. A good hobby for a grandmother, a great-grandmother. She could feel herself growing older with this wait, her hair turning gray.

At last the men above let out a new string of curses, and began hauling something heavy up. It banged and thumped on the sides of the shaft as they swore furiously. The heavy thing on the bottom of the rope swung and Madrone kicked hard to swing them out of its way. It nearly grazed them—the child gasped and Madrone squeezed its mouth closer to her. They swung wildly and crashed against the wall of the shaft. She felt the edge of the ladder bruise her thigh, and swiftly freed one hand to grab it.

Safety. That ladder, so short a time ago the most fearful, dangerous thing she could imagine, now seemed a haven of safety. She could hook one leg into it and stabilize their swing, and when it was safe, she could climb back up, one rung at a time. Salvation!

At last the men above hauled their heavy load up and over the edge and out into the lobby of the elevator. A moment of silence—then the space exploded into oaths and curses. A huge chunk of concrete went crashing down through the shaft. She hoped to Goddess that Bird had taken cover.

"Stay down there, demon-fucking roachspawn! Stupid piece of pus! Die slow, in the dark!"

"Close the doors!" commanded the second voice.

"Why? Ratspill got no wings, can't fly."

"Don't leave evidence."

Grunting and puffing, scraping ... Madrone went cold with fear. How would they ever get them open again?

"Motherfucker's stuck!" the second voice complained.

"Leave 'em," the first voice said. "Been here too long. Get the fuck out before the Lash come sniffing."

A snort, and then the soft shuffle of their footsteps receding. It was the most beautiful sound Madrone had ever heard.

"Can you hold onto my back?" she asked the child. "That's right, put your legs around my waist, and your arms around my neck. Not too tight—don't choke me! Good. Okay, hold on."

Swiftly, she climbed up the ladder, the child clinging tight to her. Her hands shaking, she clipped herself and the child tightly in, then tugged on the rope to give Bird the all clear. For a long moment, nothing happened. What would she do if he didn't respond? What if he were dead, or had lost the rope, or ... but there came a blessed, answering tug. Haul away.

She pulled up the third jug in record time, in spite of her sore arms. Panic conferred a blessed numbness. She unhooked it and dropped the rope, praying that this time it would fall down straight. It did. Soon she felt Bird give the signal—climbing. She was wondering how she'd find the strength to raise him, but to her surprise there was no weight on the rope, only a series of tugs telling her to pull in the slack and belay. He must be using the ladder, she thought. He came swiftly upwards. Only in one section could she feel his weight, perhaps the ladder had rusted away and he was obliged to shimmy up the rope. Then, to her blessed relief, the weight slackened again.

She could see something moving in the depths. A figure was crawling up the wall, like a giant spider. Now she could hear him, panting a bit. All the while the child clung to her back, silent except for its panting breath.

Finally he was just below her. She looked down and saw that he, too, had a child clinging to his back. He looked up and saw her on the beam.

"You okay?" he asked.

"Yeah. You?"

Bird climbed up until his face was level with hers. He was grinning, she saw with a sudden flash of anger. He was enjoying this!

"I have penetrated the deep shafts of the Southlands," he said. "And now ..."

"What?"

"Now I see that you're with child!"

"Shut up and get us out of here!" she snapped.

"On belay."

She braced herself as he swung onto the beam.

"How in the name of Hella did you get out here, Miss Afraid-of-Heights?" He whistled as he surveyed her narrow perch.

"Don't ask."

Gently, he loosened the tight-gripped fingers of the child on his back, and set him down on the beam.

"Don't move. You'll be okay."

Then he slackened the rope, and leapt for the door. His right foot managed to sneak through, and he grabbed both edges with his hands and wedged himself in with his elbows. Squeezing through, he pulled the rope after him, shortening it until it just reached across to Madrone's platform.

She tied the water jugs on, one by one, and he hauled them over. Improvising a sling with a loop of rock, she tied the smaller boy in, and Bird pulled him up to safety. The larger boy shook his head at her and crept confidently along the beam, levered himself onto the ledge and out through the door.

Bird threw the rope back to her. She clipped on, unclipped her safety line, and made her own way back along the ledge as swiftly as she could.

"Good thing you jammed these," she said as she squeezed through the doors. "Those men—they were going to close them. We would have been stewed."

"Don't think about it," Bird said. "We weren't. Now let's get the furry duck out of here!"

⁓

They hoisted the jugs and ran quickly through the corridors, the two boys sticking close beside them. Their flight left a clear trail through the dust and Madrone prayed that they'd make the entrance before the Lash followed it and found them.

They reached the fire door unmolested and Bird gave it a hard shove. It didn't open. He set down the jugs, put all his weight against it and pushed. It moved a millimeter or two.

"*Mierda!*" Bird said. "It's not the lock—someone's blocked it from the outside. We're trapped!"

"There's got to be another way out," Madrone said.

They hurried back through the corridors, squeezing between mammoth chunks of fallen concrete. Shards of broken glass loomed like two-dimensional mountains on either side of them.

The older child ran ahead.

"Here!" he cried.

He stood by a wall of glass, now cracked and crazed, too high to climb over. But there was a small hole in one corner. The boys could squirm through. Bird and Madrone would have to follow.

Madrone covered her hands with the sleeves of her jacket, got down on the ground and wormed her way to the other side. Bird pushed the water jugs through to her. As she pulled them out, they heard the sound of boots marching, and voices. Bird dove through himself, oblivious to cuts and scratches.

Once outside, they picked up their precious water and ran. They could hear blocks of concrete being shoved away from the fire door, which was just around the corner.

"Let's go," Bird whispered. "Hopefully it will take them a while to check out the interior—but they'll find our tracks through the dust and see where we came out."

They ran, jugs in arms, with the boys speeding just ahead. Bird directed them on a roundabout route through back alleys and across yards, away from the high-rise and away from the Refuge.

Finally they stopped in the covered doorway of a shop with shattered windows. They hushed their breathing and listened for any sounds of pursuit. But there were only the ordinary sounds of night, the rustle of rats in the shadows, the occasional soft hoot of one of the owls that had taken up residence in the ruins.

Madrone had no idea where they were, but Bird seemed to have a map in his head. He led them swiftly back through the ruins.

As the black sky lightened to indigo, they reached what they had begun to call the Gateway of the Dead. The first rays of the rising sun crept like probing fingers over the empty rib cages, the jutting jawbones and blank eye sockets. The skeletal figures seemed to come alive with the light, to glow with some eerie animation.

The boys froze, struck dumb with terror.

"It's okay," Madrone murmured. Seeing its effect on the children, she began to feel more confident that their tableau of death might actually work to frighten away intruders. "Don't be scared. The dead won't hurt you. They are our friends. Our defenders."

"As long as you're with us, you're safe," Bird said. "But don't try to sneak away on your own, or bring the police back here. The dead will know. They'll get you."

Madrone gave him a furious look. "I'm trying to reassure them," she hissed.

"I know. But we don't want them trying to escape and bringing back the Lash," he whispered in her ear.

Home, Madrone thought as they wound through the passage, the subdued boys trailing behind. In spite of everything, this pile of rubble has come to feel like home.

Chapter Twenty-Six

T HE BADLANDS ENDED ABRUPTLY IN A STARK CLIFF THAT LOOMED above them, marking the edge of a gigantic sinkhole they'd been marching through. On the west side, erosion had dumped a mountain of loose soil and upended tree trunks. On the east side, a broken-off section of asphalt lay sloped from the valley floor to the plateau above, like a tilted table-top.

They'd been marching now for more than a week and they'd developed a rhythm, a routine that Cress found himself settling into. Trudge on all day, then make camp. Set up tents and shelters, run through training exercises and target practice while the kitchen cooked them up a dinner of simple hearty stews and baked potatoes or bowls of quinoa. Eat, set the watch, and collapse into a sleeping bag or stay awake doing those things that soldiers have always done, playing cards, swapping tales, bragging about their physical prowess. Uncomfortable, sometimes grueling, sometimes boring, but oddly familiar now, as if his life in the City before the invasion was only a jumbled dream of flowers and ripe fruit and hydrological calculations.

They halted the army at the base of the slope, and Cress and River clambered up to its rim where they could lie flat on the ground and scout the lands beyond. Smokee followed and threw herself down beside them.

A barbed-wire fence marked the boundary of the cultivated farmlands on more fortunate ground that had not collapsed. Spread below them was a flat stretch of fields that shimmered with waves of heat that rose up even as the sun dipped below the rim of mountains behind them in the west. The bleached, white soil reflected the red sunset glare, and the land seemed bathed in blood.

Cress whipped out his binoculars. Lines of workers moved down the field, picking ears off the cornstalks growing out of the desiccated earth. They wore colorless rags, with tattered old baseball caps or filthy wraps

of cloth on their heads. He caught a glint of light—around each worker's wrist was a metal bracelet. That was how they were controlled. The
guards could dial up pain to keep any unruly worker in line. He saw no
other fences or bars, no physical barriers.

His eyes followed one bent old crone who bore on her back a huge
basket of corn almost as big as she was. She sank to her knees under the
weight, and for a long moment it seemed that she wouldn't rise again.
Then a young girl came over, a faded red scarf around her head, and
offered her arm. Slowly, painfully, the old woman pulled herself back up.

From across the field came a tall figure, striding with an angry confidence that showed clearly even at a distance. He swung a long baton at
the old woman. Even from the distance, Cress could hear the crack as it
split her skull and knocked her back down.

The guard slapped the young woman across the face and batted her
ass like a baseball as she hurried back to the ranks of workers. The old
woman lay, face down in the dirt, her limbs twitching like a dog dreaming of squirrels. Then they fell still.

After moonset, in the darkest part of the night, Cress and River crept
down the hill to scout the plantation. It was a small village in itself, with
a huge, metal storage barn and makeshift barracks of corrugated tin.
They must be impossible ovens in the heat of the day, Cress thought, and
not much better at night. But in the heat of the day the workers would be
out in the fields, under the blazing sun.

It didn't bear thinking about. Bare, compacted ground stretched
around them. Farther away, a row of moldering double-wide trailers
housed the overseers. They could hear gruff voices and rough laughter.

In the center, a cylindrical metal tank perched high on a rusty water
tower. Atop that was a radio tower made of metal that held a satellite
dish and a small transmitter.

Far over to one end stood an old wooden farmhouse, painted a flak-
ing white, with a long, sagging front porch where maybe once a farm
wife had rocked a baby or shelled beans in the cool of a light summer
breeze. The bosses' quarters, Cress thought. Surrounding it were the
blackened skeletons of shade trees. There was a light inside.

River led Cress in a slow crawl around the perimeter. They noted
where the fence was low, and where the transformers that kept it charged
with electricity were located. It was topped with lines of razor wire that
slanted not outwards, but inwards, designed not so much to protect
against attack from without as to prevent escape from within.

When River and Cress returned to camp, they explained their plans
to Smokee. For once, she just listened without saying much. She seemed
content to follow River's lead.

An hour before dawn, they roused the army quietly. They'd many times lectured the troops on the need for efficiency and silence, and they'd drilled to practice the silent take-down of the camp. Now Cress was gratified to see their training paid off. Down came the tents, out came packs and weapons. Platoons and affinity groups and divisions formed up, and barely a murmur of sound rode the dawn breeze.

Low hills like the knuckles of folded hands cradled the flat plantation fields. Ravines split the fingers of the ridges, and Cress took two divisions, about a hundred men, down the eastern draw. Smokee took her women and another fifty fighters down the west.

They crept silently down the dry creek bed, crouching low to avoid radar. Cress felt a mixture of excitement and dread. This was his first real command. He'd been the one to advocate for armed resistance during the invasion, but he was overruled and he'd confined himself to sabotage until the final battle when many of the Stewards' soldiers rebelled and turned on their masters. He'd faced death and danger many times, but he had never actually been in charge of troops, never responsible as he was now for lives not his own. He'd never actually killed another human being.

His hands were shaking, just a bit, and he forced himself to take some deep breaths, to practice the calming and grounding techniques they used in the City. The ravine smelled of dust, and he caught a chemical tang off the fields.

When they were in range, a sniper took aim at the radio tower with one of the long-range bazookas they'd confiscated from the warship. A whoosh, a crack—the transmitter toppled. From the barracks arose one loud, unified scream of surprise and pain, then silence. The bracelets, Cress thought. He hoped they hadn't killed the prisoners as they shorted out.

River took his hand-picked troops, recruited from his old unit, to the farmhouse. They crawled on their bellies to stay under the radar until they reached the fence of chain links topped with razor-wire that enclosed the farmyard. Threetwo, who now called himself Ace, wielded a pair of heavy bolt-cutters that snipped through the metal.

Two huge pit bulls streaked towards them, barking furiously. The door opened and a guard came out, gun cocked. One of the snipers shot it out of his hands as another shot the dogs and Ace cut open a rough hole in the fence.

The guard cried out, and another five guards poured out the door— to face a phalanx of rifles as the men poured through the opening.

River barked a command. Ace and his crew broke the lock on the great gates that opened to the fields and shoved them apart. Cress and Smokee's troops streamed through. They surrounded the trailers as Smokee and her Valkyries broke open the door to the workers' barracks.

Ragged figures poured out, carrying sad little bundles of belongings and streaking for the road. Smokee stood for a moment, helpless, not sure what to do. If they panicked and ran away, they would surely die without water or be quickly recaptured. Worse, they might alert the plantations down the way to the attack, and the army would lose the advantage of surprise.

Cress came swiftly up behind Smokee and fired a series of shots above the heads of the fleeing debt slaves. "Workers of the Southlands, don't panic!" he cried in as loud a voice as he could muster. "We're not here to harm you, we're here to liberate you!"

"Stop them!" River called to his troops, who barred the escape route.

Not yet reassured, the escapees halted with their bundles, looking warily around for other openings.

"We're not here to hurt you," Cress called out again. "We're the Army of Liberation, from the North, and we're here to free you."

There was a long moment of silence, then one of the workers let out a big cheer, and the others took it up. The noise rose up and rang off the metal barracks, filling the yard with the sounds of jubilation and rage.

Meanwhile, the bulk of the City troops had surrounded the trailers. When they were in position, Cress shot a rifle into the air and commanded the overseers to come out. They filed out—ten of them, pale and quivering in the dawn as the sun rose over the hills.

River had sent his old unit into the farmhouse, and they pushed before them five sorry guards, handcuffed and terrified.

Behind them, two of the soldiers half-dragged, half-shoved a muscular man dressed in casual but expensive clothes, real cotton and wool instead of the synthetics of the army uniforms. He writhed in their grip and spat defiance.

"You'll die for this, you demon-fucking rebel scum! I'll have your ass on a spike and your head in the dust!"

"Shut the fuck up," River told him and slapped him across the face. "Billies not in charge any more. In line to be roach food now, and a smart man be begging for mercy."

River set a double ring of his troops around the man and the overseers. The inner ring had their guns trained on the captives, the outer ring kept the furious liberated workers at bay. Then he, Cress, and Smokee held a quick conference in a dark corner back by the barracks.

"What do we do with them?" Cress asked.

"Shoot them," Smokee said.

"No," River said. "Not the way to begin."

"We don't have the resources to guard them," Cress said with some reluctance. Now that it came down to it, he wasn't sure if he could shoot another human being in cold blood. But there was a logic to the situation he had to follow. "If we let them go, they'll alert the other farms and our task will become much more difficult. More people will die—including more of us."

"Maybe they join us. Take a seat at the table." River said.

"But how can we trust them?" Cress asked.

"Gonna liberate people, gonna have to trust them." River said.

"They're the enemy," Smokee objected.

"I was the enemy, before I become a real person," River answered her. "You the enemy, too."

"No," said Smokee. "Not me."

River shrugged. "The dusters—they know which of these whips is cool and which is cruel."

Cress nodded. "Good idea. Let the liberated workers decide."

They held the trial on the bare ground between the barracks and the trailers. They cleared a ring, with the soldiers holding back the seething, simmering mob of freed debt slaves. Only the troops with their guns kept them from boiling over and ripping the overseers apart, limb from limb.

But River seemed to know instinctively how to enlist their cooperation.

"Want to burn the place down—don't blame you!" he shouted. "But best to think first. Another plantation just like this over that hill, and another one after that. Liberating this place—easy! Overseers not expectin' an Army of Liberation. Stay quiet, maybe thass gonna hold for the next place, and the next. Sooner or later, bigsticks gonna figure it out and be ready, but until that time, smarter to stay below the radar."

Cress carried on. "We've liberated this farm, and that's a success. But we can't hold this place against the Stewards' Army if they come back in force for revenge. But here's what we can do, we can liberate another farm, and another—until we have a big enough piece of land that we *can* hold. Then we control the food supply. They've got to come begging to us for chips. And then the Stewardship is over!"

Another loud cheer rose up.

Buoyed by his success, Cress expanded. "We're not a mob, we're a democracy. And we're going to show that we are by giving this crowd of scum a fair trial. You all will decide their fate!"

They dragged the first overseer into the ring. He was a hulking big man, with a black fringe of hair around a pasty face.

"Here's how we do it," Cress said. "Anyone who has anything to say can step forward. Speak for yourself—tell us what you've seen with your own eyes or experienced, don't repeat gossip. Good or bad, for him or against him, whatever it is, we want to hear it. At the end, when we've listened to everyone who wants to speak, we'll decide his fate all together. Don't be shy!"

The woman in the red scarf stepped forward. She still moved like a young girl, Cress noted, her body upright and her step elastic, but her face was lined and wizened from the sun, her blue eyes faded.

"You—you killed the old lady, just this morning," she accused him. "You're a brute. You don't deserve to live."

The overseer spat at her. "A slacker, like the rest of you scum!"

"She was old!" Now tears streamed down her face. "Mariah was the heart of this place. She was kind to me, when they brought me here. She was kind to everyone, even in this hell. She told us to help one another. And now she's dead—she never got to see the liberation."

"Do you have anything to say in your own behalf?" Cress demanded.

"Kill me, go ahead. The Stewards will hang you up in a meat locker and feed your balls to rats."

One after another, the overseer's victims stepped forward to recite a long litany of his cruelties. The sun was well overhead, and the heat growing uncomfortable, before they were finished.

"Verdict?" Cress asked the crowd.

"Death!" they shouted in a united voice.

Cress picked up his pistol, then hesitated. He had gaffed fish and gutted them. He had killed chickens, with a prayer and a quick chop to the neck. This was just the same, he told himself, only bigger. The man was puffing himself up to look hard and brave, but sweat pooled on his brow and his pasty face was dead-white. Surely there was some prayer that should be offered, to the battle Goddess Morrigan perhaps, or Huitzilopochtli, God of War....

Smokee grabbed the gun from Cress, took aim, and pulled the trigger. The shot blasted through the man's head. Blood spurted out his mouth. He died with his eyes wide open in a look of terrified surprise.

She watched him fall with a cold sense of satisfaction. One small blow for her lost child, her lost life. She was no longer a starving creature in a cage, at the mercy of every whim of power and cruelty. Now she was the one who could make the strong men cringe and beg. She felt a rush of pleasure, something like sex but more like cleaning off a really dirty stove, back when she had had a home, seeing the grease disappear, and the surface gleam white. One nasty piece of dirt removed from the enamel surface of the world.

Cress pushed his way through the crowd, stumbled into the field behind the trailers, and threw up.

Ace and Deuce, another soldier from River's old unit, pushed a second overseer into the ring. He was a giant of a man, puffed up with unhealthy fat. He was blubbering and sobbing, and the crotch of his pants were soaking.

The same young woman stepped up. It was clear to River that she was a leader in the group, and he made note of that.

"Name?" he asked her. The relinquished had names, he knew. To ask for a name was to acknowledge that they were real people who had fallen into this hell.

The woman took a moment to gather herself together, as if stating her name would be a declaration, something that required strength and a firm stance.

"Judith," she finally said.

"Judith, you in charge here. You all gonna tell us which of these suckbloods die, and which ones worthy to live."

"I'm sorry, I'm sorry. Please, please don't kill me! I never wanted to be an overseer. I only did it because they said if I didn't, I'd have to relinquish my wife and daughter! I only did it for them!" the guard pleaded.

"You weren't the worst," Judith admitted.

An older man stepped forward. "He gave me water, one time, when I was about to pass out."

"He used to slip me extra food," said a teenage girl. "And he didn't try to fuck me for it."

Others stepped forward to testify to hidden acts of humanity.

"Okay, okay," Smokee said. She turned to River, shaking her head. "You say it."

"There's a place for you at our table, if you will choose to join us," River said.

The man nodded eagerly. "Yes, yes! I can help. I'll tell you everything I know!"

Smokee was conscious of feeling a small sense of disappointment.

"Be watching you," River warned. "Unit One Oh One, you in charge of this stick. One wrong move … " He formed his thumb and forefinger into a gun and pulled the trigger.

Next the man in the good clothes from the farmhouse was led into the ring. He stared around himself defiantly.

"And what was your role?" Cress asked him.

The man simply spat. Cress turned to Judith, who shrugged.

"Never saw him before."

"I'm a businessman," the man barked. "I have no part in this operation. I am simply here to secure supplies."

"Too goodly to get your hands dirty!" taunted a big male worker who looked like he'd once been well-muscled but now was merely gaunt. "But not too goodly to take the profits!"

"He's an agent from the factories," the fat overseer said eagerly. "They set the policies and the work quotas."

"What do you have to say to that?" Cress asked.

The man spat again, and before he could make any other comment, Smokee shot him in the temple.

As the morning wore on, all the overseers were tried in the ring. Five more were judged salvageable, the others were shot on the spot. Smokee executed the first few, then River took the gun away from her.

"What the fuck are you doing?" she demanded.

"You enjoying it too much," he said.

She was enjoying it. Every bullet erased one of her child's tears. One more spot of grease gone. One small weight to restore a balance that could never be regained.

"Why shouldn't I?"

"The day you find your whelp, who you wanna be?" he asked.

After the last of the guards and overseers had been tried, Cress addressed the crowd of around a hundred liberated workers. "You have a choice. You can join up with the army, and come with us to liberate the other farms and the Southlands itself. Or you can stay here. This farm is yours, if you want it. Our soil healers and permaculturalists are on their way down, and they will help you restore it to health. Not everyone is a fighter—although we can use all who want to come. But we will also need food—real food, healthy food, not chipfodder, to feed the Southlands once we've liberated them."

"What if we don't want to do either?" A stooped, gray-haired man stood. His body was bent, and his limbs almost skeletally thin, but he was not truly old, Cress realized. Just hard-used.

"We have families, most of us," he went on. "For me, I'd be happy to join your army—but first I need to track down my wife and kids and liberate them!"

There was a loud roar of acclaim. River and Cress exchanged glances of alarm. They hadn't counted on this. Once a dozen former debt slaves started quizzing their old neighbors about their disappeared families, the Stewards would surely get wise to what was happening. But Smokee spoke up.

"I am your daughter," she cried. "I was relinquished. My family didn't run quick enough or far enough. I know what you been through."

She took a deep breath. She felt warm, glowing, as if she were filled with a fire akin to rage but better than rage. All eyes were on her. The attention was a wind fanning her flames, and she liked it, liked the clean feeling it left behind as it swept through her. It was like air when you'd been choking, water when you'd been dying of thirst.

Smokee the powerless pen-girl had been stripped of everything and everyone she loved. Smokee the fighter, the commander of Valkyries, the executioner of torturers, the defender of the weak, she had power.

"I know what it's like to wake up every day and ask yourself, 'What do I try to do today? Do I try to live or do I try to die? Which way can I hurt them more?'

"If you're alive in front of me right now, it's because you figured your death won't hurt them. A thousand deaths, a million, won't hurt them. They deal in death, feed on death!

"But if you live, then there's a chance. A fool's chance, a cheating con of a rip-off chance that will break your heart a thousand times over, but still a chance. And so, against your better judgment, you survive.

"Well now, we've got that chance. We are the survivors, and we can hurt them. We can take them down, and take back everything they took from us. Well, not everything. Not the years, and the deaths, and the hope that they stole, but we can take back our land and our lives and what's left of our families.

"But only if we stick together. If we each go off alone, we're weak and you'll be back on the work levy before a dog can fart. But if we stick together, nothing can stop us! We took this farm and we'll take another and another, until there are no more plantations, no more debt slaves, no more pens!

"We will find your families if they're still alive! Together! Only together! And we will free them. Together, only together! Not to run and hide and live a life in fear of the whips and the peepers—but to farm our own lands, raise our own babies and take them down to the beach to play in the sand, to give them day after bright new day of good memories to grow on.

"We will do that, you and I and every former debt slave and pen-girl and sojuh we can liberate. Together! Only together! And hope will no longer cheat us. Hope will be the bread that keeps us going on the road to freedom! Together!"

"TOGETHER!" echoed back the crowd. A loud roar of applause went up. Cress and River looked at each other, amazed.

"Bitch may earn her keep yet," River said quietly.

"And if we stay and farm?" Judith called out. "How much will we owe on the land, and the seed and fertilizer? How much you gonna charge for water?"

Cress stepped forward. "Water is free. Water is one of the Four Sacred Things that can't be owned—Earth, Air, Fire, and Water. Where the Army of Liberation passes, all debts are cancelled."

The freed workers stared blankly at each other for a long moment, as if they couldn't quite comprehend what the words meant. Then Judith began a tentative cheer that slowly grew stronger as other voices took it up.

Smokee sat down in the dirt. She felt weak suddenly, cold, as if some inner blaze had burned through its fuel and gone out. Had she really done that—stood up in front of people and shared intimate thoughts she'd never before admitted to another human being? But she'd seen those eyes set in grim, dusty faces light up as she spoke. And it felt good.

"All debts are cancelled," Cress was saying. "But we will need your help. If we succeed, we'll cut off the Stewards' food supplies, but we'll need something to take their place. We'll ask you to grow more than you need to feed yourselves, so that we can liberate the Southlands, not starve them to death."

"So what you're saying is that we'll pay off our debt with food production?" Judith said.

"We don't have debt in the North," Cress went on. "Our economy is labor-based, not monetary."

"What the jism does that mean?" asked a hard-bodied man with angry eyes.

"It means you get credit for your work. We all work—and we work hard, but there are no slaves and no masters."

"How's that possible?" an older woman asked.

"You put in your hours every week, and they get credited to your account. If you need more than your basic stipend—everyone gets credits to cover their basic needs like food and shelter—you draw on your account," Cress told her.

"That can't add up!" "What about cheaters?" "What if you can't work, if you're sick?" "So slackers get to do nothing?" A buzz of questions and exclamations rose from the crowd.

Cress blinked. The hot sun was beating down and sweat dripped down into his eyes. The corpses littering the ground were beginning to stink, and flies buzzed around them.

"I tell you what," he said to the crowd. "How about we bury the dead, and make ourselves some shade, and filter some water, and then we can sit down in comfort and discuss economics. And I imagine you'd all like something to eat and drink!"

Crews from the Army of Liberation were already setting up bucket filters filled with charcoal to take away the chemicals in the tap water. Others quickly erected a pavilion of shade cloth, stretching over the open ground like a giant wing. Volunteers began digging graves behind the trailers, and medics dragged the bodies away and dropped them in while chaplains said prayers.

The kitchen crew handed out rolls and nut butters and sweet jams to stave off the debt slaves' overwhelming hunger while the cooks prepared lunch. They set out jugs of filtered water, and for a long time the freed workers could only drink and munch and drink some more, tears of relief in their eyes.

But when at last their immediate needs were met, they crouched together under the shade cloth that was affixed to the north side of one of the double-wides. Much to his relief, Cress found a young economics student in the ranks. Salim was delighted to hold forth to a fascinated crowd.

"Our unit of value is the calorie. We analyze everything by the amount of energy in it—embodied energy, both from natural resources and human labor. Work is organized by the guilds. Yes, you could cheat on counting up your hours, but your guild-mates would know and all the records are open. And you can't cheat that much—because there are a finite number of hours in the day."

Salim was young and filled with enthusiasm for his subject. Cress watched him, realizing how sleek and moist and well-fed he looked, with his dark, shining eyes and even teeth. Next to him, the crowd of former debt slaves looked like shriveled, dried-up husks, their fever-bright eyes too big in their shrunken faces. They stared at Salim with a glazed look, barely fathoming what he was saying. He could have been speaking Chinese.

"We don't encourage people to store up credits," Salim said. "We want to keep them circulating, because they represent productive, regenerative work and there's a lot to be done."

"What about saving your money?" an old crone asked. "Don't you want people to save for their old age?"

"You don't need to save for much, because we took Franklin Delano Roosevelt seriously when he talked about 'freedom from want, freedom from fear.' We've removed want and fear from the system." Salim smiled kindly as she looked at him, uncomprehending. "You don't need to save for your old age—because you will always get your basic stipend and it increases every year after you hit sixty. You don't need to save for disasters, because we meet them together."

Kit was standing at the edge of the crowd. She felt River's eyes on her, sensed him moving toward her. She wormed her way inwards and sat down, fixing her eyes on Salim and trying to look interested, although in truth his words were flowing over her like a shower of soothing but meaningless sounds.

"If you get sick or injured, if you need medical care or help at home— all those hours count toward someone's credits, but they're subtracted from the City's totals, not yours. Medical care is free. Nursing is free. Education is free. Some work groups, like doctors or healers or artists, get a stipend instead of counting hours as their work doesn't lend itself to keeping track of time like that."

"That's crazy," objected a blond young man whose mouth gaped with missing teeth. "How can you afford it?"

"How can we afford it?" Salim grinned and waved his arms expansively. "How can we *not* afford it? The better we educate our youth, the more productive they will be over a lifetime and the more we will have for all."

Kit risked a glance up and behind her. She caught the shadow of River's burly form moving toward the group, and quickly looked away. He was beginning to make her nervous, with his constant talk of liking and wanting. Who was a pen-girl, even a former pen-girl, to like or to want? What did it mean, anyway? When he was near, she felt a pleasant sensation, until he got too near. Then her stomach would clench and her jaw tighten, and yet sometimes she found herself leaning towards him, or breathing in a little more deeply than necessary to take in his smell, sweaty and manly. And yet the smell made her stomach churn, reminding her of too many violations, too much pain. But at the same time, something about his big, looming presence made her feel safe.

"When your system says they can't afford it," Salim went on, "what they really mean is they can't afford to forego the profits they make on the compounded interest of all those loans over time—and that's partly because they are making virtually nothing of true value any more. Mining the natural resources, using them up, instead of conserving and regenerating them. Every hour of your labor on this land degrades its value. But our agronomists and soil scientists and permaculturalists will come down here to heal the soil and replant—and every hour they spend will rebuild topsoil and increase the earth's ability to produce. That's the real 'interest' on our investments."

River confused her. That was the word. The other girls, the Valkyries, teased her. Jealous, she thought, because River the bigstick in this army.

That was a good feeling, that bigstick fighter took notice of this pen-girl. No, not pen-girl. Had to stop thinking that. Valkyrie. Val. This Val. Me. He likes me. But do I like him? What's *like* mean, anyway?

Liked the sweeties. Liked the babies. More than liked.

The first one, that sweet little boy. She remembered his warmth and milky smell and the tiny mews of pleasure as he nursed. Almost worth living for that. But the billies took the little pup away. Kit had wanted to die, then, but she didn't. Still, second one wasn't the same. A girl, for one thing. Didn't get the boy bonus, the extra time on hiatus, the extra rations of chips and sweeties.

But more than that. Every sweet minute held a shadow of what was to come.

Like her? How could tubo like her? Didn't really even know her. Didn't really know herself. Didn't know who was her mare, whether the poor rag had cried when they took her away. Didn't even know when she was born or how old she was, or which sojuh had spawned her, or why she'd come into this cruel and hateful world. Like her? Who was a pen-girl to be liked?

"We direct our labor regeneratively, and we create far more true wealth than we draw upon," Salim was saying with a confident smile. "At the end of every year, we do an accounting to see where we are. We've yet to have a year where we draw out more hours than we put in—even during the big epidemics. Mostly we have a surplus, which we invest in long-term projects—planting trees, building soil, creating art."

The cooks interrupted the lesson, setting out big pots of chili and cornbread they'd baked in solar ovens. The liberated debt slaves lined up and fell on the food with cries of delight.

"Go slow!" the cooks warned. "Got to get your stomachs used to eating real food again!"

But the freed workers had not been raised on chips, but on such food as their families could earn or scrounge until at last the debts overwhelmed them and they were taken to the work plantations. They were thrilled to eat real beans, the sweet, moist cornbread with little chunks of soft kernels in it and, wonder of wonders, real butter and honey to put on it. Salim sat at a table and continued to answer questions from those who could tear themselves away from the tastes and smells of the dinner.

Cress took his bowl of chili and wandered away from the crowd. He squatted for a moment in the shade of the barracks, but a crew was digging graves nearby and tossing the corpses of the overseers into them. The sight turned his stomach.

He no longer wanted to eat, but he knew he had to keep up his strength, so he took his bowl and crouched in the narrow strip of shade on the sagging porch of the old farmhouse. He was ashamed of his reaction to the killings, as if he had failed some basic test of toughness and resolve. He'd been okay in the actual battle, prepared to fight and even to die. But he had not been prepared for those cold executions that River performed so perfunctorily and Smokee with such glee.

Yet he didn't see another option. He would have to toughen up.

—————

River took his plate of food and looked around for Kit. She was sitting at a makeshift table, plywood laid atop empty water drums, in the midst of a crowd of Valkyries. There was a space on the bench beside her and he set his plate down.

"Okay if I sit here?" he asked her.

"Don't see no sign sayin' it saved for a good-lookin' man," said a red-haired Valkyrie, and they all broke out in a chorus of snickering and giggling.

He gave them a grimace of a smile and sat down. Kit's eyes were on her plate. The eyes of five other Vals were on him. He felt them, hot and searching, like the sights of laser guns.

He took a spoonful of chili, chewed, and swallowed. They wouldn't get to him.

"Like this stuff?" he asked Kit.

She shrugged. "Eatin' it."

He took another bite. The eyes followed him. They were beginning to irritate him, but he decided not to show it.

"Cooks say, dip the cornbread in the beans," he told Kit as he pushed a lump of his bread into the bowl. It came up red and dripping, and as he shoveled it into his mouth a little smear of chili dribbled down his chin. Red-hair giggled. He ignored her.

"Doin' okay?" he asked Kit. "First real fight today. Scared?"

She shrugged again. "This girl stay back with the cooks."

"Tubo scared?" asked the redhead.

River shook his head. "Bred to fight. Born for it, trained for it. Trained to be a weapon, not a man. Now that weapon turn against them."

She snickered again, and River finally lost patience.

"Never seen a man eat before?" he asked.

"Call that eatin'? Or droolin'?"

Rage flashed over him. How dare a pen-girl talk to a sojuh like that! His arm moved involuntarily up to slap her, but Kit caught hold of it. He shook her off roughly, grabbed his bowl, and stomped off. Laughter rippled behind him.

He stalked over to a stump on the other side of the barracks, still shaking with rage. Some part of him hoped that Kit would follow him, but she didn't. Instead he sat alone, trying to breathe deep like Maya had taught him. Stupid fucking slits! He didn't have to put up with that shit.

But that wasn't really what was making him mad, he realized. It was Kit. Did she like him, or didn't she? Couldn't fucking spit three words out of her mouth? "I like you." Or not. Was she using him, her ticket to get her fucking precious baby back—a baby that was dead, most likely, sold off to the pleasure pits for those who got their hots from pain.

And suddenly he was lost in a place of such bleak desolation that he wanted to scream himself, if only to break the silence. But his own suppressed screams, his own stifled cries, were the very fabric of that silence.

His chili had grown cold. He dumped it into a bush. Fuck it, he was no limpdick to cry over a slit. He was a fighter, with a job to do.

———

When darkness fell, the techies set up a screen and a projector and showed movies that the Entertainment Guild had prepared before the army left the City. While the freed workers took a virtual tour of the North, scouts went out to recon the neighboring farms. Cress, River, and Smokee met in Council with the reps from different divisions and units, using the living room of the old farmhouse. It stank of old cigarette smoke, spilled beer, and moldering food, but with all of them working together with brooms and mops and rags, they made it livable in half an hour.

"Gotta push on," Smokee said as they pulled up chairs or sank into badly-sprung couches. Her eyes were glowing and her face flushed with excitement. "Strike the next farm tomorrow—maybe even tonight, before the thrashers figure out what hit 'em."

"We've got a hundred liberated debt slaves to consider," said Lee from the Medics Guild. "They may be willing to fight, but they're in no shape to march out of here. It's a miracle they're still standing."

"And they'll need training," Cress said. "You don't become an army just by wishing it so."

"Got plenty units ready to go," River said. "Take the breeds and the squabs, leave the dusters here to feed up and train."

"Don't call them dusters," objected Erik from the Farmers' Guild. "Or debt slaves. That keeps them victimized. Call them *liberados*."

"What's that mean?" Smokee asked.

"The liberated."

"In the forbidden tongue," she said.

"Not forbidden any more," Cress said firmly. *"Vivan los liberados! Viva el ejército de liberacion!"*

Chapter Twenty-Seven

WE'VE GOT TO FIND THE SPRINGS," MADRONE SAID. SHE'D JUST been warmed into waking by the high sun overhead. Bird was stirring next to her in the concrete alcove where they'd laid out their pads and sleeping bags on one side of the plaza.

The boys lay asleep in a huddle nearby. Their arms and legs were curled as if even in sleep they were guarded.

"We need to find the springs," Madrone repeated. The sun's warmth felt good on her sore shoulders. Her arms ached and her whole body felt bruised and battered. "I can't do that again. *You* can't do it, regardless of what you think you can do. In any case, we'll never be able to collect enough water that way to grow a garden. Not to mention washing."

Washing had risen higher on her list of priorities after a night spent in close proximity to the rescued boys. Madrone longed to clean them up, cut their hair and bathe away the caked dirt. Underneath the filth, they might be rather attractive children, but for now they were too dirty to tell. She wanted to hold them and mother them, but now that the adrenaline was gone, her nose rebelled at their sour, rank smell and her stomach retched. Not a good way to establish a bond of trust—fighting down nausea.

Bird roused himself, stretched, and set a pot of water to boil for porridge.

"The springs," he agreed. "Top on our list of priorities!"

He added ground acorns and a handful of their precious oatmeal, and stirred the mixture together. As it bubbled, the boys woke, sitting up and looking at them with wide eyes.

"Breakfast!" Bird said cheerfully. He dished the porridge into a couple of the old cans they'd scavenged for tableware, and handed the boys each a spoon from their camping gear.

The boys stared at the porridge blankly.

"Whazzat?" asked the older one.

"That's food. Porridge. It's good. Eat it."

"Got chips?" he asked.

"No chips," Bird said decisively. "Chips are slave food. This is real food."

"Don't like it," said the younger boy.

"Try it."

"Sick!"

"Look, you wanna eat? This is what we've got."

The younger boy took a bite, made a face, and spat it out. The older boy followed suit—but spat at the younger. Within a minute they were embroiled in a food-spitting fight.

"Stop that!" Bird thundered in a deep voice of command. Madrone looked at him in surprise, suppressing a smile. The Voice of Dad, she thought. It was a whole new side of him.

"Look, you wanna eat, we'll feed you," Bird said sternly. "You don't wanna eat what we feed you, go ahead and starve. But we don't have food to waste."

He took the bowls of porridge away and set them up on a high ledge. The boys began to whine.

"What are your names?" Madrone asked. The boys stared at her blankly. "Where are you from? Do you have parents?"

All these questions were met with the same staring silence. Madrone sighed. "Well, we'll have to call you something."

"You name yours, and I'll name mine," Bird suggested.

Madrone looked closely at the small boy she'd snatched from the air. His wary face glared from under a snarl of matted hair. He had sullen brown eyes under crusted lashes, and all she could tell of his skin was that it was not darker than the layer of dirt that covered him.

"How about Zapata?" she said. "A good, insurrectionary name."

"Great," Bird said. "Then I'll name mine Montezuma. We can call them Zap and Zoom."

"I'm serious!"

"So am I. Zap and Zoom, first citizens of the City of Refuge."

Zap and Zoom were not cuddly children—even had they been clean enough to cuddle. They stared a lot and rarely spoke. When they did speak, they whined, and fought, and called each other names in the rough slang of the Southlands. They didn't eat for a full day, demanding chips. Finally, they got hungry enough to try the bean soup Madrone made for dinner, gobbling greedily, then throwing up. They pinched, hit, and bit each other, and only fear kept them from doing the same to Madrone and Bird.

Zap had a suppurating sore on his shin, which Madrone cleaned and bandaged, but he picked at the bandage and tore it off. Zoom had oozing ulcers on his neck, but he jerked away whenever she attempted to clean them and cover them with healing salve.

At night they didn't want a story or a hug or a kiss goodnight. In any case they were crawling with lice and Madrone was less than eager to hug them until she could wash and disinfect them. She only hoped that she and Bird had not picked up any hitchhikers during the boys' rescue. The very thought made her head itch, and she had to stop herself from scratching.

Madrone told Bird, and herself, that these were all the result of trauma and deprivation. Bird simply started referring to them as the Nasty Little Boys.

They spent the next few days hunting for the springs. From the topo maps and the historical record, they knew they had to be somewhere below, but the entrance could be anywhere, under fallen blocks of concrete, buried deep under tons of debris and fill. Still, when Harmony Village was built, one of the great attractions was the spa with its natural hot springs. They had to be close to the surface.

If they couldn't find the springs, they would not be able to build the Refuge—that much was clear. Even Bird was not eager to set out on another water raid. They rationed their water, and made it last as long as they could, drinking minimal amounts and scrubbing the cooking pots with sand. But by the end of the week, they were down to half a container, and a decision had to be made.

"Either we find it today," Madrone said, "or...."

"Or what?" Bird scraped the porridge pot with a stone, wiped the inside clean with a bandanna dedicated to the purpose, and then immersed the bandanna in a handful of water, squeezed it out, and hung it out to dry. The rinse water was rapidly becoming more porridge than water.

"We give up?" Madrone suggested, a slightly hopeful tone in her voice.

"How do we do that?" Bird asked.

"What do you mean?

"What does giving up look like?"

"We go back to Beth's?" she suggested.

"What do we do with Zap and Zoom?"

Madrone couldn't answer. There were no helpful households of Sisters here to take them in—any that existed would be swamped, drowned under the onslaughts of unwanted children. They were not attractive, in their unwashed state. None of Sara's former friends were likely to want to adopt them. Nor could they turn them over to the hill-boys, who were a band of guerrilla fighters, not nursemaids. Nonetheless, she couldn't in good conscience turn even Nasty Little Boys out on the streets to fend for themselves.

"All right, we can't give up," Madrone said. "Unless we go back north and take the NLBs with us."

"Is that what you want to do?" Bird asked.

It so was what she wanted to do that her whole body ached with the desire of it. Her skin craved the moisture of the City's foggy air, her dry throat ached for the sweet waters of its flowing streams.

"No," she said firmly. "Not until we do what we came to do. And what do you want?"

"I want a bath," he said lightly. "A long, hot soak in a hot tub, with you. And Zap and Zoom safely occupied somewhere far away."

"So we'd better find those springs," Madrone said.

In the end, it was Zoom who found them. He had a terrifying habit of disappearing into small holes, diving down into crevices and exploring enticing cavities. Madrone issued warnings, Bird ordered him to stop, but he ignored them both.

"Why would a child who was forced to do all this terrifying hole-diving for the water thieves go back to it on his own?" Madrone asked. "You'd think the last thing he'd ever want to do again is to go spelunking in the ruins."

"But you do go back," Bird said quietly. "You go back because the fear outside is easier to face than the residue it leaves inside you."

Madrone took his hand. He gave her that rueful smile, and squeezed her hand in reply.

They were exploring a new area of the ruins, farther east than they had gone before. A collapsed building stood alongside an open, park-like space, now brown and desiccated. Grecian pillars framed an entrance-way that was packed with concrete rubble.

"It kind of looks like a spa," Madrone said hopefully.

"Or a funeral home," Bird countered.

Zap scrambled up a mountain of rubble while Bird and Madrone picked out a careful path between hollows that could trap a foot or break an ankle. In places, concrete slabs had stacked themselves into a giants' stairway. On other slopes, small chunks of rubble lay like scree, waiting to be dislodged and slide down in an avalanche.

Zoom dove into a promising-looking hole and disappeared.

"Get back out here!" Bird yelled. "Montezuma! This mound isn't stable. It could shift and crush you like a bug!"

But Zoom ignored him, and Zap scampered up and followed the older boy into the dark.

The crevice was too tight for Bird and Madrone to enter, so they waited at the entrance, annoyed and a little scared.

From below, they heard Zap making strange sounds, gurgles that for one sharp moment Madrone feared were choking sounds. But as she listened, she realized that he was doing something she had never heard before. He was laughing.

"Over here!" Bird called. He'd found a stack of debris that included a few two-by-fours and a section of a steel beam. Together they carried them back and very carefully excavated a wider entrance, shoring it up with the beams.

When they finally squeezed through the narrow passage, they stepped out into a hollow space of darkness. Their crystal lights played over a wide, cavernous room, floored with cracked marble, studded with benches and pools. Above, as if some earthquake angel had decided to guard the waters, a great slab of a concrete wall had fallen but remained intact, forming a new, pyramidal roof that protected all that was below.

Pools and baths and fountains lay before them, some of them cracked and empty, but many still filled with water that bubbled up from below and spilled over the low marble-lined edges. One pool was steaming hot and smelled of sulfur, others were cool and clear.

In the center was a large, rectangular pool, big enough for swimming, and Madrone knelt beside it. She sniffed the water, tasted it with her bee senses. No chemical tang, no hint of pollution, no nasty beasties. Just water—pure, earth-filtered spring water. Abundant, beautiful, life-saving water.

She murmured a prayer of thanks as she plunged her hands in and scooped it up to drink. A broken tile jabbed into her knee and the rough edge, the pain, felt good to her. It proved that this was real.

Bird began to sing a water song, his voice echoing through the chamber in thanksgiving. Madrone rose and held his hand, adding her voice to his. They had water. They would live. The vision would go forward.

The boys were lying on their stomachs, their heads in the pool, gulping water as fast as they could get it down. Madrone called them back.

"Take it easy. You'll make yourselves sick. Just drink a little bit now, and don't worry. We can get more later."

They filled their water containers, went back to the surface, and made a good dinner of soup and tea, and as much water as they wanted to drink. Then they faced the challenge of bathing Zoom and Zap.

"It's the old recipe book—how do you bathe a Nasty Little Boy? First, catch him," Bird said. Zap and Zoom, having presumably never been bathed in their lives, were not eager to undergo the experiment. At first they had helped Madrone ferry buckets of hot water up to the surface. She had prepared an old washtub they had found in the ruins of a hardware store, and a few trips had easily filled it with a mix of hot and cool water. But as soon as the boys realized that the purpose of this exercise was immersion, they disappeared.

"Which do we catch first?" Madrone asked.

"Zoom. If we do him, Zap will go along. If we do Zap first, we may never see Zoom again."

They lured Zoom down with a packet of crackers Madrone had found in her supplies, promising him something very close to a chip. He came toward Madrone cautiously, and Bird swooped from behind, catching his arms and pinning them. It reminded Madrone of the many times they'd recaptured errant chickens who'd gotten out of their pens. It had been one of their chores when they were youngsters, as soon as the flocks built up after the Uprising. They'd named the most expert escape artist Red Emma.

"An anarchist love of freedom is not a desirable quality in a chicken," Maya used to say. Nor in a Nasty Little Boy, Madrone thought to herself.

Zoom kicked and screamed, but Bird held him firmly as Madrone reassured him over and over again that he was safe, and they weren't going to hurt him, only get him clean. But he yelled and wriggled and bit until Madrone began to fear that they would have to hurt him if only accidentally.

It was a dire struggle to wrestle his clothing off, and each layer that came off released a more putrid odor and revealed new festering sores. But finally they got him into the warm tub of water. He screamed, then, that they were boiling him, that he was being cooked alive. Bird simply held his shoulders down in the water, and after a while, he actually began to calm down. Madrone gave him soap and washcloth, and showed him how to scrub himself. She washed his hair with a natural enzyme from her medkit that killed lice, and brought out a scissors to trim it. She told him to wash his own small penis and buttocks.

After the bath Madrone rubbed ointment into his sores and dressed him in a new pair of jeans and a shirt, part of the haul they'd found in the shopping bags of the dead. She found herself looking at an attractive small boy with rough blond hair, gray-blue eyes, and a pasty skin. He appeared to be around eight years old, but it was hard to tell. He was far too thin, with prominent ribs and knobby vertebrae. But he looked now like a real child.

Once clean and dressed, Zoom strutted with pride. He taunted the still-unwashed Zap and called him dirty penspawn. Zap, not to be outdone, went quietly to his bath and submitted without a struggle, for which Madrone was devoutly grateful. She was exhausted from the battle with Zoom, and sadly in need of a bath of her own.

Zap, beneath the dirt, proved to have dark curly hair and wide, black eyes. His olive skin was piebald, unevenly tanned under the patches of dirt. He, too, was undeniably male, and just as skinny and malnourished. He seemed younger than Zoom, maybe six or seven years old. But they could both be older, and stunted in their growth—or younger. They had no idea when they were born, and no memory of how they came to be with the water thieves.

With the boys clean, they made up new pallets for their beds. Madrone blessed the ghost shoppers—the bags had yielded many treasures. She said a small prayer of thanks to the woman who had bought herself numerous pairs of new sheets that she had never got to take home and put on the bed. That made Madrone sad. Maybe she had broken off a love affair. Maya always said she bought new sheets whenever she shed a lover. Maybe those sheets were meant to be the start of a brave new chapter in a life she never got to live.

At any rate, they were a start now—she could take the boys' clothing and burn it, wash the blankets in hot sulfur water, and keep the vermin at bay.

With the boys bedded down, she and Bird descended to the springs. They lit votives from their gift-shop trove around the pools. From the hot pool, they drew buckets of water to sluice themselves clean, then lowered themselves into a warm tub and soaked away their aches.

"So this is how you wage revolution down here in the Southlands," Madrone said.

Bird smiled and nuzzled her, letting his hands wander over to cup her full breasts, uplifted by the water.

"This is it," Bird said. "This is the refuge. Heart of the city we build inside the city."

"And how will we defend it?" Madrone murmured.

"The Dead will be our defenders."

"Who will come to it?"

"The lost. The desperate."

"How will they find it?"

"We will tell the story. We will sing the song."

Chapter Twenty-Eight

THE ARMY OF LIBERATION WAS REWARDED FOR ITS MERCY TO THE overseers by a flood of information. They were debriefed over the next day by the army Council, composed of River, Cress, and Smokee as well as representatives from all the key support services—cooks, tech, medics, logistics, communications, and restoration, and Judith as a rep for the liberados. She was rapidly showing a talent for leadership, and Cress suspected she would run the farm after the army moved on.

"You've got to deal with the chips." Ron, the plump first overseer they'd spared, spoke up ardently as they sat in the front room of the old farmhouse. He had watched the videos of the City with rapt attention, and now was eager to please, his pale blue eyes blinking constantly as if the light of liberation were almost too much for them to bear.

"Chips? Like the food?" Cress asked, confused.

"No, the other kind of chip. Computer. We chip all the debt slaves, so if they run away, we can find them. Or destroy them. Put a burst of power through the chips, burn 'em up from the inside out."

"*Mierda!* You mean they could be tracking all the liberados?" Cress said in alarm.

"Soon as Central Command finds out about the raid, they will be," Ron said.

"Fuck!" Smokee said. "How far can they reach?"

"Maybe ten miles."

"We've got to get the chips out!" said Susan, the chief medic. "Right away!"

She ducked out of the meeting without waiting for confirmation, and ran to the medics' tent.

Judith's hand went up to the back of her neck. Her eyes darted nervously to the door, but she stayed in the meeting.

River noticed her agitation.

"Not likely they get a message out to CenCo just yet," he said calmly.

"Not likely, but possible?" Cress asked, worried.

"Possible," River acknowledged.

"Go get that fucking thing out of your neck!" Smokee barked. Judith scurried out. Smokee turned to Ron. "What other little surprises you got that we should know about?"

"Every command post has a central coms area," Ron went on. "It's always well-protected, in the heart of the officers' quarters, most often underground, if there's a basement or something. That's where they got the computers. They can communicate with other plantations, and with Central Command. They got a map screen that shows the location of every volunteer and every officer."

"Who are the volunteers?" Cress asked. "What do they volunteer for?"

"That's what they call the debt slaves," Smokee said.

"Officers are yellow dots, volunteers are red. Click on one, and you find the name or the number," Ron explained.

"Kind of like a high-tech version of the enchanted map of Hogwarts," murmured Topaz, one of the techies. "Cool."

"They got a day watch and a night watch and two swing shifts," Ron said. "Two guys, always on the screens, always scanning for escapes. They see a dot out of place, they slam it with juice. A little bit, and you fall to the ground screaming. Too much, or you got a weak heart or somethin', and you're dead."

"So we took out their coms and personnel, but if they're in contact with other plantations, or some central command, we could lose our edge of surprise on the next one," Cress said anxiously.

"In the field, we each got a muck," Ronald went on. "That's a M-U-C—stands for mobile unit for communications. We can call in, or we can access the map screen if we need to track a runaway."

"Anyone still have theirs?" Topaz asked eagerly.

"I do," Ron said. "Don't work, now that the mainframe's dead."

"It will," Topaz said. "It'll work for us!"

By the time the others emerged from their meeting, the medics had already set up a field hospital to remove the chips. They sat close to the surface of the skin at the base of the skull, not deeply embedded, but it was sometimes a delicate matter to locate them if they had been in for a long time, and infection was always a worry. But the liberados were tearfully grateful to have them out.

The techies cleared away the debris of garbage and bottles and sad little splats of used condoms from the rec room, and set up a circle. The room still smelled faintly of urine and blood, even after they smudged it clean, but the techies lit some incense and closed the doors. Because they were short-staffed, with only five of them accompanying the army south, they asked Cress to attend and scribe. It was a huge honor, and he had always been curious about just what they did, but it was also late after a long day and he would have liked some sleep. But there would be no sleep for any of them until they came up with a strategy that could move them forward and safeguard what they'd already achieved.

The techies set up their equipment in a big space they'd cleared in the center of the room. They laid out a silk carpet and placed a huge crystal in the center.

Topaz handed Cress a bamboo pole wrapped with silk. "Hold this," she said, and proceeded to unfold a geodesic dome with a frame of bamboo and panes of silk, like a giant tent that filled most of the room. Beneath it, they arranged pads and pillows and a low folding chair for Cress with an arm rest that held a keyboard.

The techies were unnaturally pale, as if they rarely saw daylight. Even Jet's mahogany skin had an underlying pallor. Their bodies were too perfectly sculpted, as if they honed them in a gym doing orchestrated exercises but rarely engaged in physical work. Their hair was clipped short or shaved off, and aside from adornments of jade or amethyst or rose quartz stones in earrings and bracelets, their clothing was loose, simple, and neutral in color. They sported crystalline tattoos on their foreheads, intricate webs of lines and angles. It was hard to tell what gender they were and to them, that seemed to matter very little. They referred to one another not as "he" or "she" but as "they," singular or plural, and indeed their individuality often seemed submerged into the whole.

"You'd think you'd have some higher tech way of recording your findings than me typing them into a keyboard," Cress said.

"Oh, we do," Jasper assured him. "But we need to introduce you to the crystals. You're one of the commanders of the army, the only one we judge can handle this. We want them to know you and respond to your commands at need."

"I'm not a commander," Cress said. "I'm first rep."

"Right. As we were saying," Jasper went on, "by accompanying us and recording what they say, you show respect. It's a ritual."

Cress took a deep breath, and hoped he could stay awake as the lights dimmed. The techies handed him a cap to put on his head. It was crocheted of some sparkly synthetic fiber, like a web that hugged his scalp. Jet carefully parted Cress's thick black hair so the nodes could make contact with his flesh.

"Now you see why we keep ours short," Topaz murmured.

The others were fitting on their own caps. They lay down with their heads in a circle, their bodies radiating out like a five-pointed star, and began breathing in a slow, unified rhythm to bring themselves into trance. Cress synchronized his breathing with theirs, and forced himself to relax.

The lights dimmed and the dome above took on a pearly glow. Beams of light appeared, streaming out in all directions, in pure optic colors—red, yellow, violet. He was inside a sphere of light with shafts extending out like sea urchin spines. Then they began to fold back upon one another in a jumble like a cosmic game of pick-up sticks, a three-dimensional maze, a rat's nest of rays.

He saw five speeding globes of light that carried him in their wake. They were confident, familiar with this strange world. He forced his body to breathe, to not panic as they towed him along at unimaginable speeds. Light speed.

You'll be okay. The reassurance was not so much words but a burst of feeling-tone, a color of soft, leafy green that enveloped him even as their speed increased. They were racing along lines of force, tracking their way through a labyrinth of pure colors, trails of reds and blues and purples that were brilliant and clear, the essence of light. On and on they went, and Cress wondered how in Hella's name he was supposed to identify anything at that speed to record, let alone write it down. But at last they halted in the center of a glowing chamber where questing fingers of light played upon the walls like the beams of a searchlight.

You okay? Again it was not so much a question as a wave of contact, checking on him. He forced himself to breathe again. Dimly he could remember one of his teachers warning them about techie-tripping, a fad among the teens when they had first begun to explore the use of intelligent crystal technology. You need training and preparation, Ms. Winslow had warned. Otherwise, it's easy to get so distracted your body literally forgets to breathe.

The beams radiated out from a glowing, pulsing sphere. Cress could hear it, like the harmonics of a crystal singing bowl, pulsing in rhythms that began to form music. They journeyed toward it, and the tone divided into strands of sound, notes weaving around one another and merging into chords. The sphere was singing to him.

Music. The music of the spheres, as the ancients called it.

The song was itself made of light, multiple filaments woven and knotted with incredible complexity. He couldn't imagine how anyone could ever grasp the intricacies of that tangle, yet the techies began searching, trying and discarding paths with amazing rapidity.

Write this down! he heard a voice command. He took a breath again and felt for his fingers, for the hard plastic of the keyboard beneath them. The voice read out a string of numbers, and Cress struggled to record them accurately. He couldn't tell if he was hearing the voice with his physical ears or simply in his mind, but the effort to listen and type kept him tethered to his body.

On and on they went, trackers on the hunt, until they reached the heart of the glow and found another pulsing, singing globe of light. This too was composed of multiple intertwined filaments, and the techies dove in without hesitation, pausing only now and then to reel off a string of numbers. Down through one nexus to another and another, until Cress felt as if they had been speeding through eternity. Globe within globe, chord within chord, world within world, down and down forever.

And then they were facing a hard-edged, glowing crystal. It beamed out a brilliant white light that broke into rainbows against the prisms of the crystals that surrounded them. Cress and techies were six globes of light in a chamber studded with crystals, like the heart of a geode. Their reflections in the facets of the crystal sent rays bouncing and zinging around them, giving off pure tones like a celestial carillon.

Cress looked at his five companions. They too were knots and tangles of filaments, harmonies, and melodies, each one a million times more complex than the nodes they had explored.

Was he like that? he wondered. He sensed that the techies were showing their minds to the crystal heart. They were speaking, not so much with words but in images and tones and bursts of emotion.

Suddenly he felt himself on display. The other lights dimmed around him and he could see rays spreading out from his own center, some of beautiful, bright colors, others the clotted dull red of blood or pain. Well, that's who I am, he thought, a little ashamed. I didn't choose that pain—it chose me.

He was a chord, a song, the deep tones of his grief giving weight to the blue rippling notes of flowing water.

He had wanted to be a musician once. Bird had actually encouraged him to apply to the Musicians' Guild. He felt a flash of anger, remembering Bird's smug smile, his unquestioned assumption that he, of course, was in a position to judge. But music was a luxury, Cress had believed. Water was a necessity.

Was that really it? a little voice whispered. Or were you afraid, afraid to be rejected, afraid of having to display your talent and falling short?

Fuck it! He didn't need Bird or anyone else to tell him whether he was good or not.

His anger, his resentment, and yes, he admitted, his jealousy wove around him like dissonant chords, shrill and grating, so different from the sad but beautiful tones of his grief for Valeria and the child, his older grief for his mother and sister. This was like a needle scratch on an old-fashioned record, setting his teeth on edge. He wanted it to stop.

Then why do you keep digging it in deeper and deeper? Why do you worry it over and over, like a sore tooth?

Was that the voice of the crystal, or some voice of his own? Some half-remembered admonition of his mother's? Was he getting lessons in forgiveness from a fucking machine?

But he could let it go, he realized. After all, he and Bird were not in competition. He had turned his life to the service of something far more primal and vital than music, and he could do things that Bird could never do. He could bring dead land to life.

And with that thought, the screech died away and instead he heard the roar of a river in flood, the liquid notes of an ocean-bound, rushing stream, the quiet chant of still pools sinking into parched land.

Then the five globes with him congealed, pulling him into their midst. He felt one moment of sheer terror as threads interwove with his own mind strands, a panic that they would tangle forever and he would never again pull free and be himself.

But then he let go. *Breathe,* something said to him, and his body did, and the linked globes began to pulse and vibrate in a great ringing tone like a bell, calling everything to awaken.

A wave of light broke over him. He was washed clean, absolved, forgiven. The air rang with song like an angel chorus rejoicing.

Breathe again. Don't stop breathing, that was the thing. Breathe and humbly ask for help. Not in words, but in images, feelings, song.

He remembered the old woman falling, beaten to the ground. He saw his wife lying in a pool of her own blood, held again the limp thing that would have been his living daughter. He heard his sister's cries.

And then he thought about water, clear, sweet water. He heard the gurgling of the streams running through the streets of the City, saw the lush green of the gardens, the splash of a fountain, the children illumined in sunlight playing in jets and sprays. And he sent that forth as a plea. If he could have formed words, they would have been *Help us, please! Be on the side of that!*

Hours later, he awoke with a splitting headache. The cap was off his head, he was lying under the dome, and Beryl was holding up a cup of some herbal concoction for him to drink.

"Sip," they said. "It'll make you feel better."

"How'd it go?" he asked.

"Good. We've woken the heart of the network, and it likes us. It liked you. It doesn't much like the Stewards, who made it serve them without ever recognizing there was a consciousness there. It will work with us. We had to put you under for awhile, for your own protection and so that we could work at speed. It's a bit slow going, with only five of us."

"That's what you call slow?" Cress asked.

"You should see what it's like when we get a meld of fifty, or five hundred."

"Don't. It makes my head hurt worse, just to think." He sat up. "So now what?"

"So now we need a mainframe, or a board, or something more. Next raid, see what you can capture for us. We understand how this works now, but we need to get into their main system if we're going to look for records or play games."

When the scouts returned, in the early hours of the morning, they reported that the surrounding farms still seemed oblivious to any danger. Before dawn, they set out to do multiple raids. Cress took one division, Smokee took another, River took a third, and they hit the three closest farms—close being a relative term when each plantation could cover hundreds of acres. During the day, they rested their troops, then set out again at twilight to hit another plantation after dusk.

By the third day of the campaign, the troops of the North controlled almost a thousand acres of farmland.

The easy part was over.

Chapter Twenty-Nine

THE *DAY OF VICTORY* HAD NEVER LOOKED BETTER, ISIS THOUGHT as she surveyed the windspinners humming and the new solar sails shimmering like sheets of crystal. Her hull was repaired and repainted and she looked sleek, like a slender woman trembling with the tide. Like a particular slender woman, trembling with ... but she wasn't going to think about Sara any more. She had put the bitch firmly out of her mind. Isis was mistress of her own ship, her own fate, admiral—or first rep, as the City called it—of a navy. She didn't need distractions.

All right, she admitted, maybe it wasn't much of a navy. A motley collection of sailboats, tugboats, and requisitioned ferries, with a few old cruise ships and, following in their wake, the captured warship, newly christened the *Harvey Milk,* now refurbished and repaired. Not much, but it was her navy and that was something to be proud of.

They'd spent weeks training and preparing, loading supplies, practicing emergency drills. Refurbishing ferries and fishing boats into a fighting navy took time. Meanwhile, as reports arrived from the Central Valley, and messages came back via the hillboys' networks that Bird and Madrone had begun their Refuge, Isis grew more and more impatient to join the fun. But now, at last, they were off!

The sun glinted off the waves as they pulled out from the docks. The smaller boats embarked from the reconstructed San Francisco piers, the ferries and tugs steamed over from the East Bay, the warship from its deepwater anchorage down near Hunters Point. Like a flock of gulls they converged and headed out toward the Golden Gate.

It took all Isis's concentration to navigate them through the treacherous currents and the tidal pull, and that was good because it meant she had no time for thinking, no time to regret the empty space at her side where Sara might once have stood. Alone and free. That's who I am, she thought. Who I want to be. Free. And alone.

Out they went, past the rock of Alcatraz, past wild Angel Island where generations of the City's children went to learn how to camp and build a fire without matches and paddle a canoe. Out under the ruins of the Golden Gate Bridge, where the repair crews interrupted their tasks to let out huge cheers. Then through the channel, the green hills of Marin on their right, the City's secluded beaches and walking trails on their left.

Out onto the open ocean, rocking on the swells. And then south, catching the stiff wind that whipped them down toward new dangers and adventures.

Free and alone, the way a pirate should be.

Sara reached for a fresh sheet of paper and stared for a moment at its blank surface. In front of her on the small desk in her tiny cabin her crystal projected a hologram of a calendar. "Hours," she commanded, and the days broke themselves into 24 slots.

Right now, her team of divers were getting settled on the small cruise ship that they'd requisitioned and christened the *Toypurina*, after a Gabrieleño healer who'd led a revolt against the missions of the Southlands, back in the nineteenth century. It had been caught in the City during the Uprising, decades before, and allocated now to the divers because on deck was a swimming pool where they could practice underwater maneuvers.

The other divers were busy lugging their packs to their cabins, choosing their bunks and bunkmates, or simply standing on deck to watch the ship pass under the ruins of the Golden Gate Bridge and out of the bay. But Sara had work to do.

Tomorrow, first thing in the morning, her crew of thirty divers would begin the last phase of their training regime, and she was in charge. She was making a schedule—dividing them into pods of ten who would cycle through three stations: the gym for fitness training, the pool for practicing maneuvers, and dive practice off the side of the ship. Then there were all the chores of maintenance and cooking and cleaning to be divided and shared. They had a head chef and a team of experienced cooks, but all the divers would take turns helping with prep and dishes. That was the City's way.

Yes, she was busy, and she would be far too busy to think about that idiot Isis. Eventually, she was sure, the pig-headed pirate would come around. She'd get lonely, all those nights alone on her little boat, when they could have been together. She'd admit she was wrong. Until then, Sara had plenty to do. Plenty to think about.

She sighed and turned back to her timetable.

The fleet anchored in Half Moon Bay for the night. It had been a short trip that day, but they had planned for that, wanting plenty of time to get everyone going and organized and to practice moving as a convoy. Tomorrow they would reach Santa Cruz, where they would pick up another contingent before they headed farther down the coast. They could expect little in the way of opposition until they were much farther south.

So tonight was a night to relax. It would have been a perfect night to split a bottle of wine with Sara on the deck, under the waning moon, watching the stars. But this was no pleasure cruise, and how much better, Isis told herself, to have no such diversions.

Isis could have stayed for dinner on the big warship. She'd rowed the dinghy over and come aboard for the Naval Council meeting, a fancy name for a group that consisted of her, Livingston, Sara, and reps from the other boats. She could have asked Sara to come back with her, but she didn't want to give the bitch the satisfaction. So when the meeting ended, she'd jumped back into her dinghy and rowed herself back to her own private refuge. No one bothering her, no one to worry about.

She sat now, enjoying a well-deserved glass of wine. The stars were no less beautiful when she was alone. She could enjoy them more without some skinny-lipped filly trying to nuzzle her neck. She could appreciate the silence of the night, broken only by sounds of partying carrying over the water from the destroyer, and the lap of waves, and the thump of . . .

Thump of? Isis sat up, suddenly alert. There were sounds down below in the cabin, a thump, and a soft scraping. Someone was there.

Fuck! Her gun was below, hidden as always next to her pillow. That would teach her to relax, even here where it seemed to be so safe. She looked around for a weapon and grabbed a short metal bar that was used to turn the capstan. Gripping it tight, she sidled down the short flight of steps that led to the cabin and kicked the door open, bursting in with a yell and brandishing her weapon.

"Die, you motherfuckin' landslime!" she yelled and swung at a dark figure who dove into a corner.

"Stop, no! Isis, it's me! Rosa!" the figure cried.

Isis pulled out of another swing, just in time, and let the bar clatter to the floor.

"Rosa! You out of your fuckin' mind?" Isis glared down at the bunk that sheltered the girl. "Tryin' to get yourself killed?"

Cautiously, Rosa peered out from below the bunk.

"I'm sorry."

"Sorry? What the rudder are you doing here?"

"I want to come with you," Rosa said staunchly. She slid out from under the bunk and brushed dust off her fuchsia sweat pants. Isis, hands on her hips, head cocked, observed her.

"Last I checked, the navy don't recruit children," Isis said.

Rosa stuck her chin up. "I'm not a child. I'm fourteen. Almost."

"Yeah. Over the hill," Isis snorted. At that same age, she'd been running three races a week and servicing the big betters by night. "You're a City girl. Your people say you're still a child."

"Well, I'm not," Rosa said, plopping down on the bunk. "Not any more." Her head was down and suddenly she looked purely miserable.

"Okay, I give you that," Isis admitted. She felt sorry for the girl, and she understood exactly how a long, dangerous voyage as a stowaway on a pirate ship might seem preferable to staying in the City where everything would remind her of her violation. "But what about school, and learning?"

"I hate my Learning Group!" Rosa said bitterly. "They all hate me."

"Can't be true."

"It is true. They blame me for everything."

"Then they're stupid," Isis said. "Don't worry about what turtlebrains think! How in hell did you get in here?"

"It was easy. While you were meeting with the Naval Council this morning, I just got on board and hid in the sail locker," Rosa told her.

"What'd you do when you had to piss?"

"I did that when you went to the evening meeting," Rosa said smugly.

Isis shook her head. "You eaten anything today?"

"I'm not hungry."

"Yeah, and I'm a polar bear. Come on, fix you some eggs."

What to do with the girl? Isis wondered. Send her back, the Council would say. No doubt about it. But maybe I look at things in a different way. Thirteen years old—where I come from, that's no child. Old enough to know her own mind.

Isis scrambled eggs and made toast in the little toaster oven that ran on the electricity generated from the night breeze by the line of sensitive windreeds on the cabin's roof. Rosa ate hungrily and kept silent. But she seemed brighter, somehow, than she'd been since her ordeal in the hands of the Stewards. Her shoulders were set back with pride, not hunched over. Her head was higher.

She'd wanted something, and thought about how to get it, and set out to do it, and she'd done it, Isis thought. And that had to be an improvement over the head-hung slinking and hiding she'd been doing. Madrone had noted the girl's depression, even with all the worries she'd had during Maya's last days and the preparations for the trip south. She'd asked Isis to help the girl, but Isis hadn't found anything much in the way of an opening.

But now Rosa was here.

"What you expect to do in the navy?" Isis asked.

"I can help. I'm a really good sailor," Rosa said. "You need someone to help you sail this boat—you can't do it all alone."

"I been sailin' this boat alone since before you was a bloodspot in your mare's panties!"

"But not when you were commanding the navy at the same time. What if you need to go to a meeting while you're underway? What if you need to run a mission and trim the sails at the same time?"

Girl had a point, Isis admitted. But there were dozens of good sailors in the navy. She could get a mate who was grown up, if she wanted one. She didn't. Ship was too small for company, unless that company was— stop that! She wasn't going there!

Still, it was good to see Rosa looking hopeful and eager.

"Got to run it by the Naval Council," Isis said. "I doubt they'll agree to keep you on. But I'll give you a trial, tomorrow."

She made up the second bunk for Rosa, and the girl dropped to sleep as soon as she pulled the covers over herself. Isis sat for a moment, listening to her soft breathing. It was a sound. It was company.

"Reef the sail! Then make fast the sheet!" Isis barked commands at a rapid-fire pace and Rosa sped across the small deck to keep up with them. She was a good sailor, Isis had to admit. She reacted quickly and accurately, without getting flustered or losing her head. When Isis let her take the tiller, she steered a straight wake, no waggles. She kept the sail trim and seemed to have an instinctive feel for how to use the slightest shift in the wind. She cleaned up the breakfast dishes and stowed everything away ship-shape, without being told.

Of course, she's trying to impress me, Isis thought. But swablet was succeeding.

"We got a problem," she told the Council. They were meeting in the captain's dining room of the old cruise ship, on chairs with now-shabby chintz cushions crowded around a circular mahogany table. Sconces on the wall shed a soft light over the charts and papers spread out before them.

"Already?" asked Miguel, who captained one of the ferries.

"Stowaway," Isis informed them.

"What, on your boat? Hardly room to stow away a kitten, let alone a person!" exclaimed Belle, who was a tugboat pilot and felt superior to anyone who didn't know the tricky currents of the bay.

"Rosa," Isis told them. "Hid in the sail locker. Found her last night. She wants to go with us, help sail the boat."

"She's a child," said Bronwyn, head of the kayak crew. "What is she, twelve?"

"Thirteen. Almost fourteen."

"So we drop her at the harbor in Santa Cruz this afternoon, and they can get her back to the City," Bronwyn said.

"What if she doesn't want to go?" Isis asked.

"We don't do child armies. Or navies!" Miguel said firmly.

"You'd think she'd been through enough trauma and danger. Why does she want to come look for more?" Bronwyn asked.

Isis looked around at the faces. They seemed so sure, so secure, with that City smugness that got on her nerves. She understood why Rosa wanted to get away from them all, from the places where she'd once been happy and the places where she'd been so hurt.

"I sat with the girl last night," Isis said. "Girl's lookin' happy now, on the boat. On the land, her head's always down, won't meet your eyes. On the water, got her chin to the wind, hand on the tiller, eyes lookin' ahead."

"She should be in therapy," Bronwyn said.

"Therapy don't make it better," Isis said.

"It helps you cope." Bronwyn said.

"Maybe this is her way to cope," Sara suggested. "That's the thing about trauma. When you've been through enough of it, your old life doesn't fit any more. Safety can feel more painful than risk."

She stole a quick glance at Isis, who turned away from her.

Livingston sat silent, slightly annoyed at all the time they were taking up with this peripheral issue. Meetings! The squabs were in love with them, scheduling dozens a day, short ones, long ones ... by gentle Jesus's hairy balls, how they loved long ones!

"Suppose we let her stay for a while?" Isis suggested. "No real danger for days yet, maybe weeks. Send her back before we hit a combat zone, but let her sail the boat for a bit?"

She happened to glance over at Sara, who flashed her a quick smile of complicity.

"She could have an adventure that she chooses herself," Sara said. "One she can be in control of, and survive."

"There's no guarantee that we won't run into patrol boats or opposition farther north than we anticipate," Miguel objected.

"There's no guarantee that she won't get hit in the head by a gondola back in the City," Sara said.

Bitch, trying' to get back on my good side, Isis thought, and shot Sara a dagger-like glare just to let her know it wasn't working. Or at least, she meant it to be a dagger-like glare. She felt her eyes lingering over Sara's face, and forced herself to look away.

Time to intervene, Livingston thought. Or we'll be here forever.

"The navy never patrols north of Point Sal," he assured them. "Just don't have the capacity. They concentrate on the shipping lanes into Angel City. Won't be expecting trouble."

"Bring her in," Sara suggested. "Let her speak for herself."

Rosa stood and faced the Council. She wouldn't hang her head, she'd decided. She would look them in the eye and show them she wasn't someone to pity.

"I want to stay with the navy," she said. "I can sail. I like to sail. I can help."

"But you're too young, *mi vida*," Bronwyn said. "You're too young to go into danger."

"Well, I wasn't safe in the City!" Rosa snapped, and that silenced them all.

She looked around. Isis was impassive, Sara looking at her with an encouraging smile. Some of the others looked guilty, some merely bored. Like the guy who stood in the back, his arms folded, a knowing half-smile playing on his lips.

She shivered. Something about him was creepy to her. He seemed somehow familiar, as if she'd seen him before. Where? Who did he remind her of?

And then suddenly she knew him. The creepy guy from the races, wearing sunglasses in the fog, and smelling like a sojuh!

Livingston was trying to place her. Where had he seen that curly cap of hair, that child's face with haunted eyes?

Her eyes bored into him for a moment, then shifted away abruptly.

Shit. That day at the race. She'd been the girl who ran from him.

Had she recognized him? Hard to say. If she did, he had a story ready. He'd been contemplating defecting, took a little scouting trip to help him make up his mind. Impressed with what he saw. Who could argue with that?

Rosa's was hardly listening to what they were saying about her, she was too taken up with the man. She had to force herself to ground, to keep her breath slow and even. What should she do? Should she tell them he'd been spying in the City? But who would believe her? For a moment she found herself wishing Bird were here, even though he was one of the people she was glad to be away from. But he *did* believe her. Who else would?

Isis. Isis would. But what did that prove—that she'd seen him at the race. He could say he'd just been looking around. Maybe that was true. But maybe he was a double agent, still working for the Stewards? What if he was leading the whole navy into a trap?

She should tell them, warn them all! Or maybe it would be better just to tell Isis, secretly. Then, if he was trying to trap them, maybe they could trap him instead.

They were all talking again, and she wished they would just hurry up and get done with it. Sara, who saw how uncomfortable she was looking, suggested that she go down to the galley and get some lunch while they finished the discussion.

In the end, but not without another half-hour's debate, the Council reluctantly agreed to let Rosa stay until they reached a danger zone.

Isis and Sara stood leaning over the rail of the old cruise ship, watching the breeze tease little ripples on the backs of the swells like a puppy worrying the skin of an old sleeping dog.

Sara had loved her old dog, a Rottweiler they'd kept to guard the house back in the days when she was a Prime's Trophy. A savage beast, with a ferocious bark, but she had found his sweet side. She wriggled imperceptibly closer to Isis.

Sara was so close Isis could feel her heat, smell her scent like spice and flowers in little whiffs amidst the greater tang of the sea air.

"Can't we be friends?" Sara asked.

"We are friends," Isis said.

"You know what I mean. Can't we just, like, hang out? Talk? Like girlfriends." Sara's voice was low, throaty and seductive.

Isis shrugged. "Talk."

"I think it's a good thing you're doing for Rosa," Sara leaned back against the rail, stealing a small glance at Isis's face, which remained turned away, her eyes fixed on the waves as if something vital to the fate of the world were happening there.

Isis shrugged again. "It's what she wants."

"Sometimes, when you've been happy, and then you aren't happy, you just have to get away from where you were happy."

"That's why I have a boat."

"I call it the 'Run Away with a Beautiful Pirate' cure." Sara offered up one of her amazing smiles, slow, sweet, her lips languidly curving into a crescent, her left cheek sporting a dimple. "Should be in all the psychology texts."

"We aim to serve." Isis turned away. If she kept on looking at that smile, she'd be lost.

They fell silent. Sara turned again to watch the play of sunlight on the waves.

"Got to get back to my boat," Isis said.

Sara reached out an arm, took her hand.

"Isis," she drew her close. So close, their lips nearly touched. A magnetic field lay between them. Isis could feel herself drawn in, smell Sara's musk, feel her warmth and the tide of her own desire rising.

"I still love you," Sara whispered. "I always will."

With a sharp effort of will, Isis pulled away. Yield, immerse herself in the perfume and the warmth, and it would be all the harder to do what she had to do.

"Better this way," she muttered, and fled.

Isis found Rosa in the canteen, sitting at one of the long stainless steel tables eating a bowl of vegetable soup the cook had dished out for her.

"Gonna let you stay for a while," Isis told her. "Livingston says there's no danger of intercepts till we get down into their shipping lanes, farther south. At that point, you go back north with one of the courier ships. Understand?"

Rosa nodded. It would do, for now. She could think about what would happen later when the time came. Right now she had a more pressing worry.

Rosa glanced around her. No one was nearby. The cook was back in the galley, clanging pots and whistling a jaunty love song that was popular in the City.

"Isis, I saw him!" she said. "That navy guy. I saw him in the City."

"Yeah, he's been staying in the City," Isis said, sitting down across from her. "So what?"

"I saw him before ... before you captured the warship."

"When, before?"

"At the race. The day of the big race."

"What was he doing?"

"Just—watching people. He asked me questions, and I thought he was creepy."

Isis looked at her sharply. "You sure?"

"He smelled wrong," Rosa said. "Like the ... like the sojuhs. I told Bird."

Why hadn't Bird told them, warned them? Isis wondered. Was he ... but no. He had warned them there could be spies in the City. He'd have no way of knowing it was Livingston that Rosa saw. If she did see him. Girl was bit unraveled in the mind, but Isis didn't think she'd make up a story like this.

No, Isis thought, Livingston bore watching. If she thought about it, she didn't fully trust him. He'd defected so easily, so thoroughly. Granted the attractions of the City were powerful, but he could have family in the Southlands, interests to protect.

If she hadn't been so snarled up in her feelings about Sara, she would have been more suspicious, less eager to take the whole navy, such as it was, back into the jaws of the Stewards on his word.

But the girl had that haggard, worried look again. Damn Sara! If bitch wasn't so stubborn, they could have been together again and talked this through.

"Okay," Isis said. "I hear you. Good job, spotting him."

"What are you going to do?"

"Take it under consideration. Meantime, you keep out of his way!"

Alone in the wheelhouse on the midnight watch, Livingston looked around to make sure that nobody else was within earshot. He took out his own small coms unit and quietly dictated a full report. Edited, to be sure, but complete nonetheless. He covered the strength of the navy, the plans of the army in so far as he knew them. Alerted by Bird's warning of spies, the commanders of each branch met separately, no longer sharing their strategies in full open Council. But no matter. He knew they would be heading down the Central Valley, and he knew their objectives.

He also expressed his alarm that Kline had disappeared. Never turned up for their last rendezvous. Hoped he'd decided to return home, and had made it back safely.

He spoke it all into coms, then thumbed a button and sent it in one, encrypted burst. Better that way. Safer from interception—and he was protected from having to listen to any blowback.

The night was cold, but clear. The stars were bright. He was at the helm of his own ship, at last!

So many pieces on the board for him to move this way and that, maneuvering them where he wanted them, keeping his options open.

He gave a cheerful wink to the north star, and steered the boat toward the south.

Chapter Thirty

I am a breath of wind.
I am a coal in the heart of the sun.
I am the receding tide, waiting to turn.
I am food for the million hungry mouths of earth.
I am memory.
There is so much that I am forbidden to tell you.
I am a half-remembered story, the ghost of a song.
I have been a convicted word-monger, habitual namer,
*   addicted to nouns.*
I have tried to fence inchoate forces that escaped
*   like birds through a net.*
I have followed after them, wind to my wings,
*   spiraling on the updrafts, ever higher....*
I am not yet ready to land.

Now that the Refuge had a source of water, Bird and Madrone began to build and plant. They scavenged pipes and fittings from the ruins, and jury-rigged a solar pump from the innards of an old washing machine they found in an abandoned apartment. Madrone had always enjoyed plumbing and carpentry. Pipes and valves were so simple and straightforward compared to the subtle workings of the body's systems. Pipes did not suffer, or cry out, or look at her with imploring eyes.

Many times a day, she blessed her grandmother for her varied and practical education. Once Johanna had taken over the schools after the Uprising, there were no more long days sitting at desks. Johanna believed in learning by doing. Children, she maintained, needed to know what would be useful to them in interpreting and maintaining their environment. All the academics would come from that.

They'd made gardens and grown food—and so learned math and geometry and biology and organic chemistry. They'd learned to maintain every system in their homes, from the plumbing to the solar panels, and so learned hydrology and physics. When they needed to memorize something, the formula for converting yards to meters or the key dates in the anti-slavery struggles of the nineteenth century, they made songs and dances that fixed the facts effortlessly and indelibly in their minds.

Bird had learned carpentry from his father, who was a handyman by day, a jazz musician by night. From the time he could toddle, he'd followed his dad around, first watching and fetching tools, then learning how to use them. He thought of his father as he measured and sawed and hammered. He had died in the Uprising, but his voice lived on in Bird's shoulders and arms and hands. "Don't press down on the saw, just move it back and forth. Let the motion do the work." "That ain't the hammer of Thor you swingin', son. Get the action in your wrists. You got to go for accuracy, not raw force."

Those were some of Bird's happiest memories. He found himself now trying to impart some of the same skills to Zoom and Zap—the simple things, like how to hammer in a nail. He found he had to keep close tabs on the hammers, to prevent them from swinging at each other.

Their attention span was short. Five or ten minutes of focus, and then they'd be off, punching each other or running off into the ruins to play hide and seek. Bird learned quickly never to say, "That's wrong," or "That's not how you do it." Any correction sent Zoom into a frustrated rage, while Zap simply shut down, dropped the hammer, and sulked.

"You're doin' great," he'd say instead. "Now, try it this way and it might be even better ... loosen that wrist. That's right! You've got a natural feel for this."

With copious amounts of praise and patience, he could sometimes get them focused for all of fifteen minutes.

The soil in the small patches of open space was rock-hard and almost white. But Madrone and Bird were eager to start a garden. They chose an open area, close to the plaza. A few cracked concrete planters indicated it might once have been a small park.

Bird improvised a digging bar from a scrap of iron, and Zap discovered a tool shed behind one of the ruined apartment complexes that held a couple of spades and, wonder of wonders, a digging fork. Madrone and Bird enjoyed long discussions in the hot pool about how best to prepare the ground. It felt good to be talking about something so ordinary, so hopeful.

It took them three long, hard days to get a small patch ready. Bird pounded away at the cement-like crust with the digging bar, and Madrone followed with the fork. They lacked compost or anything to enrich the ground, but aerating it was a start.

Making compost was a challenge, as they had little or nothing in the way of organic materials or scraps. They had set up a small composting toilet, covering their deposits with torn-up scraps of paper, but the humanure would need to digest for a long time before it was safe to use on a food garden. Their meager meals of ground acorns and carefully hoarded beans left little or nothing in the way of scraps.

Bird's pack contained a jar of cherished red compost worms. All the way down, he had fed them carefully, making sure they had moisture and air and shade. Now they built a bin out of a plastic storage box and layered it with cardboard and shredded paper. They fed the worms on duff and ailanthus leaves and they began to multiply, but as yet they produced only a tiny amount of castings. They used them homeopathically, dissolving a teaspoonful in a bucket of water and sprinkling the ground to inoculate it with the beneficial bacteria the worms carried in their guts.

Madrone found dandelions in the edges of old ornamental beds. With their new source of water she could steam their greens for a vegetable and offer the stems to the worms. Plantain pushed up through cracks in the cements, and she made poultices for the sores on the boys' skin and let the worms dispose of the used leaves. But it would take time for the worms to produce significant amounts of fertilizer.

In the early morning and the cool twilight, they dug. During the hot noonday hours, they went underground, exploring the ruins, clearing pathways, collecting useful tools. Bird built benches from scrap lumber, and tables for their campsite and for the plaza he could envision near the sacred tree. Sometimes they just napped, collapsing in the shade away from the blazing sun.

Zap and Zoom were not good workers. Indeed, they resisted all expectations that they do any kind of work or pitch in on any project needing extra hands. They tended to run off, giggling, and then get into a brawl. Madrone tried asking nicely, pleading, cajoling, and commanding, but at most she could get a grudging assist when something needed to be moved.

"I'm not saying I would ever hit a child," Madrone said in exasperation as she and Bird settled into their sleeping bags after another long day. She had asked Zoom to help her clean up after lunch, and he had dawdled and avoided and poked at Zap until she lost patience and ordered him to do the dishes. Whereupon he'd yelled at her that she was a worthless, wormy slit and run off.

"I'm not saying I *would* whale the living daylights out of him. But I understand now why someone might want to."

"Well, they don't really have to help," Bird said. "They're only little children, after all."

"It's not so much for us, it's for them. They're bored and restless, and if they would work with us, they'd learn things just like we learned from doing things. And maybe they'd start to develop some pride, some sense of accomplishment."

"Give them time. Maybe it'll be like it was with the soldiers in the City—remember how they just sat around at first, and it took them time to join in the rebuilding. The boys have never had a chance to be kids. Give them a little time to adjust."

The soil, once dug, was still not rich enough to support much life, in spite of having lain fallow for so long. They needed compost. They scoured the village for anything that once was alive—dead leaves, scraps of paper, old shopping bags. Paper and cardboard they could find in abundance, and it would make an excellent mulch to keep weeds from coming through, should there ever be enough rain to support weeds. But the materials they had would not break down quickly in that dry climate, or contribute much in the way of nitrogen to nourish growing plants.

They also needed more hands to do the work. Bird began to see the rebuilt Refuge in his mind—but he and Madrone alone could not lift the heavier chunks of concrete. And they had not come all this way to carve out a refuge for themselves alone, or even for their rescued urchins. The time had come to venture out and recruit.

"We've been water thieves," he told Madrone as they soaked in the warm pool late at night. It had become their daily ritual, their reward for backbreaking work all day. The two boys often joined them. After their first panicked resistance, they discovered that being clean felt good, and soaking in the warm pool felt even better. They had learned to scrub themselves in the bath Madrone or Bird made for them nightly, and after they rinsed off they were allowed to relax in the pool. The water was over Zap's head, and he clung tightly to the rim, but slowly Bird was encouraging him to let go, and teaching him to float. Zoom could just touch his toes to the bottom, and Madrone had him practice holding his breath and ducking his head in the water. Soon, she hoped, he would learn how to swim.

"And I devoutly hope that phase of my life is over!" Madrone said.

"Well, now we have plenty of water. We could become water traders," Bird suggested.

"How?"

"We could fill our containers, put them on the bike trailer, pull it around ourselves and offer it for trade. Water for garbage?"

"Vegetable peelings, paper, uneaten food ... "

"There won't be much of that!" Bird said. "They sell the scraps off your plate to street kids for sexual favors, I understand."

"Maybe we can find a celibate restaurateur," Madrone said. "Anyway, once people know our route they'll scavenge for us."

Bird became a showman. They fashioned him a costume out of the scraps they found in the mall, and he set out, pulling his chariot: the wagon they'd decked out in rags of many colors that Madrone and the boys twisted into braids and flowers. While they resisted digging and dishes, Zap had proved very interested in watching her braid rags and ribbons.

"Wanna do that!" he said.

"Say 'I,' Zap," Madrone corrected him automatically. "'I would like to do that. Please.'"

"Pease."

So she showed him how to tie the ribbons onto a rail and braid three of them together. She watched him as he worked, his tough little body bent over in concentration, his tongue slightly out. For a moment she caught a glimpse of the boy he might have been, had someone cared for him and nurtured him. Maybe someone had—surely at some time somebody had given him some mother's milk, some loving arms, or he wouldn't have survived. She wondered what calamity had befallen his unknown mother. Was she a wretched creature of the pens, or perhaps a young girl from a poor family who had gotten pregnant and lost her immortal soul? Was he stolen away from someone who had his rough dark hair, his deep brown eyes?

She was filled with pity suddenly, for that unknown woman who had borne him, and flooded with a sudden rush of love. He was really a dear boy, in spite of everything, and she would do anything within her power to repair the damage done to him and give him the chance to be what he was born to be.

Zoom at first scorned the braiding and decorating, and made fun of Zap, calling him a filly and a poke-pony. But when Bird began sewing his own costume, Zoom watched with a mixture of fascination and confusion.

"Why you doin' that? Thass for your filly to do!"

"Why?" Bird asked. "It's my costume. And I'm pretty good with a needle and thread."

Actually his stiff hands were not as supple as they once had been, and his stitches were more crude than he would have liked. But they did the job and held the fabric together. And it was good exercise for his fingers, he thought. He had no piano to practice on here, no guitar, but the sewing helped limber them up and kept the stiffness at bay.

When they were finished, and he dressed up, he looked like a medieval minstrel. The cart, decked with colors, could have graced the cobblestone streets of ancient London or Paris. Madrone had transformed the Avenging Christ from Beth's basement into a flower angel, covered over with ribbons and daisies and lilies all cut and stitched from scraps of the clothing of the dead. Under a bank of fabric blossoms, they hid the containers of water.

Zap and Zoom demanded to go with him. Zap wanted a jacket to match Bird's, decked with a rainbow of ribbons. But Bird suggested that instead they could scout. They could run ahead of the wagon, and keep an eye out for the Lash. He made the suggestion with some trepidation, for he feared they might simply run away and perhaps sell them out to the first bidder. But he couldn't see them running to the authorities, or that any authority worth his chevrons would believe the wild tale of a ruined enclave guarded by skeletons and run by powerful magicians.

"Absolutely not!" Madrone objected. "They're children. They stay here, and we keep them as safe as we can."

"Wanna go with Bird!" Zoom insisted. Madrone gave him a stern look, and he quickly corrected himself. "I wanna go. Please."

"They could be useful," Bird said.

"What—like child soldiers? We're not going to do that!" Madrone's hands were on her hips, her mouth was pursed, her eyebrows raised, and she looked remarkably like Johanna as Bird remembered her, delivering a scolding when they'd trespassed in some way.

"More like kids in the Warsaw ghetto fighting in the last stand," Bird said. "It's their battle, too."

"Absolutely not!"

"Madrone, do you remember the day of the Uprising?"

"What about it?"

"Do you remember how hard my parents tried to keep me out of the fighting, and just how much success they had?" he asked.

"You were a bad boy," she declared.

"I was an angel of obedience compared to Zap and Zoom."

In the end, the boys went along because there was no practical way, short of tying them down, to keep them back. And although Zap and Zoom were reluctant workers, they proved to be natural scouts. They were happy to slather some dirt back on their faces and run ahead of the wagon in a wide arc, eyes peeled for cops and the Lash. They were little, and quick, and they blended in perfectly with the crowds on the street. So Bird could sing out his patter and trade his water for rags in some relative safety, knowing he'd have warning if trouble were on the way.

"Get it here, never fear—water pure, water clear!" he sang out. "What do I want in exchange? Well you might ask, dear lady. Not your virtue—as if you had any! Ha! Not your immortal soul—if you had one of those. Not even your cold cash. No—I'm a fool, and fool that I am, I want only your garbage. Peelings from your potatoes. Hair from your head."

He stood on a corner in the depths of the slums, a neighborhood where even the Lash rarely ventured, and then only in packs. Half-crumpled buildings were shored up with the fallen beams of their less fortunate neighbors. Behind him, a cracked plateglass window held together with duct tape displayed a few pairs of second-hand shoes and a pink satin ball gown with brown stains on the skirt. Across the street, a vender offered a cart-full of worn, plastic toys, armies of khaki and gray-green soldiers, a princess with a battered crown, a Mickey Mouse with the color rubbed off his ears. All of them dated back to before the Collapse. The Stewardship produced nothing so frivolous as toys for the lower classes.

Farther down the street were a few food carts selling packs of outdated army surplus chips and dusty bottles of sugary soft drinks. One or two offered limp onions or scabby oranges, others held cheap underwear and shabby T-shirts.

Crowds hurried by. The lucky few were on their way to work, the others scurrying to secure a good place in some queue vital to their survival. They shuffled along in flip-flops; real shoes were rare as ring-tailed quail. The men wore faded T-shirts emblazoned with Retributionist slogans, or even more faded shirts that still held some relic corporate logo from the old world. The women favored drab, front-buttoned shifts, except for one or two in short, hip-hugging skirts and fishnet stockings, heading home from a night's work.

Everyone seemed to walk with their heads down, their eyes fixed on the pavement. They bent forward, as if some crushing weight sat on their shoulders, and they barely looked up at his patter.

"Water for garbage! Such a deal! Step right up—you'll know it's real!"

"Why?" A young man stopped in front of him. His lank brown hair fell around a thin face with the dusty patina of the chronically dehydrated, and he looked at Bird with suspicion. "Why sell water for garbage?"

"I'm a magician—I turn garbage into gold." Bird said, reaching down and whipping out a small cupful. "Here, have a sample."

The man sipped slowly, cautiously, holding each drop on his tongue and letting it swirl and wet his mouth. Like someone from the hills, Bird thought. By the time he finished his cupful, a woman stood beside him, one child perched on her hip, another in tow. She was dark-skinned and her body was heavy with that false fat that chronic malnutrition sometimes produces. The baby was wailing and the older child scuffed his feet in the dust. He was wearing mismatched flip-flops, and one was at least two sizes too big. His scalp was crusty under his tight-cropped curls.

"Givin' out water?" she asked incredulously.

"Free samples today," Bird said with sudden inspiration. "Tomorrow, I'll be back to trade. And what do I want? Only your garbage. No plastic, please! Just anything that was once alive, or is made from something once alive without too many steps in between."

"Crazy man!" she pronounced, but she took the cup he handed her and gave it to the child, who held it solemnly as a prayer between his two hands and drank it down. He gave her a cupful for herself, and one for the baby. And by then he had a line of the destitute, crowding and shoving and arguing.

"Listen up!" he called out. "You want my wares, you got to play nice. You start brawling and bring down the Lash, and I'm outta here. But I'll sing you a little song while you're waiting."

He sang as he doled out water, a tune that had come to him in the springs, the core of the song he hoped would bring recruits to their Refuge.

> *"Come you who thirst,*
> *You who hunger,*
> *All you longing to be free.*

> *"Find your way*
> *Through the paths of ruin*
> *To the hearth*
> *And the sacred tree."*

The line was still growing at the end of an hour when he heard a sharp whistle. It was the signal they had taught Zap and Zoom, and he quickly packed his wares, grabbed the handle of the wagon, and apologized to the waiting line.

"I am so sorry, ladies and gentlemen, but I find myself with an urgent appointment elsewhere! And my magician's intuition tells me the Lash is on its way. I recommend to you that you practice your own form of magic, and disappear!"

At the mention of the Lash, the crowd melted away. Bird slipped into the shadows, stripped off his colorful jacket and replaced it with a faded tee proclaiming Repent and Be Free! He tossed a gray sack over the flowered adornments of the wagon, and was winding his way through side streets and back alleys before the Lash reached his corner.

"You're enjoying this!" Madrone accused him when he ducked back into the Refuge to resupply. Zap and Zoom had met him at their prearranged rendezvous, blending into the crowd until he arrived. Together they trekked back to the Refuge to eat lunch and wait out the heat of the day.

"Is that a crime—that I should have maybe one moment or two of enjoyment in my life?" Bird asked.

"No, it's just ... "

"Just what? Would we be better at this if I was miserable? Would we win some extra martyr points? Believe me, Madrone, if you're looking for opportunities to suffer, they'll turn up!"

But she couldn't tell him what it was that so irked her when he came back through the Gateway of the Dead, whistling and grinning. It was not that she wanted him to suffer, just that she couldn't help but remember how he had suffered at home, among the gardens and the running streams and the kind and laughing people. He had glowered and brooded and closed himself off. And here, among the ruins and the thirst and the unrelenting, grim work, he was like the old Bird, laughing, playful, as if some weight had been lifted.

And that made her afraid—afraid that he would never return with her to those gardens, that they would never be at peace together, watching a child of their own play.

But he was happy. Happiness, Maya always said, was not situational. "There's a certain type of person—organizers. Activists. Fighters. Doesn't matter how grim the situation, or how bad the odds. As long as they can see something before them they can do, they're happy!" she would say.

Bird and the boys ventured forth again in the evening, when people were returning from their daily search for the means of survival. Again he gave out water, and hummed his tunes, and succeeded in evading the Lash on their rounds.

The next day they revisited the corners he had staked out in his first foray. A few shy people came, bringing scraps of onion peels or burnt beans. Few people cooked, he realized, and those who did used every edible scrap, but one enterprising youngster had ripped up a bagful of weeds from an empty lot, and when Bird accepted them with praise, others followed suit. He still gave out the odd free sample, especially to children, but often they returned with a handful of dried Bermuda grass or a fistful of purslane.

Back in the Refuge, they layered the greens with shredded paper and built a compost heap, reserving some scraps to feed to the worms. The dried grasses and desiccated scraps of weeds they laid down as mulch. The outlines of a garden began to take shape.

Bird's forays out into the world served another purpose, too. For as he walked his route, he would sing tunes from the North, old popular songs of the last century, hymns to the Four Sacred Things. But always, he came back to the Song of Refuge.

It was a strong tune, a bit sad, yet hopeful, solemn as a hymn, but "sticky"—one of those tunes so catchy that it sang itself over and over in your head. People no longer sang like they once did, before records and radio and mp3s and iPods. But the music players were no longer cheap and ubiquitous—in this part of town, they were worth a year's supply of water for a poor person. And so people hummed and sang, tunelessly sometimes, out of key, hoarse or squeaky. Bird knew he was having success when he heard a young boy in a crowd whistling the Refuge Song.

Madrone, meanwhile, began to work on creating the healing center. One of the buildings close to the springs seemed structurally intact. It had a large room at the entrance, then a long corridor with many cubbies that had once been treatment rooms. She found massage tables still intact under mounds of dust and concrete chips, and moldy pillows and mildewed sheets.

"If it hasn't fallen down in twenty years, chances are good that it can make it a few more," Bird said when she showed him the building.

She began clearing away the rubble and the old furniture while Bird and the boys were out, and exploring deeper into the ruins. Not far from the entrance to the springs was an old supermarket. Its shelves had toppled in the quake, and its floor was knee-deep in chewed boxes and rodent droppings. Everything perishable was long gone. But she tied a rag around her face to keep out the dust and the mold, and grubbed through the remains.

She was rewarded by finding a trove of cleaning supplies. The labels on the jugs were cracked and faded, but she found dish soap and cleanser and laundry soap, a couple of brooms intact in plastic wrappers, as well as cups and dishes and kitchen pots.

Although she worried about Bird and the boys, she welcomed a little time alone. It had been far too long since she'd had any solitude. And she welcomed the simple and satisfying task of cleaning. It kept her from fretting, wondering what was happening to Bird.

She shifted heavy loads, hauled water, and scrubbed walls and floors on her hands and knees. Physical work made you tired, she thought, but compensated with endorphins. Healing took a different kind of energy and led to a different kind of exhaustion, as if the effort pulled life force out of her. With all the demands of the work and the stress, she still felt that this time in the Refuge was a reprieve.

It took her a long afternoon to get the big room even moderately clean. In the end, it fell far short of the immaculate standards of the healing center back home. But she judged it would serve.

Darkness was falling, and Bird and the boys were not back yet. She told herself not to worry. She would start dinner, and brew herself a well-deserved cup of herbal tea. She was catching a spark from the fire drill when she heard the rattle of cartwheels and a cheerful whistle. Relief washed over her like a warm bath.

Bird and the boys hauled the cart in through the entrance passage. He grabbed her in an intense hug, and she pressed against him as if to drive away even the memory of separation. She was hungry for him, now—she wanted, needed their singing flesh to affirm that they were both still alive. She could feel him grow hard against her, feel the answering heat rising in him.

Titters and giggles broke the spell. Zap and Zoom were watching them closely, smirking.

Reluctantly, they broke apart.

"Good day?" Madrone asked.

"We wandered, we sang our song, we collected thirteen New Empire dollars and forty-seven cents along with a chariot full of compost-to-be, we successfully evaded roving guards and policemen. What more could you ask of a day?"

"I could think of something," Madrone said wistfully. "But it doesn't look like we're going to get much of a chance for that."

In the small hours of the night, Bird woke. He could hear soft snoring from Zap and Zoom. He felt Madrone nestled into the curve of his arm, and suddenly he wanted her, needed to feel her soft skin against his, her mouth on his. But she was so tired. Was it right to wake her?

He kissed the top of her head softly, and gently stroked her back. She sighed, and arched like a cat being stroked, and suddenly he knew she was awake. Her hands caressed his buttocks, her mouth found his, and they began the dance of arousal and passion, stifling every gasp and moan so that they wouldn't wake the boys. The enforced silence lent intensity to the pleasure, as if it had become something secret and dangerous and thrilling. She was moist and ready—he was eager and rampant—and she rolled over to ride him....

Tittering broke into their rhythm. Madrone looked over to see the boys watching them, eyes wide and grins on their faces.

"Go back to sleep, you little brats!" Bird yelled, as Madrone grabbed the blanket and pulled it back over them.

***

"Parenthood is ruining our sex life," Madrone complained as they soaked in the pool the next night.

"It's been rumored to do that."

In the middle of the pool, the boys were ducking each other, shrieking and sputtering. They had progressed swiftly with their swimming lessons, and now both could float like dolphins and make their way around the pool with a combination of dog paddling and sheer thrashing.

"I can't stand it." Under the cover of their noise, she moved closer to him, letting her body press against his. "Every time you go away, I want you more and more, and then when you come back ..."

"I know. Isn't there a nice orphanage somewhere we could send them to? Like something out of Dickens, perhaps. Gray linsey-woolsey, and gruel."

A huge splash left them both sputtering. Bird launched himself off the wall and chased Zoom around the pool, splashing him while the boy giggled uncontrollably.

It was good to see them laugh, Madrone thought, remembering the terrified urchins they had been just a few short weeks ago. It was worth some sacrifice to see them becoming real children. But high on her list of priorities was finding somewhere with a door they could shut.

A few days later, she ventured up to a second level in a solid-looking ruin and opened a door to what must have once been an apartment. The hallway ended abruptly in a sheer drop where the back rooms had fallen away, but there was an intact living room complete with a mildewed sofa, and a kitchen alcove furnished with silverware and blue stoneware china, matching plates and mugs and a big teapot, still usable although its spout was chipped.

The kitchen walls were tiled in slate and the counter was a long slab of polished granite. Someone had taken thought for this kitchen, carefully chosen the dishes and the flatware, admired the deep tones of the blue against the silver-gray slate. Someone who liked clean lines and natural colors. Madrone could imagine the woman who'd cooked here, decisive, no-nonsense, a young professional, perhaps a doctor like herself. She wondered what her fate had been.

One closed door led off the hallway, and Madrone tried the handle. It opened to a bedroom—dusty and musty but remarkably free of rodent droppings or damage. A patchwork quilt covered a real bed. Though clouds of dust rose from it when she sat down, there was no smell of mildew or rot. She guessed the room was well-built enough, and the door closed tightly enough, to keep out the vermin. Under the quilt were natural wool blankets, marred by only a few moth holes, and pink sheets.

Above a desk, shelves held books in good condition: a high school biology text, a few math books, a dictionary. A student had lived here, someone neat, well-organized, with slightly romantic tendencies. On the wall was a giant poster of the pop group Zanadu, widely popular back in the '20s, and a blown-up photo from *Vogue* of Soleil, who had been America's top model back in '26 when there still was an America. The posters were faded and one corner of Zanadu had pulled away from the wall and hung free, slightly curled.

Below the textbooks was a whole shelf of sci-fi and fantasy—treasures to savor if she ever had time and leisure to read, or more likely, a stock for the healing center when she had patients lingering in recovery. Another shelf held a collection of well-read children's books which Madrone noted with joy—something to read to Zap and Zoom should they ever become civilized enough to sit still and listen.

She took down a copy of *The Velveteen Rabbit* with a torn and stained cover. Inside was an inscription, "To Sherine on her fifth birthday, with lots of love, Mom." A much-battered stuffed rabbit, patched and worn, sat next to it.

She wondered if Sherine and her mom had survived the 'quake and the aftermath, and why there was no dad on the inscription. Had they lived? If so, she had never come back to reclaim her books and her well-loved rabbit.

Best of all, the door had a button lock that could be set from inside. She tried it—and it worked!

She sat gingerly on the bed and leafed through the old, familiar tale of the toy that was loved so much he became real.

Maybe that's our challenge, she thought. With Zap and Zoom—if we love them enough, will they become real boys? Instead of bruised, abused little orcs-in-the-making?

Well, she would love them all the better for a door that locked!

⁓

She kept the room as her secret. The next day, she worked all morning, stripping the bed and laundering the pale beige curtains by hand in the big washtub. While they were drying in the sun, she pulled out the throw rugs and swept the floor. She wiped down the walls and washed the windows. It would be a surprise for Bird, and even though part of her feared she was tempting fate, she went ahead.

At the end of two days, she was ready. Bird and the boys jockeyed the biggest load of compost materials yet through the passageway, and Madrone helped fork them out into the appropriate piles. Then she ushered them up the stairs and revealed their new quarters. She'd cleaned out the living room and made up pallets for the two boys there, with chests of drawers to hold their meager belongings. On each bed, she had placed one of the scavenged stuffed animals.

"Whazzat?" Zoom asked, picking up a brown bear that guarded his pillow.

"It's a present for you," Madrone said. "A toy. Something to play with."

He looked at her as if she were speaking a language he didn't understand. Zap picked up the worn rabbit that lay on his bed, swung it hard, and whacked Zoom in the head with it. A battle followed that sent tufts of stuffing flying around the room. Bird finally grabbed Zoom and pinned his arms as Madrone took hold of Zap's wrist.

"Enough! You want to use your toys to hurt each other, we'll take them away!" Bird thundered, and confiscated the battered animals.

"Come look at our room," Madrone said to Bird. She flung open the door, and watched his face light up in amazement.

"A real bed! And no rats?" he said hopefully.

"Not a one! And best of all . . . " She demonstrated the lock on the door.

"Now I see how you earn your reputation for working miracles!"

He examined the bookshelves, the desk, the fresh curtains hung on the wall. She flung open the closet door and showed him hangers ready for clothing, when they acquired a wardrobe. At the foot of the bed was a chest, filled with fresh-washed linens.

But as she pointed out more and more of the room's amenities, his grin slowly changed to a frown.

"What's wrong?" she asked. "I thought you'd be happy to have a room of our own, a little privacy and comfort."

"I am happy," he assured her. "But you're nesting."

"Why shouldn't I nest? Isn't that part of creating a refuge?"

"Just don't ... " He stopped.

"Don't what?"

He was looking down into the linen chest. He let the lid drop closed with a thump. "Don't forget this is a war."

"I'm quite well aware of what this is," Madrone said, angry. She had worked so hard on the space, and she'd expected him to be pleased. "You don't have to tell me."

"Don't get snitty."

"I'm not snitty! You want to bitch—fine, go sleep in the rubble. Don't risk losing your hard edge!"

"I don't want to sleep in the rubble." He came over to her, slid his arms around her.

"Alone!" She pushed him away.

"I definitely do not want to sleep alone, when I could sleep here with you. Behind a door that locks. It's just ... " He turned away, looking out the window.

"Just what?"

"Just that everything precious is a risk," he said in a low voice. "Something more to lose."

"Deal with it!" She stomped out of the door, slamming it behind her.

~~~

She was chopping a precious foraged onion with the air of an executioner chopping heads. Bird squatted down and blew on the smoking fire until it caught a flame.

"I'm sorry," he said.

"How sorry?"

"I'm kneeling at your feet."

"Grovel!"

"I'm groveling! I apologize. I have failed to adequately appreciate the wonderfulness, the awesomeness, the incredibleness, the amazing, astounding, and absolutely fabulousness of your ... "

"Okay, okay," she cut him off. "That's enough!"

"I could do more. Now that we have a door that locks, I could do almost anything to get back on your good side."

"Just don't shut the door between us," she told him. She was still holding the knife and gesturing as she talked, and she looked fierce as a warrior Goddess. A healer, he thought, is not just a comforter. A healer does battle. She would never just slap on a bandage. She would always lance the wound.

"You can close down, and try to protect yourself from getting hurt," she went on. "Or you can open up, and live as well as you can. And if they want to take that from you, make them fight for it. Fight for every inch of your life they want to expropriate. Don't hand it over to them for fear they'll come and get it!"

"I'm here," he said. "I'm with you. I'm not running away."

"Then be with me!"

He took the knife out of her hand, laid it down, and kissed her. "Okay, mama bird. Make us a nice, cozy nest. But no baby birds, okay? Aside from the two little crows we've got."

"Do you ever want babies?" she asked in a low voice.

"Do you?"

"I've delivered so many for other women. Yes, yes, I want my own." She snuck a glance up at him to see how he would respond to this admission.

"Here?" He kissed her on the forehead. "In the midst of the rubble and the rat turds?"

"No. But somehow, someday. Don't you?"

He pulled away from her. "I can't think about someday. I have to think about now. If I start hoping for a someday—I won't be able to do the things I need to do. It's bad enough having you to think about."

"Oh, thanks!" She pulled away, and tumbled the onions into the hot frying pan, where they hissed like an angry cat. "I'm sorry for getting in the way of your warrior focus!"

"You know what I mean."

"No, I don't!"

"If something happened to you—if they got you and I had to watch you being hurt ... "

He was shaking and sweaty now. Back in the room, with little Rosa, seeing her rictus smile of pain and terror. Who do we work on, you or her?

Madrone set down the knife she was holding and took his hand. She would do all she could to ease his pain, but she would not be held hostage to it. That would not help either of them.

"You can't keep me here, Bird, like the nice little housewife cleaning up while the men go off and take the risks. I have to take my own risks."

"I know," he nodded.

"I do want kids," she said. "Someday. When I don't have to worry about them being taken and broken in the pens. When there are no more pens. There's nothing I want more than to see them running through the streets on the learning tracks, and you teaching them how to ride a skateboard."

He was staring at the fire with that shuttered look on his face, and she could tell that her words were somehow hurting him, pushing him to stare into that well of pain he carried just below the surface. The cap he kept on it was brittle and thin, like a skim of ice. Was she right, she wondered, to so constantly smash through it, to keep churning the waters and refusing to let it form?

But wise or not, she was a healer. She knew what happens when a scab forms too soon over a deep infection. Was she pouring salt on his wounds, or saline solution to cleanse them and release the pus?

"I want your kids," she went on. "Not just your seed—I want us to enjoy them together, watching them grow and say their first words and take their first steps, and being thrilled together every time they do some perfectly ordinary thing that every child does. I want to find out what kind of father you'll be."

"I know what kind of mother you'll be," he said in a low voice.

"What?"

"Devoted. Selfless. And scary."

"Scary?"

He looked up and grinned at her. "'You be good now, little Johnny and Janie. Clean your room, and whatever you do, don't piss Mommy off! Because Daddy doesn't want to come home and find you've been stung to death by a swarm of bees!'"

~~~~~~

They bedded the boys down in their new room, and Madrone opened the book she'd found that morning. It had taken threats and bribery to get them quiet enough to listen. The concept of "story" was foreign to them.

"Whazzat?" Zoom asked suspiciously as she sat down with *The Velveteen Rabbit*.

"It's a book."

"What's it for?"

"It's for reading. I'm going to read it to you."

They looked at her suspiciously, as if she were going to inflict something painful upon them.

"Why?" Zap asked. He'd begun asking "why" a lot, and she took that as a sign of health, as if he were becoming something more like a normal boy.

"It's a good story," she said.

"What's a story?" Zoom asked.

She didn't know how to answer. For a moment she was overcome with bleakness. How have they done this? she wondered. How have they taken away not just the myths and the songs, but the very concept of what a story might be?

She remembered Johanna sitting at her bedside, reading from a book of African tales. And Grandpa Rio, who started with the first of the Harry Potter books, and read her at least three of them before she was old enough and impatient enough to finish the rest of the series herself. And curling up on the couch with Maya, listening to her weave tales out of her own rich imagination. Suddenly a sharp memory came to her from long before that, before she had come to live with them in California. She was small, and she nestled into a warm body, and a low voice murmured while dark hands turned pages in a bright-colored book. There had been a bird, with blue and red and green feathers, and a monkey....

She had so few memories of her own mother. Each one was precious. She blessed the boys for evoking this one.

"A story is ... it's fun," she assured them. "It's like telling about something that happened to somebody. It can be real or imaginary."

"Whass 'maginary'?"

"It's something you make up out of your own head, that didn't really happen."

"Like a lie?" Zoom asked. Bird had lately been trying hard to impress upon them the value of telling the truth.

Maya had always said that writing fiction was telling the truth in the form of lies. But how to explain that to the boys?

"It's not like a lie, because people know it's not true," she said.

"Then why tell it?"

"Because ... because even if it isn't true, it might teach you something about the world. About people."

"How, if it's a lie?"

"Let's just read the story, and maybe you'll see."

"Don't wanna!" Zap dove into his blankets and covered his ears.

"Then you'll miss a good story," Madrone said calmly, and began to read. "Once there was a velveteen rabbit, and in the beginning he was really splendid ... "

"What's splendid?" Zoom asked.

"Great. Fantastic. Wonderful."

"Whass velteen?"

"It's a kind of material, like a soft cloth. He was like those stuffed toys I gave the two of you, that you were hitting each other with."

"Whass a rabbit?"

"A little animal, with big ears, that hops around on its big hind feet. But a velveteen rabbit is a toy, a pretend rabbit."

By now Zap had poked his head back up from under the covers. "Why?"

It had seemed to take forever to get through the first page, because she had to explain about Christmas, and stockings, and presents, and aunts and uncles, even parents.

But over the course of the story, they grew interested. It amazed them to think about a boy fortunate to have parents, and things that were just for him to have fun with. And yet every page seemed to illumine more clearly their deprivation. Before, they'd had no idea of what they had lacked in their own small lives, no concept of family or wealth or comfort, and so they didn't miss it. They did not feel deprived or inferior. But as they learned more, the "why's" would grow. Why don't

I have a mother? Why was I born to be beaten and misused? Is there something wrong with me, that I was destined for this fate?

By the time the velveteen bunny finally hopped away to join his flesh-and-blood companions, Madrone was ready to join him. She closed the book with a sigh of relief.

"Go to sleep now," she said, planting a kiss on each of their foreheads. Zoom immediately rubbed his off and, watching him, Zap followed suit. "Bird and I will just be in the next room, not far away. But you sleep here, in your own beds!"

They closed the door and locked it. Madrone slipped out of her jeans and shift, pulled down the covers and invited Bird into the softness of a real mattress and clean sheets. For a blissful hour, they made good use of their new privacy, rediscovering each other.

Then they heard giggles at the door, and the handle rattled.

"Ignore it," Bird murmured, nibbling on her ear. And they did.

But later, as they lay spent in each others' arms, the giggles turned to cries.

"Mado! Mado!" she heard Zap's plaintive voice. Her heart turned over. He had never called her name before.

She pulled on her shift and went out to him.

"What is it? What is it, baby?"

"Stinky rabbit shit!" he screeched and careened off, laughing maniacally.

"The time of penitence is over. Retribution draws to a close, and the time of regeneration draws near. Find you a refuge, saith the One!" Bird varied his singing and his water trading with a bit of prophecy. Madrone, who had announced that morning that she was done with being a stay-at-home mom, poured water from their jugs into the cups and bottles of the long line of people eager to trade.

Zap and Zoom were somewhere not far away. They raced around like jackal pups going out to forage and scout.

They had ventured out farther afield that day, setting up the wagon in what had once been the parking lot of a big box store. Now it was a makeshift camp of the homeless who fashioned crude shelters out of old pieces of siding and pallets. But they were out of the worst of the slums, and in the surrounding streets workers and professionals still lived with their families in homes and apartments. True, many of the backyards were now crammed with jerry-built rental units, overcrowded with families on the downward slide. And many of the houses were boarded up, with faded For Sale signs on paved-over front lawns.

But there were still working families here, children with their knapsacks full of books, purposeful men dressed for the office, women in skirts and suit jackets and nails cut short on their typists' hands, others with hair in scarves and the rough hands of cleaners.

They timed their arrival for early morning, when students and teachers headed for school and the day shift workers arrived at the factories that recycled old electronics into new vidscreens.

"Oh, my people, you have been lied to and oppressed but the time of change draws nigh ... "

"You're a little inconsistent in your seventeenth-century English," Madrone told him. The morning rush had died down and now the streets were empty. "If it's 'saith,' it should be 'draweth.'"

"'A foolish consistency is the hobgoblin of little minds.' Emerson said that," Bird hissed back.

"Iseth."

"Ith."

"Haveth," she countered.

"Hath," said a voice. Standing before them was a thin man in his early forties, his close-cropped dark hair beginning to thin on top, his slacks casual and slightly frayed at the hem but of good make, as if they had once belonged to a business suit. His sweater had been carefully darned at the elbows, his leather, well-made loafers were scuffed. Everything about him spoke of a professional or even a Subprime manager, lately come down in the world. His long face was drawn, his dark eyes looked haunted.

"Hath," he repeated. "I used to teach seventeenth-century drama. You can trust me on that."

Bird nodded and smiled. The man's eyes darkened. His fingers trembled as he took the cup of water Madrone offered.

"I commend your performance," he said. He drank, slow and deep, then gathered his courage. "Tell me, is that all it is? Or is there truth in prophecy?"

"The prophet speaks with the voice of truth," Madrone said with certainty.

His voice lowered to a whisper.

"Does it exist? Is there a refuge?" He looked around quickly, as if to catch anyone who might be eavesdropping.

Bird and Madrone exchanged worried glances. He could be an agent of the Lash, sent to trap them. But if they were ever to populate the Refuge with others beside themselves, sooner or later they would have to tell people where it was.

Bird began to sing.

> "Follow the ancient way of freedom,
> Traverse the wood of Christmas green,
> The legacy of the Latin poet,
> Will be your guide to a world unseen."

The man looked dismayed. His face crumpled, as if the last hope that had propped him up had suddenly collapsed. And then slowly, a new realization began to dawn.

"The ancient way of freedom ... " he breathed, and his face broke out into a wide grin.

"Traverse the wood of Christmas green ... " Bird said with a wink.

They sang the verse over and over, until the man had memorized it. Then Bird taught him two more. Just as they were going over the song one last time, they heard a sharp whistle.

"So sorry, my good man, but my prophetic voice tells me the Lash draweth nigh. And the time to reveal these teachings to the unworthy has not yet come."

Madrone had the wagon packed almost before he finished speaking. The man turned and hurried away down a side street, humming softly to himself. They faded back into an alley that led in the opposite direction.

"Do you think he got it?" Bird said. "Is it too obscure?"

"We'll see," Madrone said. "If he has an old map, he should figure it out."

Chapter Thirty-One

A ND HERE'S TO THE ARMY!" MATTHEWS RAISED HIS GLASS, A HARD light in his steel-gray eyes, his face immobile, the skin with that taut sheen of a recent lift. His gray hair was perfectly waved, but Wendell thought he could determine the pinprick pattern of implants on the dome of his skull. He felt conscious, suddenly, of his own receding hairline. Should he have something done about it? Or let it stand as a mark of his concern for more important things?

Matthews's family owned the docking facilities where ships from the Gyre unloaded their cargo, and Wendell couldn't even speculate on the extent of his wealth.

"To the army!" Culbertson echoed, and the three of them clinked glasses.

Around them circulated most of the top Primes of the Southlands, inheritors of armaments factories and chip plantations and vidscreen empires. All men, for this was not one of those social occasions where wives and Trophies were invited. Scantily-clad waitresses circulated with the drinks, and in a roped-off corner of the pavilion a group of Pets played on a climbing structure, their see-through shifts barely covering their children's bodies.

Wendell sipped his drink cautiously. It was single-malt whiskey, a rare, incredibly expensive relic of the old world, and he savored the smoky flavor on his tongue. But possibly laced with ... something?

It was an honor to be invited to this party, to be taken into the Primes' private world. Or was it a test?

Culbertson fixed him with a laser-like gaze and raised his glass again.

"To the army ... which has let a gaggle of treeboffers from the North actually take six plantations? Or am I misinformed?"

Wendell gulped a much larger swallow of whiskey than he'd intended to take. A test. He raised his own glass, made himself sound hard and confident. "According to plan!"

"What sort of plan?" Matthews's voice held a snakelike hiss.

"Lure them deep into the Valley, let them think they're succeeding—then wham! Close the trap."

Matthews and Culbertson exchanged glances.

"Costly," Matthews said.

"Not nearly so much as engaging them too early, when they can regroup." Wendell hoped he sounded solid, assured. He feared there might be a petulant note in his voice, a tone of the complaint he bit back. *And when we wouldn't have the troops to pursue and finish them off—the troops you refuse to provide.*

Just then came a burst of music. Spotlights played over the vast, landscaped yard, the wide view beyond, and converged on the infinity pool that seemed to spill directly into the sea of lights far below them.

Culbertson nodded and they walked forward to the pool's edge. From the loudspeakers came the dulcet tones of an orchestra playing Swan Lake. One by one, the Pets who had been playing ran out on the diving board and launched themselves, arms outstretched. They had traded their shifts for tutus of swan feathers that tipped up in a titillating way over their childish bottoms. It made Wendell sick, yet there was also a tiny spark of heat in his loins. Something about their perfect beauty, their complete submission to the leering eyes of the men who watched them....

Once in the water, they began a ballet. Wendell desperately wanted to look away, but he knew that he couldn't. *This snake rising in his netherlands ... that wasn't him. That's not who I am. It's the drink,* he told himself. *It's something they put in the drink.*

Culbertson raised his hand.

"In a moment, gentlemen, we will distribute the party favors." There was a round of polite applause.

Not me, Wendell told himself firmly. *I'll find a way out of it. Test or no test.*

"But first, I'd like to ask our honored General of the Army to say a few words to us all."

And then Wendell knew why he was there. They'd heard the rumors. Every Prime worth his station had his own set of spies and informants. They knew the war wasn't going well. His job was to reassure them, convince them, that it indeed was.

He took another gulp of whiskey for courage. "Gentlemen, I bring you greetings from the victorious Army of the Stewardship! A toast!" They all raised glasses, and he sipped again. He felt the whiskey warming him, sliding through his veins like liquid fire. "You may have heard rumors of packs of rebels and deserters making their way south. Like rats deserting a sinking ship, they are fleeing from their humiliation at the hands of the army! And just as you bait a trap for a rat, we have set out the bait. Even as we speak, the jaws are snapping shut! I give you the Southlands, secure forever!" He raised his glass again to a loud chorus of cheers.

"And I give you, General Wendell!" Culbertson cried. "General, the first pick is yours!"

He smiled, and in his eyes Wendell saw cold satisfaction. This is not a test, he thought. It's discipline. He knows. He knows that all of this horrifies and sickens me, that it goes against the teachings of my church. And now he's put me in this position to show me, as if I had any doubts, that he holds all the power here.

For I can't possibly say no. A dozen excuses ran through his mind. I'm not worthy of this honor. I have a sudden case of stomach flu. Even simply saying, Sorry, I'm happily married and not into this.

But there was more at stake than his own moral comfort. There was his army, the lives of his men.

And his church. Culbertson could override their protection with a word, calling out the Retro hounds, arresting upright old Reverend Barr as a heretic....

Surely he could steel himself to this for their sake.

At the thought, the heat began to rise. The drug. The whiskey had to be drugged.

He stabbed at the figures in the pool at random. "That one."

Culbertson again gave him that cat-playing-with-mouse smile. "Excellent choice! It will be delivered to your playroom."

The crowd around the pool dissolved into laughter and arguments over who got which of the Pets. Culbertson put an arm around Wendell and led him away.

"Don't worry about the remains," he said as he took Wendell to the door of a cabana. "They will be disposed of."

⁓

As the Army of Liberation moved southward, Cress found himself each night walking the land, trying to envision it reclaimed and healed. Sometimes he was alone. Some nights he and Erik Farmer walked together.

"How soon do you think we can bring this back into production?" Cress asked as they looked out over a wide stretch of fields they'd liberated in the first week of the campaign. Gentle, rolling hills rose beyond the dry, flat ground where sickly stalks of corn struggled up through the whitened, tortured earth.

Erik shook his head. He bent down, scooped up a handful of dirt, sniffed it, rubbed some between his fingers, spat on it and tried to roll it into a ball.

"This isn't soil," he said. "It's a chemical desert. And without a constant infusion of more chemicals, nothing's going to grow in its current state. If anything did manage to eke out an existence, there wouldn't be much nutrition in it."

Cress nodded. He wasn't a farmer, but every child of the City knew the basics of organic gardening and food production. As a man of Water Council, he could tell that this land had a deeply damaged water cycle. The dust-dry soil seemed to absolutely repel water, not hold it in. Around him in the hills he could see arid draws that once had filled seasonally with the run-off from winter rains, and would have held underground moisture all year. Now shriveled vegetation and blackened skeletons of trees lined the routes where, in happier times, springs would have gurgled. Ripples of soil over bare rock escarpments told him that when rain did come, it ran off the landscape in sheets, taking the topsoil with it.

"So what do we do?" Cress asked. "Are we going to have to abandon the whole Central Valley? Then where the jacks will we get the land to feed the people?"

"It's not hopeless," Erik assured him. "But it's also not instant. Luckily the rains are still to come this year. As soon as you tell me it's secure, we'll bring in our keyline plows and break up the hardpan. We'll inoculate it with micro-organisms and infuse it with biobrews. Then we'll plant a hardy cover crop we can disc in next spring. We can graze some cattle intensively to manure and add beneficial disturbance to the land. And we'll plant trees—we've got lots of starts for some fast-growing acacias and Siberian pea shrubs. They're hardy—they can grow on almost anything. You all in Water Council can contour the land so water can sink in and we can start to refill the aquifers."

"Okay, okay, I don't need to know every last recipe for the compost tea!" When Erik got started on land regeneration, his favorite subject, it was hard to stop him. "How long do you estimate it will take?" Cress asked.

"Not as long as you might think," Erik assured him. "We'll start to see improvement within a year. In five years, this could be a paradise."

"But how are we going to feed people through that year? That's a long time to wait for dinner."

"Aquaponics!" Erik proclaimed with enthusiasm. "We set up fish farms on a mass scale, produce proteins and greens from the plants that clean the water."

"Is there enough water for that?"

"It uses about ninety percent less than conventional farming. It all recirculates. We'll raise worms for feed, and mealy bugs. And with the excess, there's always meal patties."

"Yuck!" Cress made a face.

"They got us through the year after the Uprising. Taste pretty good, as long as you don't think about what's in them," Erik went on cheerfully. "Protein and greens, we can provide, and as for wheat and corn, well, I'd say we build up windrows of mulch and plant potatoes. Should do okay over the winter here, and they're nourishing. Plus they're easily made into chips."

"No more chips, please!" Cress objected. "It's been hard enough weaning the breeds and pen-girls off them."

———

Midnight, and a low moon rose over the flat waste of desert where River crouched behind a sagebrush. The moon curved to the left and he thought to himself that it was waning, and that once he wouldn't have noticed or cared but now he knew, thanks to the children of the City and the Learning Track of the Moon. It would set next morning, and be skinnier tomorrow and the next day and the next, until it went completely dark. Useful information for a sojuh planning ops.

Before his defection to the City, he had never thought about the moon. He had barely noticed most of the world—there had been worlds within worlds within worlds around him that he'd been blind to. Plant worlds, animals, bugs, and the mysterious worlds within the heads and hearts of other people.

Now he knew so many more things. He knew that some people worshipped the moon as a Goddess. Called her "Maiden" when she was a skinny little thing like a pen-girl. "Mother," big and round and full. "Crone" when she skinnied down again to a sliver, old woman like Maya had been.

He wondered if he could talk to this moon like he'd once talked to Maya, and if the moon could hear, and how he'd know if she answered.

But he knew other things about the moon, too. It was a place of bare rock, a place of extremes of heat and cold, with no air to breathe. Long, long ago, it had spun off from the earth, when the earth was only a glob of molten rock and metal. The children had explained orbits to him, and how the earth turned on an axis, although he was still trying to wrap his head around that.

And was the moon a Goddess, or a ball of rock? How could it be both things? No one had been able to quite explain that to him.

"It can be both or neither, more and less," Maya had told him when he'd asked her. That had been one of the last conversations they'd had around her old kitchen table. "The moon doesn't change, only the window through which you view it."

He hadn't understood that at all, but she had sunk back into silence and the waking dream in which she walked in those last days.

Men had walked on the moon, nearly a hundred years ago now. He pondered, for a moment, how those long-ago people had had the power and the knowledge for that great adventure, when nowadays they could barely survive here on earth. The army had not bred him to wonder, but now that his mind was awake it seemed to be working all the time.

And pondering passed the time as he was doing what sojuhs *were* trained to do: waiting. Around him, ten of his unit waited with him, sheltering behind clumps of brush or plastered down into slight depressions in the earth. The landscape of rolling hills was behind them now, and this section of the Valley was flat as a parade ground and bone dry. Aside from the blistering white fields of corn, lined up in military rows, nothing grew but desert scrub.

Waiting. Sojuhing was mostly waiting, and that held true for the Army of Liberation as much as it ever had in the old days. He could smell the crispness of the clear night air that carried the sharp, chemical stink of the fields, and an earthier, pungent scent of sage. The air was chilly, and he hunched his jacket up around him. In the silence, the woosh, woosh of his own breath sounded like a jet engine with a missing cycle. He opened his mouth, trying to breathe more softly.

He hated waiting. At the best of times, it was boring and uncomfortable, hard to keep still with the juice in his veins pumped for an op. But tonight something felt more deeply wrong to him, like the scary movie music that played when the shit was gonna hit the fan.

Everything had gone well, so far. Maybe too well. They had taken plantation after plantation, without much opposition. But those earlier farms were the outliers, poor and badly guarded. Their equipment was patched together and their command was the turdballs the rest of the army shat out, losers and failures that couldn't cut a real command.

But now they were hitting the core of the Stewards' agricultural operations, plantations long established and well-defended. Surprise was no longer on their side, and sooner or later retaliation would come.

It could be tonight. This could be his last night to look at the moon, that comforting source of light, to reassure himself that after it waned to darkness it would begin to grow again.

Far away, a dog barked. He heard the squeak of a key in a metal lock. Someone had let himself into the slave quarters, probably for some fun and games. After a while, he heard something between a scream and a moan.

Then he heard the tromp, tromp of marching feet. The sentries were talking softly as they passed, kicking up the chemical dust that got into River's nose and threatened to make him sneeze. He pinched his nose. One step, another step. The murmur of voices began to resolve itself into words.

"Beaner's like a dog in a shit-pile, rollin' in slime."

"No slime in those duster cracks. All rough and dried up."

They were approaching ... then they were level with River's hiding place, then past. He let out a low bird whistle and sprang forward, dropping a blanket over the sentries. They cried out, disoriented, then the cries died away as the sleepgas the blankets were soaked in took effect.

River grabbed a leg of one sentry, Ace took the other, and they dragged him off back behind the line as other troops followed with the second sentry. Quickly, they tied their hands together, bound their legs and gagged them. Then River whistled the all clear.

Ace cut the fence and he and his band rolled it away. Cress led two hundred of the army's best troops swiftly to the gap in the wire. They streamed through, a runnel of silent men and women in the dark. River joined Cress at the front as they encircled the farmhouse that served as headquarters for this plantation.

When they were in place, Cress fired a shot into the air. He raised the bullhorn and called out:

"Citizens of the Stewardship, we hereby liberate this farm in the name of freedom. Come out and surrender, and you will not be harmed."

A bullet whizzed by his ear. He dropped to the ground as a barrage of fire came from the overseers' quarters. They were shooting from every window, in all directions at once, and many of the River's troops were hit, falling down groaning or screaming if they were not killed on the spot.

"Down!" Cress yelled, a bit too late. Around the circle, troops flung themselves down to the ground, but the bullets and laser bursts hit lower. "Back!" Cress screamed.

It was a trap. A wall of firepower hit them from every side. The barren yard, the flat ground offered no cover. Some troops made it to the metal barracks, and sheltered behind them. Others crouched behind the legs of the water tower as bullets kicked up dust and laser traces lit it up in lines of bright color.

Cress and River plastered themselves to the ground in a hollow behind a truck where the great wheels concealed them. Someone crawled toward them from the fence line. It was Smokee, snaking through the dust.

A window opened in the metal shack, and a strong beam of light played over the ground, littered with the dead and wounded. As they watched in horror, a barrage of bullets poured out onto every body that moved or showed signs of life. The corpses jumped and twitched in a final, terrible dance.

From inside the slave quarters, screams were heard.

"Withdraw!" a voice thundered over the camp loudspeakers. "Surrender, or we will continue to inflict pain on our rightful property."

"Shit," Cress said. "What do we do?"

"Blast our way in!" Smokee said.

"At what cost?" Cress said. "I'm not fighting World War One all over again—over the top, men, into the rain of bullet fire!"

"Limpdicks!" Smokee snorted.

"Only one thing to do," River said.

Before Smokee could object, he whistled the retreat.

They poured back through the gap in the fence, under fire all the way, new casualties mounting as fast as they could drag the wounded through the barbed-wire fences. River led his old unit, what was left of it, to hold a rear guard as they retreated across the bare, flat lands to the shelter of a ring of low hills that surrounded the last farm they'd liberated. Here at last the pursuers fell away, and the night grew quiet except for the moans and cries of the injured.

Medics quickly set up a healing station, while River doubled the sentries to keep a lookout in case the Stewards tried to retaliate. He and the other commanders held a hurried conference in the back of the old overseers' quarters.

Cress couldn't speak. He was shivering. The units were still counting up their own, assembling a roster of the dead. But those bodies that lay twitching and jerking as the bullets thudded into them were his old friends, Cityfolk he had grown up with, argued with, laughed with. Opinionated Brook of Water Council would never again sit in a meeting and debate with him. Blowsy Jennie with her ample figure and loud voice, his neighbor for decades on Bernal Hill, would never hold another wild dance party, blasting music until dawn. Never again would bright-eyed Salim expound on the City's work credits and labor allocations with his keen enthusiasm.

Cress had made decisions, made the call, and they were dead. His hands were trembling, and he clenched his cup of chai tightly to conceal their shaking. Not since that first night, that first execution, had he given in to the need to run to the bushes and purge. He wanted to, now. But he was in command.

He forced himself to think about water, how it could tremble, and shiver, and then come back to stillness and calm. I am made of water, he told himself. Seventy per cent, if you want precision. I am water.

"Knew we were coming," River said. "Waiting for us. Party time's over."

Smokee was smoldering with rage, pacing back and forth, perching for a moment on the arm of an old sofa then springing up again to stalk around the room. If they hadn't physically pulled her back, she would have dashed in, guns blazing, all by herself, and been shot to pieces. Which would have solved a problem, Cress thought, though created other ones. Smokee was trusted by the sojuhs and the pen-girls, more than he was.

"We go back in, stronger," Smokee said. "We need more manpower."

"Personpower," Cress corrected her automatically.

"Fuck you!"

"Don't got it," River said quickly. "Billies dug in there strong. Expecting us. Whole fuckin' army go up against that, just get mowed down."

"We have to be like water," Cress said, with just a small quaver in his voice. He took a deeper breath, focused on slowing his pounding heart. "When you block a flow in one direction, it goes over, under, around, or seeps below. Or it pools up until it gets high enough to overflow the dam."

"So we hold them under siege," Erik suggested. "We can't get in, but we can make it so they can't get out."

"Take a long time," River said. "Likely that bunker well stocked inside with chips and water. Meanwhile, billies torture the slaves. Run the juice through the jewelry from the main boards. No radio tower to take out, there. Got it wired underground."

"Any way to cut off the juice?" Cress asked. "Something like an electro-magnetic pulse?"

"Sure," Beryl said. "If we had a nuclear bomb. A small one would do."

"I have an idea," Topaz said.

"If at first you don't succeed ... " Cress said as they snaked over the flat ground one more time. The MUC fit into his hand like an old-fashioned smartphone, and if its screen was correct, most of the guards were gone from the facility, chasing an illusion east, in the wrong direction.

The techies had stopped the medics from smashing the chips they removed from the liberados. Instead, they had embedded them in the necks of a flock of hardy desert sheep the Farmers' Guild had brought down with the army. The chips needed contact with a living, warm-blooded body to transmit their pulses. Shepherds drove the flock east, expecting that the guards would follow, eager to retrieve at least part of their lost labor force. And, hopefully, walk straight into an ambush that River's buddy Ace and his picked troops had prepared.

While they were gone, the Army of Liberation would make a new attempt on the plantation.

"Ready?" Cress asked, although truthfully he didn't feel ready him-self. He felt a sick coldness in the pit of his stomach, which had sent him over and over again to the compost toilets most of the night. He wished he could be like Smokee, who wrapped the cloak of rage around her like a shield of invincibility. Or like River, who seemed impervious to emo-tion. But his own rage seemed to have bled away into the rocky ground with the lives of his *compas*. He was no battle-hardened veteran, not yet. He couldn't look at himself or his friends as tools or weapons, useful but expendable.

"Ready," River replied.

Cress and River crept cautiously around the fence line toward the back of the metal warehouse that sheltered the overseers' command center. This plantation had no old farmhouse, only concrete and metal bunkers for staff and debt slaves alike. But the staff warehouse showed a patch of damp green moss underneath the dripping exhaust of the air conditioning. That was their target.

They moved carefully. Understaffed as the command post might be, they would still have sentries and watchers on the lookout for move-ment. And the watchers would have infrared scopes as well as eyes. Cress and River were wearing insulated wetsuits to conceal their body heat.

Unfortunately, Cress noted, that meant their body heat stayed in and made them torturously uncomfortable. But just for a little while, if they were lucky.

Strapped to Cress's back was a bow. Silly, maybe, going up against guns with bows and arrows, but it had seemed like the best plan and he had been archery champion back during his university days.

A burst of gunfire shattered the air. That was Smokee, who was finally getting her wish. She and a few other equally crazy commandos attacked from the front—mostly to pose a distraction. More shots—and the boom of a sound bomb. It was harmless, but would sound like a shell that had fallen short of the command post walls. It might worry them.

"Now," Cress hissed, and he and River made a run for the wall. They abandoned concealment for speed, and made it two thirds of the way before laser fire started zinging past them. They dropped and played dead for a long five minutes before River jumped up and ran an erratic course toward their goal. He had covered quite a bit of distance before the firing started up again. Meanwhile Cress crawled forward as quickly as he could.

River flung himself to the ground as bullets whizzed over his head. Cress lay still, his heart pounding. They waited a long moment—then an explosion sounded on the opposite side of the building. Cress prayed that would draw their attention as he raised himself to his knees, fitted his special payload arrow and drew back the string of his bow. It was still dark, and he would only have one chance. He was a good archer, but not fraggin' Robin Hood. He took a deep breath, muttered a prayer to someone, eyed his target, and fired.

Bullseye. Praise the Flow! The arrow went directly into the intake system for the air conditioning. Now, if all went well, the capsule of sleepgas it carried would burst, and in a short time, it would be nightynight for the guards.

He flung himself back down to the ground just as a bullet whizzed by so close he could smell the stink of scorched rubber from his wetsuit. He lay still for a long, long ten minutes. Then slowly, cautiously he raised his bow up. Nothing. His hand followed—then his head and torso. Whistling to River, he ran toward the building, slapping his gas mask on.

River followed. He was limping slightly, and there was blood seeping out from a gash in his wetsuit at his thigh.

"Hurt?"

"Scratch. Go! Go! Go!"

River shot the lock that held the metal door shut. An alarm screeched, but no one responded with shots or laser fire. They kicked in the door and quickly looked around. In each corner, a lookout station stuck out like a bay window with bulletproof glass on three sides. Each held gun emplacements and firing vents. And in each, two guards were slumped unconscious.

River and Cress tied them up and cautiously surveyed the rest of the building. They found and secured ten or more guards and overseers altogether, some in the mess hall and more in their barracks.

It all took time, and the first of the guards were beginning to moan and stir when they'd finished. There was still one more door, reinforced and heavily locked, that Cress suspected led down to the command center.

Careful, he signaled to River. The door could have protected the men below from the gas.

River grabbed a laser rifle from one of the unconscious guards and shot the lock out. They opened the door slowly and cautiously, keeping it as a shield between them and whatever might come from behind it. It led down to a stairwell, and at the bottom was another locked door.

Cress checked the MUC, and silently slid the screen over to River. There were two dots still blinking, two living men in the bunker below.

River went first, shooting the lock from above. They pushed open the second door, flattening themselves against the wall. A bullet zipped by them, ricocheting around the stairwell. River leaned forward and fired a two-handed blast of shots, laser from his left hand, bullets from his right.

Cautious silence, then the gunfire was returned.

The bunker was designed to be defended. The passageway curved and zigzagged to bar intruders from storming in. They traded shots again.

A buzz. Smokee's voice sounded in his earbud.

"What in fuck is going on?" Smokee asked. "You two dead or what?"

"We've cleaned out the upper levels," he told her. "But we're having trouble getting down into the bunker where the coms center is. It's well-defended."

"Coming right down."

"No, don't!" he protested, but she had signed off.

The stairwell was blazing with gunfire when Smokee reached the top. She sheltered behind the door and peered around, observing. Lasers zinged around corners, and bullets ricocheted around the concrete walls. One laser rifle, one automatic, she thought. There could be others behind them, but somehow she doubted it.

She was aflame with anger. The Valkyries had burst into the worker barracks, and what she saw there fueled her rage. These barracks were the worst yet, stifling ovens of metal, with the people reduced to dried-out husks, barely alive on their meager rations of chips and water. Some of them were too dull-eyed even to look up as the Valkyries pushed the door down and proclaimed the barracks a liberated zone. If these poor sticks died, Smokee thought, they wouldn't stink and rot, they'd just fall to dust and blow away. But a few of the livelier folks let out a feeble cheer.

In the back of the barracks was the pleasure room. Some overseer had been interrupted by the attack, caught literally with his pants down. A belt still lay on the floor where he had dropped it as he ran out to join the defense.

On the table, strapped down, lay the remains of his victim.

Smokee looked down at the mangled piece of flesh, and suddenly she was back in the pens, shrieking and bound and helpless, raging and fighting to the end of what was endurable, and then enduring more. She shook her head, blinked her eyes. A strap held a bound wrist to the table, so tight the hand was swollen and blue. She could feel that strap on her own wrist, the ache and throb, hear the voice begging to loosen it just a little, promising anything to relieve the pain. And then the numbness, as that pain was eclipsed by a larger pain.

She could hardly bear to look at the other injuries. Setting her gun down, she loosened the strap. It was one act of tenderness for the thing on the table, one small kindness. Then she picked up her rifle, her equalizer, her instrument of justice and revenge, and went out.

Now the anger filled her. She was alight with it, she felt herself glowing like a beacon. Nothing could stop her, not the prickheads in the bunker nor the jellydicks on her own side. Fucking men! The best of them were useless and the worst ...

There was a lull in the firing and Smokee propelled herself down the stairs with a banshee yell, laying down a storm of bullets ahead of her. She grabbed an incendiary from her pack and her arm was rising up to toss it through the open door when River snatched her back against the wall.

"What the jacks do you think you're doing?" Cress screamed at her.

"Let go of me! What are you two diddling around for?"

She was strong and wiry, and fueled by that instinctive rage that would let no man pin her down. River outweighed her, and he pushed her back against the concrete. She kneed him in the groin, and as he staggered Cress dove for her feet and pulled them out from under her. She fell hard, and dropped the incendiary. It rolled away, out into the firing line of the open doorway. As they watched in numb horror, it rolled into the bunker just as a burst of laser fire came through the door.

"Holy fuck!" Cress yelled and shoved River up the stairs, grabbing Smokee's arm and pushing her ahead of him, moving with a speed fueled by sheer terror. They were almost up the stairwell when a fireball exploded behind them. A blast of heat and wind knocked Cress into the others. He fell, but Smokee yanked him up and out into the hallway as a burst of fire roared out the door. The fire subsided but left smoldering papers and stinking, noxious burning carpet behind.

"Out!" Cress cried. "Hold your breath!" The fumes filled the air. His eyes were watering so hard he could barely see, but he found the door as much by luck and memory as by sight. The three staggered out, coughing, eyes streaming, into the yard and kept on running as the building behind them erupted into flame.

River was limping. He had a laser burn across his thigh. The hair on the back of Cress's head was scorched, and the skin on the back of his legs felt sunburned. He took a deep breath of cool, sweet air, only slightly tinged with smoke. For one moment he was struck dumb with the sheer wonder of being alive. His lungs still sucked in air. His heart still pumped. A miracle!

"Slime-headed shit-for-brains!" River yelled at Smokee. "What the fuck was that about? Wanna get sorry bitch's ass killed, okay, but do not fucking interfere with the mission!"

"What the fuck were you two doingin' around for?" Smokee returned fire, but underneath she was beginning to feel gray and sick. The blaze had passed, and it left behind cold ashes and a dull fear.

"The techies wanted the equipment intact," Cress said in a calm voice that was scarier to her than all of River's shouting. "You knew that. That was one of the main objectives of this mission."

She did know that, somewhere deep inside, but the knowledge had fled in the heat of her wrath. Her anger ebbed away and she fought to hold on to it, to clench her righteousness because without it she was a cold, shivering thing in a cage who couldn't even die.

"And there were men tied up in that building," Cress went on. "Maybe some of them deserved to die. But no one deserves to roast alive, bound and helpless and staring death in the face. That's cruel and inhuman, and you've made me complicit in it."

"You relieved of command!" River finished off a string of inventive profanity.

That kindled a new, small blaze, and Smokee welcomed it gratefully. "You can't do that!" she retorted. "We're all three equal!"

"Oh yes, this commander can!" River said. "Two over one. This a real army, you be shot!"

"Fuck you! Fuck you and your army!"

"You already did," River said.

"Stop it!" Cress said, stepping quickly between them. "River, you better go find the medics, have that burn seen to.

River started to object, but Cress gave him a look that silenced him and he went off.

Cress looked at Smokee. She glared at him defiantly but he noticed she was rubbing her wrists, wringing them as if she were trying to massage life into numb hands.

"You okay?" he asked.

She nodded.

"You hurt your hands?"

She dropped them to her sides, as if caught in a shameful act. Cress sighed. His own anger was draining away, suddenly, leaving an exhaustion so deep he could barely stand erect.

"We aren't going to shoot you," he said. "Or even fire you. We need you, Smokee. The liberados trust you, more than they ever will River or me. They trust you because they know you're one of them.

"I don't want to take away your command. I want you to rise to it. And that means you've got to get control of your anger."

She nodded. She didn't trust herself to speak.

Cress was remembering a young boy, new to the City, stomping through the streets with his head down. The streets were still streets then, just before the Uprising, not yet gardens, but they were bright with murals throughout the Mission where his Dad had brought them to stay in a crowded flat with his uncle and five cousins. They still had regular schools, and Cress had been in trouble every day, mouthing off, talking back to his teachers, yelling at the other boys and getting in fights. All so he could hear some noise in his ears that could drown out his sister's cries in his head.

"I know about anger," he told her. "Sometimes anger is all you've got to keep back the deluge. But you got to get on top of it. You can't let it ride you, or it'll kill you. And bad as that would be, what's worse is that it could take a lot of those folks who trust you along with it. You understand? You're not just a pen-girl any more, Smokee. You're not just you. You're more than you. You're a leader, someone people trust. You got to step up and deserve that trust."

She nodded again. He couldn't tell in the dark, but he thought he saw a tear leak out of her eye. Some instinct told him to walk away, to leave her alone to think about things. He turned away and headed out in the yard.

He found River at the triage station the medics had set up outside the barracks. A medic was dressing his wound and covering it with a large gauze pad.

"That hurt?" he asked.

"A true fighter don't feel pain," River said.

"Of course not," Cress nodded.

River grimaced. "Hurt like a screamin' bitch!"

"So what do we do now?" Cress asked.

"Lay Smokee out and skin the rag alive."

"No time for that. I've been thinking."

"Oh no! Trouble ahead!"

"If we'd captured their equipment, our techies could have gone to work on it. But we didn't, and we have to assume they sent a message out while we were attacking. The other bases will be warned. The next missions will get harder."

River shrugged. "War was easy, everybody be a fighter."

"But they'll expect us to go back to base, to regroup. They won't be expecting another attack tonight," Cress went on.

"Ever heard of sleep?"

"I'd like to sleep," Cress admitted. "I'd like to sleep for a week, or a decade. But there's another plantation not three miles from here, and if we can take that out, it'll be our best chance to capture some equipment intact. That trick with the gas and the vent holes might work one more time, tonight. By tomorrow, I suspect we'll find them plugged. And this time, we bring gas for the bunker, too."

River sighed wearily. "Okay, trugger-boy. This fighter too dumb to lie down, anyway. And Smokee?"

"She's feeling remorseful," Cress said. "We can't shoot her, for a number of reasons, not least the impact on morale. So let's give her a chance to redeem herself instead."

River shook his head sadly. "Squabs! Lickin' all that dirt bad for the brain!"

———

The second attack went off smoothly, in spite of the fact that Cress was so exhausted he felt like he was moving in slow motion. The plantations were built from the same blueprints, and on the broad flat plains of the Central Valley there was little variation in the terrain, so the blueprints could be executed as drawn. This farm, too, had a larger barracks and a combined overseers' quarters/command center.

Cress and River were able to approach the command center without raising any alarms, and deliver their payload of sleepgas. Entering the building, they were able this time to lob in the gas to the bunker and capture equipment and personnel intact.

"That probably won't happen again," Cress said. "But now the techies can have their day, and we can have some sleep."

Chapter Thirty-Two

I am coming down now,
Cycling, spiraling,
Beginning to land.

Coming down ...
That's what we used to call it
After some trip into the astral stratosphere with a bit of chemical aid ...
Memories.

Memories like the frayed shreds of some old pair of underwear ... the
kind I used to keep in the back of the drawer to wear on laundry day
when all the rest were dirty. Panties of last resort.
    I, the "I" that holds together these frayed scraps. I feel it beginning
to form again, to recover from the shock of the passage.
    I have been the heart of a star. The dust of galaxies. I have cycled
back to the place where time began, and out through the other side.
    Yet somehow here I am again. Not corporeal, yet coherent, as a
story is coherent.
    Yes, the story. Stories are the band of elastic that holds together
front and back, perpetuating a garment out of scraps and rags.
    I tell the story of myself, and so I am.

THE JAGGED BLACK TEETH OF BROKEN SKYSCRAPERS PIERCED A
glowing inferno of sky. Bird, Madrone, and the boys had climbed
up on the walls to watch the sunset. It was their evening ritual. Zap and
Zoom were quiet, sometimes for minutes at a time, as they sat together
and watched the sun blaze and dip below the skyline. The stillness, the

silence seemed a portent of things to come.

"It's kind of beautiful," Madrone admitted. "The ruins of the old world."

"Sunset over the empire," Bird said in a deep, pretentious voice.

Madrone made a face at him. "It's peaceful."

"Like the end of a tragedy, when all the main characters are dead."

Zap had scooted himself up close to her and cautiously she let her arm slide around him. He didn't squirm away, and she felt him very slightly relax as he allowed his body to lean against hers. She hardly dared to breathe as he nestled against her, a half-wild animal slowly beginning to trust.

A furtive movement far below caught her eye. A dark figure darted from shadow to shadow. Hesitant as a bird venturing from cover to snatch a seed, it cocked a head, turned, then stopped dead with a sharp, indrawn breath. The honor guard of skeletons, candles flickering at their base, danced in the darkness.

Bird began to softly hum the Song of Refuge.

A shaky echo came back, venturing a few brave lines.

"The way is long, the way is dusty,
The gate is guarded by the dead."

Bird's clear tenor rang out.

"But those cold hands will never harm you,
When by faith, your heart is led."

Quickly, he and Madrone abandoned their perch and headed down to the gate, followed by the boys. They ranged themselves as an honor guard just in time to see the thin man they'd spoken with that morning step through. He was singing as if he were trying to convince himself.

"Come all who by fear are driven,
Come to the place where all are free ... "

And Bird and Madrone answered together:

"Here all debts will be forgiven
At the hearth and the sacred tree."

"Welcome," Madrone said. "Congratulations on deciphering that song!"

"So it's real?" he asked hesitantly.

"It's real!" Madrone assured him. "And you are most welcome!"

"It's real, but what is it?" he asked with slightly more confidence. "And who are you?"

"I'm Madrone. I'm a healer."

"And I'm Bird." He stepped forward, grinning, and pumped the man's hand. "A singer, of sorts. These are Zap and Zoom. Professional mischief makers."

"And this is?" the man asked again.

"A refuge." Bird said. "A beginning."

The man looked up at the skeletons doubtfully.

"The dead guard us, but they won't harm you," Madrone said.

"Neither will we," Bird assured him. "We're not some bizarre death cult. We're from the North."

"Oh, the North," the man said, as if people from the North were well known to travel with an entourage of skeletons. "Are there a lot of you?"

"Just us," Madrone said before Bird could stop her with a warning look. Okay, she thought, maybe that wasn't wise to let him know they had no backup. But she felt no threat in him, no deception, just desperation. "You are the first to join us."

The man shook his head. "Everyone said I was out of my mind. But I thought I could hear directions in the song, and we followed them, my family and me. I left them back a ways back while I went on to see if it was safe. I have two little girls...."

"I'll come with you to get them," Bird offered.

By the time they returned, Madrone had a pot of stew bubbling, and with some reluctant help from Zap and Zoom, she'd opened up one of the family apartments they had cleaned so laboriously. Bird and the man, who said his name was Anthony Springer, each carried a tired young girl, while their mother, Emily, pulled a wagon with a bundle of their belongings.

They sat around the big round coffee table in the center of their lodgings. Madrone dished up stew and herbal tea on her scavenged china.

The two girls ate hungrily, slurping the stew in their eagerness to fill their bellies, ignoring Emily's stern looks. The eldest looked to be about ten, the younger about seven. They had pale blond hair, delicate features and a softness and confidence about them, the look of children who were cherished and protected.

Emily's straight blond hair fell around her face in wisps. The sharp bones of her face jutted out under ashen skin that held the pallor of chronic hunger. Her finely-drawn features were delicately beautiful but haggard, as if she were a movie star playing a dust-bowl farmer's wife. Like Anthony, she wore clothes that were worn and patched but had once been good, brown Capri pants and a white lawn shirt over a cinnamon tee. She looked as if adversity had come upon her suddenly, while she was dressed for an outing in the park.

Bird was filled with barely controlled elation. A big part of it was relief. He had begun to fear that no one would ever come, that the song was too obscure. But it had actually worked!

"So, you found the way from the song? It was clear enough to follow?" he said eagerly.

"It might have helped that I did my dissertation on the symbolic poets," Anthony said. He still looked a bit wary, like an animal on unfamiliar ground, but the hunted look was no longer in his eyes. "I used to be a professor of literature. I'm accustomed to digging for meaning. But the directions were crystal clear, once you realized that's what they are. 'The ancient road of freedom'—never heard a freeway called that before, but why not?"

"I was skeptical," Emily said. "We might have come weeks ago if I hadn't resisted. I was a math teacher—I like things quantified, certain. But yesterday the one thing that became certain was that we had to go somewhere, or ... "

She glanced at her girls, who were stuffing stew in their mouths. "Slow down, Heather! Hannah, manners, please!"

"Or what, Mama?" asked Hannah, the older girl, who'd been following the conversation intently.

"Or bad things would happen," Emily finished. "You never mind what."

Zap and Zoom had turned up their noses at the stew, until they saw the girls digging in, whereupon they demanded full bowls. They inhaled theirs with loud, smacking sounds.

"It's not polite to make noise while you eat," Hannah informed them.

Zoom stuck his tongue out at her.

"Fuck you, dogface," Zoom replied.

"Zoom! We don't talk like that to our friends!" Madrone turned apologetically to Emily. "I'm sorry."

"Not my friend!" Zoom proclaimed.

"She will be," Bird said sternly. "Say you're sorry."

"You're sorry," Zoom said, and he and Zap broke into a fit of maniacal laughter.

"All right, leave the table," Bird said. Madrone glanced at him with a smile that she concealed. There was something about him when he employed the Voice of Dad that she found both sweet and absurd. Zap and Zoom scurried off.

"May we be excused?" Hannah asked.

"I want to play with those boys," Heather announced.

Their parents nodded, and the girls ran off.

"I'm sorry," Madrone said. "We're trying to civilize them, but it's a long process."

"Are they yours?" Emily asked.

"Yes," Madrone said. "No," Bird said, simultaneously.

"They're sort of ours by default," Bird said. "We rescued them from water thieves. About a month ago." He told them the story.

"So far we've gotten them to eat actual food, not just chips, at least some of the time," Madrone said. "And to bathe fairly regularly—that was a battle."

"Did you say 'bathe'?" Emily asked. "As in, 'take a bath'?"

"I did!" Madrone smiled.

"You have that much water?"

"Wait until after dinner. You'll see."

When they'd finished eating and cleaning up, Madrone led Emily and the girls down to the springs. Emily stood trembling at the edge of the pool. She gripped Madrone's hand, and Madrone could feel her shaking.

"My God, I never imagined ... "

She sank down on one of the old marble benches that Madrone and the boys had scrubbed. "Look, girls! This is something! This is really something! Like it was in the old days, remember? Probably you don't remember. But there's ... you sure there's enough water?"

"Plenty of it," Madrone assured her. "Here, we'll draw baths for you and the girls—we like to wash ourselves clean before we soak in the hot pool, keeps it from getting scummy. And we bucket all the used bathwater up for the gardens, so don't worry about wasting it. Next project on the list is building a pump!"

Emily scrubbed the girls and rinsed them, then let them explore the pool. At first, they entered gingerly, lowering themselves inch by inch as if they couldn't trust what the alien element might do to their bodies. Emily slid down and let out a deep sigh that soon turned to tears.

"I'm sorry," she sniffed. "I don't mean to be silly ... it's just. Oh God, it's been such a nightmare!"

"It's okay," Madrone said. "Go ahead and cry if you need to."

Emily shook her head. "If I really let go, if I let it in, I'd be screaming and shrieking. And that would scare the girls."

The girls were fully immersed now, laughing and splashing each other.

"You protect them well," Madrone observed. "They have that air, that look of children somebody loves and cares for. Like kids in the North."

"Oh God, if you only knew!"

Madrone waited, with her midwife's patience, for the story to come out. "What do you do?" Emily asked. "Do you love them and raise them the way you were raised, the way every child has a right to be raised, keeping the harshness away from them? But then when the harshness triumphs, they are so unprepared. They would never survive...."

Her eyes took on that haunted look, as if she were picturing her lovely girls in the breaking pens.

"Don't think about it," Madrone said. "Don't torture yourself with those pictures. You're here now. Whatever happens, it won't be that."

Emily shook her head, as if to chase away the nightmare images.

"So what is this place?" she asked.

"Bird and I, we come from the North," Madrone said. "There, we threw the Stewards out twenty years ago, and we turned back their army again this summer."

"Vidscreens said the invasion was a huge success," Emily interjected doubtfully.

"Yes, well, they would, wouldn't they? But believe me, it was a rout for them. For us—they destroyed a lot. Good people died. We paid a huge price, but we defeated them and protected what we've built.

"But they'll be back. We can't just sit back in our beautiful city and wait for the next attack. We can't truly be free while the Southlands are enslaved. So we held a Council and decided we had to bring the fight down here. Some of the Stewards' Army, the ones that came over to us, they're heading back down to fight. Some of the people from our City have joined them.

"But Bird and I, we wanted to fight in a different way. I don't believe we can liberate the Southlands by force. But if people can see a new possibility, they might rise up and liberate themselves."

The youngest girl came over to her mother, nestled against her for a moment.

"Mommy, this is nice!" she said.

"Yes, sweetie, it is very, very nice!" Emily kissed the top of her head.

"Can we come here again?"

"We're going to stay here. Here with these people. So we can come down here every night."

"But what about our house?" the older girl came over and stood, a worried look in her wide blue eyes. "What about school?"

Emily shook her head sadly. "Our house is gone, sweetie. But I brought Grumblebear and Peaches in the wagon. And we're together, that's what counts."

"Were you going to have to relinquish us?" the older girl asked quietly.

"Hush, sweetheart. We will never let that happen!" Emily spoke with assurance, but her eyes still looked haunted.

＊

Later that night, Bird read the beginnings of another story to the boys while Emily tucked the girls into their new bed in their quarters nearby. Then the adults sat around in the Springers' new living room, on plastic lawn chairs they'd salvaged, and drank dandelion tea.

"I guess it's our turn to tell our story," Anthony said. "It's not so heroic—pretty common, really. The only uncommon part of it is how long we managed to maintain the belief that it would never happen to us!"

Emily patted his arm. "You did the best you could. The best anyone could."

"And that wouldn't matter one flying fig in the end, if 'best' didn't translate into 'good enough,'" Anthony said, tipping back his flimsy chair and propping his feet up against one of the milk crates they'd brought up to serve as tables. "I taught literature at the university. I'd wanted to major in history and political science—that was back before the Collapse and the Changes. But when the Stewards took over, I could see the hand-writing on the wall.

"I couldn't stomach the Retributionist bilge, so I switched to English literature. I had a notion that there would be less scope for trouble in dead poets than in live political theory. And above all, I'm a man who likes to avoid trouble. I'm not your hero, or your gunslinger. Nature and nurture both fitted me to be a peaceful scholar in an ivory tower. My misfortune to be born at precisely the wrong time for it!"

"Oh hush, you idiot," Emily said, nestling close to him. "You didn't do so badly. You brought us here, didn't you?"

"Even a pale, unworldly scholar might access his inner warrior when he's desperate," Anthony said.

"How about you?" Madrone asked Emily.

"I was just eighteen when the Changes came," Emily said. "I'd been planning to go on to college and major in economics—I'd always liked math. I got one year in, while the Stewards were consolidating their power. That was where Anthony and I met. But then they began passing the Family Purity Laws. Girls could no longer go on to grad school, or work in a whole lot of fields. They held a big ceremony where all the lady professors had to burn their diplomas."

She paused for a moment, and her eyes took on a faraway stare. Her voice lost its resonance.

"I'll never forget that day! They made all the students line up and watch, like a gauntlet the women had to walk through. And some of the kiss-ass frat boys, they were scowling and spitting—it was disgusting. I wanted to cry but I knew I couldn't let down because already they had half the class informing on the other half. Our teachers had to walk through that jeering crowd, go up to this big, blazing bonfire and throw their diplomas in. Then the chancellor stepped forward. He went up to each one and ripped off her robes. And then, there was this big Jesus on a chariot with a whip ... why am I talking about this?"

She shuddered, and Anthony squeezed her tight.

"Because it is your story," he said. "A seminal event. Go on. These people need to know."

"They had to walk up, in their little, light shifts that you could almost see through, and kiss the whip, and say, 'Purify me of my sins of pride and arrogance.' And then stand, with their arms out like Jesus on the cross, as the lash came down. And the blood, sometimes it wouldn't come on the first blow, or even the second, but with the third, or the fourth, or the fifth, first there would be little spots of it, staining the mus-lin, and then a dark line of it, and then a crisscross of lines like marks from a hot griddle...."

She stopped. In the silence, Anthony took up the tale.

"And those who resisted, who still thought that education and intel-ligence and innocence of wrong-doing would shield them, who clung to some erroneous belief in a world of sanity and human rights, they were stripped naked in front of us all, and lashed to death. I watched my mentor, a brilliant woman who was like a grandmother to me, who opened up the world of poetry and metaphor and symbol—I watched her die like that. Struggling to hold her head up, to the end, while the whole world stared at her aging, sagging breasts and her stretch marks, trying desperately to maintain some shred of dignity as the body voided itself in extremity and turned into nothing but meat. Dead, raw meat."

No one spoke for a long moment. Silence sat on the room like a shroud.

Then Emily let out a small, bitter laugh. "So I switched to elementary school teaching. It was that, or nursing, or something they called 'domestic science.' We waited to get married until I finished my degree, because married women weren't allowed to attend the university. But at that time, we were still allowed to work. So I began teaching school, and Anthony finished his dissertation and got hired to teach at the university.

"That was a pretty happy time, in spite of everything. Anthony and I, we had each other. I enjoyed teaching youngsters, even though that hadn't been my first choice in life. Anthony was doing well, we weren't too badly in debt from our student loans, and we were even able to buy a house near Anthony's work.

"We kept to a very modest house, with a mortgage we could afford on our salaries, because we knew the dangers of getting in over our heads. But still, there was no way to really live without taking on some debt. College was expensive, and the only way to go was to take out loans, unless you're a super-rich Prime. Everybody did it. We wanted to have a family, and we wanted to have a home for them, with a yard to play in and a swing in a tree, like we'd had when we were growing up.

"Anyway, we were married, we had a house. After some time, we had Hannah, and then Heather. We didn't have a lot, but we had work we enjoyed, and our kids and each other."

"But then the interest rates went up," Anthony said. "We were still making the house payments, but we had to cut out some things, like ballet for the girls. And dinners out. But we were eating, not going hungry, unlike a lot of people."

"And that was okay, until the rates rose again," Emily said. "Anthony tried to get extra hours, or a second job—but there weren't any. We were still eating, but not as much. Then I lost my job. The Retributionists waged a campaign, claimed everyone was lax on the Purities, and they decided that when Paul or whoever said 'A woman should not speak in public' that included teaching.

"So all the women teachers were fired. But they had passed another law, that said you couldn't enroll your child in school if you had debts in default, so that eliminated a whole lot of the student body, anyway."

"But we hung on," Anthony said. "We both did tutoring, and made a little apartment in our basement and rented it out to another family that was in even worse trouble than we were. We kept up on the payments, and we kept on eating."

"Even if it was mostly potatoes," Emily admitted. "Or beans."

"Nothing wrong with beans," Anthony said stoutly.

"Not in a nice stew, with carrots and tomatoes and a bit of meat," Emily agreed. "But alone, day after day—it wasn't what we were used to. I was raised to consider a meal meant vegetables, a protein, and a starch. We tried to grow a garden but the water rates went sky-high and we couldn't keep it alive. At first we used our bathwater, just like you do, but then it got so we couldn't afford more than a sponge-off once a day.

"Then last month, Anthony lost his job. They sold off the university to a private consortium, which allowed them to fire all the teachers who had tenure. And three days ago, we found a notice posted on our front door that we had been cited for maintaining an illegal living space. It's not allowed to rent rooms out, as we had done, without applying for a permit which is always incredibly expensive and very limited, anyway."

"We'd used up our savings in this last month," Anthony said quietly. "We didn't know what to do. We knew that we'd soon be defaulting on our loans, and that would mean consequences we didn't want to think about."

"They could come and take our girls!" Emily said in a whisper.

"And with the notice came a fine—far more than we could pay. We would have to take on more debt, debt we couldn't possibly pay off. It had happened to us—what I always swore I'd never let happen to my family! We'd slid down the slope and the next stop was the pens for the girls and the work farms for us."

Emily was sobbing, and Madrone hugged her.

"It's okay. It's not going to happen now. You came here instead."

"I can't tell you how grateful we are," Anthony said. "When I heard your song, it gave me hope. A crazy hope—I thought I was probably out of my mind, but we had nothing left to lose."

"Don't be grateful," Bird said. "Just help us. There are probably thousands of families, just like yours, out there."

"Tens of thousands," Anthony agreed. "A city full."

"They can't all come here," Emily said.

"Some can," Bird said. "And when enough do, then . . . " he hesitated.

"Then what?" Anthony asked.

"Then we move to the next phase."

Chapter Thirty-Three

E MILY, IT TURNED OUT, WAS A NATURAL-BORN ORGANIZER. THE FAMILY had slept for a day, stunned and exhausted, and she spent a second day just following Madrone around. But on the third day she woke up full of energy, pulled a notebook out of her bag, and set up a schedule. Mornings, they would all salvage and clean, preparing new spaces for others to come. Afternoons, Bird would go on his rounds. She and Anthony would take turns teaching the children. The girls were well advanced in their studies, and they would help teach the boys to read and do simple figures.

Whether it was her years of teaching a classroom full of eight-year-olds, or just some innate authority she carried, the boys actually obeyed her, at least some of the time. When she ordered them to sit down and be quiet, they stared up at her with big-eyed amazement, but did what she said.

Anthony wasn't much of a builder, but he was strong and willing to learn. With Emily on the cleaning patrol, Madrone could devote more time to the gardens and to construction, which she enjoyed, and to scavenging supplies and setting up the healing center.

"That's the sacred tree?" Emily asked skeptically, observing the rather straggly ailanthus in the center of the plaza.

"It's a survivor, like all of us," Madrone said loyally.

They were beginning to clear the central plaza. With four adults working together, they could shift heavier chunks of rubble. Madrone rigged up levers and Bird made rope slings to haul off some of the larger boulders.

While the grownups worked, the children were set to stomp clay and sand together into a kind of natural cement called cob. They required supervision, mostly because the boys liked to turn the work into a mud fight. But the girls were learning to hold their own. The first time Zap rubbed mud into Heather's hair, she cried. The second time, she beaned him between the shoulder blades with a mud ball.

"We need a ceremony," Anthony said, looking at the tree. "The song says, 'All debts will be forgiven at the hearth and the sacred tree.' We need a ceremony to wash us clean of debt."

"I'll write the songs," Bird said. "You all can build the altars."

"No way, lazybones," Madrone told him. "The Goddess in her infinite wisdom gifted you with testosterone for one sacred purpose...."

He leered at her. "And I'm ready, willing, and waiting to serve in that capacity."

"Hauling rocks!"

They set up altars in the four directions, built of chunks of rubble that Bird called urbanite. They were topped with the cob the children made, and Madrone taught them how to apply it, slapping it down and pushing each layer into the ones below for strength and stability. They sculpted each altar to honor one of the Four Sacred Things: Air, Fire, Water, and Earth. The tree, the hearth, and the entrance to the springs would represent the Fifth, the sacred Spirit.

In the bowels of a yard goods shop, they'd found a stash of yarn and ribbons. Anthony suggested that each new person who came to the City of Refuge should take a ribbon and tie it onto the branches of the tree. As the city grew, the tree would become decked in color.

When all was ready, they held hands in a circle.

"I'm an agnostic," Anthony admitted. "You all will have to come up with the liturgy."

"But you're the one who wanted the ceremony," Madrone said.

"Ritual is for the people," he said. "Ultimately it has little to do with the Gods."

"Who do you pray to?" Emily asked.

"To whom," Anthony corrected her, and she kicked him gently.

"We call her the Goddess, although she has many aspects and her gender can be quite fluid," Bird said. "The living being that is the earth and all her creatures, including us. The great forces of creation and transformation."

"She's the wheel of birth, growth, death, and rebirth, and all the ways that cycle plays itself out in nature and our human lives," Madrone added. "And we honor the four elements: Earth, Air, Fire, and Water, and the fifth, which arises when the four are in balance. Like our altars."

"Archetypal," Anthony nodded his approval.

"Sounds good to me!" Emily said.

That night they lit the sacred hearth. Madrone made a fresh fire drill. She prided herself on her ability to light a fire with just sticks and tinder. It was yet another useful skill they'd been taught when their Learning

Group went to the mountains. She loved the feel of the stick twirling in her hands, the smell of charred wood, the excitement—when would it get hot enough to spark? Would the spark catch? Of course, she also remembered ruefully a number of occasions when her skill had deserted her just at the crucial moment when they were cold late at night after a long hike.

But this time, it worked well. She drilled herself a tiny spark, caught it in the tinder and delicately added twigs until the hearth came alive with a warm blaze.

They each fed the fire with papers that symbolized their debts, moral and financial, and watched them burn away, transforming back into pure energy.

Bird had sat with his paper for a long time. Could it be as simple as this—burn away his transgressions, his failures? The moments when he had given in, the times that his captors had been just too strong for him. Drop his failings into the fire, and be free?

He didn't believe it could really work that way. But he remembered something from one of the books in Maya's library. He'd read through her occult collection when he was thirteen, and he'd especially loved Dion Fortune, her novels *Moon Magic* and *The Sea Priestess*. She'd been fond of quoting Ignatius Loyola, founder of the Jesuits.

"Put yourself in the position of prayer," Loyola said, "and you will soon feel like praying."

Or as Maya had put it, "Fake it until it gets real."

Maybe going through the motions, even if he didn't believe he merited forgiveness, would somehow evoke in him some release. Maybe the fire could cauterize some wound in his soul even if it could not erase the scars.

He tossed his paper into the flames. It landed just at the edge of the fire and lay there unburned. Like my sins, he thought.

Then a spark caught, and an edge of the paper began to glow with a line of red. It died away to a sullen, black char. The paper lay there until Zap, poking at the fire with a stick, pushed it into the glowing heart. It blazed up and turned to ash, a severed, blackened wing that wafted upwards and then fell apart.

Bird sang the Hymn of Forgiveness he wrote for the ritual:

> *"Lay down, lay down your burdens,*
> *Lay down your failures too.*
> *Don't blame yourself for the hands you lost*
> *When the deck was stacked against you.*

> *"Be kissed by Air, be cleansed by Fire,*
> *Be healed by Water and Earth,*
> *And open your hearts to your true desire,*
> *At the tree and the sacred hearth."*

Together they all went down into the sacred springs, dipped clean water from its pool, brought it back up, and let the girls pour it over all their hands.

"We wanna do the water too!" Zap said.

Madrone gave them the Look—the pursed lips, the intense, piercing eyes.

"Gently," she said. "Slowly. Over hands, only. No splashing, no fighting!"

The boys nodded and for once they complied. The solemnity of the occasion impressed them, and they carefully poured water over Anthony's outstretched fingers and Emily's palms, as the girls ministered to Madrone and Bird.

"You are cleansed of debt, and of sorrow and bondage," Anthony said.

"I am cleansed," Bird repeated. And maybe I am, but I can't feel it, he thought, looking at his battered, twisted hands. Bondage goes deeper than the skin, in me. It has twisted my very bones.

"Now choose your ribbon, and tie it to the tree, committing yourself to this new city and its work of refuge," Anthony went on.

"For an agnostic, you make a darn good preacher," Emily told him.

"Comes from studying all that symbolism," he said. "We respond on an archetypal level. It has nothing to do with faith."

"Madrone first," Bird said. "It was her vision that brought us here. And there's no vision comes to fruition without healing."

She tied a green ribbon onto a branch, and Bird tied a deep purple strip of cloth to the base of a limb.

Anthony added a ribbon of blue, Emily of clearest yellow, and the children tied on bits of a rainbow-colored cloth.

"It is done," Anthony said. "The hearth is lit, the sacred tree is honored, the debts are cleansed. City of Refuge is open for business!"

"Will we always keep the sacred fire lit?" Hannah asked.

Madrone smiled. "Maybe, in time. For now, we'll put it out in a sacred way, and relight when we need it."

"Why can't we just keep it going?" Heather asked.

"Someone would have to watch it, all the time, and we have so much else we need to do."

"I'll watch it," Hannah offered.

"I'll tell you what, you watch it now, as long as you want to, and when you get tired, or when your Mama tells you it's time for bed, I'll come and put it out," Madrone said. "Okay?"

"I'm going to quote my grandmother, Maya, who was one of the spiritual leaders of our city," Bird said. "She always liked to say that religion is something people thought up to make a whole lot of unnecessary work for themselves."

"Work, maybe, but not unnecessary," Emily said. "People need to feel something is special. People who've been beaten down need to feel like maybe it could be them. That's worth working for."

⁓

The day after the ceremony, Bird dressed Anthony up in Atonement Seekers' robes. He and Bird sang the Song of Refuge through the neighborhoods where the last remnants of a middle class clung to a meager existence. They wandered through the 'hoods of the factory workers and the restless, angry streets of the hopeless and the unemployed. They traded water for garbage until the water ran out, and then they just wandered and sang.

In the late afternoon, they made their way back to the Springers' old neighborhood. Anthony had promised a few trusted friends to let them know if the promise of the song proved to be real. As Bird spouted his patter, Anthony kept an eye out for former neighbors. He spied the teenage boy of the family who had rented from them illegally.

"I have found a refuge!" Anthony proclaimed. "I take refuge in the Lord!"

The boy gave him a startled look, then ran off. Soon he reappeared with his father in tow.

"Springer!" the man said. He was a redhead whose pale skin hung lank over broad bones, as if he had until recently been beefy and strong. It gave him the air, Bird thought, of a limp balloon, and his eyes held some of the same barely contained panic that Anthony's had when they first met.

"Take refuge in the Lord!" Anthony proclaimed again. "Oh sinners, seek the way to refuge in the bosom of Jesus!"

"How do we find the way to redemption?" his neighbor asked.

"Ah, where might one find a roadmap of the soul's journey? What hymn might be the guide, to the heart of the pure soul's habitation?"

Bird obligingly struck up the song. Anthony's neighbor listened intently, but simply looked confused. He gave a quick glance around. There were no others immediately nearby.

"Latin poet?" he asked. "I don't get the bit about the Latin poet."

"The old Hollywood freeway, Virgil off-ramp, head south, right on Third," Anthony hissed, and Bird increased the volume of the song as a group of factory workers headed toward them.

"Delay not, for the Day of Judgment is at hand!" Anthony proclaimed. Bird sang:

> "Come all you hungry, all you weary,
> All who toil without reward.
> Come take the road to the place of Refuge,
> Though the way be long and hard.

"Find the spring of endless water,
Where all people can be free.
There all debts will be forgiven,
At the hearth and the sacred tree."

And people began to come.

~~~~~~~~~

At first it was a trickle—Bob, the Springers' red-headed tenant, came with his wife, Marjorie, and their fifteen-year-old boy, Tom. Another teacher from Anthony's college arrived with his pregnant wife. Emily organized them all into homes and work groups, and every night they performed the Ceremony of Forgiveness at the sacred hearth. Everyone who came was invited to tell their story around the fire, and again and again they heard variations on the same tale: "We worked hard, we were just making it—then they raised the interest rates, or closed the schools, or changed the laws...."

Some of the families were still paying interest on debts accrued by their grandfathers who had had the temerity to aspire to an education. Some had worked hard all their lives; others had never found a job, or had been fired when they were too old to work back-to-back twelve-hour shifts. Three young girls arrived, none older than fourteen, who had somehow managed to escape from the transport taking them out to the breaking pens. There were tragedies: mothers who had not found the Refuge in time to save their children from the pens, children who had lost parents to the work farms or the prisons. The trickle became a stream.

~~~~~~~~~

"Here," Madrone said. She took the pickax from the hands of a pale young man who'd been weakly scratching the ground with it. His arms looked like they'd never done a day of physical work in their life. "This ground is hard as a rock, but you can get through it. The secret is to use your hands as a fulcrum. See—the right hand slides down to the head as you lift it, and the left hand pushes down." He was staring at her with blank eyes, but she went on. "Then when you swing it, you let your right hand slide down to the end, so the weight of the pick does the work. Like this."

She let it fall, putting momentum behind the swing. With a thunk it embedded itself deep in the hard ground.

"It's easy, once you get the hang of it. Kind of relaxing."

"Relaxing?" He shook his head. "What do you call work?"

Ignoring all her instructions, he gripped the end of the handle and whammed the pick down on the baked earth. It landed sideways, skidding harmlessly across the ground.

Madrone took a breath. Patience, she told herself. Poverty, in the Southlands, was not always the life of endless, grueling physical labor of the work farms and slave camps. For many, poverty had meant a lifetime of enforced idleness, standing around and waiting in lines. Hard work was something that benefited someone else, never you.

The result was that many of the new *refugistas* had no idea how to use a tool, or use their bodies. Their muscles weren't developed for swinging picks or pounding with a digging bar. Their attitude to physical labor was to avoid it whenever possible.

It was far more exhausting for her to supervise and teach them than it would have been to just dig the ground herself.

For she did like swinging a pick. Compared to chasing the oversoul of a virus through the astral, or holding the hand of a dying child's mother, it was indeed relaxing.

"Let me show you again," she said gently, but he gripped it hard.

"I can do it! Let me alone."

She walked off and left him to his struggle.

⁓

They were planting a small, open space near the entrance to the springs, which Madrone had commandeered to make a garden for the healing center. Over the last month, the Refuge had grown to about fifty people, and they were hard-pressed to feed everybody. Some of the refugistas had a bit of cash that they pooled to buy some bulk millet and sacks of beans. Some of them brought their own stores of potatoes or cases of chips they'd hoarded for emergencies. Still, supplies were constantly running short.

It was Hijohn and his hillboys who'd saved them thus far. She and Bird had been curling up together to sleep when they heard a coyote call from the plaza. For a moment Madrone thought a real coyote had somehow wandered down from the wild hills and found its way into the Refuge. Then she recognized the hillboys' signal.

Bird was already rolling out of bed and throwing his clothes on. Madrone followed him down to the plaza.

"Hijohn!" Bird clapped him around the shoulders. Hijohn was contemplating the sacred tree, hung with its ribbons. A three-quarters moon shone down into the plaza and his wizened face with its bemused smile.

"Merry Christmas," he said, jerking his chin at the ribbon-bedecked tree.

"That's our sacred tree," Bird told him. "Don't be snide, or the spirits'll bite your ass!"

"Is everything okay?" Madrone asked anxiously.

"No worse than ever," Hijohn assured her. "Brought you all a present. But we've got to open it, quick!"

The present turned out to be a hijacked truck full of potatoes. Madrone woke Emily, who organized crews to wake everybody up and get them to work unloading. All night long, they ferried wagon-loads and buckets of potatoes into a hastily constructed storage bin the carpenters threw together.

"Any news from the North?" Madrone asked as she and Hijohn took a short break at the hearth, where Emily's girls were serving cups of what they'd come to call wild weed tea.

It was one of the hardest things about their exile in the Southlands, that getting news from the North was so difficult. The hillboys' networks passed on messages, but that was slow and uncertain. The living crystals Madrone and Bird carried could not tie into the Net from down here. There was no radio contact, no satellite nets like in the old days. Madrone spared a stray thought to wonder what had happened to all the satellites after the Collapse. Would they continue to spin in their orbits, unmaintained, unwatched. Did they have a lifespan? Would they fall to earth in a fiery blaze and land on the Refuge? Is that one more thing she should worry about that she couldn't control?

But the hillboys had their own runners and messengers, and they coordinated with the pirates in their small boats. Older technologies still worked, if slowly.

"Katy sends love," Hijohn said. "She sent me another picture of the baby!"

He pulled a small box out of his pocket that held a thumbnail-sized photo of the smiling infant, who now sported two teeth. Hijohn beamed at it with pride.

"You should go north," Madrone told him. "You should see the baby before it gets much bigger!"

Hijohn sighed. "Your army's coming south. Your Refuge here's starting to attract folks like honey calls the bees. Things are stirring. It's not the time."

He took one last look at the picture, then closed the box and put it away. Madrone watched him, a hard little walnut of a man with a softness in his face. She wanted to hug him suddenly, to cuddle him and wrap him up in feathers and whipped cream and see what he turned into. Once, long ago, there had been an attraction between them. Now she'd learned that indulging such things outside the bowers of the City made more trouble and pain than it was worth. And what she felt for him wasn't lust, but rather a sadness that she could never share, a sense of loss for all he'd given up, the sweetness and comforts and joy that everyone deserved. But it was a grief that he probably never felt himself, and she wouldn't pry open those floodgates.

"Thanks for the potatoes," she said instead. "Of course, they'd go all the better with some eggs and greens and a bit of bacon. But hey, I'm not complaining!"

By dawn the truck was unloaded and the hillboys were gone.

Madrone stood in the early morning light, eating a baked potato that Emily handed her. She looked over her healing garden, pleased at what they had accomplished. They'd cleared away the rubble, using some of it to build beds and the bases for benches. Trays of seedlings were growing under gauzy cloth that sheltered them from the blistering sun. The beds were getting dug, or rather chiseled into the hard earth. With a little time, and some rain, they would have a garden.

Alongside the entrance to the springs, they'd cleaned out the big, open room Madrone had chosen for the healing center. It still had intact windows, and work crews had made up beds and pallets and placed them to get natural light. The newly formed Explorers' Guild who continued the work of probing the ruins had found the buried stock of a wrecked pharmacy. While all of the drugs were long outdated Madrone could sniff them and taste them and her bee senses told her if they still harbored any potency. And there were stocks of other useful things: bandages and gauze pads, tape and rubbing alcohol.

They screened off alcoves to make examining rooms, and patients they had aplenty. Most new arrivals had some complaint, and few if any had had much medical care. Many of the children were simply undernourished, but others were abused and a few arrived with open wounds or deep infections. Some recruits came with old injuries, and the hard physical labor of building the Refuge resulted in its own share of scrapes and sprains.

Madrone had put out a call for anyone with nursing or first aid experience, and assembled a small team of aides. But there were no medical doctors or healers who had yet found their way to the Refuge, and her presence and judgment were heavily in demand.

She sighed. The young man she'd tried to coach the day before was back with his pick. He was finally making some sort of impact on the dirt, using five times as much energy and muscle as he needed to use. But at least the pick was going into the ground point first. That was progress. It was time to start her day.

She brought her bowl over to the dishwashers at the hearth and turned back toward the healing center, where there was already a line of patients waiting for her. Anna, the young girl who had volunteered to be her helper, had a basin of warm water waiting for her to wash in. She splashed her face, scrubbed her hands and arms, and went to work.

Bird presided over the ceremony that night. He and Madrone and Anthony took turns playing preacher/priestess. The sacred tree, now decked with colorful ribbons, looked less scraggly and more impressive, as if it basked in the attention it was receiving, and held up its head with new pride. The water it was receiving also deserved some credit, Bird thought.

As they ran out of room on the branches of the tree itself, they'd begun tying ribbons to ribbons to make long streamers that waved gaily in the breeze, making a whap, whap noise that formed a gentle accompaniment to the discussions in the amphitheater.

There were five new recruits that night, a family of four who shared the common story of debts that kept multiplying, and a young single woman. A chorus of voices took up the Hymn of Forgiveness. After the ceremony, the new refugistas introduced themselves.

"My name is Tianne Liu," the young woman said. Her black silky hair was dyed to give it a blue sheen. It was cut with square bangs to frame a round face with wide-set, half-moon eyes that peered out intently as if they were so used to staring at a screen that focusing on anything else required a conscious effort. Her body was soft and heavy, like a pampered cat that had never had to forage or hunt. "I was a game designer for Vidmark, until I got too successful. I created the new incarnation of Sinnerslayer."

There were gasps of awe from some of the teenagers.

"As you probably know, it comes on the market next week—which meant that I was supposed to get a bonus. But one of the Primes decided I would cost them too much money—so they trumped up a reason to fire me for insubordination. And that's why I'm here!"

Bird grinned at her. "You are welcome here. Insubordination is our middle name!"

"Well, I want to propose a campaign," she said. "I'm an artist. I suggest that we adopt a new slogan. Make Something Beautiful! And whoever comes to join the Refuge will be invited to make something beautiful. Angel City is full of creative people. We should put them to work."

"That's the stupidest thing I ever heard!" a man shouted from the back.

"Hey!" Bird thundered. "Remember we agreed to speak respectfully to one another!"

"I don't remember that!" a woman called back.

"I say what I mean!" The man strode forward. He was whip-thin, black-bearded and tight-bodied, and Bird had noted him before as a troublesome element, always angry, always ready to shout down a suggestion. "Why respect a stupid idea?"

"Let's hear it before we condemn it. Let the woman speak!" called out Maddie, one of Emily's friends.

"Yeah, Frank, close your gaspipe and let the lady have her say!" said Bob, the big red-haired man who had been the Springers' tenant.

"How 'bout this for a slogan: Grow Something to Eat!" Frank countered.

"We can do that," Tianne went on, unperturbed by the attacks. "But we'll do it all the better if we have some room for creativity. Art is not a luxury! If we want this Refuge to stand out as something different from what the Stewards offer, art is a necessity. Believe me, I've been in the propaganda industry all my life. We make this place beautiful because everything the Stewards touch is butt ugly."

"That's the truth!" came a chorus of agreement.

"So we have an opportunity to make the contrast clear. And we invite everyone to be part of it, because we all have the ability somewhere inside us to make something beautiful. Most of us here, we've been told our whole lives by the Stewards that we're useless, worthless. Make something beautiful, and right away you prove them wrong."

"Make something to fight with!" Frank called out.

"A weapon can be a beautiful thing, it save your life," cried a stout woman.

"Let's just find out who wants to do it," Bird suggested. They hadn't yet instituted any kind of formal Council or governing structure, but whenever possible he liked to pass decisions on to the group. "Raise your hands if you want to Make Something Beautiful."

A large proportion of the group raised their hands, including almost all of the teens.

"Okay, let's do it," he said. "Those of you who object, you don't have to do it! Just don't interfere with those who do!"

Bird regretted his commitment to democracy the next day when half the teens deserted the digging crews to scavenge art supplies with Tianne. To him, she seemed slightly awkward and nerdy, stumping around with her stiff-legged gait as if her limbs weren't used to motion, issuing orders to her crew with a serious air. But the teens followed her around in a trance of hera-worship. Of all the deprivations in the Refuge, they seemed to most miss their vidscreens and the fantasy games in which they used to immerse themselves for hours each day.

"But this is better than a game!" Tianne told them. "This is real. And now we all become architects of the alternate reality."

By the third day, he was beginning to concede that she might have a point. The artists' crew concentrated their efforts first on the small open area at the opening to the Gateway of the Dead. Tianne found moldy, weevil-ridden flour, not fit to eat, and made wheatpaste for papier mâché. Her helpers unearthed stashes of cement and grout and scavenged broken tiles and crockery for mosaics. They sawed off lengths of twisted rebar to form into armatures for sculpture. Some of the most resistant teens, those who had dragged their bodies unwillingly to work each day and feebly tapped their shovels into the hard ground, were now working up a sweat with eagerness.

"We will concentrate on this entrance first," Tianne said. "So that after the passageway through death, you will come into a place of welcome, the Womb of Rebirth."

For her, concrete walls were blank canvasses crying out for painted murals or mosaics. She had her own special recipe that mixed ground-up paper and weeds with clay, a little cement, and old paint to make a sculptural medium that was lightweight and waterproof. Out of this, she fashioned what she called the Angels of Welcome.

"This city is called Angel City," she said. "But where are they? We will provide them!"

They were great sculptural figures with upraised arms that reminded Bird more of the figurines Maya had collected on her travels, ancient bird Goddesses of Greece and Crete with upraised, crescent-moon wings, pre-dynastic Egyptian figures in postures of strength and victory. A huge colorful mural was in progress on one wall, in which suffering ancestor figures in grays and blacks and browns framed a passageway into a light-filled, colorful garden full of bright flowers and fruits. It reminded him of the murals that covered almost every blank wall back home, some brand new, some of them dating back to the Latino Pride movement of the seventies, patterned after Diego Rivera and the Mexican muralists and carefully renewed whenever they grew faded and chipped.

He missed the murals, he realized. He missed strolling down a street where with every step there was something new to see.

Suddenly he was struck with a pang of sheer, raw homesickness so strong that he had to sit down on chunk of urbanite that Tianne was eyeing as the base for a bench. He missed the color, the life, the sound of streams flowing through garden streets, the fruit hanging ready to hand everywhere you turned. He missed the throngs of people in their colorful clothes and wild fashions as if they were competing with the flowers for admiration. The snatches of music from street-corner performers or dance platforms rolling by on the busses transformed into giant dragons or sailing ships or imaginary beasts. That sense of constantly being showered with the gifts of creativity, a thousand artists making works to please your eye, singing songs to please your ear.

He missed it, and he resented it. Could he ever go back? He didn't belong to the garden any more. He carried the grim ancestors within him; he belonged to the shadows, the grays and the blacks and the browns, not to turquoise and viridian and plum.

On the opposite wall, Tianne and her circle had begun a huge mosaic. The Garden of a Thousand Flowers, she called it, and she invited everyone in the Refuge to make a flower of their own, to leave their mark on the wall. Now she came over to Bird.

"Are you going to make a flower?" she asked him.

"I'm not really much good at the visual arts," he replied.

"That is the beauty of mosaic. You don't have to have talent. The material itself will create the beauty, out of its very brokenness. Come on! If you do it, others will follow your leadership." She took his hand and led him over to the wall, showed him how to apply the cement and press the tiles into it.

And what are my colors? Bird thought. He chose a black heart, pressed chips of red and purple into rough petal shapes around it. It was strong and bright and more hopeful than he actually felt.

"Now you have left your mark on the City of Refuge," Tianne said solemnly.

*   *   *

Bird looked around at the circle. The plaza around the hearth fire was crammed now with people. Every night they held new Ceremonies of Forgiveness, and heard more and more stories of desperation.

"We can't take this. People are going to sink under the weight of all this pain," Anthony said. He and Emily often ate with Bird and Madrone and some of the others who were emerging as leaders.

"What do you suggest?" Bird asked.

"We need to lighten up. We need entertainment. Some of these people have got to be able to sing songs or tell jokes. Half of them were probably aspiring actors!"

"We could put out a call for entertainers and musicians," Bird suggested.

"No," Madrone objected. "With all due respect to our representative of the Musicians' Guild here, I don't think professional entertainment is what we need. Everybody has some talent, something they can do. We need to let them show it. We hear all their stories of failure and despair—but that's not all of who they are. Let them each have a chance to shine."

Bird favored her with an evil grin. "So you're going to get up and tell a joke, too!"

"Me, no!" Madrone responded with alarm. "I can't remember jokes!"

"I can," Hannah piped up. "What did the door say to the window?"

"I don't know," Madrone said.

"Don't try to fool me, I can see right through you!" Hannah and Heather dissolved into giggles.

*   *   *

The next night, they followed the ceremony with an impromptu talent show. Everyone was encouraged to step forward, to share a song or a story or a poem. Madrone was pressed into service to play straight man to Heather and Hannah's routine of riddles and jokes. While she couldn't deliver a comic routine to save her life, she had a well-developed ability to look blank and confused, and she found to her surprise that she enjoyed the laughter.

Laughter is healing, she thought. And once they'd seen her onstage, looking silly, they'd be more comfortable with her if they needed her services as a healer. Bird had taught Zap and Zoom to sing an old Woody Guthrie song. But when they stepped up to the front, Anthony put a hand on his shoulder.

"We have something for you," he said.

Bob, Anthony's neighbor, came up to the front and thrust forward a guitar. Bird reached out for it, felt its weight and balance, tried its tone. It was a good one, an old Gibson.

"This is for you," Bob said. "I brought it, but I don't really play much anymore. We want you to have it, because we're grateful for all you and Miss Madrone have done, starting this place."

Bird swallowed hard. There was a lump in his throat. He knew what a sacrifice the instrument represented—a guitar, like anything portable that could be sold, represented a core part of a family's savings, their security. Undoubtedly Bob had brought it to sell, not to play or give away. It was indeed a magnificent gift!

His hands cradled it, stroked it with a kind of lust. He slipped the worn strap over his neck, plucked the strings and tightened the pegs to tune it. His fingers were still stiff and a bit awkward, but they found the chords with a sense of deep familiarity, as if the guitar were a part of himself that he had long missed.

"This land is your land, this land is my land,
From California, to the New York islands ... "

He and the boys sang, and others joined in. They sang the chorus as an anthem, an affirmation, as if they were finally beginning to believe it.

"This land was made for you and me.... "

By the second night, some were creating little skits or offering their audition monologues, for many were indeed frustrated actors who'd once hoped to star in the vidscreens. The gatherings went on long into the night, and people saw one another in a different way. Not just a victim, but a poet; not just a runaway debt slave, but a singer. Not just a grief-stricken father, but a comic.

The work of clearing rubble and building shelters was relentless, and went on through the day, but Emily decreed that work should stop in the late afternoon, so that everyone could have some hours of leisure. Some used it to be with their families, others to practice a new song or to craft a poem. Musicians got together to form bands. Eve McDaniels, who'd directed a choir until the Retributionists outlawed the Catholic Church, formed up a chorus and wrote plainsong to accompany the Ceremony of Forgiveness. Anthony found an old volume of Shakespeare in an abandoned apartment, and started up a theater group to perform the plays.

Tianne herself was possessed by a vision. She scavenged deep into the dangerous zones, looking for wood and metal and scraps of fabric. She cajoled the mechanics to borrow the welding rig that they had salvaged from an old body shop, and hoarded every spare rod and rusty piece of iron.

They planned the unveiling for Solstice morning. Madrone and Bird kept vigil through the longest night, and many of the refugistas joined them. At sunset, they ritually doused the hearth-fire, and took turns whirling the fire-drill to light it anew. They'd reserved the hot springs that night for ceremonial bathing, for now the Refuge had grown so large that baths were rationed to once a week, in a rotation that went by neighborhood. It took hours to get everyone through. Meanwhile, those who were waiting their turn or who were already cleansed sat around the fire, chanting and drumming on upturned buckets, singing songs to the returning light.

"We are all midwives on this night," Madrone proclaimed, "keeping vigil with Mother Night as she labors to give birth to the new sun, the new day. Gaze into the fire and ask yourself, what will you birth in this new year? What new day will we bring to the light together?"

She remembered so many vigils, back home. They would begin with a plunge into the bay or the ocean, at sunset, and a bonfire at the beach, everyone dancing wildly around the fire, naked and ecstatic. They'd come home to feast on winter squash and smoked wild boar and chestnut cake. Maya would mix up a huge batch of bread dough, and they would knead in their hopes and wishes for the coming year. While it rose, they'd go up to the ritual room, decked with greenery and bright with beeswax candles, and sing and chant and trance together. Then they'd come back down, for the kneading and baking, for more feasting and rounds of destiny tarot and storytelling.

Here in the Refuge, they used some of their precious store of salvaged candles to light the baths and the plaza. They lacked flour to bake enough bread for everyone, but they'd constructed a clay oven at the hearth and used it to bake potatoes. At dawn, they led a procession through the Refuge to the eastern gate. Portal of the Rising Sun, they'd called it, and Tianne's crew were in the process of decorating it with a golden mosaic. They climbed up onto the walls, and Bird led them in the Song of Rising as they sang up the newborn sun.

> *"Open your hearts,*
> *there's a new day waking,*
> *Freedom will rise,*
> *like the rising sun ... "*

That day was devoted to celebration. It began with a work party, to erect and unveil Tianne's sculpture. A hundred people gathered to lend their strength. Together they lifted huge sections while welders scrambled to attach the pieces. Finally, when it was ready, they attached ropes and pulled, all together, one massive tug-of-war, and the sculpture rose.

It rose high above the rubble, over the walls surrounding the plaza, and as Madrone looked at it her heart lifted. It seemed to be a convocation of wings, framed in heavy steel but weightless, reaching upwards to sky and sunlight. Up and up it soared, shape upon shape in a delicate, impossible balance. At the top, a gleaming figure raised her hands, wings sprouting from her back, crowned with rays like the sun, the moon at her feet.

"In the forbidden tongue," Tianne announced, "This city was called *El Pueblo de Nuestra Señora la Reina de los Ángeles*—City of Our Lady Queen of the Angels. The Stewards tried to chase her out. They forced her into hiding. They thought they had killed her dead. But they were wrong. She's back! She's here with us now. She's watching over us!"

Surely the mission fathers who'd founded the city were thinking of Mary, Madrone thought. But what they got was something older than Mary, the original Mother of Gods, Goddess herself, Lilith with talons and great bird wings, progenitrix of all the angels who came after her. She was earth yearning for sky, encircled by sun and moon, radiant in her blue cloak of water. An emblem of hope, on the morning of rebirth.

The musicians played and everyone danced beneath the Queen of the Angels' gaze. Madrone looked around at the faces around her, too thin, etched by lines of worry and care, but alight now. They brought out rusty smiles like some relic of the old days they'd kept hidden away and rarely used.

Tianne was right. It was worth it, devoting the time and the resources to art. People's hearts were lifted by the wings.

We're no longer just a bunch of refugees, huddled in the ruins, she thought. We have a culture. We are a city.

Chapter Thirty-Four

W E NEED TO FORM A COUNCIL," BIRD SAID. "THE REFUGE HAS grown beyond just us giving orders and Emily organizing everyone."

He and Anthony were preparing a meal in the apartment. The two families enjoyed escaping from the big communal hearth and getting a bit of a respite from constant questions and demands. They'd rigged up a small stove that burned scraps of wood with great efficiency, and a hand pump to bring water up. Madrone would join them when she got a break from patients at the healing center. Emily would come as soon as the day's work was complete.

They'd had a week of celebrations, Solstice blending into Christmas and Hanukah combined, and then New Year's, with the teens and former techies deejaying an all-night dance party. But now he felt it was time to get back to work.

"It works to have her organize everyone. That's what she was born for," Anthony said. "She's been trying to organize me and the kids for years."

"Be that as it may, people have to organize themselves," Bird added a pinch of their precious salt to the quinoa.

"None of them ever have before," Anthony said, splitting an onion in two with a sharp knife. "They don't expect to."

The Refuge was not yet producing longer-term crops like onions, but it was growing greens and herbs they could trade in Angel City's black markets, and crafts they could sometimes sell. Their diet was much improved from the early days of acorn gruel and stale waybread.

Bird found responses leaping to his lips like, But that's the way we do it in the North. He stifled them.

"What's wrong with leadership?" Anthony asked. "As long as it's fair and accountable? Most people don't want to lead, they just want to be well led."

"But people need to have a say in the things that matter to them," Bird protested.

"Why?"

He didn't know how to answer. It was one of those unquestioned assumptions so core to everything the City was, to everything he was, that to examine it was to risk vertigo. "Because, because that's the way people become whole—by taking responsibility, by exercising their freedom. Don't you think people want to make their own decisions?"

"Not necessarily. Not in every aspect of life. I don't. I'm happy to decide who gets the lead in *Macbeth*, but I don't give a damn how you organize the food raids as long as I'm eating." Anthony tipped the onions into a frying pan lined with a smear of their scarce and precious cooking oil. "For that matter, I don't particularly want fifty people weighing in on how I interpret *Macbeth*."

The onions sizzled, and their pungent fragrance filled the room as Bird stirred them with a fork.

"But if we're trying to overthrow the Stewards and replace them with something different, we have to model that difference," Bird said. "We can't just be a kinder, gentler tyranny. We've got to be a real democracy."

"We're not used to it. Most of these people have never voted in an election—you can't vote if there's a lien against your name for unpaid debts. They aren't used to speaking in public, or debating, or making decisions. They aren't ready for democracy."

"That's the argument every tyranny has used to keep itself in power since the beginning of time."

"Yes, but in this case it happens to be true!" Anthony asserted with a laugh.

Nonetheless, Bird brought the issue up that evening, after the Ceremony of Forgiveness when people thronged the amphitheater for the nightly talent show.

"People, before we begin, we have something serious to discuss," he announced. "We've grown in size, and we continue to grow. Up until now, a few of us have taken the lead and organized things. But it's time we had a more democratic way to do it. It's time we formed a Council."

"Why?" a woman shouted from a back row. "You doin' a good job, you keep on!"

"But we have some key decisions to make," Bird said.

"So make them!" yelled Bob with a new, Refuge-born bravado.

"It's time we began to make them all together," Bird said.

"Why? You the leaders!" said the loud woman at the back.

"But we're trying to build a city where everyone is a leader. Like we have in the North."

"But we ain't in the North!"

"I'm not stepping down, not yet," Bird assured them. "But it's time for all of you to step up. How many of you are here because the Stewards raised the interest rates on your debt? Would they have been able to do that if you'd been part of making that decision? How many of you got laid off from jobs when the bosses decided to close a factory or a service center or a school? Wouldn't you like to have had some power over those choices?"

"So what we got to decide?" the woman asked.

"More and more people are joining us every day," Bird said. "Where are we going to put them?"

There was loud talking and pandemonium as everyone began talking at once.

"Salal would have people break into small groups, discuss the issue, and bring back suggestions," Madrone whispered to him.

"Fine," he hissed at her. "You want to lead this meeting?"

"Just trying to be helpful."

He turned back to the group. "Okay, people—we all want to be part of this decision, but we can't all talk at once. Why don't you find six or eight other people, group up, and talk about it in a small circle. Then we'll hear back what the suggestions are."

Madrone and Bird wandered around and listened to the group discussions. Bird immediately realized he'd made a tactical error by not telling people *how* to talk to one another. In the North, they'd automatically go around in a circle, giving each person a chance to speak. But here they had no experience with rounds or councils. Some of the groups sat in silence. In another, one person held forth in a long tirade about the messages he heard from the angels of Retribution, who were calling on the Stewards to repent. In most, one or two people were loudly arguing while the others looked on.

"This isn't working," Bird said when he and Madrone met back up at the hearth.

"I think you have to give them more specific instructions."

Bird let out a piercing whistle. "People, try this!" he cried. "Go around your circle and give everyone a chance to talk without being interrupted. The quietest people sometimes have the most important things to say."

The discussion seemed to go better after that. When the groups reported back, several of them had come up with the same idea. They suggested that the old-timers move to the outlying areas and families could fix up their own quarters to suit themselves. Each new neighborhood could have its own hearth. That would let the newcomers take over the developed areas at the center and get oriented to the ways of the Refuge.

The major disagreement was about which way to expand. Some of the groups wanted to move east, others to fill in some of the destroyed buildings to the north, back towards the old freeway. A huge argument broke out, that threatened to escalate into a fistfight. Bird did his best to keep control of the meeting, but it degenerated into a shouting match.

"Shut up!" screamed Miss Ruby, a stout woman of middle age who'd been a teacher at Emily's school. She reminded Madrone of Johanna, with a bright red head-scarf bringing out the mahogany tones of her skin, and her feet planted, ready to stand her ground. She placed her hands on her ample hips, cocked her head, and fixed the crowd with her black eyes in her own version of the Look. "Everybody, just shut right up!"

"And Azrael came down in a thunder of glory, and his trumpet resounded over the multitudes. You who claim to speak in the name of the great Retribution—you know not what Retribution is! For you have fallen into sin ... "

The speaker was Prophet Jed, a tall man with a black beard and wild, staring black eyes crowned by brows that trailed off in long tails. He was dressed in a gray robe and carried a shepherd's crook, and looked for all the world like John the Baptist come again.

"You too, Jed!" Miss Ruby told him firmly.

"Would you silence the voice of the prophet?" Jed thundered back.

"Let him speak!" someone cried out from the crowd, and other voices rose in support.

Miss Ruby was undismayed. She raised a hand. "I'm not going to silence him, but I'm going to put him on 'pause' for a moment. Now, people, we got to find some unity here. We fight among ourselves, we'll all be in the slave pens before you can crunch a chip!"

There was a disgruntled murmur throughout the crowd.

"Why don't we expand in both directions?" Anthony suggested. "We'll need the extra space soon enough if we keep growing at this rate!"

"Do we have enough manpower to do that?" a young man asked.

"We did this area, at first, with just two of us," Madrone answered.

There was a murmur of assent, and Bird suggested they break into groups for planning. The crowd split into three—an eastern contingent, a northern group, and a base of people to hold the center. They talked and argued long into the night, not smoothly, for there were bitter disputes and a couple of fistfights and a constant stream of the disgruntled simply walking away from the meetings. But by the end, each group had a plan. And in the morning, they began the work of building and moving.

The Refuge now had neighborhoods.

It was a week later that a young couple stood up after the evening meeting was over. They couldn't have been more than twenty. He had the coloring that they'd come to call newgen—the new generation, a mix of heritages that in his case produced dark caramel skin and a wild thatch of intensely curled hair. She had a delicate, heart-shaped face with a waterfall of silky, dark hair and eyes like two black crescents. They held hands and their eyes caressed each other.

"Madrone, will you marry us?" the young man asked.

"But this is so sudden," Madrone said. "We've only just met!"

The crowd laughed. I made a joke! Madrone thought with some surprise. It worked. It was funny. She was trying to lighten up, to not always be dead serious, but she didn't have Maya's wit or her cynical sense of humor. Still, she could almost feel the old woman nodding her approval.

"You know what I mean," the young man went on when the laughter died away. "We want to get married. We love each other. Under the Stewards, we can't, because we come from debtor families. But we don't care. Will you marry us?"

"I'm a healer," Madrone protested. "I'm not a priest."

"You're the closest thing we've got to one—one that we could trust," the young woman said.

The young man turned to Bird.

"You could do it," he said.

"Me? I'm a musician."

"You're like a captain, a captain of a ship."

"We're all captains on this ship," Bird asserted.

"I know, I know," the young man said. "But you're like the captain of captains."

"Who marries people in the North?" someone shouted out.

"You don't have to get married in the North," Bird said. "Not for sex, and not to be sure that any babies are cared for. We all make sure that every child born is cared for. But if you want to get married, to make that commitment, you can. We don't have debt, or debtors, or debt law in the North."

"So who marries you?" the young woman asked.

"If you're part of a religion that has priests or ministers or rabbis or imams, they do it," Bird said. "If you're a Pagan, you get your circle to help you do a handfasting."

"What's that?"

"It's like a Pagan marriage ceremony. You say vows in front of the community—vows that you write yourself. You share bread and salt, and drink from the same cup. Then the community ties your hands together and you jump over a broom. You can add a lot more to it, but that's the basics."

"I like that," the young woman said. "I wouldn't want to be married by any bankersnot Retro, anyway. Can we do that?"

"Why not?" Bird said.

"Anyone got a broom?"

"Why not do it tomorrow?" Madrone suggested. "The moon will be full, and that will give some time to prepare. Bird didn't say it, but generally there's a big party that follows."

"We want to get married, too!" Another young man cried out.

A chorus of voices joined in the clamor.

"Tomorrow, then," Bird said. "Mass wedding day!"

There was a buzz of happy excitement in the plaza that fell to silence as two young women stood up, holding hands. They were dark and light, chocolate and butterscotch, both with that slim-skinny body that spoke of years of short rations, both with delicate features that were nonetheless hard and remote as if they had armored themselves long ago.

"We want to get married too," the dark girl said.

"We love each other," said the blonde.

In the dead silence that followed, someone in the back of the crowd cried out, "Abomination!"

The crowd erupted with a mixture of cheers, boos, and catcalls. Bird called for quiet, but it took a long time before even his resonant voice could be heard over the din.

"Quiet! Can we talk about this like civilized people?" he yelled.

The only bubble of quiet, Madrone noted, surrounded the small contingent of steely-eyed blonds with perfect features, the Angels, uneasy allies of the Resistance. They didn't live in the Refuge, for they had their own long-established safe havens in various 'hoods and sectors. But they often sent a small contingent to the meetings to watch and listen.

The Angels had been bred to service those Primes whose tastes mingled sex with torture and pain and the exquisite pleasure of killing something tiny, perfect, and helpless. Those who survived and escaped banded together, and took exquisite pleasure in revenge. They made Madrone feel uneasy, standing silent in the back of the crowd, arms folded, their perfect faces betraying no expression except possibly a mild contempt for anyone naïve enough to believe in love.

"Abomination!" another voice called out.

"That's Retributionist bullshit! They're the abomination, not two people who love each other!" came another voice.

"The Bible says ... "

"Oh, it does not! Who the hell told you that, anyway? Some blood-sucking Retro preacher who probably never actually even read the thing? There's a whole fucking book in the Bible about David and Jonathan, and you know what it says about them? It says, 'He loved him like a woman.' That's what the Bible says!" the caramel woman shot back at him.

"David was a sinner!"

"What about Ruth and Naomi?" another voice called out.

"They were just friends!"

"Says who? What, you were there?"

"Naomi was old enough to be her mother, for Jesus's sake!"

"Can we please stop arguing about gossip that's three thousand years old?" Bird thundered. "We've come here to do something different from the Stewards and the Retributionists. We've come here to build a different world. They say—'You get to do this and you don't.' 'You're worthy and you're not.' I say, we're all worthy. If one of us gets to get married, we all get to get married!"

"I thought you said that we all get a say!" shouted a tall man.

"Why on earth did I ever think that was a good idea?" Bird muttered, but only Madrone heard him. She slipped her arm into his.

"Yeah! We should vote!" a young man cried.

"We don't vote! We work by consensus," Bob called out.

"And why did you think it was a good idea to teach them that?" Madrone muttered back. They'd spent three meetings training the Refuge in the process, and she now regretted every one of them.

"I block! I block two women getting married!" a woman yelled from the back.

"Please, Jesus, rapture me now," Bird murmured to Madrone.

"You can't block that!" a tall man yelled back.

"Yes I can! It's a moral objection!"

"Well, I block your block! I have a moral objection to your suckdick moral objection!" yelled the tall man.

"Do something, Captain," Madrone prodded him. "'O Captain, my Captain!'"

Bird stepped forward and held up his hand.

"You can't block somebody else's rights or freedoms," Bird said in a loud voice that only by great effort achieved a tone of calm patience. "That's not how it works."

"What do you do in the North?" Anthony piped up quickly.

"Oh, fuck the North! I'm so fucking sick of hearing 'what do you do in the North'! We ain't the North, we the Southlands and we do what we want!" shouted the woman from the back of the crowd.

"In the North, everyone is free to marry, or not, as they choose!" Bird cried.

"Abomination!" Prophet Jed thundered as he strode forward to the front of the crowd. "Abomination! Abomination under the Lord! And the Lord sends his prophet to say to you, Repent, for the retribution of the Lord is great, and his fist is heavy. He sends the killing fire, he sends the killing drought. He will wither the grain in the fields, and blast the—"

"Oh, shut the fuck up, you buttskull idiot!" a stout woman cried.

A fistfight broke out in one section of the plaza. Others rushed in to break it up.

"You're losing control of the ship, Captain," Madrone said. "Shall I call in the bees?"

"Abomination!" Bird cried out, his singer's voice carrying over the crowd. "Abomination! Abomination! Abomination!"

The noise quieted as people turned to stare at him.

"We are surrounded by abomination! It's all around us. It's what brought us here. Real abomination! Like taking peoples' homes, and sending their daughters to the pens. Like keeping people short of food and water. Like breeding up diseases to kill people and breeding soldiers to keep the order. We all know plenty about abomination!

"But two people loving each other? I'm sorry, that is just not in the same league. If we know our history, we know how the Stewards and their forerunners used that issue to keep people apart who should have stood together, to keep people weak who should have been strong. And if we let ourselves be divided, we will fall!

"We're growing. We're growing fast, and we're growing strong. That's a good thing! But we're growing beyond the bounds of invisibility. Any day now, the Stewards may get wind of us. Any day now, they could march in here with their drones and their jackboots, and we need to be prepared for that.

"We don't need to vote on any two people getting married, whatever gender they might be. Any more than you'd want the whole assembly to vote on who you marry, or sleep with, or eat your fraggin' supper with. Freedom means these things are personal. Your personal choice.

"So tomorrow, anyone who wants to marry, we'll get a broom, and we'll have a party. Write your vows tonight, and we will all witness. And if you don't approve, that's your choice. You don't have to come. Of course, it's gonna be a hella good one!

"I'm going to come, and I'm going to witness those vows. Not as your captain, but as one free citizen of the City of Refuge, to honor and celebrate others who want to exercise their freedom. To honor the Goddess of love, who says, 'All acts of love and pleasure are my rituals'!"

Loud cheers rang out.

"And now, can we get on with the talent show?"

"Nice save," Madrone told him afterwards as they pushed the blessed lock button on their bedroom door. Zap and Zoom were presumably asleep, and the city was bedded down for the night. "O Captain, my Captain."

"Would you stop saying that?" Bird shook his head with annoyance as he pulled his T-shirt off.

"What, you don't like Walt Whitman?"

"It was a poem he wrote for Lincoln after he was assassinated, remember? It's bad magic." He tossed his shirt at the clothes basket in the corner, but it missed and fell on the floor.

"I see your point." Madrone picked it up and dropped it onto the pile of laundry.

"Anyway, we didn't completely solve the problem," Bird said. "There was still a grumbling contingent going off with Prophet Jed."

"There's always a grumbling contingent, no matter what we do. And there's always somebody stark raving bonkers who feels compelled to get up and speak at great length."

"I try to rein them in. But there's no force on earth can stop them. And Jesus never raptures me, no matter how many times I ask him," Bird lamented.

"Kegels," Madrone smiled. "That's what Maya used to say she always did when slightly cracked people were going on and on in meetings."

"Kegels?"

"The vaginal strengthening exercises. Contract, contract, contract … release. You just sit there while some idiot is blathering on and do your strengthen exercises. She used to credit the movement for the fact that even in old age, she never had to worry about incontinence."

"I so wish you hadn't told me that," Bird said.

"Why?"

"Because now, every time I look over at you in a meeting, I'm going to be thinking about your muscle tone."

"You could help me work on it, you know." Madrone's smile deepened.

"Oh? You think I could provide some … stimulation?"

"Let's work out."

After, when they lay in that glow of satisfaction and affection, Bird turned to her.

"So, do you want to do it?"

"We just did it." She nipped his nose. "How quickly they forget!"

"Not that. Well, yes, that. Do you want to jump the broom tomorrow?"

"Are you proposing to me?" Madrone asked.

"Just asking."

"Get down on one knee."

"I'm too comfortable here," he said, nestling his back into the curve of her body, feeling her breasts press into his shoulder blades.

"Lazy! I'm certainly not marrying a lazy man!"

"So you're turning me down?" He rolled off the bed, crouched on one knee beside it, and took her hand. "Madrone, would you do me the honor of becoming my wife?"

She kissed his hand, felt tenderly the scarred and broken fingers.

"No."

"No?" He looked up at her in surprise.

"No."

"Why not? My prospects are good, and I come from a good family."

"If we do it, I'd like to do it back home, with our friends and families," she said.

He took his hand back and sat, leaning against the bed. There was a long silence, full of all they didn't say. The North is still home to her, Bird thought. And I don't know if it is for me, or if I'll ever be able to feel at home there again.

"But it's not just that," Madrone said at last. "And it's not that I don't love you like life itself. It's these people here. Marriage means something different to them than it would to us. If we were home, I wouldn't hesitate. But here—I'm afraid that they'll stop seeing me as myself, and start seeing me as your appendage. Captain."

"There's some truth in that," Bird admitted.

"Besides, though I hate to be selfish, when we do it I'd like to have a ceremony just for us."

"With a white dress?"

"For you or for me?" she asked him.

"Fair is fair—if you get one, I get one!"

"And Zap and Zoom as ring-bearers. Can you see them in Little Lord Fauntleroy suits?"

"Holybear would make a beautiful bridesmaid!"

———

The wedding itself was a joyful occasion, a peak of the hope and optimism the Refuge had fostered. In all, they had thirty-three couples who decided to get handfasted that day, most of them male and female, but also women marrying women and men marrying men. People took a break from their usual work routines to decorate the plaza with all the greenery and flowers they could find, along with bunting made of scavenged sheets and lace canopies for shade.

The happy couples were arrayed in an amazing collection of rags and finery. Tattered old jeans with a lace blouse on top, or a white silk toga with a flowered belt holding it on. They shared cups of sweet water, broke loaves of bread they'd scraped up scarce cash to buy, and read their vows to small groups of their close friends. Then they lined up and jumped a hurdle course of every broom the Refuge could provide, held by pairs of children.

Crazy Janus, a small woman with a tangle of dark curls and blazing black eyes, stepped up and delivered an impromptu sermon.

"The great mother spaceship has her spies—her eyes are on us, eyes on the prize! Surprise! Love each other, she says, and I will take you home. Love belies the lies, no wise, no way, love lies bleeding, love is the answer. The question is ... the quest, the rest, the best, the pest, the pest of love is hate, don't wait, watching her weight, we are the heavy burden of the angels of light, but love will enlighten, frighten, brighten!"

Far off in the distance, they could just hear the heavy chords of a Retributionist hymn. It was a low drone, like the hum of bees working up to a war party. It made Madrone feel uneasy.

But the crowd around her was laughing and clapping, and drowned out all ominous undertones.

"Rejoice and make a happy noise unto the angels, the angels of the City of Angels, the winged ones await," Janus proclaimed. "They await us above, angels of love ... "

The party afterwards was legendary. The refugistas brought out all the food they could scrape together for a feast, and the scavengers produced a case of champagne, decades old and very mature. There were songs and poetry and skits galore.

Janus had climbed up onto a plinth of broken concrete, and she raised her skinny arms and turned her face skyward in exaltation. "Angels to carry us, carry us off, carry us up, up and away on their great beating wings ... "

The sky was streaked with fine clouds that did look like wings, lacy and delicate, or like bridal veils stretched out against the blue. The sun dipped low, the veils glowed with a golden radiance like a bright promise that deepened as blue dimmed to indigo and then to the orange and crimson of fire and blood.

Chapter Thirty-Five

H E'S CREEPY," ROSA SAID AS SHE TUGGED ON THE LINE TO HOIST the mainsail. "Creepy, creepy, creepy!" With each reiteration, she gave a sharp pull to the line, and the sail rose.

"I hear you, sailor," Isis said. She was overseeing the operation, leaning back against the rail, her arms folded. "But now let's see how fast you can lower and stow that sail."

She was rehearsing the girl over and over in all the necessary operations to sail the *Victory*, against the day when they would move into action and Rosa would take the sailboat north to safety. For now, they were anchored with the bulk of the navy in the lee of the Channel Islands. A few of the faster catamarans headed out into the shipping lanes to reconnoiter.

"I don't trust him," Rosa said as the sail jerked down.

"Slowly, slowly!" Isis cautioned her. "Soft as a Trophy's tit!"

"Well, I don't," Rosa asserted, paying out the line more smoothly now. "What if he's a spy? What if he's just trying to tie us up here, keep us from doing anything?"

Isis had had the same thought herself, but she didn't want to feed the girl's suspicions. It was Livingston's plan, this halt, and it had gone on for weeks now with the bulk of the navy lying low while shipping went on unmolested. High time to see some action.

"He's full of himself, grant you that," Isis admitted. Damn, but she wished Sara were here to talk it over with. She didn't want to get the girl all jacked up and frightened, so she tried to downplay her own suspicions. But it would really help to run them by someone else.

She'd taken Miguel aside, after Rosa shared her story. They'd briefed Bronwyn and Belle, and Belle had said she'd talk with Sara. While they considered confronting Livingston, they'd decided instead to watch and wait, for really they had no evidence that he'd done anything except visit the City ahead of the warship's surrender. Undoubtedly he'd claim that he was just reconnoitering, perhaps considering whether or not to defect.

No, better to watch him closely, and not let him know they were watching. Verify all his information as best they could, and second-guess his motives.

Still, she longed to talk it over with Sara. What harm could that do?

"He's dangerous!" Rosa said with conviction.

"Enough training," Isis said. "Stow that sail, and let's get some grub."

"So how did you become a pirate?" Rosa asked.

They were eating dinner on the deck. Rosa had made them quesadillas with tortillas she patted out herself, and some salsa she'd requisitioned off the main kitchen on the warship. She liked to cook, and Isis liked to let her earn her keep. Her own days were often taken up with meetings that felt more and more frustrating and fruitless. No matter how much they trained and scouted, Livingston always managed to postpone the day they might actually take action, block a ship, and turn it back. Yeah, jib-girl had a point about him.

The meetings were frustrating, too, because Sara was there at so many of them. Isis had to maintain an invisible wall, a barrier like a thick sheet of glass between them, because otherwise she felt the heat and the desire and it drove her crazy. But not-feeling, that took energy, too. Really, why couldn't the damn woman just have stayed safe in the North, where Isis could dream of her without the fear that gnawed away at her guts.

"You lookin' for a career?" Isis countered.

"Just wondering."

"I was bred to be a racer," Isis told her. "The Primes, down in the Southlands, some of the really rich ones, they own teams. Not a bad life. We stay with our mamas late, till six or seven. Eat good, special diet formulated to build muscle. Get the 'roids and the 'boosters, training every day. You think I'm strong now, shoulda seen me in top condition. Every muscle like a sculpture. Run like the wind."

"Did you like it?" Rosa asked through a mouthful of dripping salsa.

"Never thought about whether or not I liked it. Wasn't a question a racer was encouraged to ask. Just did it, cuz that was how it was," Isis said, biting into her own quesadilla with appreciation.

"I was top of my team in the junior division," she went on. "Then, when we get to be twelve, thirteen, we graduate. We were gettin' hormones and 'roids to control our development, you understand? Time a normal girl starts to bleed, they shut that off. But the Primes, they like a little bit of breast action, not too much, just enough to jiggle when you run naked."

"Naked?"

"Not in the big public races. Then we had little bits of uniforms, a scrap of cloth across all the pertinent parts. But after, for the big Primes, they like to watch a private race. Just the top winners and a few big-sticks. And then we got to service the big betters."

"What do you mean?" Rosa asked.

"You know what I mean. Ain't gonna spell it out for you."

"Disgusting." Rosa set her quesadilla down.

"It was what it was," Isis shrugged. "Some of the Primes, they'd take a special liking to one filly or another. That's what you hope for, cuz then they give swag. Maybe set you up on a private preserve so you don't go to be a breeder, after you're too old to race."

She leaned back and stole a glance at the girl. Time she learned a bit more about the world, Isis thought, put her own troubles into perspective.

"Had me a Prime, he liked to go out on his own little boat. He bet on me. Win, we go sailing. Get us out there in the ocean, away from the Trophy, the shore—well, like I said, ain't gonna spell it out for you. But I liked the sailing. Liked the wind, and the ocean, and I watched everything he did to sail that boat. Sometimes he'd let me hold the tiller. I learned.

"But he was a twisted fishstick, with a mean streak that got meaner and meaner. One day, out there in the ocean, nobody around. He starts in on me with some of his evil shit, and I had me a thought. Thought was—I know how to sail this boat . . .

"Came at me—liked to chase me around the deck, you know, part of the game, and I just let him come, and then when the mallet had momentum, whammed him in the shoulder and the prick went sailing over the rail. Deep water, there. Sharks. Kinda far to swim back to shore."

"What did you do?"

Isis shrugged. "Started up the engine and headed out to sea."

"Wow!" Rosa's eyes were wide. "Did you feel bad after? Like guilty?"

"More scared than bad," Isis said. "No, if ever a squirt deserved a watery grave, that one did. Jesus himself could only thank me for tidying up the world.

"But I didn't know where to go or what to do. Didn't know nothin' about the world or anything in it. Just knew enough to see where my life was headed onshore, and that was nowhere.

"Now I had me a boat. That was a prize no racer ever expects to win! Figured when we didn't get back, his Trophy or his office would raise the alarm, and so I headed north. Into the wind.

"Knew enough to know the salts kept a cordon on the sea lanes around the Southlands. Had to get out beyond it before they put out an alert. Sailed all that day and all that night, by the next day I was starting to nod away at the tiller. Kept on until I found a little cove to anchor in.

"I was too scared to sleep, but too tired to keep awake. Kept pass-ing out, then some sound would come in the night, jolt me up, heart

General Wendell lay in a lounge chair by the side of his own modest pool, watching his children play a game of water volleyball. They'd stretched a net from side to side, and they were laughing and splashing, occasionally ducking each other.

"Hey," he cried out as a particular vigorous splash sent water perilously close to contaminating his martini and the reports he was supposed to be reading. He picked it up and swigged it down. Was he drinking more lately? No, he'd always enjoyed a martini on a Saturday afternoon. Nothing wrong with that.

"Sorry, Dad!" Palin called as she slammed the ball over the net. Watching her, Wendell tried hard to erase the memory of that other pool, the children in it, what had followed.

Not children, he told himself firmly. Pets, with no immortal souls. He remembered those dull, staring eyes.

He'd had to do it. He'd had no choice. He was a soldier, and there were a lot of unpleasant things he'd had to do in his time. Let it go. Put it behind, and move on.

But he couldn't forget about it. Somehow it continued to taint him, to contaminate the simple pleasure of watching his own children cavort, to sully the purity of his marriage bed. He found himself showering longer, soaking in a bath so hot it turned him beet red. When he'd scalded himself enough to feel cleansed for the marital act, in the midst of it he'd find unwelcome memories coming to the surface, and suddenly his own wife would start to look old to him, her skin crepey and dry, her breasts sagging.

It would never happen again, he told himself firmly. He would refuse to be put in that position.

Yet some part of him suspected that it might. They would maneuver him into it, and he would be as helpless to refuse as any of the Trinkets they might offer. The thought sickened him. And yet even in that sick revulsion was a tiny core of heat, of excitement, as if he craved that discipline, deserved it. The illicit pleasure and the exquisite punishment, both.

Things were not going well. They had sprung their trap on the army of the North, and that ragtag band of rabble had sprung right back, going on to capture both the plantation in question and another one. At this rate, they'd soon be making an impact on supplies. And while the Primes were quick to blame him, they were dragging their heels when it came to coughing up the money he needed for more troops and equipment.

And Livingston! A whole fucking navy, poised to interfere with their shipping! Sure, the man claimed to have them mired on the other side of the Channel Islands, but Wendell didn't trust him. Were they truly entrapped, ripe for scuttling, as he claimed?

Or were they Livingston's own private threat, his blackmail?

He set the reports down and stood up, too frustrated to lie there relaxing any longer. The shrieks from the pool were making his head hurt, and his martini glass was empty. Where was the damn pool girl? She was supposed to keep on top of these things.

Here she came now, with a fresh martini on a tray. No child Pet, she wore her dark hair in a decorous bun and her modest uniform buttoned up to her chin. The wife had hired her, trained her, and she kept her eyes modestly down. Nothing about her to excite a man, to make him want to backhand her or flip that dress up and bend her over. Would she squeal in terror, or would she secretly enjoy it? Maybe under that prim downward gaze her eyes were scanning his manly regions, wanting it.

Enough! There were important things on his mind. Disturbing reports from the city. Disappearances. Children who didn't show up to school. Parents who didn't show up to work. Defaulters who weren't there when the Relinquishment Squads came to collect. Deadbeats who should have been working off their overdrafts with honest sweat on the plantations but instead were nowhere to be found.

Of course, some of that was normal, but this was getting beyond that point. Something was up. But what? It was as if there was some secret poison at work, creeping through the veins of the Stewardship.

He would have to find out what it was. He would root it out! He strode into his dressing room and began to throw on his clothes.

The Primes might be stingy with the troops, but they were generous with supplies of drones. Culbertson came from the family that made them. He would order drone surveillance, set up an aerial grid, and get a picture of every street in Angel City.

If there were anything amiss, he would find out what, and destroy it.

Meanwhile he would use the troops he had to fortify the home farms.

Chapter Thirty-Six

EMILY STARTED A SCHOOL. AS HEAD TEACHER, SHE RECRUITED MISS Ruby, whose solid presence conveyed a strong sense of security.

But although Miss Ruby continued to remind Madrone of her grandmother, her educational philosophy could not have been more different from Johanna's. She had the children sit in rows, feet under their chairs, insisting on quiet concentration. The work crews had scavenged a few children's books, and she had the older ones copy out the stories for the younger ones to practice reading. Emily came down and drilled them in math, and for hours each day they were expected to sit quiet and still.

Some of the children thrived in the atmosphere of calm and order. Zap and Zoom, however, were constantly in trouble. They had too much energy to sit still for long, and too little concentration to focus.

Bird liked to walk the boys over to the school each morning, mostly to be sure they actually went to class. Once deposited there, they generally stayed. But he also enjoyed having a few moments with them before the day began. It was quiet in the lanes of the Refuge, and he could observe the progress of the gardens and bask in a moment of private pride without dozens of people clamoring for his attention.

"Behave yourselves now, okay boys? I want to hear a good report!" Bird called after them as they scurried off into the classroom. Just for one moment, he heard his own voice and it brought back to him a vivid memory of his own father, walking him to first grade and leaving him at the door with a stern warning. He'd hated first grade, with that pursed-lip prune of a teacher always making them fold their hands on their desks.

He remembered his own parents fighting bitterly about whether to keep him in the public school or send him to a private one. That was before the Uprising, before Madrone's grandmother Johanna transformed the schools.

"If we believe in the public schools, we got to keep our kid in it," his father had said.

"But Bird is too smart for them. He's gifted!" his mother Brigid objected. "He's bored. They can't meet his needs."

"Then we got to press them on it—not just for him but all the other smart ones that need something more."

"But he'll hate school. They'll ruin him—all that beautiful curiosity! You're sacrificing our own son for politics!"

He'd heard the fights, and he'd seen his opening to wage his own campaign, which as he recalled involved mimicking the teacher when her back was turned, and doing anything she asked very, very slowly, as if he were moving underwater, and making up songs about her that spread through the playground. The end finally came when he brought a jar of spiders to show-and-tell that accidentally-on-purpose escaped and spread through the classroom. They were harmless, but enough people were terrified of them to evacuate the room, including the teacher—what was her name? Miss Darly, that was it. He'd gotten suspended for two weeks and by the end of them, his dad gave in and sent him to Johanna's academy, where there were no desks and every day was an adventure.

A six-year-old insurrectionary, that's what he'd been. Come to think of it, those weeks might have been better preparation for this work than all the wonderful learning experiences that followed. He'd learned a lot about power—and how to counter it.

And now? Now he was still making songs about the powerful. But as far as Zap and Zoom were concerned, he'd become his own father. Maybe that was inevitable. Maybe it happened to everyone—that parental voice that reproduced itself, passed on down the generations, encapsulated like the mitochondrial DNA. Sometime long ago an ape-in-evolution had dropped down from the trees and said to his offspring, "Behave yourself! I want to hear a good report." And they'd been saying it ever since.

Miss Ruby cornered Bird as he dropped Zap and Zoom off for their morning lessons.

"Mr. Bird, I got a bone to pick with you," she accosted him.

"If it's about Zap and Zoom, we're doing the best we can," he said hastily.

"It's not about them—it's about that low-life preacher and the den of snakes he's cultivating!" She planted herself in front of Bird, her hands on her hips. "You've got to do something about it! We came here to get away from that Retributionist bull manure, not to reproduce it."

"He's got a right to worship as he pleases, Miss Ruby," Bird said in a tone of reason. "You and I may not like it—but that's what freedom of religion is all about."

"Yeah, well, he ain't preachin' the love of Jesus, I'm tellin' you. He's preachin' the hatred of Mr. Bird and Miss Madrone. Saying you're agents of the Devil, sent to seduce us into the ways of abomination. And this whole setup is so you can get all of us to fight the Stewards for you, and then you take over and rule us all."

"He can say whatever he wants," Bird responded sharply. "People aren't going to believe it."

"Oh yes they will," Miss Ruby assured him. "People are generally not too bright. Repeat a lie long enough, it begins to sound true."

"What about believing their own eyes and ears? About the twenty times a day people come to me, saying, 'Bird, you decide this' and 'Bird, tell us what to do about that,' and what do I always say? 'I'm not the leader here, we all are. What do you think?'"

"That's part of the problem," Miss Ruby said. "You don't take control, and some resent you for it."

"They'll have to stand in line behind the many who just simply hate me."

"You got to address the lies, take them head on," Miss Ruby advised.

"But if I do that, I'm just rewarding him. I'm giving them credibility."

"You don't pull out the weeds, they gonna take over the garden."

It was later that morning that Zap and Zoom skipped school, only to be corralled by a work crew and brought back. They spat at Miss Ruby and called her a shitassed cunt, and then ran off again. But she managed to catch Zoom, and she turned him over her knee and applied a paddle.

Madrone was livid. When she heard about the spanking, she was filled with a rage so strong that she stomped out of the healing center in the midst of examining a pregnant teenager and stormed off to confront Miss Ruby. She found her collecting up the textbooks and putting them carefully away on the shelves they had built in the ruined storefront they'd cleared for a schoolroom.

Madrone planted herself in Miss Ruby's path, her own hands on her own hips, her eyes flashing.

"Don't you dare ever hit my kid!" she yelled.

"He needed a good wallop on the backside," Miss Ruby said calmly.

"No child needs to be hit!" Madrone spat back. "Especially not that poor abused boy! What in Hella's name were you thinking of?"

"He was rude and disobedient." Miss Ruby stood her ground. "You need to teach him some manners!"

"Manners! We've been trying to teach him for bloody months how to have some minimal trust in other human beings, how to eat people food, not chips, how to expect more out of life than constant abuse and an early death! And now you go and hit him!"

"He'll survive."

"You won't, if you ever lay a hand on one of them again!"

Miss Ruby widened her eyes. Madrone herself was surprised by the intensity of her anger. Breathe, she reminded herself. Ground. She took a step back.

"He needs to learn focus and concentration," Miss Ruby went on in her maddeningly calm voice.

"He's bored out of his skull with your archaic teaching methods!" Madrone snapped.

"I've taught school for thirty years, I think I know what I'm doing!" Now Miss Ruby was getting angry. Her lips tightened and her eyes flashed. She clutched the books to her breast like a shield. "How many classes have you taught?"

"My grandmother started the whole educational system in the North!" Madrone countered, her eyes flashing.

"Well, we aren't in the North!" Miss Ruby said with a decisive jerk of her chin. "We're here, and this is how these children learn, with some order and discipline."

"*Caca de toro!* That's how they learn to be good little slaveys!"

<hr />

Bird had intercepted a tearful, angry Zoom on his way to dinner and heard the story. He marched off to the schoolroom immediately just in time to hear Miss Ruby yelling.

"Don't you come down here with your snitty ways and start throwing the North back at us! Go back there, if you love it so much. You aren't doing us any favors!"

An ominous buzzing filled the sky outside the classroom. Bird looked up in alarm.

"Madrone!" he shouted.

"Stay out of this!" she told him.

"Stop it! Get hold of yourself! Call them off!"

She looked up to see a swarm of angry bees plummeting out of the sky outside, heading for the open door.

Where had they come from? she wondered. Had the gardens drawn them, were there hives somewhere in the depths of the Death Zones, subsisting on memories of flowers?

They were like grace, an unexpected gift, and she radiated out to them love and appreciation and welcome! For a moment, she forgot her rage, then it came to her, amplified ten-fold by the hive's wave of alarm and anger, and her human self was dissolving in one great overwhelming need to protect the brood.

"Madrone!" Bird's voice barely reached her, but it broke the spell. She gulped in a deep breath and tried to calm herself.

Bird slammed the door shut. Miss Ruby opened her mouth for another salvo but Bird silenced her as furious bees hurled themselves against the glass of the display windows. One or two of the insects had made their way into the classroom and they aimed themselves at Miss Ruby like bullets. Bird shielded her, swatting at them, and for his pains got stung on the ear and the lip. Madrone's eyes were closed, she was deep in concentration.

The swarm hovered in a spiral, a small whirlwind of bees, and then flew off.

"What in Jesus's name was that?" Miss Ruby asked.

"Stay on her good side," Bird advised.

~~~~~~~~

"If you want people to make their own decisions, you have to let them make their own decisions. If you put them in charge of something, you have to let them take charge." Bird was speaking through lips that had swollen to twice their normal size, in a head whose left ear sported a bulge the size of a grapefruit. He lay on a platform bed in one of the treatment rooms in the healing center, and a contrite Madrone applied clay to his stings. "*Mierda*, you could have killed her! Me too!"

"But these are the children we're talking about!" she objected. "This is our whole future generation. They're not going to learn like that. They're going to hate school and learning too!"

"Well, now you've got Miss Ruby so riled up that there's not much chance of discussion about it—at least not for a while. Just back off for a bit, okay?"

"Bees, Bird! There are bees here, and that gives me hope!" she said, stroking and coating his ear with clay.

"That doesn't give you license to use them as your personal hit squad! Madrone, you've got to get hold of this thing!"

"She hit our kid! She hit our kid—and you don't care!" Madrone charged.

"I care! But admit it, you've wanted to do the same exact thing hundreds of times. Ow!"

Madrone slapped on the clay with motions that were far from gentle. "I've never wanted to hit them! Kill them, maybe, but not hit them!"

She held onto her anger, cherishing it like an ember she could blow into a blaze. Because as soon as she let it die away, she knew she'd start to feel embarrassed and ashamed. Bird was right. She had to get on top of the bee-mind, not let it take her over. But how? There was no one to guide her, train her. How was she supposed to train herself when the demands of the Refuge drained her of every ounce of energy and gobbled up every moment of her time?

She found herself getting angry all over again. Anger was better than whining, she told herself. But more than that, her anger represented some deep, primal, mother-bear instinct. Those annoying, nasty little boys that she herself had thought of as brats, somehow they had become dear to her in spite of everything. Her rage was a measure of her love.

"They're just little boys," she said. "Little boys who carry big bundles of hurt inside. They need love and patience to open up and lay those burdens down. Not violence!"

"But you can't go off on people like that! You're the healer here—what if they need to come to you for help?"

"What, I'm supposed to be some calm, emotionless, saintly vessel?"

"Ow!" Bird cried out again. "How come I always end up being the one who gets hurt in these brawls?"

"Maybe because you don't have sense enough to stay out of them!"

"You think it would be better if Miss Ruby were lying here turned into a buzzer's pin cushion?"

"No," she admitted.

"How about saying, 'Thank you, Bird—your quick reflexes and fearless, selfless action saved the day!'"

"How about I just brew you up something to take down the swelling?" she suggested in a softer tone. "Unless you'd rather go to Council looking like a space alien from Planet Edema."

She leaned over, tried to kiss him but he turned away.

"I'm not done," he said. "I'm not ready to make up. Or even to make out."

"This is purely medicinal," she assured him, tasting a bead of sweat on his forehead. She closed her eyes, let her bee senses work on the taste, the signature of bee venom and racing hormones. A drop of honey sweat formed in her bee spot.

"You can lick that off," she told him. "Or I can make it into a tincture."

He bent over and touched his tongue to her forehead. Her closeness, her scent, the warmth that radiated from her body washed over him and suddenly he wanted to hold her, to kiss her and enfold her, all that mingled sweetness and sharp sting. He let his arms follow their own volition, and they pulled her close.

"You get to have feelings. You even get to have opinions," he whispered. He felt the swelling start to drain from his face, but it was counterbalanced by a new swelling, a sweet throbbing he felt down in his shaft. Goddess, he wanted her! He would be happy to spiral upwards, chasing her in a mad nuptial flight. Even if the consummation ripped his guts out.

"Oh, thank you, Great Father," she murmured.

He forced himself to pull back and put a hand's breadth of distance between them. Because this is important, he told himself. Not just to us, but to this Refuge. This could undo all our work.

"But take some care about how you express them," he went on. "Ever since you did the bee thing, you've had a temper like a wasp!"

"I do not!"

"Do."

"Don't!"

"Do!"

"I am incredibly sweet tempered, considering what I have to put up with!" she snapped back, although somewhere deep underneath she knew he was right.

"Name one thing."

"You! You, with all your sulking and your glowering and your stalking around like Heathcliff on the moors!" she counterattacked.

"I do not sulk!"

"Do!"

"Don't!"

"Do, do, do! You sulk and you close down and wallow in your PTSD!"

"I do not have PTSD!" Bird yelled. He pulled away from her, the mood shattered.

"Case in point!" she said with an air of triumph.

"And if I do, I've come by it honestly! Now leave me the fuck alone!"

"Sulking! Glowering! Shutting me out."

"I am not fucking shutting you out! Just go away!"

"No, I won't!"

They stood, yelling at each other, eye to eye. He was so angry it was all he could do to control his hands, to prevent them from grabbing her shoulders and trying to shake some sense into her. They had screamed at each other for a good long time until suddenly, as if a squall had passed, they both fell silent. There was a red flush under the cinnamon of her cheeks, her dark eyes were blazing but they were also wet, as if she were being pulled away from him, sinking in the waves of their fury.

Instinctively he reached out for her and suddenly a smile began to play with the corners of her tight-pressed mouth. What were they fighting about, anyway? An answering smile began to animate his lips, and then they were laughing, laughing so hard that tears sprang into his eyes, and he closed his arms around her and pressed his lips to hers. He held her tight, tight, and now he wanted more than anything to open, to let her infuse every cell of him, to penetrate him as he did her when they made love. To open up those dark, festering wounds, the ones he let no one see, not even himself.

Something was breaking open in him, Madrone sensed. She couldn't let go, not even for a moment. But she managed to lock the door of the healing center and to steer them both to one of the beds. They clung together like slow dancers. She drew him down, and somehow they wriggled out of their clothes and held each other, skin to skin.

He was warm against her, hot, as if their skin could fuse, and then he was in her, and she surrounded him and rocked with him and milked him of sorrow. Closer and closer, as if they could dissolve every boundary and separation in the great, burning heat.

When it was over, she still held him, and he began to sob. Great, deep, choking sobs, as if they had to force their way out past a barrier of concrete. She held him as he cried out the tears she knew he had long, long needed to cry. She would hold him and touch him in the deep, wounded places and with her love wash away the pain and the shame.

He was trying to speak, but he kept choking back on the words.

"What is it? What is it?" she murmured. "You can tell me anything."

"I can't ... I can't." He choked—for a moment she feared that he would stop breathing altogether. But he forced the words out.

"I can't go back there."

"I know," she said.

"I can't go back, and sit in the garden, and give you the baby that you want. I let them down, Madrone. I let them all down."

No, no you didn't, she wanted to say. She wanted to argue with him, and reason, and make him see sense. But she was wise enough to stay silent.

"I gave into them. They broke me."

She just held him and let him cry. It was a deep wound, and while it was far from healed, at least now it was lanced, debrided by his scalding tears.

"The City will not forgive me," Bird pronounced the words like a judgment, one that he had spoken over and over in his own head.

"I forgive you," Madrone said.

He patted her shoulder. "That's sweet."

"It doesn't make it better," she acknowledged.

"It doesn't make it worse," he said.

"Do you forgive yourself?"

"Maybe. In time. When I've done something to deserve it."

"No. It doesn't work that way. You'll never do enough to deserve it. You could liberate the whole Southlands, and the Heartlands and the East Coast and the Gyre and Panasia to boot, and it will never be enough." She pulled back and looked at him, with all the intensity of the bee gaze, observing the energies that swirled around him and within him, his bright red courage and his dark pain. "Forgiveness isn't something you earn. It's something you give. Are you brave and generous enough to give it to yourself?"

"I don't know," he admitted.

"We are here, at the heart of the City of Refuge, where all debts are forgiven. All debts! How can you lead us if you won't forgive your own?"

She took his hands between hers, clasping them together as they did during the Forgiveness Ceremony. "Take the pledge. Say the words after me, even if you don't believe them. I, Bird, forgive myself...."

He was silent for a long, long moment. He was going to balk, she thought, and cling to the pain because in some way to let it go was to finally accept it, the loss and the failure.

But at last, he spoke.

"I, Bird, forgive myself ... "

"For being human ... "

"For being human ... "

"And susceptible to pain ... "

"And susceptible to pain ... "

"I know that, faced with intolerable choices ... "

"I know that, faced with intolerable choices ... "

"I did the best I could."

"I did the best I could."

"Just keep saying that," Madrone whispered. "Whether you believe it or not. Keep saying it."

"The City won't forgive me. They won't forget," Bird whispered.

Her only answer was her arms around him, a small, warm circle of absolution.

Chapter Thirty-Seven

THE FARTHER SOUTH THE ARMY OF LIBERATION WENT, THE CLOSER they came to Angel City, the better defended were the plantations. Guards patrolled the perimeters in double shifts. Radio towers were no longer exposed on roofs, but buried underground. Compounds were not protected with just a few strands of barbed wire, but with concrete walls and barriers of razor wire.

"Stewards got it ass-backwards, if you ask this sojuh," River said. "Oughta fortify the outlying farms, not the ones close in. Then they'd be protection for the home farms. Devil himself couldn't dig them out."

"You've got a strategic mind," Cress told him. He was amazed at how someone who'd only learned a couple of months ago how to read more than a memo could grasp so many essentials of tactics and strategy. River seemed to have an innate feel for so many things, how to marshal his troops to best advantage, how to use the terrain, how to create the element of surprise.

As for himself, he was tired. Tired of the grind, tired of pushing himself beyond endurance, pumping himself up to face the grim fear of each raid, relaxing into safety only to know that he would have to rev up again tomorrow and tomorrow. He was ready to go home, or better, to stay here and work with the Farmers' Guild to restore the land. He looked at the desert, with its subtle swells and contours, and saw swales to capture water, and swaths of acacia and mesquite. He soothed himself to sleep at night imagining harvest parties where they would grind carob and mesquite into flour and make pancakes sweetened with jelly from the fruits of prickly pears. He would pull out his old guitar and sing songs for the children, and they would be his children, some of them, his by a smiling woman whose face was not yet clear....

But no, he wasn't ready for that.

For it wasn't true that he couldn't see the face of his dream woman. She had a face. Valeria's face. He wasn't yet ready to give her up.

He'd said goodbye to Flo back in the City with a mixture of mild regret and relief. There were women in the ranks who gave him smoky looks and plied him with cups of tea and hopeful glances. But here, on this dusty road with the Army, he preferred to keep his focus clear.

Focus brought rewards. Tired as he was of the fighting, the results were exciting. After a month and a half, the first of the liberated zones were just beginning to produce fish and micro-greens. More members of Farmers' Guild and a horde of teenagers on their gift year of service had come down to plant trees and cover crops that sprouted from the sprinkles of winter rain. Flocks of desert sheep were intensively grazing the new grass, eating down the thatch, churning the ground, fertilizing it, and then moving on to the next paddock. The Builders' Guild dug into the earth to make new dwellings that were sheltered from the summer heat, and taught the liberados how to build their own thick-walled homes of clay and straw.

Now, when they approached a new operation, Cress scouted the land with double vision. One eye saw its military possibilities and challenges, the other was planning rain catchment and run-off diversions and swales.

It might be an advantage, he thought, having a military commander who was also a key hydrologist with Water Guild. When they dug trenches for cover, he put them on contour so that when the rains came, they would capture water and infiltrate it into the land. When they needed a bunker, he built it to become an ephemeral pool after the fighting ceased. When they sited a lookout post on high ground, he ran tunnels out to it that could channel water toward the ridges and rehydrate them. When they dug out buried power lines, he had them toss the loosened dirt into downhill berms to catch runoff. It pleased him that even in preparing for war they were already watering the peace to come.

"So, how do you think we attack this one?" he asked River. They were lying on their stomachs on a low rise looking over the plantation that was their next target. It was strongly fortified and sat in the middle of a flat stretch of ground that offered no helpful cover.

River shrugged. "Could go to the gate, ask nicely to let us in."

"Or?" Cress swept the area with his field glasses, taking in the strong, reinforced gate, the high fences. He handed the glasses to River.

"Could climb over the wall, wasn't for all that razor wire on top. And the snipers." River handed back the glasses and pointed to a pair of tall towers that sported crow's nests where guards stood watch.

"Yeah, can't forget about the snipers," Cress agreed. "Don't want them to feel slighted in any way."

"Could dig under."

"There's the snipers, remember?"

"Could dig from way back, be under cover when we get to the wall," River suggested.

"That's a lot of dirt to shovel. And in this sand, tunnels won't hold up well."

"Could rig some kinda shield. Could take the tops of some of them junk cars. Four men to a hood, two hold it up, two dig below. Tunnel under enough of the wall, maybe it'll collapse. Or tunnel just a bit, blow the fucker to paradise."

"A 'turtle,'" Cress said. "The ancient Romans used a formation just like that. Told you, you have a strategic mind. And when we get in, then what?"

"Ask them nicely to surrender." River smiled.

"Or?"

"Or, take the barracks, free the debt slaves, surround the central command, and wait them out."

"And if they don't come out?" Cress asked.

"Wait some more. Or blast a way in."

"And if they radio for reinforcements, meanwhile?"

River shrugged. "Let them call. Been callin', all along. No army come. Maybe Stewards don't got an army to come no more. Half the army down here with us. They got trouble down in Angel City, trouble in the hills. Army do come, got to come over the pass and down that road. This army be ready for them."

In the end, they devised a plan.

Cress felt naked and vulnerable as he strode up to the gate, trying to project a confidence he didn't feel. He was sheltered from above by a metal hood off an old BMW, held aloft on poles. He carried one corner post, and three other fighters carried the others. But he didn't feel sheltered. He'd volunteered for this job because he didn't trust Smokee to keep cool, and because he *did* trust River to be better at commanding the strike force than he would be. The plan was dangerous, reckless even, but he didn't mind that. What he minded was the suspicion that it might turn out to be terminally stupid.

The gate was a grill of metal bars set into the concrete face of the wall. It opened in the center halfway for walkers, full width for cars and trucks. His fist made a hollow, metallic noise as he banged on the bars.

"Open up!" he cried in as loud a voice as he could muster. "Open up and admit the Army of Liberation! We declare this plantation to be a liberated zone. Surrender, and there will be a place for you at our table."

Laser fire answered him. The shield glowed red-hot. He and his *compas* ducked below it. When the firing ceased for a moment, Cress darted forward to pound again on the gate.

"Open up!" he called. "This is your last chance!"

A new burst of laser fire punctuated his cry. He heard the sizzle as it hit the shield, and then a cry of terror and a thud. Something heavy landed on the red-hot shield. Screams split his ears as the shield was knocked aside by the blow. He and the soldiers scrambled to get behind it, as the screams grew louder, and then subsided into a rhythmic, terrible moaning. Cress peered out from behind the hood, which they'd stood up as a barricade in front of them. On the ground lay a young woman, in the rags of a debt slave, her right side terribly burned and blackened, her left leg bent back on itself, one hand clawing at the dirt as if it sought a handhold to let her climb out of this hell.

He looked up. Atop the wall stood a line of debt slaves, their hands bound. A guard or overseer stood behind each one.

"Liberate this!" a guard called out, and pushed an old man off the wall. He fell, screaming in terror, his legs flailing. There was a sickening thud as he hit the ground and lay, moaning, with red foam gurgling out between his lips.

"Now fuck off, dirtlickers!" the guard called down. "Or liberate a pile of bones!"

"*Mierda*, what do we do?" hissed the soldier next to Cress.

"Let's buy time," Cress said. He felt sick. The woman was still moaning, though faintly. The old man had fallen silent, his eyes glazed over.

Holding their shield before them, they crept slowly backwards.

"Faster!" cried the head guard.

"We're retreating!" Cress called back. Step by step, they fell back to the long trench the Army of Liberation had dug into the base of a low rise in the ground. To call it a hill would be an exaggeration. Its gentle slope might collect a bit of rain in a storm but it offered little in the way of advantage for an attacking army.

Just before they reached the trench, they heard a whine and the crack of rifles being fired.

"Dive for cover!" Cress shouted and they scrambled into the ditch, but not fast enough to escape the pursuing fire. Cress heard a gurgle, and a strangled cry, then a spray of blood and something gray showered him. He flung himself behind the low barricade as the body of the *compa* who had just been standing beside him crumpled to the ground. Cress snorted, sneezing out blood and flecks of gray matter which he realized with horror were the man's brains. *Diosa*, he was going to be sick again! But he couldn't give into that now, he had to keep on shouting out commands.

"Under cover! Shields overhead!"

Bullets pinged off their shields, and laser fire turned the metal white-hot. They propped up the hoods with rocks and shielded their hands with the rags of their uniforms. A hail of bullets hit the shields like an evil rain. A few found chinks and landed in living flesh, and the cries of the wounded split the air.

Cress plastered himself into the wall of the ditch. He felt sick with terror, immobilized although truly there was nothing he could do even if he'd been able to muster the will to do it.

"*Madre de Diosa, por favor,* please, please, please!" He wasn't sure if he was praying inside his head or aloud, couldn't hear anything anyway except the whiz and ping of bullets and the screams of the unlucky. He wasn't sure who or what he was begging, all he knew was that he couldn't stand this. In a moment his thudding heart would explode. He fought down a mad urge to leap out of the trench and offer his body to the rain of fire, just to get it over with.

And then the bullets stopped.

The moans and cries continued, but there were no more rifle cracks or zipping laser fire.

He heard a shouted command, and another loud scream followed by a thud. Cautiously, he peeked out from under the cover of his shield, and saw another body fly off the wall.

Then the bound prisoners on the wall and the guards were swaying together, pushing back and forth in a macabre dance.

Suddenly the head guard himself let out a cry, and fell backwards. There was a pause, a moment of stillness when everything seemed to stop and even the moans of the wounded were suspended between breaths.

One by one the guards fell back, dropped their weapons, fell to their knees, and crawled away off the wall.

Then the gate was flung open, and River and his troops beckoned. "All clear!" he called.

It worked, Cress thought.

River and his troops had dug through the night, shoring up their tunnels until they were almost at the fortified walls. Then, while Cress and his crew posed a distraction, they had broken through.

He vaulted out of the trench and ran forward, the army streaming behind him.

They flooded into the compound where River's platoon had the guards corralled and tied. Other fighters climbed up on the wall to release the hostages who still lived and help them down.

This compound was no makeshift collection of old shacks or refurbished farmhouses. The barracks was a giant concrete bunker, windowless and roofed with metal sheeting topped with razor wire. The command center was a low concrete dome, dug into the ground, with a metal gate that sealed off the opening. A ring of gun emplacements circled the dome, but River had already sent his troops to seal them shut and to smash the glass eyes of the cameras that surveyed each direction. Command might be safe inside, but they were also immobilized.

"Good job," Cress told River.

River shrugged. "Plan worked. But this—a central command like this, got to have a bolt hole somewhere. Maybe tunnels lead out."

Cress nodded. "We'll send scouts to look for an exit, catch them when they escape."

"Maybe. Could be anywhere. A mile away. Ten miles. Could link to the next plantation."

Suddenly they heard a shrill screech. A young woman who had been rescued from the wall clutched her neck, her mouth drawn back in pain. Screams rang out around them, and from the concrete barracks there echoed a great cry, magnified rather than dampened by the walls, as if the very rocks themselves were being tortured. As they watched in horror, the woman writhed and arched, her body jerking in convulsions, her very terror and pain lost in the agony of death. Before they could move, she shuddered and fell still, a black, smoking hole burned into the nape of her neck.

"What the Jesus was that?" one of the Cityfolk recruits breathed.

River and Cress streaked toward the barracks. Smokee was already there, her Valkyries battering down the door with a post they had ripped from the surrounding fence.

They entered into a horror chamber. The dorms were packed with new-made corpses, each face twisted into a grimace of pain. Each body was frozen in its last grasp for life, some of them clawing at their burned necks where the chips lay embedded, some grasping another's hand in a futile last embrace.

Cress pushed his way out between them and stumbled to the bushes to vomit.

Even River seemed stunned, standing gazing at the carnage, unspeaking.

Smokee looked at the bodies, and felt the sick horror. But beneath it was something else, almost a sense of triumph, of vindication. As if her own secret pain were now made visible for everyone to see.

Yes, this, this is what it looks like, she thought. It's not something in me. It's here, outside of me.

She knew what she had to do. She called for the prisoners to be brought in, those guards they'd taken from the wall. Their hands were bound, their weapons confiscated, and she lined them up against the wall, where she knew one of the last undamaged surveillance eyes would capture their pasty faces and their fear-filled eyes.

"You know, we're a kind bunch, here in the Army of Liberation," she said conversationally. "We don't like to hurt anyone, don't really like to kill. We capture a farm, we let the liberated tell us who deserves to live and who to die. But that's no option here."

She drew out her pistol. It felt good in her hand, comfortable, familiar. She held it up to the forehead of the first guard, who was young and blond, with blue eyes that rolled back in his head with terror.

"This is for the woman on the wall," she said, and pulled the trigger. He dropped, and she stepped back to avoid the spray of blood. She walked up to the second guard, whose bronze skin now held a gray undertone of fear.

"This is for the old man," she said, and fired.

As he fell, she stood before the third soldier. She looked into dark brown eyes that seemed to retreat and withdraw even as she raised the muzzle and said, "This is for what we see around us."

Should stop her, River thought, but he couldn't seem to move.

The fourth soldier was young, younger than she was. His creamy skin had gone dead-white, his freckles stood out like stoplights. His eyes were closed.

"Open your fucking eyes," Smokee told him. "Jellyballs. You happy to deal out death, take a good look at your own."

He blinked, and stared at her with blue eyes that seemed to hold not just fear but an infinite sorrow.

"This—this one is for Ellis and Mary Carmen Dawson," she said.

She never knew what made her hesitate, just a second, before firing, what made her look one more time into those eyes. Maybe it was the anticipation of pleasure, that rush of power that came when the lights went out and the fear emptied into the dark. But the eyes that looked back at her were suddenly not afraid. Instead they seemed surprised, confused.

"How do you know who my parents were?" he asked.

She stopped, suddenly cold.

"Your parents?" she said, outraged. "Not your fuckin' parents! Mine!"

He looked at her again, intently, as if seeing her for the first time.

Her hand was quivering and suddenly her whole body was trembling. River shook himself out of his trance, and grabbed the gun out of her unresisting hand.

"Enough," he said. "You made your point."

"Smokee?" the soldier whispered tentatively, and then again, with sureness, "Smokee!"

She was tumbling through time, running on the beach with a small boy with a galaxy of freckles across his white, white skin and his blue eyes mirroring the sea.

"Travis?" she said softly, not able to believe it. He nodded.

She didn't know what to do. She wanted to take his hand and run with him, out into the desert and the faraway stars, away from all the death and killing until they were young on a beach again. And she wanted to slap him and demand from him how he had turned into an enemy, a killer.

At the same time, she knew. She knew he hadn't had a choice, any more than she had had a choice. She was suddenly flooded with shame.

What had she done? Who had she become? How had her own little brother come to find her in the moment she had become a killer of brothers?

River pulled out a knife and cut Travis's bonds, and the young man grabbed Smokee in a hug. She clung to him, feeling almost dizzy, as if different versions of herself were reeling around her. There was a young girl, once, who was surprisingly good at algebra and had a crush on Danny McIvern. She had a mother who had helped her sew flower patches on her old, stained bedspread. Her family shared one big room with a stove and sink along one wall, and she'd always kept her own corner very neat, with everything put away in its own place. She'd had a pair of pink sneakers her mother had salvaged from a dumpster and scrubbed clean. Her father worked a night job on top of his day job so that she could stay in school. She had a red sweater that her mother had crocheted out of an old afghan. She'd had a best friend named Mary Lou and an annoying little brother who sang himself to sleep every night with the jingles off the vidscreens and got in fights with the boys down the hall.

And she was a creature in a cage, a rag to mop up the sojuhs' spills, a used-up piece of garbage who couldn't even die.

And she had erased all that, with the gun in her hand. She was a Valkyrie now, a fury, an avenger. She had taken back her life and her power.

But she couldn't get back the girl with the pink sneakers. This freckle-faced killer before her, how could he be both the enemy and the boy on the beach?

———

"So, now what do we do?" Cress asked. He sat with Smokee and River around a small campfire just outside the compound. They were watching the army dig graves on a swelling of higher ground that Cress had identified as unlikely to flood or leach toxins into groundwater.

They gently laid each corpse to rest with prayers and sorrow. There were a number of priests, priestesses, rabbis, imams, ministers, and chaplains accompanying the Army of Liberation, and one by one they administered last rites and said the services for the dead while the sad parade of bodies went on.

The guards who had been spared had been only too happy to pay for their lives with information. The Command Council now knew that less than ten guards held the bunker.

But they would not be easy to pry out. The techies had gone to work on their systems, but had not as yet been able to breach their firewalls.

"They're in there calling for backup," Cress said glumly. "And who knows what else they got planned. For all we know, they could push a button, blow us all sky-high."

"Let them call," River said. "Bigsticks already know the plantations been hit. Sooner or later, got to send their army, and this a good place to meet it. Built like a fuckin' fortress."

"Not with a nest of snakes buried in the middle," Cress objected. "If we can dig them out, then yes, it could be a great forward base. But with them in there, controlling *Diosa* knows what technology, we could all wake up dead in our sleep.

"In fact, I think we should have the bulk of the army camp outside, leave a skeleton crew here to guard the bunker. For all we know, the whole place is mined."

Smokee sat silent. Her head was still whirling. News of her reunion with her brother had spread through the camp, and the liberados were excited. It offered hope to everyone who had lost their families.

She didn't know what to feel. Or rather, she knew what she should feel—happy. But somewhere she seemed to have lost the capacity. All she could muster up was a blank amazement, that drained away some of the hot rage that had sustained her. Inside, she felt cold, tired, and deflated. Her brother was not the little boy she remembered with shining eyes, running down the beach.

In fact, he barely remembered the beach. They'd sat together, over cups of chai the kitchen brewed for them, and tried to talk.

"Do you remember," she'd asked, hesitating, as if she were about to expose the most precious, vulnerable part of herself. "We went to the beach once."

He'd just looked at her with blue-marble eyes, blank as stones.

What he recalled was their mother's pancakes, which she'd forgotten about. Or if she did remember them, it was only that sometimes for weeks at a time that was all they ate, pancakes for breakfast, pancakes with a little chopped, questionable meat or a few grains of cheese for lunch and dinner—her mother called them "crepes" but they were pancakes, made from a lucky twenty-five pound sack of flour her father had acquired at a bargain price.

But Travis remembered that their mother made them into shapes, pouring them with rabbit ears or kitty-cat faces, and that sometimes she sprinkled them with a precious dusting of sugar. He'd smiled at that memory, and just for a moment the ghost of that little boy scampered across the sand.

He didn't know what had happened to their parents. On the terrible day when she'd been hauled off to the pens, he'd been thrown into the army. He didn't want to talk about it, but she knew from others' stories how that went. They beat the new recruits to teach them respect—Travis the little boy who'd never been struck in his life by their gentle parents. They got the boys to beat one another. Sometimes they picked someone small and effeminate and forced the boys to beat him to death. After that it was all drills and training and chips and, when they grew old enough, the rec room.

He'd been so young, only twelve. And she'd just turned fourteen. And now he must be, what? All of fifteen. A young man, but still a boy, really. A boy in a cohort of boys, like the ones she had so cavalierly executed, with barely a fringe of hair on their chins. But that was an uncomfortable thought; she pushed it away.

"We can dig them out, we can smoke them out, or we can wait them out." Cress was saying.

"Can't dig. Them foundations solid concrete, go down deep," River objected.

"Smoke them out?"

River considered. "Blast the door, toss in sleepgas, then go in. Could have masks. Could be a bloody mess."

"Then we wait," Cress said. "Leave troops behind to keep a guard, and move on."

River shook his head. "Don't like it." He turned to Smokee. "What you think?"

"What?" She looked up, her mind still clearly miles away. "Sorry."

"Why don't you take a break?" Cress said. "Go spend some time with your brother."

"I spent time." They had taken an hour of that long afternoon, walking out in the desert. But after their first round of Do you remember?, they found it hard to find something to talk about. She couldn't tell him about her time in the pens. It was still too raw. But seeing him brought it all back, what she had lost, who she had been before.

She was not that blithe big sister. And he was no longer her sweet baby brother. She was a killer, and he'd seen that. But he didn't seem to blame her or hold a grudge.

After all, he was a killer too.

She felt sad, so sad, for that boy and girl on the beach. They felt more lost to her now than ever.

"No help for it," River said at last. "Got to smoke them out. Maybe costly, but got to do it. Can't take the risk of leaving them in there, and this the best place yet to stage a defense when the army comes."

Cress nodded. He looked at Smokee, who was sunk in her own thoughts. "You and me?"

River shook his head. "Beyond that point where you and me do all the ops. Army need a general, and you better at that than ops. No offense. But you not trained for it like a sojuh."

"You're a better general than I am," Cress objected.

"Don't know that swale shit."

"That's not strictly generaling. That's more environmental engineering. I do it because I just can't help myself. But you're the one with the strategic mind."

"I the one trained to go in and take out the enemy, too."

But when River tried to recruit his old unit to back him up, he faced rebellion. They were just finishing up the evening meal at the kitchen tent, lingering over warm cups of herbal chai the cooks brewed. At first the former sojuhs had made faces and spat it out, but over time they'd gotten used to it and some of them even enjoyed it, something hot to warm them when the nights grew chill.

"Bad idea," Ace said. He set down his own cup and pointed a long, thin finger at River's chest. "Commander. Got to start acting like one." He pointed a finger at himself. "Sojuh. These tubos do the op. Time these fighters got to have some fun."

"No fun," River said. "Likely some sojuhs get killed."

Ace shrugged his bony shoulders. "No danger, no fun. Sojuhs born to die. Everybody born to die. But commander die, campaign go to shit. Trust the unit."

River shook his head. "No commanders here. Democracy!"

Ace laughed. "No army a democracy. Somebody got to be the big-stick, give the orders."

"Okay. I order you to do the op with me!" River grinned.

"Commander don't lead ops. Got to stay alive to give the orders."

River recognized that he had lost the argument. And deep inside, he knew Ace was right. He just didn't want to admit it, for that would mean he had indeed become more of a someone than he had ever bargained for. Not only a real person, but an important one.

That felt wrong. Big headed. Not what he was supposed to be.

He was supposed to be the one to face danger, if there was danger to be faced. He was supposed to bear the pain if there was pain to be borne. If there was a nasty, dirty job to do, he was supposed to be the one to do it.

Sojuhs did not become leaders in the Stewards' Army. Not breeds, anyway. Leaders came from the Primes and Subprimes, or once in a great while, a gifted conscript might rise through the ranks. But breeds remained what they were bred for—subordinate, expendable. Tools and weapons.

But he was in a different kind of army now, where he *had* become a leader. Someone the fighters trusted and would follow. Someone responsible to more than just himself.

So he nodded at Ace. "Okay. You do the raid. You plan it." Ace grinned, pushed his long, skinny body back from the table, and ambled off to find the rest of the unit and make his plan.

River waited with Cress as the men blasted a hole in the metal gates that sealed shut the bunker, and lobbed in sleepgas. Masked up, armored in Kevlar vests they'd taken from the dead guards, they went in.

And River waited. He paced the perimeter of the walls, checking in periodically on his radio to listen to the coms. But the concrete walls of the bunker blocked transmission, and all he got was static.

River hated waiting. He would far rather have been with the unit breathing gas and dust and dodging laser fire than to be shut outside, not knowing what was happening.

The tension built and built, until he couldn't stand it. He would suit up and head down into the bunker himself, find out what the fuck was happening.

"Can't take this," he said to Cress, who'd come out to the walls to pace with him. "Gotta go in, find out what's wrong."

Cress grabbed his arm. "No, you don't."

River shook his arm off roughly. "Don't fuckin' paw this fighter!" he warned.

"I'm just saying," Cress took a breath and stayed calm, "you made a decision, you got to stick to it. Ace was right. You can't do every dangerous op. You've got a different role now."

"Don't wanna role," River said and kicked a stone against the wall and strode off into the empty wastes of farmland, away from the bunker.

He hadn't realized he was searching for Kit, but he doubled back into camp and found her in the kitchen, peeling potatoes for dinner. He loomed over her, stumbling around the kitchen tent, knocking over a tray of peppers. He couldn't say what he wanted to say, which was, drop those, come talk to me, hold me, I need you. Not even to himself. All he could do was stomp, and swear, and sigh heavily until she finally looked up.

"Fighter got the crabs?" she asked. "All itchy?"

"This fighter like to fight," he said. "Not wait."

"Waiting better than fighting," she said. "Fighting get a sojuh killed, sooner or later."

"Would you care?" he asked hopefully. "Would you care if this fighter get killed?"

She shrugged. "Why not?"

"Not 'why not?' Just fuckin' say 'yes' or 'no'!" His voice rose.

"Army need its commander alive," she said.

"But what about you?"

He was talking loudly, almost shouting. All the other cooks were staring at them, some with avid interest, some glaring with annoyance. Kit put down her pan of potatoes and stood up.

"Take a walk," she said.

They walked out together into the deserted fields, flat and white and barren. Above them the cloudless sky seemed to press down on their heads.

"Still waiting for an answer," River grumbled.

"What tubo want?" She observed him closely. He was electric with tension, his skin shiny with sweat, his breathing rapid. She knew what that meant. A fighter has needs, she'd been told all her life. Would it really kill her to fulfill them? She didn't desire him, she couldn't imagine really desiring anyone pawing and huffing at her, but he wouldn't be the worst she'd endured, and she would like to do something to make him happy, something to repay his efforts at courting and kindness. And after all, that must be what he wanted from her, in the end. Why not give it to him?

"Fighter jumpy as tick," she said. "Need the rec room, maybe."

"No more rec room."

"There's the bower," she said. That was what they called it here. A different name—and the key difference, really, was that no one was forced to go. It was a big tent, set aside, and she had never been in it. But she would go with him if that would calm him down.

"Do you want to go with me?" he asked hopefully.

"Won't hurt me."

"Don't fucking say that! Just tell me, do you want to go with me?"

"This cook say she will."

"Say 'I,' damn you! Just fuckin' say 'I'!"

"I."

"I, what?"

"I. I will."

"But do you want to?"

"Want to, want to—what that matter? I say I go, I go." She didn't understand him. What was wrong with him? She'd offered what he wanted, what he had to want. What more could there be?

River glowered at her, frustrated. In this mood, he could throw her down and take her right there on the desert floor, needles in her backside, just out of frustration. Why couldn't she simply answer a fucking question, say Yes, I like you, or No, I don't. Maybe because she didn't, really. She was just putting up with him, as she had been bred to put up with men, or using him to get her baby back, or because he was the commander and the other girls looked up to her. Fucking bitch!

He had been so careful with her, treating her as delicate as a bomb squad disarming a mine, not pushing her or pressing her, wanting her to come to him, like the women in the Temple of Love, to see him and know him and confirm him with her desire. But she didn't see him. She only saw another sojuh, another user. Well, fuck her! He would use her.

He grabbed her and thrust his hands down her loose trousers, gripping her ass, thrusting his pelvis into hers. She stood, passively, not resisting but not responding, and that made him even more angry. No, this wasn't what he wanted, even though he could feel his cock begin to swell with the sense of power. He felt himself sliding back, sliding down into who he used to be. And he felt a sudden sense of panic. If he let himself go there, he might never come back to the slow and difficult climb to personhood. She was pulling him down, with her offer, with her stoic placidity.

He shoved her away from him. Too roughly, so that she fell hard, right into the side of one of the spiny cactuses. She let out a small cry, then stifled it as the pen-girls did when they felt pain.

"Kit," he said weakly. "Kit—I'm sorry!"

But she turned away from him, no longer looking at him for help. He offered his hand, but she ignored him. He didn't know what to do. Should he pick her up bodily, and violate her more? Or let her sit there in her suffering? Shit, what had he done?

Just then Cress came running up. "They're back," he called, then saw Kit. "*Diosa*, what happened?"

"She fell," River said. He felt simply wretched. He turned away, leaving Cress to help Kit up. "Gonna go get a medic." He walked off, then broke into a run, as if he could run away from the scene, from her pain, from himself.

The raid had succeeded, but at a cost. The guards inside had indeed been prepared for gas, and the sojuhs had had to battle their way in. The guards were all dead, and three of River's old unit joined them. Ace had a deep laser burn in his right thigh, the flesh blackened and shriveled down to the bone, and a scorch across his face and his left eye. The medics had him sedated and iced down, preparing to transport him back up north to the City for treatment.

River came and stood by him, looking down at the unconscious form. Had it been fun? He wondered. Ace was as close as River had to a friend, he thought, and now he was going, and he had messed up his thing with Kit beyond repair, and he was alone. Or maybe he had always been alone, since that moment they ripped him from his mother's arms. Maybe he always would be alone, stuck somewhere between breed and person, almost real but always at risk of sliding back, able to choose sometimes and other times unable to do anything but react.

Or maybe this was what being a person meant. The loneliness.

Chapter Thirty-Eight

For an interlude, I would be a bee, plunging into the sweet-scented velvet heart of a flower. Or a raven, wheeling and diving, turning tricks midair, flying upside down. Or an albatross, soaring on the great air-currents of the far oceans, sleeping with a head tucked beneath a wing. So peaceful, so restful, though I suppose I would have my storms, my wild gusts of wind.

I would be something light, with feathers, a songbird on the great migration routes over the continent.

Or maybe just a simple meat bird. A Cornish Cross, like we used to raise from time to time. Born to eat. Staggering out of the nighttime chickpile to gorge all day, sleep again. Soon growing too heavy to do much else.

Yes, that would be a vacation after my last life. No dieting. No deprivation. A few short weeks of it, then whop! Off with her head, and on to the next adventure.

But I gave my allegiance to a Goddess for whom death leads to rebirth, decay to regeneration. Not an end, but a cycle.

And so I find that even in death I have responsibilities.

It's the task of the ancestors to watch, to warn.

B AD AS THE SITUATION HAD BEEN WHEN THE PROPHET-HEADS HELD services during assembly time, it got worse when they switched their meeting dates and began attending assemblies. A little knot of them seemed to obstruct any decision from going forward. They objected, they blocked, they argued endlessly. They picked on minor points and made them into major issues, and seemed bent primarily on preventing anything from being decided or moving ahead. Meetings which were already challenging became exercises in frustration.

"We were discussing the Declaration of the Four Sacred Things," Emily said. She was facilitating the big general assembly in the main plaza. "Bird and Madrone gave us its history, how it brought people together after the Uprising around things they could all agree upon. And the suggestion has been made that we might want to adopt it. I'm taking discussion now. Questions and concerns. Prophet Jed, I see your hand. You don't have to smack your neighbor in the face with it. But first I'm calling on people who haven't spoken often."

Prophet Jed stood, folded his arms, and glowered, while a thin, balding man stood and spoke.

"With all due respect, I'm a scientist. Where's the evidence that the earth is a living being, let alone a conscious one?"

Madrone looked over at Emily, who nodded at her. She rose.

"I'm a scientist, too. I know the folks who came up with the Declaration drew on their own mysticism and a lot of indigenous wisdom. But scientific rationalism is its own belief system. And there are many things it doesn't account for. My own forms of healing incorporate western medicine, but something more, something that works with energies and awareness. You don't have to deny the rational. You don't have to believe in the Declaration. But if you could just suspend disbelief and try it out, see what we do with it."

The slim man nodded thoughtfully, and sat down. Far in the back, a buxom woman with jet-black hair and cinnamon skin stood. Her name, Bird remembered, was Faith Prophet, and she was one of Jed's followers, possibly part of his harem.

"Where is God?" she asked in an accusing voice. "Where is there room for God in your Declaration?"

That was Janus's cue. She leaped up and began to declaim. "God, Goddess, God is odd and Goddess is oddest. God is everywhere, every care, every bear, a bear of very little brain, bare your skin and we're all the same ..."

"Thank you, Janus!" Emily cried loudly. "Now sit down and give someone else a turn to speak. Remember what we talked about?"

Janus had been sternly warned by Miss Ruby that she would be thrown out of Council if she spoke out of turn. She scrunched up her lips, as if to trap words inside, but she sat down.

Emily nodded to Bird, who stood up and spoke. "God is wherever you want to put him. If you want to believe in a Creator who made the earth and the air and the waters, that's up to you. We just don't want to legislate what people *have* to believe. For myself, I think that if God went to the trouble to create the world, he'd want us to honor the forces that sustain our lives."

Prophet Jed had had enough. "Abomination!" he cried.

"You're out of order," Emily objected.

"Let him speak! Let him speak!" yelled his supporters.

"Let him wait his turn like everybody else!" cried Miss Ruby.

"Wait your own turn! You're out of order!"

"Where's Jesus in your Declaration?"

As the argument went on, Madrone noticed a dark presence standing silent at the edge of the gathering. Rafael, one of the Angels, surveyed the crowd, his stance relaxed but alert, like a cat ready to spring. Every curve of his sculpted muscles was accented by his tight-fitting dark jeans and black T-shirt. His perfect features were impassive, his blond hair gleamed like pale sun seen through a frosty window.

He attracted a lot of covert glances—admiring ones from the teenagers, wary and frightened looks from their elders who hustled them away. The crowd parted around him like filaments of water avoiding a boulder. He stood in his own clear space amidst the throng.

When he spied Madrone, he nodded slightly and beckoned. She approached him with caution, not sure exactly how to greet him. Rafael was one of the Angels who had saved her when the Stewards raided Katy's version of a refuge. And they had deserted her when she most needed help, leaving her alone with an army of cops and guards thundering after her. Did she thank them, or condemn them?

But Rafe gave her no opening to do either, no greeting, no "Hey, Madrone, glad to see you after all this time!" Instead, he simply gestured with his perfect jaw and barked out three short words.

"Beth says come."

She quickly said a whispered goodbye to Bird, left him hurried instructions for the boys, and followed Rafe out the back tunnel of the entrance and onto a zigzag path through the shadowed streets to a black van that waited in an alley. A silent Angel drove them. She and Rafe squatted on the wheel casings as the van made its way through side streets and down alleyways to avoid the checkpoints on the main thoroughfares. Rafe was silent, and Madrone didn't try to engage him in conversation.

She was grateful for the transport. It was a long walk to Beth's, or a dangerous bike ride. But she was relieved when the journey was over and the van stopped on a corner of a street a few blocks away from Beth's home. She could understand why the Angels were who they were, but they still made her deeply uneasy.

The woman was hunched on Beth's spare bed, doubled over in fetal position, her skin pale and clammy as an oyster, but burning hot. Her silver blond hair was plastered to her neck in limp strands, and she was moaning in pain, beyond communication or comfort.

"Can we roll her over?" Madrone asked. She and Beth stood together at the woman's bedside. Beth nodded and gently unclenched the woman's hands from her knees. Together they turned her onto her back.

She was a girl, really, Madrone thought. She looked hardly older than fourteen, which meant she was probably younger still, for the silver hair, the perfect features and porcelain-white skin proclaimed her to be a Pet, bred and raised for pleasure and pain, and they were mostly used up and done by the time they hit their teens. Unless, of course, they were rescued first and taken to join the Angels. As they'd rescued this poor child, bringing her to Beth for help when her pains had started.

"It's going to be all right, sweetheart," Beth murmured. "Don't be afraid. The healer is here, and she'll make you better."

Madrone hoped fervently that that was true. She laid a hand on the girl's belly, felt for her life force through a stained, peach-colored chiffon shift.

"She's had some bleeding, but not too much," Beth said hopefully. "But this terrible cramping ... "

Madrone nodded and closed her eyes, feeling with her inner senses. Brilliant colors, crimson and gold, but weaving through them an ominous stain of gray-green. A tiny globe of light, trapped in a narrow tube, and battering its way against a grayish mass.

"I'm suspecting an ectopic pregnancy," Beth was saying.

Madrone pulled her awareness into the room, and drew Beth aside into the kitchen, out of the girl's hearing.

"Ectopic," she agreed. "But she's a mass of infection and venereal disease. Gonorrhea, maybe? Chlamydia? I don't know, we rarely ever see them in the North. I'm not so familiar with their signatures."

Beth sighed. "Probably all of the above. Can you do anything for her?"

"Here? Or in a sterile, well-equipped operating room?"

Beth just shrugged. They both knew that a hospital was not an option for an illegal Angel.

Madrone considered the options. An ectopic pregnancy was one where the fertilized egg failed to move down the tube. The growing fetus had instead implanted in the tube itself, where it was trapped. Even in the North, with all its resources, it was a difficult situation to handle. They would operate, remove the fetus, and try to save the ovary and the tube. But here, in unsterile conditions, and given the level of infection she sensed the girl already carried, that would be a death sentence.

Better, maybe, to spare her that and just let her die, trying to ease her pain. But she resisted the notion. It went against the grain, to give up so easily.

Back in the room, the girl had again curled into a ball, wrapped around her core of agony. Madrone laid a gentle hand on her back, while Beth crooned to her. She tuned her awareness to *see* with her healer's vision.

That little ball of light was emitting a sharp, high whine, a squeal of fear and frustration. Not yet human, not yet conscious, just life force itself in desperate resistance to death.

Well, I can help the baby-spark pass, she thought. She herself was light, a sphere of turning colors, and she wrapped herself around the spark, cradling it like a mother rocking a baby. Then she began to move toward the greater light.

"Mama, Johanna, Great Mother, help me," she murmured. "Receive this vessel for a soul and help it to make the passage."

There were two great pillars, one black, one white, and beyond them was a source of radiance, bright and hot as a fire on a cold night. It was too bright for her, she couldn't look at it, but she felt warm hands holding her, smelled the scent of women's bodies, felt their comfort and warmth. Closer and closer she moved toward the gate, until she stood on its threshold, and opened her embrace. The spark flew from her grasp and dissolved in the greater light.

But the damage was done. The tube was shredded, and within it the bean of forming flesh was already starting to decay. Gray, buglike creatures crawled over it in a feeding frenzy.

Reluctantly, Madrone pulled her consciousness out. She opened her eyes and shook her head.

"We can try antibiotics, if you have some broad-spectrum," she said. "I don't like to use them, but in some cases, it's the best option. Maybe if we can knock back the infection her body will reabsorb the fetus. Not likely, but there's a chance. Meanwhile, let's give her what you've got for pain."

Madrone backed up the antibiotics with honey laced with a drop of her own bee brew. Beth gave the girl a sedative, and she relaxed and slept.

They retired to Beth's small kitchen in the next room, and Beth put the kettle on for tea.

"I'm sorry," Madrone said.

"You did all you could."

"Just another poor rag whose life was hell anyway," Madrone said bitterly. "Most people would say it was no great loss. And I worry about myself. I worry that it's becoming too easy for me to feel that way."

"It's that or go nuts," Beth said. "No one can carry all the pain."

"I'm getting jaded. I've heard too many horror stories. I don't even feel the outrage, just a sort of deadness."

"That's called survival," Beth assured her. "You can't go around in a state of perpetual rage."

"And when it does come to the surface, I have trouble keeping it under control," Madrone admitted. "Bird says that ever since I went through the bee initiation, I've developed a vicious temper."

"Possibly." Beth filled the teapot from the boiling kettle. The scent of mint filled the room. "Of course, there might be few other factors at work. Like the invasion, and the war, and the general level of cussedness we deal with every day."

"There is that," Madrone admitted. "Life hasn't exactly been calm and peaceful. Just when it was beginning to settle back down in the North, we came here."

"Do you miss it?"

"I think I miss this, most of all," Madrone smiled at her. "Girlfriends. Someone to talk to who understands, and doesn't try to fix it."

"Not every patient can be saved," Beth said. "Not every injustice can be remedied. You learn that early on, and accept it, or you'll lose your mind."

"There's always people around me, always wanting something, clamoring for my attention," Madrone said, feeling the relief of letting it all spill out. "And I'm in and out of the bee-mind and the astral half the time, and I'm always getting jerked back to tell someone the proper dosage of lomatium or how to wrap an ankle bandage. But I shouldn't be complaining. I'm grateful for my healing powers. Really!"

"I prescribe a regular dose of complaining!" Beth smiled. "It's one pleasure they can't ration. Don't you have friends who would listen to you, among the refugistas?"

"I just pissed off my best friends," Madrone said. "The temper thing again."

Beth set a cup of mint tea down before her. "Aren't you a healer? Heal that!"

Madrone sighed and took a long sip of the hot, pungent brew. "We could be friends, don't you think?" she asked Beth.

"I think we are friends."

"You know what I mean—the kind of friends who go out for walks and talk over their difficult cases and their love lives. I long for that! I long for normality. I'd be happy to be the bold revolutionary hera for the rest of my life if I could just have a break. A few weeks of tea and chats and comfort, in a different world."

Beth patted her hand. "Even here, people carve out little spaces of the normal for themselves. In a sense, that's what we live for, what we cling to when everything else is taken away. So let me refill your cup, and you can tell me all about your love life. I wish I could reciprocate, but it's been a long, long, dry spell."

Madrone smiled. "That would be sweet. But it would probably be more relevant to tell you about the Refuge, and the help we need. We're growing day by day, and the medical needs are just beyond the scope of what I can handle. We've got a few other nurses, but not nearly enough. And no other doctors, as yet."

Beth nodded. "Doctors are too valuable, still, to the system—they tend to make sure they don't go completely under. So, you want me to recruit for you?"

"Surely you must run across some medics who need a refuge. I'll tell you how to find us—and not in poetry."

"What if I came myself?"

"You could head up the healing center," Madrone said eagerly. "You could be a doctor again."

"My skills are rusty."

"Probably not that rusty. I know what you do. Anyway, we aren't doing brain surgery, mostly first aid, nutritional support, care for wounds, that kind of thing."

"I'm useful here. But maybe not for much longer. I think the house is being watched. You weren't followed, were you?" Beth asked anxiously. "After the Angels dropped you off?"

Madrone shook her head. "For an innocent young healer girl, I've gotten very good at things like making sure I'm not followed."

"It's probably best if you don't come often," Beth said. "Much as I would enjoy those walks and cups of tea.

Madrone nodded.

"Beth, I can't promise you that the Refuge will be safe forever. I can't even promise you that we'll win down here. But if you think you need refuge, don't wait too long to come. If you wait until the last minute, when the soldiers are at the door, it may be too late."

———

The girl died before they finished a second pot. They checked on her every quarter of an hour, and found her breathing growing more faint, her skin more flushed and hot. But she slept, and was no longer suffering. Beth and Madrone each held her hand, and sang to her as she slipped away. When Madrone closed her eyes, she again saw the gates. And the girl was a small girl-child, wide-eyed, dressed in white, young and happy as she'd never gotten to be in life.

"Don't be afraid," Madrone murmured. "You are going to be rocked in the arms of the Mother. Let go, and give yourself to love."

The girl-child let go of their hands and ran forward into the radiance. The girl on the bed gave a last, harsh gasp, the death rattle, and she was gone.

"May the wind carry her spirit gently . . . " Madrone began the prayer for the dead.

"We eased her passage," Beth said. "If the Angels hadn't brought her here, she would have died discarded on the cold streets, in terrible pain, frightened and alone."

"Is that worth risking your life for?"

"Oh, yes."

———

Madrone left with Oldjohn, one of the hillboys, just before dawn. He'd turned up in the night, asking for her to come back to the camp with him and look at some critical cases.

Oldjohn was so named because of his bald head and grizzled beard, although he was not yet forty. But the hillboys' lives took a heavy toll. Like some Paleolithic tribe, their lifespans were short and anyone over thirty was an old man. Nonetheless, Oldjohn was fit and strong and he scaled steep hillsides without even breathing hard, while Madrone panted behind.

She sat around the fire late that night, sipping a meager ration of water and munching on a cupful of acorn stew. I'm growing soft, she thought, used to our abundance of water in the Refuge, the fresh greens, the occasional bite of fish from the aquaponics system they'd set up in one of the courtyards. Now she felt the old familiar twinges of hunger, the harsh dryness in the back of her throat that sips of water could not ease.

She was tired. After the long day climbing the back trails she'd spent hours crouched over the pallets of a new rash of flu victims, in and out of bee-mind, sensing what plagued them and brewing up antidotes. Now what she wanted, more than anything, was a long soak in the Refuge's hot pool.

And I'll get that, she thought, even if not tonight. Unlike these staunch fellows who have probably never had a long, hot bath in their lives.

Hijohn sat across from her, chewing every bite of his stew a dozen times, making it last. How does he do it, she wondered, year after year? Of course, this was normal to him, he'd been only a child when his parents fled the Stewards' takeover and took to the hills. He'd been raised as a hillboy.

She tried to imagine him visiting the North, what those green streets would look like to him with their flowing streams and their murals and the fruit hanging heavy to hand. His face was deeply lined, his skin sunbrowned and leathery, as if the tannins in the acorns were working their way outwards. His muscles were stringy and tight, his eyes made periodic sweeps of the periphery as if he were always alert for an attack. She tried to picture him in a hot pool, eyes closed, relaxing, a soft hand rubbing lotion into his weathered skin. Impossible to visualize.

"Army's making progress," he was saying. "We get regular reports. Made their way down through most of the Central Valley."

Madrone nodded. "That's good news."

"Stewards're starting to feel the pinch. 'Course it'll be next year when the shortages hit. Got warehouses full of stockpiled chips and supplies. Not too worried, yet. And you folks?"

"We're doing well. Getting the Refuge built and organized. You should come visit, Hijohn. It's beautiful! We could get you well and truly hydrated, for once."

"Maybe," Hijohn said. "Or maybe we've got work to do. Like I said, Stewards got stockpiles, won't feel the pinch till next year. But if those stockpiles go away ... "

"And now's the time," Madrone said thoughtfully. "While they still haven't rebuilt the army."

"You've had a little time to build your Refuge," Hijohn said. "Stewards're mostly focused on the army, and us. But they've stepped up the drones, lately. Seem to be flying a surveillance grid all over Angel City. Starting with the rich 'hoods, of course, and they're always over these hills anyway. Gives us a chance to shoot them down, make a dent in their inventory. But sooner or later, they'll get around to the Death Zone. Be prepared."

His words fed her own sense of uneasiness. Inside the Refuge, the demands of the day-to-day work and planning and building were almost overwhelming, and distracted her from any questions about what its ultimate destiny would be, or how they could defend it if it were attacked. But from here, it seemed like a beautiful bubble, iridescent, shiny, easy to puncture.

They talked into the night, and then Hijohn told her that a small team of hillboys could escort her back down to the flatlands on the following day. But she shook her head. Now that she was here, with the scent of wild sage on the air, she knew that she had yet another mission.

She warily approached the Melissas' hive at dawn the next morning. The bee priestesses did not encourage drop-ins. When she had entered or left the hive in the past, she had never been in a state of consciousness to register landmarks or remember directions. But with the morning sun warming the blooms of the wild lilac and releasing their scent, she found that she had no trouble identifying where the hive lay. She could smell a pathway to it, and everywhere in the hills she could hear its underlying song, a sweet murmur of abundance and increase and honey.

The bees escorted her. They came to her as to a long-missed friend, circled her and flew off in the hive's direction, as if urging her to follow. She traced a route on deer trails and fox tracks, snaking through thick stands of coyote bush and ceanothus, far into a deep cleft in the hills where a trickle of stream flowed out of a hidden canyon.

Far back she went, balancing on stones and making her way upstream between steep cliffs of sheer rock that loomed above her. At last they opened out into a wide meadow dotted with horsetail and woodwardia ferns that marked springs. Steep slopes rose up behind, covered with black sage and coyote bush. A cluster of bee-hive-shaped domes nestled at their feet. Some stood singly, others huddled together in threes and sixes. All were plastered with a reddish earth, and encrusted with hundreds of smaller clay skeps molded into the earthen walls. Swarm after swarm of golden bees went busily in and out, creating a hum that rang through the glen like the overtones of a Tibetan bell.

In the center stood a particularly large and imposing dome, with hexagonal patterns decorating its portal and a family of hives clinging to its sides. As Madrone drew near, the door opened and the Melissa stepped out.

She was not an old woman, but her dark eyes were shadowed and her hair was stark white, hanging down to her waist in long, shining strands. She wore a simple white sheath. As she stepped forward, swarms of bees descended on her until they formed a living cloak of whirling bodies and buzzing song.

The Melissa gazed at Madrone. She said nothing, but Madrone could hear her question inside her mind.

"I need help, Sister," Madrone said in a low voice, trying to match the pitch of the bees. "I know you told me that you couldn't help me, but I need your wisdom, if not your advice. I'm getting lost in the bee-mind. I'm losing my ability to shift, losing perspective. Losing control."

Slowly, almost imperceptibly, the Melissa shook her head. "That is not what we teach," she said. Madrone jumped, she was so startled to hear the Melissa's physical voice, resonant, deep, humming in the priestess's throat. "We give ourselves to the hive, and do not reserve a part of ourselves for a half-life in the human world. If that is your choice, we cannot advise you, for our advice you have already discarded. But you may ask the sisters directly, yourself."

Behind the hive was a small hollow in the south face of the hillside, lined with wild lilac, coyote bush, toyon, and madrone. It was carpeted with wildflowers where the bees were hard at work, and fragrant with blossoms. Spring started early in the Southlands, and now, in early February, it was well underway.

"We call this the Dreaming Glade," the Melissa said. "Lie here, take your questions to the bees, and perhaps you will find an answer."

Madrone settled herself on the ground in a patch of dry grass that carpeted the feet of a great boulder. She leaned back and felt it radiate a gentle warmth. The air was fragrant with the scent of early wildflowers and plum blossom. The bees sang of plenty.

She nestled against the rock, the sun warm on her face as she closed her eyes and opened her bee senses.

What am I doing? she asked the bees. Am I following my true purpose, down here? How do I balance your sweet song with the cold reality of the human world?

Sweet honey and singing gold. The scent, the perfume, entered into her. The world shifted, as her mind merged with the hive mind.

Filaments of scent flowed through the air like currents of a rainbow stream, pungent coyote bush and musky oak. Scents were trails. Each was a journey, an epic. In this world of color and fragrance and touch, she tracked them, discovering the sources of sweetness, diving head first into glowing rose-red and golden pollen.

But below lay something else, not gold, but gray. Not sweet perfume, but putrid, unnatural. Its trail led into cold toxic places that scorched her wings, matted the delicate hairs on her abdomen, coated her fine probing antennae with a nasty gel.

She kept on. What was the heart of this thing, how had such wrongness come to be? On and on she went, until the stream became a sluggish river, stinking and gray-green as pus. She wanted to retch.

Why? Why did the Goddess allow this? Souls were drowning, dissolving, strands of crimson in the pallid mud, turning the stream blood-red. She was being carried down to the underworld, like Inanna on a visit to the realm of death.

Two great pillars of stone loomed above her, one on each side of the river, one deepest black, the other purest white. The Gateway. She passed between.

The river dissolved, like a window breaking into shards of glass, and each shard splintering into smaller fragments that shattered again and again, glinting with flashes of purest color. Until there was nothing left but light and the play of light: red, purple, green.

That's all we are, she realized. Splinters of radiance. Pulsing light, and behind, velvet dark. Black like a panther's coat, black like moonless sky between the stars. Light in the heart of darkness, darkness in the heart of light.

Shards of light vibrated like strings, threads of the great web thrumming. Then suddenly there was a different hum, a whining buzz that split the glowing web like a sharp knife splitting flesh. A silver-haired young girl in a white shift was running, not in joy now but terror. A copper-skinned child with a cloud of dark hair crouched beside a woman's body.

"*Despierte*, Mama! Wake up!" Madrone knelt over her mother's body. But her mother would not wake up. No, it was she, Madrone, who needed to wake up, to remember to breathe, to gulp in air.

She had not been able to save her mother, murdered by death squads when she was just a tiny child in Guadalupe. But that memory—that visceral child's experience of the heart ripped out of the world—she would never stop trying to somehow make that right. It was the core of who she was. It would never allow her to rest in the bee-mind, or the perfection beyond suffering. It would keep her continually striving to ease suffering, soothe pain.

So help me in that purpose, she said to the bees, to her mother, to the great inchoate forces of spirit around her. I committed to it at my mother's side when I was too young for it to be conscious. But I commit to it now. With consciousness, and recognition that all healing has its limits. So help me, please, bees, ancestors, spirits. What is it I need to see?

And suddenly not just bee-mind but other minds were open to her as well—the busy ants with their smooth-lacquered bodies, the web-weaving spiders, the cawing ravens and screeching jays. The trees were speaking as they waved their branches above her, the flowers calling out enticements, the rock she lay nestled against singing a slow, crystalline chant.

She understood then that bee-mind was just a beginning. What she had learned from the bees could open the doorway to unimagined alliances with fur and feather, scale and chitin, with stones and stars.

And who will I be then? Who will we all be, when science and magic merge?

Same pig-headed stubborn child you've always been, I imagine.

The voice sounded a lot like her grandmother, Johanna.

Where are you, Grandma? Are you still a note in the harmony, or am I making this all up?

Just for a moment, she could hear it, the single song of all that is, the weaving harmonies and melodies and counterpoint, the dancing rhythms. All speaking, all singing, each with their own voice, and she was part of it too, the harmonics of each in-breath, the rhythm of her pulse.

But then there came again the high whine.

You can go all cosmic, child. But if you want the harmony, you've got to create harmony.

Yes, that was her grandmother.

Then she heard another voice, husky and full-throated as an ewe's chuckle, one she had missed so much since Maya's death.

The only way out is through.

What did she mean? Madrone heard the dissonant chord echo around her. She felt a premonition of danger that shocked her back into her body.

The whine grew louder, a furious hum.

Madrone opened her eyes. She was human again, finite and fragile, lying in a warm meadow under the sun.

And above the skeps and the swarms, dark gray against the blue, a V of drones flew overhead, on their bellies the digital orbs that captured everything below.

Chapter Thirty-Nine

ISIS PULLED SARA ASIDE AFTER YET ANOTHER ENDLESS MEETING IN THE canteen of the *Harvey Milk.*

"Gotta talk," she'd said and Sara had followed her out to a private spot by the rail with such a hopeful look in her eye that Isis had to turn away from her.

"What is it?" Sara asked, laying a soft hand on Isis's arm.

Isis felt the touch through the sleeve of her sweater, a warmth that rode her veins back to her heart and then down to her belly and thighs and all that lay between.

She moved her arm away.

"What you thinking about Livingston?" she asked sharply.

Sara, disappointed, turned her face to the sea. "Livingston is not who I think about."

Isis ignored the bait. Stay focused, she told herself.

"Still trust him?"

"I never trusted him. He looks out for number one. But he seems to have genuinely decided that the City's victory would be best for number one."

"Why this delay?" Isis asked. "How long we gonna watch and wait?"

"What are you saying? You think it's his plan to keep us immobilized?"

"Suppose it is. Keep us stuck. Out of action."

"Neutralized, at very little cost to the Stewards," Sara said thoughtfully. "Could be his strategy. Or vulnerable. It could be a trap."

"So what do we do?"

Sara grabbed Isis's hand and drew the pirate around to face her.

"Break the stalemate," she breathed, so close Isis could feel the warm, moist touch of her breath. "Change the situation. Push for action!" Her lips were so close, her eyes wide and hopeful as a puppy's.

"See what happens if we do," Isis said abruptly and fled, striding off down the deck.

But to their surprise, when they brought it up at the next day's meeting, Livingston had simply favored them both with that wide, charming smile.

"Just what I was thinking myself," he said. "High time! We've got the shipping lanes mapped, got a sense of what's coming in where. There's a plastics delivery due from the Gyre three days from now. Be coming in to unload, then pick up a load of debt slaves to take back. What do you say we have some fun with it?"

In the pearly predawn light, Isis watched as the big ship steamed into view. This time the warship lay squarely across its path, the other smaller boats of the Califian Navy ranged in a crescent that could close like the jaws of a trap.

Isis had left Rosa in command of the *Day of Victory*—with strict instructions to stay far from danger, and to run back north should anything go wrong. Now the bigger boats closed in on the ship from the Gyre.

She herself stood on the bridge of the warship, scanning the horizon. A white dot, a gleam of something catching the sunlight, a flash. Slowly it grew until she could see a toy ship, a miniature that grew and grew as it approached. The graceful sweep of the foresails, the high, proud mainsails all gleaming in the sunlight as if they were spun of glass, transforming sunlight into energy even as they caught the wind—the sight made Isis catch her breath. Beautiful! She hoped they wouldn't have to sink it.

She considered where it had come from: the Gyre—an area the size of a continent at the center of the spiral where the global currents swirled. For a hundred years or more, it had been collecting debris, the trove of plastic bottles and fishing floats and radioactive wreckage of the nuclear disasters of long ago. Isis had heard all kinds of rumors about it—of teeming cities built on floating islands vast enough to withstand storms, of huge plastic mining factories jerry-rigged from old ships where unfortunate slaves toiled to their death, of outlaw organ farms and breeder boats conducting experiments even the Stewards would find horrifying.

Maybe, after this war was over, she and Sara would get back together and sail on out there, see it for themselves. Yes, she would like that, out in the wild, open ocean with Sara at her side....

Stop it! The ship was approaching. Closer now, it looked less like a vision of a proud clipper and more like something cobbled together out of a collision between a junkyard and a circus tent. It had the long body of an old container cargo ship, patched and rusted under those shining sails. Its prow sported a leering mermaid wearing giant plastic goggles, with huge balloon-shaped plastic breasts and a skirt of plastic rings. It flew a gigantic black flag, with what looked like the pirate's emblem of a skull and crossbones. But as it drew closer, they saw the bones were an X of plastic bottles.

"The fabled flag of the Gyre," Livingston said. "Shall we hail them?"

"Do the honors," Isis handed him the coms mic, as Sara slipped back to the far side of the boat to ready her divers, should they be needed.

"Ship ahoy!" Livingston called out. "I hail from the Navy of Califia. We have placed the Southlands under embargo. Identify yourselves and state your business."

"Identify your ass!" came the reply over a screechy bullhorn.

"Now, now, sailor, no need to be rude!" Livingston replied cheerfully. His handsome face held that little secret smile that so annoyed Isis. Clearly the man was enjoying himself.

She was watching him closely, feeling a deep sense of uneasiness. Livingston was doing a good job, and he had the confidence and innate authority to treat with the Gyros, who were far more likely to respect a white man in a uniform than an ebony heeshee pirate like herself. She had no quarrel with him negotiating, as long as the rest of them were there to watch, Miguel and Bronwyn and herself.

That smile ... like a cat with a mouse under its paw.

But were the Gyros the mouse, or was it the Navy of Califia?

"What you want?" the Gyro Captain barked. "My men eager to make port."

"The port is closed. The Stewards are under siege. We will no longer allow them to pay for goods with blood money!" Livingston proclaimed.

"No? We have a contract!"

"We'll make you a better offer."

"What you have that we might want?"

"Wood."

"Don't need wood! We mine plastic!"

"Technology. We have advanced systems the Stewards have never heard of."

Loud laughter came back at them.

"Technology! You grubbers decades behind us! More likely we have what you want!"

"What do the Stewards pay you?" Livingston asked, unperturbed.

"Provide us with guests. Guest workers, for the mines. And lucky girls and boys for entertainment."

"That trade is over, I'm afraid," Livingston said firmly. "But we are willing to compensate you for your lost trade and profits."

"With what?"

"Send your representatives to come aboard and negotiate, and we will guarantee their safety."

"How?"

Livingston nodded toward the gunners, and they sent a shell flying over the head of the ship that burst in the water beyond.

"With that. We can blow your ship out of the water if we want to. But we don't. We'd rather negotiate and settle this peacefully. So trust us, and we will work out a deal."

The parley took place in the conference room of the warship. The Gyro Captain looked like someone who'd decided to dress the part of a pirate, with high sea-boots over baggy sweat pants, a gray sweatshirt topped by a canvas vest decorated with many pockets, and black, greasy hair that hung down to his shoulders. He had a long face, an oily beard covering sunken cheeks, and steely blue eyes under sallow skin. His first mate was beardless, his dark head shaved, a row of rings from ancient pop-top cans through his ear-lobe, and he wore a scarlet shirt over Hawaiian print shorts.

"So the guest-worker trade, as you call it, is done," Livingston stated calmly. "No longer will we allow the Stewards to pay for plastic with lives, or carry out their vile trade in human flesh. But we are willing to compensate you with money, or other goods."

Oh, I'm good, he had to admit to himself. I was born for this. Hitting the perfect tone, a man disgusted but working hard not to show it. Calm and unruffled as I take my moral stand.

"Money?" the mate snorted. "Worthless. Need guest workers to get the job done."

"By that I assume you mean slaves," said Livingston. "And as I said, that trade is done."

"Gotta have workers to work our mines," said the Captain.

"Try feeding the ones you have, so they last more than a few weeks."

The Captain shot him a deadly cold look. "Gyros doing a service for the world. Cleaning up the wastrel mess."

"And we are deeply grateful for that service, and willing to trade with any company that can certify it treats its workers fairly," Livingston said. "Califia will compensate you for your cargo, but we won't buy materials extracted with slave labor."

"Then don't buy materials."

"And that, I'm sure, is our loss."

At that moment, Isis felt her crystal vibrate. It was Rosa's ring pattern, but it was interspersed with the old Morse code of dots and dashes for SOS. She slipped out of her chair and, with a nod of apology, headed out the door.

"Having got along perfectly well without your plastic for the last two decades, Califia will just have to man up and suffer," Livingston was saying as she left. "In the meantime, we're willing to provide you with a cargo of chips to take back, or real food if you prefer."

Rosa had had every intention of staying out of trouble. But she had no intention of staying safely moored in port, not when she had a chance to sail the *Victory* all by herself on a day with a perfect stiff breeze. She had waited until the fleet pulled out, and then hoisted sail and nosed out of the bay.

It's just practice, she told herself as she pulled out, not too far. She would hug the jagged coastline, improve her skill at running close into shore, compensating for the way the wind spiked and ebbed around the outcroppings of land, setting the depth probes that would alert her crystal to any unseen shoals.

She did truly love to sail! Alone on the boat, she felt alive and free. She enjoyed using all of her skill to ride the currents, getting every bit of speed out of the slightest shift in the wind. If she couldn't go with the fleet to challenge the freebooters of the Gyre, well, this was compensation.

She had rounded a promontory and pulled in close to an outcropping of rock, where the depth sounder assured her there was deep water below. From the open bay outside, she heard the thrumming of engines. A largish, fast boat was going by. Then another. And another.

Grabbing the binoculars, she peered out through the entrance to the cove. One by one they streaked by. Navy cutters, emblazoned with the chariot seal of the Stewards' Armed Forces.

They were heading toward the bay where Califia's navy had been anchored. Then, with a whine and a grinding of gears, she heard them turn and saw them head out to the open sea, in the direction the navy had gone.

She grabbed her coms unit, punched in Isis's code, and the SOS.

The warning gave them a little bit of time. Isis streaked across the deck, across the wide plain of the old aircraft carrier, calling on every bit of her racer's speed. Sara! There she was, on the stern, with her team of divers ready to deploy.

How lucky they were already suited up, standing by in case they were needed to handle the Gyre ship, waiting until negotiations were complete before they would stand down. Sara was issuing orders, her blond cap of hair shining in the sunlight. Even in the urgency of the moment, Isis couldn't help but notice how lithe her body looked under its slick wetsuit.

They called over the other team leaders, huddled together, and quickly formed a plan. A plan she wouldn't share with Livingston, Isis decided. Where had those enemy patrols come from? Who had alerted them?

Within minutes, the teams were scrambling down long rope ladders they flung over the side of the ship, diving into the waves and submerging just as the drum of the Stewards' engines began to reverberate through the water.

Sara herself was the last to go down. As she swung her legs over-board and gripped the ladder with her hand, Isis suddenly ran forward and placed her own dark hand over Sara's.

"Sara!" She was gripped with a sudden, overwhelming panic, a ter-ror that she might never hold that hand again. There was so much she wanted to say, but she couldn't choke the words out of her clenched throat, and there was no time to say it anyway. "Sara!" she said again, and gulped in a breath of air, swallowing hard.

"Take care of yourself," she finally spat out. It wasn't what she wanted to say, but it was something.

Sara smiled.

"I love you, too!" she said, and scrambled down the ladder.

Isis put on all her speed again and ran back across the wide deck to the gun turret, where Miguel was on duty. She dashed up the metal stairs, panting. Damn, she was gonna have to start working out again, if that little run had her winded. But it wasn't the run, she knew, it was the breathlessness that came from watching Sara sink below the side of the ship.

Swiftly, she filled Miguel in on what was happening. They sounded the alarm, and its whoop, whoop echoed over the deck of the ship as crew ran to their battle stations. Miguel flipped the switch to power up the laser guns and the shell launcher, and he monitored the radar as Isis pulled out the binoculars.

The lead combat ship swung round. It was a menacing vessel, riding high above the waves like a pyramid of gray metal armor, crowned with a tall gun turret that swiveled to point a shell launcher at them.

"Incoming!" Isis called.

"They're launching now!" Miguel called back.

A boom, and the Stewards' big gun sent a shell whizzing through the air. It exploded about a hundred yards in front of the bows of the lead Califian ship with a sound like thunder and a spray of water. Isis prayed the divers weren't underneath. Especially ... no. She wouldn't think about her. Anyway, she wouldn't be out there with the attack squads. She was supposed to stay close to this ship, in one of the zodi-acs, out of the water so she could keep track of coms and give orders, mobile and fast in case she needed to rescue survivors, and suited up in case she needed to dive.

The *Harvey Milk* was not designed for fast maneuvers. It had two original purposes: to transport troops and materiel, and to fight. They trained their big guns on the Stewards' combat ships, while around them the smaller tugs and ferries of the Califian Navy churned through the water, drawing fire and returning it. A loud crack, and laser fire ripped through the *Milk*'s gunwale, leaving a jagged scar. Another boom, and one of the combat ships exploded in a fountain of fire.

Then there was no time to think, no time to worry or wonder how a little rubber boat would fare in the midst of this hellfire. Only time to aim, shoot, and maneuver.

~~~~~~

Below decks, Livingston and the negotiators from the Gyre were jolted by the first explosion. The sounds of detonation and impact reverberated through the hull.

"Fuck!" cried the Captain from the Gyre, leaping to his feet. "Fuck your bullshit and your deals. Ship under attack!"

"Gotta get back!" cried the mate.

"And how do we know you won't join in the attack?" Livingston asked, still cool and unhurried. "Give us some assurance that you will leave the zone, and we'll be happy to escort you back."

"Fuck that!" the mate cried, and he whipped a knife out of his boot, grabbed Livingstone in a choke-hold, and pressed the blade into his neck.

"Assurance!" he said, as Bronwyn and the other Califians sat petrified in shock for one long moment; then Bronwyn launched herself at the Gyros. The Captain slashed at her face. She stumbled. The Gyros sped out the cabin door and up the ladder, taking Livingston with them.

~~~~~~

Sara clung to the tiller of the zodiac as it pitched and bucked like a rodeo bull. She was watching the coms screen on her wrist unit, trying to keep track of the green pinpoints that represented her divers and all the while steering a zigzag course that would make her harder to target, provided she didn't zigzag into a shell meant for somebody else. Shells were falling all around, the water erupting in cyclones of froth and blood. No time to count the pinpoints, to track how many winked out.

This was a bad idea, she admitted to herself. She should have stayed on the *Harvey Milk*, taken her chances there where she could have focused on running the mission instead of running a watery slalom.

But she was here. Deal with it. Okay, Red Team was in position. She barked out the go ahead to try and mine one of the Stewards' ships. Blue Team—Blue Team had been close to that first explosion. Don't think about it now. Yellow Team—there they were, closing in astern of another combat ship. Yes, do it! Go, go, go!

She was pushing the throttle with one hand, yanking on the tiller with the other, and desperately trying to get her wrist radio up close enough to her mouth to bawl out a report to Isis on the bridge and still command the teams.

"Red Team reported, mission complete. Taking evasive action!"

Isis was so relieved to hear Sara's voice that her knees nearly buckled under her. Can't afford this! she told herself sternly.

"Red Team complete," she snapped at Miguel.

"Give them time to clear out," he said.

At that moment, they heard a whistle and a wrenching screech, as if the boat herself were screaming. The tall mainmast came crashing down on the bridge, shattering the glass portholes and the lights, crushing the starboard side into a pancake of jagged metal.

Isis and Miguel dove for cover. Isis clutched her handheld control unit to her heart and rolled, taking the fall on her shoulder. The ship lurched, and threw her against the housing for the wheel, then lurched back again as she slid into the map table.

She braced herself, held the unit, and thumbed the command to detonate, praying that the damn thing would still work.

Then she struggled to her feet. Miguel was trapped under a metal beam, groaning. She shoved the coms unit back in her jacket, braced herself, and staggered to him.

"You okay?"

"My arm!"

His arm was pinned down by the beam and lay at an unnatural angle. Fuck! She couldn't shift the thing by herself, and now the ship was still pitching and tossing, desperately needing a hand on the wheel. And a hand on the gun—fuck! Where was Livingston, he might be a dickhead spy but he knew how to steer this thing.

"Blue Team complete," barked the coms from inside her shirt. She dug it out and thumbed a command as she grabbed hold of the wheel. Then she flipped it to ship's coms, and her own voice echoed out of the walls.

"Livingston to the bridge! Medics to the bridge!"

She glanced at the radar. It was frozen, nothing on it moving. Fuck! She whammed her fist down on it and for a moment the beam circled, the lights came on. Then it went dead again. What the fuck was happening? There was so much debris now in front of the bridge that she couldn't get much of a visual.

"Lost radar," she barked into Sara's channel. "Whadda you see?"

"One enemy ship took a shell, nothing left. Two have damage from the divers' charges, limping back to the south. Two still coming at us. Gyro ship turning tail and running toward the west."

"Let it go," Miguel croaked, his voice in agony. "All that fraggin' plastic—sink it and every seabird from here to Hawaii'll be dead in a week!"

"Where the fuck is Livingston!" Isis barked into the ship's coms.

The medics told her, as they came pounding up the stairs to minister to Miguel. Isis struggled with the wheel to get the ship under control.

It seemed to be listing to one side, and something was wrong with the steering mechanism. It responded in a sluggish, sullen manner.

"Yellow Team complete," she heard Sara call. Again she thumbed a button. Again, from faraway, she heard a muffled roar.

"Another enemy taking damage," Sara spoke with a note of satisfaction. "That makes four of them heading for home, and yes, looks like number five is turning as well."

"I'd call that a draw," Miguel said as they finally regrouped in the meeting room at one in the morning. His arm was plastered against his chest in a tight sling, and his head was bandaged. Isis herself was bruised in a dozen places, but she'd been lucky. Nothing was broken.

Sara had had the devil's own luck, too. Thank ... whatever. Jesus, Goddess, fucking Neptune, God of the Sea.

"I'd call it a disaster," Sara said. She was sipping hot tea out of a cup held in shaking hands, still trying to warm up. But there was a coldness inside her that had nothing to do with the hours she'd spent half-submerged in spray and the backwash of explosions. She had lost five of her divers. Five out of thirty. Friends. Friends whom she had trained, taught, commanded.

"Could have been worse." Miguel shrugged, then let out an involuntary cry of pain. "We took some casualties, but they took more. Had to withdraw. We lost the Gyro ship, but it didn't make it into port with its cargo."

"It'll try again," Bronwyn said. She had a long cut down her left cheek that she'd gotten in the fray with the Gyros, and a scorch mark through her bright red hair. "And we'll be in no position to stop it for a while."

"But we've served them notice," Miguel said, still stubbornly trying to look on the good side. "Their shipping cannot go through unmolested."

"What about Livingston?" Bronwyn asked.

"What about him?" Isis said. "How'd the Stewards know where to find us?"

"What are you saying?"

"Could have been a spy."

"Could have been a distress call from the Gyro ship," Bronwyn said.

She was right, of course. It could have been. But if Livingston had betrayed them.... He could have arranged beforehand with the Gyros to take him hostage. A way to jump ship, maybe go back home and report, without being suspected, should he want to return and spy some more. Funny that none of the combat boats opened fire on the Gyro ship. Or maybe not funny. Why should they? Leave it alone, and they could still do their trade.

"Shouldn't we try to rescue him?" Bronwyn asked.

"How?" Sara asked.

Bronwyn didn't answer.

If he was a spy, Isis thought, then the Gyros were in on the plan and they'd let him go. He'd turn up again, in the Southlands.

If he was innocent, it was an awful thing to be shanghaied out to the Gyre. But they had no boat they could spare that was in shape enough to pursue the Gyro craft, let alone fight it when they got there.

No, honest or not, the man was like a cat. She believed he had every chance of landing on his feet.

Chapter Forty

As Madrone approached the Refuge, she felt a sense of deep relief. It had become home, this surreal place with its honor guard of skeletons, who now to her looked welcoming and friendly, more like amiable *Catrinas* from a Dia de los Muertos procession and less like grim harbingers of death.

She wrapped that sense of safety around her like a blanket as she nervously glanced up. The Gateway of the Dead had been subtly embellished with higher walls and awnings to become a dark tunnel. But small gaps allowed patches of sky to be visible. They were clear, now, devoid of even a cloud to mar the sapphire strips. But for how long? How long would it take for the drones to find them? What would they see below them as they flew overhead—patches of green where no green should be? Gatherings of people in the midst of the zone supposed to be empty and dead?

Beams of light poked through the openings above to shine on a skeleton with its arms upraised, its bony hand outstretched as if to say, Stop! Other shafts were directed at niches filled with skulls. At night, candles would be lit, and if anything the bones would look even spookier. But the impact was that of walking through the dark, in a narrow, enclosed place, menaced by death . . .

. . . And then suddenly emerging into the light of Welcome Plaza. The square was lavishly planted, full of life and color. The winter rains had arrived, and now everything was bright with the colors of spring, which came on top of winter here in the Southlands. Yellow and orange nasturtiums tumbled over the pavement. Jasmine crept up the north-facing wall of the courtyard, emitting a sweet scent, while on the south-facing wall early peas raced for the sky behind a patch of collards. Mustard with bright yellow flowers marched beside broccoli with fat, fractal heads. Boxes on high poles held swallows' nests, and a pink-flowering columbine hosted a feeding butterfly.

And everywhere the flowers drew bees. They had planted all the spare crannies with rosemary and lavender and sages which all required little water, and set up skeps in east-facing niches in the higher levels of the ruins. And the bees had come, down from the hills or in from the wild deserts to the east, scouts from rogue hives that'd survived, somehow, the years of pesticides and diseases. The plaza was alive with their song of abundance and health.

Madrone stepped from darkness into light and color, from hell into paradise.

The Welcoming Angel stretched out colossal arms to gather in the needy. Bright mosaics glittered in the sunlight. Above her head, a batik banner proclaimed Welcome to the City of Refuge.

This has got to endure somehow, she thought. We've got to find a way to shield it.

A bright canopy stretched from the north wall, creating a patch of shade. Under it sat comfortable chairs and a chaise longue salvaged from a garden shop. With a wrought-iron table, they made a welcome station that was staffed day and night.

A black-haired teen leapt to her feet, grasped Madrone's hands, and greeted her warmly.

"You're back! Praise creation!"

The young woman was dressed in the height of such fashion as had already taken hold in the Refuge, art making the best of necessity. She wore loose trousers and a tunic made of the gray cloth that was a ubiquitous product of the Stewards' remaining factories, one of the few things they did produce in quantity, for uniforms. But it was embellished with a bright yellow overshirt, decorated in scraps of salvaged prints, like flowers covering a concrete wall.

And the Refuge was developing a language of its own. Praise creation—where Madrone might have said praise the Goddess, and her great-grandmother would have said praise Jesus. But the Retributionists had given Jesus a bad name—unfair to him, Madrone thought, and the real Christians among them. Praise creation was a fair compromise. After all, that's what they were doing, creating to counter the destruction. God's creation, human creativity—all were worthy of praise.

She passed into another inner plaza. Forming the Refuge out of the rubble had resulted in an odd, organic city plan of small, open squares linked by narrow corridors, like a walled medieval town or an ancient casbah. It offered surprise after surprise, like opening a set of nested boxes, each revealing a new mystery. This next plaza was wider, and someone with a strong sense of geometry had divided it into a mandala of alternating patches of quinoa and bush beans, surrounded by beds of the extremely drought-tolerant chia. Surprising, really, how much they could actually grow in this space.

Through another corridor, and she was greeted by the music of flowing water, gurgling through pumps and splashing into the aquaponics pools that teemed with tilapia and catfish. Their waste-water circulated into floating beds of greens that were fed by the fish waste which, in turn, purified the water before it went back into the tanks.

The older systems were built of scavenged plastic tanks and chains of old bathtubs—beautiful in a certain way with plants and fish. But a new system was in progress, of sculpted flowing pools and plant trays like round, suspended lily pads, the work of Tianne's crew. They had mixed up vats of Tianne's special sculptural mix and the artists were going quite nuts with it.

But they were in Hollywood, after all, or not far from it, Madrone smiled to herself. Within her own lifetime, this had been the worldwide center of the entertainment industry, and even after the Retributionists shut most of it down, they maintained studios to produce their own propaganda films and the endless bread-and-circuses of reality TV. So the Refuge had received an influx of craftspersons and scene designers who were thrilled to turn their talents into a living set for a new way of life.

Ducking through a low-ceilinged passage, she emerged into the Central Plaza. A meal was in progress at the hearth. They had rapidly established a cooking schedule and most of the people of the Refuge took their meals here or at the other communal kitchens in the newer sections of the city. They simply had no way to supply fuel and water for hundreds of individual kitchens.

The guild the cooks had formed was kept busy training new members in the skills needed to provide for a huge crowd with the limited and sometimes odd supplies that they had. Recently, smaller pop-ups had begun to spring up in other corners of the city, where some group of friends would create a spontaneous café for a few nights, often when they wanted to play music or perform. The Refuge was starting to develop a nightlife: a sign that they had passed the point of mere survival.

Madrone felt a warm glow of pride. Her dream, her vision, that little seed, had grown into this. Maybe a mother felt this way, watching a child grow into an adult with a mind and mission of her own.

But underneath was still that growing worry, a discordant note in the harmony. How long would they have to rejoice in their creation? What would it mean, if all this beauty and sweat were to end in blood?

A meeting was in progress around the hearth. Voices were raised in argument, as if to prove that with all we've accomplished, there's still trouble in paradise, Madrone thought. She stopped to listen.

Crazy Janus with her wild, dark hair sprang up onto a bench, and began to declaim.

"Now, you listen to me, brother and sisters. This is the eye of the cosmic awakening. We are the eye, and we are being watched by the eye. Eye in the sky. Pie in the sky. But She hovers above, above is love. Love one another, Jesus said, and though the Retributionists have forgotten it, the Mother has not. She comes, she comes for her children. Out of the stars, out of the night. To counter the might. Will you be ready? Or will it bite? She'll be coming' round the mountain, when she comes, when she comes.... She'll be drivin' six white horses, she'll be roaring in on the cosmic tides, ride the tide, the tidal bride, hold onto your pride cuz the old world died. Died for your sins. Repent and win. Let it begin."

Madrone skirted the edge of the crowd and headed for home. Janus could go on like that for hours, and she didn't envy whoever was running the meeting. But that was not her problem tonight, praise creation!

Yet she did have a point, in all her craziness. Eye in the sky. Drones fly and people die.

Now I'm starting to sound like her. Stop it! Bring it to Bird, or to Council, but don't let it spoil your homecoming. Because if we let worries and dread infect these moments, then we have nothing, not even sweet memories to comfort us when the fears come true.

She approached their apartment. A small, wet, naked body burst out the door and sped down the corridor. He stopped dead in his tracks when he saw Madrone, then threw his small arms around her waist and gave her a long, fierce hug.

Madrone knelt down and gathered him into her arms.

"Oh, Zap, sweetie, I'm glad to see you!"

It had taken so long for him to be willing to hug her, and she wanted to cry with joy every time he did. She held him close, cherishing him, the wild little boy, his body marked by old scars and the recent bruises of a hundred tumbles. He was filling out, she noted, no longer so pitifully thin, becoming the sturdy boy he was meant to be. "Oh, Zap!"

The door to the bathroom was closed. The Plumbers' Guild, one of the most highly valued and respected groups in the city, had surprised them a few weeks ago by running water up to their apartment, as a special thank-you for all their work. From the sounds inside, Bird was immersed in the continual struggle to get the boys into the bath.

"Get in there, or I'll put you in."

"No! Why do I need a stupid bath, anyway?" she heard Zoom's muffled voice.

"Because you haven't had one in a week, and you stink!"

"I don't care!"

"I do! I have to live with you."

"You aren't the boss of me!"

"Oh yeah? I'm bigger than you, I'm stronger than you, and when it comes right down to it, I'm meaner than you!"

Thumps, the sound of something smashing, a thud and splash.

"Frag it! Don't you dare get out of that tub! You're barefoot and the floor's covered with broken glass."

"Mado'll be mad when she gets home. You broke her soap dish!"

"Mado'll be mad if you don't deploy that soap in the tub to wash yourself. Now get to it!"

Should I rescue him? Madrone wondered. But Zap was still hugging her, and she rocked back on her heels and let him nestle into her arms. Maybe there was hope for him after all, hope that he could yet be just a child, a small boy able to accept comfort and let in love. In another few minutes, she knew, the spell would break and he would go back to being just as wild and annoying as ever, but for the moment, she would treasure this sweetness and hold it close.

After a long time of splashing and shouting, the bathroom door opened.

"Don't you move from that tub until I get back with the broom!"

And there he was, dripping wet as if he had bathed himself fully clothed, glowering and grumbling. He stopped when he saw her, took in the sight of Zap curled up and pressed into her lap, and a huge smile lit his face. She smiled back at him, and he stood there for a long moment, just taking her in with his eyes, the two of them grinning at each other in a wave of pure happiness. Then Zap rocketed off, and she rose up gracefully and he clasped wet arms around her. They stood together, dripping and kissing.

A cry from the bathroom drew them back.

"I'm drowning in here!"

"Got to get the broom," Bird said.

She followed him into the bathroom as he swept up the shattered, rose-patterned soap dish that had been in the apartment when they found it.

Zoom was lying on the bottom of the tub, immersed in the water, his lips pursed tight and his cheeks puffed out with the effort of holding his breath. She leaned over him, and he blew out the air with a burst of bubbles and sat bolt upright.

"You're back!"

"I am. Glad to see me?"

"He made me drown!"

"I don't think so."

"I was tempted," Bird admitted, smiling. "Okay, you can get out now and dry off. We'll get you dressed and we can all go down to the hearth and get something to eat."

Zoom was out of the tub and off to his room in a flash. Madrone perched on the edge of the tub and pulled out the drain. The water gurgled out, off to the graywater system and out to the gardens. She watched Bird mop up the floor. Something inside her had shifted, she realized. She was no longer fretful, angry at the precariousness of their happiness. She could appreciate it now, the precious moment, this sweet, shining, ordinary moment with her genius prophet hero mopping the bathroom floor. The kind of ordinary evening that was the very fabric of normal life: bathe the kids, feed them, get them to bed.

In a different world, she might expect a lifetime of such nights. She might have gotten bored with them, chafed at their dullness and the lack of excitement. But in this life with the threat of attack always on them and drones wending their way across the sky, this ordinary happiness was infinitely precarious and all the more precious.

The towel mopped up water, leaving a streak of jeweled drops behind. The boys' voices were raised in shouts from the next room. She heard Zap yell in outrage. Bird's head was bent. Atop the coiled springs of his close-cropped hair were sprinkled shining drops of water, jeweled beads of radiance. He grunted, and the sound held the music of the world.

⌇⌇⌇

They sat at a table under the stars, feasting on dishes of quinoa stew and pots of collard greens. Zap and Zoom were off somewhere playing with other children. The meeting around the fire had broken up, but couples lingered in the mild air, chatting or strolling or leisurely finishing a meal.

"I wonder if we could brew beer from quinoa or amaranth?" Bird said idly.

He was watching Madrone, thinking how beautiful she looked in the flickering light of candles, letting the relief of her return flood through him.

Madrone snorted. "We have enough problems with the moonshine the teens smuggle in and the bootleg vodka they brew up from potato peelings. Accounts for a high proportion of our work in the healing center."

He basked in the sound of her voice. It didn't really matter what she was saying. For the moment she was back, and as safe as any of them were safe. Whatever had happened before, whatever was to come, this was the secret of happiness, to savor the moment and keep it unstained by regrets, untainted by fear.

"Bird," she said abruptly, "they've got surveillance drones patrolling the city. I saw them."

Moments pass, he thought. And the fear returned.

"We knew it had to happen sooner or later," he said. "We need a strategy."

"Or a cloaking device," Madrone said.

"There's a thought."

"We should call a Council."

Bird gave a pointed look toward the table not far away, where Emily, Anthony, and Miss Ruby sat. They hadn't spoken since the fight, and Anthony had greeted her with only a cold nod. They couldn't bring the Refuge into unity to deal with the drones if she was feuding with the other key leaders.

With a sigh, Madrone stood up. She knew what she had to do.

"I'm going to apologize," she told Bird.

He nodded, and rose to follow her as she slowly walked over to Miss Ruby's table.

Miss Ruby met her with a glare. Madrone glared back, only to see Bird give her *his* best imitation of Johanna, his eyebrows raised, his lips set tight.

Madrone took a deep breath and forced herself to smile.

"I'm sorry I lost my temper," she said.

Ruby folded her arms and gave her own version of the Look, at which she excelled, Madrone thought. Her head was cocked, her lips pursed, her eyes piercing. Well, to hell with her! Madrone folded her own arms and Looked right back at her, her own head at an opposing angle, her own eyebrows climbing toward her hairline.

"Just don't hit my kid," Madrone said. Bird coughed behind her.

"Apologize!" he hissed.

"You need to get that child under control," Miss Ruby said.

Madrone's Look intensified. Bird stomped on her foot.

"Ow!"

Bird unfolded Madrone's locked arm and brought it down to her side, holding her hand.

"Miss Ruby," he said in a conciliatory tone, "we know the kids have problems. They were scuts for a gang of water thieves. They had nothing in their lives besides violence and terror until we rescued them. Yeah, they're wild. They're still afraid. We can't break them of that by hitting them. And underneath it all, they have good hearts."

"Hmmph. That remains to be seen."

"I'd love us all to sit down and discuss the educational philosophy of the school when we're calmer." Madrone made a great effort to keep her voice neutral—not least because Bird was pinching her.

"After thirty years in the classroom, you think I don't know how to handle a bunch of problem kids?"

Bird pinched harder. Madrone wrenched her arm away.

"I'm sure you do. But Miss Ruby, you had a different job in that classroom. A difficult job—an awful job. I don't envy you—I don't know how you managed it. You had to take kids who were born into a rotten system and teach them how to survive. They were going into a rigged game, and you had to prepare them to navigate it as best they could. I'm sure you were the very best kind of teacher a kid could have in those conditions."

Miss Ruby's eyes narrowed and her lips tightened.

"I mean it!" Madrone assured her. "You, Emily, too—you had to teach them to be quiet and shut up and put up with things they hated, to work hard and not expect too much. Am I right?"

Miss Ruby didn't reply, but her head shifted oh so slightly, cocked at a new angle. She was listening.

"But now we have a different challenge. We have to encourage them to want more, to want everything—and to fight for it. Their job here isn't to survive a rotten game, but to make a new game, a new world. They have to be able to think for themselves, and challenge authority—even ours."

"And what will happen to them if we fail?" Ruby asked. "You think the Stewards gonna let this place be, once they find it? And that's just a matter of time."

A silence fell.

"They may die," Madrone said softly. "We all may die. It's the most likely outcome, isn't it?"

"Then why are you here?" Emily snapped.

"Because there's always a chance. Because if we don't change it here, sooner or later it will come back after us in our gardens back home."

"You talk about dying as if it was just that simple." Miss Ruby shook her head. "But in fact, people don't die. They adjust. They do what they have to do to survive. So isn't it better to take this opportunity to teach them a few more things they might otherwise never learn, to give them a better chance?"

Madrone looked at her bleakly. "I don't know. Maybe there are things that it's better not to endure."

"Don't you say that!" Miss Ruby snapped. "Look at you! You and me and Mr. Bird there, every one of us had some ancestor who endured. Tied up in the slave ships, rolling in their own wastes, chained up in bondage—they endured and you are here because of it! You're trying to tell me that wasn't worthwhile?"

"No," Madrone said. "I'm grateful for it. I try to be worthy of it. But ... "

"Don't 'but' me!" Miss Ruby said sharply. "But nothing!"

"But I don't want to settle for it," Madrone went on. "Those ancestors who survived the slave ships weren't raised to be slaves, they were raised to be villagers! They stayed alive because they knew in their bones how decent people were supposed to behave and they held onto some hope that they could create that wherever they landed. They passed it on to their children and their children's children. I'm not willing to condition the next generation of the Stewards' future slaves for them. Let's raise them with a real experience of freedom and nurture their curiosity and creativity and trust that whatever happens, they'll carry that seed forward."

"As you do, Miss Ruby," Bird quickly interjected. "We know that you're trying to teach the kids how to behave like caring human beings. And that you've never given up hope. Isn't that why you're here?"

"I'm here because I had no other choice," Miss Ruby said.

"There's always a choice," Bird said. "If you'd turned informant on your neighbors to keep your home, that would have been a choice."

"Not for me!" Miss Ruby stated emphatically.

"If you'd done nothing," Bird went on, "if you'd waited until they came and took you, that would also have been a choice. Instead you chose to take a chance and come here."

"I'm here because if there is even a chance, like you say, a hope of making a different game, well, that's a chance worth taking. And I do thank you—for offering it," Miss Ruby conceded.

"So can't we be friends?" Bird pleaded. "After all, we're supposed to be the grownups here."

"Tell me about your schools in the North," Miss Ruby said. "You might have an idea or two."

"A certain amount of discipline is not a bad thing," Madrone admitted. "These kids might need a strong structure."

They ended up talking long into the night, trooping up to Bird and Madrone's living room. Madrone brewed them up tea and Bird produced a rare, treasured bottle of real beer that someone had slipped into his cart one day while he was busking. Madrone told Miss Ruby and Emily all about the system her grandmother Johanna had pioneered, the Learning Groups, the lessons based on building and gardening and exploring and fixing things, the Learning Tracks through the City, the way older students were encouraged to help and teach the younger.

"My grandmother always talked about the three Cs instead of the three Rs," Madrone said. "Connection, creativity, cooperation. She said kids have to connect with the material, with their hands and hearts and bodies, not just have it spoon-fed to their minds. They need to have their creativity encouraged and nurtured, and that means an environment that encourages cooperation, not competition. And I truly believe she laid the basis for everything we have in the North—the abundance of food that comes from working together with the land and the plants and the microbes and the animals, the chemistry that cooperates with molecules and figures out how they want to combine, the energy that we get by cooperating with the sun and the winds and the tides, the Net that cooperates with the crystals in silicon, all put together in new and creative and joyful ways. That's the kind of education these kids need, to heal the damage that's here."

"I like the idea of learning through doing," Emily conceded.

"Work 'em in the mornings," Miss Ruby suggested. "Tire them out—then maybe they'll sit quiet and learn in the afternoons."

Eagerly, they planned. They would engage the children in building the first Learning Track through the City of Refuge. And then, in a central area, they'd enlist the children's aid to build their own Learning Center. The children would work together in the mornings, and in the afternoons, they'd read and research and get formal lessons to address the questions they came up with in doing the work.

They'd help Madrone plant healing herbs, and learn their uses. Emily and Madrone would enlist others from the community to come and share their knowledge. Anthony would direct them in plays that the children could present at the hearth fires.

The conversation went on long beyond midnight, until Emily finally rose and stretched and remembered she had an early class to teach in the morning.

"All friends again?" Bird said.

Miss Ruby nodded.

"To be truthful, I am sorry I whacked the boy. Jesus knows he had it coming, but it's not the way I want to be."

"Goddess knows I want to whack him twenty times a day," Madrone agreed. She reached out and gave Miss Ruby a hug. Emily joined them, and Bird wrapped his arms around them all.

"We got to have each other's backs," Miss Ruby said, her eyes moist. "We have made something beautiful. But I got a feeling the hard part is still to come."

Madrone nodded. She'd been so engrossed in their plans, so pleased to be friends again, that she had shoved the threat of the drones to the back of her mind. She just couldn't bear to say: And now that we've come up with all these beautiful plans, you should know that we might have a very short time left to realize them.

Tomorrow, she thought. Tomorrow they would bring it to Council.

Chapter Forty-One

S O WE'RE DISCUSSING WHAT TO DO ABOUT THE DRONES," EMILY SAID. She was back in front of the big general assembly that night, fortified by a pot of herbal stimulant, a grounding, and a lucky stone that Madrone had administered before the meeting. "Who has ideas?"

A short woman in the back eagerly raised her hand. "I know where there's a supply of camo cloth. We could rig it over the plazas and the gardens."

"But the gardens need light in order to grow," a young man objected.

"We could mount patrols, shoot down any drones we see," cried out one of Tianne's teens, and a shout of agreement rose up from the crowd.

Bird stood and held up a hand. "They're not easy to hit," he said. "Granted, we could get a few rifles from the hillboys, but think for a moment. You're a drone operator. Every time you send one to a certain part of the city, it gets blown away. What are you gonna do next?"

"Go see what happened to it," Anthony said in a quiet voice.

"If we had some of our techie crew from the North," Bird mused out loud, "they could hack into the system maybe, feed them false information."

Tianne stepped forward. Her black silk hair now hung in a hundred tiny braids, each bound with a different color of thread. She had a thin, cold smile on her face.

"What's wrong with the techie crew you have right here?" she asked. "With all due respect to the North, I'd say we have hackers here who can hold their own against anyone!"

Another cheer rose up.

Bird stifled his urge to protest, to say: but you don't talk to the crystals, don't communicate with them, cooperate. You just manipulate numbers. Instead, he simply said, "Do you think you can get into their system?"

A tall thin man with hair like a blond wire brush stood up. "I used to work in security," he said. "I still have friends. We can get in. We can do a lot. But how long we can remain undetected—that depends on a lot of factors that are not under our control. If they're on high alert, and clever, they'll notice right away. If they're lazy trolls, it'll take them longer. But sooner or later, they'll realize the data is being manipulated. Then they'll know there's definitely something to look for."

"So you can buy us some time," Emily said. "Good. Do it!"

"And let's not discuss it any further in Council," Anthony chimed in hastily. "I'm all for an open Council, but if they have drones in the sky they could have other spies and agents right here among us. No, I'm sorry, it has to be said! Best keep the hacking details to those who need to know."

There was a buzz of both agreement and anger, and Emily had to shout multiple times for quiet.

"So we can have some time, with luck," Bird said. "But we do need a plan for what to do if that luck runs out."

"Do we fight or do we run?" yelled one of the teens.

"Ain't no place to run to," cried a woman from the back. "We all here cuz we runnin' from what's out there!"

There was laughter, but it had a serious undertone. She was right, and they all knew it. Our Refuge, our last hope, our death trap, Bird thought grimly. Yes, defend it, but how? Can we win? Or are we doomed to become another hopeless last stand, our own Masada, our Thermopylae, our St. George's Hill, our Warsaw ghetto.

"We need to stockpile some weapons," Tianne said. "And learn how to use them."

Miss Ruby bridled. "This Refuge was founded on the principles of nonviolence!" she proclaimed. "We're following in the footsteps of Martin Luther King!"

Blank looks met her pronouncement. The Stewards' educational system didn't feature heroes of nonviolence, or any revolutionary heroes at all later than 1776.

Tianne's thin smile tightened into a hard line. "Please, Miss Ruby, there's no point talking about Martin Luther King. We're fighting the Stewards!"

Her crowd of supporters broke into laughter, but she waved a hand and silenced them.

"I prefer to fight with art, myself," she said. "I believe that beauty is stronger than ugliness, and violence is ugly. But I'm a practical person. When the Stewards discover we're here, and that we're more than just another homeless camp, they are going to come after us. And not with a bunch of limpdick croots ready to desert. They'll send their crack troops, the breeds and the lobsters climbing over the backs of their betters to get up a bit. And their military drones. We're not going to win them over with our pretty Welcome Plaza and our angel statues. We're going to have to fight."

"With what?" Bird asked. "We have exactly eight rifles, three laser rifles, and fourteen handguns in the Refuge." He knew, because he was enough of a hillboy still that he had made it his business to know.

"I thought we'd agreed that newcomers had to hand in their weapons!" Miss Ruby was outraged.

Bird shrugged. Yes, they'd agreed. Just as they'd agreed to no drinking and no drugs. But not everyone complied. He could look around in the crowd and count dozens of pairs of bleary eyes, and some of the loudest voices were amped up on more than natural adrenaline.

Still, weapons were scarce and most refugistas had only a sharpened kitchen knife or a pen knife for defense. The gangs outside, of course, were well-armed, but they were also beyond the Stewards' immediate control and so rarely found themselves in the kind of desperation that would lead them to seek refuge.

"There are families here," Emily objected. "Children!"

Bob, her old neighbor, stood up to answer her. "And that wouldn't stop the thrashers from using lethal force for one minute. You know that. We all know that. That's why we're here, with our families, because we know the Stewards don't give a rat's ass for our lives."

There was a loud murmur of agreement.

I need Lily, Bird thought. *Or Maya, or someone with a clear devotion to the nonviolent ideals. I'm not doing a good job of standing for them, because part of me agrees with Tianne. We're not going to win the bastards over. So how do we win?*

The fortress falls when the ground beneath it shifts, he heard in his deep memory. *But what in Hella's name does that mean in practical terms?*

Tianne turned hopefully to Rafe and the Angels' contingent. "Can we get more guns?" she asked.

Slowly Rafe nodded his elegant head. Starbursts of light gleamed in his cornsilk hair.

"A few," he said in a low, calm voice. "Not many. Too dangerous, raiding the armories. Not what Angels like to do."

"But you can get us some?" Tianne asked eagerly.

"Not enough," Rafe said. "Not enough to defend against a full assault."

A heavy silence settled on the crowd. Bird could feel hopelessness seeping up from the ground. They had been raised on it, all these Southlanders, taught from the moment they could focus their infant eyes that dreadful things could happen and they could not stop them. They could stave it off for a time, immersed in building and organizing and creating the Refuge, but always, just below the surface, it was there, a cold wind blowing from underground, a ghost voice whispering, *What's the use?*

Prophet Jed jumped up. "The Lord is our defender. The Lord is our avenger! This saith the Lord, 'Allow abomination to flourish, and I will smite you!'"

At least he woke people out of their stupor, Bird thought, as a ripple of annoyance spread through the crowd. Anger is more mobilizing than despair.

"Jed, you're out of order," Emily said firmly.

"Let him speak! Let him speak!" cried his supporters.

"Shut him up! Shut him up!" came a counterchant.

"Think not that we will hold this Refuge if it becomes a refuge for sin and filth. Our defense is in our moral purity!"

Janus leapt up on a bench. "But when do we begin to sin? To sin is to win, to need to win, winners take all. To lose is to choose, choose to lose and not to win and there is no sin, but losers are boozers, bleeding refusers, I am not amused, the Great Mother says. Hear what I say, the wings of the angels will bear you away. No need to defend, open your hearts to love and I will descend."

"The Great Mother is the Whore of Babylon! Deceiver! Handmaid of Satan!" Jed roared back.

"What is a whore? We've heard that before! To whore is to be more."

"Thirteen demons possess you, scarlet woman! Lying harlot!"

"Scarlet harlot, harlot starlet, blood flows scarlet. Scarlet A, letter of shame, no blame, we're all the same."

"What do I do?" Emily whispered to Bird.

"You could think of it like a symphony, point and counterpoint. Just let it wash over you," Bird said grimly.

"I'm stickin' with the Kegels," Madrone hissed.

"Burn in the flames!" Jed screamed. "The flames of hellfire will consume you!"

"Silence!" Bird roared.

But the prophet's supporters chorused back. "Do not silence the voice of the prophet of the Lord!"

"You shut up!" yelled a slurred voice from the back, where a bottle of something was passing from hand to hand. Something flew from that section of the crowd and landed among the prophet's followers, who roared in outrage.

Emily gathered up all her determination. "He's got to take his turn, just like anybody else! He can raise his hand, and he can shut up from time to time and let somebody else have a chance to speak."

A hand shot up and she pointed at it. Unfortunately, the young woman it belonged to was Faith Prophet.

"You're just trying to silence Prophet Jed because he's speaking truths you don't want to hear! There's an anti-religion bias in this place, and those of us who come from faith never get a fair hearing!"

"You can have your hearing," Emily said, "but you've got to keep on topic. That's the only way we can get anything decided."

"The only decision that counts is the decision to turn to the Lord, or against him!" Jed interjected. "For he who indulges in sin in this world will pay in the next."

"Shut him up!" cried out the bulk of the assembly. The contingent of drinkers took it up as a chant.

"Everyone shut up!" Emily yelled.

"That's your answer to criticism—be silent! Shut up! That's always your answer!" cried Faith.

"No, you shut up! We got important things to discuss!" yelled a man.

"What are you people, anyway?" an older woman demanded of the prophet's contingent. "Agents of the Stewards, sent in here to create discord?"

"Oh, that's your answer to any criticism. You don't agree—so you must be an infiltrator!"

"Just seems suspicious to me that every time we try to talk about defense, you all come in and disrupt!"

"There is no defense against the vengeance of the Lord! No safety in sin! No security but in the arms of Jesus!" Jed intoned.

"People who accuse other people of being agents are usually agents themselves," his supporter snarled.

By the end of the meeting, Emily was screaming in fury. Miss Ruby had slapped Faith Prophet across the face, and Bird had had to jump in and use all his skill at martial arts to keep a couple of the prophet's more ardent followers from socking her. A brawl had broken out in the back, and medics had treated a cracked head and fractured jaw. The meeting broke up with nothing accomplished.

"Christ Jesus Savior, if they aren't agents of the Stewardship, the Stewards are missing their best bet," Miss Ruby said as they met back in the apartment for a late-night debrief.

"The Stewards aren't that subtle," Bird said, rubbing his elbow where Prophet Jed had attacked him with a tire iron.

"You okay?" Madrone asked. He nodded. The blow had been a glancing one, and he'd ducked and rolled with it, come up behind and grabbed Jed by the knees to knock him off his feet.

"Clearly I'm in a state of sin."

Miss Ruby shook her head. "Sin isn't a state with them, it's a nation. A universe. Those folks aren't Christians—they're Sinians. They've done away with Christ and everything he stood for. Left nothing *but* the sin."

"We've got to do something," Emily said. "Every day brings us closer to the moment the Stewards move in on us, and we've got to have a plan."

"I wish Salal were here," Madrone said. "She's good with meetings. I'm not, particularly."

"What would Salal do?"

"She'd take them aside, one by one, and reason with them."

"That would work, if they weren't impervious to reason," Anthony said.

"We should expel them all!" Miss Ruby said.

"Right, and have them go straight to the Stewards and denounce us," Bird said.

"What would Lily do?" Madrone asked.

"She'd say we need to be better healers than they are disrupters."

"I have an idea," Miss Ruby said. "I'll facilitate the next meeting. It'll be a short one."

———————

Miss Ruby took the dais.

"Okay, people, listen up. I'm facilitating this assembly, and this is how it's gonna be. I taught seventh grade for thirty years, so don't mess wit' me. You understand?

"Now, we're all going to listen to each other, and we're each going to take our turn. We're going to call hands. Anyone gets out of order, anyone disrupts, and that's it. Meeting over. We all turn our backs and walk out. You hear what I'm sayin'? We are no longer rewarding bad behavior."

A pimpled, freckled teen started to object, and Miss Ruby fixed him with her eye. "You got something to say, young man? Raise your hand!"

Dutifully, he did and she nodded at him.

"But we need to meet, Miss Ruby! We've got important things to discuss."

"And just how far have we gotten discussing them in these meetings? No, we've got to train ourselves how to behave, and then we can meet. Now, here's what's on the agenda—how do we defend ourselves if the Stewards come?"

Prophet Jed recognized his cue. He leapt to his feet, pounded his staff, and began his rant.

"We cannot defend ourselves in a state of sin. Only God can defend us, and he will not save the unrepentant. There is no refuge from the wrath of the Almighty."

Without a word, Miss Ruby strode off the dais and marched out. Bird, Madrone, Emily, and Anthony followed her. After a moment of hesitation, so did the majority of the crowd, leaving the prophet surrounded by only a small coterie of followers.

"Told you it would be short," Miss Ruby said.

Drones were attacking, spitting death from the sky, buzzing over the courtyards and the plaza. But in the plaza, they were having a meeting, and every time Bird tried to tell them about the danger, someone interrupted.

"The drones ... look out! Take cover!" he shouted, but no sound came out of his mouth, only the roar of Prophet Jed's voice.

"Repent! Repent!"

One by one, they were dropping, but nobody noticed. Blood flowed into the plaza, pooled, rose like the seas, higher and higher....

Look out! he tried to cry, but what came out of his mouth was "Repent, repent!"

Someone was shaking him....

He opened his eyes to meet Madrone's anxious gaze. The room was dark, and he'd been having another nightmare. Or was it a prophetic dream? Better not to think about that.

She wrapped her arms around him. They didn't need to speak. There was nothing to say. He breathed in her scent, felt her warmth. She was warm and alive, and they were together, in this moment. Stay in the moment. That was the way. Don't think about the pattern of the past, or what would come after. Just stay in this moment when she was there with him, offering comfort in the dark.

Chapter Forty-Two

LIVINGSTON AWOKE TO DARKNESS WITH A THROBBING HEAD AND a strong feeling of nausea. He was lying on a hard surface that was pitching and tossing, and every lurch made his head hurt more. The room felt small to him, though he could only see a dull grayness around him, and it stank of stale piss and old shit, which didn't help his stomach.

Fuck. Where the fuck was he?

I am Adam Livingston, formerly intel officer of the Navy of the United Stewardships, he told himself.

The bottom dropped out of the room and he crashed down, then it rose up again and slammed into him. The floor was rocking.

I am a navy man, he repeated. The motion, the nausea felt familiar. He knew, now. I am a navy man, and I am at sea.

With that, the memory of his mission rolled back to him. Yes, he had succeeded in leading the Navy of Califia into the trap prepared. And getting himself extricated, as planned. Then what the fuck had happened?

Saints' balls! How he wanted to vomit! Was there even a bucket in this stinking hole? To find out, he would have to move, and he couldn't, not just yet, couldn't raise that pulsing sack of pain that was his head without spewing all over himself.

Yet he was going to have to move, or end up lying in his own vomit.

An involuntary groan escaped his lips as he slowly turned himself over. Start with that, just rolling the head was painful enough. Something must have smashed into it. What the fuck had happened?

Had the squabs figured out his game? But no, they wouldn't do this. Would they? More likely lock him up in some cushioned lounge with an odorless composting toilet and a tape of meditation music.

He was on a ship. He was not seasick, he told himself firmly. Adam Livingston did not suffer from seasickness.

He had a concussion. Someone must have hit him on the head. That was why it hurt.

But what ship? Why? There was a sick feeling in his gut that had nothing to do with the concussion. Something had gone terribly wrong.

Another groan, and with a huge effort of will he contracted his stomach muscles, brought his head and torso upright. He clamped his jaws shut to hold down his gorge.

Now his eyes were adjusting to the dim light, although everything still seemed to spin and divide itself into multiples. A small metal room, like a sail locker. No portholes, but a dim light filtered into the room from under the door. It was about five feet square, long enough for him to stretch full length only if he lay diagonally. A small bucket stood in one corner, and that was some kind of mercy.

He lurched toward it, pulling himself along the metal floor with his hands, got his chin to the edge of it, and vomited.

Relief. But Mother Mary's twat, what he wouldn't give for some water!

He lay his head down, pushing himself feebly away from the bucket, and let the merciful darkness enclose him again.

When he woke again, the light filtering through the cracks seemed a little brighter. How long had he been out? He felt a raging thirst, his throat raw and his mouth filled with acid and the taste of bile.

The floor was still moving, with the long pitch and roll of a fast ship in a following sea. He could hear thumps from above, as if someone was moving about. And now he began to remember.

The battle, the explosions, the Califian ship under attack. The parleyers from the Gyre. The knife at his throat.

The Gyre freebooters had hustled him out of the saloon, up to the deck, over the side and down the boarding ladder back to their zodiac. The knife at his throat had somehow morphed into a gun at his back. He'd scrambled down with alacrity and they'd streaked back to the Gyre ship, with shells bursting all around them and the zing of lasers and bullets in the air.

Then they were climbing a ladder up to the deck, the Captain barking orders, the crew leaping to furl the sails and rev up the engines. They raced away from the battle zone as fast as they could maneuver.

Livingston remembered leaning against the gunwale, watching it all. One of the Gyros had remained by his side, continuing to press a pistol into his ribs. The man had greasy black locks, a ring through his nose, and smelled like unwashed socks that had been stuffed too long into seaboots.

"Uh, thanks so much for the extrication, but I don't think that's strictly necessary any longer," he had said, nodding at the pistol.

The man's eyes were blank as steel shot. Maybe he didn't understand English?

It had been a long wait for the Captain to come back. Not until they were safely out of the danger zone, the thunder of explosions now a dull murmur far behind them, did the Captain emerge from the bridge, striding across the deck, flanked by two heavily armed mates.

Livingston had offered up his most charming smile.

"Mission accomplished," he said. "I am in your debt. Now, if you gentlemen would be willing to furnish me with a zodiac or something like it, I'll head back to shore on my own and won't trouble you any longer. I'm sure the high command will see to your reward."

The Captain had smiled back, but his had definitely not been a charming grin. More like the baring of teeth of a cobra before it strikes, Livingston thought. The sooner he was off this ship, the better.

He remembered a low snick, the sound of a safety on a pistol being released.

And the sudden cold feeling in his gut.

"No trouble," the Captain said. "Guest."

In his mouth, the word had an ominous tone.

"Charmed, I'm sure," Livingston had carefully kept his tone casual. "But I do have a duty to make my report."

"Relieved of duty," said the Captain. Suddenly there were three more guns aimed at Livingston's heart. "Guest, for voyage back to Gyre."

Livingston's mind had worked at top speed, assessing his chances if he tried to run—not good. Could he back flip over the gunwale into the sea without getting shot? What were they, ten miles from shore? Too far! Overpower one of the mates, grab the gun? Jammed into his ribs, need to be fast. Super fast. Worth a try?

"My pleasure."

Twisting, chopping down at the gun, grasping—barrel in his fingers, almost in his grip, trigger ... fist in the gut....

Then darkness.

Fuck!

Did they really think they could get away with this? A blatant kidnap! The General would have their heads.

Surely he wasn't worth so much as a slave that they could risk displeasing the high command. Sooner or later they'd recognize that.

It was a comforting thought. But it was soon displaced by a thought much less comforting.

No, they wouldn't risk it.

Therefore ... therefore ...

Shit, his head hurt. He couldn't follow a thought to its logical conclusion.

Didn't want to.

Because the logical conclusion was ... they weren't displeasing the high command.

This was what Wendell must have ordered.

Fucking double-crossing pus-squirt!

I must have pissed him off, somehow. Never trusted me. You'd think delivering him back the warship and the Califian Navy would be proof enough....

But once he'd delivered the navy, he'd be expendable. His job done. His potential as a threat or a competitor neutralized for good.

Fuck!

Of course, he had to admit, he had delivered the navy but he hadn't *delivered* the navy. He'd reported their location, destination ... but he hadn't incapacitated the ships or destroyed their steering or cut the ropes. Could have, but he liked to keep his options open.

Okay. What were his options now?

Roll over, vomit again, pray they would eventually bring him some water at least. They would have to, if they intended keeping him alive to reach the Gyre.

Then what?

Try to bribe whoever brought him food?

With what?

Overpower him, hold him hostage, force him to bring me up on deck. Use my amazing superhero judo powers to take out the entire crew, capture the boat, sail her myself to ... where?

If only I had superhero judo powers, that could work.

Surely even that fucking prick of a general couldn't have meant for him to end his life as a slave in the plastics factories of the Gyre! Maybe this was only temporary. A lesson to be learned. A disciplinary measure. General Prickface would need him again, call him back. He had to. The alternative was unthinkable.

He went round and round the possibilities for a long time. He had nothing but time, after all. More galling even than the pain in his head or the fear in his gut was the thought that he'd been bested by that dickhead, pompous, rotten little sausage! That was just wrong. It couldn't be. Not him, not Adam Livingston, smarter than the average bear!

After a long, long time the light grew slightly dimmer. He heard footsteps. A clang.

The door opened a crack. A hand shoved in a glass jar full of water, and a couple of packets of chips. Then the door slammed shut again, before he had time to react.

He would worry about that in a minute. For the moment he had water, blessed water, sweeter than Mother Mary's tits! He allowed himself one precious mouthful to rinse his mouth, then made himself sip slowly. One sip. Two sips. Eat a chip or two—vile things but they would sustain life. Then another sip. Another.

There was nothing much he could do while they were on the open sea. But would they head back to the Gyre? He didn't think so. Not with a cargo to unload. Not if the Califian threat had been neutralized, as he was sure it had. Hadn't it?

No, they might steam away from the battle, but they would return, head down to the Port of Long Beach or the transfer terminals at Saint Kat's. Anchor close in. He'd be able to tell, from the ship's motion. Or lack of it.

Then, then he would make his move. What move? He wasn't sure, but he would find some opening. Lie low for now, get his strength back.

Get off this godforsaken hellcraft, and then ... then ...?

What should his game plan be?

Chapter Forty-Three

IN SPITE OF THE DANGER—THE SURVEILLANCE DRONES PATROLLING the skies, the chaos within the Refuge itself—or maybe because of it, Madrone made regular visits back to Beth's. Foot patrols were fewer these days, as the Stewards' resources were stretched thin by the army's advances in the Central Valley. Sometimes she risked a bike ride in the night. Other times she went with Bird and Anthony on their busking rounds and then split off to snake through the quiet streets and knock on Beth's back door.

"This place is a refuge for me," Madrone told Beth over yet another pot of steaming herbal tea.

"A refuge from the Refuge?" Beth said with a smile.

"Exactly."

"Everyone still fussin' and fightin'?"

"The techies have rigged up some sort of scrambler that seems to be keeping the drones away for now. But how long it will last, or what we'll do if they attack.... *Diosa*, I never imagined it would be so hard to work together!"

Suddenly, over their heads they heard three loud knocks, echoing down through the floorboards. Beth stopped, cup halfway to her mouth, her face pale.

"What is it?" Madrone asked.

"Our signal." Beth's hand trembled as she set down the cup. "They're here. The Lash!"

Three more knocks came from the back of the house.

"At the back door, too." Beth sprang up. "Let's go!"

"Go where?"

"The side door, obviously! Damn, I have to pee. But no time. The girls'll try to delay them, but we've got to get out!"

Madrone slung her pack over her back. Beth grabbed a small pack of her own, and snatched a pair of Atonement-Seekers' robes from hooks in the warren of dusty basement rooms. Within the space of a few short breaths, they were out the side door and onto a short flight of cement steps that led up to a tunnel of green, creeping through the dense tangle of shrubbery that pressed up against the side of the house.

The tunnel led to a hole in a brick wall that bordered the neighbors' estate. Beth wrenched away the board that closed it and pushed Madrone through the narrow opening. The rough boards scraped against her denims. It was a tight squeeze that required effort, like being born.

Madrone grabbed Beth's hand and pulled as she squirmed through, panting. Her hand was cold and clammy.

"Getting too stiff for this!" Beth pulled the board taut against the opening again.

They followed the line of the wall, screened by small trees and shrubs from the windows of the next-door house that looked out onto the open lawn. At the far corner, another opening led to a broad backyard, this one edged in climbing roses and fragrant jasmine. A narrow path was hollowed out behind the bushes, but it was overgrown and Madrone found her cloak catching in the thorns.

She slipped out of the cloak, bundled it up and pushed through the brambles. Now her skin took the brunt of the scratches, but she could move more easily, and adrenaline was the best anesthetic, Doctor Sam always said.

The next opening took them into a broad belt of ornamental trees bordering a wide lawn. A party was underway in the house. Music blasted through french doors open to a wide, brick patio where couples danced. Madrone could smell the barbecue and hear shouts and laughter. She also heard a soft whizz behind her as Beth lifted up her skirts to pee.

"Had to do it, even if I die for it," she whispered. "Slowly, now."

They crept along the wall. The bright lights of the patio would blind the partiers' night vision, Madrone knew, but motion, especially quick and sudden, would stand out. The trees they hid behind were only a partial screening, with much open space around their trunks and only low hostas covering the ground. They moved as if they were underwater, every step measured, in slow motion. A dog barked, and they froze. A small dog, by the sound of it, someone's pet who sensed or smelled intruders.

The dog yapped louder.

"What's he on about?" came a young man's impatient voice.

"He's got a squirrel fetish, old Petey. Someone shut him up!"

They heard the yaps receding into the distance, and a door closed. Breathing quiet sighs of relief, they resumed their slow stalk.

At last they reached the board fence at the opposite end of the yard. Beth pushed the third board from the end, and it swung in. She squeezed through, with Madrone following. There was a party in progress in that yard, too. Every window in the huge mansion was alight and the thundering bass of loud music echoed through the walls.

"Fraternity row, big party night," Beth hissed.

This fraternity seemed less affluent than the others. The lawn was shaggy, and there was no convenient screen of landscaping along the wall, only some big monkey-puzzle trees with piles of fallen needles below, littered with beer cans.

"Unfortunately, here we've got to get out the side passage," Beth murmured. "Bunch up your robe, and run!"

Beth took her hand and they made a dash across the yard. They had almost made it to the side wall when the sliding glass doors opened and the flood lights came on.

Beth and Madrone hit the ground and lay still. They were half-hidden in a pool of shadow, but half-exposed.

"Party under the stars!" a somewhat slurred male voice cried out. "Back to nature, baby! Come on!"

He lurched toward the trees, but a hand pulled him back.

"Let's go inside, Jimmie."

"What, you donkeyin' out on me?"

"No, I just want to go back inside."

"Me, king of the jungle! You, tasty piece of jungle meat!"

"Jimmie, there's bugs under those trees."

"Oh, precious baby scared of buggie-wuggies? How about snakey-wakeys? Like that—feel that!"

"You're drunk."

"Gloriously! Come on, don't be coy. You're no virgin."

"Jimmie, wait! There's something out there—look! Maybe it is a snake!"

"Look at what? That's just a piece of garbage!"

"No, it moved! Jimmie, go see what it is!"

"What, you think I'm crazy?"

"I'm going to get security!"

Beth rolled on top of Madrone. "Moan!" she whispered. "Pant like you're liking it."

Madrone began moaning, panting, and for good measure threw in a hoarse "Please, Jesus! Give it to me!"

Jimmie laughed. "There you go, darlin'. Not everyone's scared of bugs!"

"Let's find somewhere more private," the girl pleaded.

They heard the door close again. Beth made a dash for the side yard, Madrone close behind her. They ducked through an opening in the fence, and out to the street.

A taxi was pulling up to the door of the frat house, and Beth steered Madrone in the opposite direction. Private cars cruised, but no one was walking along the sidewalks and there were as yet no signs of active pursuit. But farther down the street, in front of Beth's house, an ominous dark sedan was parked, flanked by a pair of humvees.

Beth took Madrone's hand and pulled her into a narrow alley.

Halfway down was a locked shed. Beth pulled out a key and wiggled it in the padlock. The lock stuck, and she swore, but finally got it open.

Inside were racks of bicycles. Beth grabbed her own, and pulled out a blue one for Madrone.

"I hate to steal Cissy's bike, but she'd understand," she said. "We've got to get out of the neighborhood before they cordon it off!"

Madrone nodded, bundled her robe into her pack, and held the bikes as Beth relocked the shed. They sped off down the alley, away from the party houses onto dark, winding streets where big houses overlooked wide lawns. Beth led them on a labyrinthine route, sticking to quiet back streets but always heading out of the hills and down to the flatlands. They crossed a major thoroughfare and then wove their way through a neighborhood where the houses grew successively smaller and the lawns were replaced by concrete.

After about an hour, they found themselves back in the vast areas of rubble-filled slums. Madrone's back was beginning to hurt—the bike was just a bit too small for her and she either had to ride standing or crouch at an awkward angle.

"I think we can rest for a moment," she said.

Beth was breathing hard, clutching the handles of her bike as she stood astraddle. Madrone walked her bike over and took the older woman's hand. It was shaking.

"It's okay," Madrone said. "It's going to be okay."

"I was so calm, until a moment ago."

"It's when you stop that it catches up with you."

Beth was breathing hard now, almost hyperventilating.

"Take a deep breath," Madrone said. "That's right, in ... count to five ... and out. Slow and easy."

"Oh God! I knew it might come, someday—I thought I was prepared...." Beth gave a shaky laugh.

"I'd say you did an exemplary job of preparing," Madrone said.

"That basement door suggested it," Beth said. "We just let the shrubbery grow until it took over. We've used that route for patients before. Now, I suppose, they'll find it. I hope the girls will be okay. They know to play innocent—and most of them genuinely are."

"Ready to go on?" Madrone asked.

They turned their bikes and headed down in the dark across the silent nighttime streets.

Chapter Forty-Four

ONLY THE TECHIES WERE TRULY HAPPY, CRESS THOUGHT. RIVER WAS moping around like a sad-eyed donkey. He himself was as nervous as a newt on an electric fence. But the techies, they were like pigs in mud.

They were taking apart the consoles and the wires of the command center, burrowing into the system, trancing into the database, and examining the firewalls from every direction. On the rare occasions when they emerged, they seemed to have grown even paler and leaner than before, as if they were becoming wires, or the vibrating-string stuff that underlay the cosmos. Their eyes glowed like fluorescent bulbs, their skin looked fragile and bone-stretched as if flesh itself were merely an afterthought.

"You got to eat," Cress told Beryl. "Can't have a bunch of skeletons walking in the victory parade. Southlanders'll think we starve our techies."

Beryl just nodded and took the tray of soup and sandwiches Cress handed her. He followed her down and delivered a cask of fresh water.

"You all need to drink more," he told them. "Eight glasses of water a day. You dry up and blow away in this desert wind, then where will we be?"

"Thanks, Mom," Topaz said.

"I'm not nagging," Cress said. "I'm giving you a military order."

"Sure you are, Mom," Topaz smiled, and then they proceeded to chat on about backdoors and trapdoors and algorithms and highways, and Cress couldn't understand a word of it. But in the end, he gathered that they were working out a way to hack into the Stewards' main system, and to do it invisibly.

"All wars are ultimately wars of information," Beryl proclaimed. "Someday we won't bother with all this sweaty marching and bloody mess, and it will just be us, hackers against wardens, fighting it out in cyberspace."

"That day can't come too soon for me," Cress said. "Now let me see you eat something."

⁓

They had decided to reinforce the base against the day when the Stewards' Army sought them out. They called it "the Castle," for it had something of a medieval air with its high wall and secret chambers. They called the bunker where the techies worked "the Dungeon."

Cress set himself to strengthen the fortifications, clearing the ground all around the wall so there would be no cover for diggers. He hated tearing up the scrub, the spare and precious growth the desert provided. He had the troops chop it fine and layer it into the swales they'd dug, and he mulched the graves with it, so that when water did flow it would begin to break down and feed the soil. Not far away, the Central Valley came to an end and a range of mountains rose to bar the way to Angel City. There had to be water in those mountains, he thought, hidden springs, secret lakes of it. Soon, very soon, they would take those hills and begin to channel the water down, to infuse and renew the land.

And then ... just over those hills lay the ruins and habitations of Angel City, spread out like a tattered blanket over a dry land. What would they find when they got there? Did the Stewards still have the strength to mount an avenging army to come dig them out? And then repopulate the Valley with new conscripts and slaves? Or would the Army of Liberation find Angel City crumbling, burning from its own contradictions, ready to fall?

⁓

There was a movie River saw back in the City at the Old Movie Club, where everything was in black and white—and then the girl stepped into another world and suddenly it was all in colors, blues and yellow and greens. He felt like the opposite, as if suddenly his world had gone gray. Ace was gone, back to the City on the transports for the wounded, and he couldn't help but think if he'd been with them in that bunker Ace would still be whole, even though he knew that was probably not true. But if he'd been down in the bunker where he belonged, he wouldn't have been up shoving Kit into the spiny bushes and wrecking all his chances with her. The medics had fixed her up, carefully extracting each barbed thorn, but nothing could fix the mess he'd made of their relationship, and he felt simply wretched.

"You ever had a ... a woman?" he asked Cress. "I mean, not just a slit or a priestess, but like a girlfriend?"

"I had a wife," Cress told him. He stopped. He'd actually not been thinking of Valeria, he realized. The older griefs, for his mother and his sister, had covered over the fresher losses. But all griefs were the same grief, didn't the psychologists say so? All losses emptied the same deep well.

"She was pregnant with our first child," he told River. His voice was neutral, staccato. Just the bare facts, not the pain underneath. "Then she died in the epidemic."

"Sorry," River said.

But I can't touch that grief now, Cress thought. I can't let myself remember how happy we were, how excited for the baby, can't relive that bloody moment when Mama and baby slipped away. Let it stay underground, like the deep, subterranean flows of magma that press upwards to shake mountains.

"Look, River, if you're having problems with Kit, just go talk to her," he suggested. "Apologize. That's what people do—they have fights, even in the best of relationships. They make up. They get over it."

River shook his head. "Hurt her. I hurt her."

"So say you're sorry!"

Kit was back in the kitchen, peeling garlic, with little dots of band-aids on her arm. She glanced up as River walked in, then cast her eyes down again.

He stood and watched her for a moment.

"You real quick at that," he said.

She nodded.

"Kit ... just wanted to say, sorry. Didn't mean to hurt you."

"Been hurt worse," she muttered to the garlic.

He waited a long time, but she said nothing else and she didn't look up. Finally he walked away.

Been hurt worse. He knew that was true. She'd been hurt, and he'd been hurt. Two wounded animals butting at each other with bleeding heads, that's what they were. He'd looked to her to ease his pain but maybe she couldn't. Maybe she'd been hurt too bad, as he'd been hurt in ways he couldn't even feel. Maybe that hurt went too deep, down into his bones, his foundations. Maybe it could never really be repaired.

⟋⟋⟋

"Talked to her," River said. They were hunkered down over their dinner rations, up on the walls, supposedly having a strategy briefing before the nightly meeting of Command Council. "Didn't do no good. Hates this breed."

"Well, you can't make her like you," Cress said, dipping a tortilla into a stew made of beans and quinoa. The kitchen must have received a big supply of chili powder, he thought. Be nice if they made something other than variations on chili, just for a change.

"Can't do nothin'," River said sourly.

"Nothing?" Cress laughed. "What about liberating about ten thousand miserable debt slaves? I wouldn't call that nothing."

"Wasn't me done all that," River said. "Not alone."

"You're our strategic commander," Cress told him. "You've got a gift for it. Me, I'm the mulcher. I don't mind—I play my part. But without you, we wouldn't be here."

River shrugged. "A sojuh bred to fight."

"But not to think," Cress countered. "The thinking and the planning, the decisions you make every day—those you can claim. They're yours. They're you. But here's the thing, you can liberate the farms, you can command the army, you can conquer the whole fraggin' Southlands, but in the end, you still can't make one sorry little pen-girl like you if she doesn't want to. And that's the sad truth of the human condition."

"So, this breed doomed to be just a sojuh all his life?" River said.

Cress shook his head. "Unrequited love—that doesn't make you any less of a person. In fact I'd say it's likely that there's hardly a person on earth throughout history who didn't at least once fall in love with somebody that didn't or couldn't love them back. Welcome to the ground of tragedy and the inspiration for ninety percent of the world's love songs. 'I love you, you don't love me. It hurts!'

"But meanwhile, there's still a campaign to plan. A revolution to conclude. So, have a good cry, then buck up, bite the stiff upper lip and soldier on. Now can we go to the meeting?"

River nodded, and stood up. He would go to the meeting. He would soldier on. And if it turned out that was his doom, that he would never be more than the weapon they'd bred and trained, he'd get his revenge. He'd be the most deadly fucking weapon they'd ever forged.

There was a large room in the bunker where the guards had kept a coffeepot and a supply of chips, with a few beat-up tables and chairs. The Council met there, sitting in a circle, reps from all the army's divisions and working groups, trying to hammer out a strategy for the next assault.

River's head hurt. He ached with a physical pain that rang through his bones, but he was a sojuh, and he set pain aside and tried to focus. But there was a thrumming in the air that reverberated in his head, throbbing and pulsing.

"What's that?" Jasper asked.

Suddenly River realized what he was hearing. His body reacted almost before his mind could form the word and his mouth could shout out "Copter!"

He was out the door, screaming at the bugler to sound the call to take shelter. He pelted across the yard, running in a zigzag pattern as the thrumming grew louder. Lasers streaked across the yard, and he plastered himself against the wall, then ran on to the armory. There was a map in his mind, lit up like a vidscreen: where the big bazooka guns were stacked against the wall, where the shells were. He found them, and loaded one, then another and another, faster than he could have issued an order. Behind him came some of the men from his old unit, Deuce and Trace, and he tossed them loaded weapons and then followed them out.

The copter had strafed the camp, and he heard moans and screams but he blocked them out of his mind. The medics would take care of that. Instead, he looked for someplace he could take cover and still shoot, as the copter banked and turned over the desert and headed back for a second run.

"Cover the gate!" he screamed to Deuce. "North wall!" he barked at Trace. "Don't fire too soon! Wait to see the numbers!" Old training, still engraved in his nerves and muscles.

He dropped to one knee, half-sheltered in the doorway of the bunker.

"Stay back!" he yelled down to the reps who were still scraping back chairs and staring blankly at one another as the thrum grew again. The copter was riding low, leaving a trail of fire and blood. He saw it swoop down over the cooks' camp, and the urge to fire and scream was almost unbearable. He had to shut his mind, close out the image of Kit and her friends, and focus.

He was a sojuh. He was trained for this. He heard a blast—Deuce had fired, but too soon. The shell went wild, the copter banked, and now it dodged and zigzagged, making it harder to hit. But he locked onto it, and waited.

Wait, the instructors had told them, wait until the ID numbers painted on the underbelly were clear.

He waited, while the thrum became a throbbing roar, a sound that cut off all thought. He waited, as the copter swooped low again, as its backwash kicked up a cloud of choking dust that obscured his sight, as laser fire zinged past him to catch a writhing, wounded sojuh who burst into flame. He waited, the stench of burning flesh in his nostrils, until the copter was above him, the lasers trained on him, each number distinct....

He fired. The gun roared—the kickback slammed him into the wall but he braced himself and fired again and again. A spurt of flame in the copter's underbelly—the thrum lost its rhythm, the great tail began to spin, out of control....

"Take cover!" he screamed although no one could hear him over the roar. He pushed himself back into the doorway as the great beast plummeted. Its rotor smashed against the guard tower and spat out sparks of flame. The huge undercarriage skidded and crashed into the courtyard wall. A roar of flame—then a sound hit him like a club as the thing exploded into a blazing tower.

Cress pushed past him, yelling for water. From everywhere, survivors of the attack came running with buckets, pots, fire extinguishers grabbed from walls. But the copter continued to burn.

⟶

Hours later, when the fires had subsided to smoldering, they reviewed the dead. The kitchen staff and the medics had been hardest hit, and the bodies laid out in a sad line on the desert were mostly women, support staff, many of them former pen-girls who had followed Smokee down but taken roles that were supposed to be safe.

Smokee walked the line, looking down at the bodies of girls she recognized from stolen glimpses in the pens, from the days in the City when she had organized her Valkyries. She should feel sad, she thought, or filled with rage, or something, but all she felt was empty, as if she couldn't find that core of herself that *did* feel. Ever since she'd met her brother, she didn't quite know who to be. It was as if she'd split into multiple Smokees, like a photo copied and recopied, altered a bit each time. Travis brought back the young girl with all the painful hopes and fears she'd thought were buried in the concrete of the pens. There was that free and happy child who had run on the beach, and there was pen-girl Smokee, despairing and trying to die, and mother Smokee, fierce with rage and longing for her child, and warrior Smokee, on fire with desire for revenge, and there was the slow-budding leader of the Valkyries Smokee, struggling to bank the flames and turn wild revenge to careful strategy, responsibility. And she didn't know which one to be, or how to honor them all.

⟶

River walked the line in a state of numb despair. There was Deuce—he had forgotten his training, fired too soon, and missed. The gunner in the copter had followed the shell's trace back, and laser fire had scorched him to the bone. A sojuh's life, a sojuh's death, River thought. Where was he now? Did he go to the ancestors, as the Cityfolk believed? Or to some Retributionist hell? Did he even have a soul, the poor dumb breed? Or was he simply extinguished, a bug crushed under the Stewards' heel?

He was putting off the moment when he would reach the end of the line, where the cooks and kitchen staff were laid out. No one had come running to him to tell him she was alive. Those who might know had looked down, failed to meet his eyes. But he was a sojuh, bred to face the hard shit. He walked on.

She looked peaceful, he tried to tell himself. Her eyes were closed, she was at rest. But there was a huge laser burn running down from her right eye to her heart, the skin blackened and curled, the white bones of her face exposed. He stood above her and suddenly he couldn't breathe. It was as if a giant weight pressed down on his chest. He didn't feel grief or sadness, or anything, just the weight of a cavernous emptiness and a reluctance to inhale or exhale or to let his heart beat.

It was over. He would never hold her now, or teach her to take her own pleasure as the Temple of Love had taught him. He would never know whether or not in some deep part of herself she had dared to like him. He could have been kinder to her, could have understood her deep wounds. He could have just taken up her offer, had her in the bower, filled her with his seed and given her a child to replace her lost ones, a child she could keep.

He dropped to his knees, took her hand one last time. How cold it felt, that small, delicate hand in his own huge paw. She was only a pen-girl, and she had infuriated him half the time and left him angry and frustrated, but how much better it was to have her to think about, to swear at and wonder about and bitch at and even nearly hate sometimes, than to have only this great, echoing emptiness.

A tide of rage rose in him, dense and slow-burning as lava, searing through the nothingness. His body moved of its own volition, as it had during the attack. He grabbed a rifle and emptied it into the smoldering remains of the copter. But that was not enough, not nearly enough. He swung it around by the butt, smashed it into the metal hulk again and again, shattering every pane of glass that was still intact, banging against the nose as he let out animal grunts, anguished cries. Until even that was not enough. He dropped the rifle and used his own fists, pounding on the unyielding metal, punching dents into the side, welcoming the pain that drove out the deeper pain.

Cress didn't know what to do. River was hurting himself, and he should stop him. The techies were murmuring with alarm—they wanted the electronics kept intact. But River was a raging fury. No one could get near him.

Instead Cress stood looking at the dust on his boots, how it made patterns that were almost ripples, the false illusion of water. He remembered how he'd felt when Valeria died, and the baby with her, how he'd suddenly become someone else, not the proud, expectant father, the beloved husband, but the angry, lonely, bitter man who somehow felt more deeply familiar, as if he'd never really trusted the joy. Grief was like the underworld of the Greeks, a dark place of shadows and no one could guide you out of it. Anyone who tried, who looked back too longingly at those memories, got turned to stone.

It was Smokee, of all people, who went to River when the first wave of his fury was spent. He stood looking blankly at the copter and down at his own bloody hands. She came and stood beside him and picked up his bruised paw gently.

"Hey," she said, over and over again until she got his attention. He was staring into the empty abyss she knew only too well.

"You think you can't bear it," she said softly. "But you can. You gave that girl something nobody else in her poor life ever offered, your precious love. Maybe she was too dumb to take it, but it's with her now. If she goes to heaven or back to the ancestors or wherever the fuck dead people go, they're gonna know she was a real person. Somebody who was loved. That's all you can give to her. That's enough."

And as she said it, she knew that it was true. That she had always known it, somehow. Love had kept her alive in the pens—love and the memory of love for her parents, her brother. And then love for her child, who had surely loved her back. Love was the fuel that fed her rage, and love was why her Valkyries followed her and the liberados respected her—not because of her anger, not because of her power, but because they sensed the fierce love that drove her and craved the heat of that smoldering fire.

And the kaleidoscope of Smokees shifted and settled into one. One ruthless lover willing to kill or die in the service of searing, cleansing love.

"Now you got to lift your head and go out and love your army," she told River. But she was really telling it to herself.

She covered his hand with her hand, prying him gently loose from the cold grip of the dead with her own warm heat. They stood together for a long time, as night fell and the desert air grew chill. At last she was able to lead him away, to tuck him into a pallet in the bunker and cover him with a blanket as she might have covered her own child.

"Sleep," she murmured. "Sleep, River." She stroked his head and began to croon a lullaby, the song her own mother had sung them, the song she'd hummed to her own lost child and thought she'd never sing again.

"*Hush-a-bye, don't you cry,*
Go to sleepy little baby . . ."

Her own voice sounded small and uncertain. The desert wind crooned back at her, as if to outdo her and show her up, as if to assert that grief and desiccation were always howling around the edges of every tent. Yet she sang on, staking a claim with each note, marking out a territory that even death could not assail.

"*When you wake, you shall have*
All the pretty little horses . . ."

This is who I am. You can take my family, my body, my child. But this you can never take, never touch again. This lullaby. Pancakes with rabbit ears. A sandcastle. Not just memory, but power, and I am stronger than you because of it. My power. My victory. My love.

Chapter Forty-Five

L IVINGSTON HAD TRIED TO KEEP TRACK OF TIME, TRIED SCRATCHING A line on the metal walls of his cage with the edge of the metal button on his jacket. But he was not entirely sure his count was accurate. Three days, he thought it had been. But he might have lost a day, or a night. His head still ached, and he had bouts of unconsciousness. He counted packets of chips, but sometimes they brought him two, sometimes only one, and he had yet to find a pattern in it. He lined up the wrappers, rearranged them against the wall, folded them into paper airplanes and zoomed them around his cell. Of all the torments—pain, hunger, fear, helplessness—the sheer boredom was hardest to bear. At times he thought he'd simply go mad.

But he couldn't go mad. He had to stay alert. Watch for his chance. He fucking had to get out of this!

Now, at last, he was hearing a change in the engines, feeling the difference in the ship's motion. Yes, praise Jesus! He was certain of it. They were heading into shore.

That meant they would be unloading cargo, taking on more cargo. That meant change, and opportunity!

He spent a long time examining the door to his cell. Not a cell proper, he realized, just a small locker repurposed. The lock itself might be pickable. If he had anything to pick it with. But it was bolted from the outside. He could hear it sliding back and forth.

He had so little to work with. They had taken his gun, his knife, his wallet, and the crystal the City squabs had given him. Too bad—it probably wouldn't have worked for coms. Too far out of range. But it held a whole library, and that would have alleviated the boredom. He could have read *Moby Dick*, which he'd always meant to do and never quite gotten around to. Or *Two Years Before the Mast*. Or *Twelve Years a Slave*. Picked up some pointers.

But he still had a few tricks up his sleeve. Literally. A paper clip and a couple of safety pins concealed in his cuffs.

He spent the day crouched by the door, waiting, ready. Like a tiger coiled to spring, he told himself. Well, maybe that was an overstatement. Like a mousetrap ready to snap, more like it. But the engines had stilled, and today had to be the day. They would be unloading cargo, and close enough in to shore that if he could somehow get off the damn tub he could swim if he had to. He was still a little woozy but nothing was going to stop him now.

He waited, moving and stretching from time to time to keep himself limber. He would have prayed, if he'd been a religious man. Instead he spent the time rehearsing his options and cursing. General Snotrag. General Butt-fucker.

This was it! He heard the bolt slide. He took a long, slow breath, let it out silently. He would have an instant, no more. Stay relaxed, on the alert....

The crack of light widened, the door opened. He struck like a tiger, jabbing his safety pin deep into the hand that thrust chips at him. A howl—the hand jerked back and he followed, jamming his arm into the door, shoving it open, grabbing for the wrist, the arm, the neck of the Gyro. He grabbed the freebooter's jaw with a yank and twisted, snapping his neck.

The sailor slumped, and Livingston shoved him into the cell and bolted the door shut.

They had taken his shoes, so he ran in his bare feet, silently as a cat. Down the corridors, scarcely daring to breathe, into the hold where a mountain of gray plastic pellets were being loaded onto skips.

Two swabs were shoveling plastic, their greasy hair tied back with bands, their faces covered with sweat. Livingston plastered himself against a wall, crouched down behind a mound of pellets. Would they take a break? Would they turn their backs?

It seemed to take an eternity, waiting, crouching, his left foot going to sleep on him. They made their way down the huge hold, laughing and joking in some language he did not understand. How long would it be before someone missed the scut he'd killed, and came looking? He had to make a move.

Could he take two of them at once? But that might make a disturbance, raise an alarm. No, he could see a better way—risky, but every way was risky.

They were down at the end of the corridor. Their backs were turned. They were talking to each other, not expecting trouble. Now—now was his moment.

He launched himself up, leaping for the top of the skip. Grabbed it with his fingers, gripped it, and pulled himself up, over the side, his sore muscles screaming. He had lost weight in these last days, good thing!

He somersaulted over the top and into the skip, dove down into the pile of pellets. Plastic dust filled his nostrils and for a moment, he panicked. Can't breathe! But he managed to pull his shirt up over his nose, breathe through it. Yes, it was okay. Enough air circulated down through the pellets, he wouldn't suffocate. If he inhaled some of the dust and died of lung cancer twenty years from now—that would be a far better fate than what awaited him at the Gyre!

Now all he had to do was lie still, pray that he didn't have to pee, and wait.

It was an hour or so later that he heard another loud scraping. The light that filtered down through the gray of his pellet mound grew lighter. He heard new rough voices, the screech of skips scraping on the metal decks, the beep, beep of a forklift backing up.

Yes, yes. Please, Jesus! I'm sorry for every bad name I've ever called you!

Then he felt a scraping of metal, a shudder running through the metal down below him. The whole huge crate was lifted, higher, moving, banging down onto rails, now sliding with a screech like a fork on a saucepan ... oh, beautiful sound!

A clang, and the skip banged up against something solid and stopped.

Jesus God, Holy Mary, had he done it? They would have some kind of barge to ferry the containers to shore. Or possibly a crane?

What would happen to them once they got ashore? Hopefully they'd sit somewhere, waiting to be transported to the factory. Wait. Just wait.

Chapter Forty-Six

B ETH JUMPED INTO THE WORK OF RUNNING THE HEALING CENTER LIKE
a pony let out to pasture.

"You save your strength for what you do best," she told Madrone. "Me, I enjoy being in charge."

She organized shifts and rotations. She recruited from all the newer arrivals to the Refuge, and soon found everyone who had medical experience or first aid training. She supervised procedures and shepherded those who needed it through booster withdrawal. She organized the pharmacy and wrote out requests to be conveyed to the raiding hillboys.

Suddenly Madrone had regular time off, time when she didn't have to feel vaguely guilty and anxious. Best of all, she had someone to talk to over a tea break in the afternoon, while setting out supplies in the morning, or reviewing cases at night. Someone who wasn't just looking to her to make miracles, but knew the dull details and grueling routines that healing actually required.

"My skills are truly rusty," Beth told Madrone in a quiet moment as they shared a cup of herb tea in the patio outside the healing center. "Comes from twenty odd years of practicing in the basement. Can't get used to actually seeing what I'm doing."

"Your skills are fine," Madrone assured her. Around them, the garden of healing herbs perfumed the air. The indigo flowers of the gray-leaved sage glowed in the afternoon light and filled the air with their pungent fragrance. Greenery crowned the rubble with blue-studded rosemary and pink-flowered thyme. The Gardeners' Guild tended it now, and Madrone felt a small pang of regret for the era when she'd had time to hack away at the hardened earth and plant her tender seedlings.

"I haven't kept up with the research," Beth said. "Didn't have access to the journals."

"Most of the Stewards' research was stuff you wouldn't want to keep up with, anyway. 'Comparative methods of torture on uncooperative subjects.' 'Effects of virus 32109b on the aging primipara female.' That sort of thing. And if it was useful, it probably required drugs and facilities we don't have, anyway. We're not going to do cardiac bypass surgery or kidney transplants here. Just mostly treat wounds and injuries, and try to keep people as healthy as we can."

With Beth there, they decided to form a Healers' Council. There were about fifteen people altogether with actual medical training. Aside from Madrone, Beth, and Thomas who had been an anesthesiologist, the other twelve were all young women who had been nurses or aides. Three or four more among the refugistas knew some first aid. Madrone got a work crew to haul in an old cement satellite dish that made a perfect fire pit in the center of the patio, and they gathered around what soon became called the healers' hearth every night to discuss their patients, share information and skills, and make plans.

"We need more training." Hepsie, one of the nurses' aides spoke up. Generally they kept silent, waiting for Thomas or Beth or Madrone to speak. They referred to the three of them as the Doctors, in reverential tones. But gradually over the days they were getting bolder. "We should be improving our skills—in case something happens to one of the Doctors, Jesus forbid!"

There was a little moment of silence, breath indrawn as if she expected God himself to blast her with lightning for her impudence. The moment passed, and nothing happened except that Madrone beamed encouragement at her. Emboldened, she went on.

"And if the Stewards find this place, and we have to fight, we're going to need lots more people trained in first aid."

"That's a really great idea!" Madrone said. She was so happy to hear one of the women actually speaking up, taking initiative, that she would have applauded if the suggestion had been that they all learn to juggle. But the proposal was truly a good one. After some discussion, they decided to offer some bit of basic first aid training at every big meeting. Beth also volunteered to train a corps of lay medics to be prepared in case the Refuge was invaded by the Stewards.

"We used to do that for protests, back in the day," she said. "The Red Cross wouldn't go into a riot zone, but we did. In fact, that's how I got interested in going on in medicine in the first place."

"And we need to train more skilled people," Thomas said. "Madrone, I think that's your job. You have the most relevant knowledge. We should run a class for the older students in the school."

"You do that," Madrone said. She and Miss Ruby had achieved a truce, even an alliance, but better not to test it too closely.

Madrone suddenly found herself longing for the hills. She spent her days in the healing center and her nights in meetings, surrounded by concrete ruins. Dotted with plants, to be sure, but she was starving for true wild nature. Or home, where the City was a sea of green, its parks and gardens a riot of herbs and shrubs and flowers, and real forests lay just across the bay, with redwoods and tanoaks and arching, red-barked madrones, her namesake.

She was losing vitality. For hours every day she journeyed in the trance-worlds, healing, and that drained her energy slowly but surely, like a pin-hole leak in the liner of a pond. For balance, she needed to fill up again, to immerse herself in strong elemental energies.

If there was a source of elemental power here, it lay in the springs. She took to spending time alone down where the water seeped from the ground and pooled into deep reservoirs—not without pangs of guilt. She had to force herself not to jump up after five minutes of meditation to check on some issue at the healing center, or make sure Zap and Zoom were all right. And the drones, coming closer every day—how could she indulge herself like this when they were on the edge of destruction?

The only way out is through.

That was Maya's voice again. She heard it like a deep echo in her mind. What did she mean?

Maybe the only way she could truly integrate the bee-mind was to go through it into deeper mind, water-mind, rock. To where mind dissolves altogether.

At the edge of the pool was a jumble of concrete ruins, but within them the slabs had fallen so as to form a crack. One day she squeezed through, and found that a passage led downward. She wormed into a tunnel that grew narrower and narrower until she had to cram her shoulders through. Should she keep on, and with luck, find a place to turn? Or begin the laborious process of squirming backwards upslope?

The only way out is through.

Her headlamp cast a narrow beam forward. Through the crack ahead of her she caught a gleam of light, a bright reflection off still water. The tunnel constricted even more, so that she could just manage to twist her shoulders through, wriggling like an ill-positioned baby twisting in the birth canal. She popped out, nearly plunging head-first into a pool ten feet below her.

She clung to the narrow ledge above it, listening to the musical note of water falling drop by drop, ringing like a bell in the deep silence. When she switched off her headlamp, the dark closed around her like the sheltering flesh of a womb.

She was in an earth-womb. Well, not earth exactly but concrete was a form of earth, and solidity embraced her. The silence and darkness felt pregnant with possibilities. In such caves the ancient shamans traced outlines of the spirit herds to birth the beasts into abundance. She was a midwife—could she not draw something forth from here? If she could commune with the bees, losing herself in the hive-mind, could she not commune with the springs?

She slowed her breathing, quieted her mind, and let the boundaries and divisions disappear. She was a vessel. In her veins coursed the living memory of primal seas streaming in circular currents and swelling with the moon-called tides.

Just as rock was frozen consciousness, water was awareness on the move. Every drop was alive. Each carried its own memories, traces of where it had been and what it knew. Each sought another like itself.

Water calls to water. Raindrop calls to raindrop. Molecule cleaves to molecule.

Water seeks the embrace of earth, seeps into her secret places, as if the whole world were enfolded by a great love, and water the visible and tangible flow, the sacrament, the outward sign of grace.

And I'm just a raindrop. A fleck of ancient stardust, the pearl that congeals around grit. A standing wave that arises where a stone cleaves the current.

The flow would continue, whether they won or lost, whether she lived or died. Yet each riffle added to the river's music.

She was filled with a river of love, for this Refuge that they'd built, for Bird, and Zap and Zoom, and efficient Emily and outspoken Miss Ruby and dreamy Anthony and crazy Janus and even their crackpot Prophet Jed.

For just a moment, she thought she could hear Maya's chuckle.

Love. What is it, really, but the great delusion that this other person is special, uniquely precious in all the universe? And yet it's a delusion we crave. We can't live without some base of it, some eyes that mirror back our infant smiles with amazement and wonder, as if no child had ever smiled before.

Delusion, and truth. For we are, each of us, unique and precious. We are special, every lumbago-ridden old geezer or lumpy, stolid lug or bustling, bossy matron, as radiant as the blazing stars.

Love peels back the veil, the Big Illusion, the lie that we are expendable, interchangeable. Love is grace, shed by the divine onto the ordinary world. And in the act of loving, of cherishing, we become real.

But then she was back, no longer a filament but merely a woman crouched on cold concrete above a dark pool. Some internal clock alerted her that Zap and Zoom would soon be out of school for the day, and they might be scared if they couldn't find her.

That is also love, she thought. I have become a mother, not by giving birth but by taking on the care of these boys. Just as you mothered me, Maya. When you taught me how to roll out a piecrust, when Grandma Johanna sat with me through my nightmares, whenever I hand Zap a sandwich or scrub Zoom's face, we channel the forces that birthed the stars.

Surely if we can do that, we can somehow hold and protect this Refuge. We can defend one small island of caring and healing in this vicious world. Surely, in spite of all evidence to the contrary, we can continue to believe that the powers of life and love and nurture will, in the end, prevail.

Chapter Forty-Seven

THE LIGHT FILTERING DOWN THROUGH THE MOUND OF PLASTIC slowly dimmed to dark. The chill of night settled on Livingston in his hiding place. He shivered. Maybe he had slept for a few hours, or possibly just passed out. Dangerous! His head felt like it might split open—the intense activity of his escape had not helped his concussion. Plus he was now dangerously dehydrated. His mouth was dry, his throat parched.

Nighttime. Time to go. But where? How? Lie still for a moment, and make a plan.

He'd escaped from the ship, and that had to be a good thing.

But he was alone in the bowels of Angel City, injured and battered, fiercely hungry, desperately thirsty, with no ID or money and nowhere to go.

Just for one moment, he was struck with a fierce pang of nostalgia for Califia, with its green streets and flowing waters and overhanging boughs heavy with fruit. Ah, to plunge his aching head into those cool waters, drink his fill! Pluck a peach from a branch and suck its sweet flesh.

No use wishing. Action! That's what he needed.

Best to make his escape now, in the darkness, before morning came and some officious inspector of cargo came along, or before they tipped the skips into the melting vats. Long Beach was his hometown. He had friends there, or once had. Now was the kind of moment when a man needed a friend. Who could he turn to?

He hauled himself up and over the side of the skip, shaking the plastic off him. He itched horribly, as if little grains of it had stuck to his skin, but there was nothing to do about that. If he lived, he'd make sure a shower was in his near future, no matter who he had to fuck or kill for it.

He heard a sound and a low growl, and suddenly a furious barking split the air. Oh fuck! Guard dogs! He could jump back into the skip, but suddenly he felt an aversion to that plastic tomb that made even the teeth of Rottweilers seem preferable. Instead he sprinted for the fence, terror propelling him despite his throbbing head and stiff limbs. He leapt, higher than he would ever have imagined he could, and managed to grip the chain links and pull himself up as the dogs growled below him and ripped at his heels. He felt his pants rip, and something sharp grazed his calf as he scurried up higher.

The ten-foot-tall fence was topped with razor wire, but it was designed to prevent thieves from getting in, not shanghaied sailors from getting out. It leaned out over the pavement at an angle, and he steeled himself, sacrificed his shirt to cushion the barbs, and crawled out onto it. The shirt was only a partial help—he could feel his skin tearing and little streaks of blood dribbling out. Damn, he couldn't afford to lose the moisture! But the barking, slavering beasts beneath him—and the guards who might at any minute come out to check on what the commotion was—that was enough to dull any pain.

There was no way to really grip the wire. All he could do was slither off the edge of the barbed angled panel, and let himself fall.

He'd often fallen ten feet in jump school, and he knew the trick was to relax and roll. Easy enough to say, harder to do with a fanged werewolf just a few yards away raising a commotion loud enough to wake a zombie army. He landed with a hard thud that jolted his sore head so hard he had to bite his lips to keep from screaming. For a long few moments, nothing existed in the universe except for blinding, all-engulfing pain. Each deep bark from the dogs set his brain ricocheting against his skull.

But he had to get out of there. Long before he was ready, he set off.

⁓

"Marilee?"

A shrill scream pierced the night.

"Shhh, please! It's me, Adam. Adam Livingston!" He was crouched against the wall of his old high-school girlfriend's house, only slightly concealed by a desiccated skeleton of what had once been a shrubbery. It was still shrubby enough to scratch, but that was the least of his worries.

"Adam?"

The window slammed down. He barely snatched his hands away in time to avoid getting his fingers broken.

All right, it's true he had ditched her at the senior prom and gone home with Betsy Ferguson, Betty of the Big Boobs, the guys had called her. But that was a long, long time to hold a grudge.

A piercing light assaulted his still-throbbing skull. The high-powered beam of a flashlight streamed through the window. It opened a crack, and Marilee's face peered out. He was too blinded by the light to see her clearly, but her voice sounded older, harsher than he remembered.

"What the fuck do you want?"

"Marilee, it's a long story. Can't I come in?"

"Are you kidding? My husband's in the house. I have children. I'll give you to the count of three to explain yourself before I call the cops."

"I've done nothing wrong, I swear it! Please ..." Livingston was aware of a kind of cringing whine in his voice. Shit!

"One ..."

"I was kidnapped by a Gyre slaver—managed to escape ... injured ... just need to clean up, rest a bit ... water...."

"Two. And try the truth!"

"Marilee, I swear, that is the truth!"

"Three!" The window slammed down again.

Fuck. Heartless fucking bitch. Why did he even take her to the prom in the first place? She was a dog!

He opened his mouth to yell it at her, then stopped himself. He was a man on the run, no time to get into a shouting match.

Then the window opened. Her hand reached out, placed a plastic bottle on the ledge.

"Take that, just on the off chance some part of your fable is true. Then go, and never bother me again!"

The window slammed.

She had left him a plastic juice bottle full of water, precious water! It wasn't much, but it slid smoothly down over his rasping throat like a blessing.

You're an angel, he wanted to call through the glass, but he didn't let himself do that either. Or at least, only a partial fucking dog-faced bitch.

Okay, old girlfriend, no go. But he had a brother.

~~~

His brother, Tom, and his wife, Millie, lived in a small apartment just a few blocks away from the house where the Livingston kids had grown up. Its living room had sliding glass doors that faced a small, walled patio about eight feet square that Millie had crammed with potted plants, Livingston remembered. Should make it easy to pick out. Livingston wondered why she bothered, and how they could afford the water. Or maybe that was why she bothered, to flaunt that they could afford to squander water on ornamentals.

Fuck. If they were so god-cocked affluent, why didn't they rent a bigger place?

Their diminutive patio backed onto the alley where Livingston cautiously scouted. Yes, that was the one, he recognized the bougainvillea. There was a wooden door that led onto the alley, but it was locked and bolted. He upended a garbage can and used it as a launching pad to vault over the wall.

He landed heavily with a jolt that set a new roller derby of pain racing around his skull. Lie still for a moment. All these plants—would they have a spigot out here, to water them? No, that would be like leaving your cash out for thieves to help themselves.

Livingston's eyes had adjusted to the dark, and there was enough light filtering in from nearby houses and streetlights that he could pick out the small table and two chairs, the pots of flowers. A small, green watering can was set back between two pots, and he picked it up eagerly. It was heavy—something sloshed inside it. Eagerly, he gulped down the liquid within, although it tasted a bit like used bathwater. Probably was, even though that was against the law. Maybe that was how she maintained the plants, an illegal water-abuser. Was that soap he was tasting? Never mind, don't think about it. It was wet.

Now what? The sliding doors were, of course, locked and bolted and even if he picked the locks, they'd have a bar at their base. In any case, sneaking into his brother's home was a bad idea. Tom might think he was an intruder and shoot him.

It was close to dawn, and the patio was concealed from any prying eyes or patrols. Best to wait, and when daylight came, try the direct approach.

He squatted down, leaned back against the concrete wall, and closed his eyes.

A click woke him. Something cold and hard was pressed into his aching forehead.

"One move, and you're dead," said a cold voice.

Livingston opened his eyes.

"Tommy! I love you, too!"

The cold, hard barrel of his brother's pistol moved away, to be replaced by another blinding beam of light.

"Adam? You're supposed to be fucking dead!"

"Sorry to disappoint you."

"What are you doing here?" Tommy lowered the light and stared down at him, his eyes cold. He was starting to lose his hair, Adam noted, and hoped that wasn't a sign of his own future. Always assuming he had one.

He tried for a warm, fraternal smile. "Hoping for a bit of brotherly love. Can I come in?"

Tom eyed him suspiciously. "Are you in trouble?"

"Who, me?"

"What'd you do, defect?"

"Not exactly," Adam was beginning to lose patience. "Tom, I'm hurt, I'm thirsty, I've got to piss, although Jesus only knows how I have enough water in me to piss out, and I haven't eaten since the Lord pronged the Virgin."

"Piss in the flowerpots." Tom lowered the gun. "I do, all the time. Adam, you can't come in. I'm up for a security clearance, they'll have biometric sensors planted all over the house. Jesus God, if you've screwed that for me ... "

"Tom, I've done nothing wrong!" Adam declared.

"Somebody apparently thinks you have," Tom said. He sounded regretful, but determined. "And your family is the first place they'll look for you."

"You've got to help me!"

"Wait."

As if I had anywhere to go, Adam thought bitterly.

After a few moments Tom came back, shoved something into Livingston's hand, and unlocked the back gate.

"There's a sandwich and fifty bucks. Get yourself a room somewhere and sleep it off. And don't come back—it's too dangerous!"

He yanked Livingston up to his feet and propelled him out through the gate.

"And don't go home!" he hissed. "Don't bring this down on Mom and Dad! Whatever it is. They think you're dead. Maybe best to stay that way."

Home. He'd avoided even thinking about home, because he preferred almost any other port in a storm. At best, his father would wring his hands and lecture, and his mother would tie herself up in knots of anguish. But they were his mother and father, and fifty bucks wouldn't get him much more than a sleazy, skuzzy hole-in-the-wall for a night or two. When what he needed was quiet, and rest, and good food, and about a month of sleep.

But if Tom was right, and they were looking for him.... What would Wendell have done? If he'd been reported dead, they wouldn't be looking for him. But if the General had charged him with some crime....

Fuck him. He'd done nothing wrong. Nothing but what he was charged to do.

Well, maybe not quite the way he was charged to do it. But his little transgressions ... a killing here or there ... they had no way of knowing about them!

But they didn't need to know. If Wendell wanted him out of the way, he could just make up anything he wanted to.

Fuck!

Livingston was not a man given to self-pity, but a little twinge of it crept up on him now. Was there nobody in the world who cared for him? Who'd be happy that he'd turned up alive?

Well, there was his little sister. Mallory. She'd be fourteen now, a student in Miss Frances's Finishing School for Girls, being groomed for a match slightly above their station, maybe even for Trophy status. Not that she had Trophy looks, she had always been plain-featured, her eyes too wide, her face too broad, her blue eyes too watery behind her glasses. But she had a kind heart, his sister, and hopefully life had not yet knocked that kindness out of her.

Of course, Miss Frances's was guarded like a caliph's harem, but in his own schoolboy days, he'd considered it a challenge to the honor of St. Anthony's Naval Academy to get past those defenses and drop in on his girlfriend of the moment. If luck was with him, he'd still be able to.

He knew which room his sister had. It was on the third floor, fourth door down the corridor. Out of old habit, he'd noted last time he visited that the old oak tree which had furnished him with entry and exit routes in his younger days was still there, and not far from her window. Of course, last time he'd done this, he'd been fifteen years younger, twenty pounds lighter, and without the dizziness and intermittent agony of a concussion. But he couldn't at the moment think of a better plan.

He made his way swiftly through the streets, eyes alert for the Lash who might be patrolling, looking for curfew breakers. Miss Frances's grounds were surrounded by a high, spiked iron wall, but he balanced on a trash can to get leverage and then climbed over with only a few new bruises and gashes to add to his collection. It was the hard drop onto the ground below that once again sent his head throbbing and spinning. This time he allowed himself time to recuperate.

But not much time. Already the eastern horizon was turning from black to indigo. Once the sun came up, he'd have a much harder time staying hidden.

He quickly found the old oak tree, planted long before the Changes and now stretching tall and majestic toward the sky. It wasn't hard to climb, and he hauled himself up to the big crotch at the height of his shoulders and from there clambered up a ladder of huge limbs until he reached an upper branch as thick as his waist. He used to be able to walk out on it. Now he felt shaky and dizzy, but still, how hard could it be?

Harder than he would have imagined. With every step he felt his vertigo grow worse, until he had to give in, crouch down, and crawl along the limb. But he made it out to end, to the spot where it was only a short leap onto the ledge that ran along the Academy's brick wall.

He couldn't do it. His head was spinning and his legs were buckling and he just couldn't make himself stand up and jump.

Okay, think of your options, he told himself. You can stay here, and get discovered in the morning, and probably arrested. You can end up in the pens or back on a slave-ship, Gyre-bound.

Or you can jump. And hope that, if you miss, you land on your head and that's the end of it.

There was no hope for it. He had to do it.

Just get to your feet, he told himself. That's the first step.

He pulled his knees under him. Carefully, waving his arms to find his balance, he stood up. The branch rocked and swayed beneath him like a ship. He used to enjoy that.

The wall. It was a narrow ledge, only about eighteen inches wide, but if he landed right it held him easily and if he landed wrong, there was a downspout he could use to help stabilize himself.

No more thinking, he told himself with a glance at the lightening sky. Now!

He jumped. His judgment was woozy, and he landed hard, his head screaming again, overbalanced, grabbed for the pipe, and slipped. He slid down the face of the wall, but managed to just grasp the pipe in sweaty fingers. He was slipping ... his free hand groping ... whap! His other hand connected with the pipe. Now both gripped the downspout as he hung plastered against the wall, his legs flailing, his head a ball of agony. He couldn't completely stifle a deep groan as he found a purchase on the wall for his feet and walked them up, back to the ledge. With a twist, he righted himself.

Then it was an easy walk for a fit young boy to the fourth window. Unfortunately, it was a torturous, terrifying ordeal in his current condition. But he did it, moving along the wall inch by inch, always aware that sunrise was near.

Finally he was there. The sky was light enough now to let him see a bit, and he cautiously slid the window up and slipped into the room.

He was concentrating so hard on being silent that he almost forgot to breathe. He heard a soft sound coming from the bed that he fervently hoped was his sister's. Yes, there was the portrait on the desk of their parents, another of him and Tom. Thank calumny, the girls at Miss Frances's each had their own rooms, not shared dorms. He heard another sound, and suddenly realized that under the covers, someone was sobbing.

"Mallory?" he breathed. "Mallory, don't be frightened, it's Adam. Your brother, Adam."

Another sound, like a snort or a sob choked back. The blanket flew off, and in the pale dawn light he saw a look of such amazement and joy on his sister's face that for a moment he almost broke down with happiness.

"Adam? Oh Jesus, Adam! Everyone thought you were dead!"

She propelled herself off the bed and hurled herself into his arms, jolting his sore head even more. But he didn't mind. His arms closed around her and she began to sob in earnest, but now for joy.

"Not dead yet," he said. "But Mal, I need your help."

She pulled back then and looked at him. Joy turned to shock and worry in her eyes.

"What happened to you?"

"Oh, that's a long story. And you shall have it, but if it's at all possible, I need a place to rest and sleep and some food and water. And a wash."

"What about a doctor?" she asked with concern.

"I'll be okay, if I can get the rest of it."

She didn't ask him for explanations, she didn't quibble or make excuses.

"You can stay here," she said after a moment's thought. "The maids just did our rooms yesterday, they won't be back until Thursday. If anyone comes, you can slide under the bed. I'll sneak some extra food from breakfast, and we get all the water we want here. The wash might be another problem, but I'll think of something."

"Mallory, I always said you were a princess!" Livingston said.

"Not really."

She got out of her bed, he got in, and sank down onto the thin mattress. She wet a cloth from her water pitcher and gently began to sponge the blood off his head. Livingston let out a long sigh, and passed into blessed unconsciousness.

Chapter Forty-Eight

O KAY, A, B, C, WHO REMEMBERS WHAT THAT STANDS FOR?"
Madrone stood up in front of the evening Council. Starting off with
first aid training proved to be a good idea. For one thing, it brought
everyone together in a common activity they didn't need to argue about.
For another, it reminded them of what was at stake.

A teenaged girl jumped up and called out, "Airway, Breathing, Cardio!"

"Right! Let me hear it...."

"Airway! Breathing! Cardio!" the crowd thundered back.

She'd recruited Zoom to be the unconscious patient, a role he thoroughly enjoyed, and as he lay prone in the center of the amphitheater
the same smart teen demonstrated how to check for obstruction of the
airway, see if he was breathing, and check for a heartbeat.

Then Madrone had them break into pairs to practice, and to practice
doing cardio compressions and mouth-to-mouth breathing on the dum-
mies she and Beth had fashioned out of cloth stuffed with rags.

This is a good thing, Madrone thought as she made rounds among
the practicing pairs. People were engaged. They had that alert, focused
look that told her they were paying attention, not the bored glaze that
often went with meetings. Every skill they learned, every new thing they
mastered, built that sense of confidence and helped construct that self
that so many of them had never been allowed to form. Who am I? No
longer merely a debtor or a pen-girl in waiting. I am a person who knows
how to save a life.

Bird stood watching her, smiling. This was one of the good moments,
when he could believe the Refuge would yet come together and learn to
work in harmony. He'd gotten news from the hillboys just that morning.
Califia's army was making headway, coming south. Their navy had won
a victory. If the techies could continue to buy them time, the Refuge
might actually become the nucleus of the uprising he imagined it to be.

But suddenly Prophet Jed strode into the plaza, his contingent of followers close behind. "Jesus is the only healer!" he cried in his thunderous voice. "God is our only defender, protector!"

"Where was Jesus when they took my child!" A gaunt woman leapt up and began screaming. "My baby, my Annabel, my beautiful little girl!"

She pushed her way through the crowd toward Prophet Jed, nearly tripping over the patients who tried to roll quickly out of way. "Where was your fucking God then!"

She was new to the Refuge. Bird had seen her come through the passageway just the day before. He liked to take his turn staffing the welcome center when he wasn't out on his rounds, liked seeing the wide, frightened eyes of the newcomers turn to wonder as they entered the plaza. But this woman had been shaking with a grief and an anguish so intense that her whole body trembled and her hands shook as she thrust forth a picture of the child that the grips had stolen from her kindergarten class.

"Annabel, her name is Annabel," she kept repeating over and over, as if the name could call the child back to her. "We were current on our debt, they had no right to take her!"

Bird had taken the picture from her and given it a long, thoughtful look. She was a particularly beautiful child, blond and delicate and innocent-eyed. A perfect plaything for some jaded Prime. He restrained himself from saying much, for what could he say? There was no comfort for such a loss.

"We weren't behind!" the woman kept repeating, as if it would have been somehow less odious if they had actually been late on their payments. Her husband had gone to protest to the authorities. That was two days ago, and he had not returned.

Bird had brought her to Madrone, although even she had no true healing to offer for such a loss. She'd given the woman an herbal sedative, and tried to get her to sleep. But how could you rest when your child was likely being raped and tortured? How could you not try to follow every imagined agony, trying to take them onto yourself? How could rest not feel like abandonment and betrayal?

He'd asked to borrow the picture of the girl, thinking he'd take it to the Angels. It was a forlorn hope, but they did raid the breaking pens and the pleasure pots, and it was better than no hope at all.

Annabel's mother—Lila, her name was—slapped Prophet Jed across the face. "Where was Jesus?" she shrieked. "You tell me, goddamn you! Tell me! Where was he?" She slapped him again. The force of her pain and fury was so great that he simply stood there, shocked into immobility.

Faith Prophet tried to grab her arm and Lila shook her off and wheeled on the crowd.

"This is all we've got!" she cried. "This is the last place! It's all we have left! How can you stand there bullshitting and arguing when this is all we've got!"

Madrone hurried through the crowd to reach Lila's side. She wrapped her arms around her, swaddling her in a great hug. Lila broke into tears, and Madrone just held her and let her cry.

The meetings had gotten slightly better once Miss Ruby instituted her walk-out regime. Once again, the prophet-heads and the worst of the disruptors simply stopped coming. But with a sizeable contingent boycotting the organizing of the Refuge, disorder began to disrupt all of their daily routines. Work shifts didn't get done. Watches were not all kept. There was a die-off in one of the big fish tanks because no one checked the pump, which had clogged. Children were cranky and Miss Ruby brought out the paddle more than once. When Madrone protested, she got a look that said, You aren't in charge here any more!

More of the homebrew liquor was circulating, and Beth was called upon to set broken noses and sew up split lips from a number of fights. Bird suspected there were other drugs in circulation as well. There were no locked doors in the Refuge, and they had never been needed. But now people began to come to Council with complaints of missing belongings. Late one night Bob heard screams from a dark corner and chased off two men who had cornered one of the teens and were proceeding to rip off her clothes. After that, many of the women became afraid to walk around at night alone.

Madrone went from feeling angry and heartsick to frightened. Were the Stewards to attack now, they'd destroy the Refuge and no one would be unified enough to stop them.

Bird was glad to escape the conflicts in the Refuge to go on his recruiting rounds, although he'd begun to wonder just what he was recruiting people to. That day, he was a blind singer. He took his guitar down to the "mall" in East LA, a labyrinth of small storefronts that sold necessities to the poor. On weekends, it became an impromptu street market.

Not much was produced in the Southlands, but such goods as there were vied with the lively trade in salvage. Vendors set out tables full of used clothing and worn shoes, mixed with linens still in their packages of twenty years before and battered toys and repaired appliances "guaranteed to work."

Bird put on a pair of dark glasses, took a white stick, and tapped his way through the market, looking for a good spot. There was a small, open space in the center of the crammed tables, but he rejected it. It was too confined, with no easy exit. He liked a spot on the edge of the crowd, where a side street was joined by a narrow alley.

He scouted the street and the alley behind for potential escape routes. Zap and Zoom were no longer functioning as his lookouts, now that they were in school. If trouble came, he would have little warning and no one near to help.

He checked to see if anyone was around. The alley was empty. A dumpster leaned against a concrete wall that was topped with barbed wire. Behind was a low, flat roof. Beside the dumpster lay a pile of someone's broken belongings, as if a room had been shoveled out. Torn, dirty sheets, a ragged blanket, ripped pillows and a couple of smashed chairs lay in a small heap atop a moldy sofa with broken springs. An old garden chair with its back broken off lay on its side. He righted it, and tested it. Sturdy enough, he thought. He leaned it against the dumpster and sat for a moment, as if resting.

Chair to dumpster to wall to roof. The barbed wire would be an obstacle, but the ripped and mildewed blanket could cover the spikes. He pulled it out from under a sad, stained, pink teddy bear and bunched it by the side of the chair. Step up on the chair, toss the blanket over the barbed wire, climb over, and run across the roof. He rehearsed the moves in his mind until he was satisfied that the route would work for him.

Then he tapped his way back to the market and stationed himself on a low wall running alongside a concrete building at the corner. The wall formed a small courtyard that was filled with vendors selling a sad array of shriveled oranges and misshapen lemons for inflated prices. He set out his hat for coins, and began to sing and play. While he would never be the guitarist he once was, hours and hours of practice had restored some facility to his shattered hands, enough to do a simple accompaniment for his songs.

He tested the crowd with a few Retributionist hymns while he carefully observed the pair of patrolling scourges, officers of the Lash. Once he was familiar with their patterns, he waited until they were at the far side of the square and launched into the Refuge Song. That drew a crowd to hear him. They stood gazing at him with a kind of hunger in their eyes, as if they desperately wanted the song to be true. His cap filled with coins, albeit mostly pennies.

This was good, Bird thought. It was something. But it was no longer feeling like quite enough. He was haunted by Lila's tortured eyes, by the endless arguments in their Councils and the feeling that things were coming apart at the seams. Something more needed to be done, and yet it was hard enough to keep what they had already built together.

But now the Lash were turning and heading back across the plaza. He quickly shifted to old love songs, early Beatles, "Michelle" and "Norwegian Wood." The crowd began to drift away.

The two scourges strode up to him, looked him up and down while he carefully pretended not to see them. In a loud voice, they demanded to see his permit, and he pulled out a battered piece of paper, expertly doctored by the Documents Working Group of the Refuge.

The larger of the two scourges took the permit and scrutinized it suspiciously. Bird forced himself to breathe slowly, but he began to mentally plan his escape route. Drop the guitar—that would be a sad, sad loss but he couldn't run fast with it and it would hamper him if he needed to climb or jump. Through the courtyard, between the old lady selling lemons and limes and the wall. Around the side street, into the alley and over the roofs. Adrenaline was pumping through his veins but he forced himself to stand calmly as the second officer picked up his hatful of change and pocketed all but a few coins. He was blind, he couldn't see it although a truly blind man would have heard the jingling and known he was being robbed. But a blind man would have done exactly what Bird was doing about it—nothing. No one argued with the Lash.

The scourge handed the paper back to him. Bird just stood there, carefully not seeing the outstretched hand.

"Take your permit," the Lash barked, and Bird reached toward the voice. The scourge slammed the paper into Bird's hand, and the two marched off.

Bird allowed himself a long, silent breath of relief, and resumed singing hymns until they were far away.

The rest of the morning passed uneventfully. Bird sang, and when the Lash was otherwise occupied, he shifted into the Refuge Song, and then, if the audience seemed receptive, he sang the Song of Rising. He was rewarded by murmurs and knowing glances, and side conversations that started up around the edges of the crowd.

When he stopped to retune, an old woman pressed an orange into his hand. He felt with his thumb along its waxy skin, and glanced down behind his glasses to see a symbol carved into the layer of orange outer skin. The white pith below displayed a spiral crossed by a horizon, crowned by the rays of the rising sun. The symbol of the new dawn, the new day.

Quickly he peeled the orange and ate it, resting his voice and grateful for the moisture and the energy. It was a long day to go without sustenance or water, and probably he should take such coins as the Lash had left him and buy himself a drink and a bowl of soup from one of the venders, if only to maintain his cover. Soup should be safe enough to eat, if it was hot. Once he'd made the mistake of buying a hot dog from a cart, and he'd had the runs for three days afterwards.

The afternoon wore on. In another hour, he'd pack it up and call it a day. The Lash were on the other side of the market, sampling the beer, and he decided to risk one last round of song, and this time, add the patter. So when the crowd gathered for the Song of Rising, he launched into his best imitation of Prophet Jed, albeit with a slightly different message.

"Thus saith the Lord, the first shall be last and the last shall be first. There will come a day, a judgment day, when the greedy shall be punished and a new day will dawn. Then will arise the army of justice and justice shall be done! Then will the mighty be cast down and the least among you rise to take your place among the great. All debts will be forgiven for those who march with the army of justice. All will be equal, each a captain of his own soul!

"Ask yourself, Am I ready? Will I be of that company? Am I prepared? For justice demands great sacrifice, but justice offers great reward. Prepare yourselves!"

He was feeling just slightly smug. He hadn't listened to Prophet Jed for all those hours without picking up a few tricks. But a little trickle of uneasiness began to crawl down his spine. He felt a sense of menace somewhere in the vicinity. Turning slowly, he scanned the crowd as well as he could while keeping his head down and his blind persona intact. A closed-faced man stood sentry in the back. He was a little too well-dressed for this part of town, and his hard-edged aura smacked of military or Intel. His cold eyes were fixed on Bird.

"But enough of my blathering," Bird cried out. "Time for a song!"

He launched into the old Retributionist favorite, "This Sinful World." But the crowd wasn't having it.

"Sing about the Rising!" a child cried out.

"The Rising Song! The Rising!" people clamored.

Suddenly, there was silence. The hard-faced man stood directly in front of Bird, staring down at him.

Bird willed himself not to react, but to keep tuning his guitar.

"Just what is this Rising you sing about, ratspill?" the man asked. His voice had an interrogator's dead lack of tone. Bird pushed down his fear, willed himself not to sweat, and said in the prophet's voice:

"Jesus rose from the grave on the third day. And with his rising he conquered death and opened the gates to immortal life."

The man reached forward, in a gesture swift and deadly as a rattler striking, and whipped off Bird's glasses. Bird saw a flash of light, even as he tried to roll back his eyes, and with his peripheral vision saw the man reach under his coat.

He moved quickly, grabbed the man's elbow, pivoted, using his leg for leverage, and tossed the spy over his shoulder. He crashed among the oranges, and Bird leapt to the top of the wall, pausing only for an instant to call out to the crowd.

"You are the Rising! We are! We will be the army of justice! We bring the new dawn and the new day!"

Then he was over the wall and pelting down the street. He ducked into the alley. His chair was still there, where he'd placed it, and he grabbed the moldy blanket, vaulted up onto the high wall, tossed the blanket over the barbed wire and rolled over it onto the roof. He pulled himself up and was off.

Below him, he heard sirens and shouts. Frantically, he scanned the roof for a good route out. They would pick up his trail quickly, he knew. He ran, dreadfully aware that he had to get out of the area before they threw a cordon around it. The block was like an island surrounded by streets too wide to jump. He could leap from one roof to another, but to escape he would need to get down to the street and across a wide boulevard, quickly.

His bad leg was beginning to pain him, and soon it would slow him down. Where to go? Somehow he had to get off the rooftops. As if to confirm his thought, a laser zipped by his head. He threw himself down and crawled. There was a trap door, leading into the building, held by a flimsy lock. He wrenched it open, and dropped down into a dark hallway that smelled of piss and stale liquor. He ran past doors with peeling paint and shoved aside a bleary-eyed old man who accosted him at the stairwell.

"Hey!"

Into the stairwell and down, down, leaping the stairs two and three at a time until he landed too hard on his bad leg and it gave way beneath him. He grabbed at the banister and just caught himself from plunging down, head first. Now his leg screamed at him as he carried on at a slower pace.

At the first floor, he hesitated. They might have guards already in position at the front door, even at the back. The hallway was lined with doors to tiny rooms. He tried one after another—all locked. But halfway down, he found a handle that turned.

He burst into a tiny bedroom, hardly more than a cubicle, where a couple of whiffsters lay in blissful stupor. They looked up as he shut the door behind him and pushed in the lock.

"Just passing through," Bird said as they lay, mouths open in surprise. The one window was small. He jammed it open, got his head out the opening and wriggled his shoulders to squeeze through. For one awful moment he thought he was stuck. The guards would find him in this humiliating position, and there would be nothing he could do about it. He pushed harder, scraping the skin off his shoulder, and then he was out. His hips and legs shot free, and he dove for the ground, rolling into a ball to cushion the fall. Something sharp cut through his shirt and ripped into his back. He was in a garbage-strewn courtyard enclosed by the building. Another trap. But there had to be a way out, some way they could let themselves into this space.

Dark was falling, but he let his eyes adjust as he looked around. There—a door. It had a lock on it but the lock was busted, praise the Goddess. He slipped into the narrow side passage crammed with garbage cans, and forced himself to move carefully and silently. A doorway led out. It locked from the inside, and cautiously he turned the lock and slowly pushed it open a crack.

He was in the middle of a long block. He could hear sirens, and see the reflection of flashing lights down at the corner, but in front of him, all was dark and quiet. He heard shouts and a shot rang out from the opposite corner, but the door blocked his view of what was happening. He could risk opening it slowly, but no. Better to do it fast, and get out of there.

He didn't hesitate, but pushed it open, stepped out, and closed it behind him. He forced himself to walk across the dark street at a normal pace. If anyone was looking, running would alert them that something was wrong.

The other side of the street was a rubble field of ruins. *Gracias a la Diosa!* From a dark patch of shadow, he slipped into a darker patch. He threaded his way through the labyrinth of fallen slabs and half-standing walls, heading away from the marketplace, moving as silently as a cat. He had made it outside the cordon, but there was no time to stop and relax. The danger was still too great.

It took him another full day to get home. He kept on the move, all through that long night, and at dawn found a hollow cave under a half-fallen brick wall where he could shelter through the day. The Intel guy had flashed something at him—most likely a biometric face recognition program. They'd be circulating his description, if not his picture, so he would need to wait until darkness to move. Lucky he still had his pouch, with his bottle of precious water, and what was left of the orange. He burrowed deeper beneath the wall, making sure he was entirely hidden, and then he slept.

He woke at sunset, ravenously hungry. As the sky darkened, he crept out of his den and sheltered behind a standing wall to relieve himself. The night was quiet, no sounds of pursuit, and he made his way back without incident. But it took him a long, long time, for he at first didn't know exactly where he was, and it was three hours before he found a familiar landmark. Then he made a wide circuit, to approach the Refuge not from the entrance but from the hidden passage on the north side.

The boys were asleep when he slipped into their apartment. The bedroom door was closed, but when he quietly pushed it open, Madrone sat bolt upright on the bed.

"Who's there?" she demanded.

"It's me. I made it back."

"Thank Goddess!" She threw herself into his arms and held him close. He smelled of sweat and rot and fear, but she didn't care. They held each other for a long time, without speaking. They didn't need to speak, Madrone thought. Better not to. Not to burden him with her fears, with the cold dread that had crept up on her when he didn't return the night before, with her determined efforts to force herself to sleep through the night. But she'd woken, again and again, from uneasy dreams, to reach for him and find only empty blankets. And then she'd lain back down again, heart pounding, using every breathing technique and meditation she knew to shut off her mind and calm her body.

No, if she were to voice out loud the fears, she would be fit for nothing but to cringe and hide.

"I knew you would," she said, instead.

"Someday I won't," Bird said.

"Don't say that!" she protested, squeezing him tighter. "Don't think that! That's bad magic!"

"It's just what is," he said in the old, cold voice. He was beginning to feel the reaction now. The exhilaration that he'd made it back, and the icy certainty that he was drawing down his store of luck with each foray out into the world. After today, it would get harder. They had him marked now, photographed.

"No it's not!" Madrone said firmly.

"Well, I'm back now," he forced himself to smile. "And thank Goddess, back to a place with our own bathtub! I'm going to go soak in it, and if you really loved me, you'd make me something to eat and bring it to me."

"Is that the test of our love?" she smiled back up at him.

"Well, you could crawl in with me and scrub my back, but I'm probably too tired to do anything about it right now anyway."

That was the way, he thought, keep it light. He was giddy with relief, and light-headed with hunger and the backwash of adrenaline. Slam the doors on all those alternate realities where he didn't come back, where he lay once again in a locked cell somewhere, his world reduced to pain and its resistance, his only question how long he could stave off the ultimate betrayal. And yet he knew that he would never give into them again. Whatever price they exacted, the long-term torment he inflicted on himself was worse. So in the end, he would have to count on his own body to end it, its breath refusing to fuel his blood, its heart refusing to beat.

Chapter Forty-Nine

L IVINGSTON YAWNED AND LAY BACK ON THE BED WHILE HIS EYES traveled over his sister's room. The bookshelves were crowded with books that spilled over onto the desk and stacked up on the floor. Her closet, on the other hand, was sparsely furnished with clothes. The dressing table was covered with brushes and mirrors, the drawers had an adequate supply of mascara and lipsticks all neatly organized. But it was nothing like the overflowing cornucopias of beauty supplies he remembered in the boudoirs of his paramours.

He had plenty of time to examine the room in detail, between bouts of napping. He'd slept, exhausted, until early afternoon, then awakened to discover a tray of sandwiches and a pitcher of water that Mallory had left him. With her usual organization and thoroughness, she'd also provided him with a pot to pee in. An admirable girl!

He inspected her books. She favored heavy subjects—tomes on biology and psychology and philosophy—some of them dating back to the old regime and most probably contraband. Not for her, the fluffy romances most girls favored. He looked for something to pass the time with. *Human Sexual Deviation* looked promising, but when he took it back to bed with him it proved to be a dry medical text. He read a few paragraphs and promptly fell back asleep.

When he woke again, dusk had fallen. He lay on the bed, not daring to turn on a light, contemplating the room and what it said about his sister. He realized now that he barely knew her. She had always been a favorite of his, a cute little toddler who followed him around and gazed at him adoringly, but she had been born a year after he left home for the naval college and their contact had mostly been at holidays when they were surrounded by the demands of family.

She was smart, he knew that. Always top of her class. Socially, a bit shy. It had worried their mother, who had insisted on sending her to Miss Frances's in the hopes it would break her out of her shell. Truthfully, there weren't many other choices. She could go to the university, later, but girls were limited to nursing and home economics as majors. There was no scope in the Southlands for a girl who wanted to read Kierkegaard and *The Biological Basis of Consciousness*.

In the North, now . . . ah, there was a dangerous thought. Had Mallory been born in Califia she would face no barriers or restrictions. She could indulge herself in deep thinking until her brow wrinkled up like a peanut, and no one would say a word of reproach. She could study any damn thing she pleased, become a scientist or a philosopher or a fucking engineer.

Would that be better for her than being some Prime's favorite Trophy? Or more likely, some junior officer's slavey in a tiny dive, surreptitiously watering her plants with bathwater in order to prop up her status.

He wondered how she was faring at Miss Frances's. She had been crying when he came in—what was that about?

Again, he dozed off. The click of the door opening woke him. He smelled something rich and meaty.

She favored him with a smile, and from under her jacket she pulled out a napkin-wrapped packet.

"Chicken tonight. You're in luck!"

She'd brought him two drumsticks, a handful of broccoli spears, and a hunk of bread, and he gobbled them down. Jesus God, was he ever hungry!

"Thanks!"

"Feeling better?" she asked as she gathered up the napkin, opened the window, and shook out the crumbs.

"Much, much better. You are a pearl among women."

"Glad somebody thinks so." She plopped down in the easy chair by the window, suddenly looking sad.

"What's up? Why were you crying before?"

"Nothing. It's just . . . I got kicked out of the Trophy Prep Program."

"Why? You've always been the top of your class in every subject." Livingston swung his legs over the side of the bed and turned to face her. Yes, his head was still sore but not nearly as bad as it had been. He was beginning to feel more like a man and less like a walking disaster.

"Said I'd never be pretty enough," she said in a low voice.

"Toad's balls!" Livingston swore. "Fucking piss for brains! Pardon my French. But can't the old prunes see how smart you are?"

"'Men don't like women who are smart, men like women who make *them* feel smart,'" she said in a simpering voice. "That's what Miss Frances says."

"Miss Frances is a hog-titted old bat!"

She giggled. "You're awful!"

"I'm your big brother. I'm supposed to look out for you." In truth, he could see Miss Frances's point. Mallory's features were on the plain side, her sense of style undistinguished. Not really Trophy material, unless some Prime wanted conversation and not just window dressing. He would, if he made Prime status someday. Or would he? In truth, his women had always been more decorative than deep. On the other hand, he'd always gotten bored with them after a short time. Part of the reason he had not yet married. But these were muddy waters for a man in his condition to tread. "I should go in and give her a piece of my mind. But ... maybe not just at the moment."

"What happened to you?" Mallory asked.

He gave her a carefully edited version of the truth. "So you see, only the General knows what my true mission was, and everybody else'll think I've defected for real. Somehow I've got to stay out of jail long enough to report back in."

"Why didn't you?" she asked abruptly.

"Why didn't I what?"

"Defect for real. I would."

"You would?"

"Why not? I could be a doctor up there, they say. And not have to marry some zitface Subprime bean counter!"

He arranged his face into a look of mild disappointment. "Mallory! The Southlands are your homeland."

She stuck out her tongue at him.

"Just promise me one thing," he said, serious now.

"What?"

"Don't ever say that to anyone but me!"

Chapter Fifty

I HAVE SOMETHING THAT MIGHT INTEREST YOU."
Wendell looked up. Standing before his desk was Ravitch, one of the faceless Intel men that he had sent to rove the city, looking for the source of his own unease. Something was rotten, something not right. He felt it, the taint, the creeping scent of decay. The drones had not yet brought back anything conclusive. But human eyes could ferret out anomalies the mechanical orbs would miss.

Ravitch had the cold, gray eyes of a killer, the bland, gray countenance of the born Intel agent. Nothing about him stood out or was distinctive, unless it was a certain chill that seemed to surround him.

He laid a sheaf of photographs down on Wendell's desk. They were of a young, turd-colored black man, a mongrel, in multiple incarnations. There he was, his woolly hair in a puff around a thin face, in hillboy camo. And there, his face thinner and drawn with lines of pain around the eyes and mouth, his eyes curiously blank, in a prison uniform. And here, now again, in the uniform of the Stewards' Army.

Him! Wendell recognized him suddenly, and glanced down at the files. Bird was the heathenish name he went by. Bird Lavender Black Dragon, if you could believe that. He read avidly through the file. His father had been a Durrell Parker, sometime musician. His mother, Brigid Greenwood—daughter of a notorious witch and heretic. He'd been given a Christian name, apparently: Charles Parker, but hadn't used it.

And he'd been at the center of the insurrection in the North.

Oh yes, Wendell remembered him. Two-timer, traitor, he'd been notoriously insensitive to torture but ultimately persuaded to cooperation when they'd threatened some little Pet of his. But he hadn't stayed persuaded. When all hell erupted on the fatal day they were driven out, he'd been at the center of it all, croaking out some demonic incantation, spewing his poison filth.

Now he was here! Yes, that explained it, explained so much of it! He was here, and now Wendell knew the source of the infection, the origin of the disease. Him!

It had to be rooted out. And he, Wendell, was the one to do it. Yes, now that he knew the source, he could destroy it.

The thought excited him, set that fire pulsing in his loins. But this was a fire he could stoke without guilt, the fire of purity that would burn away those other smoldering embers. What would it be like to have *him* back in Wendell's power, to play on the instrument of that body, a body that deserved the discipline and the pain, that cried out to heaven to be broken to the will of God?

The scum had gotten away this time, but not for long. Yes, Ravitch would find him, and bring him to judgment. Wendell would not simply kill him, although that would come in time, but would drive the evil out of him, purge and purify, and in so doing he would drive out the taint, the stench, and redeem himself.

"We'll put out an all-points bulletin," he said. "Ravitch, good work. I'll put you down for a commendation."

"Thank you, sir."

He turned to his own aide, blond, earnest young Finch. "I want his picture up on every vidscreen, $1000 cash and all debt wiped away for information leading to his capture. I want his stats fed to every surveillance camera, stationary and mobile. When he's caught, I want him brought to me. I'll interrogate him personally."

"Yes, sir!" Finch said eagerly. "Which picture do we use, sir? The most recent?"

Wendell contemplated the gallery, then plucked out the one of Bird in the Stewards' uniform.

"Oh no. This one! He looks the best in it, and if he has followers in his rebellion, it will give them something to think about."

~~~

Bird slept through the day, waking just in time for assembly. But when he walked into the crowd that had gathered in the amphitheater, something felt wrong. People who usually smiled at him turned their heads away. Friends who always greeted him looked elsewhere in silence.

"What's going on?" he asked Emily, who stood close to the front dais. Corrina, one of the other teachers, was facilitating.

"You're back!" she said. There was a note of doubt, almost of accusation in her voice that he found puzzling.

"Evidently."

"Your face is plastered on every vidscreen on every corner of Angel City."

"Yeah, they got a snap of me," Bird admitted. "But I'm a hundred percent sure I wasn't followed back."

"Your picture," she went on in a stony voice, "wearing the uniform of the Stewards' Army."

Bird felt cold, suddenly, flash-frozen.

Someone he didn't know was shouting up front. "He's a traitor! He's an agent working for them, just like Prophet Jed said! They've led us all in here and here we sit, like cattle waiting for slaughter!"

"All the time, all the time he was working for them."

Madrone saw him age before her eyes, his spine shrinking, his chest caving, imperceptible maybe, except to her eyes. He was growing more and more remote without moving an inch from where he stood, as if a receding tide sucked his life force away, leaving a husk in the sand.

"What do you say to it, Bird?" Emily asked coldly. "Or should I say, Sergeant Parker."

Bird turned his back on her and walked away, out of the crowd. Madrone started to follow, then stopped.

"So it's true," Emily said, her voice full of dismay.

"No, it's not true!" Madrone snapped at her. "*Diosa*, after all he's done for you, this is the trust he gets?"

Her words rang out in a sudden cold silence. Eyes turned to look at her.

"You've all worked with Bird for months now! You've seen what he's done and what he's given to this place, and the risks he's run. You're going to toss that all away because of one picture and a bunch of Stewardship lies?"

"Why doesn't he answer the charges, then?" Anthony asked. "Why did he run away?"

"Because he's hurt," Madrone said. "He'll be back. Just give him some time."

"How much time?" Emily asked. "How much time do we have, before the thrashers march in here?"

Madrone couldn't answer. She turned away to follow Bird.

Bird locked himself in the bathroom and ran the hot water. Might as well enjoy it before they hounded him out of here and ran him out of the Refuge on a rail. The sound of the water running brought a sort of oblivion. He could lose himself in it and forget thought. Liquor would be better but none of the rotgut hawkers would be likely to share it with him now. Better to trust to water, just water, pouring into the tub, hot, so hot it was close to scalding, as if he could scale away the guilt and the shame.

He submerged himself, welcoming the pain. It was a distraction intense enough to chase away thought and memory. As close as he could get to reproducing the effect of a neural probe. Pain without injury. Nerves shrieking, a pain like no other. Welcome it. Within its grace everything was simple. No thought, no questions, nothing to decide. Only endurance.

He was, if nothing else, durable. That is, what was unendurable, he could endure.

A loud knocking and a banging disturbed his reverie.

"Bird," Madrone cried, "let me in!"

After a long time, when the banging began to make his head ache, he called out, "Go away!"

"Let me in!"

This was it, Madrone thought, the core of their relationship. Go away! Let me in! It was the real reason, she realized, that she wouldn't yet marry him.

"It's my bathroom, too!" she called, aware that that wasn't at all what she wanted to say.

Zap and Zoom were staring at her, wide-eyed and frozen with anxiety. She tried to calm herself for their sake.

"Come on, Bird. You're scaring the children."

Silence. Zoom tugged at her arm, and handed her a stiff piece of plastic. She stared at it blankly. He sighed with exasperation at her dimness, took it back and slipped the plastic into the crack between the door and its jamb, sliding it up and tripping the lock. Madrone planted a light kiss on his head, then slipped in and locked the door again behind her.

"Go away. I don't know how you got in, but just leave me alone," he said, his eyes fixed on the opposite wall.

"I'm not going to leave you alone."

Silence. He submerged himself under water.

She waited a long moment. When he didn't rise to the surface, she reached down between his legs and pulled the plug.

"Hey, don't do that!" He sat up, reached for the plug but she held it away from him. He stopped the drain with his heel.

"Give that back!"

"Not unless you talk to me. Why did you run out of the Council?"

"I didn't run."

"You did. You ran. And you have no reason to run. You have nothing to be ashamed of!" she said desperately.

But he did. That was the crux of it, he thought. Rational or irrational. He knew how it worked. They did terrible things to you, and then left you feeling the shame of it. The guilt. But knowing didn't help. He did have things to be ashamed of. He had worn their uniform. He had served them.

"Bird, you've just got to explain it to people. When you tell them how it was, they'll understand," Madrone pleaded.

But he couldn't. It was his most private, painful place, and he couldn't expose it to the searchlight of scrutiny by people hostile to him.

He vaulted out of the tub and left her with Zoom clamoring for a bath and Zap whining that he had to pee. By the time she'd settled them and followed him out, he was gone.

Chapter Fifty-One

THE FORTRESS STOOD WHERE THE OLD INTERSTATE 5 MET HIGHWAY 99. It rose up, a solid block against the starlit sky, towering above the ditch where Cress and River crouched amongst the tumbleweed. Strong and impregnable, it straddled the roadways at the junction, surrounding the old off-ramps with barriers of concrete and razor wire. Above, sniper towers kept guard.

Within lay barracks big enough to hold a thousand or more troops, and giant warehouses where the grain from the Valley was stored, to be sent on to the factories that made the chips. Viewing the enormous structures, Cress understood how the Stewards were able to withstand the cutoffs of supplies from the plantations that the Army of Liberation had already freed. There must be enough stores in the silos before them to last for a long, long time.

Concrete ramparts stretched out to either side, and beyond them, steep-sided ditches were carved into the dry land, making it impossible to bypass or go around. Armories and helicopter launch pads were surrounded by a twenty-foot-high wall of concrete topped with razor wire. The road to Angel City was securely blocked.

"The place where three roads meet," Cress murmured. "The crossroads. Sacred in ancient times, you know. To Hecate, the Goddess of the Underworld. Goddess of death. The place has a Greek sort of quality to it. Like a Greek tragedy, where everybody dies in the end. But who the jacks were they expecting to invade? The zombie army?"

"Stewards not so worried about invaders coming in," River said. "Worried about bloodyback dusters gettin' out."

"Either way, it's not going to be easy," Cress said, surveying the stout walls and the vicious razor wire that topped them. "What do we do? Surround it, and hold it under siege?"

"Take a long time," River said. "And this army be exposed to their fire, or a copter attack."

"Can we go around it?"

"On foot, sure. With transport for an army, stuck like a drill in a snatch-trap."

"So what do we do?"

"Why ask this tubo? You the educated City squab."

"You're smarter than me," Cress said. "In this way, at least."

"Got to take it from the inside," River said thoughtfully. "Not possible to go in from outside—engineers too smart. Got to get in."

"We need a Trojan horse," Cress said, his mind still on epics and archaic myths.

"A what?"

"It's an old, old Greek story. Homer, the poet, wrote about it. The Greeks had been ten years besieging the city of Troy—couldn't get through the walls and the gates. So they pretended to be leaving, but they left a gift—a huge, wooden horse that the Trojans brought in. But it was hollow, and inside were soldiers. In the night, they came out, opened the gate, and took the city."

River beamed at him. "Like I said. Me—smart, but ignorant. You—kinda dumb, but educated."

"You want to build a giant wooden horse?" Cress asked. "I doubt that the breeds have read the *Iliad*, but some of the commanders may have."

"Whass the modern-day horse?"

"You're thinking! Didn't I warn you about that?"

The line of transports came down from the north just after dark. The guards at the northern gate were surprised—they weren't expected. But their papers were in order, and when they radioed back to Command, and Command texted the Northern Outlier Command that had presumably sent them, all the responses checked out. NOC had more troops than it needed, so it was sending five transports down to reinforce the base, as Intel reported a potential enemy force in the area.

They checked in the transports, and easily found space for the hundred sojuhs aboard. The barracks, River noted as they hefted their duffels and chose their bunks, were half empty. Good! Between the defections in the North and the reported troubles in Angel City itself, the Stewards' forces were stretched thin.

Although he had never been there before, the place was eerily familiar. All the Stewards' barracks were built on the same plans. Two long lines of bunks, with a common shower room at the back. He lay for a moment on the hard thin mattress, contemplating the bottom of the top bunk, and wondering how many hours of precious life he had spent like that, knowing nothing more, expecting nothing more. Familiar as his skin, the drill, the routine, the evening count and the dinner line, the meager chow of chips and stimulant-laced "coffee" brewed from roasted waste grain. There was a card game in the mess hall, the men sitting together in their units, making the same crude jokes and trading the same insults he had heard all his life. He could slip back into this life, and his whole sojourn in the City would seem like one long, fantastic dream.

Or he could play the part he'd volunteered to play. Oh, they'd argued about it, and Trace did his best to try and persuade River to stay back with the army, to protect his life and his command, but he'd had enough of that. The truth was, he didn't know if Trace could pull this op off, and he didn't know anyone else he could trust, who had both the experience and the sheer, raw guts to do it. He'd thought of it, all right. He would carry it out.

He didn't feel fear, exactly, just a heightened sense of awareness. He felt the blood pump in his heart, the breath whistle in and out of his lungs, as if they were asking to be noticed, to be appreciated in case they met their end. He observed the bare metal tables, the cold chairs, the slight stench of men in groups, sweat and unwashed socks and sour breath. It felt good to smell, to feel his heart pump, to be alive in a body still intact and unhurt. There was a hollow feeling in his gut and he had no appetite for chips but he forced himself to munch through them, for no sojuh ever turned down a meal. He sipped the coffee slowly, wishing for a cup of clear sweet water instead. Too many stimulants would make what was coming just that much harder to bear.

The meal ended swiftly, and the men gathered for their games and a precious hour of relaxation. The top braids ate in a separate dining room, he knew, where they were served real food. But the noncoms ate with the men, and they were sprinkled around the room. It wouldn't take them long to react. Just wait a little longer. One more sip. One more breath.

Suddenly the fear of missing his moment grew far stronger than his fear of what that moment would bring. He couldn't wait too long or the men would be sent back to their barracks and he would lose his chance. Now was the time!

He stood up, cleared his throat, and began to speak.

"Sojuhs of the Stewardship, listen up! This fighter ... *I* come down from the North, with a message. Sojuhs, the bigsticks, they lyin'! Stewards didn't win the war, the North drove them out like a pack of limpdrill curs with tails draggin' in the dust! And why? Cuz we fighters, we saw what they had in the North—a place where we could be free! That's right—croots and breeds and all! Free to be a more than a tubo clone, free to be a real person."

They were listening, he realized. Eyes turned and locked on him like a battery of rifles. He had to go on, had to use this chance to reach them. And he would address them not as sojuh grunts but as real persons, he decided. He would use "I" and "you."

"You there, maybe you a croot got caught stealin' water, you don't wanna be here. You there, maybe you sold to the army to pay your family's debts? You, over there—you a breed? I'm a breed. Yeah, that's right, I, me, born and bred for the army, Ohnine fivethirtythree sixteen-hundred, Unit Five. But in the North, I—you heard me! *I, me*, I'm not just a breed. I can be whatever I want to be.

"They got streets in the North where water runs free, free and open for anyone to take what they need. They got gardens in the streets, fruit hangin' down so you just reach up a hand to eat, tastes like nothin' you sorry chipsters ever put in your froghole! They got women like sweet heaven—shit, I can't begin to tell you! And you can have it all, taste it all, cuz they don't want war and they don't even want revenge. They just want peace."

A big noncom stood up. "Shut up, lying filth!" he yelled. He strode toward River.

"Ain't shittin' you," River cried out quickly. He had little time left, how to use it well? "Telling you the honest truth! Why'm I down here? Cuz you my brothers, every sorry jellydick tubo and crawler and breed! You got a choice now. You can be free! Just open the gates and walk out. Army of Liberation, they take you in. Open the . . . "

The big noncom smashed him in the head with a chair.

When he came to, he was tied hand and foot, laid out on a steel table in an interrogation room, staring up at a bright light that stabbed into his brain.

"Comin' round," a harsh voice said.

"Give the slime a wake-up call."

Okay, River thought. Now this sojuh get to experience the other side. He felt calm. Only the hollow feeling in the pit of his stomach told him he wasn't. But all he had to do was hold on. Hold on, hold out. He was still in his uniform—they hadn't stripped him. And that meant that his mission was accomplished. He would have smiled, but just then they touched the neural probe to his neck, just under the jaw line.

The pain was beyond anything he remembered from his training days, beyond imagining. His every nerve shrieked in rebellion. Pain took him—he was nothing any more, not a person, not a breed, just one shrieking nerve.

Hold on, hold on, he told himself. All I have to do is just hold on. Easy.

But it wasn't easy. He wanted to shiver and blubber and beg, as the pain receded. Beg them never to do that again.

He thought about Bird. Shit, he went through weeks of this, months, years. Worse. Iron man. What would Bird do now? Clamp shut the jaw. Shut the mind down.

"That was just a warm-up." It was a bigstick standing over him, not just a noncom or a juicer tubo, but one with braid all over his shoulders.

"Or it could be the end of it, as long as you tell us honestly why you're here, and who is with you."

River licked dry lips. Safer to stay clamped, he knew that. But "safe" wasn't why he was here. The noncom raised the probe again, he opened his mouth and gasped out, "Wait!"

"I'm waiting," the bigstick said coldly. "I won't wait long."

"You're my brothers," River gasped. "Even you. I'm here to free you!"

This time the pain was even worse, if that were possible. Maybe I can get used to it, River thought. But it wasn't designed to let a body get used to it. Maybe I just deserve it. This one for Kit, for hurting her. But that way lay true danger. Better to just surrender, but his body instinctively braced against it and that bracing made the pain even worse. To let go into it would be to accept it, accept all the unacceptable things. And yet, there was a strange relief in it. While he was in it, everything else fell away. Even that larger, deeper pain, the abyss of emptiness, of Kit's death and his own betrayal of her.

"I can't believe that even a breed could be that stupid," the bigstick said. "Not even one corrupted by the Northern demons. Are you going to continue to shield your masters? They aren't shielding you, are they, sending you in here when even a demon-crazed soakhead could predict this is what you'd get."

The probe again. Made death look sweet. Nothingness, to feel nothing at all. But hold on, he told himself. Can't die, got an army to look after. And there was a thought there, if the pain would release him for even a moment to follow it. An army that needed him, River . . .

The pain seemed to go on for an eternity. When the probe at the neck started to become too familiar to him, they changed and went for other sensitive parts. Under the arms, the base of the testicles. They could change the quality and the tempo—now he was burning, burning from the inside out, now it was an itch that couldn't be scratched, an irritation that built and built until it was worse than extreme pain itself. Bird had sent his mind away. But he, River—he had something to track . . .

"Who else is with you?"

"How did you get into the ranks? Who forged your papers?"

. . . An army that needed him. Him. River. So there was a "him." This, this burning, this raw scream of nerves, was a choice. He, River had made it. He had done it. He had become a person, a chooser. The mounting crescendo of pain was simply proof.

Suddenly, instead of resisting it he welcomed it. Bring it on, he thought. Turn the dial higher. Every screaming nerve cried out that he was real. This agony was his tribute, the birth pangs of River the Real Person. Make it strong, make it hot, bring it to the intolerable edge, and he would be born all the stronger for it.

And then it stopped. They shoved the probe into the hollow at the base of his throat . . . and nothing.

The juicer looked at the monitor with surprise.

"No juice," he said.

The bigstick slugged River across the mouth. The ordinary pain felt like a love tap, a welcome distraction against his still-shrieking nerves.

Then the lights went out.

They did it, he thought. The techies came through. Took them long enough.

In the sleeve of his jacket pulsed the transmitter that had allowed them access to the system. That was the plan, to get it into the heart of the Stewards' fortress, and it had worked. At a cost. Now if only he wasn't hogtied and helpless here. And if only his dear brothers remembered not to toss down an incendiary . . .

A sweet smell began to waft through the doorway. The bigstick opened his mouth to issue an order, but his head drooped and he slumped to the floor. The juicer followed him, crumpling like a piece of tissue. And River was nodding, his eyes closing, his pain easing into welcome insensibility . . .

⁓

Darkness. Cold clean air, sharp in his lungs. Darkness, but when he opened his eyes, the darkness was not complete. In a hazy glow deflected from the searchlights, a medic was bending over him.

"You okay?" the medic asked.

He pondered the question for a long moment. He was alive, and his body felt like his own again. His jaw was sore and his head hurt like the devil's throbbing balls, but he could move. All his limbs seemed intact.

"Got to go command the unit," he said.

He sat up. The medic pushed him back down again. "Got to rest, regain your strength."

Around them were the sounds of battle. They were lying against a wall, outside the central command, and he could hear shots and running feet and the boom of explosions.

"We're winning," the medic told him. "Techies opened the gates, we stormed in, your transports marched straight up, threw down their arms in a dramatic gesture and joined up with the Army of Liberation. A lot of the other soldiers followed suit, and we're just mopping up the rest. Got the bigsticks rounded up and hogtied, just like you said. Nice work! Hope it didn't cost you too much."

River sat up, and instantly wished he hadn't. "Wouldn't wanna do it every day."

"Getting up now," he insisted, in spite of his throbbing head, and the medic gave in and helped him to his feet. He staggered a bit at first, but soon found his balance.

He made his way cautiously along the wall, staying out of the line of fire, until he found Trace in command of a unit exchanging shots with troops dug into a bunker.

"The croots, they come over big," Trace said. "Got us a nest of breeds, though, hard to burn out."

"Let me talk to them," River said.

Trace rolled his eyes. "Wanna be a tigerfucker, get your head bit off, go ahead!"

"Kill the searchlights," River ordered. "Don't wanna stand out like a target in the practice range."

Trace nodded, and barked into his coms. The harsh light dimmed. Now there was just enough light from the snipers' towers to see shadows and motion.

River crouched behind a concrete pillar for cover, peered around it, and called out.

"Sojuhs of the Stewards' Army ... "

A shot pinged by him, narrowly missing his chin, but he went on. "Who you fightin' for? Got the bigsticks rounded up. Got half the army come over to our side. Why die for nothing? Put the guns down, join us, and be free!"

"Put the guns down and be dead!" someone called back from the other side.

River took a deep breath. "I swear on the bloody pouch of this sojuh's dam!" It was the breeds' strongest oath. "No slaves in the Army of Liberation. No breeds, no tubos, no bigsticks. Everybody equal. Like they say in the City, 'There is a place for you at our table, if you will choose to join us.'

"Gonna step out of the shadows now, where you can see me. Look me in the eye, see I tell you the truth. Shoot me if you want. And I say 'you,' cuz you a person, not just a weapon. Every stinkin' last one of you. Not just a breed, not just a sojuh or a fighter. Equal to the biggest braid, the stiffest-ass Prime in the world—equal to everybody!"

He stepped out into the cool blue light, and never had he felt more naked and vulnerable. There was a cold pit of fear in his stomach, but he pushed past it, and suddenly he was feeling strong and light, as if he could sail over the fortress on the high wind with the scudding clouds. It didn't matter, suddenly, whether they shot him or listened to him, whether he lived or died even though he was loving his life right now, his thumping heart and the bite of cold on his skin and even the rank smell of his own fear-sweat. The whole world felt new, and he was new, this "I" who was feeling and smelling and making this choice.

"Ohnine fivethirtythree sixteenhundred, Unit Five," he called out. "I was that. Now I got a name. River Black Dragon. I got a family. I a—I *am* a leader of the Army of Liberation. And I seen wonders in the North that you don't even know exist, but they can be yours, too. Water that flows free through the streets. Fruit you never even tasted, fallin' from the trees, free to pick. Knowledge the bigsticks keep from you, there it's free to learn. Thass your birthright too, if you're brave enough to take it."

It was the longest moment of his life, under the cold desert sky. A crazy throw of the dice, risking it all, all this new life that had opened up for him, all his grief and losses that were part of him, too.

Yet he also sensed that this was how they would win, in the end. Not by strategy, not by weaponry, but by making real people out of breeds and croots and debt slaves. Not by killing men, but by creating them.

Offering a choice. And he made himself that offering.

A late, gibbous moon rose over the concrete wall. A soft light illumined the yard, the huddle of men behind their bunker, the crowd plastered against walls and sheltering behind posts, watching the drama. A cool, gentle light that bathed everything it touched in a silver beauty. And suddenly he felt joyful. He remembered dancing in the Temple of Love, giving himself to the music.

This was just another sort of dance.

The great gaping hole within him, the abyss of loss and grief, all of that filled up with the moonlight and spilled over until the hard-packed dirt before him seemed a silver sea.

A sound, a soft scraping of the dirt, and one of the sojuhs stepped forward. He was dark, darker than River, and he looked around him warily, as if he expected any moment to be shot or captured. He clutched his rifle like a toddler clasps a blankey. But he walked forward.

"Threeforty seventytwo ohsix eleven fifty," he said. "Head of Unit Thirty, Division Seven."

River stood and looked at him, the wary stance, the eyes black holes in the night. He thought about Kit, suddenly, her wariness, her suspicion. But her memory was touched now with this same soft glow. He would like to honor her, to remember her.

"I name you Lion," he said. He gently took the rifle out of the unresisting sojuh's hand. "Welcome to the Army of Liberation."

One by one, the men stepped forward, handed over their weapons, and received a name. River ran through Tiger and Wolf and then ran out of inspirations. There were more big cats and fierce animals, he knew, but he couldn't remember what they were called. But then Cress was beside him, whispering him suggestions.

"Lynx." "Panther." "Jaguar." "Coyote."

"Welcome to the Army of Liberation."

Chapter Fifty-Two

B IRD DODGED FROM SHADOW TO SHADOW. HE WAS BEYOND THINKING, beyond feeling, without really knowing what he was doing, only that he'd had to move, to get out of the Refuge, away from accusing eyes and Madrone's worried glance. He was in danger out on the streets, but he didn't care. Worse than that, he relished the danger, the adrenaline pumping through his veins, the challenge of dodging from one dark corner to the next. Looking out for the Lash, keeping his eyes down so as not to glance into one of the security cameras by mistake. A pure animal wariness that took up all of his mental space and left no room for feeling.

He didn't know how long he'd been walking, or where he was going. It was a dark night, with no moon out yet, and he was deep in the zones where streetlights had been shot out long ago.

But far ahead was a glow, as if searchlights lit the hazy air, and he found himself headed that way. These streets were black and deserted. The Lash rarely patrolled here and there was nothing to secure, no biometric cameras dotted the burnt-out poles and bullet-scarred walls. He loped along, without knowing why he was running, just that he needed speed and air pumping through his lungs.

The searchlights lit up a huge compound surrounded by chain-link fences that enclosed acres of asphalt paving and a collection of concrete barracks. And suddenly he knew where he was.

The Stockyard, they called it. The Angels had described it to him. The transport site for pen-girls and racers and Trinkets and all the pleasure-pups that serviced the bigsticks and the Primes. On the outskirts lay the Pet Shops, and deep within, the breaking pens.

He thrust a hand into his jacket pocket and felt something there. A piece of paper. He drew it out. It was the picture of Lila's lost child, Annabel.

He'd shown the picture to the Angels, early in the morning before he'd set out on his ill-fated blind singer's mission. Gabriel had shaken his golden head.

"Hard to pick out one bauble from the toyshop," he'd said.

"Be with the wildings," Rafael had said. "That young—worth more unbroken." A long discussion had followed, but in the end they'd handed the picture back and declined to make any promises.

No matter. A sudden crazy idea took hold of him. He would find the girl. He would save her.

It was a reckless idea, probably suicidal, but he didn't care. More than that, he embraced it. It would be his release, his way out. Maybe he would die, but that would be okay. More than okay, it would be a sweet oblivion achieved with some small measure of honor. Maybe he would end up back in their prisons, back in that hell of pain and torturous choices. But no, he would not. He made up his mind. He would never again allow himself to be taken. He had no gun, but he had a knife. They would have to kill him to take him, or he would do the job himself.

He squatted down in the dirt. He'd run out without thinking or planning, just throwing on his darkest clothes and slipping away before Madrone could stop him. But he had grabbed his daypack and within was a precious jar of water. He spilled a little out now, on the ground, scooped up the mud and blackened his face and his eyelids. He would become a shadow.

His mind felt unnaturally sharp and clear. In the darkness, with so little for his physical eyes to see, his inner senses took over and he could *see* the lines of electric force running through the wires. *See* them, but could he do something about them? If he'd had a laser gun, he could have blasted through them, but that would undoubtedly set off some greater alarm. Staying in the shadows, he followed along the fence, tracing the lines until they converged together and dove underground.

See them, could he *hear* them if he put his mind to it? Light was vibration, vibration was sound. And tonight he was immortal, possessed by something larger than himself. The lines of force hummed to him, each with its own note. Together they made a chord.

What would happen if he sang the music back? Matched vibration to vibration, tone to tone? He hummed a note, let it reverberate in his chest and make his lips buzz. Cautiously, he reached out a hand and touched the fence where he knew the invisible wire ran. A deeper hum ran through him, not pain but pure energy.

In an instant he was over, humming his way past the wires, padding the razor wire on top with his jacket, grabbing it off, and leaping down. His bad leg screamed, but held him. He was inside the Stockyard.

He crouched in a patch of shadow next to the fence and watched the searchlights play over the wide stretch of asphalt that stretched before him. He counted out the timing, singing it to himself as the Song of

Rising, one verse for the light to pass, two verses of shadow. If he stayed in dark places, his eyes lidded, his teeth concealed, he would be very hard to see, even in the light. He picked out a route, pool of darkness to patch of gloom. Ready, set, run.

Bad leg hurting, ignore it, don't let it slow you down. Stop. Crouch. Hold still as the light passes. Ready—and run again. No room for any other thoughts. Down. Still. Up. Move!

He'd made it. He plastered himself into a cranny between two buildings. Wait. Deep, calming breaths. Meditation to slow that racing heart. Watch, and catch the rhythm of the patrols. Think of nothing but the moment, the breath, the heartbeat.

And just for a moment, he realized that he was happy. Fully alive, every doubt and regret and human tie cast aside, just present here in his body, his heartbeat, his breath matched against the danger.

A wide street stretched before him, lined with the blank walls of what looked like concrete warehouses or windowless barracks. It led on for a few hundred yards, then butted into a well-lit avenue. The market, he recognized. Where buyers for the clubs and the top Primes came to replenish their stock.

It would be lit and patrolled, and busy even now in the last hours of the night. There was one shop, he knew from what the Angels had told him, that was reserved for "wildings," meaning children who were not bred as playthings but were captured or confiscated from their parents. They had not yet learned not to cry or scream, or make futile attempts to fight back. That added to the thrills, and the price.

If he had any chance at all of finding Annabel, it would be there. He needed a vantage point, a way to survey the street and find it. A rooftop.

There was a locked gate between the street he was on and the bright-lit avenue, and another high fence. He waited until the patrol passed him, then slipped silently out of his nook and dodged from cranny to cranny, heading back behind the vast warehouse that lay nearest the gate. The rear of the building was unlit, *gracias a la Diosa*! He had cover to reach the fence and swing himself up and over. From the other side, he leapt onto a metal fire ladder on the back of one of the shops and swiftly scaled it to the roof.

He threw himself down flat and crawled to the edge, where he peered over a parapet and looked down on the market below.

The light dazzled his eyes. Vidscreens above shop windows glowed with full-color displays of the wares inside, sequin-clad women with painted eyes and lolling tongues, dancers slithering up poles or draping themselves over a succession of wild beasts, posturing figures in high heels and corsets. There was something for every taste: women with perfect bodies, muscular men bound and chained, costumes of every sort from parlor maids to police, naked toddlers romping in a kiddy pool. Like a toxic version of the Temple of Love, he thought, and shuddered, feeling suddenly sick.

Across the street and down the avenue, he saw his target. The Wild Side, it was called, and the vidscreen showed a live-stream of a clutch of young children, some sleeping, some sobbing. One of them, he thought, could be Annabel.

It could also be any blond kid, and Annabel could be already sold and suffering her fate. But it was his best shot.

How to get across the well-lit street and into the shop? And what to do when he got there? He was beginning to formulate a plan, which as long as he didn't stop to calculate the odds might seem like a reasonable plan with a chance of success.

Carefully, he lowered himself down the ladder. He shifted his vision again to follow the lines of electric force, down to their underground cables. Somewhere there would be a transformer, a power box. Underground, no doubt, but if he could determine the cable that led to it. . . .

There, praise the Gods, close to him on the fence. He lay down on the ground, put his mouth as close to the cable as he could, and hummed a tone that brought him into the meld of currents. Then he began to sing a dissonance, a disharmony. He couldn't always summon the wide-open consciousness that allowed him to channel the power, but tonight he felt the energy flowing. His mother's power, she who'd taught him to sing to metal and trace the lines of electric force through solid walls. When she wasn't nagging him to do the dishes and stop pestering his brother.

The wires protested. They screamed back at him. Feeling slightly guilty, he nonetheless sang louder, with more intent.

The lights on the street flared sharply and went out.

The Southlanders were no strangers to power outages, he knew. They would see nothing out of the ordinary in it, and they would have a backup generator.

Before it could come online, he slipped through the sudden darkness over to the opposite side of the avenue and back behind the shops. Fire ladders ended a good ten feet above the ground, but he was pumped tonight and his strength felt superhuman. He leapt up and caught the lowest rung of one of the ladders with his hands, pulled himself up to slide his legs through, and scrambled up to the top where he could scurry from roof to roof. The buildings lay close together, with at most a three-foot gap between them. Not an easy jump with his bad leg, but if he was careful to launch himself off his good one, he could do it.

He'd noted carefully how many roofs he would have to cross to reach his target, and was onto it before the lights below began to flicker.

There would be a trapdoor, he knew. Thank Gaia, it had an electronic lock. Sealed shut with the blackout, but he sang it just enough of a sweet chord to flip it open. Down the stairs, quietly, quietly. There would be guards, and mams. He hadn't thought yet what he would do. He had once sworn his hands would never kill again, but that seemed like a different Bird from a different world. Now he was not thinking, but doing.

Some instinct stopped him just before the narrow stairway opened out into a dark hall. Someone was down there. He sensed rather than heard someone breathing, waiting....

He dropped to the ground just as a burst of laser fire raked the air where he'd been standing a moment before. He slid down the stairs and dove for the feet of his attacker, knocking him off balance. The guard fell with a crash and a cry, his laser rifle skittering out of his hand and clattering on the floor. Bird was on him with a chop to a pressure point on his spine that knocked him out and might have broken his neck. He didn't think so, but he didn't have time to care.

A door burst open at the end of the hall and bullets were blazing. Bird ducked, rolled, and came up to a boot that landed on his jaw in a powerful kick. He reeled with the pain but grabbed the leg and brought the guard down. He fell with a thud on top of Bird and grappled for his throat. Bird twisted but the hands were on him, squeezing. He was gasping, almost blacked out....

He kneed the thrasher in the groin. The hands loosened and he twisted free, groped along the guard's belt and grabbed his gun. Before he could think, he laid down a blast of fire.

The guard fell, limp. Down the hallway, he heard another cry and a thud.

He kicked the nearest door open, saw the light of the streaming cam above and smashed it with his gun barrel.

Minutes, seconds now. He heard a child's cry. He risked a call.

"Annabel?"

As his eyes adjusted to the dim light, he sensed a child look up.

"Annabel? Your mama sent me to find you." He struggled to make his voice soft, gentle.

A small child hurled herself at him and plastered herself to his leg. He reached down with his left arm and hoisted her up, keeping the gun ready in his right.

"What about my mama?" another small voice asked from the corner. There were eyes all over the room, trained on him.

"Any of you kids want out of here, come with me!" he called. "But now! Gotta move!"

Small feet scrambled and tiny bodies hurtled through the door. He shepherded them up the narrow stairway and out onto the roof. Holy fuck, he hadn't thought this out! How in Hella's name was he going to get them down and out of here?

When the last of them was through, he blasted the lock shut. Might buy them a short delay. The power was still out in half the street, might confuse things.

"Hold onto my back," he told Annabel, and placed an even smaller girl on his shoulders. "The rest of you, follow me."

He swarmed down the ladder, swung from the low rung and dropped into a deep squat. *Mierda*, his bad leg did not like that! But he was down, and now came a small boy after him.

"Swing from the low rung," he directed. "Now let go. I'll catch you." With a grunt, he caught the boy. Two little girls followed. The last clung long to the rung with fear, until he finally barked, "Let go, or we're leaving you here!"

She dropped, and motioning to them all to follow, he sped along the dark alleyway behind the shop fronts, carrying the smallest girl.

There was a deep niche behind a garbage bin, and he shoved them in one after the other.

"Stay there," he ordered. "I'll be right back. Don't make a sound."

He ran, his bad leg sending shoots of agony up his hip with each step. But he ignored the pain, speeding along the alley and a short stretch of asphalt until he reached the perimeter fence. He aimed the laser gun, and blasted a huge hole in the wire barrier.

There. If the guards went looking for his escape route, they'd start there.

Then he ran as fast as he could make his legs go back to the children.

They were whimpering with fear but he had no time to soothe them. He grabbed the tiny one again and she clung to his back. He grabbed Annabel's hand in one hand, his gun in the other, and with the other three following behind they ran in the opposite direction from his hole.

When they reached the fence on that side of the compound, he took the gun and thumbed it down to the lowest setting. Carefully, delicately, he popped wires one by one to make a doorway. He pushed it open and the children popped through. He followed and pulled it shut behind them. In the darkness, it was almost invisible.

"Let's go," he whispered, and they ran, dodging through back streets and alleys until he found an overgrown bush with space behind it to huddle together and hide.

Behind them, alarms were shrieking and searchlights sent streaks of light down the alleyways and set the sky aglow. But it was already lighter, no longer black but indigo.

Breathe. Calm the racing heart. Breathe again.

Five pairs of eyes looked up at him trustingly.

Then the mad ninja spirit that had possessed him suddenly deserted him. It was as if all the adrenaline drained from his veins at once, leaving him exhausted and terrified.

Oh Goddess, what had he done? He was out here alone, with five lives in his hands and all the forces of hell bent on tracking them down. He didn't have a glimmer of a plan. No escape route. No exit strategy.

And the sky was growing lighter.

Chapter Fifty-Three

S LEEP," MADRONE TOLD HERSELF. "I HAVE TO SLEEP. I HAVE WORK to do tomorrow, and healing, and my not-sleeping can't help Bird in the least."

But she couldn't sleep. She was filled with alternating fury and terror. The *cacacita* idiot! Running out like that, putting himself and all of them in mortal danger, because whatever he believed about his heroism, if he got caught they might torture him enough or twist the right knife to make him reveal the Refuge. Hella take him for dodging out and lending weight to all their suspicions. Let him die! Serve him right!

But oh Goddess, what would she do without him? How would she survive, if they took him again?

And what would happen to the Refuge?

Zap and Zoom had sensed her mood and been unnaturally well-behaved—a symptom of their own anxiety. She would have preferred it if they were their usual rowdy selves. It would have given her something else to cope with and think about. But they dressed themselves in their pajamas and went quietly off to bed.

Which left her all alone, with nothing to do but pace and rage at her own helplessness.

She down went to the springs. The boys were asleep, and if they awoke with some need, Anthony and Emily were not far. She needed some solace, some way to find that place where everything was perfect. Because everything so clearly was not.

Deep in her cave, she lay still. She calmed her breathing, tried to dissolve into the flow. In and out. Nothing but the breath, and the sound of water.

But thoughts of Bird kept intruding, sharp little waves of fear. He was in trouble, somewhere. She could feel it. No, that was her own panic. Let it go, and be part of the oneness. That was the work of the mystic. It would revitalize her, give her strength for whatever was to come.

Ah, but that's not the work of a Witch!

Maya?

The surrender into the ultimate—that's not your task. No, leave that to the gurus and the mystics on the mountains. Yours is a different challenge.

What? What can I do?

You can learn the geography of the otherworlds and to navigate among them, finding the right level for the work to be done. That requires intention, not dissolution.

Please, *madrina,* what the jacks does that mean?

And here I thought she was the brightest of my grandkids!

She's your only grandkid.

That explains it. The bar is low.

Johanna? Grandma? Oh dear Goddess, why does being dead mean you can't talk sense!

Let me put it to you this way, then.

Rio?

If you can commune with the soul of the hive, why not commune with the soul of the Refuge?

What do you mean?

If a virus has an oversoul you can wrestle with, so does the Refuge. Go hunting.

And so she did. She made herself a little anchor back to physical space and time, an energy thread she envisioned that connected her to the rock-solid concrete of her cave. Wherever she went in the otherworlds, she'd be able to follow it back.

Then she mentally dove deep into the springs' flow to replenish her own vital energy. Slowly she brought her awareness back up again, like a scuba diver coming up in stages to avoid the bends. If reality were a multilayered cake, then she was going not for the bottom, nor for the top tier, but for something in between, some layer of icing or fruit jam or heavy cream.

Here, she realized, was the layer of the hive-mind, the bee level, golden and sweet like honey. Up just a bit more, into a level that felt more human somehow. Like a colored image made of many dots. In the bee-mind, they were one solid mass. But here, she could see the individual dots and still see the field of color, the picture they made together.

The Refuge. A living green glow in a field of gray. A mist that congealed into something like a veil, or a banner flying in the wind, stenciled with shifting scenes of their mutual history. Here she was with Bird and their bicycles, and there was the charnel house of the Dead, and there were Anthony and Emily arriving....

If she watched long enough, she could see everything that had happened. And perhaps, if she watched even longer, she would see what was to come.

A brave but tattered banner, a threadbare flag. A gust of a breeze worried it, and the wind whipped it around whuffing and flapping. She could see the threads fraying, strained by the enormous forces that tore at it. There were gaps and holes and brown spots where mildew had eaten the fabric away.

Back and forth it flapped, and she began to fear that it would fly apart.

The holes, she realized, were wounds. They were empty, but a shimmer of pain like a heat haze rose from them, and a stink like gangrene.

All our wounds, she thought, all our wounds are eating us alive. How do we weave a new world with broken threads?

Pour a little love on it.

That was her grandmother's voice, what she used to say when someone had a skinned knee or a cut on their finger. She'd bring out the iodine and say, "Don't be afraid, now. I'm just going to pour a little love on it."

Madrone dipped into the flow as if she were drawing up water from a well. Water to wash that tattered flag, to shift the patterns of probability that governed its fate as she could bend the fate of an illness.

Filaments and currents spun themselves into threads, caressing and reweaving the fabric.

And there in the middle was a great black bird, its wings torn, blood dripping from its eyes. She cleansed its lacerations and set its bones, but its worst injuries were internal. To heal, it would have to drink.

You can lead a bird to water, but you can't make it drink.

That was Maya, sitting on a high peak with the flag flying above.

Horse.

Rio looked well and strong, his beard full and white as it had been when he'd first come to bring her back from Guadalupe after her mother was shot.

Mule, more like it. Johanna looked strong and capable, not young but full of a quiet dignity and power. *Boyfriend always was stubborn as a mule.*

"What can I do?" Madrone asked. "I can't reach him. Can you?"

We can knock at the door. That's what we do. The Dead, the ancestors, we're always knocking at the door.

Maya's voice sounded sad.

You can reach for him, and we can knock. But he's got to let us in.

Chapter Fifty-Four

CRESS AND RIVER STOOD AT THE BASE OF THE GRAPEVINE, LOOKING up at the road that climbed the hills ringing the Central Valley. To their left stood the remains of the old pumping station, now in ruins, where once the water from the North had been lifted over the mountains to feed the maw of Angel City, back when it was still Los Angeles. Now the aqueduct lay in ruins, never repaired after the Collapse and the quakes of the twenties. The great pipe was full of huge gaps where its metal had been mined to be melted down. Its concrete tubes lay on the sand like the emptied shells of a giant sea worm on some antediluvian beach.

They'd made their camp at the bottom. At the top of the rise, on the crest, stood a fortress ten times larger and stronger than the one they had captured at the crossroads. It commanded the high ground. They couldn't see it, but the scouts' reports had described it all too well.

It wouldn't be easy to take, Cress thought. Even the Greeks had only worked the Trojan Horse once. They would have to attack from below, with no cover. They couldn't besiege it—for there was no way to surround it and the fortress itself commanded its own supply line, the road to Angel City. Yet if they didn't take it, the Stewards could use it as a powerful base from which to launch an attack on the whole Central Valley. All the lands they had liberated could be taken back.

River had pushed them to move swiftly to this point. He wanted a forward post while they refortified the fortress they'd nicknamed Troy behind them. More troops were on their way down from the North, where liberados had been training and Cityfolk had been streaming in as word of their victories travelled home.

But now they'd been encamped here for a week, dug in with trenches and swales for cover, antiaircraft bazookas staffed day and night. They were waiting, and Cress was tired of it.

The sun was setting. River watched it sink behind the hills, wishing that Kit could see it. Wishing he could show her the Valley, the long stretch of land they'd conquered, lay it at her feet. See, he would say, this for you. All for you, and your babies and your babies' babies.

He wondered if she could hear him, in whatever strange place she had gone to. The old lady, she talked to the Dead all the time. But maybe it took a while, when you were dead, to figure out how to use the coms. Maybe that was why Maya never talked to him.

Suddenly he didn't want to look at the sun any longer, to see it sink behind the rock and be gone, gone like the old lady was gone, like Kit was gone. He could talk to her, but even in life it had been hard to get her to talk to him. And now there was nothing but the sadness. However many hard-won victories lay ahead, she would never see them, never hold her child again, never throw her arms around River's neck in the exuberance of a victory kiss.

He nodded to Cress and headed back to camp.

"So now what do we do?" Cress asked later at the Command Council meeting. They sat around a campfire in a large round pit dug into the desert soil. Someday, Cress told himself, it would be an ephemeral pond— maybe someday long after that, if they won, if the healing process were allowed to go on for generations, maybe in some far future it would hold precious water year round. But for now, it offered a bit of shelter, and the low earth walls reflected back the campfire flames and held the heat against the cold desert night.

"We've now got hold of a significant part of their food supply," Erik Farmer stated. "They're bound to come back after it. Our scouts are reporting food riots already in Angel City."

"We've got to take the Grapevine fort," Jasper said. "Techies can give you support, but they're building firewalls as fast as we can knock them down. So what we can do is limited, unless River wants to take a transmitter in a second time."

"No!" River said. He shuddered involuntarily.

"It wouldn't work a second time," Cress said. "Only worked once because they didn't expect it."

"We can't take it easily from below," said Beryl.

"We can't take it," River said flatly. All eyes turned to him, and he stared them down. "Can't take it. Air power could, or more bombs than we got. But with what we got, no. Not possible."

"So what do we do?"

River smiled. "We make like water. Go around."

Within a day, the first wave of transports rolled out. Every food truck, supply van, and captured vehicle they could find or make serviceable was filled with troops organized into platoons. Mechanics worked round the clock to make them operational, and the cooks stayed up all night, baking waybread and pemmican, and filtering water for the canteens.

River went with the lead vehicle, an open jeep reclaimed from the fortress's motor pool. He'd been up all night, too, organizing the line of march and supervising the troops as they checked weapons and readied their gear. He'd consulted with the coms techs to make sure the convoy had good communications and could stay together. He'd fended off the medics who wanted to dose him with painkillers to stay the ghost pangs that assaulted him in periodic spasms, residue of the neural probe. The pain would pass, and he needed a clear head to keep track of all the pieces of this operation.

As they crested the ridge, he halted the jeep for a moment, rose up out of the seat, and turned back. Behind them flowed a river of lights, evenly spaced, orderly. His troops. His men. His orders.

He had done it, he realized with pride. He had thought out the system and put it in place and made it work. Not Cress, not some techie from the City, but him. Maybe it was all those years of marching in formation and going on training maneuvers, when real kids were in school or playing with their toys. But he was good at this.

⁓

Cress climbed up one of the foothills, following a sandy trail over the rocks until he could look back over the whole, flat expanse to the north, all the land they'd fought for and liberated. In the golden glow of the low sun, the Valley looked enchanted, a place full of promise where wonderful things could happen.

But he knew better. This was the dry, cracked land he was born in. Whole sections had collapsed into sinkholes from the quakes and the emptying out of the water table below. Vast stretches had become barren badlands, and even the flat and featureless plain that still supported agriculture was salted and dying from the poisons with which the Stewards drenched their fields.

Yet he remembered his father telling stories of the days when the air was clear, and you could see the High Sierras rising up in the east. He remembered the play of the wind in the fields, how they would ripple like the waves of the sea, tossing the light back and forth like foam.

He was a man of Water Guild. He could feel the waters, retreated now deep below the earth, crying out to be replenished. His vision rippled and he saw how the land could be gently carved with swales and berms to capture every scarce drop of rain, to guard and cherish every dribble, infuse every trickle back into the earth. Then, once again, springs would well up, and vernal pools harbor delicate, ephemeral wildflowers. Wetlands would form, with cranes and herons coming to feed and wild geese resting on their long migrations. Shelter belts of fruit trees and nut trees would enclose green fields, and on the hillsides, meadows would clothe themselves each spring in brilliant tapestries of wildflowers, pink and orange and blue. Free farmers would till rich soil restored to health, dark and alive and fertile, and their children would swim in blue jewels of lakes and feast on peaches and almonds, free and unafraid.

And he was crying, suddenly, hugging a rock in the red-gold light of the dying sun. Under this land lay his mother and sister, and nothing he could do would bring them back or ease the terrible thirst of their passing. But he could bring water to their graves.

The rage and drive that had fueled him for so long seemed to sink into the land like the runoff from a storm, leaving him spent and tired. Tired of the raiding, the killing, the fear of being killed. Tired of that edge where fear disappears into a kind of silent clarity, where everything slows and the whole world seems outlined by a cold, blue light.

Bored, even. They had reached the end now. From here, the rounded hills rose and then tilted up into the steep sides of mountains, range after range of them, until they opened out into the broad valleys surrounding Angel City. A climb, and a last push, a final battle, or more likely, weeks or months of fighting, house by house and street by street. But in the end, the Southlands would be free.

Once, he had lived and breathed for that day; now he simply felt weary. What he craved now was only the land, and a shovel to sculpt it into an open hand, cupped to receive and cherish water.

Chapter Fifty-Five

T HE SKY HAD LIGHTENED FROM INDIGO TO GRAY, AND THE SUN would soon be up. People would be out and about in the streets, and the search would be on. It was vital that Bird get himself and the rescued children to safety.

But where was safety, and how could he get them there? A wanted criminal and five wanted children?

Oh Goddess, he'd been stupid. He'd been on some kind of a binge, an adrenaline bender, high as a kite and not thinking at all, not following any of the basic rules he'd taught to others a hundred times. Think. Plan. Don't go in without an exit strategy.

Guilt and recriminations hung above him like a pile of loose bricks poised to fall. Relax his shoulders, breathe too hard, and they'd bury him. He couldn't afford that now. He had to think. He had to get them out of there.

But he couldn't think. His head was buzzing and it ached where the guard had kicked him and he was so tired he could barely hold his eyes open. Johanna and Maya and Rio were all having some stupid argument, and he was drifting into sleep. And he couldn't fall asleep. He had to think, and act. But he didn't know what to do.

It's a classic. One of the great musical works of our time.

That was Maya's voice.

It's popular crap.

And that was Rio. He swore he could hear Johanna snort.

White folks' music.

Led Zeppelin sang behind in a high falsetto.

Why are you plaguing me with this right now?

"Stairway to Heaven." That was the song. Why was this argument playing in his head?

Stairway to Heaven.

Heaven.

Where Angels lived.

He closed his eyes, willing a map to appear in his head. Wait, there was his crystal. Think, idiot. He spoke a word, and it cast forth a holo. It couldn't pick up a signal to tell him where they were, but he could figure that out for himself. Yes, there was the Stockyard, there the alley, here is where they must be.

And Heaven was not far away.

⸻

"Rafael!" Bird said, giddy with relief and fatigue. He'd hurried the children along the alleys from bush to bush, gap to hideaway, until they'd reached the concealed doorway where he'd given the password to a steel-eyed Angel guard. The guard sent them down to this cavernous concrete chamber filled with mattresses arranged into little coves separated with velvet draperies. Lithe blonds were draped over velvet cushions, sharing pipes or plates of cookies. It was just after sunrise, but several were already sipping glasses of wine.

Safe, he thought. Against all odds, they had made it to safety. Thank you, Maya! Thank you, Rio and Johanna, and all the ancestors and allies and guardian angels of all sorts who had absolved him from his idiocy and let him rescue these innocents.

The Angel in front of him uncurled from his couch like a snake and stood looking at Bird and the children through cold, marble eyes.

"Dickhead," Rafael said coldly, and socked Bird in the stomach.

Bird gasped and doubled over, and by the time he straightened up, Angels had the children's arms pinned behind their backs. Gabriel had Annabel in a headlock and Rafael had a knife at her throat.

"No!" Bird screamed. "Don't hurt them! Kill me, do whatever the fuck you want. Whatever it is you think I've done, it's not their fault!"

The knife flicked. Annabel screamed.

Something small and silver glinted in a bowl of blood.

The other kids were screaming now in terror. Bird dove at Gabriel, who kicked him hard in the leg. He went down while the knives flashed again and again.

He rolled into a crouch, trying to rise on legs that didn't want to carry him.

The kids were still alive, screaming in pain. A younger Angel slapped pads of rags on their bleeding necks.

"Shut up!" Rafael barked at them, holding up the knife. They swallowed their cries and stood staring at Bird with eyes bleak with betrayal.

The other Angels moved to surround Bird with a ring of ice-blue eyes and frozen stares.

"Dickhead!" Rafael said again, and spit on Bird. "Slime!"

"What've I done?"

"Working for them!"

"No! No, never."

"Vidscreens show different."

The knife was still out. Bird knew that Rafael could flick his wrist and send it flying into his heart. Strange how little he'd cared about living just a few hours before, and how much he wanted to go on living now.

"Please don't hurt the kids," he said in a quiet voice. "Please get them back to the Refuge, whatever you do to me. The little girl's mother . . . "

Gabriel kicked him in the kidneys. "The little girl's mother," he mocked. "That make a wild-caught worth so much more than an Angel-breed?"

"No!"

"Nobody gives a dead rat's ass for the Angels."

Rafael held up the bloody bowl. "Tracker chips," he said. "That the plan, lead the thrashers here?"

"No! I didn't know."

Rafe handed the bowl to one of the crowd of younger Angels. "Get rid of them. Use the cats."

He punched Bird again while the slim blonde girl aimed a vicious kick at his bad leg. It buckled and he fell, and then they were on him, kicking him hard as Gabe yelled at him.

"Wanna do a rescue, come to the Angels! Wanna go on a rampage, ask the Angels! Wanna piss or fart or jerk off this side of town, fucking ask the Angels!"

Bird rolled into a ball, clasped his hands behind his neck, and endured. He couldn't fight them, not with the lives of the children at stake. Whatever they did to him, he deserved.

At last Rafael raised a hand and the blows stopped. He grabbed Bird's wrist and yanked him up to a sitting position.

"Now talk. Wanna live, explain!"

Well, he did want to live. But explain? He'd rather they just started kicking him again. But he didn't have that option. There were five innocent kids he'd dragged into his own madness. Their fate depended on his willingness to justify himself to these judges.

Yet he was his own harshest judge. He couldn't justify himself to himself. And that was the heart of the problem.

"They forced me," he said. It sounded weak, whiny, a little kid complaining, he made me do it!

"It wasn't the pain, or the torture," he began again. "*Diosa mia*, you of all people should know that sometimes you do things you're ashamed of in order to survive!"

Something shifted in the energy, a ripple in the steel.

"Or not even to survive," he went on, and in spite of himself he was shaking, some part of him back there, Rosa's eyes looking out at him through Annabel's. And now the words were spilling out, jagged, his voice breaking. "To protect ... to try and protect. And you can't. No matter what you do, how low you fall...."

"I put on their uniform. I sat in the plaza, day after day, handing out their water ration cards that nobody took. Can you imagine what that was like? I pretended, I never really served them, but they made a show of me, and I let them. I let them. I wasn't strong enough...."

He'd been weak, as he was weak now, too weak to keep back the sobs, although he knew that was exactly the wrong tactic for the Angels, who would only hold him in contempt. Contempt he deserved.

Was that what this night was really about? A way for him to erase that weakness with an act of such crazy bravado that no one could ever again accuse him of cowardice? Except himself.

One by one, the Angels turned away. Rafe threw him a blanket. It was rough, scratchy, and smelled like mildew and old sex. The fragrance of forgiveness.

"Get some sleep," Rafe growled, and walked away.

The children were curled up in a pile on the mattress in the corner. Bird lay down on a velvet-covered mattress that smelled faintly of spilled wine and wet dreams. If only he could sleep! Just go unconscious, into oblivion, with no thoughts, no nightmares.

It was dark in this Heaven, perpetual twilight. Ghosts twittered around him, as if he'd become an open channel to every ancestor who'd ever found themselves in hopeless circumstances. Every slave who bowed to the lash, every inmate of a death camp forced to load corpses into the ovens, every priest who'd ripped out a captive's heart to feed a greedy war God. *Diosa*, he had too many ancestors, all complicit.

What had he done? Running out like that, everyone in the Refuge would take it as an admission of his guilt. All they'd worked for, everything they'd built—had he destroyed it? Had he toppled Madrone's vision, as if it were less important than his personal pain or pride?

Some guys just get drunk.

It was Rio's voice in his head again.

Maybe that would be better.

Rio shrugged. He was sitting on the mattress that faced Bird's, his face lined and craggy but still strong, his hair white, the stubble of his beard grizzled.

Rescuing the children, that wasn't a bad thing.

I was trying to die. My suicide mission. But when it came down to it, instead of dying I killed, which I'd thought I would never do again. Bang, bang, bang, just like that. Without a second fucking thought. Who the fuck am I?

A dickhead!

Maya joined Rio on the mattress.

Ah, but he's our dickhead!

Johanna chimed in, nudging Maya with her hips to gain a little extra room.

Fuck you. You aren't real! You're in my imagination!

We're in your blood and your bones.

We formed you.

How real is that?

I thought there was somewhere I could go where I wouldn't have to carry those memories and bear those mistakes. But now they've followed me, and there is no refuge.

Johanna favored him with a little smile.

You can't take refuge from yourself. You can't hide away from your past and your choices. But you've done some good along the way as well. You aren't a total dickhead.

Well, that's something.

Rio's eyes were on him, luminous blue as if they were holes the sky shone through.

Regret can eat you alive. And if you let that happen, then they've won. But you can do something else. You can take that shame and regret, and step beyond them, and go on.

How do I do that? How are they ever going to trust me again?

Johanna gave him her Look. *Ever thought of telling the truth?*

Chapter Fifty-Six

WHEN DUSK FELL, THE ANGELS BROUGHT BIRD AND THE CHILDREN to the Refuge in the bowels of an Atonement-Seeker's cart. They'd quarreled over the four other children. Rafael wanted to keep them with the Angels. Bird wanted to bring them to the Refuge and find families to adopt them. In the end, he prevailed with the argument that if their families were still alive, they might be at the Refuge or someone there might know what had happened to them.

He arrived just as the Council had started. He brought the kids in through the back entrance and steered them toward the Central Plaza. In the end, he'd slept for a few short hours, but he hadn't had his wounds tended to or even had a chance to wash the mud off his face, and he imagined that he looked as bruised and battered as he felt.

When he reached the plaza and threaded his way through the crowd, kids in tow, the buzz began. Surprise, shock, accusations. The crowd parted like a gauntlet and he walked between rows of hostile faces. Then a small figure hurled himself at Bird like a missile, nearly knocking him off his feet.

"Dad! Dad!" Zap clasped his knees, and Bird knelt down to hug him. Zap pulled away. "You stink! Stinky pants!" He ran away cackling.

Bird stumbled back up to his feet. Zoom stood in front of him, his arms folded across his small chest.

"Mado's mad at you!" he announced. Then he turned away.

It was a long, long walk up to the front. He got himself through it with the comforting fantasy that he was walking up to a firing squad. A few more steps, the blindfold, please—and it would all be over.

But when he reached the front, all he faced were eyes—accusing eyes, curious eyes, a few pairs of eyes that were warm and friendly, more that were glaring at him with cold suspicion.

The children he'd rescued waited behind him as he stepped up to the speakers' place and turned to face them all. This was it, he thought. If he were going to ask these people, his people, to accept him, he had to accept himself. Not the impervious hero, not the visionary, selfless leader. Just the man that he was, human, susceptible to pressure and pain.

All debts will be forgiven,
At the hearth and the sacred tree.

The song ran through his head. Suddenly he believed it. He could lay down this burden, let go of his failures and his shame, and simply tell the truth.

"I'm sorry I haven't stepped up before this to explain some things," he began. "The truth is, this is hard for me to talk about. It brings back the most painful time of my life."

There was dead silence in the crowd as Bird struggled for another breath. He felt short of air, as if he were surrounded by vacuum.

In the silence, Prophet Jed called out in his deep voice, "Pain is the wage of sin! Pain is the wage of betrayal! Thus saith the Lord, 'He who forsakes me shall have endless torment, while he who—'"

"SHUT UP!" chorused most of the crowd, and this time no one, not even Jed's most devoted follower, clamored to let him speak.

Steady, Bird told himself. The pandemonium at least allowed him a moment to catch his breath. The chaos didn't quiet until Prophet Jed and his followers stomped out in a fury so tangible it left a scent in the air behind it, like the residue of smoldering plastic.

Again the crowd quieted, and Bird went on.

"It's painful for me to talk about this, but I owe you an explanation. I was in prison, here in the Southlands, for many years. I stood up to the beatings, the torture, the despair. I suffered, but I never gave in. They broke my hands—you may think I'm a musician now, but it's nothing, nothing compared to what I was or could have been. Anyway, I finally escaped and got back to my home in the North, just in time to prepare for the invasion.

"When the invaders took over, I got captured. I was tortured again, but that—that I could handle. But they threatened to kill and torture the people I loved most. And so I did what I had to do to protect them. Or I tried. I don't know if I made the right decision, or the wrong one. But I wore their uniform. And yet I never served them. I made huge mistakes, I know that! But I did everything I could do to undermine their rule.

"You don't have to believe me. You're entitled to have your doubts and your suspicions. If what I've done here over the last months with all of you hasn't earned your trust, well then, I'm sorry.

"You ask if I led you here into a trap. Believe me, I ask myself that every day. Maybe this wasn't the wisest or the most strategic thing to do. But I tell you this—we didn't begin this Refuge as a place to be safe. We started it to have a base, a base to spark a new Uprising.

"Every time we try to discuss our defense strategy, we end up embroiled in some bullshit argument. Well, maybe there's a reason for that.

Maybe we're not supposed to just defend this place when the Stewards walk in—which all of us know in our hearts we can't do if they really decide to go after us. Maybe we're supposed to have an offense, to bring the struggle to them, and bring them down. So that we don't need a refuge any more.

"And we can do that. I believe that if we come together, and act together, we can do it. I wouldn't have come here and risked myself and someone I love more than myself, if I didn't believe we can do that.

"I ask your forgiveness, now. And I ask you to trust what you know of me, how you've seen me behave. If we let the Stewards destroy that, our ability to come together and to work together, that's all the weapon they need.

"Most of all, I ask you to trust yourselves and each other. If we carry this struggle forward, we're going to face bigger dangers and more painful choices. We won't always make the right ones. Sometimes there won't be any right ones.

"But I believe we can trust the great forces of creation and compassion in the universe to work with us and through us. In the end, that must be our refuge, and our hope.

"Are you with me?"

There was a ripple of motion at the back of the plaza. Someone was hurtling through the crowd, plowing her way forward, calling out in ragged gasps as she ran.

"Annie, Annie, Annabel!" she cried, and the child ran forward, sobbing, "Mommy! Mommy!"

Lila grabbed the child in a fierce hug. Bird watched as Lila cried tears of joy and relief. This was his moment of reward, he told himself. Whatever came after, this was one small reparation for his failings and, hard as it was to open and feel it, he forced himself to breathe, and stay present in the moment, and let some of Lila's happiness trickle in.

The other rescued children stared out hopefully into the crowd, as if their own parents might be waiting there. Lila turned to Bird in wonder. "You did it!" she cried. "You found her, and you brought her back to me!"

She turned to the crowd. "Open your eyes, people! Can't you see that, whatever they made him do, this is a good man! I trust him, and I say that we all should!"

A roar of approval went up from the assembly. They chanted Bird's name, over and over again.

"Bird! Bird! Bird!"

> "Open your eyes,
> there's a new day waking,
> Freedom will rise,
> like the rising sun ..."

The Song of Rising swelled out of a hundred throats.

I should go up to him, Madrone thought. When Bob had rushed in to the healing center with the news that Bird was back, she had dropped the bandage she was applying to a sprained wrist and dashed to the plaza. Now she was caught in the back of the massed assembly.

She wormed her way forward until she was close enough that he could catch her eye. He gave her a little sheepish smile. She could see the bruise on his chin, the black eye, the way he stood as if his back hurt and his bad leg was about to crumble. Oh, she wanted to bind his wounds and slap him upside the head all at once!

She pushed on, and made her way up to him.

He looked heavy, as if he still carried the weight of all his mistakes. And yet they no longer seemed to bow him down. The boyish lightness she loved was all gone, as if he had grown up overnight. But he held his head high and his shoulders were straight and strong atop a back that could bear the weight of all their hopes and fears.

Gravitas, they called it. He had it, and she did, too.

He picked up the mic, and began to sing with the crowd.

> "Open your hearts,
> There's a new day waking.
> Freedom will rise
> Like the rising sun!
>
> "Now it starts,
> The dawn is breaking.
> Open your eyes,
> A new world's begun!"

Bird looked out over the crowd, their faces now bright with hope and determination. No choir of angels, no chorus of Gods, could sound sweeter, he thought. Whatever comes at us now, whatever we face next, we stand on this ground.

Madrone stood by his side, and reached out to take his hand, giddy with relief and a renewed sense of hope. The Song of Rising pealed up through the plaza, echoing on the concrete rubble they had turned into a city, and she could feel it binding them all into one whole again. The wounded and the healers—they all were both. Cowards and heroes, the weak and the steadfast, a rainbow of threads, all of them frayed and flawed. Yet together they wove one brave flag of defiance to raise against the tyranny.

Zap and Zoom wriggled through the crowd to clutch at her waist. Anthony and Emily and Miss Ruby made their way up and joined them. Tianne and her teens climbed up on the walls and even some of the prophet-heads joined in on the chorus.

They sang. And when the song was done, when the last chorus had trailed away, they sat back down to make their plans.

The next morning, Prophet Jed and the bulk of his followers were gone.

PART THREE

WHEN THE GROUND
BENEATH SHIFTS

Chapter Fifty-Seven

How to Make a Revolution: II

Revolution, you must understand, is a form of magic. A sleight-of-hand trick, an illusion we make real.

Breathtaking, heady, like riding along with a mad Egyptian who is just learning to drive, who accelerates and halts in a jerky fashion, makes sudden turns across lanes of traffic, steers as best he can but is never in complete control.

Or maybe it's always seemed that way because I got lessons in revolution from one of the mad Egyptians who made the Arab Spring back in '11. Ahmed Salah was his name, and he was in exile here in the teens. I gave him driving lessons in the worst car in the world, a creaking old stick-shift Ford that stalled out and died incessantly.

Ironic, I thought, that my contribution to the revolution amounted to parallel parking. Yet both demand that you set your marks, apply both fuel and brakes judiciously, watch your timing. Know when to start and when to stop.

In between inches-away collisions and near-death experiences, Ahmed told me how they made the revolution. He and his friends had been working for years, decades, to bring down the dictator Mubarak. They had been arrested, tortured, outlawed—and seemed to have little hope of success.

Then the call came out over the internet—not from the groups who had been planning and organizing, but from some loner at his late-night computer: January 25 would be the day!

The organizers were dismayed. Nothing was planned. In no way were conditions ready. But they felt obligated to organize something.

Ahmed and his friends posed as journalists. They interviewed people and, when they found someone who admitted that they were opposed to Mubarak's regime, asked them if they intended to take action. And most said no.

People were afraid. They felt action was futile. Or they were so poor, so desperate, that they could not afford to take even a few hours off work, or their families would not eat.

But there was one set of conditions under which everyone agreed that they would come out to the streets:

When everybody else came out.

The task of the revolutionary, Ahmed realized, was to be the stage magician, the illusionist, the Wizard of Oz: To make people believe that now was the moment.

He and his friends started rumors. They went to markets and advised housewives to stock up because soon martial law would be declared. They told lies that became predictions. They planned small marches for narrow streets where a few people looked like a swarming crowd.

On the morning of the 25th, Ahmed awoke in fear. Not of getting arrested. Not of getting beaten or tortured. He had experienced all of those.

His fear was that the whole thing would be one enormous flop.

But instead, that was the day when everyone came out because everyone came out. The streets were full, throngs crowded Tahrir Square, the barricades were raised, and tyranny toppled. A great day, when the world changed.

The compromises and betrayals came later. But no disappointment can remove the memory, the possibility inherent in that heady moment when fear falls away, and the people rise to burst their chains and open their arms to a bright new dawn.

How to make that happen? Ah, that is the mystery.

All I can tell you is this: for people to believe an illusion, someone must spin it. To make a vision real, someone must create it.

For the story to unfold, someone must tell the tale.

A Century of Good Advice:
The Autobiography of Maya Greenwood
Yerba Buena: Califia Press, 2049

THE SUN ROSE OVER ANGEL CITY, OVER THE BROAD AVENUES AND THE
narrow sidewalks and the acres of ruins. A soft glow illumined the
worn faces of workers scrambling to do their shopping in the crowded
markets before their shifts began. It beatified the worried faces of young
mothers walking their kids to school and wondering how long they could
keep afloat. Sunlight kissed the brows of domestics grabbing a quick stim
as they lined up for transport to the better parts of town, and tickled the
chins of serious Subprime accountants hurrying to their desks.

Fingers of light stroked the pavement, and where they touched, as
if by magic, words appeared. A blue shadow, at first, faint as a whisper,
then deepening with the growing light to an outline of a rising sun that
enclosed a message of hope and insurrection: Arise and Unite! Cancel the
Debts! We Relinquish No One!

All over the city, the messages appeared. Outside the water distribution
sites, at the entrance to the factory canteens, beside transport stops, on
the corners where day laborers waited in hopes of a job, on the sidewalks
where beggars sat with eager hands outstretched, and beneath the walls
where sullen hookers leaned, the rising sun appeared emblazoned with
the slogans of liberation.

The Office of Public Order dispatched an army of street cleaners to
remove the offending graffiti, but the stain penetrated deep into the concrete and could not be scrubbed off. They resorted to painting over the
slogans, leaving white splotches everywhere that attested to the hidden
resistance.

The Council erupted in cheers that evening as one scout after another
reported in. Tianne, who was wearing a hat crowned with a rising sun
and a stuffed, felt fist swept it off and bowed low in homage to Bird.

"I admit, that was brilliant!" she said.

"Thank my great-aunt Gisela, who was in the German Resistance,"
Bird said. "She told the story to my grandmother, who put it into her
autobiography." He had combed through Maya's book, projecting it
onto the wall from the library in his crystal at night, eager for practical
tidbits and strategies. "Gisela's husband was a printer, and he fitted out
a suitcase with type on the bottom and ink that stayed invisible until it
was hit with sunlight. He used to wander around Berlin at night, setting
his suitcase down here and there, and in the morning—shazam! Down
with Hitler! appeared all over town."

That was Maya's idea of a good story, Bird thought. She put them
to bed at night with tales of resistance and revolution. It was only when
they grew up that they'd learned the grimmer parts, the torture in the
camps, the death transports.

You should have told us the whole story, he said to the Maya in his memory. You should have prepared us for the cost.

But that was the thing about revolution, and heroic acts of liberation. Nobody tells you the price.

⁓

A few nights later, another team fanned out from the City of Refuge, wandering the streets of Angel City with heavy bags that they set down often to rest. And the next morning, again, the rising sun and the words of hope appeared. Dissent Cannot Be Silenced! End the Stewards' Tyranny!

On the streets, people raised their heads and looked each other in the eye. They caught sight of the blazons and winked with a sense of conspiracy and possibility, as if anything might happen. In the long lines waiting for water or a few hours of paid work or a handout, people whispered to one another. They muttered under their breath, growled their hatred of the relinquishments and the endless debts. The city rumbled with discontent.

After the first week, the signs began to change. No More Relinquishment! Make a Noise! At Curfew, Every Day!

It started each night when the sirens howled for the nine p.m. curfew that the Stewards enforced in the more downtrodden neighborhoods. From the windows of every crowded tenement room or hovel in a crumbling high-rise came the clanging of metal spoons on pots. Just a few, at first, then more and more. Every day the clangor grew, louder and louder, until the echoes rang even down to the City of Refuge.

⁓

"This is great, but it's all symbolic. It's not going to hurt the Stewards if a few folks bang on pots and pans," Anthony said. They were in the midst of what Madrone called a meta-meeting, a meeting to plan the next Council meeting. Ten of them sat crowded into Madrone and Bird's living room, while Rafael and Gabriel leaned against the doorway to the hall, relaxed as cats, arms folded, eyes expressionless. Like gargoyles, Madrone thought, or twin icicles. Zap and Zoom were afraid of them, and that had its advantages. While they warded the door, the boys would stay where they'd been put, in bed in Madrone and Bird's room.

"It's drowning out the nightly newscast!" Tianne said, her eyes shining.

"It's more than that," Bird said. "Symbols hold power. Everything people do is a message. It says that the regime can be resisted, that people are not helpless victims doomed to passivity. They can act. They can have a voice. That alone is worth the risk. But it's not all we'll do, it's just a beginning."

"So where do we go next?" Anthony asked.

"What are the pillars of support for the regime?" Bird asked. "We figure that out, and then we knock them down, one by one."

"Hey, you copied that out of my book report in our Theory of Revolution module!" Madrone poked him.

"Diligently," Bird poked her back. "Gene Sharp, *198 Methods of Nonviolent Resistance*. 'No system of force can sustain itself if it has to use force to enforce every decree.' Or something like that—I'm sure he phrased it more gracefully. But force is costly, that's the point."

"But it's always the top item on their budget," Anthony said. "They don't hesitate to pay that cost."

"Take relinquishment, for example," Bird went on. "They can do it in part because people are afraid to oppose them. If they had to fight their way through a street riot every time they tried to take away someone's kid or home, they couldn't do it on a mass scale."

"So is that our campaign?" Emily asked. "Relinquishment?"

"Let's look at the pillars. Debt is certainly one of them, with relinquishment as its ultimate enforcer. What are some of the others?"

"Control of water," Madrone said.

"And food," added Miss Ruby.

"And boosters," Beth said.

"Control of all the information systems," Anthony said.

"Control of the imagination," Tianne added.

"Stop, I'm getting depressed!" Anthony said.

"No, it's hopeful," Bird proclaimed. "It's what the military would call a target-rich environment."

"You have a unique definition of 'hopeful'!" Miss Ruby told him.

"Not at all. The fact that they need to control so many basic aspects of life shows just how shaky the foundations of their system are."

"Yeah, but they *do* control every basic aspect of life," Tianne said. "Except for imagination, but they silence any evidence of it."

"And how do they keep control?" Bird went on. "With the army and the police. Well, there's two parts to the army. The croots and the breeds. The croots don't really support the regime, they're forced to join up or go to the plantations themselves. Once in, they're controlled by the boosters. They should be easy to turn."

"That still leaves the breeds. And the police," Anthony said.

"Police are a mixed bag," Emily said. "Some are in it because there aren't a lot of other job opportunities."

"And some because they're corrupt, sadistic bastards," Anthony said.

"The breeds are another story," Bird said.

The conversation went on for a long time. But in the end, they agreed to make relinquishment their first campaign. Of all the Stewards' policies, it was the most feared and hated. If they could succeed in protecting people from relinquishment, they would have a powerful success to mark up to their credit, and the people might take heart and be ready for other struggles.

All the while they debated, Rafael and Gabriel simply stood and watched. Make your plans, their silence seemed to say. Spin your fantasies. We know the grim and bloody truth.

⁓

Bird ran trainings in the plaza every day, running people through hassle lines and role plays, teaching them all he'd learned from Lily and Maya about how to stay calm in a tight situation, how to de-escalate violence, how to protect the vulnerable in a crowd. Madrone and Beth trained medics—how to stop bleeding, how to move an unconscious patient safely, how to treat tear gas and bullet wounds and laser burns. Emily organized affinity groups—small groups that would take action together in the streets and support one another. Anthony and his favorite troupe of actors created street theater skits with insurrectionary messages, while Tianne and her crew built props. The Refuge was abuzz with a sense of excitement that overlaid any unspoken fears.

By the third week, the sidewalk messages read: March Against Relinquishment! 5 p.m., Saturday!

Preparations for the march went on for a week. The artists raided the ruins of department stores and fabric shops, cut up sheets, and made stencils for banners that could be rolled up and hidden until the crucial moment. They made T-shirts with slogans and Tianne's own symbolic design—two fists, one black, one white, rising up, breaking the chains that bound them and curling in to form a heart.

Bird pored over Maya's autobiography. It was comforting. She was still with him, advising, offering helpful tips. As he read her words he began to feel her come alive again, as if his attention, his gratitude, fed her spirit.

From Lisa, one of her old organizing buddies, he learned how to keep the tail of a march connected to its head, and how to take a street in the face of police opposition. From Stella, veteran of a million meetings, he learned how to streamline decision-making. From Ahmed, Maya's old friend from the Arab Spring, he learned how to hand out flyers in the midst of a tyranny. They put his advice into practice, sending out teams with scouts and backup, and the leaflets disappeared faster than they could scavenge paper to print them on.

The Stewards controlled what was left of the internet in the Southlands. They had a lock on all the vidscreens and the few remaining radios. But there was a network they could not control, the word-of-mouth network of rumor and gossip. The refugistas went back to their neighborhoods and alerted trusted friends to the plans for the march. They warned neighbors to stock up on food and water.

"Everybody's going to come out for it," they hissed. "This is the big one! You won't want to miss it!"

"There are two basic human drives," Maya wrote. "The drive to stay safe, and the compelling desire not to miss out on the action. Play to the second, and it will override the first."

The plan was for Anthony and Emily to lead the march. Because Bird and Madrone were both on the Stewards' wanted list, Bird in more danger than ever since his near-capture, they had promised to stay in the midst of the crowd, in relative safety. Miss Ruby and Emily had tried to persuade them to remain in the Refuge, but that they had refused to do. They compromised by agreeing to leave if arrests seemed imminent.

Miss Ruby went back and forth in an agony of indecision. She was terrified, but also exhilarated at the thought of marching as her grandmother had done during the era of civil rights. One day she'd decide she was going, the next day she'd persuaded herself that the children and the school needed her to remain free and safe.

But in the end, as they assembled in the entry plaza on the morning of the march, she was there, head high and smiling proudly. Under her sweater she wore one of the T-shirts stenciled with a bright rising sun that read: All Debts Will Be Forgiven in the Bright New Day!

About fifty of the refugistas assembled in the plaza to review their plans. More wanted to come, but they'd decided it was better not to risk the whole community. Either people of the city would join them, or not, and if not, making up the numbers with refugistas would be far too risky.

Bird had gotten up at three in the morning to organize the crews that went out to stash crucial supplies in strategic places, and he'd been too keyed up to get back to sleep. He'd have to count on adrenaline to see him through the day.

"Remember the plan," he said to the gathered crowd. "Take your time today. Don't rush. You're shoppers, or job seekers, or the unemployed just killing time. Meander, don't go straight for the area. Plan to get there by four or four-thirty, not earlier. Don't worry if you see police there. Just keep an eye on the exit route."

"What if the Lash are already there?" a young woman asked nervously. "What if they keep us from marching?"

"There will be cops," Bird assured her. "But they won't keep us from marching, if people want to march." He sounded more confident than he felt.

"Can we say a prayer?" a young woman asked. Her voice held a quaver and her eyes were frightened.

"At the tree!" called out one of the older teens. "Let's tie a ribbon onto the tree, for our march."

A clamor of agreement, and someone ran for the storeroom, returning with a long length of red ribbon. Bird thought it was an unfortunate choice: the color of blood, but he didn't say so. The assembly formed a circle with it, holding it in their hands so it linked them all. The tree seemed to stretch up with pride, holding its beribboned branches high, its fine, silvery leaves glinting in the bright sunlight. It was a beautiful day, as most days were in Angel City, the sun now dipping low and shining golden in a cloudless, limpid sky. A day when everything could change.

"Who do we pray to?" a pimply young man asked.

"To the Four Sacred Things," Madrone said. "May the Air bring us clarity. May the Fire give us courage and protection. May we flow through the streets like cleansing Water. May the Earth keep us grounded, safe, and calm. And may the fifth sacred thing link us together in love."

"And let's pray to the angels," Tianne said.

"Better pray they don't show up!" Bird said in alarm. "Not if we want to keep this march nonviolent."

"Not those Angels," Tianne said. "The real angels, the ones the city is named for. May the angels of Angel City spread their wings of protection over us!"

"What about the Queen of the Angels?" Bird suggested. "*Nuestra Señora la Reina de los Ángeles.* Virgin Mother of God. Where the Christian and the Pagan meet. Shall we pray to her?"

"Queen of the Angels," Miss Ruby thundered suddenly. She looked a bit surprised as if her own voice were coming forth not entirely of her own volition. "You are a mother. Hold us in your mother's heart and wrap us in your arms, you hear? We're callin' on you to keep us safe, to open the way. Hear our prayer!"

Bird raised his arms and sang one of the Samhain hymns to the Changemaker.

> *"I am the change,*
> *I am the tide that's turning.*
> *Your love and your rage,*
> *Passion for justice burning!*
> *And when you take a stand,*
> *I'm the courage that guides you.*
> *I'm in the streets, I take your hand,*
> *I'm marching beside you."*

"Be with us, Goddess of Change," Madrone called out. "And may we be in the right place at the right time in the right way, with all the protection, luck, strength, and courage we need to do the work."

A mixed chorus of "amen" and "blessed be" filled the air.

———

Bird and Anthony walked casually around the big intersection at the corner of Sunset and Cheney. They'd chosen the spot because it was not too close to the Refuge, but not too far away either. And there was a straight route down Sunset to the Relinquishment Center. The streets were wide, built in the days when almost everyone had a private automobile. Now cars were a scarce luxury, but there were enough jitneys and army transports and delivery trucks and police vans to make crossing the street an adventure.

There were also enough police, stationed in the street, directing the traffic, and peering suspiciously down the side streets, to make Bird wonder how in Hella's name they were ever going to get into the street, let alone march up it. About fifty cops in full riot gear stood in formation in the parking lot of the burger joint. Another twenty or so prowled the crosswalks.

Bird and Anthony made low conversation and tried to look casual as they made their way to a small sidewalk stand where Madrone sat with Emily and Miss Ruby on battered plastic chairs around a greasy table. Miss Ruby was drinking a soda. Madrone pursed her lips and toyed with her straw, trying to pretend she was enjoying the cloying sweet stuff.

"This was a bad idea," Anthony announced as he and Bird grabbed chairs away from a neighboring table and sat down. "It's never going to work. The cops know we're coming and they're ready for us."

"We've just got to go ahead anyway," Miss Ruby said. "The cops knew Martin Luther King was coming to that bridge outside Birmingham, but that didn't stop them."

"Yeah, and they all got clubbed within an inch of their lives," Anthony muttered. "When did I sign onto the martyr brigade?"

"Don't listen to him," Emily said. "Grumbling makes him feel better."

"The news teams are out," Bird said. He'd spied a small enclave of reporters, and down on La Brea a covey of vans with transmitters on their roofs lay waiting.

"That's something," Emily murmured.

"They're only here to show how futile this march is bound to be. That's if anyone shows up," Anthony said. "If it's successful, the censors will suppress the footage." He dug into the last of his change and bought them each a bag of chips, surplus from some army depot, and another drink.

"Our last meal," he said.

"Oh, don't!" Emily said. "We're scared enough, okay? You can go back home, you know."

"These are vile," Madrone bit into a chip and made a face. "I can't believe people live on these."

"They'll keep you on your feet," Bird said. "Nutritionally complete." He reached over and snatched her bag.

"Hey, that's mine!" She snatched it back.

"You aren't eating them." He grabbed for it, and she held it behind her back.

"It's the principle of the thing. Ask first! Nicely!"

"Please, Miss Madrone, can I have the chips you aren't going to eat?"

"You are?" In her astonishment, she lowered her guard and he plucked them out of her hands.

"I ate them for years in prison," he said.

"Ah, the happy memories!" Anthony said.

"Now I have to pee," Miss Ruby lamented.

"Let's do it now, and then we go," Anthony said.

They all took turns at the filthy toilet behind the shop. By the time they'd finished, it was five o'clock. They didn't see anyone obviously there for a march, although the crowd did seem dense. They couldn't see any of the other refugistas.

"Should we wait?" Madrone asked anxiously.

Bird shook his head. "We made a plan, we put out a time. Best to stick with it!"

"Here goes," Anthony said.

"Do it," Bird said. "Do it big, and fast, and with confidence."

Behind the fruit stalls on the corner was a little space between the back of the stall and the wall behind it. Anthony pushed his hand in and drew out the bamboo poles that held the canvas banner that they'd stashed there the night before. Moving swiftly, he unfurled the standard that proclaimed in big red letters: End Relinquishment! Miss Ruby took the other pole. Emily marched in front with a tall flag that was also stashed behind the booth.

"Hey hey, ho ho!" Anthony shouted out loudly. "Relinquishment has got to go!"

Emily and Miss Ruby took up the chant, and they started off, the three of them, a sad but brave little protest. Madrone moved to follow but Bird put a hand on her arm. They had agreed that unless they could merge into an actual march, even a small one, they would simply fade back into the crowd and make their way back to the Refuge. They looked at each other, at the brave, sparse figures of their three friends, and without speaking they both moved forward to back up the banner. They couldn't let Anthony and Emily and Miss Ruby carry the flag alone.

"We'll be a march of five," Bird thought, with a sick feeling in his stomach. He and Madrone would be caught with no crowd to shelter them. But he didn't feel afraid. He felt, more than anything else, embarrassed, waving a flag, chanting a chant with three other people. Well, if he had to die, he would die a fool.

The cops, in spite of patrolling the intersection for hours, still seemed to be caught off guard that a march was actually happening. They began moving in on the banner, but slowly, and the banner gained some ground.

"At least we made it into the street," Bird muttered. "That's more than any other march has done down here for the last couple of decades."

They were, in fact, about twenty feet into the avenue that led toward the Relinquishment Center. Suddenly a new voice joined in the chant. Fred and Bob from the Refuge unfurled a banner of their own. All Debts Will Be Forgiven in the Bright New Day! it read. Ten refugistas marched behind it.

Then, in the midst of a crowd in one of the crosswalks, a teenage boy peeled off his overshirt to reveal a T-shirt that read No Debt Slavery! and dashed toward the banner. Behind him came a middle-aged woman, waving a flag she took from her purse, and then a chanting man in a sunburst shirt, and then another, and another.

The tide of people swarmed around the surprised cops and flowed into the street, and the march gained yet more ground. Suddenly Bird and Madrone found themselves in the midst of the flow, with fifty, a hundred, two hundred people crowding around them.

From a side alley, Tianne and a group of her artists pulled a wagon with one of the papier mâché angels on it, her great wings upstretched, her face beaked like an archaic bird Goddess. On the angel's breastplate was written: Dignity and Freedom Are Our Sacred Rights!

"*Diosa mia,* it's working!" Madrone breathed. Bird grabbed her hand and squeezed it tight.

More and more people joined them—all kinds of people. Some were poor and ragged, others looked like they had just finished a day's work in a clean office. They were all colors, and all ages—some old enough to have marched against the Stewards' rise long before the takeover, some young teens born under the Stewards' rule. All of them had a light in their eyes and a look on their faces that seemed to say, "Look at me—I'm really doing this!"

The police spread out to block the intersection behind them, but people spilled around the edges. Someone found a way into the big discount store on the corner and a mass of people poured in and then out the double doors that opened onto the street. The cops surged forward, pushing the crowd back with their nightsticks, but suddenly more people appeared, and more, until there was nowhere for them to be pushed. People were getting knocked into one another. An older woman was shoved off her feet. A young man took the brunt of a club in his face and stumbled to his knees. One of the cops whacked him on the head.

Bird grabbed Madrone's hand and started weaving through the crowd, like a salmon swimming upstream, squeezing between people and trying to keep his footing in the currents of the river that continued to swell and rush past him. A few refugistas Bird had trained made their own way up to the line of cops.

A stick-thin teen huddled on the ground, arms wrapped over his head as the cops clubbed him. A teenage girl with a long, blond braid threw herself over his back. A man with a gray ponytail and a skull tattoo on his arm dove on top of her, then another and another, until they had a tall pile surrounded by a surging crowd.

Frustrated, the cops began peeling people off, shoving them roughly back into the crowd. Although the front of the march kept moving on, more and more people surged into the melee and the crowd continued to grow.

Madrone knelt at the backside of the puppy pile, found the arms of the victim at the bottom, and gave him a tug. He squirmed out from under, and she gave him her shoulder to lean on as they hobbled away, protected by the throng.

Bird blew a shrill note on the whistle that hung around his neck. He was in the midst of the melee, close to the line of cops, and while he was aware that the situation was dangerous, he had moved into that state beyond fear, the clear calm where he could watch the situation and assess what to do. In some faraway part of himself, where he could still feel emotions, he was radiantly happy. They had done it—they had really done it! They were marching, and all the might of the Stewards had not been able to stop them!

The puppy pile dissolved, and the refugistas quickly sprang to their feet, linked arms, and formed a line facing the cops. The cops grabbed their night-sticks to push the line back. The refugistas fell back before the onslaught, slowly, taking one small step, then another, speaking to them all the time.

"You don't have to do this. You could join us. How much debt does your family owe?"

"My father was a cop. I remember, back in the day, when police had a union!"

"What kind of pension do you get?"

"What happens to your family if you get injured?"

One of the cops pushed back his riot helmet to reveal his face.

"I'm on your side," he mouthed.

But others were simply enraged, prodding and swinging with their clubs. Bird took a jab to his stomach, though he twisted to let the blow glance off. Another cop smashed a gray-haired woman in the face, bloodying her nose. She remained calm and kept on talking to him.

"Why did you do that, young man? You had no call to do that. Would you do that to your grandmother?"

He faltered. Two of the cops on either side of him moved together, squeezing the bully back out of the front line.

> "Bankers and Politicians,
> Tell us what we owe!
> They say, Pay Up!
> We say, No!"

The chant echoed and thundered through the streets. The march carried on, trailed now by a tame line of police who made token efforts to keep pushing the line.

"March!" Miss Ruby yelled in her schoolteacher's voice that carried far above the crowd. "March on!"

They marched. Down the broad avenue and east, toward the Relinquishment Center where the desperate were taken. Teams from the

Refuge appeared along the route to hand out more flags and T-shirts. People were joining now, some of them frightened and hesitant, looking behind them with every step, a few of them prepared with their own homemade placards. Refugistas came out of the doorways of fast food shops and the corners of alleys, and unfurled banners they'd stuffed into backpacks or hidden under their shirts. Bright colors flew above them.

> *"You say we owe you*
> *All of our pay!*
> *But all debts will be forgiven*
> *In the bright new day!"*

They marched, and they gained confidence. Their numbers swelled as more and more people along the route gained courage to join them. It was a great thundering wave, a beast let loose, and Madrone found herself suddenly lifted with a sense of joy. This was why people sat through a hundred grueling meetings, why they took such terrible risks. All to feel this great sense of hope and exhilaration, as if they were aswim in a river that could sweep away all injustice and water the banks of a new world.

The police let them march. In truth, she realized, they were probably caught by surprise. Nobody expected the size of this crowd. When they topped a small rise and she could look behind her, she was awed to see people filling block after block with their signs and their presence. More than hundreds—thousands had come out.

The Relinquishment Center lay just a couple of miles down Sunset Boulevard. Once it had been a Hollywood studio. Now the gates were lined with barbed wire and armed guards, and inside, the old sound stages were packed with miserable families held until they could be assigned to plantations or army units or pens.

The front of the march reached the entrance, almost too quickly, Madrone thought. She could have marched another ten miles, or twenty, or kept on marching forever. But they arrived, and stationed the banner in front of the entrance, facing the gate where massed lines of riot cops stood guard.

Scouts quietly moved away to circulate through the crowd and patrol the surrounding streets. They would alert Anthony and Emily if the police began to close in. A refugista brought up a sound system that one of the techies had rigged from some scavenged parts, and Miss Ruby took the microphone.

"Friends!" she cried in her ringing voice. "We have done a beautiful thing today! We have taken our first steps toward freedom on these streets. Let's hear a big cheer for our courage!"

A thundering roar came back at her.

Madrone made her way quickly to the medics' station, strategically placed in the midst of the crowd, but not too far from an escape route. She checked in with the others. So far, there were few injuries and most of the medical need was for water, which dedicated refugistas had brought in their packs.

"Someday we will take these gates down, and set the prisoners free!" Miss Ruby cried. "Someday those brothers in blue who today guard the prison will join us to make a bright new world!"

Bird came up and squeezed Madrone's shoulders. She leaned into him, letting herself savor the moment. Terrible things might still happen, would happen, sooner or later. There would be wounds and blood and death to win this liberation. But right now, the sun was shining, the medic station was nearly empty, the streets were filled with chanting people, Miss Ruby was discovering her talent for oratory, and she and Bird were together.

"Miss Ruby is having the time of her life!" she said.

"Mnnn. She's a natural-born speech maker. But I think this is when we remember we're wanted criminals and make our exit. You okay to leave?"

Madrone nodded. "Demand is light and the other medics got it covered. You really think we should go now?"

"We agreed to keep the rally short, not press our luck if we made it this far. And the end of these things is always the most dangerous time for arrests."

"Maya did always say that part of her survival strategy for being a lifelong activist was 'Skip the speeches.'"

Bird smiled. "Yeah. Although she'd always add, 'Unless, of course, I'm the one making them.'"

They slipped through the throng of people, away from the makeshift stage at the front. The crowd was bigger than she'd realized, stretching on for blocks and blocks, far beyond the reach of the sound system. But that didn't worry people—they were staging makeshift rallies of their own, led by some of the refugistas who set up soapboxes and called for a "people's mic." A speaker would call out a sentence or two, and the crowd would repeat it for those farther back to hear. People were telling their stories, and as she and Bird moved back, they caught snatches of tales like fragments of lives.

"I was a teacher, until they closed the school."

"I wanted to train as a nurse, but we had no money ..."

"My father couldn't make the payments on the farm, so they took ... "

"My brother and sister-in-law and my two nieces were relinquished when they couldn't make their house payments. I tried to help, but I could barely ... "

It was like a ritual, Madrone thought, with the crowd chorusing back each person's tale like an affirmation of their suffering and courage. It was far better than speeches and she wished she could linger and listen. But Bird was probably right. The most difficult part of the day was still ahead of them, finding a way to get back to the Refuge without being stopped by patrols.

The crowd filled the streets encircling the huge block occupied by the Relinquishment Center. But as Bird and Madrone threaded through the press of marchers, back toward where the ranks thinned out, a gate in the chain-link fence opened. Here the crowd was thin enough that a bus could pull out—only to find itself stuck in the midst of a mass of people.

The bus was painted gray and had windows covered with metal grills—a transport bus, filled with the relinquished. As the crowd spied it, someone let out a great shout, and suddenly a swarm of people surrounded it, pounding on its sides, chanting and yelling. A loudspeaker warned the crowd to move away, and the engine gunned.

There was a flash of light, and a white-blond head streaked through the crowd, followed by another, and another. The Angels, Madrone realized, their perfect features masked by scarves, their perfect bodies swift and lithe. They formed up on either side of the bus and began to push it to and fro. The crowd joined in, rocking the bus back and forth, wilder and wilder, until at last they tipped it over with a great crash.

The Angels leapt up, wrenched the door open, and started to pull out the prisoners.

But the prisoners were writhing and screaming in agony from the bracelets that shackled their wrists. One of the Angels dove through the door, tackled the guard inside, and tossed him out to the crowd. Bird and Madrone were already running toward the scene. The guard was unarmed now, and screaming in terror. People were pulling on his arms and legs and the fury was so great Madrone feared they would tear him apart.

"Don't hurt him," she yelled, but her voice was lost in the din.

Bird put on a burst of near-superhuman speed, and reached the crowd as they lifted the guard up and tossed him up in the air like a giant cat playing with a mouse. They threw him up, then stepped back and let him fall crashing hard to the ground. Bird dove on top of him.

"Don't fucking protect that scum," someone screamed at Bird in fury.

Someone else swung a tire iron at his head, but Madrone was there, and blocked his arm with a chop she'd learned in martial arts class. The tire iron spun away, the man swore at her, and Bird stood up with the guard's thumb pad in his hand.

"Silence!" he yelled with all the power he could put behind his singer's voice, and Madrone and a few of the refugistas took up the cry. The crowd fell quiet, a deadly, cold quiet.

Inside, the prisoners were still moaning and screaming. Two men pushed the guard up to his feet.

Bird faced him with the thumb pad.

"Turn off the pain," he said.

The guard tucked his hands into his armpits.

"Do it, and I'll try to save your miserable ass," Bird said.

Reluctantly, the guard held out his hand. Bird shoved the pad at him, and he thumbed it.

The screams stopped, to be replaced by sighs of relief.

"Now open the bracelets," Bird commanded.

"In your dreams. You think you can get away with this?"

"Doesn't matter. You think you can survive this crowd playing tug-of-war with your body parts while we find out?"

The guard looked around at the sea of seething fury. He thumbed the pad again.

"Bracelets off!" came a yell from inside.

"Bring out the driver!" Bird called.

Rough hands shoved out a skinny, gray-haired man, his pants wet with urine stain.

"People's mic!" Bird called.

"I know we're all angry," he cried out, and the crowd roared an echo.

"*I'm* angry!" Bird cried.

"I'm angry," they cried back with one voice.

"But we got to think, people."

"We got to think ahead."

"Now we could kill these two slime."

"They deserve to die!"

"But we got fifty folks here we've rescued."

"Who deserve to live."

"And we got to give them that chance."

"And we aren't here just for one march."

"Or just for one day."

"We're here to usher in ... "

"... a bright new day!"

"A bright new day!" the crowd cried, over and over again, cheering and roaring. Finally Bird raised his hand, and called out over the noise.

"We got to think ... "

"What that day's gonna bring."

"If we begin it with murder."

"So I say, we hold them hostage ... "

"... while our friends disappear ... "

"... and find refuge!"

"And then, I say, we send them back."

"But we send them with a message."

He turned to the driver. "Pull up your shirt," he hissed.

The driver stared at him.

"Just do it." The driver bared a pale and bony back, studded with pimples.

Bird pulled out a marker from his bag and wrote in big letters: No Debt Slavery!

Laughter rippled out into the crowd. Someone else pinned the guard's arms and pulled down his pants, pushing him over to thrust his bare cheeks to the crowd.

"Now what message should we write here?" Bird called out.

Hoots and hollers and a variety of obscene suggestions came back at him. He parried them, and kept the discussion going while the prisoners in the bus were helped to discreetly blend into the larger crowd.

The exodus from the bus seemed to take forever. Bird kept up a patter, but inside he was tense with anxiety. Surely the cops would have called for backup, and time was short to get the crowd dispersed before the troops closed in. Meanwhile he invited up some helpers to decorate the guard and the driver.

"Gonna pay for this," the guard warned.

"I already have," Bird said quietly.

From his vantage point, he could see movement behind the gates—ranks of cops forming up. At last the bus was empty. Bird blew a blast on his whistle, then a pattern to alert the coms team that meant: "Declare victory—get the hell out!"

"Okay, people!" he cried. "Our message is prepared! But I can see that our friends in blue are preparing something for us, too! And unless you want to fight off laser guns with rocks and bottles, I suggest we call this day a victory! Are you with me?"

A cheer rang out.

"Then let's send these dogs back to their keepers, and go home!"

Another loud cheer.

"When you go, stick together in groups. Watch out for each other—don't let your friends disappear. Go home today, but know that this is not the end. This is the beginning! We'll see you again, and again, until the day comes when we tear this place down!"

A huge cheer. Many in the crowd began to heed his advice, and melted away down side streets and back down the avenue. As the group thinned, a group of refugistas came up and took the guard and the driver.

"Get them as close to safety as you can," Bird said. "Don't risk your lives. They can run a bit if they need to."

They nodded and spirited the hostages away.

Madrone ran up to Bird, pulled him down and into a huddle. When he emerged, he was wearing a different colored T-shirt. His hair was bundled under a cap, his skin was three shades darker, and they were walking calmly but quickly back down the avenue, staying in the thickest part of the crowd.

"If you weren't wanted before, you sure are now!" she said. "But good job!"

A tall, lean man, his head swathed in white, came up behind them.

"Come on," he said. "Your guardian Angel is with you."

Behind them, a sizable contingent apparently *did* want to fight cops with rocks and bottles. A battle was underway, and Bird caught a whiff of tear gas. Soon, they'd have the area cordoned off. Movement through the streets would be very, very difficult tonight. But the Angels had bolt holes and safe houses and secret passages.

"Let's go," he said.

That night the *cacerolazo,* the cacophony of banging pots and pans, echoed through the streets as if the city were a liberty bell, ringing out a warning like the old song said. Metal has a resonance, and so do structures. Through the bang! bang! of the pots sang a vibration that could bring down walls, shatter barriers. Bird heard it as he and Madrone sheltered in the bowels of an Angel safe house. It sounded like the death knell of the old order. Exciting and ominous, filled with the promise of the new.

Chapter Fifty-Eight

WENDELL SAT ALONE IN HIS INNER SANCTUM, WATCHING THE debacle on his vidscreen. He had a bottle of whiskey with him, a gift from Culbertson after the last party. Old and irreplaceable, like his precious collection of vases that surrounded him. Something left from a kinder world.

Yes, the parties went on. After each one, Wendell told himself that was the last. Next time, he would be stronger. He'd have an ironclad excuse to say no.

But deep inside, he knew that no mitigating circumstance would ever excuse him. For the parties were simply one more way for Culbertson to exercise his control. The stronger Wendell got, the more he rose to command, the more respect he was offered or victories he won, the more Culbertson would need to demonstrate his greater power, not just over Wendell's appropriations and armaments, but over his innermost fantasies, his very soul.

Although he was not winning a lot of victories these days.

He prided himself on never drinking alone. But Jesus himself wouldn't begrudge him a drop or two of comfort right now, as he watched the riot on the vidscreen.

At the beginning, it seemed to be all going according to plan. Police deployed, news crews poised to capture the mess it was bound to be for the rebels when their ridiculous little band was crushed like a cockroach.

But cockroach-like, they had somehow evaded those bumbling idiots of cops, and then suddenly it was no pathetic troop of a dozen losers but wave after wave flooding through the streets, far outnumbering the cops sent to control them.

The censors quickly killed any public broadcast, but not quickly enough. Not before shots of a huge, surging crowd were carried to every vidscreen in the area. Bunglers! Like the city cops and the fucking Lash!

Wendell did not command the Lash or the city's police force. Bannerman, the sharksucker who did, had muffed the response. Afraid he'd look bad if he fired on "peaceful" protestors! Next thing you knew, the "peaceful protestors" had captured a bus full of plantation-bound workers, terrorized the guard and driver, and staged a bloody insurrection!

But that was not what set Wendell to pouring himself a second drink as he watched the private broadcast from the network of security cams. No, it was *him*. Standing there in the middle of the crowd, smug as a fly in shit, spewing his stinking propaganda to his brainless followers. Egging them on to more blind destruction, infecting them with his filthy hatred.

Him!

Wendell had sworn to root it out, this rot. He would do it, if he did it with his last breath. Find the foul hole where the rebels went to hide. Step up the drone surveillance, send out the Intel and the Lash, do whatever it takes to end the infection before it continued to spread.

And the infection in his own soul? a little voice whispered.

Purge the greater disease, and that would relieve him, too. He would no longer be so dependent on the Primes, so obligated to please them and do their will.

At the thought, he felt just the tiniest trickle of disappointment. Images flashed through his mind, memories from those back rooms where he went so unwillingly and yet performed so well.

Him! He stood up, focused all his fury at the vidscreen where Bird was scrawling slogans on the guard's fat ass. Focus that rage, blow on those embers when it died low, let it become a roaring fire that would burn away everything and anything impure.

He glanced up at the most precious of his vases. A red-figured kylix from Athens in the era of Euripides. A beautiful thing, infinitely valuable and irreplaceable. An historic work of art.

Depicting debauchery. He grabbed it off the shelf and without stopping to think, smashed it into the vidscreen, into the crowd and the evil at its heart. Vase after vase, the amphora from Thebes and the Delphi kantharos, cups and bowls and vases, hurling them, smashing them down, crushing them underfoot.

As he would crush them all, the cockroaches, the vectors of contamination, spreaders of filth. Starting with *him*!

~~~~~~

River sat scrunched uncomfortably in the jeep as it lumbered up the dirt road, its engine groaning with the steep climb. Four of them were crowded into a seat meant to hold three, and the back was packed with troops, hanging over the edge and clinging to the roll bars. River's knee was bent at a disturbing angle, and whenever they hit a rut, which was about every forty-five seconds, Erik Farmer's elbow was shoved into his ribs.

They had left Cress at Troy, with enough of the Army of Liberation to maintain the illusion that they were contemplating an assault on the Stewards' fort at the top of the Grapevine. The fiction wouldn't hold for long, and it was always possible the Stewards would take the offensive and attack. River hoped that wouldn't happen, or that if it did, Cress and the others would have sense enough to hunker down in the base and wait it out. But now there was no more he could do about it, except to lead this strike force on to the heart of the Southlands, hoping to cut the defenders of the passes off from aid and reinforcements.

The scouts had plotted this route, looking at old maps and running it themselves first with their electric bikes. It avoided the main highway, with its checkpoints and troops, and would bring them over the mountains and into St. Ferd's Valley from the east. But the road had not been used for a long time, and it was as pitted and rocky as the Road of Righteousness the Retributionists preached about. The night was dark, and they were running with minimal lights, so it was hard to see the potholes and the boulders. A light rain was falling, but as they climbed higher and the night grew colder, the rain began to sheet down as an icy sleet, and then a curtain of white.

The truck stopped.

"What's this shit?" the driver complained.

They piled out. It was a welcome relief to stretch his legs, and River decided that when they got back in, he would maneuver for the window seat. The night was icy cold, and he shivered, hugging his sides against the sharp wind. Before them stretched a carpet of white, and as his eyes adjusted to the dark, he saw that a thin silver dust brushed the sides of the hills and coated the brush.

He reached out to a coated branch and touched it. It burned, and he jerked his hand away.

"This some chemical shit!" he said in alarm. He risked a light, and shone his powerful flashlight around at the hillside, the road ahead. It revealed a landscape of death. The white stuff blanketed the hills farther on, lying deeper. The road ahead was buried in it. Nothing showed above it. Nothing looked alive.

Erik Farmer smiled. "This, gentlemen, is what we call snow."

"Snow?" River said. "In the Southlands?"

"Snow in the mountains, at the higher elevations," Erik assured him.

"In March?" asked the driver, incredulously.

"It's not unusual."

"But this shit burns! Chemical shit!" River exclaimed.

"That's just cold you're feeling," Erik said. "It won't hurt you, not unless you stay out in it so long your toes freeze. Basically, it's water."

"Whatever happened to fraggin' global warming?" the driver grumbled.

"This is it," Erik said. "'Warming' was probably always a misnomer. Think extremes. Hotter heat waves. Freakier freak storms."

"So how this army gonna get through it?" River returned to the immediate question.

"We could wait, and it might melt," Erik suggested. "Could take a few days."

"Don't got days."

"We could shovel, if we had shovels."

"Don't got shovels."

"We could plow, if we had a snowplow. Or a 'dozer might do."

"Take time to get it, bring it up here. Don't got time. Any minute now, Stewards could spy us out."

"Or we could leave the vehicles, and trudge on foot," Erik concluded with an irritating smile.

They halted the convoy and sheltered in the trucks for warmth while they made a plan.

The scouts from the City improvised snowshoes with bent branches and rope. They were experienced with snow, for as children they were all taken up to the mountains each winter. There they learned to ski, to snowshoe, to winter camp and even, when conditions were right, to build igloos, all the techniques of survival. At night they sat around campfires or in warm cabins with woodstoves, and learned about the land and peoples and ecology of the old Arctic, before climate change had ruined so much. Snow didn't worry them.

But it worried River, and the rest of his troops, who had never seen the stuff before. His feet were damn cold in their thin boots. He stomped on the ground, and went over to see what the squabs were up to.

A few of the Califian troops who were good with an ax had felled a sycamore from a crowded stand. River watched them split it into planks and whittle them into rough spades with lashed-on handles. Meanwhile, the troops pulled out the warmest clothes from their packs, or put on layers of their lighter gear. The tubos and croots from the Stewards' Army had their boots. The Califians from the North had sturdy hiking boots or work boots. But most of the liberados had only flimsy canvas shoes or worse, sandals.

The scouts soon returned, and the platoon leaders held a hurried council. The snow was deep ahead, but it extended for only a couple of miles along the highest parts of their route.

They would go on foot, rotating the lead platoons who would break trail, digging out the roadway behind them so the trucks could move through. As troops tired, fresh troops chosen from those with good footwear would take their places.

It was a long, cold tramp all through the night. The wind came up and fresh snow swirled around them and soaked through their thinner garments. Snow melted on River's neck and trickled down his back. His toes grew colder still, then numb, and he wondered if they were frozen. His feet felt heavy and clumsy, like blocks of ice.

But they pushed on. He took his own turn at the front, jamming his makeshift shovel into the snow and heaving it out of the way, kicking it aside when he didn't have a tool to use. The marchers who came behind had it easier, trudging through the tracks the trailblazers had made.

The trucks, lightened of their heavy loads, lumbered up the steep hills. Where the snow was too hard-packed to move, the troops beat down a solid, wide trail and shoveled dirt on top to give the wheels something to grip. From time to time, a call went out and marchers jumped onto the backs of the trucks to give them more weight and traction. Slowly, slowly, they made forward progress.

Smokee and her Valkyries marched as a unit toward the rear of the line. Once she would have fought for their right to be up front, to take their turn breaking trail just as the men did. But she felt strangely subdued, reluctant, as if the rage that had fueled her were siphoned off. Where was her anger, her fire? She could use the warmth right now, she was shivering in her three sweaters and a light jacket that didn't completely close over them.

She found herself regretting that she hadn't spent more time in the City exploring its offerings and enjoying its beauty, that she hadn't stored up more days like pearls on a string of memories to tell over in the night. She found herself entertaining unwelcome thoughts—like, if River could fall in love with a pen-girl, maybe someone, someday, could love her. There was another kind of warmth, arms around you, as her mother's arms had sheltered her in the long ago past. But that was too, too risky to even think about. She didn't want it. She wouldn't know what to do with it.

She just wanted warm feet right now, and a hot cup of tea, and her own little apartment back again. How generous the City was, to have given her that. How wonderful it would be right now, to have a room and a door to shut, to close everyone out and curl up with a blanket, and not have to talk to anyone for days at a time.

Her brother had joined a unit of the Stewards' Army deserters, and marched ahead of her. They were still shy with each other and awkward, not quite knowing what to say or how to fill in the gaps. Smokee thought she ought to feel a flood of warmth for him, but what she actually felt was astounded, and kind of numb. He wasn't the little boy she remembered. He was a stranger she barely knew, as she must be equally strange to him.

But he was there, and if she had found him, she might find others, her mother, her lost child. And yet she couldn't muster up the driving mix of hope and rage that had propelled her for so long. She felt only a great weariness, and a heartsick grief at the killing and the suffering. She had come back to herself somehow, and her real self was not the bitter victim nor the raging fury, not the instrument of justice nor the spearpoint of vengeance. Just a girl with cold feet, trudging through a long, cold night, her heat reduced to an ember longing to be a simple hearth fire.

At last the long night passed. They struggled up over the crest of the hills, and the road began to head downwards, not consistently, for there were ravines to cross and canyons to climb down into and up out of. But the overall trend was down, and as they went farther down the snow grew less and the going got easier.

The sky grew light, and the first rays of the sun kissed the white tops of the mountains, turning them to a gleaming gold. The lead platoon clambered up to the top of a rise, and then stopped. River and Erik Farmer hurried up to the overlook.

Below them stretched a blue lake, its arms snaking back into the embrace of the mountains. The sun hit it and the water gleamed with gold.

Around it, small fires glowed. It wasn't a hillboy camp, he knew that, but in the hills there were other encampments of the lawless and the refugees who'd escaped the debt levies and the Southlands prisons. He'd been sent often enough to root them out, back in his sojuh days.

Suddenly he heard a sound, the snick of a weapon being primed.

He scanned the road below, then looked up to the hills above. He caught a gleam of metal, another....

"Ambush!" he cried. "Fall back!"

Instantly their own snipers had their rifles primed, trained on the brush around them. But they were in a bad place, vulnerable to their enemies on the higher ground. If the shooting started, it would not go well for them.

River took a breath and stepped forward with his arms up. If this were an outpost of the Stewards' Army, he was dead. But he didn't think so. The haphazard pattern of campfires was not that of the military.

If this were an encampment of the lawless, he might have a chance. He wished Smokee was here. She was the talker. He could speak to the breeds and the conscripts—they understood him and he understood them. But for the ones who had been real people once, the relinquished and the renegades, she had the gift. He was painfully aware of his own limitations, the crude and simple words that were all he knew. But there was no time to send for her, and it was up to him.

"Lakefolk!" he cried out. "Hold your fire! Let this fighter talk a minute."

"What you got to say?" came the sneering response.

The voice, the accent, the use of "you" told him he was not dealing with breeds. He relaxed, just a millimeter, because he could still die here. Yet what he needed to save his life was not firepower or force or the sheer ruthless brutality he knew how to muster up. What would save his life were words, the right words, if he could find them.

"We're not the enemy!" he called out. "'We' still didn't come easily to him, but he used it deliberately, because a breed who was still part of the army never would, and the snipers in the bush would be listening to every nuance, trying to decide who it was they were facing. "Not here to drive you out or round you up. Just passin' through."

"Through to where?" called a gruff voice.

"Through to liberate the Southlands!" River cried in a ringing tone.

A cynical laugh was the response. "You and who? Jesus and the band from Mars? What the fuck you talkin' about?"

"Talkin' about you," River said. Words began to come to him, and he let them flow. "You people, why you here? Cuz you had nothin' and nowhere to go. Right?"

"Right," came back a cautious voice of agreement.

"But why?" River asked. "You strong, or you wouldn't survive. You smart, or you be debt slaves sweatin' in the hellhole plantations. Why you have to run, and hide, and scrape the dirt for a few bites to eat?"

"Tell you why—cuz the Primes take it all. They suck blood like vampires. Feed on sweat and flesh. And Primes got the army to keep order.

"But what happens when the army wakes up? When the people wake up? We here *are* the army, army sent to take over the North. But when we got there, we say, wait a minute. Here in the North, they got no Primes. No debt slaves, no relinquishment, no breeds, no pens. Here, everybody got a right to be whoever they want to be. Maybe we in the wrong fuckin' army!"

He couldn't see his audience, but he heard a light snicker. He sensed he was getting through to them—at least they hadn't shot him yet. He took a breath and went on.

"So now this the Army of Liberation! Along with our friends from the North, marchin' together, liberating debt slaves and plantations all down the Central Valley. Marchin' to Angel City to join the insurrection there. Gonna throw the Primes out on their fat swollen asses and take back our land and take back our people!

"So join us! We succeed, this place be yours, free and clear. No debt. No more hidin' and skulkin' and scrapin'. You got a right to live free, on your own piece of land, raise your children in the sunlight without the shadow of the pens or the plantations. Gonna fight for that!"

Cheers came from behind him, and he thought he heard a faint cheer in the hills.

"How we know you tellin' the truth?" came the challenge. "How we know this ain't a trick of the Stewards?"

"Stewards don't do tricks," River called back. "Wanna root you out, move in with a couple tanks, shell the place. Or wait for a clear day, bomb it from the air. If we the Stewards, you already be dead."

A long, long moment.

Then the answer came.

"Okay, let's talk."

Chapter Fifty-Nine

How to Make a Revolution: III

Be like mushrooms.

Spread your mycelial threads underground, and connect them out of sight. Extrude them, extend them, clamping one to another in a pattern with no center to destroy, no head to cut off.

Then exude. Sweat out the revolutionary fervor that dissolves old structures, that breaks toxins apart.

Extend your reach, link root to root. Trees feed their young through subterranean fungal webs. Be a conduit. Take in. Share.

Be ephemeral, mostly invisible. Pop up everywhere, overnight, and then disappear.

But also be like trees.

Grow slowly. Push up from below, when you're ready.

Draw from deep sources, but also take in light.

Build structure. Flex and strengthen your fiber so when the storms hit, you can hold your ground.

Feed on light, on air and water. Grow.

Grow so tall that you can be seen from everywhere, a brave silhouette that shapes a new skyline.

And don't grow alone.

A Century of Good Advice:
The Autobiography of Maya Greenwood
Yerba Buena: Califia Press, 2049

S TRONG AND IMPENETRABLE, THE HUGE WAREHOUSE PRESENTED A
blank, concrete façade to the outside world. Before the Collapse, it
had been a big box store. Now weeds poked up through the cracks in
an acre of pitted asphalt, a parking lot for cars that would never come
again. A newly repaved pathway like a dark river led to a receiving dock
where trucks backed up to be loaded with chips. Surrounding it, in the
darkness, stood low-slung, crumbling houses that had once been prosper-
ous suburbs. Now their stucco fronts were falling away in chunks, their
lawns bare hard dirt, or infilled with shanties and jerry-built apartments.

A river of fire flowed out of the surrounding darkness. Torches flared
and angry voices cried out a chant. In the lead were cold pale flames, the
avenging Angels, their blond hair gleaming red with reflected fire. Behind
them, the mob, some armed with guns and rifles, others with sticks and
broken bottles, others simply with their rage.

A line of soldiers guarded the entrance bay. They raised their riot
guns and opened fire, but the press of bodies was so great that the leaders
couldn't stop even if they'd wanted to. The crowd stampeded over soldiers and casualties alike, trampling them under a thousand angry feet.

The front lines of the rioters were in danger of getting crushed
against the walls. Uriel sprang up on the shoulders of Gabe and vaulted
onto the ruins of the old marquee that had crowned the entranceway
when shoppers had thronged here. She blew a blast on a trumpet and
cried out in her loud clear voice, and the crowd halted.

Rafael swarmed up a lamppost, attached a rope, and leapt down as a
hundred hands grabbed hold of the rope and hauled away. With a great
crash, the post toppled. Six burly men picked it up on their shoulders,
pushed through the press of people by the gates, and rammed the doors
of the receiving dock. Bam! Nothing.

"Harder!" someone yelled. BAM! A dent. A crack in the opening
between the bay and the deck. Bam! Bam! The door began to buckle.
Another few swings, and it caved. The crowd pressed in, far too many to
squeeze through the doorway.

Uriel organized a line and soon cases of chips were pouring out and
packets were being opened and munched. Thirsty rioters punched holes
in cans of soda and swigged down the sweet dark brew. Some sat down
to enjoy a picnic, while others ran home with their spoils to feed their
hungry families.

When the warehouse was nearly empty, the Angels held a hurried
conference.

"Celestial!" Uriel said with satisfaction, looking around as a last
handful of looters stripped the shelves. "Now what?"

"Next target?" Gabe asked.

Rafael shook his head. "This mob done for the moment. Grunts gonna attack, sooner or later. Time to fly home to heaven!"

By the time the riot squads arrived, the looting was complete. A few desultory scavengers were all that remained. At the sound of tromping feet, they fled. The Angels watched from the shadows as the soldiers took command of an empty warehouse and the sad corpses that littered the ground. Meanwhile, the mob were back home, enjoying their spoils. For some of them, this would be the first time they'd eaten in days.

An Angel brought the news to the Refuge, announcing it in Council.

"Food riots happening in the streets. Mob attacked a warehouse—looted it. Won't be the last. Don't have enough of the army to control them."

Loud talking and pandemonium broke out. Emily was facilitating again that night, and she did her best to bring the crowd back to some semblance of a group conversation.

"What's this mean for us?" Bob raised the question.

"They'll be looking for us!" a young mother cried in alarm.

"Lash searching for the Refuge," Gabriel agreed. "Won't be long."

The techies with their scramblers had bought them precious time, time to organize the marches and the protests, which had grown in the past weeks until Angel City seemed a vat bubbling with ferment. But no scrambler could fool the living eyes of a cop or a thrasher.

"Do we flee, or do we defend it?" Bird stood. "That's what we've got to decide."

"Defend it!" came a loud cry from the crowd.

"We have nowhere to flee to," Tianne said. "This is the place we've built. Even if we die defending it, that will be more than we had before."

"That's all very well for us," Emily said, slipping out of her role as facilitator. "But what about our kids? We can't sacrifice them!"

"Maybe we could send them to safety," Madrone suggested. She felt a cold knot of fear in her gut for herself, but overwhelming it was a greater terror. She imagined looking down at the broken bloody bodies of Zap and Zoom, and the other bright-faced children they played with. No, it was unthinkable. They were barely beginning to be children again now. How could she let their lives be stolen?

"Send them where?" Miss Ruby asked.

"To the North," Madrone said.

"How?"

Bird thought quickly. Yes, with the help of the hillboys and the navy—it was possible.

"We'll figure out the 'how,'" he said. "The question is, is that what we want to do? Send the children to safety, while we stay and defend the Refuge?"

"Yes!" came the thundering reply.

Madrone volunteered to contact the hillboys, reluctantly because she really wanted to stay and ready the healing center for the battle. But the hillboys knew and trusted her, and Beth was quite capable of setting up triage areas and inventorying supplies.

She was scared. That was the real source of her reluctance. Although she wasn't sure whether she was more afraid of getting caught outside the Refuge, or being caught inside when it was under siege. But at least then she'd be with Bird and the others.

She cycled up to the hills, pushing herself to do the journey faster than she had ever done before, and reached the camp at dawn, sweaty, breathless, and thirsty. A hurried conference with Hijohn secured them a truck for that very night. While he and the other hillboys plotted a route, she hiked away from camp, up to a high ridge where she could radio out to the navy without fear of the signal being tracked.

"Copy," came a young girl's voice.

"Copy, Red Tree here," Madrone said, using her code name.

"Copy Red Tree. Big Pink here."

"Big Pink?" Something about the voice, even over the crackle of the radio, sounded all too familiar. In alarm, she broke all codes of protocol. "Rosa? What the jacks are you doing down here?"

"Big Pink," the girl replied calmly. "I'm staffing coms. Did you have someone you wanted to talk with?"

Madrone had a thousand things she wanted to say, but she bit them back. Now wasn't the time. Still, when she saw Rosa and Isis and Sara too, she would say them! Loudly!

"Pirate Girl," she said.

A hurried conference with Isis secured help from the navy.

"Suffered some bad damage and a lot of casualties," Isis told her. "But we got an old ferry or two we can deploy to do this."

Quickly, they hammered out a plan. Not until all the details were covered did Madrone say, "How in Hecate did Big Pink get on this mission?"

"That's a story," Isis said. "Better told at another time. But don't you worry about her. We'll keep her safe."

"Send her back with the transport!" Madrone pleaded.

"That is the plan."

Madrone, after a fitful hour of sleep in the sun, spent the afternoon ministering to the hillboys' illnesses, and the wounds they'd acquired in raids. She brewed them up a good supply of the booster withdrawal elixir and the general antiviral, antibiotic brew. Then she set off after dark, to make her way back to the Refuge.

"I'm out of shape," she thought. "Too much healing and trancing, and not enough aerobic exercise." But the way back was mostly downhill and she made good time, fueled by anxiety. Would the place be surrounded? Would they be able to get the children out?

She avoided the main entrance and went to one of the secret back ways, the tunnel that led down through a labyrinth of ruins and came out in the east sector. No one seemed to be watching, and the guard recognized her and let her through.

They called a special Council at dawn, and spent the day preparing the children. It was a tearful, awful day that Madrone never wanted to relive. She was in the thick of it, packing for Zap and Zoom, making sure they had their favorite clothes and that Zap had his little stuffed bear which she knew he slept with secretly. She and Bird set the boys down to say goodbye.

"Boys, I have something serious to tell you," she began. "You know that we're expecting the Stewards to attack this place any day now. When they do, we're not going to just go away."

"We're going to fight," Zoom said with satisfaction.

"We are," Bird said. "At least, we're going to defend this place, hopefully with weapons other than guns. But we want you boys to be safe, and all the other children too. So we're going to send you to a safe place."

"I don't wanna go," said Zap.

"I know," Madrone said. "I don't want you to go. But I want you to be protected."

"You said you'd never send us away," said Zoom, his lip quivering.

"Oh sweetie, we're not sending you away because we don't want you! We want you. We love you! That's why we want you to be safe, away from the battle."

"We'll come find you again," Bird promised. "You're going to the North, where we come from. To the beautiful City. We'll come find you there and we'll show you all the parks and the playgrounds and the Learning Tracks."

"Not if they kill you first," said Zap.

"Well, we hope they won't," Bird said. "But if they do, we'll die easier knowing that you are safe and others will look after you."

"I don't wanna go!" Zap repeated stubbornly.

The conversations and the arguments went on in a hundred families that day, with tears and shouting amidst the frantic packing and the ongoing preparations for a possible siege. The scene in the plaza that night was heartbreaking, with parents hugging their children for possibly the last time, and issuing frantic last instructions. Emily's face was gray with worry as she said goodbye to Hannah and Heather. Lila had elected to go with the convoy, and Annabel clung to her as she took charge of the other rescued wildings and frightened children.

At last midnight drew near, the last goodbyes were said, and as Beth administered calming teas to distraught parents, Madrone and Lila and the scouts led the children out in groups of twenty—some from the front entrance, some from the back—to the two rendezvous points they'd agreed upon. Both were within blocks of the Refuge, but in different directions, in case one was spotted.

Madrone led one of the first groups, then came back to the Refuge for another round. Some of the scouts would go with the convoy, along with Lila and a couple of the other adults who had volunteered to help escort the children rather than stay for the fight. The first wave went through without a hitch, and the second wave followed close behind. Zap and Zoom were in the third wave, and Madrone had decided to let someone else conduct them. Better to say goodbye in the Refuge, like all the other parents.

But when she went to the plaza where the last of the children were gathered, she found Bird frantically searching.

"Zap is missing," he said. "He's hiding out. Damn it!"

"Did you check ... "

"I checked everywhere. His room, our room, the school, his favorite hideouts. But he's not stupid, that boy. If he doesn't want to be found, he won't be found."

"The convoy is heading out," Madrone said. "It can't wait."

"It's got to go, then," Bird said.

"I'm going!" Zoom said proudly. "I wanna sail on a boat and see the North!"

Madrone gave him a tight hug, holding him so closely he squirmed away in protest.

"You're choking me!" he complained.

"I love you," she said, realizing how much she did. This wounded, cocky, irritating little boy they had saved from death—how dear he had grown to her.

"I love you, too," Bird said.

Madrone knelt down and gave Zoom a kiss on his cheek. Much to her surprise, he threw his arms around her, hugged her, and kissed her back.

He had never done that before.

Then the line of children and scouts moved off, and he was gone.

Zap emerged in time for breakfast, grinning and unrepentant. Madrone was so angry she let loose and yelled at him.

"Don't you smirk at me like that—you disobedient little brat! Don't you know what you've done?"

But of course he did know, and he sat calm, stoic, and self-satisfied under the barrage. The convoy was gone, and there was no way they could send him on now. She was shaking so hard with anger that Bird finally pushed her gently into the bedroom and closed the door.

"I'll deal with him," he said. "You're going to have the bees on us in another minute."

Bird squatted down to catch Zap's eyes, and opened his mouth for the lecture on safety and obedience. But he couldn't help remembering another young boy, ten years old, sneaking out of the house with his skateboard on the morning of the Uprising.

He had been so different from Zap—a beloved, innocent child who had never really known fear or grief until that morning. He remembered it so vividly, rummaging in his closet for his baseball mitt so he'd be equipped to lob back hot tear gas canisters. He'd grabbed his skateboard, and then towed a reluctant and terrified Madrone down to the makeshift emergency clinic in their basement garage and abandoned her there. He felt a little bit guilty about that. But that was where she'd demanded to go. She'd always said she wanted to be a doctor, like her mother, and she lost her fear as she helped the medics wash out the eyes of the tear gas victims.

He remembered seeing her in the doorway of the makeshift clinic, backlit by the sun, her unruly hair a halo. A line of patients kneeled before her like worshipers, as she tended to their eyes, a small angel of mercy.

Maybe it was that moment that had made her a healer. It was certainly the moment when something shifted in him, when he saw her not just as his annoying little friend, but something far, far more.

Then he'd run back out to the street—the noise, the chanting, the crazy excitement of it all. Maya and Johanna and the other old women were in the center of a huge crowd, swinging pickaxes at the pavement and planting little saplings of trees. Behind the crowd were the tanks and soldiers of the army. Gas swirled around them in misty clouds, but they raised bandannas and kept on.

He had watched his grandmother, awed with admiration. Then something had caught his eye. There was a gunner in the ranks of troops, sitting on an armored personnel carrier. Bird saw him swing his rifle, take aim at Maya and the women. For a long moment, time seemed to stop. All he could think was, She's going to die and there's nothing I can do.

Then a tear gas canister flew by him. And suddenly there was something he could do.

He'd leapt and caught it in his mitt, hopped onto his skateboard and raced toward the APC, gas streaming, screaming at people to get out of his way. He had some crazy memories of jumping steps, skimming along curbs impossibly narrow—but it was all happening in less than a moment, and then he was in range, and he threw.

After twenty years, he could still feel that lob in his pitching arm, with his eyes fixed on the gunner, his mind trusting his body to send the can on the right trajectory to hit its target.

And it did, hitting the gunner in his stomach, spoiling his aim so the shot went wild. Better than that, it tumbled down into the APC, belching gas, and all the soldiers manning it came streaming out.

He was flooded with pure joy and pride. He still felt it, twenty years later, remembering that throw. Maybe that was the moment that had made him a warrior.

Then his dad, among the medics, had spied him and yelled at him, and Bird had yelled back, "Look what I did!" His dad turned and stepped forward....

A bullet exploded in his father's chest, and Bird watched as he sank into a pool of his own blood, and died.

And maybe *that* was the moment that had made him a warrior.

He sat for a moment, staring at Zap who now had set his jaw into a stubborn line. His own dad should have locked him in the basement, he thought. A ten-year-old had had no business in the midst of a battle. Zap was only six or seven, as far as they could guess. But there was no safe basement here to lock him in. Safety was gone with the convoy, and Zap had made his choice.

"You know," Bird told him, "I was just a little older than you during the Uprising in the North. On the day the tanks rolled in, my parents absolutely forbade me to leave the house. I was supposed to stay home, take care of Madrone. But I wanted so badly to go out in the streets, get into the action. So I know how you feel."

"What you do?" Zap asked, stealing a look up at him.

Bird smiled. "What you think? I snuck out. I had my skateboard, so I could run messages. I had a catcher's mitt, to pick up hot cans of tear gas. I may have saved my grandmother's life. I probably caused my father's death."

"You shoot him?"

"No. I distracted him, made him be in the wrong place at the wrong time."

Zap shook his head. "Bad luck kill him, not you."

Was that true, Bird wondered? Or rather, how was it not true? Had he been carrying the guilt for his father's death all these years, rightly or wrongly? Had Zap, this stubborn child far too familiar with death, just offered him the absolution he hadn't known he needed.

I should feel lightness, release, he thought. But what he actually felt was a sudden sense of vertigo, as if he were teetering on a narrow ledge above a deep abyss. His guilt had been his tie rope, his safety line. It kept him tethered to something solid, some sense of structure. Without it, he could tumble into this vortex where there was no cause, no agency, no control, only impersonal forces of luck and chance.

Yet try as he might, he couldn't call back his sense of culpability. He would have to free climb without it. Battle was looming, and whether he and his loved ones lived or died was not, never had been, under his command.

"Well, you're in it now," he said to Zap. "So try to have good luck."

Chapter Sixty

GENERAL WENDELL SAT HUNCHED OVER HIS DESK IN HIS COMMAND center, drafting a memo to the top Primes and politicians. He was sore and tired after a long night on his knees, a night of penitence and prayer. God was punishing him for something, he thought. Or was it the devil himself, sending his minions after him? Was that why *he* kept evading capture—demonic aid?

Purity. That's what it took to fight demons. Purity of mind and body, but even more important, purity of purpose. He was putting his career on the line with this memo, but that was okay. He was done with toadying and cajoling and pretending to go along with their decadence. A military man kept his focus on the goal and ignored distractions.

And the situation called for a military man at the helm. So he was recommending that they put Angel City under martial law.

Then he would control the police, the Lash and the riot squads, and all the rest of them. He could coordinate with his own troops and the drone squads. He would be the one to bring the city to heel!

And he would not be weak about it! This job was too hard to be done by a sentimentalist. He'd do whatever it takes to win.

For if he didn't now, there would be nothing left.

The rabble was roused, the army of the squabs was on the march, and thanks to Alexander's failures, troops were thin on the ground. But bring all the forces together under one command, and they would strike like a fist.

Finch, his aide, entered quietly and snapped to attention.

"Sir."

"What is it?"

"Sir, they've attacked Distribution Depot 113 and opened it. Guards were calling for backup when they went down...."

"They? Who are they?"

"A mob, sir."

So it had begun. Maybe this would play well for him—show the Primes just what was at risk.

"What backup do we have to send them?" Wendell asked.

"We could call the 101st off the search for the rebels' hideout...."

"No!" Wendell shook his head vehemently. They needed to find *him*, take out the leaders of this insurrection. The first rule of warfare. Cut off the head of the monster and the monster falls.

That was far more important than contesting every liquor store the rabble might decide to loot. It took a leader with a strategic mind to see it, to keep the focus clear.

"But I don't want to go back to the North!" Rosa tightened a rope around the mainsail cleat as if she were strangling a mortal enemy, her lips tightening into a sulk.

Isis watched her, hands on hips, and sighed. She didn't have energy for this argument, not least because if it were up to her, she'd let the girl stay.

"We had a deal," Isis told Rosa firmly.

"So a deal can change." Rosa turned and tried on a sweet, engaging smile. "I like being part of the navy."

Better than the sulk, Isis thought, but she wasn't going for it. "You part of the navy, you under orders. Orders say, you gotta get back to the safe zone. You already been too close to fire."

"That's age discrimination!"

"Absolutely."

Rosa opened her mouth to argue, but Isis just stared her down, stone-faced and hard-eyed. Rosa fled down to the galley, where she relieved her feelings by banging pots and pans and slamming them down on the stove. The rice was slightly burned and the fish overcooked, but Isis didn't say a word when she made her own way down for supper. She just sipped her wine and smiled at the girl.

After half an hour of silence, Isis finally lost patience.

"Look, you old enough to be in the navy, old enough not to sulk and whine at orders. Gonna be doin' a job for us, accompanying the transport back north. If it wasn't you, some other salt gotta do it, and they don't get to complain."

"It's a made-up job," Rosa complained.

"Not! It's a rule. Every ship gets an escort, in case of trouble."

"So what do I do in the *Day of Victory* if the *Winstanley* sinks? Cram all the survivors onto the bowsprit?"

"You run for help," Isis told her.

Her role was not so bad, Rosa admitted to herself a day later. Of course, she'd never admit that to Isis. She'd followed the *Winstanley*, a reclaimed ferry that had once plied the bay from the City to Marin. They headed back up the coast, a tame ride but still, she acknowledged, it was fun being the captain of the *Day of Victory*, making her own decisions, setting her own sails. She knew Isis trusted her, otherwise she wouldn't have let her go off in the pirate's own boat, her pride and joy.

Anyway, the rest of the navy was still licking its wounds, making repairs to the warship and scouting the shipping lanes all over again. Livingston had not returned from the Gyro ship. Everyone else felt sorry for him but she still didn't trust him. Maybe he'd paid the Gyro Captain to pretend to kidnap him. Maybe he'd been the one to set the Stewards' navy on them!

Whatever. He was gone, and that was a relief. She'd avoided the gatherings on the warship, the common meals and the parties, staying alone on the *Victory*, out of his way. But now when they anchored at night she rowed over to the *Winstanley* and ate dinner with the crew. That was nice too, having company, with someone else cooking for a change, and hanging out with the sailors, playing cards and swapping tales. They didn't look at her with pity or accusations, just accepted her as one of them.

The rendezvous was scheduled for three in the morning. The sky was cloudy, and only the dim light of the stars cast a soft glow through the veil of haze. The hillboys had picked a deserted stretch of beach where the coastal mountains came down to the shore. They'd trucked the kids up into the hills and were marching them down the last miles, carrying the youngest ones, on a secret trail through the scrub that only the Resistance knew.

The *Winstanley* anchored far offshore. Every dinghy, rowboat, and rubber raft in the flotilla was gathered, ready to run shuttles back to shore.

Rosa took the *Day of Victory* in close. With its shallow keel it could anchor in water merely fifteen feet deep. They waited, as the boom of the waves began to relax and soften as the wind died down. And they waited ...

At last—a flash of light on the hills. Rosa strained her eyes to see through the dark as little boats plied the waves around her.

"Ahoy!" she heard a cry, and tossed the rope ladder down. A dinghy scraped against the side, and she winced for the *Victory*'s paint job. One by one, five small figures scurried up. Then the boat pushed off with another painful scrape, and a soft-sided zodiac grabbed hold.

As the deck filled with boatload after boatload, she hauled up the anchor to be ready to go. When the decks were crowded with thirty or more children, she fired up the silent electric engines and headed out.

"Hurry, hurry," she urged the kids as she expertly pulled the *Day of Victory* up alongside the *Winstanley*. The crew on board threw down rope ladders, and a few of them climbed down to carry the ones too young to climb.

As soon as they were safely aboard, Rosa again revved the engines even as the crew pulled the ladders up. She had furled the sails. There was plenty of juice in the batteries and this was a mission that needed speed and efficiency, not the vagaries of the wind. Back she went and held the boat steady as a swarm of zodiacs surrounded it, with children scrambling up the sides and over the rails. She packed them in, sent some down to the galley while others clung to the rails and swarmed over the deck.

She felt exhilarated. This was dangerous after all, and exciting, and she knew that her skill with the boat, her efficient steering and navigation, helped shave precious minutes off the time needed to transport more than a hundred kids from shore to ship. Every moment increased their risk of discovery.

One trip, two trips. A third—and there were kids stuffed into the cabin, sitting two deep on the bunks, hanging on the rails.

"One last load," cried a hillboy, pulling up in a rowboat with seven children aboard. "Can you take them? Then we're outta here."

Somehow she'd find room. So far their luck had held, but she really wanted this shuttle to be her last. She tossed him a rope and he pulled the rowboat in close alongside the ship's ladder. The bigger children scrambled up—then the tallest boy leaned down to grab a toddler as the hillboy hoisted her. But he wasn't a seaman, Rosa realized, stifling a cry of warning as he leaned too far, overbalancing. He caught himself just in time before the boat tipped over, flung himself back and crashed down on the gunwale with a loud cry, leaving the tiny girl dangling in a ten-year-old's grip.

The girl was screaming, her feet kicking frantically as the older child clung on, screaming back at her. All the kids were shouting and crying, forgetting the need for silence, and the sound echoed over the water.

Rosa froze. She needed a moment to kill the engine, to rush over to the scene of the disaster. But before she could get there, a young boy vaulted over the side, scooted down the ladder, and grabbed the toddler around the waist. He held her tight against the ladder and the side of the boat as she wailed. Then the helpful hands of some of the older, stronger kids reached down and drew her up. The boy scrambled back up like a monkey.

Somewhere far down the dark beach, a light went on, as if the noise had woken some Primes in their oceanfront estate.

"Loose the painter!" Rosa called down to the hillboy who was rubbing his sore arm. He looked up at her blankly.

"The rope! Untie your boat!"

"Broke my fuckin' arm!"

She heard a humming sound, coming from the air. A recon drone?

"I don't care. Just cut yourself loose!"

She didn't wait to see if he complied, just revved up the engine and darted back out toward the *Winstanley*. Her heart was pounding. What if the drone set trackers on them? What if it wasn't just recon, but armed?

The child was still wailing. Noise—a drone could pick that up!

"Take her down to the cabin," Rosa called. "Shut the blasted door!"

The cries became a more muffled wail, then slowly faded. Someone, she hoped, was comforting the girl as well as stifling her. She gripped the tiller tightly and took some deep breaths to ground and calm herself. She couldn't afford to panic—after all, hadn't she argued for her right to be part of the dangerous missions? Did she want to prove they were right, that she was too young for this?

She made herself stay calm and follow the bearing back to the ship. There it lay, and again she swooped up alongside, roped in, and helped propel the kids up the ladders, one after another.

They were almost all up when the humming sound grew louder. A beam of light swept over the sea, and a hot hiss of a laser scorched one of the zodiacs, which burst with a loud bang.

Then a shot rang out from the *Winstanley*'s deck, and the drone exploded in a starburst of flame.

"Move!" she yelled at the last two children on the ladder. They scurried up, terrified, and she desperately wanted to follow them into the relative safety of the big ship. But Isis had entrusted the *Victory* to her. She couldn't leave it.

With shaking hands, she cast loose, revved away from the *Winstanley* and quickly hoisted her sails to catch the breeze. She had some battery power left, but not enough to carry her through a long night evading pursuit and following the big ship. She needed wind. Goddess didn't provide much, but she would use what she had. The *Winstanley* set a course north, and she followed.

"Great Mother Night," she murmured, "spread your cloak of darkness and hide us. Flap it gently and fill our sails with wind."

It was the first time she had prayed since her own mother died. "She's in the arms of Mother Mary," the nuns had said. "She's in the arms of the Great Mother," Allie had assured her. Frack that! She wanted her mother's arms around *her*, to shelter *her*. What kind of stupid Mother let mothers and babies die? Let men do the things that had been done to her....

She shivered. A light breeze picked up, as if the night and the ocean were answering her prayer.

I can't always protect you. I can't keep you from harm. But my arms are always open, and I have never stopped loving you.

The wind in the sails sang with a woman's voice. Was it her mother? Or the Mother? Or just some great mothering force in the universe that lifts the spray from the waves and sends it back to shore as life-giving rain?

She didn't know. She didn't really care. She just let it enfold her and carry her into the embrace of the night.

Chapter Sixty-One

How to Make a Revolution: IV

How do you build a fire?

Know what your tinder will be, how you will make a spark, how you will capture it and feed it into flame.

Lay kindling, a bit of paper, small twigs, pine needles, things that are light, that catch fire easily but have no staying power.

Position the larger twigs, the thin branches. They will need encouragement to get going, and burn out quickly. But that's their purpose: not to sustain, but to ignite.

Place the bigger branches, those that burn hot and intensify your small fire into a blaze.

Last of all, the logs. Those that need great heat and are slow to catch fire. Have patience, for when they do they will burn for a long time, steadily. Now you can cook: now you can make the true transformation.

When the flames die down, and nothing seems left, stir the coals.

The deeper the ash, the more likely you are to find something smoldering: a last ember, a spark to ignite the next conflagration.

A Century of Good Advice:
The Autobiography of Maya Greenwood
Yerba Buena: Califia Press, 2049

THE TRUCKS CAME DOWN OUT OF THE MOUNTAINS, PACKED WITH recruits, new volunteers crammed on their roofs and hanging off the sides. Below them spread the wide panorama of Saint Ferd's Valley, a flat stretch of land that had once been orange groves and farms, then suburbs and shopping malls. Now it was reverting back to swaths of farmland studded with warehouses, divided by more densely populated strips around the old freeways.

Red flares of burning buildings studded the plain, and smoke billowed out from them, settling into a dull haze as if it didn't have quite the spirit it needed to rise. It blotted out the few visible stars, but reflected enough light so that the red glare of the fires and the white of artificial lights combined to create a pink, glowing haze.

Smokee sniffed. The air carried the harsh reek of fire laced with chemicals. She savored it—the perfume of insurrection. Smoky, like her name.

Far across the Valley a lower range of mountains held the haunts of the hillboys and the gated canyons where the elite of the Primes built their mansions. Beyond that, in the flatlands below, lay the urban heart of Angel City itself.

But first, they had to cross this plain, covered with red flares and swirling clouds like visible rage, dark against the ruby glow.

Suddenly she felt a great longing for something else. A clean fresh wind off the ocean to sweep it all away and leave the air clear. A salt-tanged breeze in her lungs, blue skies, and the golden sunrise of a new day ...

Enough brooding. They were moving out.

They swept down from the hills, marching along the old freeways. Now they began to hear the roar of the crowds. Below them, they could see swarms surrounding one of the big box stores that served the Stewards as warehouses. All over the Valley, they were ablaze.

For days now, mobs had been attacking the storehouses, looting the stocks of food and goods the poor could not afford to buy. The Stewards' police and troops between them were hard-pressed to keep any semblance of order. As soon as they quelled one riot, another broke out in some other part of town. A hundred fires raged below, as if an army of giants were encamped on the broad plain.

The Army of Liberation rolled down an old off-ramp and paused on a slight rise of ground that looked over the scene of chaos surrounding one of the warehouses. Knots of determined men were battering down the doors and bashing holes in the walls with sledgehammers. Yelling rioters danced on the hood of some Prime's private car, which bowed under their weight.

An old car hurtled toward the warehouse wall. Just before it collided, the driver bailed out, leaving it to crash through the wall like a missile.

A crowd poured in. They could hear the weak report of a few shots, fired from the entrance, but they were soon silenced. Nothing could withstand that flood of rage.

Smokee, watching, felt both exhilarated and frightened. This fury dwarfed even her own, and left her feeling small and empty. What could she do in the face of this? How could any words be heard over this deafening roar?

And yet Erik Farmer was handing her a microphone, the gift of the City with its love for processions and outdoor festivals and mass meetings, its technicians who'd spent twenty years perfecting their sound systems for addressing crowds. Her voice could carry over the thunder. But what would she say? What words could change this mob into a spear of liberation?

Some instinct told her to simply match the energy. She cried out a chant:

> "*No more slavery, no more debt!*
> *Stewards ain't seen nothin' yet!*"

Behind her the army thundered an echo, and slowly the crowd below began to take it up, just a few at first, then more, and more. The stompers on the cars began to jump up and down in unison. A group of men with a telephone pole were now working on a new stretch of wall, and they swung it in rhythm, pounding against the concrete.

> "*NO MORE SLAVERY, NO MORE DEBT!*
> *STEWARDS AIN'T SEEN NOTHIN' YET!*"

It was an affirmation, a cock-crow of pride and defiance, that dissolved into a huge cheer as the ram smashed a second opening through the wall itself. The crowd surged forward, and Smokee raised her voice and cried out above them.

"People of Angel City," she cried, "this is the hour of victory! The Day of Liberation has come! So let's don't die now! We all crowd into that goody-box, we gonna crush each other like roaches in a bottle. So let's stay strong, stand your ground, and let the bashers inside throw the shit out to us!"

She had little hope that her words could stem the flood tide rushing in, but enough people felt the sense in what she said, or saw the danger for themselves, that slowly the crush began to ease. Swiftly she improvised a new chant:

> "*Throw the food out*
> *To the people!*
> *Throw the food out*
> *To the people!*"

It didn't rhyme, but it had a rhythm and it said what needed to be said. And when they chanted together, she realized, they unified. The chant made a whole out of the angry parts. She heard yells from inside the big box, and then cans and boxes and loaves of bread began to fly out of the breach. Quickly, she came up with a new rhyme:

> "*Pass it back,*
> *Spread it around,*

> *Share the wealth*
> *All over this town!"*

She was on a roll. The army echoed her, and below, the crowd took up both the chant and the instructions. Those close to the breach tossed bread and packets of chips and cans of soup back. They flew from hand to hand, a wild confetti of plenty littering the crowd who were now laughing and cheering and occasionally howling as a flying can connected to an unprotected head.

"People of Angel City," Smokee cried out. "We are beautiful! We are not the Stewards, not gonna hoard and fight and starve our brothers. We're gonna share the wealth so there's enough for all!"

A big cheer rose up. Erik Farmer was looking up at her in wonder. "Go, Smokee!" he breathed. River was nodding and smiling as if he'd expected nothing less.

"The Day of Liberation is here!" Smokee cried. "The rule of the Stewards is over!"

A roar rose up. Like a lion, Smokee thought, waking up and feeling its power.

"Together, we're gonna bring 'em down! But we got more fighting ahead! We are the Army of Liberation! We've fought our way down from the North. We've freed our sisters and brothers from the slave plantations—and now they are marching with us, as free people!"

Another huge roar, as if all the lions in the world were gathered together. Then a strange silence. They were listening.

"But even now, the Stewards' Army is forming up, heading this way to crush us under their dirty heels. Are we going to let them?"

"No!" the crowd called back.

"I can't hear you!" Smokee cried.

"NO!"

"When they come for us, are we going to run?" she asked.

"NO!"

"Are we going to hide?"

"NO!"

"Are we going to fight?"

"YES!" A thunderous, earth-shaking roar.

Smokee held up her hand. "I hear you! We're gonna fight! And I know we're not afraid. We got nothin' left to lose, and everything to gain. But do you want to fight as a mob they can scatter with the first shot?"

"NO," the answer came back with a note of uncertainty in it.

"Or are we going to fight as an army, an invincible army of liberation?"

"YES!"

"An army to fight for your kids and lives and your rights!"

"YES!"

"An army to end the debts and the relinquishments!"
"YES!"
"An army to make a space for a new world, a free world!"
"YES!"
"We are the Rising!"
"YES!"
"We are the dawning of the bright new day!"
"YES!"

And the sun was rising, creeping up over the ring of hills to the east. Smokee felt it, a warmth seeping through the smoldering haze, like the heat she felt in her words, her voice. She was alight with love, incandescent. If she exploded in a rain of fire, she would rise again from her own ashes and take wing, invincible.

This rabble of rioters, crazed by desperation, they could be her parents and her brother and herself. She loved them, in all their fury and destructiveness, as she had loved her parents and her brother, as she loved this flat and wretched piece of ground and the garden it could become, as she might someday once again love herself.

She was good, River thought. She had the words, the magic touch. Meanwhile he was rapidly calculating their strategy.

He sent twenty of his most trusted leaders out to form up the mob into units. Not all the looters would come, but enough would that they couldn't all ride. They would march forward on foot, with the trucks bringing up supplies in the rear. That would make for a slower progress, but along the way they would be recruiting, preparing, training.

He quickly thought over all the possibilities, about how to counter offensives and how to protect his own ragged troops who had lots of fury but were weak on actual weapons or training. He thought about bullets, and lasers, and shells, and drones. He looked at maps. And he made his plans.

By the end of the morning, the mob had become an army on the move.

General Wendell cast a bleary-eyed gaze over the vidscreen, which showed snap after snap of mayhem and destruction all over St. Ferd's Valley. And that was just from the cameras that somehow remained intact. When he shifted to overview, there were huge gaps where cameras had been taken out. He'd ordered surveillance drones out to fill the blank spots, but half of them had been shot down. He felt a trickle of sweat crawl down his temple.

The warehouses were falling, one by one. That was bad, but Wendell still knew in his heart that it wasn't the worst of his problems. No, somewhere in the city was the nest, and from it the terrorists spilled out like ants, spreading their poison everywhere. Root it, kill the head of it, and the whole thing would die away like a swarm deprived of their queen.

Only in this case, it wasn't a queen but a king. *Him!*

He heard a soft cough, and looked up from his command-center display to see Finch standing at attention. Too young for the job, Wendell thought, but his elders were off now commanding field units. Finch annoyed him, with his plump pink cheeks, his white-blond buzz cut, and his eagerness to be helpful when his help wasn't wanted.

"At ease," he barked. "What is it?"

"Sir, the Valley is in flames. We should send every division we've got to quell the riots or we'll lose ... "

"Don't tell me what we'll lose!" Wendell snapped. "I know what we'll lose! I've ordered every spare division we've got to sweep the Valley."

"With all due respect, sir, that might not be enough," Finch said, his weak blue eyes fixed on the wall above Wendell's head. He looked for all the world like a rabbit, Wendell thought. An officious, self-important, smart-ass bunny rabbit. "There's the 101st and now the 57th..."

"They're needed for the house-to-house searches."

"But can't the SWAT teams and the civvy police handle that, sir?"

Wendell stood up in a fury, towering over his quivering aide.

"There's a rat's nest somewhere, and we're going to root it out! Whatever it takes!"

"Yes, sir."

Wendell came to a decision.

"Order drone ops to the search teams."

"We were going to deploy them in the Valley, sir," Finch said in his rabbitty squeaky voice.

"The Valley is a bunch of witless mobs. Show them some firepower and they'll be crawling back to their holes!"

"Sir, they seem to be a bit more organized than that. From the reports ... "

A rabbit too stupid to know when to quit. "How long are you going to insult me and question my authority?" Wendell's voice rose. "Take out their leadership, and their whole structure will crumble, riots, and all."

"Sir, I'm not sure ... "

"Enough! You want to argue, you can argue with the overseers on the work levies. You want to fight, you shut up and don't question your superiors!" Fuck it, he didn't have to defend his decisions to this little snot rag.

"Yes, sir." Finch snapped a salute and marched off.

That was more like it. But the questions made Wendell uneasy. How dare the little prick try to undermine his command?

I'm right, Wendell assured himself. He could feel the evil emanating, he had to root out the source of it. It was worth whatever they expended, drones or men.

Get *him!*

Chapter Sixty-Two

R OSA WOKE SUDDENLY, COLD AND STIFF. WHERE WAS SHE? SHE shivered and looked around her, felt the hard length of the tiller under her arm. She was on the deck of the *Day of Victory*. She must have fallen asleep.

It had been a long sail, all through the night. The *Winstanley* crew had offered to send someone to spell her, but she'd insisted she could do it alone. By midnight, she'd started to wonder if she'd made a mistake. She caught her eyelids drooping shut, her head dropping. From time to time, she'd awaken with a jerk. Once she'd even lost sight of the *Winstanley*, but a quick trim of the sail and an increase in speed had brought the big ship's bulk back in sight. She'd lashed the tiller on course, just in case.

But it seemed that sleep had claimed her, after all. The first rays of the sun warmed her cheeks as it crept over the coastal mountains. She looked around in alarm. There was no sign of the *Winstanley*, and her own sails were flapping. She desperately had to pee, and so she quickly ducked down to the galley, relieved herself, refilled her water bottle, and grabbed a roll and a hunk of cheese for a quick breakfast. Then she hurried back up to the deck, trimmed the sails, and adjusted the tiller.

The batteries had charged during the night from the windspinners atop the masts, and now the rising sun would give them extra energy from the solar sails. She revved up the engine and made all the speed she could toward the north.

It was half an hour before the *Winstanley* came in sight, and when it did, she knew immediately that something was wrong. The big ship was listing to one side, as if she were taking on water, and blocking her bow sat an armored patrol boat emblazoned with the seal of the Stewardship.

Mierda! They were supposed to be in safe waters, too far north for the navy to patrol. Isis said the Stewards' forces never ranged farther than Lompoc. It was one of the helpful pieces of information they'd gotten from Livingston....

Livingston!

Rosa felt sick. Quickly, she reefed the sails, and pulled out Isis's binoculars. She swept the deck of the patrol boat, saw menacing guns trained on the *Winstanley*. Holy shit! She tried to raise the crew on her radio headset, but got nothing but static.

She tried the hillboys' frequency, tried the main line to the destroyer. Nothing. They were too far out of range.

What to do? Her hands were shaking. Run for help, Isis had said. But by the time she got help, the ship would be gone, towed back to some Stewards' base, and the children would be.... No, can't think about that. She felt terribly guilty for falling asleep—maybe if she'd been awake, she might have.... No, don't go there. Think about now. What to do now?

Through her binoculars, she caught a glimpse of motion on deck. A scurrying, streaking figure, a child, with three big black-clad navy salts pounding after him.

One of them caught him by the collar, but he shrugged free of his jacket and ran on. Another backed him against the wall—he lashed out viciously with his foot and kicked the scrub hard in the balls. Then the boy was off, only to run into the arms of a sailor who grabbed his limbs and attempted to hold him. But the boy kicked and wriggled and elbowed him in the nose, twisting and biting like a wild thing, until suddenly he jerked himself free and leapt over the rail and hurtled down, tumbling and twisting into a semblance of a dive, into the deep sea below.

Nothing broke the surface of the water. Could he swim? Rosa wondered. Where would a child from the Southlands learn how?

A sailor leaned over the deck, sprayed the sea with rifle fire. No red spurts of blood blossomed. But something caught her eye, a hundred yards away from the boat's wake. A gleam of blond hair catching the sun. He was there, alive. He was swimming, sort of, awkwardly bobbing and then sinking again, floating on the breakers. The watch on the boat either didn't see him or didn't care. They probably figured he'd drown, sooner or later, or get eaten by the sharks. What's one slave more or less—not worth the waste of time or ammo.

Suddenly she knew what she had to do. She had to save him, and she had to somehow slow the ship down.

She lashed the tiller, reefed the sails, and set the sea anchor. Then she ran below. No time to suit up, no diving gear on board here. She wished Isis had left her a gun, but she wasn't supposed to need one. However, there was Isis's shark-fishing harpoon. That might do it—even better because it was designed to work underwater. A plan was formulating in her mind. She tossed the harpoon along with a couple of life jackets into the dinghy, threw a gray canvas tarp over the small boat, and lay flat as she pulled the cord that started the engine.

Holding the tiller while trying to lie flat and somehow peek up over the tarp at the same time was awkward, at best. She thought her arm was going to twist off at the shoulder. But if she sat up, she ran the risk that hostile eyes would spy her. While she remained under the tarp, the dinghy would look just like a piece of big floating debris on their radar. Or so she hoped.

When she got closer to the *Winstanley*, she killed the engine. The ship's bulk would hide her from the patrol boat, but undoubtedly the Stewards' officers would have placed lookouts aboard the captured ferry. She risked peering up from under the tarp, her eyes sweeping the water for that blond thatch of hair.

At first she saw nothing. *Diosa!*—had he drowned already? Was she too late? The waves were small but choppy, she could see a bird floating on the water that bobbed up one minute, disappeared the next. He could still be out there.

She swept the area with her eyes, looked again. There—there was something. She whipped up the binoculars. A gull resting on the waves. But there—no, that was a seal, she thought, something sleek and brown. Damn it, it was a big ocean and he was a small, small boy....

There. Something yellow—yes, that was it. She set a course and sped over the waves, away from the *Winstanley*. He was drifting out to sea on a fast tide, and her engine lent speed to the current that pulled her out as well. Now she was far enough away from the *Winstanley* to risk sitting up. Again she swept the waves with the binocs. Yes, that was a mat of blond hair on a small head.

She revved up the engine to its max and brought the dinghy in closer.

"Boy, over here!" she cried. The wind blew her words back at her, but she continued to close the distance between them. "Over here!"

He turned. She whipped up the binoculars, could see his eyes looking desperate and blue-shadowed. She let out a loud whistle, and tossed the life-belt toward him. It fell about twenty feet short, but he turned and thrashed his way across the waves, until finally his hand closed over it. When she was sure he had a strong grip on it, she pulled him in.

When he reached the side of the boat, Rosa hitched the rope, braced herself, and hauled him in. He lay on the bottom, gasping and spluttering. She handed him the life jacket.

"Here, boy, put that on in case you fall in again. You okay?"

He nodded, but coughed when he tried to speak. She pulled the cord on the motor and sped off toward the disappearing navy ship. It was moving slowly, towing the listing *Winstanley*, but Rosa knew that she didn't have much time. At any moment, they might decide to abandon the ferry or sink it. They might just speed off to the west with their captured cargo, or dock in one of the Stewards' ports and hand the children over for cash.

"Hold on," she said to the boy, and sped west.

"Whatcha doin'?" the boy asked finally, when he could speak again.

"I'm chasing them," Rosa said. "We've got to slow them down. Can you handle a boat?"

"I can do anything," the boy said.

"Have you ever handled a boat?"

"No. But I can do ..."

"Okay. When we get there, you can hold it steady. I'll kill the engine. But here's how to start it again if you need to...."

Rosa brought the dinghy in close to the stern of the *Winstanley*. She made the boy lie down under the tarp with her, and when her cautious reconnaissance told her they were within range, she killed the engine.

She put the boy's hand on the tiller. "Hold it steady," she hissed. "Just hold it there. Don't wiggle it or pull it to one side or move too much."

She grabbed the harpoon, and slipped over the side.

Damn, the water was cold! But moving would help with that. If only she had some diving gear, even a snorkel. But she was a strong swimmer and she could hold her breath for three minutes solid if she had to.

Rosa made her way alongside the *Winstanley*, swimming underwater, surfacing as seldom as possible to catch a quick breath. Pulling herself alongside the ship, she made her way to the prow and the tow rope that led to the patrol boat's stern.

The patrol boat was running hard, towing the big ship behind. She took a deep breath of air, dove down, and took her reckonings. The propeller churned up a roiling mass of bubbles that made it hard to see. Okay, she would fix that. She beat her way back to the surface, gulped air hard, and readied the harpoon gun. One deep gulp, another dive down ... aim, steady. Fire!

Beautiful! The harpoon slipped between the blades, nicking one of them as it passed, sending it tumbling and hurling into the mechanism, its tough carbon-fiber line tangling in the blades. The ship let out a screech like a metallic scream, and slowed.

One more harpoon. One more thing to do. The wake was still strong, but she gulped another lungful of air and pushed through it. There was the rudder, and there the delicate pins that connected it to the steering mechanisms. She was needing a breath, losing time, but she forced herself to take aim, steady....

A great shot! The harpoon jammed itself between the rudder and the stern, the rope wrapped itself around the rudder, and she propelled herself upward, reaching the surface with a great gasp of relief and striking off back toward the *Winstanley*'s stern as fast as she could. Abandoning caution for speed, she used her fastest surface stroke, hurled herself aboard the dinghy, nearly squashing the boy who squawked in protest.

"Shut up!" she barked as she revved up the engine and streaked away.

It would take the sailors some time, she thought, to figure out what had happened. They would have to send a diver down to check the rudder and the propeller, then clear them. She had bought them some time. But not much.

"Where we goin'?" the boy asked.

"Back to my ship," Rosa said. If I can find it, she thought to herself. She knew how long she'd sped west, and what the bearing was. There, wasn't that it? No—just another gull on the waves. Shouldn't they have reached it by now? What if it had sunk? What if she didn't find it?

"Why?"

"So we can go get help," she told him.

"What help?"

"The Navy of Califia."

But no mast broke the line of the wide blue horizon. Nothing showed above the swell of the waves.

Chapter Sixty-Three

FUCKING ARROGANT PRIMES! WENDELL FUMED TO HIMSELF AS HE and Finch rode upwards in the elevator from the war room bunker. Culbertson, that pork balloon! Of all times to demand a meeting—and on their turf! Couldn't they understand he was in the middle of a war? They should fucking drag their pimpled asses down here, not expect him to interrupt his duties and come report to their doorstep. Clowns!

He strode down the corridor with Finch trailing behind, gave a salute to the guard on duty, and headed out down the north stairs of the old Mormon Temple that served as Command Central for the army. It had been built as a fortress of God, with high blank walls of concrete embellished by square concrete lattices. Now it served as a fortress of a more secular, martial power.

Below, on the pavement, a car and driver waited for him. But on the steps, an altercation was underway. Two of his honor guard were wrestling a wild-eyed man with a mane of white hair who was dressed in a dirty white toga.

"Iniquity! Evil and iniquity fester, and the righteous decline!" the old man was yelling.

"Move along, grandad." One of the guards pushed him down the steps, but he leapt back up again, brandishing a tall staff.

More incompetence! Jesus God, couldn't they even keep the steps clear of the crazies?

"I have come to preach the word of God! Do not deny me entrance to God's house!"

"Not God's house no more, this the general's headquarters!" said the second guard. "Now move, or shut up forever!"

"I am the way, the truth, and the light! Admit me to the halls of power, for there is a nest of demons breeding in the heart of this land, and we must root it out."

Wendell stopped. Suddenly his full attention was fixed on the old man. "What did he say?"

The ranting old man raised his arms high and turned blazing eyes on Wendell.

"Sin and transgression run amok, while righteousness withers! Root out the evildoers, oh hand of the Lord, and he will reward you! For they breed together and conspire, out of sight, and their number grows and grows!"

It was as if Wendell's own innermost thoughts were being shouted aloud. Yet, was it possible that within them lay the information they needed?

"Let him loose," Wendell ordered. The guards dropped the old man's arms. "Who are you?"

"Who? Who will be my hand of retribution? saith the Lord. Oh, who will be the instrument of my revenge? I am Jedediah, prophet of the Lord, and I call for a rain of fire to smite the evildoers and bring them to justice!"

"Prophet Jedediah." Wendell made a small bow of obeisance. "Show us where these evildoers lie, and I will be the strong arm of the Lord's revenge!"

It was a long way across the Valley, twenty miles or more, made longer by the stops the Army of Liberation made to intervene in the looting, to recruit the mobs into a disciplined force. They bivouacked for a short rest at midday, setting guards and sending out scouts so the troops could get some fitful sleep on the hard asphalt.

They encountered crowd after crowd of rioters. Every warehouse in the Valley was under siege, it seemed. Insurrection was spreading like influenza, and the looters had now grown bold enough to attack their targets in broad daylight, trusting to a bandanna or a scarf to hide their identity, or simply smashing every security camera they could find.

Some of the storehouses had fallen and were already emptied. At others, fierce fighting raged where the authorities had massed stronger defenses. Some of the rioters were intent on their looting and resistant to even Smokee's revolutionary fervor. But at most sites, they picked up new recruits, and through the afternoon and the night that followed the army grew to be more than five thousand strong.

That was a lot of folks to feed. The kitchen distributed the looted chips to all who would eat them, but they made many people gag. The cooks parceled out their dwindling supplies of waybread and real food for the civilians. Whenever the army came across a working pipe, they halted to fill all the water barrels and bottles. It all took time, precious time, even as the scouts reported back that a full unit of the Stewards' troops was heading toward them over the old 405 freeway.

At sunset, River called a halt. They had made their way to the 405, the freeway that was the spine of the Valley and their direct route to the temple, where the scouts reported that the central command of the Stewards had their headquarters. They still had a long way to go, another two days at least, he calculated, at their present speed. But they were at a nexus of looted buildings, with easy on-ramps to the freeway close by. Here he would make their barricade, blocking the route of the advancing enemy.

For the Stewards were advancing. Scouts reported a massive force marching out from Angel City, easily three times their own numbers. River felt a cold fear in the pit of his stomach. He'd done so much, won so many battles, punched a deadly spear into the Stewards' bowels. But they could still lose it all. With the drones and the tanks and the troops the Stewards still had, they could sweep away his own rabble army quick as a boot stomps a bug. And if they emptied the Grapevine and set those troops marching south to defend Angel City's heartland instead of north to recapture the Valley, the Army of Liberation wouldn't have a hope.

His hope now was that Cress was keeping the Grapevine divisions fully entertained back at Troy. In the meantime, he set troops to collecting materials, loading it onto trucks when they could or ferrying it on their backs. Broken doors and smashed up desks, heavy chunks of concrete and uprooted poles, anything and everything they could find went into the roadblock. Higher and higher it grew, until it towered above them, a wall ten feet tall across the freeway.

Then he called a meeting of the troop leaders. They sheltered behind the towering construction, and River looked over the haggard and dusty crew. He wondered if he looked as bad as they did, bleary-eyed and gray-faced with exhaustion as they squatted in the dust on the roadway. There were all his own troop leaders, croots and tubos, squabs from the City and dusters from the plantations. Lakemen from the bordering hills squatted among them too, their faces coated with dried gray mud, and Angels, slim and cold as well-honed knives. All of them were battle-hardened and trustworthy, but the grim, desolate-eyed leaders from the looters' mobs were hastily chosen and completely untried.

"Maybe we hold the robos off for an hour here," he said. "Maybe more. Less if they bring up a tank and blow it away."

"So why are we building it?" Erik Farmer asked. His usually cheerful face was covered with grime and drawn with worry.

"Buy time. Every hour a precious bit of time."

"For what?"

"For the city to explode," said Rafael coldly.

"For the people to rise," Smokee chimed in. "Every hour we hold the troops here is one more hour they're not blowing up homes or executing rebels."

They were in an area of single-family homes, now crowded with multiple families in each room, but still low, isolated, too small to make a good base. No time to dig trenches. They needed something sizeable and solid, that could maybe withstand a few shells.

River sent scouts out to hunt for a place to make their stand. They came back with the suggestion of an office building, half a mile away. It was surrounded by the smoking ruins of a business district, and the lights and power were out, but it seemed intact.

River left Deuce and the rest of his old unit to hold the barricade, along with a few hundred of the makeshift army. They would have some help from the techies who set up speakers that would broadcast the shouts and cheers of a thousand voices, to create at least a temporary illusion that the barricade held far more defenders than it did.

"Hold it, but don't be stupid," River told them. "Bail when you can, and join us. Delay, thass all we expect."

The office high-rise they chose for their makeshift fortress was built with insurrection in mind, its bottom floor a blank façade of concrete, embossed with a bank's logo but solid and impenetrable. Windows began only on the third floor. That was a disadvantage, for it meant that they had to climb up in order to see out or shoot, but it would make the building much easier to defend in a siege.

He deployed his troops to cover all four sides of the building, and hurried back outside where the troops were massed in the parking lot. There he found Smokee contending with a mutiny from the newly recruited troops.

"Ain't goin' in there. It's a trap!" one of the recent recruits was shouting. River wasn't surprised. The looters were brave when they were jacked up to attack a warehouse, but they weren't seasoned fighters accustomed to holding ground in the face of danger. Already he saw many fewer than he remembered. Along the edges of the crowd, he noted a trickle of dark figures melting away into the dusk.

Fucking civilians! How to hold them? Couldn't hold them if they wanted to go. Fuck. But he couldn't really blame them. Chances of lasting out the night didn't look good.

Boom! A loud explosion came from the freeway. Smoke billowed up, lit by floodlights. Another loud boom—the barricade was falling. Shit. He had to get the troops inside and in position.

"What are we gonna do? The scrabblers are running back to their ratholes," Smokee said, her voice taut with anxiety. She felt a deep disappointment, mostly in herself. She'd been puffed up with pride, thinking she'd inspired them. But she should have known it was like a blaze of toilet paper, quick to flare up, quick to fade.

"Gotta let them go," River said. "Nothing else to do."

"No!" Smokee said.

"Can't stop them," River said.

"Then let's order them to go," Smokee urged. "Command them— then we stay in control. They stay in the army. Maybe they come back?"

River looked puzzled. "Not followin' that."

Smokee grabbed the bullhorn.

"Free people of the Southlands," she cried. "Today we have struck a blow for liberation! All of us, together! Let me hear you say Yes!"

A somewhat reluctant yes came back at her.

"Now the Stewards' Army is on our tail. They'll retaliate. Oh yes. They'll try to take revenge. And do you have families and friends to protect? Say yes!"

"YES!" thundered back at her.

"Then go to them!"

A huge cheer erupted, and it took her a long time to be heard over it.

"That's an order. Yes, for you remain part of the Army of Liberation! Go to them, and we who have come down from the North will try to hold the Stewards' forces here!"

Another huge cheer.

"While we keep them busy here, your homes and families and neighborhoods will be safe, for a little while. But when they're done with us, then what?"

She paused to let them think about it, and began again in a milder tone. "Then they begin the house-to-house searches, the arrests, the beatings, the executions. They'll find those looted vidboards and the bottles of booze and the cases of chips, and they'll take your children and your lives in payment."

A dead silence. Even the trickle of deserters stopped.

"But not if you come back. Go now, and run while you can. But if you truly love your lives, and your families, and your children, then come back! Gather up your friends and your neighbors, find what weapons you can and what tools you can muster, and return to this fight. We may die here, defending your homes from the Stewards. We're ready to die. But if we do, then you got to finish the job, or we die for nothing.

"But if we don't die, if we hold this place, then we will finish the job together! Meet us, at sunrise tomorrow on the 405, and we will march together and take the Southlands back! We're counting on you. Come back! And come back stronger! Bring your neighbors and your friends. Make our hundreds into thousands, our thousands into tens of thousand! With or without us, finish the job! Drive the Stewards out, and build the new world in the light of that bright new day!"

A huge cheer—loudest of all, and then the crowd melted away as quickly as it had formed, leaving only the City squabs and sojuh defectors, the dusters and the lakemen to hold back an army that far outnumbered them.

But there was nothing to be done. Quietly River deployed his forces. He set the best of the sojuhs' troops, the trained sharpshooters, at the lower windows with backup in case they fell. The liberados he positioned at the gate, the service bay in the bowels of the building, with a sheet-metal door that was the most vulnerable spot. But it didn't require a lot of training or fancy shooting to hold it, just bodies with some sort of weapon to attack any of the enemy who pushed in.

Other crews would hold each door and entranceway on the ground floor. "If the thrashers break in, make the slime fight for every inch," he told them. "Gotta run—try to run down and out. Temptation is always to run up—but thass a trap. No way out. Best to make a break for it. Go out into the 'hoods, bring back more recruits."

He sent Smokee to command the snipers, who needed little in the way of instruction. He took his place at the weak spot, with the squad guarding the service bay. Its metal door was large enough to admit delivery trucks, and although it was locked down, it was still the most vulnerable point. If he was attacking, that's where he'd start.

And then the wait began.

Chapter Sixty-Four

ROSA HUDDLED WITH THE BOY IN THE BOTTOM OF THE DINGHY. A stiff breeze had sprung up when night fell, and she had never had a chance to dry off from her swim. She was numb with cold, and the boy felt like a cold, dead fish in her arms. She was thirsty, her mouth dry and her throat raspy. She wished she'd thought to put a bottle of water in the dinghy, but she had rushed off without thinking, and now they paid the price. For hours, they'd been searching for the *Victory*, zigzagging back and forth across the sea, with no luck. She'd done it again—she'd run headlong into danger, trying to be a stupid hero, and all she'd been was stupid, stupid!

Now she was going to die for it, and the boy too. And all the children. *Don't go there, sailor.*

It was like she could hear Isis's voice in her head, suddenly. That's what the pirate would say, she knew. *Thrashers always willing to beat a girl up, don't do the job for them.*

The boy shivered, and she snuggled closer to him, although her own flesh was so cold it offered nothing in the way of warmth. But they were still alive, and he had not drowned in the ocean, because of her. If they could just hold out through the night—surely they would find the boat in the morning. Wouldn't they?

The moon hung low in the sky, a fat crescent curving to the right, dipping low toward the horizon where the waves reflected back a string of pearls. So if it curved to the right, it was waxing, Rosa thought, and it would have risen, invisible, by day and now be slowly preparing to set. In the west, that was where the moon would set. And so that way was west, she realized with a sudden flush of hope. Now we're not completely lost.

Was that something—something like a stick poking up, silhouetted against the moon's glow? Could they have come too far east, and missed it?

Excited, she sat up, took the tiller, and revved the engine. The dinghy rode the swells westward, and yes, the stick thing grew taller, and taller.

And then the engine died.

Oh Goddess! They were out of juice.

Now they were drifting, and the swell was taking them farther away from the stick thing that might or might not be the mast of *Victory*. Rosa leaned over the side and tried to paddle, but her small hands couldn't move enough water to fight the current.

No, it wasn't fair! Not when she could see the ship. If it was the ship?

She could swim for it. The thought made her shiver. She was already so cold, she didn't know if she could force herself back into the water.

It could be a mirage, like thirsty people saw in the desert. If she believed it was a mirage, she wouldn't have to go into that cold ocean and swim off into the dark.

If she did risk the swim, and that stick turned out not to be the *Victory*, then she probably would drown.

It was an elusive dark line in the moon's glow. She thought she could see something spinning on top—that could be the windspinner. Or not.

Well, there was nothing else to do. She might die, if she were mistaken about the ship. But if she did nothing, they would die anyway.

She shook the boy awake, and placed his hands on the tiller.

"Hold it like that," she said. "I'm going to swim and tow us. I see the ship."

She sounded far more confident than she felt, but why burden him with her fears? If she died in the ocean, he'd die too, a long, slow hopeless death of thirst and hypothermia, but she wouldn't have to watch it or make apologies.

She slipped over the side and into the water.

Diosa, it was cold! With numb fingers, she tied the tow rope around her waist, and struck out in the direction where she thought she'd seen the mast. At first her arms and legs felt like lead, so heavy with cold she could hardly move them. But after a while the motion began to warm her, and that was a comfort.

Stroke, stroke, stroke. Stop, look up, try to see the stick thing. Stroke, stroke, stroke. Look again.

It had disappeared. She wasn't sure she was swimming the right way, but the moon laid a silver track to the west, and she followed it.

Stroke, stroke. Over and over. Don't think about how tired you are! Just keep on. Nothing to do but keep on.

I'm trying, she told the moon. I'm not giving up.

And the moon was talking to her, in Isis's voice, cheering her on. *You go, sailor! Swim it, salt!*

Suddenly there it was. She looked up and just on the horizon, dark against the moonlight, was the silhouette of a sailboat with a windspinner on the mast.

She was near the end of her strength, but the sight gave her new hope and determination. She put on a burst of speed and swam toward it.

It was the most beautiful thing she'd ever seen, the graceful hull of the *Day of Victory* bobbing on the waves. She felt weak with relief, but she couldn't relax yet. Wheezing with exhaustion, she hauled the dinghy the last hundred yards toward the boat. It felt heavier and heavier with every stroke.

She brought it alongside where the rope ladder still lay, just as she'd left it. With a prayer of thanks to the moon and all the Gods, she tied the tow rope on. The boy was lying still in the bottom of the dingy, asleep, she hoped, and not dead. She shook his arm, and to her relief he grunted and sat up.

"We're here," she said. "Can you climb up the ladder?"

Because I don't think I have the strength to help you if you can't, she thought, but didn't say it out loud. She hoped she'd have the energy to get herself aboard.

The boy looked up. "I remember this boat," he said. "Thass the ladder the little girl got hung from."

He balanced precariously on the edge of the dinghy, but managed to grab the ladder and scramble up. Rosa followed, her arms and legs feeling heavy as stones. But up there was water, and blankets, and warmth. That was all she could think of, now.

She tumbled over the bulkhead onto the deck, and lay still for a moment, grateful for the solid surface under her. The boy was already down in the galley, and while she was still trying to persuade her shivering body to move, he came up and draped a blanket over her. He was wearing one around his own shoulders.

She wrapped the blanket close, and crawled to the galley steps, almost falling down them. It was warmer in the galley, but she needed more heat. She knew from all their survival training that she was dangerously hypothermic.

Her hands were shaking so hard she could barely hold a cup to fill it with water, but as she gulped it down she began to feel a little bit more alive. The electric kettle was full, thank Goddess! She switched it on, and soon had a cup of hot tea clutched in her hands. She sipped it slowly, feeling life return.

The boy seemed to be warmer, and full of energy. She got him to pull out the hot water bottles from the storage under the bunks, and fill them with water from the kettle. She clutched one close to her belly and put another under her numb feet. It was the best feeling in the world! Slowly she stopped shaking.

"What's your name, boy?" Rosa asked.

"Zoom."

"Rosa. A pleasure to meet you. You're a smart kid!"

"I know."

"You ever been on a sailboat?" she asked.

"No. Just that one time when you bring us to the ship."

"In a minute, just another minute, we'll go up and try to get to a place where we can contact the navy." She felt guilty, suddenly, thinking about the other children on the captured ship. She should try the radio again. In a minute. "Just gotta warm up first. There's some soup from yesterday in the cool box—maybe you can heat it?"

His head was barely higher than the stove, but he was a competent child. He followed her instructions to light the stove and heated the soup, pouring it into big mugs. Rosa drank it down gratefully, wishing she could just drop into the bunk and sleep for a week.

But not until she made contact with the navy. Already hours had passed since she'd hobbled the ship. How long would it take them to get underway again? Or start searching for their attackers?

She shivered, with a different sort of cold. Best to get up, away from the tempting bunk. She pulled on a pair of sweatpants and a warm shirt. She would try the radio, and if she still couldn't raise help, she'd take the *Victory* back to the Southlands herself.

She pulled out the radio and tried the navy channel. "Big Pink here. Mayday! Mayday!" Nothing. She tried again, on the hillboys' frequency. Nothing but static.

Okay. She was tired, but she was alive, and she had brought them this far. They weren't dead in the ocean, or slaves on the captured ship. She could force herself to stay awake a little while longer, to pull up anchor and set sail. Back to the Southlands, back into range of the hills if not the navy.

She was strong. Suddenly she felt years older and smarter than that pitiful girl who cared what a bunch of silly schoolkids thought of her. It didn't matter what they thought. She knew who she was, and the fact that she was alive on this boat, drinking up the last of the soup with the boy she'd rescued, that was all the proof she needed.

She and the boy, together, they could do anything!

Chapter Sixty-Five

CRESS'S EYES STUNG WITH HIS OWN DRIPPING SWEAT, AND HIS cheekbones were raw from the rough cloth of his sleeve wiping it away. He was crouched in a hastily dug ditch, one of a network of swales and berms that they'd carved into the side of the hill to give them some shelter from the hail of bullets and laser fire. They arched out to protect the all-important antiaircraft guns positioned in the spots that River had suggested were most strategic.

Trench warfare, Cress thought. His mouth was parched and sore, his tongue felt like sandpaper, but water was hard to resupply and so he rationed out his portion, a sip at a time. Back to World War I, but at least they were spared the mud and the rain. Instead they suffered the searing valley heat, and that combination of tension and boredom he had come to loathe as the signature of war.

"Hold them," River had told him. "Long as you can. Then fall back to Troy, hold 'em there. Mostly, distract the bastards, make 'em think the whole army dug in here."

So they were holding. Cress had placed himself in a forward trench, where he could sneak a view of the overall terrain. The Stewards had unleashed one copter attack early on, only to have it shot down over the desert, exploding in flames. How much airpower could they have?

The Stewards' troops moved out in waves, pushing moveable concrete barricades before them that gave scanty protection against the Army of Liberation's barrages. Sojuhs fell like dominoes, but each decimated wave was replaced by another, and another.

Cress felt sick. He had to force himself to shoot, closing his eyes and aiming blindly, then berating himself for wasting ammunition, which was growing scarce. And still the sojuhs kept on coming. The Stewardship didn't care how many of them were lost—they were expendable. But Cress couldn't help but think of River, and Deuce and Trace.

I thought I was tough, but I'm just a fluffy trugger after all, he admitted. A life is a life, and I can't kill without wincing. Without hating the waste of it all.

Hour after hour, wave after wave of slaughter, until he thought it would never end, never release him from this hell of thirst and stench and relentless heat that seemed to stew his very brains. And with each wave, the Stewards' Army advanced, now a few yards, now a football field's distance. There seemed to be no end to them, but there was an end to his strength and his ammunition and worst of all, to his water, which was gone now. They had not had time to dig connecting tunnels between trenches that would let him resupply safely. That was a bad oversight. To get more, he would have to expose himself to the Stewards' guns.

There were only a few yards separating the trenches, and again and again, as he grew thirstier, he was tempted to make a mad dash for it. But it would be safer to wait until dark, which was just an hour or two away. He certainly wouldn't die of thirst in an hour. But even mild dehydration might impair his judgment.

Then the world exploded into sound and flame. The desert erupted in a cloud of sand and a fine red spray rained down as a shell tore up a section of their defenses, just across the old road. He couldn't see through the dust. Faintly, through the ringing in his ears, he could hear screams. Fuck. They should have retreated long before. River would have sensed that, gotten the troops back to the safety of Troy.

Another boom. Dust offered concealment, he realized, and without another thought he scrambled up out of his trench and pelted back toward the linked fortifications that guarded the guns. He was coughing with the dust but he didn't stop to fix a bandanna, just ran for his life. He leapt over the berm and tumbled into a trench yelling out the password as a strong arm pulled him in.

"Retreat!" he barked into his headset. Was the fraggin' thing even working? But a short time later he heard the call of a bugle sounding "Fall Back." The old technology of war. Still a good backup when the new technology failed, as it tended to do under conditions of dust and heat.

He snaked through the tunnels and links until he came to the bazookas. Trace and a couple of the sojuhs from River's old unit had stayed back to work the guns.

Trace slapped a dust mask over Cress's mouth.

"Guard the airway," Trace said. "Fighter's first rule. Can't breathe, can't fight."

Cress gasped heavily and nodded at him.

"Got a tank or somethin' like it," Trace said. "Tired of the shootin' gallery."

"Can we take it out?" Cress asked.

"Can try. Got heavy armor, not like the copters."

"Try."

"Miss, take out our own folks."

"Don't miss."

Another boom, a shell landed in the trench Cress had just abandoned, plowing through the dirt and exploding with a force that knocked them all to the ground. Trace picked himself up, swung the gun around, and fired at the source of the shelling. A pillar of dust rose up with a roar, but when it cleared, the tank was still there. The shell had fallen short, but it tore up the roadway in front of the tank, heaving up great chunks of asphalt into the ridges of an impromptu mountain range. The tank was stalled, but still deadly, and aiming back at the bazooka....

"Retreat!" Cress yelled. "Move!"

Trace and his partner muscled the gun between them, hefting it up and running through the trenches. Cress and the other sojuhs followed behind, as a new explosion tore through the berm behind them.

It was a nightmare of punishing sound and fire. They ran in stark fear, as bullets whizzed overhead and shells exploded behind them. Trace and his partner shouldered the heavy gun, Cress and the other two sojuhs forged ahead to clear debris and help them over the berms and barbed wire, every second expecting to die.

Finally they came to a slight rise. Trace and his partner, in some unspoken communication, stopped, turned, and braced the gun. The dust was so thick that the air itself seemed half-solid. Cress's throat stung with the dryness and his eyes burned. He couldn't see anything but billowing clouds of smoke and dust and debris, blood-red with the light of sunset. But somehow Trace aimed behind him, fired.

There was one last explosion, a wall of sound that slammed into them, and a new eruption of smoke. And then, suddenly, silence. His ears rang—maybe he had gone deaf from the noise, but no, he could hear the patter of debris falling, his own gasping breath....

The dust settled like slumber on a weary child, and sunset spread a crimson blanket over the flats below.

"Retreat," Cress barked again. Maybe River would have pushed forward, but this seemed to him to be the moment of grace they needed to gain the greater safety of the walled fort behind them. Maybe he was wimping out—but their objective wasn't to take the Grapevine. River himself had said that couldn't be done. It was to distract them, delay them, reduce the force they could bring to Angel City's defense. In that they had already succeeded.

"Retreat," he cried again, and in the distance, a faint bugle sounded. Trace and the others nodded, and once again picked up the big gun. The enemy made no sound still, not even the ping of bullets or the hiss of laser fire. A good moment to make their move.

The sojuhs ran forward with the guns, and he swept the rear, pushing other fighters ahead of him as they navigated the labyrinth of trenches and ditches.

Back, back to Troy, where they would have thick walls to shelter them, at least for a little while. Troy, commanding the place where three roads meet, blocking the way north to the plantations they'd freed with so much sweat and blood. Troy, at the crossroads, where the fate of the Valley would be decided.

Crossroads were holy places, he thought as he ran for his life, choking on smoke and dust. Sacred to Hecate, who holds the keys to the underworld. Ancient crone Goddess.

A shell exploded, so close he could feel its hot breath shove him forward. His ears were filled with a high ringing sound like spirit voices shrieking, or maybe singing. Or pleading.

Hecate, Goddess of death. Please, Grandmother, just a little more time . . .

They ran, dodging down into trenches and up over the rims. He was feeling almost weak now from the backwash of adrenaline, and there was still a long way to go. But he was amazed and overjoyed to find himself still alive.

Life. The trenches were deep and he pictured them filling with water when the rare rains came, infiltrating it back into the earth. Desert plants would flower in the fortunate spring, a blaze of color all across the Valley. Birds would return to feed on the seeds, and their song would praise the dawn.

He had wanted to be a musician once, but now all he wanted was to be an audience for that choir, to hear the frogs' chorus in the vernal pools, the katydids' percussion in the evening thickets. He would come through this, and he would never again waste a precious moment of life chewing over old wounds and hurts and nursing his resentments. He would love again, and sow his own seed to raise children who would never thirst. And he laughed with the joy of it, the blood pumping in his heart, the breath wheezing in his still-dry throat.

The bullet caught him as he scrambled over one last trench. A jolt, a sting, a red fountain spraying up before him that he regarded with surprise. Where the jacks had that come from?

And then he knew. As he had always suspected, he was made of water. It sprayed up and pooled out from a hole ripped in his throat, sinking down again into the land. He had no time even to clap a futile hand over the wound.

If he could have made a sound, he would have cried out a great no! Not yet! Not when he had so much more to do, so many more swales to dig, channels to engineer, shelter belts to seed and mulch. That was what he was born to do. He knew it. To bring water back to this land, and fill it with life.

But his knees buckled and he sank to the ground. His lungs spasmed and gasped in desperate quest for a last breath. Flowers flashed before his eyes, flowers he would never see bloom. And faces. Children's faces. Children he would never father.

He had lost his mother, his sister, his wife, his child. He had nothing left to lose, except his unfinished task, his unlived destiny.

If he had to die, he didn't mind dying here, on his own ground. No, he didn't begrudge the land one drop, but not now, not yet.

Not when he had so much more to give.

His hands scrabbled in the dirt, hands of the land, hands the land had grown to heal itself. Eyes clouded, eyes born to see all the verdant potential of this dry country.

That was who he was, the land made flesh, flesh a vessel for water. He clutched at the dirt as if he could hold tight to that self, embrace all that made him who he was and prevent its dissolution.

Diosa, Goddess, please, please, just a little longer! Not for myself, I'm asking, but to be all that the land asks of me!

Not this. Not merely this great pump, pouring out his blood onto the land, bringing water at last to the bones of his mother and his sister.

Chapter Sixty-Six

BOOM! CRACK! A WHIFF OF SOMETHING ACRID ASSAULTED RIVER'S nostrils.

"Steady," he called to the troops. "Stay back from the door, could fire a shell right through—"

A blast split the air, noise so loud it seemed to engulf the world. He was slammed back into the wall, stunned. For a moment he couldn't breathe, his ribs ached, and his lungs and diaphragm didn't seem to work. Frantically, he gasped for breath.

He faced the metal bay door, which now had a hole in it the size of a big truck. Stewardship forces began pouring through.

With a groan, he gulped in air, full of bitter powder, and struggled up to shooting position on one knee.

"Hold them off!" he cried out and began to shoot. Bullets and lasers ricocheted around the service bay. A Steward sojuh fell, and then another and another. They let out cries of alarm and ducked for cover, but still more were pouring through the hole, and as soon as one went down another took his place.

River kept on firing. But there were more enemy troops than he had bullets for. As fast as he and the others picked them off, their ranks reformed.

"Fall back!" He barked the command into his coms unit, and shouted it out as loudly as he could over the din. A band of defenders were clustered by the doorway that led into the basement of the office building. Unfortunately, he was not among them—he was on the opposite side of the bay, and he couldn't get to them through the rain of fire.

"Fall back, then barricade the door!" he commanded, aware that he was likely giving his last command.

But I'm not dead yet, he thought. A catwalk ran the length of the bay, and he sprinted up the metal ladder that led to it. There was another door on the end—if he could get to it. Were there other options? No. So he would have to make this one work.

He turned and fired a laser blast at the ladder supports. The beam connected, and with a white-hot sizzle they melted through. The ladder crashed down into the chaos below. No retreat for him that way, but it would delay his pursuers.

Crouching low, he ran along the catwalk, slow, fast, slow again, varying his speed in case a sniper was trying to take aim and anticipate his movements. A curtain of bullets blocked his way, and he plastered himself back against the wall. Behind him, laser fire zinged so close he could feel the hem of his shirt start to burn. He beat it out with his hand and pushed ahead, running flat out now.

A burst of laser fire flashed in front of him, revealing a three-foot gap just ahead of him where the catwalk abruptly disappeared. Without breaking stride, he made a great leap and landed on the opposite side, letting his momentum carry him forward. Here the gunfire was slightly less. He snaked along the wall. Now, if only the door would be open....

It was locked. He beat a tattoo on it, the code they'd agreed on, yelling as loud as he could although he knew nobody could hear him on the other side. He put his shoulder to the door and crashed against it, hurting himself without making an impression on it. He pounded harder. If he had to, he would shoot the lock, but his ammo was almost gone and burning out the lock would make the door that much harder to hold against those who might come after him.

One more try. He knocked with his gun barrel, fingering the trigger, throwing himself flat on the catwalk just as a burst of laser fire raked the wall where he'd been standing. The metal below him felt hot. Time was up!

Just then the door opened and he squeezed inside as laser fire scorched the catwalk.

"Last man out," he gasped. "Hold that door for real, now!"

He'd told them all not to run up, but there were no other options. Anyway he wanted to get up to the third floor, to see how the defense was going there. He dashed through the corridors, hazy with smoke but clear otherwise, made a quick detour to hearten the defense on the stairwell.

"Stay to the side and back from the doors," he commanded. "They can blast through, but then you pick 'em off from the sides and above."

Pings and shots and screams down below, a thunderous roar, then blasts of gunfire. He ran up.

Smokee stood flat against the wall beside a tall, plate-glass window with a jagged hole in it. At intervals, she'd peer out, fire down at the heads of the troops pushing their way in the door of the lower floor, then duck back again for cover. But picking off a few grunts made little difference to the swarm that was flowing into the service bay.

"Smokee!" River called. She turned and saw him just as a shell ripped through the wall with a blast. Smokee was thrown to the ground, River was knocked back into the wall. He pulled himself to his feet, crawled over to Smokee and pulled her back with him toward the central stairwell. Around them, smoke was filling the room. Papers burned and flames licked the ceiling. They crawled through a thick haze that rapidly filled with a torrent of bullets. He pushed her head down, toward the slightly cleaner air near the floor, and they crawled toward the doorway. River shoved Smokee through, then followed, slamming it closed behind them.

They were in the central stairwell, the fortified heart of the building. Below them, they heard a roar and a crackle and smelled fresh smoke. The lower levels were on fire.

Don't run up, he'd said, but there was nowhere else to go. They pounded up the stairwell with the staccato pop of gunfire behind them and the shriek of alarms in their ears.

Up and up. Pounding below them now, and shouts. Smoke rising. Shit. They would be captured or burned alive. Neither appealed to River. But it wasn't a very tall building, only about six stories up and soon they'd reached the end of the stairwell. There was nowhere else to go.

All right then. It had to end somewhere. They'd had a good run. No use crying because it was over. Meanwhile he'd do what he could to keep fighting until the last bitter moment.

This floor was dark. Completely black, like a windowless cave. He groped around for something to hide under. Maybe, in the dark, searchers would miss them. Maybe they wouldn't come up this high. But he knew that was a futile hope. The Stewards' troops would have lights, bright lights, and they'd never leave a captured building without searching every cranny.

His own light had gotten smashed somehow in one of the times he'd been blown against the wall. He and Smokee crawled along the wall, feeling for any kind of shelter or escape route. Maybe there would be a second stairwell, somewhere. A fire escape. But there was nothing. Finally they tumbled into a little three-sided alcove which offered no real safety but a slight illusion of shelter.

They were alone. Quiet. No sounds of shots or explosions. The defense was broken. Well, they hadn't expected to be able to hold the building forever, but he admitted that in his secret heart he'd hoped to hold it through the night. Oh well. Below them the mopping up had undoubtedly begun. They could hear the occasional thump and bang.

Below them were dead men who had trusted him. Prisoners who had counted on him to liberate them. Sojuhs who'd believed he could lead them to victory. River felt sick.

He hadn't realized that he'd made any sound, but he must have let out something between a choke and a sob, because Smokee's hand suddenly reached for him.

"River," her voice came out of the dark, "don't blame yourself. Not your fault."

"Stupid," he said. "Mobsters right—was a trap."

"We knew that. We all knew that. But if we hadn't given them battle, they would have chased us all over the 'hoods, killed a lot of innocent people. We were willing to pay the price."

"Sorry?" he asked in a low voice.

"No, not sorry. Grateful. Grateful to you, to everybody in this crazy excuse for an army. Grateful to die fighting," she said. And to her surprise, she realized that she was. She felt no fear, only gratitude and a great, surprising love for them all, for this gruff boy-man who crouched beside her.

"Scared?" he asked quietly.

"No. Not scared of dying," she told him. But then suddenly a new fear rose up in her, so strong it nearly took her breath away. "Just scared of one thing. You know what."

Was he scared, he wondered. Dying seemed unreal, too big for him. It would hurt, but not for long, not like that time under their probes. Was he scared of that? Of enduring it again and again, until it broke down the person in him he'd struggled so hard to birth?

"River, I gotta ask you a favor," Smokee breathed. "If it comes down to it, if they're gonna take us—don't let them take me. Please! You still got a bullet or two?"

"Yeah."

"Would you do that for me?"

She was asking him to kill her. Well, one thing he knew was how to kill. He nodded, then realized she couldn't see him.

"Okay. I can do it," he said.

"Thanks. I know you'll do it quick and clean. I don't mind dying, really. I haven't had much of a life, but I've had some days at the ocean."

"Had the Temple of Love," River said dreamily.

Smokee snorted. "You can have it!"

"Wanted more," River admitted. "Wanted something different—with Kit. Like Bird and Madrone. Wanted to be more than a breed. A real person." It seemed safe to tell her, here in the dark, at the end. Good, in a way, to share it, those sad lost hopes that now would never come to be. But in telling her, in some way he honored them, honored the possibility.

Smokee laughed. "Oh, River, think about what you've done! You liberated the Valley, gave all those sorry dusters another chance at life."

"Stewards gonna take it all back now. So what good is it?"

"No," Smokee said. "They may win a few. They may kill us now. But people gonna finish the job if we can't."

"Think so? That sorry bunch of looters?"

"That's what I believe," she said with sudden faith. "Never believed in God or Jesus or Goddess or even the Four Sacred Things, not really. But I believe that the people will finish what we started."

Below them, they heard shouts coming from the stairwell, and the heavy thump of boots.

"Now, River," Smokee whispered. "Do it now. I wanna die while I still believe it."

He couldn't see her in the darkness, so he reached over and felt her face. His fingers traced her cheek, her soft eyelashes, the curve of her brow. Like he had traced Lilith's brow in the Temple of Love. It was an act of love, what she wanted from him. He suddenly felt that he needed to ask permission, like in the temple, for every step of the way.

"Smokee, I gotta get close to you. Can I put the pistol up to your head?" he asked softly. "Don't wanna mess it up, in the dark. Can you handle that?"

A long breath. "Yeah. Just do it," she said. "Don't talk about it. That'll make me afraid. Just do it."

He felt her temple, her soft hair growing out longer now. In a moment, he would pull the trigger, and that would be the end of her eyes flashing, or her voice which sometimes so irritated him and sometimes moved a mob to become one. He had pulled so many triggers, but never had he felt so reluctant. He didn't want to pound the nail with her, wasn't like that, but suddenly he wanted to touch her all over, to treasure her skin and her body and her life one time before he ended it.

There was a banging at the door. He should just do it, do it now. But something else was needed—wasn't right to just let it end without something more. What was it Maya would say? A rite. Rite of passage.

"Smokee, gotta just tell you first. So you go knowing. You—you one hella brave fighter. You got a strong gift. To move people. You say people gonna finish the job. It cuz of you. You made them people, not just a mob."

That wasn't exactly what he wanted to say—she deserved something smoother, more eloquent to mark the end of her life. He cursed his lack of words, his awkwardness.

The shouts were growing louder, the footsteps closer. He put the pistol up to her temple, reached over and stroked her hair. Gently, like he had stroked Maya's face, like maybe her mare had stroked her baby fuzz. He put his arm around her and kissed her on the head, gently. Not sexual, just gentle, like he might have stroked Maya's hand.

She put a hand up to his face. Something was wet. It was his own eyes, he realized. He was crying. He, River, hard-assed breed who never cried.

"Do it, River," she whispered. "Don't cry for me, cuz I'm not crying. Just do it. Please."

"Count to three," he said. "One."

Now they were pounding, banging on the door.

"Two." He would shoot her, and then himself. Better they didn't take him alive. He would be with Maya, and Kit.

But no, that didn't feel right. That wasn't who he was, the person he'd become. He was still a fighter, beginning and end to it. He would go out fighting, and if luck was with him, he'd take out a few more of the enemy as he died.

The door burst open and shouts filled the air, the harsh voices of man-boys pumped on adrenaline, full of bravado and fear. Beams of light played over the walls.

Now, now was the moment. No more delaying.

"Three."

A blaze of light filled the room, and the bottom dropped out of the world.

Chapter Sixty-Seven

How to Make a Revolution: V

Advice for the urban insurrectionist: the city streets are your terrain. Learn them. Be like the fox, who knows her territory, who lays trails and back trails. Learn the scent of safety, the odor of alarm.

Buildings are mountains, streets are rivers, alleys are canyons. Know where you can go to ground, burrow in, and recover from the chase.

Be like the squirrel. Plan ahead, stash nuts and food against hard times.

If you plan a march, cache supplies along the route: water, food you can grab and eat without fuss, trail mix is good, some nuts for protein, a bit of sugar for energy.

Be like the mouse. Look for the cracks, the small, unnoticeable openings. Nothing can keep you out or keep you in. Always have an exit strategy. And if there is no opening, gnaw at the baseboards until you make one.

Announce yourself, like the blue jay. Know what your message is, and cry it out loudly, with color and conviction.

Fly free, like the wild goose, but flock together. Take point, and when you are tired, drop back and let another lead.

If one of you falls, accompany her down, trumpeting your rage and grief like a bugle call to battle.

And if you all fall to earth, become seed. Coat yourself with a protective shell, and wait.

Wildfire roars through a forest, but destruction is never uniform. The fiercest blaze leaves patches of green, pockets of moisture, crevices where a seed can survive.

Conditions will change. The sun will grow warmer. The rains will return, and soak the ground. The time will come again for you to put out roots and push forth shoots.

The time will come again for you to rise.

A Century of Good Advice:
The Autobiography of Maya Greenwood
Yerba Buena: Califia Press, 2049

B IRD'S CRYSTAL WOKE HIM WITH A CHIME IN THE PREDAWN DARKNESS. He lay still for a moment, coming slowly awake, amazed and grateful that he'd actually been able to sleep in spite of all the adrenaline of tension and anticipation. He reached for Madrone, who nestled into his arms with a murmur. No time to make love this morning, but he breathed in her scent as if she could inoculate him against the losses the day might bring.

Today was the day, the culmination of all the planning and preparations they'd done since the children were sent away. For the refugistas had not sat passive in the face of the threat of attack.

"The best defense is an offense," Bird had said in the assembly where they forged their strategy. "Mobs are rioting all over the city. Our army is fighting its way through the valley. We've had marches and protests for many weeks, now. Spring Equinox is upon us, and Easter is around the corner. Seems like a good time for the Rising!"

The refugistas had cheered, and then organized. Now Bird reviewed the plans. Banners and signs had been stashed in strategic locations along the route. Tianne and her gang of artists and techies had slipped out of the Refuge two nights ago with giant sculptures in pieces hidden under tarps on Atonement carts, and were even now assembling them in garages provided by sympathizers. Food and water and medical supplies had been stockpiled for weeks in safe houses. Refugistas had circulated through the 'hoods, recruiting their old friends and neighbors, spreading rumors in the food depots and the markets, and waiting in the water lines. "Stock up—the Rising is coming!"

Everything was ready. This morning, when the sun rose, its emblem would appear all over the streets and sidewalks of Angel City, emblazoned with the call to action. Today is the Bright New Day! Rise Up!

He let his arms tighten around Madrone, bent his head to brush his lips over her brow. She opened her eyes, reached up and kissed him. For one long moment, they drank each other in. This could be the last time we wake up together like this, he thought. The last time I feel her softness and strength enfold me.

Or the beginning. The first sweet kiss of a new era. Before nightfall, for better or worse, the world would change. Everything was ready.

Then he heard the alarm.

The watchers on the walls of the Refuge had been waiting through the night. The sky was just beginning to lighten when they saw the drone plane pass over them. They barked into the coms units the techies had cobbled together from salvaged parts, and sounded the alert. Salvaged trumpets took it up, and throughout the Refuge sentinels banged out a warning on makeshift drums and metal pots.

A whistle, and by the time the bomb fell people had pulled on breathing masks improvised from charcoal sandwiched between cloths, and taken cover.

Nothing exploded. But the bomb, lying in the East Plaza, hissed out a trail of gray gas. The bomb squad threw blankets over it and rigged fans to dissipate the vapor as people fled the area.

Madrone had thrown on her clothes, grabbed Zap, who had slept in his, and run with him to her station at the healing center. Even through her mask, she caught a faint scent of something sickly sweet. Her bee senses went into overdrive, analyzing and neutralizing it. Stun gas. Not lethal, but dangerous. The Stewards evidently preferred not to murder them all, but to keep them alive for ends of their own. Death might be a better option.

The watchers sounded a new call. Soldiers on the horizon. They were keeping their distance, but they were there, hundreds of them, ringing the Refuge. Madrone felt one moment of sheer, primal panic. What if more drones came, more gas attacks? Their breathing masks were only barely effective. What if they were choking, and couldn't get out?

At the alarm, Bird leapt out of bed, grabbed his clothes and boots and streaked to the Welcome Plaza, where they'd stashed such rifles and weapons as the hillboys and Angels were able to provide. Anthony tossed him a rifle, and he quickly looked it over, felt its action. He felt slightly ashamed to admit how good it felt in his scarred hands, how familiar. He had missed this sense of augmented power, this lethal, unfeeling ally. He'd renounced it in favor of a deeper, less tangible power that now felt out of reach. He couldn't sing the drones down from the sky, or offer them a place at the table.

A buzz, an ominous whir. A bugle trumpeted out the call for Incoming. No more time for thought. Bird dropped to his knees behind a low rubble wall and aimed carefully. The damn things were so small and moved so fast that they were hard to hit. But they had to fly low, within rifle range. He wanted to bring the thing down before it dumped a load over the Refuge. Afterwards would be too late.

He laid down a spray of fire like a fan in front of its trajectory—missed! But farther down the wall, someone else's luck was better. The drone exploded a hundred feet short of the city walls. Bird grabbed his mask, a true gas mask that Hijohn had sent down for him personally. As he pulled it up, the air filled with a sweet, noxious vapor.

After that he stopped thinking, stopped worrying, stopped doing anything except struggling to breathe and to peer through the haze, watching for the telltale red laser lights of the drone's guidance systems, and calculating trajectories and firing. At times he thought he made a hit, most often he had no idea. The air, even through his breathing mask, was hot and acrid and burned his throat. But he couldn't stop, not even to take a drink of water.

Now the drones were spraying bullets, not just stun gas. And there were bigger ones behind them, shooting bursts of explosives that took out chunks of concrete and filled the air with flying rubble.

Aim, fire, aim again. Time stopped. Shoot, then run to a new hideout, before the drones' computers could calculate his position. Drop to his knees, aim, fire …

He couldn't withstand this forever. He would have to stop, eventually, to load in another clip of ammo. He began to feel a creeping sense of futility. Sooner or later they would wear him down, and he would run out of ammo or keel over from exhaustion or they'd track his shots and follow him back and he would die.

Suddenly the wind shifted. A strong breeze blew down from the west, a finger of the ocean winds. It carried the gas and the smoke up in a great pillar of cloud and rolled them back over the attackers. The square was clear, and he could see clearly. There were bodies strewn on the pavement, dead hulks who had once been his friends. He couldn't think about that now.

He pushed down his mask and gulped in the clean air, and it was as if his mind cleared at the same time. He remembered some of River's briefings, back in the City.

The drone launcher. It would be back somewhere, back in the ranks. But if they could find it, take it out …

His throat was parched. He groped for his water bottle. But it was empty. There was a wide scorch mark on its side, a hit from a laser that had melted the steel. He shivered suddenly, realizing how close that had been.

Why was there this respite? They must be moving something into position. A tank, perhaps? Would the gate go down in a blast?

The wind died, and the cloying haze closed in again. His thirst was a raging torment. Ignore it, he told himself. You've suffered worse. Try to see through the clouds, to keep alert for what was to come.

"Dad!"

A small voice called to him through the murk. He looked back.

Zap came barreling out of the fog, and shoved a new clip of ammo into his hands, and oh blessed Goddess! A bottle of water. He shoved his mask up and gulped it down. Maybe he should leave some for later, but right now all he could think of was quenching his thirst. It tasted very faintly sweet, a hint of honey, as if Madrone had laced it with one of her brews.

"Thanks!" he croaked.

"Can I stay with you?" Zap asked, leaning up against Bird's leg as if he could find safety there.

"Hell no! You get your ass back to Madrone!" Bird barked. The boy said nothing, just looked up with appeal, like a puppy asking not to be turned away.

"No arguments!" Bird made his cracked voice stern. He felt sick with worry. *Diosa!* He had to get Zap out of this hell and back to the relative safety of the healing center.

For once, Zap obeyed. He turned to duck back through the tunnel.

Bird allowed himself the luxury, just for one moment, of watching him go: that small scurrying figure that in the end was what he was fighting for.

And then suddenly the tunnel exploded in a blast of fire. A shell, Bird thought numbly as the barricade at the gate was blasted away and the tanks rolled in. Had Zap made it? *Madre de la Diosa*, holy Mother of all the Gods, please let him have made it back far enough before the hit.

But Bird knew better. Another gust of the wayward breeze lifted the smoke again, just high enough for him to see, lying on the ground, one small, severed hand clutching an empty clip of ammo.

No! No, no, no fucking no! He wouldn't believe it, wouldn't accept it, not for that little boy he'd chided and bathed and tried to give some slight chance to *be* a little boy. The air was too thick with flying bullets and gas to even go out to the broken little body, and new drones were coming in, minute by minute. No time to cry for him, to mourn.

The bloody bookends of my life, Bird thought. My father dying in a pool of blood, and now my son.

"Fall back!" he heard the cry. But he was possessed by a wave of cold blind fury and he couldn't persuade his feet to move in a backwards direction. If he could roll back time just one moment, if he could say yes, yes, stay with me, I care about you, I love you! How infinitely sad that the last words the boy would carry with him into death were shouts of rejection.

Grief pierced him. But he didn't have the luxury for grief right now. Time to put on, once again, his warrior's armor. How familiar it felt, how oddly comfortable! A carapace to shield the soft parts, to encase in impermeable chitin the lover, the father, the singer. He would not need them again.

He threw himself to the ground and began to crawl forward. Gas and smoke billowed all around him, burned his skin and made his lungs ache. Below, along the ground, the gas was denser, as if it were a heavy substance that settled and pooled. He pushed on, crawling through a miasma of poison, out through the rubble of the ruined Welcome Plaza, the litter of broken angel wings and the shattered colors of mosaics.

Here the air was a bit more clear, and he could breathe. Through the haze, he made out the wave of troops and machinery pouring in. *Mierda*, it looked like they had half the army here, at least ten tanks, rank after rank of troops. But his target lay behind them. It would be far back, like River had briefed them. Well protected.

The gate, the tunnel were blasted into oblivion. The Angel of Welcome lay headless, and the troops kicked the shards aside. Bird pressed flat against the remains of the mosaic wall, its flowers now chipped and cracked and shattered. He slid down to crawl amongst the rubble. He could only hope the others, deeper in the Refuge, had heard the blast and were getting out.

There was no withstanding this firepower. But there was one last way he could protect them from pursuit. Maybe the Refuge they had built would fall, maybe they would all die. He couldn't save them. He was no superhero to take out an army all by himself. But here was one thing he could do. And he would do it, whatever it cost.

Luckily, he thought, I'm so covered with concrete dust that I blend right in. He used a trick Maya had taught them long ago, and imagined wrapping himself in a cloak of invisibility. Invisibility is not about being unseen, she used to say. It's about being unnoticed.

He stayed close to the walls, moving slowly, except when he could shelter in some crevice and run in a crouch, or when a new blast of gas created an even thicker haze.

Out through the ruins of the old gate, he dodged from shelter to shelter through what was now a shattered burrow filled with concrete chunks and shattered debris. The skeletons hadn't protected them, in the end. They'd been blasted into fragments. Here and there he came across a finger bone, or his knee pressed painfully into the sharp splinter of a skull.

There it was. His target. His prize. With its antenna turning atop its roof like a red seeking eye, an armored trailer stood surrounded by a protective circle of APCs with their gun turrets and their armed, watchful sojuhs. Drone ops. A measure of the Stewards' technological power, and their weakness.

Once operators could have sat safely in Nebraska and pushed a few buttons to wreak havoc in Afghanistan. But now the satellites that had carried those signals were burned out or in disrepair. Now the hands and eyes that guided the hunters needed to be in radio range. They could send Seekers throughout the city to track and follow anything that lived, but to guide an attack like this, with its hundreds of drones and complex logistics, the closer they were in proximity to their targets, the greater their accuracy.

He couldn't defeat an army. But he could buy his people some time.

The gunners on the APCs were careless, sitting exposed behind their turrets. Most likely they wore Kevlar vests, but he could pick them off. He was a good enough shot for that, hitting them between the eyes or in the back of the neck. He was already forsworn of his vow not to kill, and now they had killed his child, his son. No one, not even Gandhi himself, could blame him.

But that wasn't his mission. Badly as he wanted to let loose with a spray of fire, he had a more vital objective. Do that first, then he could take his revenge.

The trailer. How the jacks to get to it, ringed by all that firepower, those watchful eyes?

He saw one possible opening. A chunk of wall had fallen and now lay at a precarious slant, propped on another leaning segment. One of the circle of APCs was close to it, close enough that if he could crawl up to it . . .

He snaked his way along the low triangular tunnel where the two walls met, praying they wouldn't choose that moment to fall and crush him. The tunnel opened out directly behind the APC. Five feet of open ground between him and his objective. He would have to cross it, to risk it. He threw himself flat in the dust, and wormed his way along the ground, moving slowly, holding that image of the cloak above him. Maya, Grandmother, help me now!

You seem to be doing okay on your own.

He almost smiled. Soon, soon he'd be with her in some unimaginable dimension. That wasn't so bad. That wasn't something to fear.

He wriggled under the APC. There was just room enough for him to move, and he prayed that they wouldn't choose that moment to start up the motors and roll out. Lying beneath it, he had a clear shot at the trailer. He gulped air, forced himself to breathe the acrid dusty stuff in slowly, to ground himself. Roots burrowing down, drawing on the power of the earth itself. Send down fear and rage and grief, calm yourself, think. How many shots could he get away with? He knew where the computer consoles would be, alongside the wall that faced him. He might get thirty seconds, maybe as much as a minute before they realized where the shots were coming from. Don't think about what would happen then.

Take out the consoles, that was the first priority. Then, maybe, aim for the fuel line. He had one clip of ammo, no more. Use it judiciously.

He poked his upper body warily out from under the chassis and raised himself up on his elbows. Positioning the gun carefully, he took a deep breath and sent a tattoo of bullets into the wall of the trailer, in a zigzag pattern that would have the optimum chance of doing crucial damage. From his new position, he had a clear view of the underbelly of the truck that pulled the trailer. Not an easy shot, but he steadied his mind and focused on his target, like his archery instructor had taught him many years before. Breathe, ground, squeeze the trigger slowly,

slowly. Ping! He was gratified to see a stream of gasoline pour out. But he had no time to congratulate himself.

Without thinking, his body was squirming backwards, his legs carrying him in a quick dash back to the shelter of the concrete wall before the gunners on the APC had time to turn and track him.

He was alive. Alive, uncaught and unharmed, for this one precious moment. Not for long, he suspected. He heard shouts, and a barrage of laser fire raked the walls, up and down. He threw himself behind a concrete block, just in time. The back of his legs burned with the heat. The next round would catch him, or the one after that. But now, he still had ammo left. He could die skulking in the rubble, or he could go out blazing the trail of his anger in their flesh.

He stepped out of the shadows and raised his sights to the nearest tank as it swung its turret toward him. For one long moment he stood poised, rifle barrel facing off against the barrel of the tank....

The air convulsed as the shell hit. A roar of sound engulfed him. Concrete cracked and split, and huge chunks tumbled down. A deep rumble ... and the Refuge collapsed around him, carrying him down into a tomb of rubble and dust, into the dark embrace of silence, as all went still.

Chapter Sixty-Eight

A SOUND LIKE THUNDER RUMBLED THROUGH THE CENTRAL PLAZA, AND a shudder ran through the ground like an earthquake. The huddled crowd looked up in alarm.

"They're shelling the gates!" cried a teen who was perched high up on the walls.

Zap, Madrone thought in alarm. He hadn't come back yet. And Bird—he was there. Oh *Diosa, Madre de la vida,* let them be all right!

The refugistas were clustered around the hearth and the sacred tree, clutching breathing masks and treasured possessions. Madrone could smell their fear, an acrid note under the sickly-sweet traces of stun gas. Not everyone had resisted the gas. Some lay slumped in the arms of friends, barely conscious. She had managed to brew up an antidote and sent it around, but those who woke up still seemed sluggish and confused.

She found the other leaders at the hearth.

"What was that?" Emily asked in alarm as another loud boom echoed through the Refuge.

"We've got to get out of here!" Miss Ruby said. "They're coming in."

"I thought we were going to stand and fight," Bob said stoutly.

"We are fighting," Anthony said mildly. "Unfortunately, we're losing."

"That was plan A," Emily said. "When we thought they might bring in a few policemen or a squad of riot cops. We weren't thinking of tanks and drones and half their army!"

"I recommend plan B," Beth said. "We get the hell out, and live to fight another day."

"But they'll destroy everything we've built!" one of the teen artists cried.

"Build it up, tear it down, we are the joke of the Cosmic Clown!" Janus declaimed.

Suddenly everyone was shouting. In a moment, Madrone thought, we'll descend into chaos and the Stewards will mow us all down while we fail to come to consensus. Where was Bird? He could move them. Miss Ruby was trying to shout for order but they weren't listening. And she couldn't lean on Bird to do this. She pushed down the fear that she might never be able to lean on him again.

Madrone stepped up. "We can build again," she cried. "We wanted to create a refuge, and we succeeded. We wanted to inspire an uprising, and we've done that. Right now, the whole city is on the march. I don't know about you, but this is the day of the Rising, the moment we've dreamed of and planned for. I want to see it! I don't want to die here in some useless suicide stand. I want to join them. Because when this is over, it won't matter if they destroy this place, even with all the love we've poured into it. When this is over, the whole city will be our refuge!"

A huge cry of approval went up.

"So you know what to do and where to go." Miss Ruby took the stage. "Let's do it! This city is gonna need us, all of us who have been here together, who have learned how to organize and rule ourselves. Let's go, while we can go. See you in the streets!"

But it was all very well to cry: See you in the streets! Madrone thought. The problem was how to get there. The main entrance was a battle zone. They couldn't go out that way. They sent scouts out to the other exits, to find at least one of their back doors or secret tunnels that would let them escape. Madrone headed back to the healing center, to prepare the wounded for transport.

She felt a growing sense of fear, but she pushed it down. No time now to wonder about Bird and Zap, or to give way to panic as the booms of explosions sounded nearer and nearer. She had patients to load onto stretchers they'd prepared beforehand from poles and blankets, crutches cobbled together from rough sticks to hand out. There were groans of pain to somehow ease, last doses of medication to distribute, new brews to conjure with her bee powers. The bee-mind demanded calm, focus. If she gave way to panic, she could not heal.

But the rumors came down to her in anguished whispers from her crew of healers, from the volunteers she corralled to carry stretchers, from the casualties who staggered in from the lines of battle. The back way was blocked. Platoons of sojuhs were patrolling the streets, rings of tanks and APCs surrounding every way out. The very air was thick with bullet-spewing drones, shooting anything that moved.

They'll find a way, she told herself as she wrapped a bandage around the bleeding stump of an arm and held a glass of water while the slender teen it belonged to gulped down the last of the morphine tablets. He'd been part of Tianne's crew, a budding artist.

They'll have to find a way. The story couldn't end like this.

Then the air seemed to split with sound, an explosion so close that the shock of it knocked her into the wall and toppled the shelves of supplies. Amidst the tinkling of falling glass she heard screams and the thunder of running feet.

Suddenly the healing center was swamped with people crashing in through the doors in panic.

"Stop!" Madrone yelled. "Why are you all coming in here? We have wounded to care for!"

But her voice was lost in the wave of noise.

"To the springs!" she heard Anthony's tenor above the roar. Miss Ruby took up the call.

"To the springs!"

Madrone pushed through the throng and managed to grab Anthony's arm as he formed up a line of volunteers to protect the patients from the stampede. Miss Ruby continued to bellow out the call as she led them through the clinic and on down to the entrance of the springs.

"Are you out of your mind?" Madrone hissed. "There's no way out of there!"

"There's no way out!" Anthony told her. "We're trapped. Maybe down there we can block the entrance, hold them off. And we'll have water ... "

It was a terrible plan. It was no plan at all. But she had nothing better to offer.

They let the able-bodied run past them, with the walking wounded hobbling after. Then she and Anthony quickly directed the stretcher crews to follow. She had to fight against her own rising panic, her instinct to dash for shelter, as if the springs would shelter them, as if safety of any sort were not a mere illusion. But don't think about that.

She cast one final glance back at the clinic as the last stretcher was carried out. Her neatly arranged shelves of precious supplies, now toppled. Her clean floor and orderly rows of cots now covered in dust. The place where she had tended and comforted and healed so many, about to become rubble. She would have liked to do some final ritual, some closure for all the magic she'd poured out in this place. But another loud boom sent her scurrying down to follow the others.

She hurtled through the door to the old spa, and a crew led by Anthony immediately blocked it with chunks of concrete, shoring it up with any old beams and sticks they could find.

Bird, she thought. And Zap. If they made their way back from the battle, looking for refuge, they would be walled out.

But she couldn't think about that. She had patients to care for, people to soothe and calm and ...

And what? *Madre de las Diosas,* what in Hella's realm were they going to do?

This was it. This was the end. One more shell, one more explosion, one blast to the pathetic blockade at the doorway, and all of these people, her friends, her patients, her allies in the vision that had brought them to this nightmare—all of them were going to die.

At best.

How do you prepare to die with everyone you care about?

Maya, Johanna, where are you now? Why aren't you guiding me through this?

She wanted to wrap her arms around her head and scream. But she couldn't. She was Madrone, the healer. Other people were depending on her to keep calm, to hold out hope.

Why did that matter? Will it buy me some credit in the afterlife if I go with healing pouring out of my hands, or condemn me to some astral hell if I'm screaming my head off? What am I supposed to do when everything is over but nothing has quite ended yet?

This was my vision, she thought. All these deaths are on my account.

I'm the healer. They'll look to me, turn to me to show them the way.

And I have nothing, nothing to give.

Chapter Sixty-Nine

Yes!" Wendell pumped his arm up into the air as his eyes darted from vidscreen to vidscreen. He faced a bank of screens in the war room in the basement of Central Command, and they all showed happy news. At last!

On one, his troops mopped up the remains of that pathetic rabble army. On another, a patrol boat towed a captured ship filled with rebel children. On a third, his army surrounded the stronghold at the gateway to the Central Valley. As he watched, a shell blew away a section of wall.

Best of all, his ultimate triumph, on the largest, central screen he watched as a tank fired a shell into that mound of decorated rubble they'd found at last, the heart of the rebellion, the fount of evil, the source of the taint.

He took a deep breath. The air in the war room was close and acrid with cigarette smoke, but he sucked it in joyfully. It felt like the first free breath he'd taken in weeks.

He had done it! The compromises, the sacrifices, all had been worth it. He'd rooted out the disease, stemmed the destruction. The sins, the iniquities, the taint, the temptations, all of that now could tumble into the junk heap of the past, leaving him free and pure once again.

"General, sir," Finch interrupted his private moment of sheer bliss. "101st is asking for orders. They're entering into the rebels' headquarters now, sir. What shall they do with the survivors?"

"Survivors?" Wendell turned away from the screen. Ah, it was tempting to think about, how they could slowly purge the sin from the survivors, apply the disciplines of punishment and pain. But survivors were like the bacteria that survived antibiotics—all the more resistant and dangerous. He was done with taking chances. Done with risking that *he* might survive and go on to spread contamination once again.

"Oh, let's not have survivors," Wendell said with a cold smile. "I think not. Blow the place to smithereens, Finch. Tell them that. Take no prisoners. Rid us of this stink, once and for all!"

Bird slowly opened his eyes. His ears were ringing and his mouth was filled with dust. I'm buried, he thought. His whole body felt sore, as if every soldier in the Stewards' Army had stomped upon him systematically.

But I'm alive. I couldn't be dead, and feel this fraggin' bad.

A spasm of coughing racked his body, and something heavy pressed down on him. He slapped an edge of his shirt over his mouth and nose and gasped for air.

He was lying in the smoking ruins of the Refuge, a huge slab of concrete tilted at an angle above him. It had sheltered him from the blast, as if the Refuge itself were protecting him even as it fell. But as he lay gathering strength, he heard an ominous creaking. The slab might shift at any moment and crush him. He had to move.

He groped for his rifle, which was still strapped around his body, rolled over and quickly crawled out.

He heard shouts and the crackle of coms. The ruins were swarming with sojuhs. But he was alive, and while he felt bruised all over he still seemed to have all his parts in working order. A miracle.

Alive, but not for long. Not with this horde of sojuhs searching the ruins, not with the gunner still perched atop the APC whom he saw as the dust began to settle. But he had done it. He had taken out the drone ops trailer, and the refugistas would be able to escape without drones dogging their tail.

He gave one last regretful thought to Madrone, to years of loving and arguing they would never have, to the baby that she longed for. But she would have babies, and her children would play unafraid in the green streets of their city, and if he bought them that safety with this sacrifice, he would be in some sense their father too.

He was not afraid. He had passed beyond fear into a place of absolute clarity, as if he were already dead. His story was over. Every moment he continued to live was simply a bonus.

But he wasn't quite ready to give up, either. Not when he was still alive and mostly unharmed, a fighter with a gun in his hand, a few bullets left, and a son to avenge.

He squirmed back under the slab that had protected him from the shell, and began to crawl deeper into the ruins of the Refuge. He knew it so well, every last hidden tunnel and cranny and hidden passageway. That was an advantage.

But half of it was blown away and there were more of them than there were of him. That was a disadvantage.

He squirmed his way through the ruins, squeezing through narrow shafts and creeping through tunnels where ominous rumbles warned him that the rubble might yet shift and crush him alive.

It was a nightmare journey. The blast had blown his second water bottle apart, and his dust-ridden mouth and throat were painful and raw. For long moments, he found himself completely lost, unsure which direction would take him deeper into the ruins and which might lead to safety. He came upon mementos, here the blown-off head of a doll, there a shoe he thought he recognized.

All the while, he could hear shouts, behind him, above, all around. The ruins were swarming with sojuhs. The voices of his pursuers bounced around in strange reverberations and echoes. He couldn't tell if they were behind him or in front of him. A few loud barks echoed through the concrete. Dogs. Could they sniff out a living human scent amid the smell of sulfur and death?

In the wreckage of one of the apartments, he lay crouched beneath a fallen stud wall while boots clacked above his head. A crunch—and the thin drywall covering gave way. A booted foot broke through, and landed on Bird's head, shoving it into the dirt. He lay, barely daring to breathe, while above him the sojuh swore loudly and tried to jimmy his leg back up. Each jerk ground Bird's head into a rough chunk of rock below him, and he lay frozen, willing himself not to make a sound.

He was lying across something soft. A sliver of light came through the edges of the hole, and he opened his eyes a crack.

Bright motes of dust turned in a slow gyre as the boot crunched down on his skull. Through them, as through a bright cloud, a face stared back at him.

Bird gulped back a scream. Sightless eyes stared into his, sad and shocked as if they hadn't expected death to catch them.

He lay across the body as if they were long-familiar lovers. It took every bit of control he could muster not to run screaming out of that death chamber.

But the sojuh's boot was still grinding a sharp piece of rock into his cheek, and the heavy tread of other sojuhs' feet dislodged new little rockfalls of pebbles and dust. He didn't dare move or squirm or cough. He couldn't give in to his urge to retch and purge himself. If he wanted to live, all he could do was lie there and stare into the face of the dead.

The skin was ashen with concrete dust, as if it were already turning to stone. But after a long, long time, he began to register the features, the black eyes staring out sightless, the heavy moustache now plastered with fine gray powder.

Bob. Anthony's neighbor. One of the first to join the Refuge.

Bob, who had given Bird his precious guitar. Bird remembered him in Council, earnest and filled with fervor. He had a family, boys who had gone to school with Anthony and Emily's girls. A mechanic, that's what he had been before he fled to this Refuge that in the end had betrayed him to death. So good at fixing things.

If Bird could just clamp his mind to those memories, just hold the living man in his head, he could keep at bay the horror, the revulsion at this lump of meat that faced him, the lips mashed, the cheeks distorted, the nostrils trickling dark blood. Only the startled eyes still belonged to something human. For it seemed to Bird that he was staring into the eyes of his own death, and there was nothing noble about it. No great white light, no radiance, no otherworld opening, no Great Adventure.

Just meat and rot.

And this was hell, this eternity lying immobilized while death ground him down from above and stared him in the face.

May the wind carry his spirit gently ... He didn't day say the prayer out loud, but he murmured it inside his head, although he couldn't in that moment believe there was any spirit in the thing that stared at him. But the prayer helped to steady him, to keep him sane. It lent some dignity to the grim visage before him.

May the earth receive him and bring him to rebirth.

We need to believe in that, he told himself. We need to believe in something to cushion the sheer stark finality of this. Some comforting fairy tale. Something to keep the children from crying in the night.

All those stories he'd grown up on—the Isle of Apples where the dead grow young again, the Wheel of Rebirth. The heaven and hell of his grandparents on his father's side. Fantasies, Bob's blank eyes said. Self-delusion. We wink out, and in a moment you will wink out, and there will be nothing left. No welcoming arms of the Goddess, no hands of your loved ones reaching for you, no great cosmic council to say, Well done! Nothing, as there is nothing left of your son, your father, this Refuge you risked so much to build.

Ha, ha. Joke on you.

He felt one moment of overwhelming temptation to leap out of this hole, gun blazing, screaming, offering himself up to the hail of bullets that would greet him, and be done. Over. One blast of pain, then oblivion.

Tell the story. Sing the song.

He heard Maya's voice. Was it her, surviving after death in some realm of the ancestors? Mocking his crisis of faith? Or only his memory of her?

It means what I make it mean, he remembered her saying long ago when someone asked about the symbolism in one of her stories.

Memory or survival of the spirit, while he could hear her voice some part of her still lived.

It means what we make it mean, with our choices, our tales, spinning meaning out of nothing, like gold from straw.

His eyes were tearing up, and Bob's face was shining now, a radiance infusing it, a golden light.

Light from above. He became aware that the boot was no longer pressing down on his head. The hole was wider, letting a ray of the sun caress Bob's face. A grunt, a final shout, and now sunlight streamed down through the hole as the leg withdrew.

Bird held his breath, praying that the sojuhs above would not look down. Or if they did, that he would appear to be just another dead body.

Slowly he became aware that the footsteps had ceased. He listened hard and heard only silence. Grace.

I've got to get the fuck out of here, he thought. He wasn't dead. His living heart was pounding and his blood racing, a rush of fear pushing him to run and fight and survive.

He grabbed hold of his rifle and bashed the hole above him open wider, so he could propel himself through. Quickly, quickly, before the sojuhs returned. He might have only a moment ...

He popped his head up, gulped a breath of air, acrid with smoke but free for the moment of grit and death.

But then he stopped. Every instinct urged him to streak and run, but he forced himself to crouch back down for one last moment and close Bob's eyes. Not so much for Bob, who after all was beyond caring. But for himself.

To commit himself, once again, to the side of the singers and the storytellers, the makers of meaning. To grace death with the one thing that could counter it, one small act of kindness, of love.

After that he became reckless, no longer creeping through tunnels. He couldn't force himself to go back underground. Instead he dashed through open spaces, pressing into crannies, plastering himself into shadows. He had lost that blessed clarity, but he made himself fight the panic that could have sent him crashing blindly through the wreckage of the Refuge into the arms of his own death. He was no longer willing for the story to be over. No, he had more chapters to write, more verses of his own to sing.

He had to think, to focus through the fear, to remember routes, to orient himself, to keep his ears open for shouts and footsteps. *Diosa*, he would give ten years of his life for a mouthful of water!

Slowly he came into parts of the Refuge that had not been shattered by the shells. He moved swiftly but warily, because the enemy would have patrols and guards spread all through the area by now. Now he came to landmarks he recognized, and at last, to a small statue of a robin that Tianne had made with the younger children from the school. It marked the way to a passage out.

He abandoned his caution and ran. They had worked so hard to build the Refuge and now all he wanted was to flee it, get out into the open streets and alleys, evade the patrols, find Madrone. Clean air blew back through the passage, the scent of freedom, and he bolted toward it.

And stopped. Silhouetted against the light at the opening was a guard, who turned and trained his rifle on the walkway.

Bird flattened himself into a cranny in the wall. For a long, long moment the guard stared down the passage.

And then he turned away.

He stood, haloed by the light, a perfect target. Now, Bird thought. Now. I have a few bullets left. Shoot, and be free.

One shot, and he could avenge his son and Bob and all of them. One shot to equalize them all, then sweet freedom. For this one moment he was a God, wielding the power of life and death.

No one would blame him. Not even his most severe critics, those who judged his failures so harshly, would blame him for this.

The gunner turned his head. And something in the gesture reminded Bird suddenly of Zap, how he would scan a street before he entered, how wary he had been, how alert to danger or pursuit. Or of River, how he scanned a crowd. Or of any of the thousand sojuhs who had joined the City. Even of himself. It was so human, that fear, that wariness.

It was like looking into a mirror.

Make meat out of meaning, or meaning out of meat? It ran through his mind like an earworm, like an advertising jingle from his childhood before the Uprising in the North did away with advertising.

They had killed his son. Now he would kill in turn. That's how it went. On and on, down through generations, millennia. Kill and be killed. Avenge the fallen and suffer the vengeance of the enemy in turn.

Or he could do something else.

Before he could think too much about it, he slung his rifle back over his shoulder and walked forward, his hands out.

"Sojuh," he said softly, but it came out from his parched throat as more of a croak.

The sojuh whirled around and trained his gun on Bird. He was wearing the gray of the croots, and that was the only shard of hope Bird could gather as he gulped one last breath of air.

They were staring at each other like two young roosters and the thought came to Bird that if this were his last thought, it wasn't much of a thought. The sojuh was young, his eyes were a watery blue, his face had that thin pallor and his limbs that stringiness of the chronically underfed.

I'm not dead yet, Bird thought. And he began to sing.

His voice was harsh, the notes rasped out of the dry passage of his throat, almost tuneless.

"Open your eyes,
There's a new day dawning,

Freedom will rise
With the rising sun ... "

Singing for my life through a sandpaper throat, Bird thought. Not my brightest idea. He stopped. The sojuh was still staring at him.

"I could have shot you," Bird said. "I didn't want to. You can shoot me. But I don't think you want to, really. If you did, I'd already be dead. I think you know that the Stewards are falling. The new day has dawned. And what I want, and what I hope you want, is for us to be together in that bright new world."

The sojuh still stood, staring at Bird as if dumbstruck. He was very young, Bird realized. Maybe he'd never yet killed a man in cold blood.

Slowly, Bird moved out from the passageway and sidled his way along the street. The sojuh pivoted, keeping the rifle barrel still pointed at Bird's heart.

"So I'm not going to hurt you," Bird went on in as soothing a voice as he could produce. "I'm going to invite you to join us. To dream it together. To build it side by side. Or failing that, to just pretend you don't see me, and let me go. Nobody else is around. Nobody else will know."

There was a wall, and if he could get around it, he might make it to cover, if the kid was a bad shot and missed the first time.

The sojuh looked at Bird, looked at his rifle, looked at Bird again, and they locked eyes.

"Let me go and I promise you that we will make a world where you won't have to steal water. Where you and your mother and your sisters will never have to fear the pens. Where we will share what we have and make enough for all."

Another step, and another. The stripe hadn't shot yet, and every moment he held off increased the chances that he wouldn't. But take it slowly, slowly, as if he were a wild beast you didn't want to startle.

"We've liberated the plantations," Bird went on. "Maybe your family are already free."

Something flickered in the boy's eyes then, as if Bird had hit a mark.

"Go!" he hissed. "Just fucking go!"

Bird ducked around the wall, keeping it between him and the sojuh in case the boy changed his mind. Then he belted out into the back alleys and passageways that surrounded the Refuge, seeking distance from its besiegers, keeping his own wary eye out for patrols.

Finally, when the Refuge was far behind him, he slowed to a walk. He was panting, and he had a stitch in his side. His throat burned with thirst. He would have given a lot to find an open tap, somewhere he could drink and soothe his gravel throat and wash off the reek. Never did he more resent Angel City's miserly way with water.

Slowly, the adrenaline seeped away and left a backwash of weariness. He realized how long it had been since he'd eaten or slept. But he forced his heavy feet to keep moving.

He had come out at the edge of the Death Zone, and he headed blindly north, toward more populated areas. Slowly, he became aware of others on the street, heading in the same direction. They looked around furtively, as if they feared being noticed or followed, but they walked with determination, not with the hopeless shuffle of the perpetually unemployed. They hurried, as if they had an appointment to keep.

No police lurked in the intersections of these alleys, where stucco flaked off the fronts of the tenements and garbage banked up around stairwells. No army tanks prowled. Behind him, smoke billowed up from the ruins of the Refuge, and the faraway thunder of explosions. Keeping the army busy.

His exhaustion was so deep it insulated him like a hazmat suit. Everything looked dim, as if a film separated him from the streets. His ears were still ringing, he was alive, but he walked like a dead man, blindly, without purpose and above all without feeling or thinking. One rent in the fabric, one crack in the helmet, and the vacuum of empty space would suck him away.

Had the others gotten out? Madrone? Would he ever see her again?

Fear turned him inside out. What if she were dead? What if he had escaped the Refuge only to leave her in its grave?

Slowly he became aware that the street was filling with people. More and more of them, heading north, pulling him along like a current.

Here came a bold young man, striding forward in a T-shirt emblazoned with a rising sun. And now a woman, looking carefully around, whipped out a sunrise flag from her bag and waved it defiantly.

The march! Holy sweet Mother of all the Gods, today was the day they had called for the Rising! In all the panic and destruction, he'd forgotten.

And with all that had happened, it was still early. The sun was still climbing toward its noon peak, and the march was beginning to form.

Now an old man passed him, carrying a placard that proclaimed End Debt Slavery Now! A young mother pushing a battered old baby carriage stopped and reached beneath the blanket. She pulled out a rainbow flag roughly sewn out of scraps of cloth, and a blessed, precious bottle of water.

"Here," she said, handing him the water. "You look like you need this more than I do!"

He couldn't speak, could only nod his thanks, and drink. The water was cool and sweet in his parched throat, and the last of his insulation dissolved.

Where was Madrone? Had she escaped? Was she alive?

The woman smiled at him, with crooked teeth and the pinched face of someone who never got quite enough nourishment. But her face was bright as she pinned the rainbow patch on his ripped, blood-stained shirt.

"All debts will be forgiven in the bright new day," she said, and pushed her buggy on up the road.

He would follow the march. If the refugistas had escaped, that's where they would go. It was a long, long way to the Stewards' headquarters, their destination. But though the Refuge had fallen, the Rising was just beginning. Filthy, sweaty, stinking as he did of blood and smoke, he yet felt clean, as if he'd passed through some test, come through some great temptation intact. With all his faults and failings, he still chose to be a singer, a maker of meaning, not a maker of meat.

Surely that had earned him something. He had been willing to die to save the others and Madrone—didn't that count for something? Surely the grace that had spared his life would allow him to come to her again.

Chapter Seventy

Miss Ruby was bellowing at everyone to stay calm. Madrone sank down, leaning against a pillar that still supported a bit of intact roof. She wanted, more than anything, just not to move, to sink into the concrete and turn to stone. She was exhausted and heartsick.

They don't talk about this in the tragedies, she thought. Sounds so simple and final, even restful. They all died. Don't talk about those moments before, when the ship is sinking, the plane going down, the monster approaching, and yet you're still alive, heart pumping soundly, all faculties working, all the systems of the miracle body still unharmed.

Can't I just skip this part? Apparate directly to the Isle of Apples, throw herself into Maya's arms, Johanna's arms, into the arms of Bird who was surely already waiting for her there. Can't I just hopscotch over the terror and the pain, the aching, wrenching loss?

But she knew better. Habit pushed her up onto her feet, and she found herself laying a soothing hand on a woman in pain, speaking a comforting word to a sobbing teen.

Whether it matters or not, this is who I am, she thought. A healer till the bitter end. Might as well die being myself.

And more than that. I am who I have chosen to be, and I continue to make that choice, whether it's for five more minutes or another fifty years.

Who I am is not someone who gives up.

Wasn't there something, anything they could do?

The only way out is through.

What in Hella's name did that mean? Through death?

Or through something else? Could there be another entrance? There was her secret tunnel, her meditation cave. But that was too small for them all to get through, impossible to bring stretchers or wounded.

But maybe it was not through the cave, but through the meditation? If she could sink into bee-mind—or rather, the mind behind bee-mind. Rock-mind. Water-mind.

She changes everything she touches ...

I am all possibility.

... And everything she touches, changes....

The chant hummed in her mind, and behind it, scraps of words....

I am the radiance of starlight, and the dust of its dissolution....

Sinking so deep she could feel the structures around them, see any passageways....

Stardust made flesh, made rock ... all form a dance of energies....

Anything was worth trying. She found a corner where she could squat down against a concrete slab, close her eyes, still her breathing....

Find the pattern at the heart....

Boom! The loudest explosion of them all echoed through the rock above them. She was seized with a wave of sheer bodily terror, her breath stopping, her hands shaking.

Breathe. Ground. Training, remember your training ...

Boom! The earth shook again. Cries of fear echoed through the chamber.

Breathe through it, go through it. Fear is the block. The only way out is through.

Dive into the wave, Bird would say in his surfer days.

She took a deep breath, like a diver, and let the fear wash over her. She was engulfed by fear, unable to breathe, her heart pumping, her blood racing....

Heart. Blood. Life.

And the fear dissolved, or transmuted. It was life, nothing but life asserting itself, the heart fighting to go on pumping, the blood racing to continue its flow. She felt the raw animal exuberance of her body, nerves firing, muscles ready to spring. She was part of that great creative force endlessly reinventing itself, a river that flowed on, whether her particular filament lasted an eyeblink or an eon.

Ephemeral flesh pressed against immutable concrete. So different, her soft and malleable body, from the cold hard stuff at her back. Yet not so different, after all. Made of the same elements. She and the rocks both, in the end, merely the debris of stars.

And then the rock dissolved, or she dissolved into rock, into layers of clay and sand that water bubbled through, and she was probing water, and she was the great gravitational pull, the earth's enfolding arms holding her lovers close.

Witchcraft, Maya was saying. *It's the practical application of mysticism.*

What are you doing here, *madrina?* Where have you been? Can you show us a way out?

Buddhist dissolution without the detachment. Utter transcendence, welded to will. Ultimate perfection of being, coupled with good old-fashioned American know-how.

Maya, *madrina*, please, just tell me in plain English what I'm supposed to do!

"Thou art Goddess," but Goddess with a mission.

A mission. A goal. Her goal. Life, pulsing, throbbing life. That was her goal. To continue. Flowing, flowing like water. Like water flowing through the cavern.

Find the pattern at the heart.

She could feel the crystalline structures of rock and cement, and through them flowed pattern through pattern, dance through dance. She could drift along with that stream, but if she held within her a single point, a focus, she could move with volition. Pulled by gravity, shifting patterns as she went, changing and shaping, like water, she could make an opening.

And the opening was there. The explosions, those bursts of energy, had shifted the planes of the crystals that held these chambers, and made a passage.

A passage through planes of crystalline concrete, precariously balanced, ready to shift again.

An opening, but a dangerous one. One blast, one creaking beam slipping down, and they would all be crushed.

But she was stardust, the stuff of rock. And rock was stardust, the stuff of mind.

If she could talk to the walls, enlist the cooperation of concrete like the techies did with the crystals that powered the Net ... hold its structure....

Was she strong enough for that? But if they stayed here, if they didn't try, they would surely all die.

Her first task was to stay in the rock-mind and yet to stand, to work those animal muscles, rise, move. A pattern moving through a pattern, a fluid through crystalline structure.

And then, a thousand times harder ... to find words. She moved awkwardly through the chambers, cries and sobs echoing around her. Hard to keep her balance. Rocking, like a drunk.

Need an anchor. Someone to hold to. Who?

Anthony? The name came to her, a slippery bundle of glowing fibers dissolving as her mind touched them. Emily, a brittle carapace of light that barely contained her own terror.

But there, there in the center of the cavern, like a rock glowing with an inner heat but still solid, undaunted by terror or pain or death, stood Miss Ruby, shouting out her orders in the face of fate. Ruby, yes. Adamant, crystalline, red as living blood.

Madrone staggered over to her and gripped her hand.

Miss Ruby looked at her in alarm.

"What's wrong with you, child?" she asked.

Madrone suddenly wanted to laugh. Oh nothing, she thought, just ruin, destruction, imminent death. She couldn't get the words out, but they brought her back into enough of human-mind to gasp.

"Anchor me!"

Miss Ruby gripped her hand tightly.

Objective. The goal.

"There is a passage," Madrone gasped. "Out. That way!" She pointed. "Not ... not stable. But I can hold it ... hold the rock. But got to stay ... stay like this...."

Miss Ruby nodded. She continued to grip Madrone's hand while she barked out a new set of commands.

"Okay, now stop your howling! Madrone, she says there's a way out of here. Now we're gonna form up in an orderly line, no panic, no pushing. Stretchers in front, then the wounded. We're not gonna leave a soul behind. Marigold, you help Marcus with that stretcher there, take the corner. Arthur, lend a shoulder to Miss Vanessa. Janus, you walk between them. That's right!"

Her words washed over Madrone like another sort of stream. Yes, she was rock now, holding a fragile geometry together, forces balanced one against the other. And through them, an opening ...

Now they were walking forward, moving slowly. Madrone and Miss Ruby in front, leading the way. Miss Ruby holding tight to her hand. A step. Then another. Muscle and bone. Bone another form of rock. Rock solid beneath her feet. Rock in balance above.

A breath could shift it, or an unkind word.

Step. Step.

"Rock is stardust, far dust, our dust. From dust we come and to dust we go, over the hills and through the dust to grandmother's house, we go, we go...."

Janus's murmuring seemed to echo her own voice. Maybe I'm as crazy as she is? The thought intruded like a shell and the world shook.

"Oh, grandmother, what big eyes you have! The better to see you with, my dear, my dear! Eyes are wise, big surprise. What big ears you have, ears to hear ... no fear, no fear in the house of the grandmother."

Or maybe Janus has a crazy wisdom. The words spun spider threads that Madrone could weave with, helping to shore up her own power, to bind the rock together. Stay in the house of the Grandmother, the Crone, the Ancient One, and what is there to fear?

Back they went through the room of the baths, vessels of water moving through a space of water. Back where her tiny passage had been, now opened into a wide crack. Wide enough to move through. Step. Step.

Darkness. Feel with feet, flesh over bone. A hole. An obstruction.

Words like waterfalls.

Miss Ruby's commentary, a lifeline. "Watch your step there!"

Life flowing through rock. Slabs of it, rocking above them, shifting behind them ...

Then it came, another explosion, a burst of fire and force that shook all the structures around them. She could feel the balance shifting, tilting....

She was pleading without words, holding without hands, bracing with no back and thighs to brace with....

It was going to come down and crush them all. In a minute—she only had the strength for a minute....

"Run!" she cried. She pressed herself back against the passage wall, into a shallow niche, and they thundered past her, each heavy footfall a new shudder in the walls, a tremble in the roof above....

"Run!" she barked at Miss Ruby, who was still holding her hand, but Miss Ruby did not let go.

Extra hands grabbed onto the stretchers. New shoulders supported the hobblers. They poured on past, stumbling ahead, running for their lives.

"Run!" she cried again as the last of them passed by, but Miss Ruby didn't understand. She didn't know that Madrone was rock and water and nothing could truly hurt her. She still thought Madrone was soft flesh, and she yanked her out of their sheltering niche and dragged her down the passage as Madrone's pure focus wavered and rock began to fall all around them.

A rumble, and behind them concrete walls were collapsing, slabs crashing down, dust choking them, and sharp splinters stinging.

And then she was back in human-mind, back in sheer raw terror, gripping Miss Ruby's hand for dear life and now Madrone pulled the older woman along, pelting down the passage as it collapsed behind them.

It led them, not up to the light, but down, deeper into the dark.

They stumbled out into a wide, dark space that smelled like death itself. Rot and decay and excrement assaulted their noses, and a wave of screams battered their ears. Madrone and Miss Ruby clung together as something ran over her feet, a flood of somethings, chittering and squeaking.

A pale beam from someone's flashlight lit the dark. Through the swirling dust, they saw a river of rats racing through the long, dark tunnel. They pelted headlong toward the huddled clumps of refugistas, who shrieked as the rats skittered around their ankles and dashed off through the foul stream flowing through the center of the tunnel below them.

Miss Ruby let out a high, shrill scream and Madrone felt a squeal escape her own lips before she clamped them shut. Her healer's soul shuddered with revulsion.

Life, she reminded herself. All life is one.

But she was no longer in the Great Flow where all was perfect. She was back in Madrone-mind where they were stuck in a sewer and rodents made her skin crawl. And the rats kept on coming for what felt like hours, thousands of them, scared out of their hollows by the shelling, no doubt.

Finally their numbers began to diminish. Hundreds of rats, not thousands, with space to avoid the feet that kicked out at them. Then dozens, then just a few stragglers.

"The sewers," Anthony remarked. "Now how the hell are we going to find our way out?"

Miss Ruby looked at him as if he were a particularly dimwitted student in her class.

"Follow the rats," she said.

They followed the rats and the pale beam of Anthony's flashlight through the long, winding underground tunnels, holding folds of their shirts over their noses and holding onto each other's hands to avoid getting lost. Again, they put the stretchers and the wounded in front, and again Madrone and Miss Ruby brought up the rear.

Madrone was exhausted, her legs shaking with weariness. The trance had drained her of energy, and she could barely force herself to move. But she would rather stagger on then sit down here in the filth and stench. If only she could breathe! One gasp of clean clear air!

Miss Ruby kept a tight grip on her, and Madrone was grateful for every ounce of the stubbornness that had once so irked her. Step by step, for what seemed like eternity, they stumbled on.

Finally Anthony called a halt. On the wall was a rusty iron ladder that led upwards. One of the younger scouts scrambled up, and pushed open a manhole at the top.

"All clear!" he called down. "No sign of the army up here!"

Madrone closed her eyes, swaying on her feet, as Anthony and Emily between them organized the ascent. They sent most of the able-bodied up first, then rigged up a rope sling to haul up the stretchers and those wounded who could not climb.

"Now you go up!" Miss Ruby told her while there was still a good crew down below to help up the less mobile. Madrone started to object, but in truth she didn't have the strength to both argue and attempt the climb. It was hard enough to haul her exhausted body up, her legs still shaking and her hands seemingly unable to muster the force for a strong grip. She had to stop halfway, to gather her will and her strength.

I can't do it! she wanted to cry, like so many of the mothers she'd helped to give birth. But they did do it, in the end, because you couldn't stop halfway, and neither could she, now. One hand, one foot, then another, and another, and yes, now she could smell open air, see the light above. Strong hands reached down for her and helped her through the opening onto the street.

Sunlight blinded her. It was just before noon, and she blinked away tears.

They were on a street of small shabby shops and apartments with crumbling stucco. And around them people were streaming with signs and banners toward some convocation somewhere.

It was a mark of the revolution that someone had opened a fire hydrant. Water sprayed into the street, diamonds of light dancing in the spray, and the refugistas were gratefully washing themselves clean of the stench of sewers and terror, gulping it down and laughing and splashing each other.

They had made it, after all. Out from death and darkness into the light of a bright new day.

Chapter Seventy-One

A BLAZE OF LIGHT FILLED THE ROOM. RIVER BLINKED, AND THEN A wall slid closed across their alcove, the light dimmed and the floor fell away. Or not away, exactly. The floor was falling and he and Smokee fell with it, glued to it, and suddenly the air was alive with the electrical hum of machinery come back to life.

He blinked, blinded, and carefully lowered the gun. His stomach lurched as they dropped.

What the fuck?

Smokee was laughing, laughing and crying, laughter that turned to gulping tears of amazement and relief.

What the fuck? What the fuck?

They fell, but slowly, as if the hands of the Gods were cushioning them, and Smokee was in hysterics, gulping for air between laughs that turned to sobs. There was a dim light around them, and now River could see that he'd been leaning on a panel of colored buttons with numbers on them, and symbols he didn't understand.

"Where the fuck are we?" he asked.

"Oh God, I'm going to wet myself," Smokee choked, then reached up past River to press one of the buttons hard. "Oh God, River, you nearly shit your pants!"

"What is this?"

"It's an elevator, dungbrains! They must have got a backup generator working."

"Elevator?"

"Takes you up and down tall buildings. You never been in one before?"

River shook his head. Army barracks were all on one level, and he'd never had cause to attend any meetings at the bigsticks' headquarters.

But they'd talked about elevators in their urban warfare training sessions. He should have remembered. Now he felt like a fool. Just a moment before he'd been all noble, ready to die, telling Smokee how much he admired her and even loved her. Now he wanted to kill her again.

She reached over his shoulder to punch a button. "Keep the door closed," she said. "Let's ride it down to the basement and see if we can get out. Who knows, we may finish the job ourselves yet!"

They descended slowly, the lights above the door blinking on in sequence, four, three, two, one, B. The elevator came to a halt, with a shivery jerk.

"Might be a guard on the door," River warned. Smokee nodded. Guns ready, they waited as the door opened.

A young sojuh stood there, peering at them open-mouthed. Before he could raise his weapon, River shot him.

"Sorry," he said as the boy fell. Quickly he peeled off his jacket and cap, slipped them on, then told Smokee to put her hands behind her back.

"What for?"

"You be my prisoner, now," he said. "Get us the fuck out of here!"

He looped a pair of plastic handcuffs loosely around her wrists, shoved her gun into his waist belt, put his gun to her head again, and together they marched down the corridor searching for an exit.

None of the Stewards' sojuhs challenged them as they made their way out. Whenever a stripe got too close River simply snarled, "High-value prisoner for interrogation," and marched on. They snaked through the labyrinth of underground corridors, through the basement, out through mangled doors and scorched hallways until they came to the shell hole that had been blasted into the service bay. Troops were streaming freely in and out, and they slipped through in the throng, out to the dark edge of the crowd around the parking lot.

"High-value prisoner," River barked as a guard challenged them at the gate in the chain-link fence at the edge of the asphalt.

"Over there," the guard pointed with the muzzle of his rifle.

In a corner of the parking lot, two guards surrounded what was left of the Army of Liberation. It was a sorry picture, maybe a couple of hundred defenders now kneeling on the pavement with their arms behind their heads.

It didn't look good to River. It looked like standard procedure for a mass execution.

"This a high-value prisoner," he said to the guard. "Not for execution."

The guard shrugged. "Orders. Bigsticks say, kill all the rebels."

"Got a better idea," River said as Smokee kicked the guard hard in the balls. He doubled over, and River gave a chop to his neck that laid him out cold. He grabbed the rifle, tossed Smokee a gun, and they ran for cover behind a dumpster where they could take aim at the guards surrounding the kneeling captives.

"Gonna do this?" River asked her quietly.

"Only a dozen guards, and there's two of us," she said. "Better odds than we've had all night."

"More guards where those tubos come from," he said.

"Got a plan then?"

"Always got a plan."

"Invite them to the table?" Smokee suggested, her tone ironic. "Offer them the chance to join the invincible Army of Liberation?"

"Good as any," River said, and he stepped out from behind the dumpster and bellowed out in his loudest voice. "Sojuhs of the Stewardship, drop your weapons. Army of Liberation got you covered! Don't make us shoot!"

There was a moment of surprise, when they wheeled and turned toward his voice. He swiftly ducked behind the dumpster as a barrage of fire turned his way. But when the dust cleared, he saw that the prisoners, as he'd hoped, had used surprise to their advantage. Some of the guards were down on the ground, others were wrestling with gangs of liberados and fighters from the Army of Liberation. He heard shots and cries of agony, but it was too dark and he and Smokee were too far away to risk a shot in return.

Instead, he ran forward and trained the laser rifle he'd taken from the guard onto the chain-link fence. He blazed a line of fire up and over and down again, carving out a blazing gateway. He and Smokee ran forward, and he rammed his shoulder against it and the whole section of fence fell out, leaving a wide opening to the streets beyond.

It hadn't taken long for two hundred to overcome the dozen who guarded them. But dark figures were streaking across the parking lot from the building, where white smoke poured out. Backup. Time to leave.

"Army of Liberation!" River called again. "This a good moment to fade away. Time for the army to disappear."

"You know when and where we meet again," Smokee cried. "Find yourself shelter now. Rest. And then come back to the rendezvous, with everyone you can bring with you! We will see you at the sunrise of the bright new day!"

"Or we all die miserable in the dark," she added in a low voice to River only. "Which will it be, I wonder?"

"Not dead yet," River said as they ducked through the hole in the fence and out to the dark streets to find a hiding place where they could wait out the long hours.

Chapter Seventy-Two

L IKE RIVULETS OF WATER FORMING INTO STREAMS, GROUPS OF FRIENDS
and neighbors converged and began to march, forming into clumps,
then crowds, then rivers streaming toward the temple. They came from
the flatlands and the rubble fields, from the vast hordes of drifters and
laborers and the desperate. A surge came from the crowds besieging the
distribution sites, scattering bags of chips as they went.

Even the ubiquitous vidscreens seemed possessed by some spirit of
liberation. They showed the crowds forming, the streams converging.

The Rising! With all that had happened, Madrone had forgotten
that today was the day. But now the streets were flowing with people,
and bright patches of sun-colored fabric began to be seen. She wished,
for one sharp moment, that she could call it off, could wait for a day,
to rest and recover, and mourn. Surely she should mourn, because how
could Bird and Zap possibly have escaped that mayhem?

But there was nowhere to hole up and hide out, no comforting cups
of tea awaiting at Beth's, no more sweet secret apartment where she and
Bird could lock a door and steal a moment together. No, she couldn't let
herself think that there never would be again. Not now, not when there
was still a long, long day ahead of them.

With all the losses, the refugistas were still over a hundred strong.
And there were others who would join them, who had left in the night
long before the assault to prepare artwork or position themselves to lead
feeder marches. They had called forth this river of marchers, and now
they would join the stream.

Madrone sent Beth off with a contingent to ferry the stretchers and
the wounded to one of the safe houses. They'd be cared for there. For
once, she decided her place was not with the medics and healers. She
belonged with the march today.

Because if a miracle had happened, if somehow Bird and little Zap had made it out of that wreckage, he'd be pulled by this same stream. She knew it.

Together with Anthony and Emily and Miss Ruby, she stumbled along in the mass of moving people. Someone thrust a flag into her hand, and she lifted the banner of the rising sun into the wind. She had gone somewhere past exhaustion into a numb trance that carried her along.

Then came a huge cheer and down from a side street came Tianne and her contingent of teens, towing the cart with the Angel Goddess statue upon it. They joined the procession amidst cries of joy, and took the lead, the Queen of the Angels gleaming in the sunlight, her arms raised high in triumph.

They had done it. They had escaped the Refuge and roused the city, and the sun was shining on the bright new day.

But Madrone could barely feel the jubilation. Inside, she felt cold and hollow. Bird wasn't there to share this triumph. Not there, to take her hand.

Bird and Zap. Would she ever even know what had happened to them? Would she be able to go back, to search the ruins for bodies? If they had been blasted into oblivion, would they find ...

No, don't think about that. Think about the sweet times they had had, the gift that had been. Watching him bathe the boys—watching them squirm and wiggle and run away. Or no, don't even think about that now. Think about this moment, the great moment of Rising, and how they could nourish it, protect it.

She was far too exhausted to risk the bee-mind, now. If she sank into it, she would not have the strength to pull out. But she voiced a silent prayer, to the bees, to the Goddess, to the ancestors, to any and every power that might be out there willing to help.

Seek, she said, as she remembered his scent, how she could breathe it in when he wrapped his arms around her, his skin, his hair. Find, if there is anything to be found. Bring them to me.

The refugistas' march came out to the broad Avenue of Judgment which was swimming with people like a river. In the distance, someone was coming toward them, walking against the current, moving against the flow. Something in the rhythm of its motion, seemed familiar to Madrone. No, it was just her imagination, her wish. It couldn't be.

But the figure came closer and closer, pushing through the crowd with the same pig-headed determination Bird would have. But he wasn't the only stubborn idiot out there ...

Now she could see—*Diosa*, it was someone who looked so much like him. Could it be? Could it truly be?

He broke into a loping run, coming toward her. And it was his slight limp, the lopsided gait that she knew so well.

She stopped, stock-still, hardly daring to breathe. If this was an illusion, please Goddess let her hold it a moment longer, let her have this instant to believe it was real.

And then it was real. He came to her and threw his arms around her. Goddess, he was filthy, covered with streaks of sweat and blood, but she had never seen anything so beautiful.

Then he pulled back, and she saw his eyes, his grim face.

"Zap," he croaked in a harsh whisper.

And she knew.

She was sobbing, now, and march or no march, he stopped and just held her, feeling her gasping as choking sobs broke from her throat. The marchers parted around them, and they stood for a moment still as a stone in a river.

He held her, hardly able to breathe with relief and gratitude and the deep grief for Zap swirling through him. He'd seen the glint of gold on the Angel's wings as the stream he was with joined in the main procession. His exhaustion had dropped away and he'd been possessed with the wild strength of the salmon thrashing their way against the current, not letting himself hope or believe, but hoping just the same.

And now he had found her. He encircled her with his arms, a magic circle, circle of protection. But that was an illusion. He couldn't keep her safe, as he couldn't keep the Refuge safe, or Zap, or Rosa, or his own father long ago.

He knew that now. He still heard the inner voices, accusing, blaming, It's your fault ... if you had kept him with you ... said yes, instead of no....

But they were weak now, like the echoes of the voices you hear from above when the boot is on your head. He no longer believed them. There was a place within him that they could no longer reach, where vines grew over the rubble and seeds took root in the dust.

He drew her closer into that shelter.

The Refuge was never destroyed, he realized. It's here, in my arms, in her beating heart. All the guns and bombs in all the world cannot destroy the refuge we offer one another.

The march had halted around them, and finally Miss Ruby came up and handed them both a handkerchief.

"I'm so sorry," she said. "He was a brave little boy, with all he'd been through. But we got to go on now. Are you ready?"

Madrone nodded.

"And at least your little Zoom is safe. And the other children."

"Yes," Madrone said. "At least they are safe."

Chapter Seventy-Three

ISIS STOOD ON THE DECK OF THE WARSHIP *HARVEY MILK* AND SURVEYED the Stewards' ship on the horizon as it grew larger in her binoculars. Apparently they had been able to partially repair what Rosa had done to it, as it was moving, but its steering appeared to be still somewhat out of whack. It traced a zigzag course through the water, lurching like a drunken sailor from an old song.

The girl had done well, slowing it down, crippling it, and allowing the Navy of Califia time to catch up. They'd needed that time, for it had taken Rosa a couple of hours of sailing before she was able to raise the hillboys on coms. They'd passed the message on to the navy, who had changed course immediately for the North, bringing up a strong flotilla—the warship, two of the reconditioned ferry boats, and half a dozen smaller craft. They left the rest of the navy in the Southlands' waters to continue blockading the shipping lines.

It was midafternoon before they spied the *Day of Victory*. Rosa and the little boy with her were sound asleep in their bunks, but they woke when they were hailed and gave a quick account of what they had seen. Then the girl had guided them on a compass bearing toward where she'd last seen the ships.

An hour out, they found the *Winstanley* abandoned and adrift, its deck littered with the bloody bodies of its defenders. They'd hooked up one of the tugs and set it to be towed north, up to Avalon Beach in the toxic zone where the Monsters and hillboys would take charge of it, and bury the dead. They had no time to do that while the living were still in jeopardy.

Isis had done her best to get Rosa aboard the tug, but the girl had flatly refused to go and she didn't have the heart to argue with her. The little boy had simply run away into the labyrinth of cabins and corridors below decks on the *Milk*. Isis gave up. She didn't have time to chase down kids who were determined to get into trouble, and to tell the truth, she sympathized with Rosa. If it had been her, she wouldn't have wanted to leave, either.

Truly the girl had been a hera. Smart, brave, and effective. If they succeeded in saving the children, it would be due to her and Isis made sure she knew it. She deserved to be present for the outcome.

The boy described how the ship had fired on them without warning, blowing a hole in the hull just at water level. As the crew scrambled to deal with the damage, armed men had come aboard, shot some of the crew, and taken the rest prisoner, shoving down them into the hold.

"Got a machine on that ship," he said. "Make you weak. Feel like a worm, all floppy. Can't hardly move. But I thought, feel like a worm, crawl like a worm. Weren't watchin' us cuz they think that machine'll keep everybody quiet. I crawled up the ladder, then at the door they got somethin' that make you hurt like a screamin' rat. But I don't care. Went right through it, and then got on deck and tried to hide. But they chased me, and then they caught me but I fought them and I got away and jumped into the water. I can swim! Mama Mado made me learn it. So I swimmed away fast as I could. But I never swimmed in the ocean before. Got big waves, crash down on your head. But then she came along, and saved me!"

He grinned proudly, a pint-sized hero. Already full of himself, Isis thought, the baby-man, strutting like a blue-ribbon winner. Well, give him that. At least he had something to strut about.

"Good job," Isis said. "Now you two punks get below. Cooks'll feed you. Then get some sleep. Gonna be a long day!"

The timing was all wrong, Isis thought as the *Harvey Milk* approached the navy ship. No cover of darkness for their divers. No storm to conceal their movements. No fog as a screen to display their ghost ship.

But they had no choice. They had to stop the Steward swabs getting away with the children of the Refuge.

She felt a soft hand on her shoulder.

"What do we do?" Sara's husky voice sent a little secret thrill down Isis's spine.

For one sharp moment, Isis imagined saying, Do what we shoulda been doing all along. Forget trying to forget you—ain't working anyhow, and I want you! Right here, right now, because I've let you go too long.

But she stifled the thought. Now was not the time. Anyway, Miguel was right behind Sara, his usual broad smile replaced with a frown of worry.

"There's the old mining-the-hull trick," he suggested. "How far can our divers swim?"

"Far as we have to," Sara said.

"We gonna sink the ship with all the cubs on board?" Isis asked.

"We can threaten," Miguel said.

"How about board and shoot?" Isis suggested.

"With the children as potential hostages?" Sara countered.

"Set the mines first, then board if we can," Miguel suggested.

"Won't be easy," Isis warned. "Probably take heavy casualties."

"Let's take a lesson from Rosa," Sara suggested. "Mine the steering mechanism and the propeller. We don't have to sink the ship, just incapacitate it."

"Good idea," Miguel said. "Then let's hope they listen to reason."

"Reason?" Isis snorted. "Jam a gun barrel down the robos' throats, might listen to that!"

"Just keep them talking," Sara said. "Buy my divers some time."

⁂

"Ahoy," Isis called over the bullhorn. "You have something belongs to us!"

The enemy boat was a larger, more heavily armored version of the cutters they'd fought off before. It loomed up, a floating pyramid of steel plates, with gun towers fore and aft, menacing and invulnerable.

A shot over their bow was the reply.

Isis snorted. "Diplomacy—can tell it's a high art in the Southlands! Here's a suggestion. Give us back the children and our crew, peaceful-like, and we let your sorry asses go."

"Here's a better suggestion!" came the reply.

A shell splintered the mainsail and mast of Ming's boat, sending shock waves through the water.

"Hold the fuck on!" Isis screamed as their warship rolled sharply with the backwash. She grabbed the wheel and struggled to turn the prow into the swell.

Ming's sailboat was caught broadside. It rolled and capsized. Small figures dove from the sides.

Isis barked the command to rev up the engine. She swore out loud, wishing she were back in the *Day of Victory*, small and maneuverable. There was no way she could turn this giant hulk swiftly enough to pick them up. But Bronwyn was ready on deck, tossing out life-belts and calling out to the lifeboat crew to launch.

"Recalibrating!" the Stewards' ship warned.

"Move out of range!" Isis yelled through the coms system as she made speed away from the enemy ship. The Califian ships began dodging and tacking, trying to evade enemy fire. Another shell exploded just beyond the deck of the tugboat. It rocked and swayed alarmingly, but remained upright.

"Come closer, we bring the cargo on deck. Pull off a few limbs, feed some hungry sharks," the Stewards' bullhorn barked. "Do the little ones first while the others watch."

"Pull back," Isis commanded. "Play for time."

Sara swam, pushing herself to move swiftly through the water against the heavy drag of her oxygen bottles. Each of the divers carried extra bottles, a four-hour supply. They moved through the water at depth, following the sonar beacon on their headlamps that gave off a low tone to guide their direction. The sonar was more accurate than lights, and wouldn't attract attention from above.

She was swimming fifteen feet below the surface, low enough to not be easily visible from the decks of the enemy ship, high enough to surface swiftly and safely if she needed to. It was a long swim, and Sara forced herself to breathe calmly and settle into the rhythm of it. Stroke, stroke, inhale. Stroke, stroke, exhale. Fast, but not so fast she would run out of energy by the time she reached her target.

She had done this enough now that it was no longer a novelty—still, she never quite lost that sense of wonder, that voice that wanted to crow, Look at me, I'm having an adventure! But this was more than an adventure. She couldn't let herself think about the children, about what would await them at the end of the voyage if they failed in this rescue attempt. They'd end up in the pens, or sold off to the slave ships of the Gyre.

For a moment, she pictured herself and Isis, together on the *Day of Victory*, sailing west on that rescue mission. Together, that was the point. Even better would be not having a mission, just heading out to find some tropical island with a white sand beach. Sailing away together, into the sunset, if that hard-headed porpoise would ever admit she'd been wrong! For just a moment, on deck that morning, Sara had sensed a softening. She'd caught a look in Isis's eyes that seemed to say, I'm sorry. I want you.

Sara had given her space. She'd waited for her to come around. But maybe that was the wrong tactic. Tonight, after this mission was over, after the kids were safe and the celebration was underway, that would be the moment to shift gears. Yes, she sensed the time was right. She pushed forward with a strong stroke, buoyed by a sense of hopeful anticipation.

It was a long, long swim, but she was strong, and fit, and if danger awaited at the other end, well, that was after all the definition of "adventure." She kept on, until her arms ached and her legs felt like lead. On and on, hoping that Isis and the rest were keeping the sailors deeply engaged in conversation.

Finally she saw the bulk of the ship ahead of her. It was an ugly thing, like a tower of steel boxes precariously buoyed up by the water, with armored hulls and weapons bristling over the gunwales.

As she reached the perimeter of the ship, she heard a deep, muffled boom. Far away, something exploded underwater, sending a shock wave that carried her closer to the ship. She steeled herself for the impact. Not far away, she could see the black-suited shapes of other divers. One of them, probably Annie, approached the ship, dove down behind the stern near the propeller and the rudder.

An echo of a sharp sound above the surface resounded through the water. A red cloud spurted from Annie's back, swirling in eerily beautiful patterns. Annie arched like a dancer, her head flexed back in a painful curve. Her breathing tube drifted out of her slackened mouth. Then her weights began to pull her down, slowly, slowly.

Sara instinctively dove deeper. They were spraying the surface of the water with rifle fire, guarding the vulnerable parts of the ship. How deep could bullets penetrate against the friction of the water, and still have impact? She didn't know, but she suspected that deeper was safer. Down, down—it was a barrage, an underwater rainstorm of death. Was Annie still alive? Could she help her?

But how could she find her, and what could she do? The water was churning with bullets and blood, and if she tried to search for Annie she might simply end up joining her in death. That could happen anyway. What was important was to plant her gel first. There were a hundred children's lives at stake.

If she could get to the hull, the ship itself would provide her with cover. She kicked her way forward, and then down.

With a thud, she clamped onto the steel-plated hull. She could plant her gel here, but better would be to get to the steering mechanism or the propeller, something that would disable the ship permanently. But that would take time, following the hull backwards, avoiding the slowly-turning propeller blades....

Down below her, she could see a form drifting. Sara pushed off and streaked downward.

Annie's eyes were open, staring blankly. Sara grabbed her, pushed the breathing tube into her mouth, tried to squeeze her lungs to make them work. She felt for a pulse. Nothing. A cloud of blood surrounded them, staining the water red. There was nothing she could do.

May the wind carry ... what was it? Carry your spirit gently, she murmured to herself. May the water cleanse you. How did the prayer for the dead go? But through the haze of blood, she could see new shapes circling, sleek, white and ominous, with triangular fins on their backs. Sharks! Attracted by the blood. Shit! She didn't want to leave Annie for them, but they were circling closer. She grabbed Annie's knife off her belt, wishing it were a harpoon or something that could kill at a greater distance. Her own knife would be a backup.

A flash, a swift lunge—teeth coming at her, sharp and fierce. The snout, she thought—that's the vulnerable place. Stay calm, focus, don't panic—now strike! She jabbed at the bulging protrusion above that vicious mouth. A red blossom, a thrashing that churned the water and tore Annie's body away from her grip. Without thinking, she kicked upwards. A sharp, burning pain tore through her calf. She looked back and saw her own blood streaming out behind her. She kicked harder, doubled back, and jabbed again at a jutting jaw. She cut a deep slice in the creature's snout, jabbed again at an eye. The shark streamed blood, and from below, its brothers attacked, giving her a moment of respite.

She fled. Kicking harder, upward and up, risking the bends or anything else to escape from the razor teeth below.

Again she reached the hull of the ship. Board and capture might not be the best plan, but she had no other choice now. She had to get out of the water before the sharks grew done with Annie and each other and went for her. But before that, she still had a mission.

She dug in her pack for a strap and tied a quick tourniquet around her leg. The blood was no longer streaming, but still seeping. She tightened the strap. Now she could hardly use the leg, but she pulled herself along the bottom of the hull.

The cut was deep and the salt water burned, but the blood slowly stopped. Still, it might open again at any moment. Back she went along the hull, and farther back, until she found the rudder and the propeller. She could see the broken stick of Rosa's harpoon still jammed into the steering mechanism. It was slowly working loose, being pushed out each time the rudder moved back and forth. Just a little gel there would do it—but the propeller, crippled as it was, created a strong backwash. She clung to the side of the ship, inched along. Hurry. Below her she saw a white shape begin to swim upwards toward the cloud of blood she'd left behind her. Not much time.

She pushed off and went for it. The propeller created a vortex strong enough to pull her in. If it had been working full speed, she would have no hope of staying out of it, but now it limped along slowly and she had just enough strength to fight free, even with her wounded leg dragging. Up, and over, and there, there was the sweet spot where the drive chain met the rudder. She slapped on the gel....

Her leg was seeping blood again as the strap worked itself loose with her movements. The propeller lurched. She gave a huge kick and escaped from its vortex at the cost of a huge spurt of blood.

The white shape streaked toward her.

Clinging to the hull, she made her way around the ship. Somewhere, surely, there had to be a ladder, a rope, something to grip onto to help pull her up along the slick sides. There, she found it—a rope hanging down over the side. It could be a trap. There could be a sailor up there with a gun, ready to kill her or capture her. But staying in the water was sure death. The thought of those teeth, pulling off more of her flesh, ripping into her belly—no, don't go there. Don't think about it.

Stark terror propelled her to the rope. She grabbed it and began to pull herself up, hand over hand. Underwater, it was easy. She was weightless. But to rise up out of the water, she would have to pull her own weight. She was carrying twenty pounds of oxygen bottles. Reluctantly, she let them go. Without them, she could not escape again through the water—but with her leg bleeding, the sea was a death trap anyway. She abandoned her pack. If she somehow lived through the next few moments, she might regret that, but with it her chances of living were that much less.

Rest for just one moment. But the white shape was just below her, and she knew how swiftly it could speed through the water. One deep breath—then she pulled herself up, hoisting herself on the rope, hand over hand, while her legs walked her up the side of the hull. Her hurt leg burned but she willed herself to ignore it, scrambling swiftly up as a white, bullet-shaped head erupted beneath her, snapping and slavering. Up quickly, before she could be noticed and shot from above—and then she had done it, pulling herself over the rail, landing in a crouch on the deck which, thank fortune, was empty.

Luck was with her. She was in a small alcove sheltered from view. She pressed flat against the wall, forced herself to breathe slowly, to reoxygenate her screaming muscles. Her leg was bleeding again, and she pressed it hard but it continued to seep.

Now what? she thought. If I were an action hero, I would take out the crew singlehandedly. But I'm only one woman, good at diving, bottom of the class at hand-to-hand combat. I don't want to die. I want to save the children and bring them home to their happy parents. I want to get off here and back to shore and find Isis and talk her out of her stupid pigheadedness and take her to bed for days and days and days.

Just then, she heard footsteps coming around the corner. She crouched low. What do the weak and powerless do? They grab a hostage. Maybe, just maybe ...

A young sailor rounded the corner. Sara leapt at him. Although her wounded leg dragged, she had surprise on her side and she knocked him down, rolled, and grabbed his arm and pulled it behind him. In seconds, she had him in an arm lock, her knife at his throat.

"Quiet," she hissed. She wondered if she would really use the knife if he resisted. Probably not, but hopefully he wouldn't guess that.

He said something to her in a shaky voice that she couldn't clearly hear.

"There's a place for you at our table, if you will choose to join us," she said experimentally. A flood of expletives came back at her.

"Captain," she said finally. "Take me to him."

He jerked his chin to indicate a direction. She frog-marched him along the deck.

Another shell whizzed over the bow of the *Harvey Milk*, exploding just beyond the deck. Damn, that was too close! Isis thought.

Bronwyn came up behind her and offered to take the wheel. Isis nodded and let her have control. The warship continued to move swiftly back from the Stewards' ship. She headed to the deck. Maybe they had a rocket launcher on board, or a sniper rifle?

"Person overboard!"

The cry came from Nick on the foredeck, and she ran swiftly up to join him at the rails. But he was already hopping over the side and diving.

Floating in the water was a black-clad diver. He wasn't moving. Nick turned him over and Isis threw him down a rope. He grabbed hold and she began pulling him up, joined by a couple of burly swabs.

They grabbed him, pulled him on deck, and a medic began pounding his heart and blowing into his mouth.

Soon he was spluttering and coughing.

"Made it to the ship," he said. "Then the explosion caught me back here."

"The mines?" Isis asked.

"A few of us got through. Some got shot. Then, the sharks ..."

Sara! Isis thought. But she couldn't allow herself to think. No. Sara meant nothing to her, no more than anyone else. The mission, that was the thing. This fucked-up, demon-plagued disaster of a mission.

She grabbed the loudspeaker.

"Hold your fire!" she called. "Your ship is mined. One more shot, and we crack you like a nut."

"And sink your precious cargo?" came the laughing reply.

"Better dead than slaves," Isis called back with a bravado she didn't truly feel.

But she was already streaking back across the deck, heading for the wheelhouse. Another shell landed, this one just short of them. Again the boat rocked and Isis danced with the motion and sped toward the red dial fixed to the wall that would set off the radio signal that would explode the mines.

Hope this works, she thought as she pressed the detonator. Nothing happened. She tried another frequency. Still nothing. One more time. Somebody must have gotten through. A boom, and water churned around the stern of the Stewards' ship. It lurched and wobbled in the water.

A barrage of shells was the answer.

Sara, rounding the corner with her hostage, gripped him tight as the boat rocked with the impact of the explosion. A sudden lurch, and they were thrown to the deck but she held on, even at the cost of a hard blow to her elbow as they landed. Pain shot through her arm, but she gritted her teeth and tightened her grip.

Then she yanked them both into the shadows of an alcove as a guard of sailors brought out two more of her divers, Matt and Harmony. The scuts jammed pistols into the bases of the divers' skulls, and shoved them forward into the midst of a rough assembly on the foredeck.

The Captain was a barrel-shaped man with his blond hair so close-cut he looked nearly bald. A younger salt handed him a bullhorn, and he barked into it.

"A trade!" the Captain said. "Surrender, and we'll spare the lives of your pathetic boarding party and yourselves. Take you all back to Angel City, where you'll get a fair trial. Refuse, they die. First. Then you all die."

Isis had binoculars trained on the deck. Oh shit, she thought. Now what?

"You shoot them, you sink," Isis countered. "Let them go, and our offer stands."

The Captain responded by cocking his pistol and pointing it at Matt's temple.

My cue, Sara thought. Don't think about it, don't think about dying or living or Isis finally realizing how much she loves me. Just do it. She stepped forward with her hostage.

"They die, he dies," she said.

The Captain and sailors turned to her. Her hostage lunged and then cried out in pain as she jerked his arm. Damn—she didn't really mean to hurt him that much. She thought his shoulder might be dislocated.

"Sorry," she murmured.

In the moment when attention turned to her, Matt ducked, Harmony rolled, both came back up to flip their guards and made running leaps off the deck, diving into the water below. They both still had oxygen. They sank deep below gunfire range, and if the sharks stayed distracted elsewhere, they had a good chance of making it home.

Good. That's one good thing she had done. She couldn't save Annie, she had yet to save the children, but she had saved them.

The Captain barked out a series of enraged commands. Suddenly rifles were trained on her.

"He dies, you die," the Captain said. "He is expendable."

It was at that moment that Sara realized she was not going to make it. Her leg was bleeding harder, a pool of blood staining the deck wherever she stood. The water was no refuge for her. She'd done well, she'd had some luck, good and bad, but she was no superhero, no action figure who could fight off a shipload of armed sailors alone. Her only hope of survival was for Isis to surrender, and Isis must be in mental agony.

Isis loved her. She knew that. She loved Isis. And while they would never make love again, never lie together in the hold rocked sweetly by gentle waves, never laugh as Isis barked commands or share a bottle of good wine and a long talk, Sara knew that she had one gift left that she could give.

Isis would never reveal to her now that sweet, soft core that she hid so well, so barricaded. But Sara knew it was there. And Sara could protect it.

Isis stood, clutching the rail of the deck, frozen to a statue. Sara, that stupid bitch! How the fuck had she got herself into that situation? And what was she, Isis, supposed to do now? Kill the bitch? She wanted to! Oh, how she wanted to, because this fucking hurt too much. But that wasn't what she wanted. What she wanted was to say, Sara, I've been so fucking wrong, and I now know that I need you. I can't go on without you!

Yet she couldn't surrender the fleet, the mission, the children to that love. She would have to do it. In a moment, she would have to issue the order and kill her love. And that would kill something inside of herself, too—something that never really got a chance to live. Count to ten. Give herself ten more seconds to live in a world that included Sara. Nine more. Eight. Seven. Six. Five. Four. Three. Two . . .

At that moment Sara dropped the knife, gave her hostage a shove, and set him free. Slowly, calmly she walked toward the Captain.

"I'm done with this game," she said. "It isn't really the game we want to play. What we want to say to you all is this—you can join us. There truly is a place for you at our table, if you will choose to join us. You can come and live in a world where there are no debt slaves and no pleasure transports, no rich and no poor, where everybody has enough."

As she spoke, she could see it. Yes, it took shape in her mind, brighter and stronger than the scene on the deck: a green world, where the streets of Angel City were overhung with orange trees, where a swarm of boats with silver sails descended on the grim factory ships of the Gyre. And she held to the thought that she was walking forward into that world. There was nothing to fear.

"We won't stop. We won't be afraid. You can refuse us, you can kill us, but others will come after us to build that world. They'll liberate your plantations and free your slaves. And those who carry out your orders and wield your guns for you will throw their weapons down because they see what the world could be. They will choose to be free."

The Captain raised his pistol.

Sara smiled and kept on walking. She had no idea if the scuts were listening to her, but she kept on talking nonetheless.

"You, Captain, now, this moment, you have a choice. Give me that gun, and I will toss it into the sea, and we will make peace and build that new world together. Put down the gun, and we will all be free."

She took one more step, and then another, and another, smiling, radiant, aglow with her vision.

The first bullet caught her between the ribs. She took a deep gasp and continued walking. The next hit her shoulder, but she had moved into some new place beyond fear, beyond pain. She was walking for Isis, for her love, giving her the only gift she now could give. And as another bullet slammed into her hip, she was filled with love. Love for Isis, love for the City, love for all the crazy idealistic Califians, and love for the possibilities of peace, even love and pity for those too shortsighted to grasp them. Yes, she knew, the day would come when ships like graceful swans would sail the oceans filled with things of beauty, when the garden streets of Angel City would weave a green net over the flat desert plains, when schools of whales would cruise clean seas again, singing the ancient whale songs.

She could hear them. She could see them, so vivid she believed in her heart that the sailors could see them too. Not the ghost ship, this, no holo in the fog, but the dream ship, the promise ship, sailing toward them in the bright light of day.

Most of all, she realized with some surprise, she was filled with love for herself, for this person she had become, this great giver of gifts, this fearless lover. Love blossomed inside her, and as the last bullet caught her in the heart, it opened like a great red flower.

One last rose to lay at Isis's feet.

Chapter Seventy-Four

IT WAS A LONG, LONG WAY FROM THE REFUGE TO THE OLD MORMON Temple, the command center for the Stewards' forces and the central hub of their government.

Tianne and her crew took the lead in the march, with their bright banners and their Angel Queen. Behind them, people continued to stream from their homes, from their makeshift shelters, from their crowded tenements. The call spread by whispers, by rumors, by impromptu speeches on street corners, by song. Tianne's techies hacked into the vidscreen network and a banner rolled out on every screen in the city:

March on the Temple. Now Is the Moment, the Sun Rises!

They held to a brisk pace, stopping every hour for water breaks and snacks. All along the route, people came forward, from the alleys and the shadows, to offer what they had, a loaf of dry bread, a handful of cookies, a pitcher full of water.

Tianne had taken a good long look at Bird and Madrone, stunned with grief and exhaustion, and made room for them to ride on the Angel Cart. For an hour or so, they rested, holding hands, drifting for long moments into sleep. But as the day wore on, their grief subsided for the moment, and their strength returned. They hopped off the cart to march alongside and make room for other tired walkers to get a respite.

Hour after hour they moved forward, and more and more people streamed out to join them. From the far neighborhoods of the city came feeder marches that converged with theirs. By the time they reached the temple grounds in the late afternoon, they had become a great river, spilling out into a sea of people that surged around the fences protecting the huge edifice.

Some of the marchers were chanting and raging, or hurling rocks at the impregnable temple walls. But many were just milling around, looking slightly lost as if they were asking, What do we do now?

Madrone looked up at the fortress-like structure. Surmounting a hill that jutted up from the wide plain, it commanded a view over the flatlands to the sea far to the west. Built by the Mormons over a hundred years before, it had served as their central temple in Southern California until the Stewards outlawed the Church of Latter-day Saints along with all the other denominations that the Retributionists decided were deviant.

The temple was a solid block of stone and concrete. A tall spire rose from its center, reaching skyward. Once it had been crowned with a golden statue of the Angel Moroni. Now an Angry Christ, whip held high, drove a brace of foam-mouthed horses that pulled the chariot of the Retributionists. Its blank façade was pierced with an oversized concrete lattice, but there were no openings that she could see. It looked solid and impregnable.

For decades it had been a worthy fortress for a militant God. Now it was just a fortress, Madrone thought. And a strong one.

The fortress falls when the ground beneath it shifts, she remembered. That was Bird's dream.

And we are the ground, she thought. Strong as it seems, the foundations of the Stewards' power rest invisibly on the consent of the people. Now the rulers anchor in shifting sands, and will fall.

The sea of people surrounded the hill and spilled out over the neighboring streets, back out to the wide Avenue of Judgment. Crowds swarmed up to the solid iron fence surrounding the grounds. Ignoring the razor wire on top, they pounded on the bars, climbing up on each other's shoulders to grip the rails up high and rock them back and forth, shaking the posts loose from their anchoring. Within minutes the barrier toppled over, and the crowd scurried back, only to swarm forward.

Behind the temple on the north side was a small army base, converted from what had once been a middle school. Its purpose was to supply the honor guard for the temple, and the rush of the crowd had rapidly overrun its meager defenses. Most of the troops were out, either trying to quell the riots and looting that were still going on, or deployed to fortify the Grapevine against the Army of Liberation. They had not expected this upsurge of insurrection at their heart.

They would be back. But for now, Madrone huddled with Bird and the other refugista leaders at a picnic table behind what had once been the gym.

A sudden realization hit Bird with a jolt.

"This is where Maya and Johanna went to school!" he said to Madrone. "Remember, when we talked about the Stewards' Command taking over the Mormon Temple, she said they walked past it every day on their way to junior high school. They might have sat at this very table, having lunch."

Madrone squeezed his hand. Her grandmother and his had grown up together, next-door neighbors, best friends, long before they became lovers in later life. She pictured them, two not-quite teens, both a bit nerdy, their schoolbooks under their arms, their heads together, giggling.

Maya in her glasses with her curly hair she'd ironed the night before and set on big rollers to flatten it, Johanna with hers processed, curving around her head like a helmet. Madrone felt warmed by their presence.

"They'd be glad to know we've liberated their old school," she said smiling. She was amazed, somehow, that she could smile, and the grief hit her again. Was she betraying Zap, with that unthinking grin?

"More likely, Maya'd just snort and say, 'Ha. Always felt like boot camp to me,'" Bird said.

"Command is hunkered down inside the temple," Anthony reported. "They can't get out, but it won't be easy for us to get in."

"So we wait them out," Bird said.

"That could take a long time," Emily objected.

"We have nothing but time," he smiled. But one of the blessings of Maya's school was a tap they could open into city water, and he'd finally been able to drink his fill and wash away some of the grime. Madrone had rubbed arnica on his bruises, and dressed the sore places where his hands and arms had been scraped raw. She'd cleaned his wounds rather more rigorously than he thought was absolutely necessary, so that they still stung from the antiseptic they'd scavenged from the base's infirmary. He'd even caught a short nap in a quiet corner.

Now, even though there was a dull lump of grief for Zap deep in his belly, he couldn't help but feel exhilarated with the sheer animal pleasure of survival. Madrone was by his side, the city was rising, and truly it was a bright new day.

"It's fucked," said Darren, one of the 'hood leaders from the south side of the city. He had giant lips tattooed on either side of his neck, as if he were perpetually being kissed, and now they were flushed an even deeper red. "Stewards are dug in like a nest of rats. We're stuck out here, natives gettin' restless. And the Stewards' Army could come back any time."

"It's a gift," Bird said quickly. "We've got everybody here—the whole city, massed in the streets or watching on the vidscreens. This is our chance to set the pattern for the new world."

"How so?" Emily asked.

"Let's get people organized. We send out our crews from the Refuge, start forming everyone in affinity groups and 'hood councils and work crews. We stay here for a few days, we can teach them how to run a council, make decisions together. By the time they go back to the 'hoods, we'll have a democracy."

Bird mounted the stage. Tianne's tech crew had rigged up a sound system. More than that, somewhere she'd found a battered guitar and stashed it beneath the skirt of the Queen of the Angels. She'd handed it to him with a smug grin, and he was more touched than he would have imagined that she cared so much about his lame and halting music, his patched-together songs.

It was an old guitar, without much tone. But this crowd would not be judging his fingering or his tremolo. A good thing, too, with his throat still raw and hoarse. He swiftly tuned the guitar, and began to sing the Song of Rising.

> *"Open your eyes,*
> *There's a new day waking.*
> *Freedom will rise,*
> *Like the rising sun!"*

His voice rose over the crowd, and thousands of voices joined in with him. People linked arms and held each other with tears in their eyes. And he felt tears in his own.

So many days, he'd sung this song on the streets. So many people in the crowd had hummed it under their breath, at work in some factory, waiting in the endless water lines, walking away from the cashiers' windows where they turned over the bulk of their wages to service their debt. They'd hummed it in defiance, as a gesture, a vision, a fairy tale of a beautiful dream that could never be more than fantasy. And now they were here, together, making it come true.

The chorus swelled and rose and filled the streets with the sound of hope. And he was glad, so glad, to be here. For this was a moment of grace, one of the great moments of his life. He was thankful to all the Gods that be not to have missed it.

When the song was done, Bird stepped back and took Miss Ruby's hand to draw her forward.

"Why me?" she protested. "I'm no public speaker. You do it!"

"You're the most charismatic rabble-rouser we've got," he told her firmly. "And if we're going to have a new world, let's have it be one where the grandmothers lead us."

In spite of her protestations, there was nothing Miss Ruby loved more than an audience. She stepped forward as Bird clipped the mic onto her collar.

"People, we're here at the beginning of a bright new day!" she cried. "Say it with me—a bright new day has dawned!"

"A bright new day has dawned!" the crowd thundered back.

"We are the sunrise! We are the change we want to see!"

"We are the sunrise! We are the change we want to see!" they echoed.

"The rule of the Stewards is over! Some of them don't seem to realize that yet, but we know. We're here, and we are not goin' back! But to go forward, we got to know where we want to go, and how we're gonna get there.

"Who's gonna lead us to the promised land? You see Moses any-where about? How about him—Mr. Bird here with the silver voice, you want him to lead us?"

Shouts of "Bird! Bird!" rose up.

"What about me? Maybe me and the other grandmothers should take charge?"

A roar of approval rose up.

Miss Ruby raised her hand. "Oh no. No, it's not Mr. Bird and not me and not some hero that'll come riding in on a white horse. I'll tell you who's gonna lead us. You. You and you and you, and all of you. Us. We're gonna make a new world, we're not gonna have rulers. We'll all be the leaders. We're gonna bring this country back to what it was meant to be and never was, except maybe way back in the Indian days. A true democracy! A place where we make the decisions together that determine our lives. Are you for it? Say yes!"

"Yes!" they chorused back.

"I can't hear you!"

"YES!"

"But this isn't gonna be easy." Miss Ruby surveyed the crowd as if it were an unruly class of subteens. She was in full stride now, enjoy-ing every moment of it. "Most of us, we weren't trained for it and we weren't brought up to it. But we know it's possible. Some of us have seen it in the North. How they run their City. Some of us have been practic-ing in the Refuge. And now, right now, while we're here holding the last dregs of the Stewards to account, waiting them out, now we can begin. Are you with me?"

"Yes!"

"So here's what we're gonna do. We're gonna organize ourselves. So look around you—and grab yourself some homies to be your posse. Start with your friends, your family—or whoever around you looks like you might get along. You're gonna stay together when we go back home, and be the first building block of the new order. So try to find the folks from your own 'hood. You'll be responsible for helping to get everyone fed and bedded down and kept as safe as we can.... "

Swiftly, she outlined the organization. Posses would meet to make decisions, and choose a spoke to go to council in the 'hood where they belonged. Councils would organize their sections, setting up hearths to feed people, and composting toilets. They'd establish shifts so people could go home and sleep, those who had homes to go to.

People with special skills formed work teams, and soon Beth had a functioning central clinic going with satellites around the area. There were crowds covering the lawns surrounding the temple, but farther back they spilled down into the street, carpeting miles of the Avenue of Judgment in both directions. Refugistas fanned out into different sec-tions to hold impromptu trainings in decision-making and tactics. They set up soapboxes every few hundred feet, where anyone could step up and harangue a crowd as long as people were willing to listen. Meetings were live-streamed over the vidscreens, and Miss Ruby made a special appeal to all those who were home to connect with their neighbors and start organizing as well.

They also formed a Defense Council. Representatives from all the 'hoods and gangs, Angels and hillboys and refugistas were on it. They organized scouting parties to report on what was happening throughout the city, as well as patrols around the borders of the encampment.

Bird and Madrone watched. He stayed close to her, sensing that she needed his presence, his comfort. Every now and then she would stop, her eyes would lose their focus, and he could feel the upwelling of grief that swept over her. He would touch her, or put an arm around her, and then it would sweep over him, too.

But it was a clean grief, untainted by false guilt or self-recrimination, like a minor chord giving soul to a symphony.

"He bought us this," Bird said. "He brought me what I needed to take out the drone ops trailer. He paid with his life, but if he hadn't done that, you would have had drones picking you off all the way from the Refuge."

"You took out the drone ops trailer?" She looked up at him. He had just a hint of a smile at the corners of his mouth, a bit of the look of a satisfied cat. "Bragging about it, are we?"

"Just saying ... "

"Think we're subtle, do we? I suppose you think that merits a reward?"

"There are women who would kiss a man for less."

"And you think I'm one of those women?"

"I can only hope."

She drew his head down, and touched her lips to his. Then suddenly she was holding him tight, their bodies plastered together. She wanted him, right there, on the walkway where Maya and Johanna had complained about algebra, with the crowd chanting and the thunder of guns in the distance. Wanted to wipe out grief with passion, erase their terrible loss by kindling a spark of some new life.

"Ahem," Miss Ruby coughed loudly. "If I might interrupt, Miss Madrone, Beth is asking for you to help at the healing center. And Mr. Bird, those Angels are plotting somethin', about to march off with a whole faction that all have guns and mean expressions."

Reluctantly, Bird pulled away. Madrone let out a long sigh.

"I'll go," she said.

"I know what they're doing," Bird said. "Or what I'd be doing if I were them. They're off to liberate the Stockyard."

"Do we try to stop them?" Miss Ruby asked.

"I wouldn't," Bird said.

"But we'd hoped this would be a nonviolent revolution."

"For the Angels, liberating the Stockyard *is* nonviolence. However they do it. We can only model. We can't impose."

By nightfall, the kitchens were serving up hot food, simple but real food that people brought from their homes, not chips. Bird turned over the mics to other singers and poets. Set the pattern of culture, he said. Anthony's players performed, and other musicians, and the vidscreens showed ordinary people sharing their gifts with one another.

At midnight, a great clamor went up, and Bird was called back to sing again. His voice was smoother now, and he sang them the Song of Refuge as a bedtime lullaby. The Song of Rising was a song for the morning, all about dawn and sunrise and a bright new day. But evening called for something else, mournful as taps to honor the fallen of the day, some tune to carry the grief of endings. He thought of an old song that Maya used to sing to him.

Zap. Had he ever sung the boy a lullaby? Had anyone? Had some lost mother crooned to him when he lay, an infant in her arms, ignorant of what was to come for them both?

I'm singing it for you, Zap, he thought. For you, and for Bob, and for everyone who won't see the sunrise. Sleep well.

"Lay down, lay down your weary head.
Lay down your task and go to bed.
Your burden shall be light.
The moon shines so bright on the hill.
The morning will be brighter still.
And wiser than the night."

Chapter Seventy-Five

S ARA ... "
It was as if the world stopped dead for a moment. One moment of silence, as if Isis could stop time, stop knowledge from reaching her like a superhero stops bullets in midair. Or like those old cartoons they used to show the racers, when some character ran off the edge of a cliff and just kept running, legs pumping in midair, suspended. She was suspended, and in a moment she was going to plummet.

Sara, beautiful Sara, pearly white and graceful as a lily, her Sara. Could have been her Sara if she hadn't pushed her away, shut her out to protect herself from feeling this. And then she hit ground, hard. Her breast was heaving as if she'd had all the wind knocked out of her. A wail was trapped inside her, battling its way out. She was screaming, without making a sound, sobbing without a tear, and her lungs locked while her throat spasmed, trying to suck in air, trying to push air out, and let her follow Sara into death.

She was dimly aware of her own voice issuing orders. Her hand hovered over a screen, thumbed a button....

Sara lay on the deck, her body twisted and broken, and yet lit with a glow, suffused with light.

A great boom rocked the Stewards' ship. Slowly, slowly it began to list to starboard as the hold filled.

"Time for bargaining is done," the sailors heard a cold voice from the loudspeaker on the *Milk*. "Surrender, or the ship goes down."

The men were staring at Sara's body, as if they were still hearing her words. Then, as one, they lifted their eyes up, where billowing clouds hovered on the horizon, as if they could see a school of blue whales swimming through the sky, or a fleet of silver ships heading west into the setting sun.

One of the men stepped forward. He raised his rifle to the sky—a salute, an honoring. Then he laid it at Sara's feet.

Another stepped forward, and another, until Sara's body was covered with rifles, protecting it like the sepals of a flower enclosing a bud.

The Captain reluctantly picked up his bullhorn.

"Tow us in," he said.

Isis felt like some imposter with her face and voice continuing in quiet, efficient command while the real her huddled inside, unseen, arms over its head, silently screaming. She issued orders. She directed her crew to hook up tow ropes to the Stewards' ship, to transfer the terrified children to the *Harvey Milk*, and secure the enemy sailors in the hold until they could be dealt with.

A zombie commander, functioning without truly living. She was good at that. She realized now that's what she had been all her life until Sara appeared: a kind of ghost, bloodless, moving among the living world without really touching it. Acting fearless, because what do the dead have to fear? And yet everything she did, every choice she made was sculpted and constrained by fear, fear of facing this moment, this overwhelming pain.

The exuberant shouts of a hundred liberated children rang over the deck, but Isis barely heard them, barely registered when Bronwyn came and relieved her at the wheel. Slowly the flotilla turned and headed back toward shore, towing the crippled ship.

They had brought Sara's body on board, wrapped in a sheet, and she lay now on the aft deck. Isis went to her, stared down at the white bundle that had once been her love. She lost track of time, barely noticed when the sun dipped down and darkness fell, when Miguel brought her a blanket to wrap herself in against the chill night breeze.

In the end, all the gunwales she'd erected hadn't protected her at all. She had only compounded the loss.

If Sara had to die, she could have gone decked with memories like a garland of flowers, this one a sweet, sweet day, this one a dark, fringed orchid of a night. They could have had a time of grace.

Now all Isis could do was to recollect each smile, each shared glass of wine, each sweet night and windswept day on the water, telling them over and over again like pearls on a string. She could have had more, so many more!

Instead, she had nothing but this abyss of loss and regret.

Not for long, she told herself. Not for long. Onshore, a battle was still raging. There were plenty of opportunities coming up to join Sara.

Even if she didn't give way to the urge to simply lie down beside her now and pull that sheet over her own head.

And suddenly she felt a little trickle of fear. Yes, it would be so easy. To let go. To give up. By land or by sea, by bullet or by salt water, there were so many ways to end this pain. No one would blame her. No one but her would know that her own adamant will had, in the end, failed her.

She could feel the salty breeze on her face, the roughness of the blanket against her skin, hear the whuff, whuff of the wind in the sails, smell the iodine spray of the water even though every touch burned and every sound seemed to scream no! No! Not in a world where Sara can no longer share this with you!

Sara beckoned, and the tide was pulling her out.

But pirates buck the tide.

Maybe, before everything else, she was just too damn stubborn to give in. To hand them that double victory—Sara's life and hers.

Sara would want her to go on. She knew that, she could practically hear the damn woman whispering in her ear. *Live! Have the adventures I don't get to have! Open!*

Open. Open to the incalculable risks and pain a heartbeat could deliver.

Find the courage to love in a world where love can die, and there's not one fucking thing you can do about it!

Or sail forever on the ghost ship, never touching shore.

Chapter Seventy-Six

WENDELL, LOCKED INSIDE THE COMMAND BUNKER DEEP BENEATH the temple, watched the vidscreen in the conference room in a cold fury. He wasn't as yet worried about the siege. They had water and working toilets, and stockpiles of chips. While they were vile-tasting things, they would sustain life as long as was needed.

But when Bird stood up to sing, Wendell went into an icy rage. How the hell had that demonic little piece of scum survived? What was he doing in that crowd instead of lying where he belonged, cold and dead in his rubble pile?

And why were the vidscreens showing this crap? Had someone hacked the networks?

He was seated at the head of the table, and before him lay the coms console. He swiped the screen and a huge, flat-screen map appeared on the wall to his left. His own troops appeared as circles of blue. Enemy targets were highlighted in red. The biggest red spot lay near the old center of the city where the Refuge had been located. It was surrounded by a ring of blue. Good. If they hadn't already been blasted into oblivion, the rats were trapped.

But if that bleating devil was here, at the temple, there was no more point in tying up his troops at the Refuge. Time to bring them home, let them disperse the rabble, and get on with business. He barked an order into his coms unit.

A crackling voice came back.

"Sir, coms is blocked. We can't raise them."

Wendell swore. With the bumbling idiots that surrounded him, it was a wonder he'd gotten anything done, ever.

"Get the damn coms back on line!" he yelled.

"Techs are working on it, sir."

Wendell felt a little wriggle of true worry in his gut. For the first time, it occurred to him that he might actually lose this battle. He brushed the thought away. A pack of rabble bring down the Stewardship? Impossible! Still, it began to seem to him more and more urgent to bring in the troops and clear the crowd.

"What manpower do we have left?" he asked Finch, who stood impassively waiting behind his chair.

"Sir, we've got a full division in the Valley headed north to retake the plantations. We've got the 101st battalion besieging the rebel stronghold, and another two brigades patrolling the hills, making sure the rebels don't come up and burn the estates."

Wendell thought long and hard for a moment.

"Order them all back here. Our first priority has got to be to clear this mob," he said.

"Sir, the Primes won't thank you for that," Finch said in a hesitant voice. "They depend on us to protect them."

"We'll protect them best by breaking the back of this rebellion," Wendell said.

As he spoke, the map began to strobe on and off.

Wendell swore. As if it heard him, the map stabilized. But now dark blank patches appeared, like mange spreading on a dog's back. Much of the Valley was blacked out, and where the Refuge had been was nothing but a giant black spot.

Coms were apparently still open to the estates, however. Within a few moments of issuing his orders to the hill patrols, his earpiece rang with a musical chime.

"How dare you withdraw the troops?" buzzed a deep voice he recognized as Culbertson's. It was a very bad sign, if he was calling himself instead of delegating the matter to an underling. "We need that protection!"

"It's my command, my call," Wendell said firmly.

"The hell it is! We put you in, and we can take you out!"

Reason with him, Wendell thought. Culbertson didn't get to be head Prime by being stupid.

"Look, sir, if the rebels succeed, no army on earth will be able to protect your property." Wendell forced his voice to sound conciliatory. "And once we clear this rebellion, the danger will go away."

"Are you telling me that you can't protect us?"

Wendell swallowed. "Not if we don't clear the mob here at our gates," he admitted.

"Then you're a worse idiot even than I imagined!"

⁓

Livingston rocked back on the heels of what had to be a priceless, hand-carved dining chair decorated with real gold leaf, and observed the three nondescript men in business suits across from him. They sat around a table that was deceptive in its simplicity, a simple slab of black wood. But Livingston recognized it as ebony. The walls of the dining room were paneled in the stuff, their carved borders of stylized flowers also gilded and gleaming.

He allowed himself one moment of self-satisfaction as he ran a finger along the smooth wood. Not a bad run for his money, from the hold of a Gyro slave ship to this elite and secluded room.

Granted, he owed a huge debt to his sister, who'd provided him with a refuge, fed him and nursed him until he regained his strength. And she would be rewarded, he'd see to that!

But he was the one who had schemed, maneuvered, called on his contacts, and interpreted the finer points of the gossip he'd heard to get himself here. True, Wendell had stabbed him in the back. No problem. He'd simply gone above Wendell, found the puppet masters who pulled Wendell's strings and who were growing more and more dismayed at his incompetence. Find the true power, and put yourself at its service. That had always been Livingston's motto.

The negotiators at the table didn't look all that different at first glance from any group of midlevel managers at a meeting. It took an educated eye to size up the subtle tailoring, the hand-tooled detailing on the shoes, the cufflinks with the glint of gold and diamonds.

They were, in fact, three of the top Primes, who controlled the sale and manufacture of that lifeline of the Stewardship—weapons.

"We have a proposition to make," Culbertson said.

"Gentlemen, I'm all ears." Livingston favored them with a smile.

The Prime spoke in a measured, cultivated tone. His voice was silky-smooth and low, as if he expected people to bend to hear him rather than exert himself to be heard. "We don't agree that the Stewardship is failing. But we recognize that there are some challenges we face right now, mostly due to the incompetence of our military, and our setbacks in the North. We didn't get to the position we hold by ignoring unpleasant possibilities. So we wish to make a contingency plan.

"We have a warship, privately refitted and maintained. We keep it docked on Saint Cat's Island. Should events warrant, we need someone to take command and sail the ship to where we want to go. In return for that small favor, we'll take as many of your family on board as wish to come. And we'll pay you in gold."

"Where do you want to go?" Livingston asked.

"We'll tell you when the time comes."

Livingston rose with an affable smile. "Thanks for your time, gentlemen. I'll be leaving now."

"Sit down. Sit down!" The order came from the second Prime, a big florid man with a shine of sweat on his face. He thundered it out in a voice used to being obeyed. Livingston considered for a moment the pleasures of disobedience. He could walk out, or remain on his feet just long enough to rouse the Primes to a state of fury.

That would be fun. But it wouldn't get him what he wanted. He sat back down.

"I need to know where we're going," he said. "I'd need to plot a course, and navigate, and stock up on enough fuel and supplies. You don't just point a ship to the west and hope you hit Hawaii."

"Who told you?" the second Prime asked.

Livingston just smiled.

They settled down to bargain.

The scouts who cycled up into the wealthy neighborhoods in the hills came back with an alarming report.

The Primes were deserting their estates, piling up their portable wealth into limos, and heading out toward the private docks in the west.

"Should we try and stop them?" Anthony asked.

Bird stifled a groan. They had moved their impromptu headquarters from the picnic table to the mess hall in the old school cafeteria, where he and some of the other leaders crowded around a table in the corner. The hard, plastic chair was digging into one of the raw places on his thigh. They'd been there for hours, it seemed, and every time he tried to get up, some new crisis developed that needed a decision. He wanted out. He wanted a long, hot shower and a long sleep. More than that, he wanted to walk outside and see with his own eyes what was happening with the crowd.

"We'd have to divert our strength, cordon off streets," said Margaret, the gray-haired rep from Westside.

"Let them go," Bird said wearily. "Better out than in, as my mother used to say."

"But they'll be robbing the city blind, getting away with the most valuable of their loot!" objected a stocky rep with a heavy black moustache.

"Where will they go?" Anthony asked.

"I don't know." Bird shrugged. "Where are there openings for large numbers of arrogant useless parasites with a penchant for giving orders and some portable property?"

"Panasia, maybe?" Anthony suggested. "Hawaii? Maybe they think they can set up a base in the Gyre? Or they could head east, to Arizona or Texas."

"Let the people decide," Miss Ruby said. "It can be a first test of our new structure."

"That could take days!" the man with the moustache objected.

"Maybe not," Miss Ruby said.

It was Madrone's turn to get on the mics and the vidscreens. They'd agreed to rotate the key speakers, to model shared leadership.

She passed a weary hand over her hair, which seemed to expand in its wiry exuberance even as she wilted from fatigue. Revolution, for a healer, meant longer hours and worse working conditions. She'd been on duty at the makeshift healing center that Beth had set up in the old school gym for longer than she could remember, catching short catnaps, but no real sustained sleep. The excitement of their success in actually sparking the Rising was beginning to sink into a morass of sheer exhaustion.

But she forced herself up onto the podium and took the crystal mic. Enthusiasm. Confidence, she told herself. Bright. Positive. Optimistic.

"People, we've got a decision to make!" she began. "We've got the Stewards' central command trapped in here. But meanwhile, we've gotten word that their corporate masters, the folks who benefit from the slave plantations and who own the interest on the debts, they're all piling into their cars and escaping with all they can carry. What do we do? If we let them go, they could get a new base somewhere else and return to attack us again. But if we go after them, we'll divert our strength.

"Defense Council doesn't want to decide this alone. It's up to you. So, we've got twenty minutes for you to meet in your posses and come up with your thoughts and questions. Then send your spokes to council, and we'll see what the councils decide. I know that's not much time, but if we're gonna move on this, we've got to do it within the hour, or it'll be too late."

The posses met. Some bogged down in bitter arguments or went off on tangents, but most came up with coherent questions, if not a plan. The councils took longer, but the refugistas sent out their most skilled facilitators, and the answer came back.

Some favored sending out small teams in hot pursuit. But most said, Let them go. Our strength is in our unity. Don't divert us.

A messenger, Wendell thought. What did armies do before coms and radios? We'll send out a messenger to the 101st, bring them back here.

Hours had passed on this demon-cursed day, tedious minutes when the mob on the vidscreens grew larger and the efficiency of his coms deteriorated. Vital to bring the troops back. Vital to clear the mob. Jesus's britches, they were the top force of the last remaining empire. How could a rabble of bark-suckers do this to them?

When technology fails, do what they did before they had technology. General Alexander, his predecessor and mentor, always used to say that. Screw the vidscreens and the coms, all he needed was one simple, competent messenger to send out to the outlying forces.

But that proved not so easy to do. The temple had been built to keep people out, but it was even more effective at keeping people in. And it was surrounded with thousands upon thousands of angry protestors, who did not look like they were going away any time soon. The vidscreens were broadcasting meals being served and tents being set up. There was a crowd of people camped in front of the main entrance, and every back door had a watch set on it.

He sent a team down to search the basements, looking for an escape hatch, anything. From what he knew about Mormons, which wasn't much, they were some sort of weird conspiracy cult with a mystical bent. Surely in their spiritual paranoia they would have provided themselves with some secret tunnel, some escape hatch.

Finally they found it, a tunnel beneath the old parking lot that led to what had long ago been the public welcome center. It was half collapsed from the earthquakes, but the messenger managed to clamber through and emerge into the crowd under cover of darkness.

It took him many long hours to make his way through the city, dodging roaming bands who were still rioting and looting without much larger agenda.

But at last he reached the 101st and delivered his message. The most heavily armed troops of the Stewards began marching toward the siege at the temple.

In the last hours of the night, the 101st reached the edge of the siege and threw up a barricade around them. From the west, three of the divisions that had been guarding the estates did the same.

The besiegers were themselves surrounded.

Chapter Seventy-Seven

THE SUN ROSE, CLIMBING OVER THE LOW MOUNTAINS THAT RINGED Angel City to the east. It shed a pale light on the ruins, the rubble, the wide avenues, and the green enclaves of the Primes in their gated estates, where limos and security vans continued to ferry the wealthy away from the conflict. It sent a curious finger up the rise where the temple stood, besieged by the outraged people of Angel City. And as it rose up in all its glory of light, it revealed around them a deep ring of glittering arms, all the crack forces left of the Stewards' Army. The uprising was trapped.

Bird, Anthony, and Miss Ruby climbed up to the highest point on the hill to observe the threatening force surrounding them. Ranks of sojuhs stretched out over the plain below and tanks prowled the higher ground near the school. The siege was an island in a sea of blue and gray.

Bird surveyed the attackers with a sick feeling in the pit of his stomach. The Stewards' Army might be decimated, but it still had enough strength left to destroy what they were building here. That would be more than a shame and a setback. That would deter every stick in Angel City from ever thinking about rebelling again.

A knot of command cars and a phalanx of tanks marked the army's central command. A small figure below stood up from the hatch of a tank and pulled out a bullhorn. Through the crackling of static, a harsh voice squawked. "Rebels and traitors, you are surrounded! Surrender!"

"If sound technology is the measure of victory, we'll win for sure," Bird said, because it was better than saying, We're fucked, we're doomed!

"Yeah, too bad they actually have guns and we don't," Anthony said.

"Then we'll just have to fight with what we do have," Miss Ruby said confidently. Bird looked at her in amazement. She wasn't daunted, not in the least. Her head was high and her eyes held the light of battle.

"What's that?" Anthony asked.

"Words," Miss Ruby said.

⁓

"Soldiers of the Stewardship," Miss Ruby cried, "we are not your enemies! Your old system is falling! Lay down your guns and join us."

She stood atop the stage, which they'd moved up against the wall of the temple, hoping that would deter the army from shelling it. They looked over the crowd to the makeshift barricades the Rising had thrown up from anything and everything they could find, uprooting the picnic tables from the school—Maya would have approved, Bird thought—and piling up the iron fences and the barbed wire. The defenders took shelter behind buildings and dug trenches into the hillside, but they were still vulnerable.

"Keep them talking," Bird had said to the emergency Council that met. "The longer we can hold off the assault, the longer we have to gather support."

They tried to send out scouts and messengers, but the ring around the temple was tight. They were able to broadcast a call for help over the vidscreens. But would people come, to face the wrath of the army, the guns and drones and lasers?

"They may kill us all, but they can't kill the whole city once it's roused," Bird had assured the others with more confidence than he felt.

"No, but they can intimidate them back into their holes," Anthony had replied grimly.

Then the vidscreens went dark.

"Join us!" Miss Ruby cried again. "Together we will make a beautiful world for everyone!"

The answer was a shell that tore into the hillside, blasting a crater in the temple's lawn.

"Surrender, or face more of that!" came the answer, made slightly less intimidating by the squeaks and static of the bullhorn.

Bird grabbed the microphone from Miss Ruby. "You surrender, and we'll get you a bullhorn that actually works!"

A loud wave of laughter came from the crowd. Sheer bravado, but it raised everybody's spirits.

"The Stewardship is over!" Bird went on. "The people have had enough starvation and slavery. Soldiers of the Stewardship, the bulk of your army has come over to our side. We don't want to kill you, we'd much prefer to welcome you to our table, to sit down together as family, and rebuild this sorry land. Put down your guns, as your brothers have done! Join us!"

A barrage of rifle fire was the answer.

"Can't say I didn't ask them nicely," Bird remarked.

The hillboys and Angels and others of the volunteers who had weapons stationed themselves just behind the barricades, and let loose a wave of opposing fire.

"That's done it!" Miss Ruby cried. "That's torn our chances of persuasion!"

"Which weren't high to begin with," Bird admitted. But now, on the west side of the temple, gunfire answered gunfire and the noise was too deafening for any more pleas or conversation. "Let's get down to a safe location."

"Safe?" Anthony asked.

"All things are relative."

Sporadic exchanges of gunfire broke out again and again through the day, punctuated by the fiery pings of lasers. Madrone and the other medics in the healing center worked like automatons to dress wounds and care for burns. As fast as they helped one patient, new victims kept pouring in.

"Why the hell don't they just march on in and finish us off?" Beth muttered as she dressed the mangled limb of a moaning girl and Madrone struggled to brew a painkilling elixir out of her own bee-sweat and nothing.

Madrone struggled to hold her concentration. They were running short of water, and she was exhausted and dehydrated. Poppies, she thought. Think of poppies, smell them, make that chemical change that can ease pain. But this broken girl before them was only one of hundreds, lining the walls of the old school gym on pallets, moaning and screaming. And I'm just about out of miracles.

The endless day wore on into a grim night. Madrone stumbled through the motions of healing, dressing wounds, binding limbs too shattered to heal, closing her ears to the cries and screams.

At midnight, the blank vidscreens let out a hideous squawk and came to life, showing row after row of soldiers.

"Go back to your homes!" a hard-faced military man commanded from every screen. "Go back to your jobs. Did you really think you could oppose the might of the Stewardship with your pathetic heresies?"

There was a screen in the cafeteria where a much-dispirited Council met. A Retributionist came on and exhorted the crowd to forego their sinful ways.

"Turn the damn thing off, would you?" Anthony begged. "We may have to die, but we don't have to die with that crap in our ears."

"Wait," Bird said. He was watching the screen intently. "Look. Do you see what I see?"

"Evidently not," said Emily, who set down a tray of waybread before them all. "Eat. Got to keep up your strength."

Bird was too intent on the screen to pick up his ration, and Emily plunked it into his hand.

"It's the last we've got," she said. "Make the most of it."

"Look!" he said. "They're showing the same ranks of soldiers over and over again. See, there's the one with the black smudge on the uniform ... and now, there he is again ... and again. They're trying to make it look like they've got more troops than they actually have. I think they're stretched thin."

"Great. I'd far rather be shot by a thin soldier than a fat one," Anthony said.

"Look hard. Do you see it? There's space behind that last row of troops. Empty space. They're like a thin shell around us. If we could break through ... "

"Then we'd be split into two unarmed factions with the guns in our midst, shooting at us from every side," the rep from a Westside neighborhood said. "No, let's just keep talking...."

They set up a mic behind the strongest of the concrete barricades, and in every lull of the fighting they talked until Bird's voice was hoarse, with no results. Maybe the Stewards had gotten smart, issued the soldiers with earplugs like Odysseus with the sirens, Bird thought. Did they teach them classical mythology in the Southlands? More likely, they had their most loyal commanders stationed behind the grunts, ready to shoot any one who looked like deserting.

At last another weary dawn came. Bird lifted a heavy head up from the concrete pillow where he'd fallen at last into an exhausted doze. The sun warmed him, but it would also make them visible, even more vulnerable.

He looked around. They were dug into the hillside. Miss Ruby sat slumped with her back to the dirt, her mouth open, snoring slightly. Anthony was awake, peering nervously over the mound of dirt, then ducking back. Bird thought about Emily, and Tianne, and Janus with her crazy wisdom, and all of them, all the fights they'd had, the work they'd done, the meetings and the meals and that exhilarating moment when they'd stepped out into the street at the head of the very first march.

They'd had a good run, and achieved so much. The sun was rising, and the bright new day was here. How ironic to die now, and let the world fall back into nightmare.

With that thought came a barrage of gunfire like a storm from hell, a hail punctuated with screams. Bullets strafed the hillside and pounded the barricades. Laser fire crisscrossed the lawn, pelted every square foot of open ground. An acrid smell of powder and burned flesh filled his nostrils. He clapped his hands to his ears and shut his eyes, overwhelmed by the roar and the ferocity, the screech of incoming shells and the deep boom of explosions. There was no withstanding it, no way to do anything but crouch deep into the dirt and endure or die.

A halt, a lull. Miss Ruby was pressed back into the wall of the cave, her eyes wide with terror. Anthony was huddled by Bird's side. Madrone, *Diosa,* let her be safe.

But there was no safety left. They had gambled, and ultimately failed. The power of the gun was indeed stronger than words, and he had nothing but words left to fight with. Words, and maybe a song.

But fuck it, he thought. It was a new day. And a new day deserved an anthem.

If he had to die, he'd rather die singing, not cowering.

He tapped the mic. It gave back a reassuring thrum. Still working, by some miracle, as he was by some miracle still alive.

Slowly, fighting every instinct of his body to cower in safety, he forced himself up. He stood up above the protection of their berm, where the sunlight could warm his face. He raised his head high, and sang out loud and clear in a voice raw and husky.

> *"Open your eyes,*
> *A new day is waking.*
> *Freedom will rise,*
> *Like the rising sun."*

He closed his eyes, and waited for the shot, for the shell, for the last burst of pain to end it all. But while I wait, he thought, I'll keep singing.

> *"Raise up your voice,*
> *Feel the fortress shaking.*
> *This is our choice,*
> *The grim night is done.*

> *"In your strong hands,*
> *The chains are breaking.*
> *Reclaim our lands,*
> *For the battle's won."*

He was still alive. Well, he still had another verse.

> *"Open your hearts,*
> *To the world we're making.*
> *And now it starts,*
> *A new day's begun!"*

And a voice came, from far in the distance but clear and deep.

"Hear the man!" it cried. "Drop your guns, sojuhs. Wanna hear you sing!"

And suddenly Bird heard other voices, joining in with his, taking up the chorus. He opened his eyes.

The army was still there, a deep ring around the temple grounds that were smoking and littered with bodies.

But around the lines of sojuhs and tanks and APCs was another, thicker ring. Row after row of dusty troops, with Califia's sigil sewed onto their denim uniforms, the City volunteers and the sojuhs who had joined the North, and behind them, legions of others, the freed debt slaves with bandannas wrapped around dusty heads, the ranks of the leather-skinned hillboys come down with their rifles and pouches of acorns, the blond, cold-eyed Angels with their perfect faces, the motley, ordinary folk of Angel City, all in a crowd a hundred thousand deep.

"So you have a choice," the voice said, and now Bird recognized it. Deep and resonant, but with a new tone in it, no longer the hesitant voice of the lowly breed, but the proud voice of a real person. River.

"Fight on, and protect the assholes that done nothing but shit on you your whole sorry lives. Or put down your guns and join us, and live free. Don't know about you, but I know which I'd choose.

"And I did choose. I was a breed, like some of you. Raised to be nothin' but a tool to keep the Primes in power. A weapon. But the weapon turned. And now I am a commander of the army that fights for you, and for me, and all of us to be free."

After a long moment, in the silence that fell upon the hilltop, came the clink of a weapon falling to the ground.

And then another, and another, a clatter like a rainstorm falling on parched ground.

Chapter Seventy-Eight

THE PRIMES HAD BROUGHT THE WARSHIP CLOSE ONSHORE. Livingston walked through it, checking the instruments and the cabins and the cargo holds. If he was going to be captain, he liked to know what he was captain of.

It was stocked with enough weapons to arm an invasion. They clearly weren't planning on a simple Hawaiian luau. But that was not his concern.

The limos came down Sunset Boulevard in convoys guarded by troops—troops that could have been better deployed, to his mind, clearing the crowds from around the temple, or at least, if he'd been in command, that's what he would have done. But the Primes called the shots, and they would, as always, look out for their own skins first.

They got out of the cars, impeccably tailored Suits, followed by their buffed and coiffed Trophies, wives and mistresses, their children like carefully dressed dolls. Some carried bags and dragged rolling suitcases behind. Others had brought servants to ferry the loot.

Below decks there were a few cabins designed for officers and crew. There were larger bunks for the enlisted men, and plenty of open cargo bays left. He and his crew had made no attempt to assign quarters, except for their own. As far as he was concerned, the Primes could fight among themselves for space.

Culbertson accosted him on the aft deck.

"Where's our cabin?" he demanded.

"Cabins are below stairs," Livingston said. "First come, first served."

"That's not acceptable," Culbertson glared, clearly expecting Livingston to quail and tremble.

Instead he shrugged. "I've got a special place set aside for you. But right now, we've got to get underway."

He dodged Culbertson, managed to sidestep another disgruntled Prime, and got himself to the engine room. They fired up the engines, the propellers turned, and the ship pulled out from shore.

Livingston had always loved the open sea. He was happy in the wheel-house, whistling to himself as he pictured the alpha males below squabbling over cabin space.

They were five hours out to sea when he ordered a change in course. By then it was dark. He had his electronic navigation system, but he loved to steer by the stars, as old-time captains would have done. Hawaii was west by southwest. Beyond it, the Gyre. And farther yet, Panasia. They had fuel and food enough for a long, long trip.

At midnight, he ordered the engines to halt.

"What's going on?" Culbertson accosted him in the corridor below stairs. The Prime was in a filthy mood, as the special accommodations Livingston had promised turned out to be a small, windowless cabin close to the head.

"Standard maintenance," Livingston assured him. "We run for a few hours, then cool it down to do our final check over. Nothing to worry about."

Culbertson eyed him suspiciously, then returned to complaining about his cabin. Livingston simply nodded and assured him that it would all be taken care of in the morning.

Then he retired to his own bunk and slept soundly until dawn.

The city had fallen. All over Angel City, refugistas and the liberados were busy organizing councils and food distribution sites, impromptu clinics, and volunteers to set up meeting places and schools.

But inside the temple, the General still held fast.

"Come out, General. It's over. It's time to end this," Bird called out over the loudspeaker. He headed a crowd massed by the main entrance to the temple, giant carved double doors where once worshippers had streamed in and out. He wasn't sure if he could be heard inside, but he strongly suspected the remaining Stewards would be watching on vidscreen even if his voice didn't carry through the doors. An ancient intercom let out a crackle of static, and an archaic speaker next to the door spit out a voice.

"I'll negotiate—with you. Come inside."

"Don't do it!" Erik Farmer said in alarm. "It's bound to be a trap!"

"I won't come inside," Bird called back through the mic. "You've got to come out. We guarantee your safety."

"No. You come in. We'll guarantee *your* safety."

"No. I'm not doing any closed-door meetings, or secret deals. I'll negotiate outside, in plain sight. Or not at all. Everyone deserves to see this. It's their Rising, not mine."

While the arguments went on, Miss Ruby put out a call to the posses, the gangs, and the Council.

"You tell us the terms we should offer them," she said.

The answer that came back was simple.

We've made our terms. We control the city. The bigsticks can stay, if they choose, and be part of building a free city. Or they can leave. But they are no longer in control.

It was not until the next day that they got an answer from the General.

"Clear a space," the intercom buzzed. "I will come out, and you will meet me. No guns, no weapons."

"No weapons," Bird agreed. "All negotiations conducted in the open air, visible to everyone, and live-streamed. Don't worry, our techies will take care of that."

"Agreed."

The newly formed logistics crew cleared a space on the north side, on the high plinth in front of the great doors. They ran a rope around it, and everyone who entered the space was required to leave their weapons behind, in a pile guarded by what was left of River's old unit. The techies set up live-streaming cameras and their crystal mics for clear sound. A row of former soldiers held the crowd back.

"Are you sure this is a good idea?" Madrone asked Bird anxiously. She had finally broken free from the demands of the healing center, at least long enough to watch this final confrontation. She didn't know why, but she felt uneasy. They had won, hadn't they? But Maya always said the most dangerous part of any action was when you thought it was over.

"No," Bird said. "I think it's probably a bad idea. But I don't have a better one, do you? It could take us weeks to dig them out of that bunker, and meanwhile who knows what kind of power they might still bring to bear. There's a huge portion of the army up on the Grapevine, River says. And another whole section still holding the Coast Road. We need to end this."

Madrone nodded, trying to ignore the sick feeling in the pit of her stomach. She leaned forward and kissed him gently on the forehead.

He smiled. "That's all I get? Kiss me like you'll never get to kiss me again."

"No, don't say that! That's bad magic!"

"Yeah, but I bet it'll make for great kissing."

He pulled her tight and they clung to each other, lips locked, tongues probing, breathing in each other's breath and smell. Madrone wrapped her arms around him, holding his solidity, feeling his warmth and the pulsing of his heart. Dear Goddess, Mother, Grandmother, Crone, Coatlicue, Death and Life, please. This is all I ask for, all I want. You've taken my child. Please protect this man. And I will serve you all of my days and nights.

She thought she could hear a faint chuckle in the air.

Ha! Like you have some other option?

The chuckle deepened to a cackle.

The doors opened and General Wendell stepped out. In spite of days of confinement and the knowledge of his defeat, he was carefully groomed, wearing a spotless full-dress uniform, and he strode forward with a sure and martial air as if he had won the war, not lost it. Bird had to admire his sheer bravado.

In contrast, he was aware that he must look like someone who had slept in a ditch. Filthy, unshaven, covered with sweat and dirt and powder burns, hair full of concrete dust and pieces of rubble, shirt ripped and pants dotted with holes made by sparks. Well, this was no fashion contest.

Wendell's hands were up and open. Erik Farmer stepped up and patted him down, as Wendell's aide came forward and ran practiced hands over Bird's waistband and pockets.

Bird walked forward. He stopped. The hairs on his neck rose up. He sensed something. A nexus, one of those knots where the lines of probability tangled and fate stepped in. There was no way to avoid such places, only to navigate them. He could be walking to a triumph, or to his death. The outcome wasn't sure.

All he could do was walk forward, eyes open, ready to face whatever might come.

"Are you ready to surrender control of the city to the people?" Bird asked.

"Never," Wendell said.

Bird gave him a long puzzled look.

"Then what in Hella's name are we doing here?" he asked.

"You think you've won," Wendell said. "But I'm not going down alone. You'll die, and your movement with you."

Something flew through the air then, from the back of the crowd near the doorway where Wendell's aides stood watching. The General whipped up a hand, snatched a pistol out of the air, and fired....

Bird caught the motion out of the corner of his eye and swiveled. He felt a thud in his side. He jerked back, leaving a stream of blood behind. Wendell fired again. A whir, and out of nowhere a drone was spitting bullets. Bird felt another hot thud in his thigh. The drone was coming at him, and Wendell was coming at him, and he felt one sharp moment of sorrow, to die at this moment of grace and victory.

Not fair! he wanted to cry. I spared a life. I closed the eyes of the dead.

What, you want a medal?

The boy's still thinking in cause and effect, reward and punishment. Doesn't work that way!

No, Maya, Johanna ... don't come for me yet!

You can be on the side of love, and still meet hate.

That was Johanna's voice. Hate met him with another hot thud, a drone strike into his thigh. And a sting in his shoulder. And shit, shit! They kept coming, and coming, and he wasn't ready. He wasn't ready!

No one is ever ready. And no one promised you fair.

Shut up, Rio! Don't take my hand! I'm not going with you!

You can offer compassion and meet only retribution, ally with the makers of meaning, and still be reduced to meat.

It's not a bargain. It's who I am.

He forced his eyes to stay open, to focus through the searing pain. Even though what they met was Wendell's staring eyes, filled with a hate that was palpable, that bored through him like a laser as the General cocked his pistol and aimed for Bird's forehead.

No! He fucking wouldn't go this way!

He felt fire in his bad hip and it buckled under him. He tumbled, grabbing Wendell's gun hand as he fell, pulling the General over on top of him just as the drone released another spray. Bullets thudded into Wendell's back, and Bird sheltered beneath him like a blanket. Wendell opened his mouth in one shocked stare, then blood leaked out and his eyes went blank. But still the drone kept on coming, burrowing through his body, seeking Bird.

A wave of drones flew out from the temple, snaked their way through the crowd, looking for their targets....

"Look out!" Bird managed to cry. "They'll be coming for the leaders...."

In a flash he understood what was happening. Everyone who had been on the vidscreens, everyone who had made speeches, whose image had been shown, could be a target. They would take out Miss Ruby, and Emily, and Madrone....

The fucking drone was burrowing through Wendell's body. It would never stop. They would never stop.

Where was Madrone? The bees couldn't help her here. Nothing could. No one could. He would happily die to save her but this was his last, his ultimate failure....

Anthony threw himself over Emily and knocked her down to the ground as a drone screamed by.

Madrone grabbed an iron spike from the barricade and ran to Bird. She raised it high and whacked down on the drone still drilling through Wendell's body. Again and again she struck, until it went still.

"No!" Bird cried, because he could sense what was coming after her. A flight of them, a semi-circle of death aimed at her, and he tried to force his bleeding body up from under Wendell's heavy weight. But he was too weak, too slow....

River, at the first sign of attack, had barked a command back to his troops. Now his old unit-mates shoved through the crowd and tossed him a rifle. He dropped to his knees, and shot. A spray of fire—one of the drones exploded in a small fireburst, and the others veered off course and crashed.

Smokee grabbed a gun and pushed through the doors and into the temple. She jammed her revolver into the head of Wendell's aide. "Drone Ops! Lead me to it."

More and more drones poured out the doorway. They were shooting sprays of bullets and spewing noxious gas. Madrone was bent over Bird, trying to push Wendell off him, oblivious as a drone changed direction in midair and headed toward her.

Crazy Janus leapt up, arms stretched wide, crying, "Welcome the Mother, the Other, sisters and brothers, the light, the light, angels take flight—" The drone hit her in the stomach. She clasped her arms around it as if embracing it, then crumpled in a pool of blood.

River grabbed Madrone by the hair and pulled her back as a new flight of drones crash-dived down on Wendell's prostrate body. She stood for one long moment of horror as a barrage of laser fire scorched what was left of Wendell's corpse, leaving streaks of fire on the concrete. Then, as suddenly as it began, the assault stopped.

Madrone ran to Bird, shoved Wendell's body off, and knelt. Behind her, refugistas and soldiers immobilized the rest of the General's staff, or simply shot them where they stood. A huge, angry roar rose up from the crowd, and people rushed in through the open door to rampage through the temple. In vain Miss Ruby got on the microphone and tried to call for order.

Bird was bleeding all over the pavement, and his left hand was scorched by laser fire. But he was breathing, and he had a pulse. She touched her lips to his, tasted his sweat, trying to calm herself to brew up something to heal these wounds. Just a moment ago, he'd been alive and well, and now ... now....

"Don't you dare die now!" she snapped.

Bird opened his eyes. Pain engulfed him. It was fire, it was ice, it was a bell shrieking an alarm so loud and so long that he stopped hearing it. Behind the noise and the roar was a blessed silence. A stillness, sweet rest. He was floating in a warm sea, the sea of his own blood pooling, cradling, rocking him to sleep.

And the light. So it isn't just meat, he thought. I was wrong. That was only the residue. Morning was breaking, and this was the true sunrise. I'm seeing it, the light of the bright new day. A dawn radiant with the wings of angels, who took up the beat that his own heart forsook, pulsing, rising. Lifting him out of his broken body, up into clouds pearly and pink and gold that opened like welcoming arms. This, this was the rising!

A sharp sting brought him back. He opened his eyes. A face, dark but touched with golden light. Bee wings and angel wings hammered the air. A wild cloud of hair, alive with the song of golden bees. She was their queen. A queen bee. *La Reina de los Abejas. La Reina de los Ángeles.* A sound, like a hum, a whirlwind. Queen of the Angels.

She slapped him again.

"Look at me, you tick-brained, moldy-headed idiot! Keep your eyes open! Don't you dare drift away! You're not dying, do you hear me! I won't have it!"

The wings were pulling him, up and up. She was their queen, but she could not command them. She was holding him back, pulling him away from the glory and the rising, down into heaviness and pain. He wanted to let go and float upward, but that would piss her off and he hated it when she was mad at him. Glorious mad, scary mad. But the light was stronger. The sun, too bright to look at.

He wanted to close his eyes, but she wouldn't let him, wouldn't let him go. And yet her will alone was not enough to hold him. He would have to join his own will with hers, and fight. But he was tired, so tired. He'd been fighting all of his life, and he was done fighting now with his strength leaking out around him. It is just light, he wanted to tell her. There is nothing to fear.

He would tell her that, and she would let him go. He would open his mouth for one last goodbye, and then the struggle would be over, and it would all be easy. His lips parted. He drew in a long breath. His senses were heightened, he could smell her, the golden honey of her skin, the musk of her tinged with acrid fear. And around them, smoke and sweat and the tang of gas. The stink of life. The fragrance.

It entered into him, deep within, through the clouds of his lungs into what was left of his blood, breath that had touched the lungs of his lover and his enemy, ancient air that in its time had been in and out of the lungs of heroes and villains, haters and lovers, dinosaurs and trilobites, and the first primal breathers of the ancient seas. Breath, gift of the ancestors. Something was pushing on his chest, a weight, a drummer pounding on his quiescent heart.

She leaned over, touched her lips to his, and blew her breath into his mouth. It was a gift, gift of life, pouring into him, and he wanted to pour it back into her, giving and receiving, carrying her with him into a rising not of wings alone but light made flesh.

"Stay with me," she said, half command, half plea.

She was the Queen. His body obeyed her, his lungs convulsing to suck in their own gasp of air. Oh, it was heavy and hard and it hurt more than he could have imagined. But he was no coward. He didn't fear pain.

This is what birth is like, he thought. This is labor.

Angels circled the temple like huge white birds, calling to him to dissolve with them into the great music. But he let them go, and turned away. His eyes met hers, dark pools that harbored life.

"I want to have your baby," he murmured. That was the last thing he said for a long, long time.

Chapter Seventy-Nine

B Y SUNDOWN, THE TEMPLE WAS CLEARED OF THE STEWARDS AND THEIR defenders. The Council moved quickly to set up satellite councils in every neighborhood in preparation for a Grand Council three days later that would establish a new government. River found himself answering a hundred questions an hour, and Smokee no less. But in the golden light at the end of the day he grabbed her arm.

"Come on," he said. "Let's go see what we been fightin' for."

They climbed the temple's tower, up and up a narrow stairway until at last they came out onto the platform high above the city. Some group had already thrown down the chariot and set up Tianne's golden angel, its wings outspread to enfold the victors and the dead alike.

They looked out over Angel City's flat plain, mile after mile of hovels and rubble threaded by boulevards with tall buildings and expensive homes. They saw the range of mountains to the north. Now the hillboys could come down from the hills, or turn their camps into true homes. Now people could build up from the rubble and plant the open spaces with real food, begin to heal the soil and harvest the rain and make the plain the lush and fertile place it could be.

"For a breed and a pen-girl," River said, "we done okay."

Smokee looked out over the plain and sighed.

"Go ahead. Feel good. Won't kill you," River said.

"Cress should be here," she said. "Coms say he's dead, defending Troy."

"He's here," River said. "Cress's here, cuz we thinkin' about him."

"So now what do we do?" Smokee asked. "You gonna stay, be the new commander of Angel City?"

River shook his head. "No commanders, just them councils. But— don't know. Know what I'd like to do."

"What?"

"Learn more things. Words. Learn more words. Talk like a real person."

"River, believe me," Smokee shook her head. "You're about the realest person I ever met."

———

Livingston awoke just before sunrise and made his way up to the deck. It was still dark as he looked out over an indigo sea, but the sky was growing lighter and the pale dawn revealed the dark mass of an island off the bow.

Culbertson was up early, too. He headed a delegation of angry Primes who buttonholed Livingston as he headed toward the galley for a much-deserved breakfast.

"Where the hell are we? We're supposed to be on our way to Hawaii!" Culbertson demanded.

"There's been a slight change in plans," Livingston said with his ironic smile.

The sun peeked up over the coastal hills and laid a golden track on the sea behind them. The air was suddenly filled with the thrum of engines. Out of the blaze of morning light came a ragtag fleet of small boats, old reconditioned ferries, sailboats and tugboats, trawlers with gun mounts fixed to their bows, zodiacs zipping about like water pups.

"What the Jesus?" Culbertson's face was livid. His hand dove inside his blazer, but before he could draw a weapon, a corps of Livingston's hand-picked men surrounded the group of Primes with cocked rifles.

"Traitor!" Culbertson spat.

Livingston shrugged. "Now there's a hard word, gentlemen. I prefer to think of myself as a man who likes to play on a winning team."

And that was only the truth, he thought, with a certain smug sense of satisfaction. In the end, he had picked the right side.

The navy had taken him back, with only a few suspicious frowns on a few faces. But they'd bought his story of capture, imprisonment, and escape, which was after all the truth. All he'd had to do was leave out Wendell's betrayal, and his own.

He'd wrestled with the decision for days, lying up in Mallory's dorm room, laying convoluted plots that would allow him to hedge every bet. It had been far from clear, at the time, that a tatty bunch of squabs and dusters would succeed in overthrowing what was still the most impressive concentration of force left on the planet. Maybe Mallory had influenced him, with her enthusiasm for his stories of the North, and her discontent at the lot of a brainy female in the Stewards' regime. Maybe those glimpses of green streets and flowing waters had sunk in more deeply than he'd realized.

But he'd found himself asking disturbing questions. Like, would he need to strive for a big estate with five gardeners, if the whole world were a garden? What would he buy with gold when water flowed free and fruit hung down for the picking alongside every path? And would he be endlessly stuck under the command of assholes in a world where everyone was free to rise?

A smart bet, yes, but he had to acknowledge that deep inside, he'd been rooting for liberation for longer than he wanted to admit.

Of course, there was always that unparalleled satisfaction that came not just from having what you want, but having more than someone else. The sweet taste of triumph and power.

Which he was thoroughly enjoying right now.

"We had an agreement," Culbertson said coldly.

Livingston smiled at the Primes like a cat smiles at a bowl of cream.

"A winning team," he repeated. "And you, gentlemen, I'm sorry to say, are the losers."

Now the deck was filling up with angry Primes and their women and children, who looked simply terrified. Livingston grabbed the ship's mic and spoke to them.

"No need to be scared," he assured them. "No one's going to harm you, or your families. We'll even feed you and support you. You don't even have to work if you don't want to—I'm sure you'll receive the same basic stipend as everyone else. If you want more than that, you will have to make some useful contribution to society. If you've committed crimes, you'll be expected to make restitution.

"Take a few minutes, folks. Chat among yourselves. You're no longer the rulers of the world. Get used to it. A new day has dawned."

A convoy went out to the Valley to bury Cress. They had laid him out in state in the fortress, but they hadn't really known what to do with him. Shakir of Water Council, who'd come down from the City, wanted to take him back for burial. But Beryl was adamant that would not be what he wanted.

"He was born in the Valley. He loved this place," she said. "He would have wanted to be buried here."

Topaz gave her a wry, sad smile. "And on contour, no doubt."

River and Smokee took a staff car, and Madrone reluctantly left Bird's bedside to go with them to Cress's funeral. Bird was still unconscious, and she wanted to be there when he woke. But the surgeons were keeping him sedated, and the distance that had taken so long for the Army of Liberation to fight through could now be traversed in little more than a couple of hours.

So they gathered around him, old friends from the City, freed debt slaves, breeds, and volunteers. They gave him a funeral, City-style, with his friends and his comrades stepping up one by one and telling stories of his life, sharing memories. They poured libations of water.

Overhead, clouds gathered, as if they had come for the memorial and clustered close to hear the tributes. Clouds, and then great thunderheads, billowing up in pillows of white with dark gray underbellies.

And the rain poured down like a benediction. It filled the trenches and pooled in the hollows of the new-made graves, it sank into the swales and ditches Cress had dug, collected in every scrape he had so carefully contoured. Then slowly, slowly, it sank into the parched earth. As if the heavens themselves were crying great tears of grief, for Cress and Kit and Sara and Zap, for all the dead. Hour after hour of a storm that was rarely seen in the Southlands, heavy, pelting, life-giving rain.

The earth drank deep, and even the white bones of the dead glistened like pearls, their thirst quenched at last. Rain that would conjure up ribbons of flowers, great bands of blue touched with fringes of white, with harlequin patches of purple and gold and swaths of the orange and crimson hues of sunrise: a promise kept, an avowal of returning life, a wreath of tribute extending for five hundred miles.

Chapter Eighty

HER EYE ON THE SAILS, ISIS MANEUVERED THE TILLER JUST SO. THIS boat was bigger than the *Day of Victory,* which had gone back to the North now under Rosa's guidance. They were both now thankfully out of danger at last.

But she missed the boat. She even missed the girl, with her stubbornness and her deep sadness. Well, she was going back as a hera, and that should erase the looks of pity and replace them with admiration.

But most of all she missed . . . she had one sharp moment of longing, when she felt Sara beside her. She could see her golden hair, whipped by the wind, her sea-blue eyes. Laughing. Maybe that was a good sign. Maybe, wherever she was, she was laughing now.

Don't think about that. Think about this boat, so much better fitted out than the *Victory*. She'd had no lack of yachts and sailboats to choose from. She could have taken a fifty-footer, with a hot tub and a mirrored bathroom and a private screening room below. But she had liked the looks of this one—not too big, easy to maneuver, sleek lines. And she was glad to be out of the bunks on the big destroyer and back on a craft of her own.

The hatch opened, and Smokee's head popped through.

"Need anything?"

"Somethin' hot be nice. And company."

Girl was one raw nerve, a churning mass of hope and fear, as they headed for Saint Cat's. Popping up and down, trying to pace the deck of the ship that was far too small for pacing.

Saint Cat's had once been a pleasure island, a semi-wild place of scrub and land preserves dotted with little tourist towns full of bed-and-breakfasts and cafés. A ferry-ride away from Long Beach, it was a place for excursions, remote and magical. But the Stewards had changed all that. Oh, a few of the top Primes still had their walled and gated estates in the far reaches of the island. But the town of Avalon had proved a perfect site for a more brutal business.

At its foot stood a tall stone tower, round and impregnable. Built as a casino in the 1920s, it loomed over the harbor. From its upper balconies, where once dancers had stepped out for a breath of air, now gunners patrolled the seas. And in its windowless bowels, slaves were kept for transport.

Here, scuts from the Gyre came to buy drudges destined for the plastic processing factories of the deep seas or the brothels that served the overseers. Outcast traders from faraway islands came here to fill their quotas for the plantations, and emissaries of distant warlords sought captives to service their armies or live bodies for the organ farms. From here, human cargo was shipped far across the oceans to ports and fates unknown.

According to the records the techies had found in the Stewards' database, here the babies of the pen-girls had been taken. That in itself was unusual—the Stews must have been hard-pressed for ready cash, Isis thought, if they were selling such young babies to the Gyre. They'd be worth more if they were a bit older, less likely to die and already broken in. Under two, they were probably destined for the organ farms.

Isis had no hope that they would find them alive. They had long died of grief and neglect, or if they survived, been shipped on to an unimaginable fate. But she was not a mother. She had no reason to cling to hope, as the pen-girls did. They crowded the commandeered ferry and the sprinkling of boats that accompanied it.

Would they find the fortress held against them? Isis hoped not. She was tired of battles, tired of fighting, tired of death. All she wanted now was to sail away, somewhere out onto the wide empty sea where she could be alone with her grief and let the ocean storms wash her clean.

Smokee waited impatiently for the kettle to boil. She felt like the kettle, with tension boiling up inside her until she thought she might let out a shrill, piercing scream. Hope, the dangerous cheater, clamored at her again. She kept trying to push it away. Everyone said it was unlikely they'd actually find the babies on the island. At most, they might hope to find records of what had happened to them, where they'd been sent.

So very dangerous to hope. Far wiser to prepare for despair.

Yet she had found her brother. Out of all the thousands of troops and hundreds of places, fate had brought them together. Maybe the same kind fate would bring back her lost child.

The kettle boiled, and she brewed some strong mint tea and brought it up to Isis.

"Stay," Isis commanded. "Talk to me. It's lonely up here."

Smokee looked at her suspiciously. From all she knew of Isis, the woman had never in her life felt lonely at the tiller of a boat out on the ocean. She was just saying that so Smokee wouldn't be alone, brooding in the bowels of the ship.

"You? Lonely? Don't think so!"

"I feel you down there. Itchy as an ape with crab-lice. Better stay up here where the wind is fresh."

Smokee tried to settle on the bench across from Isis, cradling a cup of tea in her own hands. But she was restless. She kept shifting and moving, and adjusting her seat. Finally, although she knew the question was futile and better not asked, she blurted out, "Do you think we'll find them?"

"Know soon enough," Isis said calmly. "Look!"

There was a smudge on the horizon that solidified, as they drew nearer, into a mass of land.

A blue harbor, cradled in the arms of brown hills, with a solid, round tower of stone-faced concrete guarding it. Isis whipped out her binoculars, and scanned the balconies that lined the top. She could see the gun emplacements, ugly bulwarks of metal that contrasted strongly with the graceful arches above. They looked empty. But she didn't trust it. The scouts had gone out the night before, landing a small boat on the other side of the island, hiking cross-country in the dark. But they had yet to report in.

She spoke into the coms, ordered the convoy to stop at a safe distance just outside of firing range. She hailed the tower over the loudspeakers.

No reply.

"Let's wait," Isis commanded, to Smokee's dismay. Unable to stay still, Smokee collected their cups and took them down to the galley to wash. She climbed back up the ladder and stood on the deck, then went back down where she surveyed the small cabin, trying to remember what she'd come down for. She went back up again. More tea, that's what she wanted if they were going to be stuck there, waiting. Oh, it made sense to be cautious but everything in her wanted to rush ahead, storm the gates, to know one way or another what the answer would be.

At last Isis nodded, and barked into her headset. She called out to Smokee to haul in the sea anchor while she hoisted the sails, and they were underway.

"Scouts say it looks deserted," she said. "Hope they're right."

The convoy moved into the small harbor. No one challenged them. The ferry pulled up to the old dock, but Isis called for them to send out a small recon force before they all piled out. She led it, and Smokee came with her.

They walked along a crumbling boardwalk that skirted the sea. Once, the little town must have been a charming place for a vacation. There were still fading icons of ice cream cones and chocolate treats hanging over peeling shop fronts. But now they stood waist-deep in the risen sea, their roofs falling in, the windows that were visible shuttered over with plywood and spray-painted with military numbers.

It was a sad place, eerily quiet. No one peered from the blank windows or challenged them. They made their way along a high sea wall that still protected the tower, though it had failed to safeguard the town.

The tower, when they reached it, was locked and barred. Tiles were broken or missing from what had once been a mural at the entrance, but they could see enough of its graceful lines to imagine how elegant it must once have been. The place looked and felt empty, but Isis had the techies bring up their infrared scanner. It showed life-forms within.

She pulled out her bullhorn and hailed the tower. Again there was no reply.

Still cautious, she had everyone stand back while a small crew went to work on the doors, cutting through the bolts with lasers. Smokee now could pace, and she did so, impatiently, her tension rising to a level Isis could feel as a palpable heat radiating out from the girl.

It seemed to take them forever to carve through the heavy steel of the doorways and cut the locks. But at last they were thrown open, and the troops marched in.

Steel doors and concrete walls divided up what must once have been a pleasant lobby. There were still scraps of flowered carpet underfoot that were now gray with trodden-in dirt. The lower floor seemed to be offices, and the techies went quickly to work on the computers and the physical records that were left in file cabinets. It seemed someone had begun an effort to destroy them—they were shredded and half-burned and dumped onto the floor. The tech crew carefully packed them and carried them off to be taken back to their base, where any traces of information they still held would be extracted.

Isis and Smokee, with the forward crew, made their way up a winding stairwell to the next floor. Here the space had been divided into cells, their metal doors locked tight. But inside they could hear something, a sound like a low moan.

She barked a command into her coms, and three techs brought up lasers and went to work. Expertly they cut out the locks, being careful not to let their beams extend out beyond the width of the door itself and risk frying something beyond.

At last it opened. Isis made the others wait behind. Gun drawn, she stepped in alone, and froze in horror. The stench assaulted her first, a stench of stale piss and shit and death. Amongst the low moans, she heard the squeaks of rodents annoyed at this disturbance to their feast. The floor was strewn with bodies, some dead, some still barely alive, weak with thirst and barely conscious. Rats scurried away from torn flesh.

I'm a pirate, Isis told herself firmly. Pirate don't puke at the sight of a few corpses. But she had to clamp her jaw shut to stop her gorge from spewing out over the floor.

It was as if their captors had simply fled and abandoned their slaves, still locked in. Isis felt a hot anger begin to boil.

And Smokee? She didn't need to see this.

She stepped back out and slammed the door.

"Get the medics," she ordered. "Bring water!"

She grabbed Smokee's arm firmly and hauled her away from the door.

"What, what is it?" Smokee asked.

"No babies there."

"I want to see." Smokee pulled her arm away.

"Maybe you don't need to," Isis said.

"I need to!" Smokee insisted, and jerked out of Isis's grasp. She followed as a crew went in to sort the living from the dead, and quickly stepped back out again, her face white.

Isis continued up the stairs, and Smokee stuck close by her side. Awful as it was, she would rather know. No carnage could be worse than her nightmares.

They found cell after cell of the hapless transports, some dead, some still gasping out a bare breath of life. At what point had the guards deserted them? Isis wondered. Had they mustered and gone to the temple's defense, five days ago? Or waited until it finally fell?

Slowly, they made their way to the upper levels, where once had stood gaming tables and beyond, a great ballroom. On the walls were still a few black and white pictures of the days of glory, the glass in their frames cracked. The floor was now pitted and scarred, littered with cigarette butts and ground-in smears of dirt. A rat ran squeaking out with a scrap of something bloody in its mouth.

Some of the guns had been wrenched from their mounts, a few others remained as if the deserters had run out of time to salvage them.

And that was all. Altogether they found about a hundred survivors that the medics treated with electrolytes and water, turning the ferry into a hospital ship to bring them back to the mainland. There were ten times that many corpses.

But the survivors were all teens or adults. There were no babies, not among the living nor the dead.

Isis furled the sails and dropped the anchor. They were just outside of the port of Long Beach, still in the open ocean after the sad sail back from Saint Cat's. Crews would stay there over the next days to bury the dead, but the survivors and the pen-girls and the bulk of the escorts had headed back.

Sadness permeated the little boat like an odor, and she couldn't get the stench of death out of her nostrils. She needed a few more hours on the ocean, under a waning moon, with clean air in her lungs.

"Why're we stopping?" Smokee asked. The girl sat huddled under a blanket on the deck, her eyes on the planks beneath her, her face gray.

"Need a little more time out here, away from all the clamor," Isis said. "Give you some time, too."

Smokee didn't answer. She didn't care, really. Once again, hope had cheated her, and she was angry, so angry with herself most of all, for being a fool and letting herself be seduced. Her child was gone now, gone far out of her reach into death or a fate too horrible to be imagined. The sex ships of the Gyre, or even worse, the organ farms. What else would they do with such young children, too young to work the plastic plantations, too young for any use other than the worst? She hoped, she prayed, the child had found a quick and easy death.

Then she felt Isis's arms around her.

For a moment, she panicked. They constricted her, they were like chains to hold in her grief, and she lashed out.

"Don't touch me! Don't fucking touch me!"

Isis pulled back.

"Offering you some comfort," she said. "Nothing more. Maybe I need some, too."

Suddenly Smokee felt a coldness where those warm arms had been. "Okay."

Then she was wrapped in Isis's embrace, and a deep sob worked its way up from somewhere down inside her. The sob let loose, and was followed by another and another. She was flooded with grief, sobbing as if her lungs would burst, and the arms now were a refuge, a ring to hold in this sorrow before it spilled out and drowned the world.

"S'okay, sailor. Just cry it all out."

Holding her felt good, Isis realized. In Smokee's unrestrained grief, she could let go of some of her own. She wasn't one to sob, but she had feelings, too. She could let Smokee cry for Sara, and for her, and for them all.

After a long, long time, Smokee's sobs receded. She gulped in a deep breath of air.

"They're gone," she said. "We'll never get them back. All this way we've come, all that we've done—but we'll never get them back or even know what happened to them."

"Maybe not," Isis said. "But I've always kinda wanted to see the Gyre."

Smokee sat up.

"You mean that?"

"Why not? Why not sail away with a beautiful pirate, go take a look? Maybe the Southlands not the only place need liberating. Kinda get a taste for it."

Smokee sat and looked at her for a long, long moment. There was just enough moon to trace the outline of her dark chiseled face, her sculpted neck. She was beautiful. What was she asking?

"I don't like sex," Smokee said abruptly. "Had too much of it. Don't want it ever again."

Isis raised her brows. "Who's talkin' about sex, girl? I'm talkin' adventure. You think I want you for sex?"

Smokee shrugged.

Isis smiled. "I want sex, no trouble to find it. Plenty ladies hot for this pirate, don't you doubt it!"

It was force of habit, more than anything, to boast and flirt a bit. Sara wouldn't begrudge it. Isis still felt like she was going through the motions of living, not truly alive. But just for a moment there, when her arms had wrapped themselves around Smokee, she had felt ... something. Not so much an easing of the ache in her heart, but a sense that maybe someday that pain would shift.

Smokee nodded. She found, to her surprise, that a shy smile pushed her lips up. "I don't doubt that at all."

"No," Isis said in a voice so low Smokee could barely hear. "Just wantin' a friend."

Had she ever admitted as much to Sara? But she hadn't needed to. Sara knew.

"You miss Sara?" Smokee asked softly. Tentatively, she reached out a hand, and patted Isis's arm.

More than you'd miss your heartbeat if it stopped. More than you'd miss air if your lungs stopped breathing. But she would never say that. Instead, Isis gave Smokee a long look from under hooded lids. "Course, I'm not sayin' that if you change your mind, I don't find you attractive."

"Pen-girls don't worry about that," Smokee said bitterly.

"That shit's all done! Hear me? No pen-girls here, just what I call one hot insurrectionary! If I wasn't in mourning, and you closed to it all ... yeah, I'd say something could happen. Something nice."

Isis realized that, for the first time since Sara's death, she felt the stirring of desire. Desire for Smokee, with all her wounds and her minefields of pain and the power that moved through her. Smokee's grief spoke to her own, mirrored it. She longed to ease it, to see those sea-green eyes, so wounded and shuttered, grow soft and misty with desire.

What a sweet challenge it would be, to slowly, carefully, unlock that treasure box. Not to steal its jewels, but to give them back, all those potentials of pleasure that had been so roughly taken.

"But that's okay," she murmured. "I am patient as the sea. Wait for the time to be right. If ever."

"Most likely never," Smokee said, but she no longer sounded adamantly sure.

"Fine by me," Isis smiled. "Just enjoy the anticipation."

She nestled just a little bit closer, slid her arm just a millimeter farther around Smokee's waist.

"If you decide you're ready to try," she breathed into Smokee's ear, "won't be like those dickheads pawing and hammering. A pirate knows what a woman wants. But you be the one in control. You say yes, or you say no, all okay by me."

"No," Smokee said.

"Not asking!" Isis gave her a long, slow smile. "If I was, I'd take it slow and gentle. Say, 'Smokee, how would you feel if I just touched your cheek, delicate-like, just with one finger.' Running it over your skin. You say yes, gonna feel like a feather. So light."

"Well, that might be okay," Smokee conceded.

"And if you like it, maybe I say, 'Smokee, suppose I was to just run that finger over your lips?' You got beautiful lips, such a lovely curve to them. And maybe that's all I do, for an hour or so. Just trace the edges, and maybe brush across the surface. Think you might like that? Not now, of course, but someday?"

Smokee felt something stir deep within her. Her grief and disappointment had emptied her out, but it was as if that empty place now craved to be filled. With something, anything, something sweet and nice, to take away the taste of disappointment. Something to make her want to live again.

Isis was close to her, still cuddled with her arm around her like a sister, offering comfort. But she could feel the warmth of her skin, her heat. She could breathe in her clean scent, like the ocean wind with a hint of spice.

It was daring, it was terrifying. But she felt the heat rising in that empty place.

"You could try that," she breathed. "But nothing more."

Isis gave her a long smile. "You say stop, I stop." She let a delicate forefinger trace the line of Smokee's cheek. Softly, so softly she was barely touching.

"Feel good to you?" she murmured.

Smokee sucked in a breath. It felt electric, like Isis was tracing a line of fire, a good fire, one that warmed without burning.

"And now very softly, I touch your lips."

She placed her forefinger in the cleft in Smokee's upper lip, let it glide down to the corner and come back along the full curve of her lower lip. Smokee felt her mouth tingle and come alive.

She pulled her finger away.

"Why did you stop?" Smokee asked.

"Want me to go on?"

Smokee nodded.

"What about two fingers? Would you like to see how that feels? Say yes if you want it."

"Yes."

Isis traced a spiral on her cheek, let her fingers brush across her lips and around the curve of her chin.

"And suppose, just suppose now, I was to brush your lips with mine? Think you might want that?"

"Yes, I think I might."

Isis gave her a feather-light kiss, just lips touching lips. And now Smokee's lips were burning.

"Good," Isis murmured. "Probably enough for now. Like I said, it's not just sex I want from you. Let's not push it too fast."

Suddenly Smokee knew that was wrong. Now, now was the moment, when she was empty and open and so deeply needy. Now, if she were ever going to know pleasure and not just the wounding.

"No," she said. "Let's go on. Let's do it."

"You sure?"

"I'm scared."

"Course you are."

"But try. Let's just try."

"Then I might ask if I can let my lips do what my fingers have done. And I might want to kiss you again, not so lightly, this time. I might want to taste you."

"Yes," Smokee said. And it was easy, to let go into the pleasure of that tongue-tip tracing her cheek, her lips. When Isis leaned forward and pressed her lips against Smokee's mouth, yes, she wanted it, the softness and the warmth, wanted Isis's tongue caressing her own like two mating snakes. Easy, too, because she had never been kissed before. That wasn't how the tubos took their pleasure in the pens.

"And that's enough for tonight," Isis said. "Like I said, we take it real, real slow. Don't want you getting scared."

"What if I don't want to take it slow?"

"That's good. Build up anticipation."

"Please," she said. "Go on."

"You really want to?"

"Please!"

"Okay, sailor. Feelin' the magic tonight. Got magic in my fingertips. They're like that thing on the backside of a pencil. Erasers. Gonna touch you all over, every part of your body. And every place I touch, gonna take away any touch was ever there before, unless it was a touch of love."

Isis breathed softly, blowing over Smokee's neck as her fingers swiftly unbuttoned Smokee's light cotton blouse. They ran over the soft skin of her shoulders, and traced circles around her small, pert breasts, spiraling in with infinite slowness until they reached the even softer areolas, the nipples swelling with desire.

Down, down over belly and thighs and shins. She spent a long time on Smokee's feet, stroking the soles, feeling the calluses of long marches. Then she flipped the girl over and made her way slowly, softly back up over calves and hamstrings, lingering a long time on the twin, curving hills of her ass. Smokee's back was a landscape, a journey up to neck and hair and the sweet fleshy lobes of her ears. Or an ocean, where she could skim light as a sailboat over the swells, tacking with the wind, sensing every breeze.

Back down the spine, running before the wind, a light feather touch down the crack of the ass just to the edge of the moist softness below.

Wounds, the tubos called them. And yes, that was the most wounded place of all.

Gently she rolled Smokee over.

"Got to see you," she whispered. "Got to watch your eyes. Here we go, sailor. Ready to dive?"

Smokee's lips were parted, her eyes fogged by desire, her breath coming in gusts. Isis slid her fingers down. There it was, the sea cave, the pearl in the oyster. First touch, then breath, then the softness of lips and tongue, the taste of salt and fish. They were swimming together, diving into strong currents, letting go, gliding, diving again. Until the waves took them, and they became the sea, pulsing, beating, breaking in a spray of rainbow foam.

Smokee lay on the blanket, staring up at the stars that seemed to wink knowingly back at her. She felt washed clean, like a castaway washing up on a new beach with all her baggage and memories sunk behind her.

Isis stirred. "How you doin'?"

The pirate lay beside her. Smokee's body nestled into hers, craving warmth and touch. Her mind pulled away suddenly in a sharp moment of panic. What the Jesus had she gone and done?

"Scared?" Isis asked softly.

Smokee forced herself to take a long deep breath.

"In my mind," she admitted. "Not my body."

"Sometimes the body is smarter," Isis said.

"I know."

"Gotta trust it."

Smokee propped herself up on an elbow, and looked down at Isis's strong sculpted face.

"And you?" Smokee asked. "Are you scared?"

"Terrified." Isis gave her a long rueful smile. "Love you, could lose you. Like Sara. You and me, we go to the Gyre, could both end up dead. But I lost Sara, long before the swabs shot her. Lost her cuz of fear. Pushed her away. Now I learned my lesson."

"What lesson?" Smokee asked, feeling a sudden urge to trace the pirate's lips with her own forefinger.

"Can't hold onto love," Isis said. "Can't make it safe. But when it comes, you gotta grab it, if you wanna live. And I do. I want you, girl. I think I could love you."

"I think maybe I could love you, if I could love anyone. But I don't know if I can," Smokee admitted.

"Always did like living dangerously." Isis smiled up at her, then her eyes grew serious. "I'll take the risk, sailor, if you want me to. I'm done sailin' on the ghost ship."

Chapter Eighty-One

Madrone waited by Bird's bedside. She kept vigil there, for once letting other healers and doctors carry her workload. Zoom and the other children were safe up north in the City. In a few more days, when conditions were stabilized in Angel City, they'd come back down. But now, for once, she had no other pressing demands that could pull her away from where she most wanted to be. Here. Waiting. Praying.

The surgeons had fought for his life—thank Goddess there still were a few of them left in the Southlands, and a working hospital to send him to. Lines of people offering to donate blood had stretched around the block. Now he would have the blood of the Southlands running through his veins. He'd lost a lot, and he was weak, but his vital signs were good and they expected him to pull through.

His left hand had been badly scorched, but they'd made contact with Dr. Sam up in the North and he was sending down their crack orthopedic team. Strange how that long and dangerous journey was now reduced to a long day's drive! The surgeons were surprisingly hopeful. With the worst of the old scar tissue burned away, they had a clearer field for reconstruction. It would take time and many surgeries. But with work, he should be able to regain use of the hand.

Madrone had spent the day helping to tend the critically wounded, and using her bee senses to brew up elixirs that chased away the Stewards' engineered bugs. She laid on hands, and dressed wounds, and did what was needed, all the while longing to just sit with him, to hold his hand and stroke his face and be with him when he woke.

Now she had stolen these precious hours. Maybe she'd be wiser to use them for sleeping, but she sat and waited, dozing in her chair. It was almost dawn anyway, time for her next shift.

She heard a sound, a low whisper. Eagerly she leaned close and bent down her head.

"I'm alive," he whispered.

"Barely," she murmured back, and kissed him lightly on his forehead.

His eyes fluttered open, traveled across the room, fixed on her face for a long moment. He smiled. Then he looked down to his bandaged hand.

"No answer on that yet. But there's hope for it."

"Hope. Hope sucks."

"Not always," she said, smiling back at him, allowing herself finally to relax into the sheer happiness that he was alive.

"How long have I been out?"

"Almost a week," she told him.

"A week!" He closed his eyes as if he could drift back into sleep again, then opened them abruptly. "What's happening?"

"We won."

"Figured as much. Or I wouldn't be alive. What else?"

"We've sent everybody back to organize their 'hoods. We've got a newly set up Water Guild replumbing all the pipes, the farmers setting up neighborhood compost sites and starting to plant, medic stations in every section. Councils in the 'hoods every night at five, Grand Council starts at eight in the stadium. Miss Ruby's having the time of her life, setting up the schools. Emily's running everything." Madrone grinned. "Just what you'd expect."

"When can I get up?" He struggled to sit upright, then fell back again.

"When I say so. And not a moment before!"

"She Who Must Be Obeyed," he nodded to her. His eyes were far away again now, half back in some other world. "Queen of the Angels— that's what you are. Did you know that? I saw them, all around you, wings, hundreds of wings."

She leaned over and kissed him again, on the mouth this time.

"An angel kiss?" she asked.

"Celestial!" he said, like the Angels did.

She beamed down at him. "We did it! We really did it, Bird! Take a moment, let it sink in. No more debt slaves. No more pens, or child soldiers, or manufactured epidemics, or threats of the army marching in. We can go home, if we want. Or stay here, and help Angel City transform into the paradise it was meant to be."

"What do you want?" he asked.

"What do you want?" she countered.

"I asked you first."

"I saved your life."

"All debts will be forgiven in the bright new day," he said, and then lay back down, his eyes closed, resting from the effort. After a long few moments he drifted into sleep, and she just watched him, basking in her happiness.

He opened his eyes again, grinned at her, and said, "Let's have babies. Lots of babies."

She smiled. "That's what you said. It was sweet. No man's ever offered to have my baby before."

"How soon can we start?" He winked.

"You must be on the mend!"

"A man needs something to live for."

"You've got a few holes need mending, first. And other things. We'll have to get in some practice." She hesitated. "But Bird ... I'm not so sure.... Maybe there's some things I need to do, before that...."

"We can still practice, can't we?" he said hopefully.

"Practice makes perfect," she agreed.

"I want to take a bicycle trip. I want to go sailing," he sighed. "*Diosa*, there's going to be a fuck of a lot to do!"

But it was good work waiting for them, he thought, the work of healing and regeneration. The work of war was done, and he was ready to be done with it, to leave behind the fighter and be the singer, the gardener, the lover. He drifted back to sleep, dreaming of rich earth on his wounded hands, and the trill of songbirds returning.

She sat, holding his good hand, as he drifted back into sleep, and she half-drifted with him. She could feel Maya looking over her shoulder, and her grandmother Johanna, and Rio, their mutual lover. Smiling and nodding, they were cradled by angels and ancestors.

He would heal. And they would have that great gift of time together, long years ahead in a world that they had transformed into a great refuge for all the wounded, the heartsick, the weary. They would be together, to heal, to plant, to build, to trek deeper into bee-mind, rock-mind, water-mind and see where it led, to discover what world they could create, when all of creation was alive and speaking, and they became the earth's healing hands, her voice to sing her praises.

The Primes were being held on their ship, while the Council debated what to do with them. It continued to meet, for the moment, in the cafeteria of Maya and Johanna's old school. The temple was too grim, too removed from the people, and they'd grown fond of this shabby room with its plastic chairs and Formica tables carved with initials of schoolchildren long grown and gone. Already they were nostalgic for the tense days of the siege, now that they had led to victory.

Isis suggested the Primes be formed into the cleanup detail for the slave tower on Saint Cat's.

"Let them clean up their mess," she said. "Get a taste of what they handed out."

Most of the reps from the 'hoods simply wanted to shoot them.

"No," Miss Ruby said firmly. "They're a bunch of sorry excuses for human beings, but we don't want to christen the new world with a bloodbath."

"Can we heal them?" Emily asked. "We know how to heal sojuhs and pen-girls, how to liberate the debt slaves and restore to them human-ity and dignity. But what do we do with the Primes? Are they reachable?"

Madrone had pulled herself away from Bird's bedside to join in this debate. She sat across the table from River, who caught her eye and smiled.

"We can try," she said.

"Ain't nobody hopeless," he agreed.

They brought the Primes into circles, one by one, sat them in the center of groups of freed debt slaves and the rescued relinquished and the ordinary folks who had lived so long in so much fear. One by one, the people told their stories, tales of the hunger, the fear, the long nights of grief and toil.

"Listen."

"Witness."

"This is the suffering that bought you luxuries."

"These are the bones of my children sacrificed so that your children might rule."

The stories were rich with drama and tears. The people of Angel City told them over and over again, recording them and writing them down, broadcasting the circles over the vidnet for all to see.

Some of the Primes were moved. Teary-eyed, they set their soft hands to the work of making reparations, healing and planting and building. Some remained stone-hearted, telling their own tales over and over of how they had been cheated and wronged, plotting and scheming in bitter knots of sad conspirators to the end of their days.

But as the people of Angel City listened to story after story, as the artists immortalized the histories in sculptures and mosaics, and the singers trans-muted the tales into songs, they began to realize that what was most import-ant was not what the story did to the Primes but what the telling did for the teller. It made meaning out of the suffering that had seemed so meaningless, spinning from raw loss and humiliation yarns of triumph and hope.

Anthony formed a Theater Guild to act them out. Tianne's teens gathered crews to clear out the Relinquishment Center and return it to what it had originally been, a studio with huge sound stages where they could film the tales and broadcast them and send them north with the returning Cityfolks and west with the trading ships to inspire the world.

And all the while, crews fanned out into the city, tearing up the streets, sculpting the land to capture and hold the rain, liberating the pipes for water. They planted groves of citrus and lined the avenues with date palms, took cuttings of figs and started new groves. On the drier slopes of the hills they set saplings of olives that could live for a thousand years, underplanted with fragrant hedges of lavender and rosemary and thyme. They resurrected the sad trickle that had once been a river, brought it out of the imprisoning concrete to nourish cattails and sedges and birds.

Atop the temple, the Queen of the Angels flashed golden, mirroring the rays of the rising sun. Under her gaze, bowed heads lifted. Bent backs stood proud and straight.

Come out, come out, she seemed to say. Out of your hiding places, out from the canyons of the hills and the underground havens, out of your fears and timidity. Make this place a garden where a living river runs, a warm-hearted bower of oranges and roses, a habitat fit for angels and Gods.

What comes after the revolution? You do well to ask that question before you wage one. Easier to bring the old system down than to create the new. Growth and evolution take time. We learn by trial and error, by making mistakes and trying again.

Revolution, when it comes, is sometimes swift. Rebuilding, reshaping, is always slow.

And change brings questions difficult to answer. How do we create justice? Do we hold the perpetrators accountable for the crimes? If we forgive, does that let the injustice continue? If we exact revenge, who do we become?

For my part, if I could, I would declare a general amnesty for all of us, everywhere. Forgive our debts and our mistakes, our missteps and failings and betrayals, even our occasional or devoted cruelties, all the ways we play out our inner torment on one another. We are wounded creatures, all of us, bashing away with bloody limbs. We never had a chance to be anything else. Forgive it all, and start anew.

Let us forgive all the ways we wander in circles, take the wrong path. We all lose the way. Let it go and know that all you have to do, really, is just to come back. Stand up again when you fall. When you can't see ahead, grope your way back to the trail.

That's all we ask, all we can ask. Not perfection, but course correction.

Not a symphony, but a few notes pulled from the air and shaped into something with meaning. A song, however simple, even if you forget the words and flub the harmony. Even if you think it makes no difference.

Just sing. Be on the side of the makers and shapers, the singers and the storytellers. That's all you need to do.

Not to sing with the voice of an angel, but however cracked and broken your instrument, sing anyway.

Afterword and Acknowledgments

City of Refuge is a book animated by a vision of community, and is itself an example of community in action. Without the help of many, many people, I would not have been able to write and publish it, and I'm very grateful for all the support I have received.

More than twenty years ago, I wrote a novel called *The Fifth Sacred Thing*, the parent book to *City of Refuge*. *The Fifth Sacred Thing* was published by Bantam in 1993, followed two years later by its prequel, *Walking to Mercury*. Then, for many years, I let that world alone.

In the winter of 2008, I was contacted by a Bay Area filmmaker, Philip Wood, who wanted to bring *The Fifth Sacred Thing* to the screen. So began a long journey that still continues today. In the process of writing multiple drafts of a screenplay, and later a pilot, the world came alive for me again. The characters began to clamor to tell more of their tale.

In 2011, we ran a Kickstarter campaign to fund development of the film project. Hundreds of people told me how much *The Fifth Sacred Thing* had meant to them, and kicked in their hard-earned money to help us. Encouraged, I began a sequel.

Writing a sequel to a book twenty years old is not an exercise I recommend! Especially a well-loved book. I had to continually fight those nagging inner voices that whispered, "What if it's not as good as the other one? What if people don't like it?"

But soon the characters and the story took over, and developed a life of their own. I have tried to stay consistent with the earlier books, but over the course of two decades, the world has changed, and so have I. The astute reader may notice some differences.

The most obvious difference is in the language of the sojuhs of the Southlands, which in this book has many more quirks and unique characteristics than in *Fifth*. In truth, I was never entirely happy with the

Southlands slang in *Fifth*, so here I have taken the opportunity of developing it further, as well as working on the expressions and language of the Califians and the other groups and factions. I've asked myself questions such as: "Would people who believe sexuality is sacred use 'fuck' as a swear word? If not, what?" Tolkien created whole languages for the elves and orcs in *Lord of the Rings*. I haven't gone that far, but I *have* created lexicons of alternative profanity.

A deeper difference is in the books' approaches to nonviolence. In *The Fifth Sacred Thing*, the Califians adopt a profound, spiritually-based strategy of nonviolent resistance to the Stewards' invasion. In *City of Refuge*, faced with the challenge of liberating the Southlands, the Califians take a variety of approaches, from the prefigurative creativity of the Refuge to the out-and-out gun battles of the Army of Liberation.

In part, the changes reflect my own experiences over the years. When I wrote *Fifth*, I had been deeply involved for a decade in strictly nonviolent movements against nuclear power, nuclear weapons, intervention in Latin America, and other social justice issues. I was wrestling with the question: Can our strategy of peaceful resistance work against a truly ruthless opponent?

In the decades since, and especially after 9/11, we've seen the police grow far more militarized, and their use of brutal force against even nonviolent protestors has escalated. We see continual assaults and outright murders of people of color by authorities who most often go unpunished. As an activist, I've found myself immersed in movements such as the global justice actions of the '00s that embraced a diversity of tactics rather than a pure pacifism. I've supported the nonviolent resistance in Palestine and encountered the despair and resilience of a people who have lived their lives in a war zone. I've stood in the rain on the streets with the Occupy movement, and experienced the excruciating frustration of trying to facilitate some of their meetings.

The question that animates *City of Refuge* is a very different one from *Fifth*. It's simply this: How do you build a new world when people are so deeply damaged by the old?

While I remain personally deeply committed to nonviolence, I believe the job of fiction is not to espouse a position but to deeply explore a question, through the actions and behaviors and realizations of the characters, lived through the incidents of the plot. I hope readers will understand that *City of Refuge* is not meant to be prescriptive, but rather, to experiment with possibilities that are easier lived in fiction than in real life.

Many people contributed to this book. This book would not have come into being without the support of Philip Wood—known to his friends as "Mouse"—and Katy Bell, Maya Lily, Jay Rosenberg, and Paradox Pollack, the team that has worked so diligently to pitch the book for movies and TV.

The book is fiction, but much of it was inspired by my real adventures with buddies in the Pagan Cluster, a loose group of activists rooted in earth-based spirituality who ran together on the streets through many of the global justice mobilizations of the early '00s, and still do from time to time. Bird's vision of the fortress originated in some of the imagery that have helped us maintain hope and optimism even in grim times. I could name hundreds of collaborators, but will restrain myself to thanking Lisa Fithian and Juniper Ross, core members of our organizing collective Alliance of Community Trainers.

Baza Novic and Johnny Hornung read the sea-going scenes early on and helped me with nautical information and terms. All inaccuracies in those areas, however, are my own.

Early on, a grant from the Curry Stone Foundation provided writing time for me, as did some of the funds from those who supported our 2011 Kickstarter campaign, and I am deeply grateful for their faith in this project.

Moral and emotional support came from many sources—my husband David, my core housemates Rose, Bill, Kore, and Akerah, my land partner and permaculture teaching buddy Charles Williams, Earth Activist Training administrator and teachers Jay Rosenberg and Pandora Thomas, my filmmaking partner Donna Read Cooper, and many dear friends, as well as my agent Ken Sherman who has championed my work throughout my career. Logistical support was provided by my assistant Akasha Madron, along with astute astrological consultation, and by Jodi Selene, who helped manage the complexities of all my travels, lectures, workshops, and teaching schedule.

Bird's great-aunt Gisela, who gave him the idea of the graffiti stencils on the bottom of suitcases, was based on Gisela Konopka, who was an old family friend and a mentor to my parents when they studied social work at the University of Minnesota. During World War II, she and her husband were part of the German Resistance, and the story of the suitcases is told in her autobiography, *Courage and Love*.

Ahmed Salah is also a real person, one of the architects of the Arab Spring of 2011, and he has kindly given me permission to tell a bit of his inspirational story, even though I have yet to succeed in teaching him how to parallel park. He tells his own story more fully in his book, *The Spark: Starting the Revolution*.

All other characters and incidents in this book are entirely fictional, the product of my own imagination, and are not meant to represent anyone living or dead.

This book is my first venture into the new world of digital and self-publishing, and it wouldn't be possible without the support of this summer's 2015 Kickstarter backers. Thank you so much! When the corporate publishers declined to take a risk on a sequel to a book twenty years old, you proved that there is indeed an eager audience for this story.

Alli Gallixsee helped me launch and manage that campaign, and I couldn't have done it without her. I am also so grateful to the many people who shared our links and passed on the information to their friends and contacts.

Cherise Fisher did the developmental editing. Her understanding of my core intentions for the book helped me to realize them more fully. Mary DeDanan did the copyediting, and her amazing eye for detail, ability to keep track of a thousand different strands of information, and rigorous elimination of exclamation points helped keep the language, the time lines, and the moon phases clear. Jennifer Ruby Privateer artfully managed the production aspects and proofread the book with great skill, professionalism, and grace under pressure. Jessica Perlstein created the beautiful cover image, both for the Kickstarter edition and the regular edition. Diane Rigoli did the elegant design for both the interior and the cover. And special thanks to the whole team who worked so hard to get this done on a very tight time line.

This book is dedicated to the memory of two special people.

Andy Paik stood shoulder to shoulder with me many times as the tear gas was flying and the riot cops advancing. He helped me scout the Mormon Temple in LA for the general's stronghold, and Catalina Island for the Primes' shipping base. As well, he was the originator of destiny tarot. Andy was a brave and stalwart activist, an accomplished stage magician with a wry sense of humor, and a true magician with a huge commitment to creating the world of justice envisioned in these pages.

Isis Rebecca Coble was my dear friend from our days together in high school. For many years, she was my first reader, on both *Walking to Mercury* and *The Fifth Sacred Thing*. Her contributions helped shape those stories, the characters and their voices, and I have missed her more than I can say in writing this book.

And I would also like to dedicate this book to the future, to some of those young ones who will take their places in the times this book envisions: Scarlet, Phoebe, Nolan Orion, Solas, Brighid, Skyler, Cedar William Huckleberry, and Charles Oliver Francis.

A Sincere Thank You to our Kickstarter Backers Who Made *City of Refuge* Possible

Aaron Lehmer-Chang
Adam Huggins
Adrienne Amundsen
Aileen Paul
Alex Iantaffi
Alexzandria York
Alix Davidson
Alli Gallixsee
Amanda B. McPeck
Amanda de Boer
Amber, Knox & Nakona
Amy D. Mozingo
Amy Elizabeth Antonucci
Andrea Lampersdorf
Angela Davis
Angela Sabrina Lytle
Anika Tench Dixon
Anjelica Leigh Whitehorne
Ann Corbett
Ann Marie
Anne Champagne
Anne Whitcomb
Annie Gwillym Walker
Annika Mongan & Autumn Crow
Anonymous
Apel Mjausson
April C. Taylor
April Dawn
Aria Cahir
Ariana Lightningstorm
Ashley Philpot
Aubrey Marcus
Aurora WindDancer Sanquilly
Autumn Skye Morrison
Avyn Norah Trace
Ayramaia

B.H. Lenius
Barbara L.M. Handley
Barbara Rigby
Barbara Sinclair
Barbara Woschek
Baruch Zeichner
Beatrice Briggs
Becki Harris
Bert Monroe
Beth Ann Nawrocki
Beth Ebbing Johnson
Beth Girshman
Bettie "Bells" Davis
Bex vanKoot
Blue Fire MacMahon
Bonnie Cullum
Brenda Hoard
Briana Cavanaugh
BrightFlame
C. I. Machanek
C. Milton Dixon
Caduceus Antonius
Caerrean Sunzephyr
Caitlin McCaughey
Camille Cimino
Candace Delaney
Canyon Laurel
Cara Marinucci
Cari DeHate
Carla Poppen
Carol Lee Johnson
Carol Trasatto
Carwil Bjork-James
Cascade Spring Cook
Cassandra Wildheart
Catherine Cameron

Catherine Carter
Catherine Gronlund
Catherine Mock
Chad Bowden
Charlene Elderkin
Charles Williams
Chelidon & The
Casa Chaos Denizens
Cheryl Taylor Desmond
Chris Abbott
Chris Bass
Chris Gustafsson
Cindy Arnold Humiston
Cindy Prince
Clara McCoy
Clifford Curry & Delight Stone
CMonster
CodePink
Coleen Douglas
Collene Spiridonoff
Corinne Viner
Coty Behanna
Craig A. Correa
Craig & Dustianne North Godfrey
Cricket
Cynthea Lee Rose
Cynthia Capodestria
Cynthia Cathryn Almy Savage
Cynthia Riggin
Dale Hendricks
Daniel Taghdiri
Darcy Skye Holoweski
David Brightman & Tom Metz
Dawn & Brent
Dawn Isidora
Deborah Bradford
Deborah Lynn
Debra
Deena Benson
Deidri Deane
Delia Yuhas Carroll
Demetra Delia Markis
Dennis Corvin-Blackburn

Derek Brown
Desiree' Ann Pearce
Devin Graham
Diane Baker
Diane Perazzo (Amber)
Diane-Angéline Baechler
Dmitri D'Alessandro
Donna Garrison
Dori Herrick & Cheryl Dunlap
Dory
Doug Brown
Dr. Jacqueline Zaleski Mackenzie
Dr. Susan G. Carter
Dress
Eddy
Efrat Barak
Ela & Franklin
Elaine Wender
Elga Antonsen
Elisabeth Schramm
Elizabeth A. Williamson
Elizabeth Deborah McCoy
Elizabeth Fraser
Elizabeth Stadtmueller
Elizabeth Wilson
Ellen Farmer
Ellyn Parker
Emily Copeland
Emily Jane Embers Johnstone
Emily Wilson
Emily Yost
Emma MacKenzie
Emmah Eastwind
Eric Horstman
Erica Wilson
Erik Ohlsen
Erika Lynn Feaster
Erin Grabowski
Erin Poh
Erin Rose Conner
Esmerelda CalicoFury
Esther Ellen Harrington
Eve-Marie Coyote Woman Hughes

Evelyn Clark
Evergreen Erb
Fio Santika Akheron
Fiona Heath
Flame
Flower Power
Francesco Raneri
Fredrick Trafton
Gael Fraser
Gail Bjorkman
Gene Weinbeck
Genevieve Vaughan
Geoffrey A. Rosen
Gerry Green
Grace Kirby
Green Hag Farm/
WomynSpirit Continuum
Gregory N. Buckland
Grietje Laga
Gwydion Blackrose
Gwydion Logan
Harald Griesbacher
Heather K. Veitch
Heather King (Aurora Rose)
Heidi Schultz
Helen/Hawk & Thermal
Helene Kippert
Holli Harper
Holly Blakemore
Illona Trogub
Institute for Earth
Regenerative Studies
Iyeshka Farmer
J. Chevalier
Jack Buksbaum
Jack Greenwood
Jacklyn Theoharis
Jacquie Clarke
Jaina Bee
Jan & Atlant Schmidt
Jane E. Ward
Jane from Maryland
Jane Meredith

Janet Lee Zahn
Janet McLachlan
Janette Nash-Ferrise
Jason Bushman &
Charles Herman-Wurmfeld
Jason Guille
Jax & Aidan Higgs
Jean Hegland
Jeanne Ruetz
Jen Curley
Jennefer Johnson
Jennifer F. Taylor, PhD
Jennifer Ruby Privateer
Jennifer Seligman
Jennifer Wyld
Jeremy Blanchard
Jes McCullough
Jessica Abell
Jessica Ann Myers
Jessica Gorton
Jessica Tartaro
Jessie Raeder
Jesua
Jezanna & David Gruber
Jill A. Einsmann
Jill Cohen & Stephen Pocock
Joan Haran
Joan McKinzey
Joan Stevens
JoAnne Brooks
Joerg Wichmann
Johanna Mitchell
John E. Dunkerley
John John
John Mirassou
John P. Young
Jonathan Carter
Jonathan Furst
Jonathan Waterlow
Joseph Frakes
Joseph Micketti & Jane Chandler
Joy Kirstin
Joy Schen

Judith A. Cartisano
Julia Bielefeld
Julian Kondas
Juliana
Julie Ann Koehlinger
Julie Anne Wayman
Julie Shaw
Juliet Trail
Juniper
Jürgen Piater
Kaaren Gann
Karen B. Taylor
Karen Hurley, PhD
Karen Kromer Lynch
Karen Milligan
Kari Allen-Hammer
Kat Steele
Kate Gillis
Kate Heiber-Cobb
Kathleen Lelack
Kathleen Mary Fitzgerald
Katrina Messenger
Kay Erdwinn
Kellee *krystal* Dawson
Kelley L. Grimes M.S.W.
Kelly Bootes
Kevin C. Newland
Khepe-Ra Maat-Het-Heru
Cruz-Rebeiro-Heru-AppleWhiteJohn
Kiki LeSeed
Kiko Aumond
Kim Chilvers
Kim Niedbalski
Kim Stanford
Kim Tournat
Kireth
Kirsten M. Corby
Kitty Degler
Kris McLonis
Kristin/Ivy
Kyddryn
Kylie Gifford
Kyndyll Rikard Greyland

Lane Bendis
Lanette Miller
Lanna Lee Maheux
Laura Bonella
Laura Callanan & Anne Brannen
Laura Stanger
Laurel Eastling
Lauren Kurzman
Lauren Liebling Davis
Laurie Kaufman
Laurie Lovekraft
Lawrence Neal
Le'Ann Duran-Mitchell
Lee Gelson
Leigh Ann Hildebrand
Leona L. Lauder
Leslie King
Lessie Brown
Licia Berry,
Guide to the Frontier Inside
LightningHeart
Lilyth Minnig
Linda Carol Latta
Linda S. Barnett
Linda Stout
Lindy Barnes
Lisa Brideau
Liz Highleyman
Looby Macnamara
Lora Powell-Haney
Lorelei Schroeter
Lori Ann Highley
Lorraine Brilliant
Lou Judson
Louise Lieb
Louise Tate
Lucy Bukrey
Luz & Ned
Lydia Olchoff
Lydia Ruyle
Lynn Fraser
Magali Roy-Fequiere
Maggi Joseph

Maggie Springer

Manko Eponymous

Mareena McKinley Wright

Marg Hall

Margaret L. Meggs

Margaret Pevec

Margaret Theisen

Margi Curtis

Margot Brennan

Mariah Drogitis

Marion McCartney

Marisha Auerbach

Mark Schonbeck

Mark Simos

Marlene M. DeNardo

Marsha Buck

Marshall Klotz

Mary Beth Brangan & Jim Heddle

Mary Lounsbury

Mary Rogers

Matthew J. Paulus

Matthieu Tallard

Maureen Holley

Max Penalty Magen

Maya Gutierrez

Megan Kearney

Megan Oswald

Melinda Tursky

Melissa MoonGoddess

Merry O'Brien

Michael Negron

Michael Skeeter Pilarski

Michael Tank

Michael Wiedmann

Michelle Renee Johnson Heytvelt

Michelle Schultz

Michelle Taitch Moyer

Mika Scott

Mikalina Kirkpatrick

Mimi Neilson

Moe Wendt

Monika Antonelli

Morgen Raney

Myozen Barton Stone

N'kai Moonwatyr

Nancy Abernethy

Nancy C. Alexander

Nancy M. Lewis

Naomi Stone

Nellsummer

Niamh Moore

Nic Rogoff

Nicky Lewis

Oriethyia Mountain Crone

Otmar

Pablito

Pachamama Rising!

Pamela & Rebecca Rosin Kaplan

Pamela Portlock

Paradox Pollack

Pat Hogan

Pat Ryan

Patanjali Sacha

Patricia Awen Fey O'Luanaigh

Patricia J. Menzies

Patricia L. Burton

Patricia Miller

Patrick & Sienna Fisher

Patti M. Davis

Patty & Bill Sievers

Patty Love

Patty Rodrigues

Paul de Tourreil

Paula J. Slomer

Paula Koepke

Peggy Case

Peggy Lagodny

Penny Livingston

Philip Wood aka Mouse

Pilgrim's Way Community Bookstore & Secret Garden, Carmel-by-the-Sea

Pipaluk Weinhold Andersen

Poppy Edgewalker & her Moose

Priscilla Anne Tennant Herrington

Punya Heinen

Queen Cara Pietrina Cordoni

Rabbi Mordechai Liebling

Rachel Soumokil

Rae Watterworth

Rainey Hopewell

Raixel d'Exu

Ramona Ralston

Rebecca Kelley Morgan

Reverend Two Eagles

Rissa Lyn

River Fire-Seed

Riyana, Jason & Brighid Johnson-Sang

Robert Beridha

Robin Clayfield

Robin Sol Lieberman

Rodney Balbin

Rose May Dance

Rosemary Medvedec

Ruby Berry

Ruby DeVol Berson

Ruth J. Wajsblum

Ryan Psymurai Oberfield

Sabo Weaving Wren

Sageheart

San Mueller

San Wages

Sandra Whisler

Sara Boore

Sara Lipowitz

Sarah & Maisey

Sarah Livia Brightwood

Sarah Preston

Sarah Rebstock

Sarah's Mandala

Satsi, Alli, & Cedar Jaquith

Scattering Hoffman

Scott R. Webber

Sea Raven, D.Min.

Sequoia Sempervirens

Seren Sonell

Shamira

Shand Yates

Shandie Crystal Norris Howell

Shanti Mc

Shar Inanna Molloy

Shar Stjerne

Shari Gross

Sharon E. Owens

Sharon Jackson

Sharon Lee

Sharon Quigley

Shasta Martinuk

Sheila Bracani

Sidnie

Silvia Daole

Siri Margareta Kalla

Sobey Wing

Sol Solomon

Somraj Pokras & Jeffre TallTrees

Sonja Wentz

Sophia Rosenberg

Stacy Cygnus Rockwood

Stephanie Panagopoulos

Stephen G. Daugherty

Steve Brown

Steve Stormoen

Stewedart

StormDragon

Stuart Getty

Sue Fulton

Sue Lohrer

Sue McEwing

Sue Skinner

SuEllen Shepard

Sulyn Cedar

Susan K. Matyskella

Susan L. Herrick

Susan Mausshardt

Susannah Grover

Suzanne & Neil Savage

Suzanne Vogelsmeier

Suzanne W. Nichols

Tamara Duval

Tammi Sweet

Tarin Towers

Tasnim Janice Burton

Tere Mann

Terry Shistar
Tessa Kappe
Theodora Alves Craigen
Theresa Kastorff
Theresa Vernon
Thom & Nick
Thomas Torma
Thomas Weidemeyer Jr.
Tiffany Lazic
Tim V. Johnson
Timothy J. Meng Raven's Glen
Timothy Schwinghamer
Tricia Edgar
Trisha Dee
Trudi Hayes
Trudy Lynn Taylor
Vanessa Ronsse
Vicki Toale
Vik-Thor Harrison-Rose

Vishwam Jamie Heckert
Wanda Rudzki
Wanda Stewart/ Obsidian Farm
Wendy Bennett
Wes Modes
Wesley Roe
William Hertling
Willow Toccata
WillowJune
Wolf
Wren Day
Yadina Clark
Yarrow Angelweed
Zay Eleanor Watersong
Zoë & Leo Guzman-Lanois
Zoe Blue Brown
Zofia Hausman
Zunes-Wolfe Family

About the Author

Starhawk is the author or coauthor of thirteen books, including *The Spiral Dance: A Rebirth of the Ancient Religion of the Great Goddess, The Fifth Sacred Thing,* now in development for film and television, and its prequel, *Walking to Mercury.* Her most recent nonfiction book is *The Empowerment Manual: A Guide for Collaborative Groups,* on group dynamics, power, conflict, and communications. Her works have been translated into Spanish, French, German, Danish, Dutch, Italian, Portuguese, Polish, Czech, Greek, Japanese, and Burmese.

She is one of the prominent leaders in the revival of earth-based spirituality and Goddess religion. She is a cofounder of Reclaiming, an activist branch of modern Pagan religion. Her archives are maintained at the Graduate Theological Union library in Berkeley, California.

She consulted on and cowrote three documentaries for the National Film Board of Canada: *Goddess Remembered, The Burning Times,* and *Full Circle.* Starhawk and director Donna Read Cooper then formed Belili Productions, to make documentaries on women and the earth. Their works include *Signs Out of Time* (2004), about archaeologist Marija Gimbutas, and *Permaculture: The Growing Edge* (2010).

Starhawk is a veteran of progressive movements, from anti-war to anti-nukes, and is deeply committed to bringing the techniques and creative power of spirituality to political activism. She is a founder of Earth Activist Training (EAT), which teaches permaculture design grounded in spirit and with a focus on organizing and activism. She also champions "social permaculture": the application of permaculture principles to groups and human relations.

She holds a BA in Fine Arts from UCLA and an MA in Psychology with a concentration in Feminist Therapy from Antioch University West. She is presently adjunct faculty at the California Institute of Integral Studies.

Starhawk travels internationally, lecturing and teaching permaculture, earth-based spirituality and ritual, and the skills of activism. She lives part-time in San Francisco, in a collective house with her partner and friends. But much of her time is spent on Golden Rabbit Ranch in western Sonoma County, where together with land manager Charles Williams, she is developing a model of carbon-sequestering ranching, incorporating holistic management rotational grazing with sheep and goats, restorative forestry, food forests, and perennial systems.

Starhawk's website: **starhawk.org**

Find her Author Page on Facebook at:
facebook.com/pages/Starhawk

On Twitter at: **twitter.com/starhawk17**

Earth Activist Training: **earthactivisttraining.org**

Belili Productions: **belili.org**

Made in the USA
Middletown, DE
13 April 2017